OXFORD WORLD'S CLASSICS

THE KREUTZER SONATA

AND OTHER STORIES

COUNT LEO NIKOLAEVICH TOLSTOY, the youngest of four brothers, was born in 1828 at Yásnaya Polyana, his father's estate in Tula province, about 200 miles from Moscow. His mother died when he was 2, and his father when he was 9. He revered their memory, and they were the inspiration for his portraits of Princess Mary and Nicholas Rostov in *War and Peace*. Both his mother and father belonged to the Russian nobility, and Tolstoy always remained highly conscious of his aristocratic status, even when towards the end of his life he embraced and taught doctrines of Christian equality and the brotherhood of man.

He served in the army in the Caucasus and the Crimea, where as an artillery officer at the siege of Sevastopol he wrote his first stories and impressions. After leaving the army he travelled and studied educational theories, which deeply interested him. In 1862 he married Sophie Behrs and for the next fifteen years lived a tranquil and productive life as a country gentleman and author. *War and Peace* was finished in 1869 and *Anna Karénina* in 1877. He had thirteen children. In 1879, after undergoing a severe spiritual crisis, he wrote the autobiographical *A Confession*, and from then on he became a 'Tolstoyan', seeking to propagate his views on religion, morality, non-violence, and renunciation of the flesh. He continued to write, but chiefly in the form of parables, tracts, and morality plays—written 'with the left hand of Tolstoy' as a Russian critic has put it—though he also composed a late novel, *Resurrection*, and one of his finest tales, *Hadji Murád*. Because of his new beliefs and disciples, and his international fame as pacifist and sage, relations with his wife became strained and family life increasingly difficult. At last in 1910, at the age of 82, he left his home and died of pneumonia at a local railway station.

RICHARD F. GUSTAFSON, Professor of Russian at Barnard College, Columbia University, is a specialist in Russian literature and religious philosophy. He is the author of *Leo Tolstoy: Resident and Stranger* (1986) and has edited Tolstoy's *Resurrection* (Oxford World's Classics, 1994).

OXFORD WORLD'S CLASSICS

For over 100 years Oxford World's Classics have brought readers closer to the world's great literature. Now with over 700 titles—from the 4,000-year-old myths of Mesopotamia to the twentieth century's greatest novels—the series makes available lesser-known as well as celebrated writing.

The pocket-sized hardbacks of the early years contained introductions by Virginia Woolf, T. S. Eliot, Graham Greene, and other literary figures which enriched the experience of reading. Today the series is recognized for its fine scholarship and reliability in texts that span world literature, drama and poetry, religion, philosophy and politics. Each edition includes perceptive commentary and essential background information to meet the changing needs of readers.

OXFORD WORLD'S CLASSICS

LEO TOLSTOY

The Kreutzer Sonata

and Other Stories

Translated by

LOUISE AND AYLMER MAUDE

and

J. D. DUFF

Edited with an Introduction and Notes by

RICHARD F. GUSTAFSON

OXFORD
UNIVERSITY PRESS

Great Clarendon Street, Oxford OX2 6DP

Oxford University Press is a department of the University of Oxford. It furthers the University's objective of excellence in research, scholarship, and education by publishing worldwide in

Oxford New York

Athens Auckland Bangkok Bogotá Buenos Aires Cape Town Chennai Dar es Salaam Delhi Florence Hong Kong Istanbul Karachi Kolkata Kuala Lumpur Madrid Melbourne Mexico City Mumbai Nairobi Paris São Paulo Shanghai Singapore Taipei Tokyo Toronto Warsaw

with associated companies in Berlin Ibadan

Oxford is a registered trade mark of Oxford University Press in the UK and in certain other countries

Published in the United States by Oxford University Press Inc., New York

These translations first published by Oxford University Press in the World's Classics hardback series between 1916 and 1935
First published as a World's Classics paperback 1997
Reissued as an Oxford World's Classics paperback 1998

British Library Cataloguing in Publication Data
Data available

Library of Congress Cataloging in Publication Data
Tolstoy, Leo, graf, 1828–1910.
[Short stories. English. Selection]
The Kreutzer sonata and other stories/Leo Tolstoy; translated by Louise and Aylmer Maude and J. D. Duff; edited with an introduction and notes by Richard F. Gustafson.
(Oxford world's classics)
Includes bibliographical references.
Contents: Family happiness—The Kreutzer sonata—The Cossacks—Hadji Murád.
1. Tolstoy, Leo, graf, 1828–1910—Translations into English. I. Maude, Louise Shanks, 1855–1939. II. Maude, Aylmer, 1858–1938. III. Duff, J. D. (James Duff), 1860–1940. IV. Gustafson, Richard F. V. Title. VI. Series.
PG3366.A15M38 1997 891.73′3—dc21 96–40166

ISBN 0–19–283809–1

4

Printed in Great Britain by
Clays Ltd, St Ives plc

CONTENTS

INTRODUCTION

Leo Tolstoy, known to the world for his novels, also created throughout his sixty-year career as a writer a significant body of works of shorter fiction. These fictions, like his novels, tend toward a uniqueness in form, even as they explore a set of themes common in the longer works. For example two of his most famous short stories, *The Death of Iván Ilých* (1886) and *Master and Man* (1895), differ in structure from each other and from all Tolstoy's other shorter fictions, but explore in a specific and focused way themes from his novels: life understood as a journey of the discovery of identity and vocation, the meaning of one's life in the face of death, the redemptive role of suffering and compassion. Tolstoy's four novellas, collected in this volume, share these two features with his other shorter fictions. In the complexity of their matter and manner, however, they stand closest to the novels and represent Tolstoy at his creative best.

Family Happiness (1859) was written four years before *War and Peace* was begun. In theme it shares with the famous epic an idealized view of the human potential for the happiness of hearth and home. As a first-person narrative told by a female character, it is unique in Tolstoy's *œuvre* and rare in the collective corpus of Western male authors. The narrator, however, does resemble Tolstoy's more common omniscient third-person narrators who are secure in their moral grasp of life; Másha tells her past story from the vantage point of her present and, she believes, correct understanding of the meaning of her life. The title, therefore, tends to be ironic, for this is not a story about family happiness, but about how Másha comes to discover what family happiness is. In this sense it is a tale of conversion to a meaningful life, a common Tolstoyan structure, seen for example in the two short stories mentioned above. What is different is the female point of view.

Also like *War and Peace*, *Family Happiness* draws heavily on Tolstoy's personal experience. The novella is a fictional recasting of a set of ideas Tolstoy worked out in a series of letters sent to Valériya Vladímirovna Arsén'eva, a woman with whom he had a short 'romance' several years before the writing of the story. In these letters Tolstoy instructs the young Valériya, revealing to her the proper way to live and love. He urges her toward self-development and growth: 'May God help you, my darling, to go forward, to love, to love not just me alone, but all God's world, people, nature, music, poetry, and everything attractive in it and to develop your mind in order to understand the things in this world that are worthy of love.'[1] There is, he further insists, a 'great reason' for a woman to pursue such moral development: 'Beside the destined purpose of a woman to be a wife, her main purpose is to be a mother, and to be a *mother*, and not a *female*, you need development' (lx. 122; 1856). Central to the theory of love elaborated in these letters is the notion of self-sacrifice: 'One must not love for one's own pleasure, one loves for the other's pleasure' (lx. 116; 1856). This conception of a woman's vocation and this notion of self-sacrificing love lead to a redefinition of romantic love: 'That is what love is. Not to kiss the hand of your sweetie (which is even disgusting to say), but to reveal your soul to each other, to verify your thoughts with the other's thoughts, to think together, to feel together' (lx. 140; 1856). These letters, written to his first beloved, represent one of Tolstoy's earliest attempts to clarify for himself what he meant by 'true love'.

To share his feelings and thoughts with Valériya, however, Tolstoy chooses a mode of indirection: he turns his epistolary instruction into a story of two fictional characters, Mr Khrapovitskóy and Miss Dembítskaya, who are now married. 'Khrapovitskóy, a man morally old, who did a lot of stupid things in his youth which he has paid for with the happiness of the best years of his life and who has now found for himself a path and vocation in literature, detests in his soul the *social world*, adores the quiet, moral, family life, and fears nothing in

[1] L. N. Tolstoi, *Polnoe sobranie sochinenii* (Complete Works), 90 vols. (Moscow, 1928–58), lx. 122. Henceforth all citations from Tolstoy's non-fiction (unless otherwise indicated) will be given parenthetically from this edition, the roman numeral referring to the volume, the first arabic number to the page, and the second to the date, e.g. lx. 140; 1856.

the world like the dissipated social life in which all good, honest, and pure feelings and thoughts get lost and in which you become a slave of social conventions and creditors' (lx. 108; 1856). Miss Dembítskaya enters the marriage with a different experience of life: 'For her happiness is a ball, bare shoulders, a carriage, diamonds, and the acquaintance of adjutant-generals and gentlemen of the chamber.' In the marriage these differences will have to be worked out. While the letters admit to the author's moral weaknesses, the focus is on the changes she will need to make. 'Mrs Khrapovitskáya will pursue music and reading and, sharing Mr Khrapovitskóy's plans, she will help him in his main occupation' (lx. 118; 1856). The goal is peaceful family life in the country, safely cut off from the treacherous social whirl and devoted to her moral development and his work.

Family Happiness retells this story not from the man's but the woman's point of view and after Tolstoy himself has come to a more complex sense of the quest for happiness. 'I feel ridiculous when I remember how I used to think that I could construct for myself a happy and honest little world in which I could live quietly, peacefully without mistakes, repentance, or confusion and without haste could accurately do only good. Ridiculous! *Impossible* . . . Just as it is *impossible* to be healthy without moving, without motion. To live honestly one has to strain, get confused, fight, make mistakes, begin and give it up, again begin and again give it up, and eternally struggle and be deprived' (lx. 231; 1857). This quest he gives to Másha, the fictional version of the fictional Miss Dembítskaya, just as he bequeaths his former illusions to Sergéy Mikháylych, the fictional version of the fictional Mr Khrapovitskóy.

Family Happiness opens with the 17-year-old Másha in a state of crisis. Her mother has just died and, her father being long dead, she is now an orphan in a home filled with the 'horror of death' (p. 3). Nothing matters: 'I felt that my whole life was bound to go on in the same loneliness and helpless dreariness, from which I had myself no strength and even no wish to escape.' Most Tolstoyan heroes are orphans like Másha (and like Tolstoy himself), and most come to some moment of existential crisis and despair, which urges them out of their isolation and onto a quest for meaning. But while the male characters, such as Pierre Bezúkhov and Prince Andréy in *War and Peace*, Lévin in *Anna Karénina*, and Prince Nekhlyudov in *Resurrection*, move toward the discovery of moral and religious truths, the female characters like Natásha in *War and Peace* and Kitty in *Anna Karénina* are destined to seek meaning in 'family happiness'. Másha emerges from her state of 'dejection, loneliness, and simple boredom' only when her guardian, an old friend of her father's, the stodgy bachelor Sergéy Mikháylych begins to visit. Now a possible suitor, he reintroduces her to the world of nature and art, and the sounds of music and burgeoning nature (depicted in sumptuous detail) accompany her return to life and love.

Like the fictional Miss Dembítskaya and Mr Khrapovitskóy from the letters, Másha and Sergéy Mikháylych live in worlds apart, she with fantasies of Byronic heroes from the urban social set and the romance of being swept away, he with settled ideas of country living and family values. Sergéy Mikháylych rejects the romantic view of love: 'A man seems to think that whenever he says the word, something will go pop!—that some miracle will be worked, signs and wonders, with all the big guns firing at once! In my opinion . . . whoever solemnly brings out the words "I love you" is either deceiving himself or, which is even worse, deceiving others' (p. 23). And Másha cannot accept this: 'Let him say "I love you", say it in plain words; let him take my hand in his and bend over it and say "I love you." Let him blush and look down before me; and then I will tell him all' (p. 28). So, like Mr Khrapovitskóy, Sergéy Mikháylych begins his instruction. With its focus on the woman's point of view, however, *Family Happiness* tells the story of Másha's attempts to conform to Sergéy's ideals, even as she hides from her own youthful fantasies. In her pursuit of his ideals Másha has a telling experience in church. Like Natásha in *War and Peace*, in church she comes to a sense of love for all. But Másha, who is after all very young and insecure, also discovers a 'whole new world, out of his reach and beyond his comprehension' which allows her to feel 'equal' to Sergéy (p. 31). She announces her love to him, and soon they are married, Másha believing they are of one mind and heart.

While just before the wedding she has her doubts, and after the ceremony she wonders 'Is this all?', Másha rides off to her new life feeling that she is 'wholly his' and 'happy in his power over me' (p. 44). With these words, which close Part I, Másha makes clear that she sees her romance as a struggle for power.

This struggle for power contaminates the marriage. Másha, who has no clear sense of self or purpose separate from her husband, rebels against Sergéy's rigid mode of life in their 'little world of frantic happiness' (p. 47).

> To love him was not enough for me after the happiness I had felt in falling in love. I wanted movement and not a calm course of existence. I wanted excitement and danger and the chance to sacrifice myself for my love. I felt in myself a superabundance of energy which found no outlet in our quiet life. (p. 50)

Like Anna Karénina, Másha 'wants to live'. So they move to St Petersburg, and Másha enters society where she feels herself 'the centre around which everything revolved' (p. 57). Sergéy is bored, Másha enthralled, and the struggle for domination leads to quarrels. Both become discontented and isolated. Their love fades into a sense of its failings. As later in *Anna Karénina* this psychology of failed love is represented as a complex state of guilt and resentment, projection and recrimination. Then during a summer spent in Baden Másha encounters an Italian marquis who makes an explicitly erotic pass at her: 'A feeling new to me, half horror and half pleasure, sent an icy shiver down my back' (p. 71). Tolstoy presents this central moment in a characteristic close-up:

> His liquid blazing eyes, right up against my face, stared strangely at me, at my neck and breast; both his hands fingered my arm above the wrist; his parted lips were saying that he loved me, and that I was all the world to him; and those lips were coming nearer and nearer, and those hands were squeezing mine harder and harder and burning me. A fever ran through my veins, my sight grew dim, I trembled, and the words intended to check him died in my throat. Suddenly I felt a kiss on my cheek. (p. 72)

Másha rejects this passion, but in the experience of the urge to live the life erotic she shares the archetypal Tolstoyan moment of female crisis with Natásha and Princess Mary in *War and*

Peace and Kitty, Dolly, and of course Anna in *Anna Karénina*. She rejects the life of the flesh (and hence all living for self) and returns, chastened, to her husband. They move back to the family estate where Másha recalls her former youthful love, now lost for ever. She discovers that she does not have 'a lover any longer but an old friend', who is the 'father of my children' (p. 84). Her former romantic ecstasies are replaced by her motherly rapture at the sight of her young Ványa: 'Mine, mine, mine.' Her sense of power and possession has been transferred from lover to child. With this 'my romance with my husband ended'. The 'new life and . . . quite different happiness' Másha finds in the end turns out to be not so different from Sergéy's original ideal. It has not been simple and both he and Másha have had to struggle, but he has instructed her well.

Family Happiness is Tolstoy's first attempt to write against the tradition of the novel of romance, marriage, and adultery, well represented by Flaubert's *Madame Bovary* published two years earlier. In general Tolstoy tended to connect the genre of the novel with the theme of romantic love, in part probably because in Russian the word 'novel' (*roman*) is also the word for 'romance'. When Másha says at the close of the work that 'my romance with my husband ended', one can read this as a generic inscription, for *Family Happiness* is a female *Bildungsroman* similar in narratological structure to Dickens's *Great Expectations* published a year later. It was composed, however, against the new ideas about women, sexuality, and the family that were taking shape in Europe at that time. These ideas were given specific expression in Russia four years later by Tolstoy's exact contemporary Nikoláy Chernyshévski (1828–89) who argued in his novel *What Is To Be Done* (1863) for a rational but sexual love freed from the strictures of marriage and dependence. *War and Peace* responded several years later with its conservative view of the 'woman question', and *Anna Karénina* can be read as novel written against the tradition of the novel of romance, marriage, and adultery. In his well-known tract *What Is Art?* (1896), Tolstoy traced the development of Western art from the Middle Ages to the present as a story of the loss of the 'infinite, varied and profound religious subject matter proper to it,' and the art of the nineteenth century he saw dominated by the 'feeling of sexual desire' which he believed had become 'an essential feature of every art product of the wealthy classes' and most particularly of the novel.[2] Tolstoy firmly believed that woman's great calling was to motherhood, which he considered the noble vocation of raising the next generation. By no means innocent of sexual desire or experience, however, Tolstoy himself was fearful of the power of eros, which he perceived as a threat to his freedom and control. In his fiction children seem to be of virgin birth, and sexual expression tends to be destructive. The older he grew, the more he spoke out against sexuality and the tendency to confuse the idea of 'true love' with romantic, erotic attraction. In the last two decades of his life, in response to the new ideas, he preached an ideal of chastity even in marriage. These ideas and this ideal are brought to the fore in the brilliantly strident and provocative *The Kreutzer Sonata*.

Tolstoy's life can be seen as a process of greater and greater articulation of self, of identity and vocation. He did not just live, but subjected his life to constant analysis and evaluation. He kept a diary obsessively from the age of 19. The general pattern is clear: he moved from life experience to literary image to philosophical idea. The image and the idea are usually closely related, as the process of writing *Family Happiness* makes clear and as *War and Peace* with its increasing number of philosophical 'digressions' illustrates. This process of articulation is also seen in Tolstoy's obsessive recasting of his ideas, ever attempting to find the precise statement of the perceived truth. The 'Afterword' to *The Kreutzer Sonata*, published in conjunction with the novella for the first time in English in this volume, exemplifies this urge toward clear articulation. The novella explores many of Tolstoy's ideas and concerns about sexuality, romance, the status of women, the institution of marriage, and the moral issues inherent in the social structure of his times, all expounded and explored from the vantage-point of his most peculiar hero. But already before he

[2] L. N. Tolstoy, *What Is Art?* (Indianapolis, 1960), 71–5. Henceforth all quotations from this work will be given parenthetically.

completed the story, Tolstoy felt the need to state his philosophical view related to these issues more precisely. The literary image does not so much embody this understanding as presuppose it. To perceive Tolstoy's artistry in the creation of his didactic fiction, one must confront the presuppositions on which it rests.

Tolstoy's metaphysics, like that of his younger contemporary the philosopher Vladímir Solovyóv (1853–1900), rests on an assumption of metaphysical total unity, a near pantheistic identity of the divine, human, and natural realms. In a Neoplatonic manner this unity is seen as the higher and true reality, the spiritual ideal toward which this fallen world is to strive. Every human being partakes of both this ideal world and this fallen, real world; for Tolstoy the human being has both an 'animal, personal, individual self', which he understands as a mode of 'living for self', and a 'true, divine common self', which he understands as a mode of 'living for all'. 'The human being as an animal being', what he often called a 'personality' (*líchnost'*), 'is subject to the law of struggle [for existence] and sexual striving to increase the species, but as a rational, loving, divine being he is subject to the opposite law' (li. 43; 1896). The animal self lives by sexual love for one or many, the divine self lives by spiritual love for all. The purpose of life is to clarify identity by subordinating the personality to the divine self, Tolstoy's version of that salvation the Eastern Christian tradition calls 'deification'. The 'ideal' represented by Christ's teaching as understood by Tolstoy is believed to be directly available to the clarified reason of the divine self of every human being. This is the 'ideal' of the Kingdom of God on earth, the harmonious togetherness of all in spiritual love, the attainment of which is the vocation of all. The argument of the 'Afterword', presented in the clear, step-by-step logical analysis Tolstoy wields so well, is that this ideal cannot truly be approached until the present sexual arrangement known as marriage is transformed, along with the whole sexual politics and economy that flow from the assumptions about men and women inherent in this arrangement. This transformation Tolstoy cannot imagine without the elimination of sexuality itself, which for him, given his metaphysical assumptions, is the root cause of the inequities he so clearly sees. What must be borne in mind when evaluating Tolstoy's position on sexuality is what he stresses in this essay, that an ideal is not a rule of behaviour strictly speaking, but a guide to give us direction. The prohibition against sexual expression may in our age seem extreme, even as it did in Tolstoy's time. Indeed the novella, with its explicit reference to sexuality and its extreme position, was first prohibited by the censors and then printed in an early form of *sámizdat*; it was officially published only after Tolstoy's wife pleaded personally with the Tsar. However we may now assess Tolstoy's ideas, as a minimum we can hear the pain in his voice.

This painful voice dominates *The Kreutzer Sonata* (1889). Like *Family Happiness*, written thirty years earlier, this story is also told as a first-person narrative. But in this work there are as it were two voices, a first and faceless narrator who is a fellow-traveller on the train where the primary action of the story takes place and a second narrator who is the central figure in the work and whose spoken words the first narrator quotes verbatim. Thus this novella gives us the effect of both a third-person and first-person narration, a description of the central figure and the context of the world in which he is found on the one hand and, on the other, the unreliable telling of a figure whose point of view we have to discover from his own words. These words, we learn early on, express the views of a person who, like Másha, now knows the truth, but who, unlike Másha, has learned this truth too late, as his name Pózdnyshev (*pózdnyi* means 'late') implies.

We meet Pózdnyshev in a characteristic Tolstoyan manner in the midst of a conversation about love. A pious old merchant of the Old Believer persuasion regales his clerk with tales of orgies during the good old days. A young lawyer and his modern, emancipated-woman friend (she smokes and wears 'mannish' clothes) discuss a divorce. This leads to an extended four-way conversation about marriage and divorce, love and romance, the politics of the male–female relationship. The old merchant believes in the subordination of the wife to the husband as a way of controlling the 'leaky vessel' (p. 89). He seems to uphold the principle of arranged marriages, and disparages modern education which he believes has introduced the idea of romantic love as a method for the selection of a marriage partner. His position is strict and internally consistent, even as it indulges the male at the expense of the female. The lawyer and his emancipated-woman friend enjoy no such consistency. The woman believes that romantic love, the capacity for which is what distinguishes humans from animals, sanctifies marriage, even as she seems to believe that the loss of this 'true love' justifies divorce (p. 91). At this point Pózdnyshev enters the conversation with his cutting questions: 'What is meant by "true love"' and 'if true love is a preference for another above all others, then for how long?' In the Tolstoyan scheme, of course, 'true love' is not a temporary preference for another or just some others, which can after all be found among dogs and other animals, but the ever expansive outgoing from the divine self to all that leads to the Kingdom of God. Tolstoy dismisses the modern argument by capturing the voice of the lawyer who restates his friend's point: 'She means . . . that in the first place marriage must be the outcome of attachment—of love, if you please—and only where that exists is marriage sacred, so to speak. Secondly, that marriage when not based on natural attachment—love, if you prefer the word—lacks the element that makes it morally binding.' This discussion thus outlines the social and intellectual context in which Pózdnyshev's experience must be placed. The old-world, patriarchal, and religious understanding of marriage and the modern, professional, and secular conception of romantic love are not adequate notions to deal with the relationship of the sexes in the modern world, let alone Tolstoy's exalted conception of 'true love'.

In the course of this dialogue on love the lawyer's fatuous statements send Pózdnyshev off on a tirade against modern marriages which in the extreme, he insists, can lead to suicide and murder. When the lawyer agrees that indeed there are such 'critical episodes', however, Pózdnyshev takes this as a statement of discovery: 'I see you have found out who I am' (p. 94). This is most telling. Of course we later learn that Pózdnyshev has killed his wife, but the lawyer does not know this. Rather Pózdnyshev projects this onto him, as he later consistently projects his inner experience onto others. Pózdnyshev claims that although he is 'a ruin, a cripple', still he has one advantage, he 'knows what others are far from knowing' (p. 121). But what he knows, often expressed in hyperbolical statistical terms or in meandering tirades that keep losing the point, is generated from his own isolation. He is a man wrapped up in himself, obsessed with his suffering and guilt, then and now. This obsession comes from the pain of his experience and colours all that he knows and says. What follows the dialogue on love is a series of tormenting tirades, now addressed to the faceless narrator, who keeps reminding us of Pózdnyshev's agitated, intoxicated state. The significance of this state Pózdnyshev understands in the manner of Tolstoy in his article 'Why Do Men Stupefy Themselves' published a year after this story: 'For man both salvation and punishment lie in the fact that if he lives wrongly he can befog himself so as not to see the misery of his position' (p. 126). Pózdnyshev is a ruined man hiding from the misery of his position. The tirades and later Pózdnyshev's verbal re-enactment of the 'critical episode' do not relieve him of his pained guilt, and like the Ancient Mariner, he seems destined to retell his story:

> I have strange power of speech;
> I pass, like night, from land to land,
> That moment that his face I see,
> I know the man that must hear me:
> To him my tale I teach.

Pózdnyshev is convinced that his life has been ruined by his obsession with sex. This obsession, he now believes, began with his first encounter with a prostitute, after which the divorce of sexual expression from human commitment and responsibility turned chronic. He became addicted: 'I became what is called a lecher. To be a lecher is a physical condition like that of a morphine addict, a drunkard, or a smoker' (p. 98). Sex was now the motivation for everything he did. But Pózdnyshev with characteristic hyperbolic projection also claims that in this he was not alone. Everyone in society was and is obsessed with sex. Social customs, cultural values, and industrial production all serve this ever-present, ever-needful urge to copulate. He looks at his wife or at his 'rival' and all he sees is a lurking id. This is what he 'knows'.

Pózdnyshev also believes he is not responsible for his addiction. This is what they taught me, it's good for your health, and everyone does it. Thus Pózdnyshev sees himself as an addict whose addiction is caused by others. He is simultaneously obsessed with his own actions and paranoic of what others do to him. He tells the story of his failed relationship through the filter of his peculiar version of that psychology of guilt and resentment we saw in *Family Happiness*. At one moment he wonders in resentment why his wife did not leave him and in the next moment guiltily claims that it is better that way, 'it serves me right' (p. 101). He is both victim and victimizer, and this dualistic sense of self colours his vision of the world where everyone is simultaneously oppressor and oppressed. Women are traps or bait on a hook, but they are also slaves at an auction (p. 104). In this they resemble the Jews who 'pay us back for their oppression by financial domination' (p. 105). Later, when he tells the story of his wife's alleged infidelity, he portrays both his wife and his rival as the seducer and the seduced. The whole logic of his tirades and his tale is based on this splintered vision of a world in which everyone is both evil and justified.

Pózdnyshev's tale of the 'critical episode' is significant for the manner of its telling. As the story increases, the faceless narrator takes note of Pózdnyshev's ever-increasing agitation, marked by his continuous smoking and consumption of tea, 'really like beer' (p. 95). This agitation, accompanied by the agitating movement of the train, builds to a climax as Pózdnyshev shifts from his tirades to his tale midway through the story (p. 127). The culmination of this tale commences when Pózdnyshev begins his narration of his train ride home on his way to the murder:

That eight-hour journey in a railway carriage was something horrible, which I shall never forget all my life. . . . from the moment I sat down in the train I could no longer control my imagination, and with extraordinary vividness which inflamed my jealousy it painted incessantly, one after another, pictures of what had gone on in my absence, of how she had been false to me. I burnt with indignation, anger, and a peculiar feeling of intoxication with my own humiliation, as I gazed at those pictures. . . . The vividness with which they presented themselves to me seemed to serve as proof that what I imagined was real. (p. 149)

From this moment on the time of the two train rides seems to merge, and Pózdnyshev re-experiences his original experience of the 'critical episode'. In this he ironically resembles the Tolstoyan artist as defined in *What Is Art?*: 'To evoke in oneself a feeling one has once experienced, and, having evoked it in oneself, then, by means of movements, lines, colors, sounds, or forms expressed in words, so to transmit that feeling that others may experience the same feeling—this is the activity of art' (p. 51). For Pózdnyshev this artistic expression seems to have no cathartic effect, but the aesthetic character of his endeavour is significant. It surfaces in the very title of the work.

This title refers to a turning-point in Pózdnyshev's tale of the 'critical episode', the performance of Beethoven's 'Kreutzer Sonata' by his wife and his 'rival'. Pózdnyshev's experience of this peformance leads him to a theory of music which is a key to his dilemma:

Music is a terrifying thing! . . . Music makes me forget myself, my real position; it transports me to some other position not my own. Under the influence of music it seems to me that I feel what I do not really feel, that I understand what I do not understand, that I can do what I cannot do. . . . Music carries me immediately and directly into the mental condition of the man who composed it. My soul merges with his and together with him I pass from one condition into another, but why this happens I don't know. (p. 144)

As in his addiction to sex and his intoxication through cigarettes and strong tea, with music Pózdnyshev loses touch with 'his real position'. Under the influence of the performance he sees the whole affair in a 'new light': 'I felt light-hearted and cheerful the whole evening.' The terrible jealousy which has disfigured his sense of reality and his image of his wife lifts and he feels 'satisfied'. Now this may well be the appropriate response to this performance, and Pózdnyshev's jealousy may be quite unfounded; given the mode of narration, we cannot know except as Pózdnyshev knows. But to Pózdnyshev such a view is untenable, for he needs his wife's affair in order to justify the 'misery of his position'. When he rereads his wife's letter, the filter of jealousy is restored and Pózdnyshev is ready to bring his rage to its murderous conclusion.

The irony of Pózdnyshev's self-serving theory of music, and the key to why this musical performance provides the title to the work, is that the theory resembles Tolstoy's. In *What Is Art?* Tolstoy argued that the effect of art is union:

> A real work of art destroys, in the consciousness of the perceiver, the separation between himself and the artist—not that alone, but also between himself and all whose minds perceive this work of art. In this freeing of our personality from its separation and isolation, in this uniting of it with others, lies the chief characteristic and the great attractive force of art. (p. 140)

> Sometimes people who find themselves together are if not hostile then alien to each other in mood and feeling till perchance a story, a performance, a picture, or even a building, but most often of all music, unites them all as by an electric flash, and in place of their former isolation or even enmity they are all conscious of union and mutual love. Each is glad that the other feels what he feels, glad of the communion established not only between him and all present, but also with all now living who will yet share the same impression, and more than that, he feels the mysterious gladness of a communion which, reaching beyond the grave, unites us with all people of the past who have been moved by the same feelings, and with all people of the future who will yet be touched by them. (pp. 150–1)

For Tolstoy the experience of art functions as the rite of communion in his religion of salvation through love for all. For Pózdnyshev this experience threatens his deep-seated need for isolation and hostility. Pózdnyshev cannot reach his 'real position', which in Tolstoyan terms is experienced through harmony with others. He truly is 'a ruin, a cripple', then and now. *The Kreutzer Sonata*, therefore, is not a story of a conversion or a narration by the converted. It is a painful tale told by a man who has learned too late the 'misery' of our position. Like a Tolstoyan artist he can re-experience his experience, but he cannot overcome his separation and isolation from others. His journey of discovery ends as does his 'story' (*rasskáz*) with no certain sense of forgiveness.

*

In his attempt to articulate his idea of 'true love', Tolstoy in his later years came to the conclusion that the love for others which has a certain guarantee that there is in it no hidden form of love for self can best be found in love for one's enemy. He pressed this idea, along with the prohibition against murder, into a strict argument against all war. As with his ideas about romance and marriage, this later anti-war theory had its origin in early experience. During his twenties Tolstoy spent four years in military service in the Caucasus and the Crimea. In the Caucasus he fought against the Chechéns and during the Crimean War he took part in the famous battle at Sevastopol in 1855. A number of his early short stories reflect the moral issues raised by these experiences: the romantic vision of war and heroes versus the reality of suffering and death, the significance of the masculine cult of bravery, and in general the absurdity of war. But unlike the epic *War and Peace* with its vision of the patriotic defence against the invading foreign enemy, these early stories tell of the imperialist Russian army occupying a territory inhabited by various alien but indigenous people. *The Cossacks* (1863) focuses on the experiences of one young Russian man in this alien territory, even as it explores again the Tolstoyan theme of love.

This 'Tale (*povest'*) of 1852' opens, like *The Kreutzer Sonata*, with the beginning of a journey and a discussion of love. In the small hours of the morning, as the working classes are rising for their day of labour, three young gentlemen friends are lounging about over the remains of a farewell dinner for Dmítri Andréich Olénin, a 24-year-old cadet who is leaving Moscow for the Caucasus. Olénin stands accused of a failure to love: a relationship in which he was loved by a young woman but could not reciprocate has just come to an end. His friend thinks that 'to be loved is . . . as great a happiness as to love, and if a man obtains it, it is enough for his whole life', but Olénin wonders 'why shouldn't one love' too? (p. 179). While Olénin feels guilty for what he perceives as his failure, his friend assesses the situation objectively: 'The fact is that you have not yet loved and do not know what love is.' Olénin, however, insists that he has a 'desire to love' and that 'nothing could be stronger than that desire', even as he wonders if 'such love

[does] exist'. He departs for the Caucasus, therefore, on a journey to discover love.

Since the publication of Púshkin's 'tale' 'The Prisoner of the Caucasus' in 1822, the Caucasus had become the favourite geographical location for the Russian literary exploration of the other in its orientalist guise. For the Romantic writers the mountainous region tended to be represented as a 'space for the therapeutic uses of the lyrical Russian self' whose encounter with nature, often imaged in the feminine, entailed spiritual uplift and passionate love.[3] The brutalities of the Russian conquest of the area, which had begun in the mid-sixteenth century under Iván IV and was especially intense in the first half of the nineteenth century, tended to be erased in favour of the pursuit of the exotic and the erotic. The native inhabitants, usually marginalized, were conceived as Rousseauan noble savages, violent infidels, or inscrutable Asians. Mikhaíl Lérmontov (1814–41), who spent some time in the region and had significant knowledge of its inhabitants, depicted his hero Pechórin in *A Hero of our Times* (1840) as someone who has gone native, adopting the Chechén mores of violence and commerce in women, even as he hopes for a revived spirit and harmony with nature.[4] Tolstoy writes within and against this tradition. His text quickly turns away from his hero's departure to five chapters in which the reader encounters the Cossacks. In the spirit of his times, but not of Púshkin's or Lérmontov's, Tolstoy gives precise and abundant geographical and sociological detail. He evokes this world not only by describing it, but by incorporating into his Russian text many local words, some of which he defined in footnotes. The place is demystified and deromanticized. We are presented with specific scenes depicting the characteristic behaviour and concerns of the Cossacks, represented by the figures who will play a role in the subsequent tale. These scenes play against the stereotypes. The Cossack women share concerns for the marriage of their daughters not so different from their Moscovite counter-

[3] Susan Layton, *Russian Literature and Empire: Conquest of the Caucasus from Pushkin to Tolstoy* (Cambridge, 1994), 52.
[4] Ibid. 216–21.

parts. Daddy Eróshka, who styles himself a representative of the glorious golden days of Cossackdom and speaks with his own linguistic tics (as do Vanyúsha, Belétski, and Elias Vasílich), turns out to be a complex psychological figure and a highly ambiguous version of a Rousseauan natural man. He is not inappropriately coupled with the civilized Russian hero Olénin. Entitled *The Cossacks*, Tolstoy's 'Tale of 1852' actually attempts a realistic picture of their world.

Derived from the Turkic word for 'vagrant' or 'wanderer', the word 'Cossack' originally referred to Turkish or Tatar brigands who wandered the steppes of fourteenth-century Muscovy. Soon hired as mercenaries, these Cossacks quickly found their mythic role in Russian culture as defenders of the Tsar. With time, homeless and disenfranchised eastern Slavic peoples, peasants, criminals, and adventurers, formed themselves into free Cossack communities at the borders of the growing empire, often intermingling with the local Turkic and Tatar peoples. They settled along the rivers, first the Dnieper, then the Volga and the Don, later in the Ural Mountains along the Iaik (Ural) and in the Caucasus along the Térek. By the beginning of the nineteenth century the Cossacks had become loyal vanguard soldiers of the Tsar and self-appointed defenders of Russian Orthodoxy against the Poles and Jews in the Ukrainian territories and against the Islamic peoples in the Caucasus. In 1851 Tolstoy, who had abandoned his study of Caucasian languages at Kazan University six years earlier, found himself among the Grebénsk Cossacks, a settlement located across the Térek from alien Chechnyá. These Grebénsk Cossacks shared the Chechén ethos of war, could communicate in their language, borrowed the term *dzhigít* ('warrior') for themselves, and wore the same type of tall sheepskin hat and outer coat (*cherkéska*). *The Cossacks* is set in this culturally mixed zone which intersects Orthodox Russia and Muslim Chechnyá, and its hero Olénin encounters the exotic other through the liminal mediation of the Cossacks. The focus of the tale, however, remains on Olénin and his quest for love.

The central moment in this quest occurs on a hunting expedition. Lying in a stag's lair ('stag' is *olén'* in Russian), Olénin was 'suddenly . . . overcome by such a strange feeling of causeless joy and of love for everything, that from an old habit of his childhood he began crossing himself and thanking someone' (p. 260). This moment of grace reveals to him 'suddenly, with extraordinary clarity' that he, Dmítri Olénin, is 'a being quite distinct from every other being'. He is like the millions of mosquitoes buzzing around him who are 'each one of them . . . just such a Dmítri Olénin separate from all as I am myself', and like them 'I shall live awhile and die.' This discovery of existential identity and vocation casts him into a moral crisis: 'Never mind what I am—an animal like all the rest, above whom the grass will grow and nothing more, or a frame in which a bit of the one God has been set—still I must live in the very best way. How then must I live to be happy, and why was I not happy before?' The solution rests in his discovery that 'happiness lies in living for others', and he leaves the lair in pursuit of a life of love understood as self-sacrifice. In this he bumps up against the more down-to-earth attitudes of the Cossack Lukáshka, who views Olénin's attempts to put this ethic of self-sacrifice into practice with bewildered and bemused suspicion.

Tolstoy links this existential and moral layer of his tale with the established Romantic topos of the erotic encounter with an exotic Oriental beauty. Olénin takes a fancy to Lukáshka's girl Maryánka, and much of the story revolves around Olénin's tortured pursuit of this beautiful young Cossack woman. Prince Belétski serves as Olénin's foil, showing how the untroubled Russian soldier behaves; Lukáshka and his friends understand him and like him. But Olénin cannot find happiness in flirtation and parties. He wants to love. In the culminating moment of this erotic pursuit, Olénin writes a letter, never sent, in which he describes the love he now at last has experienced:

> This is not the ideal, the so-called exalted love which I have known before, not that feeling of attraction in which you admire your own love, feel that the source of your emotion is within yourself, and do everything yourself. I have felt that too. It is still less a desire for pleasure. It is something different. Perhaps in her I love nature, the personification of all that is beautiful in nature. Yet I am not acting by

my own will, but some elemental force loves her through me; the whole of God's world, all nature, presses this love into my soul and says, 'Love her.' I love her not with my mind or my imagination, but with my whole being. Loving her I feel myself to be an integral part of all God's joyous world. (p. 312)

This love, at bottom too metaphysical and too private, Olénin cannot realize. When shortly thereafter Lukáshka is seriously wounded in a battle with the Chechéns, Maryánka ceases her girlish flirtations with Olénin, who then immediately departs. What Olénin learns on this journey may not be clear, but in his quest he develops from a man who has not truly loved to one who pursues a moralistic love of self-sacrifice for others only to find a more exalted, almost mystical sense of some 'elemental force', 'the whole of God's world' directing his will to love 'all that is beautiful in nature' and thereby making him feel himself 'an integral part of all God's joyous world'. In this quest he resembles his creator, Leo Tolstoy.

In *The Cossacks* the social and political realities of life in the mid-nineteenth-century Caucasus are subordinated to the focus on the private experience of Olénin and the realistic representation of life in the Cossack settlement. The local Caucasian people are part of the background, the Nogáy women or the Chechén enemy *abréks*, but there is little attempt to enter into their world or place their experience in its historical context. Forty years later Tolstoy returned to his experience in the Caucasus and now, with his heightened sense of human solidarity and his more realistic awareness of Russian imperialism, he wrote a very different work. *Hadji Murád* is a tragic story of the conflicting loyalties that emerge from the complex religious and political life of the native peoples of the Caucasus in the mid-nineteenth century, and that are still evident in the hostilities of the 1990s. After the annexation of Georgia in 1810, the Russians initiated a concerted compaign finally to gain control over the rebellious Muslim peoples of Chechnyá and Dagestan. In 1816 General A. P. Ermólov was appointed commander-in-chief of the Russian forces in the area. Two years later he began his 'pacification' programme, which consisted of the destruction of villages, theft of cattle and goods, clear-cutting of forests, and the resettlement of the people. This attempt at 'pacification' elicited an anti-colonialist reaction from the neighbouring Muslim powers, Persia and Turkey, whom the Russians engaged in battle in the Russo-Persian War of 1826–8 and the Russo-Turkish War of 1828–9. The end result was the uneasy subjugation of Chechnyá and Dagestan to Russian rule and the rise of a militant nationalist-Islamic independence movement. In 1830 Kazi-Mulla, Imám of Chechnyá and Dagestan, declared the first expedition (*ghazavát*) against the Russians. General G. V. Rosen, commander-in-chief of the Russians 1831–8, led the forces that killed Kazi-Mulla in 1832 and his successor, Hamzád-Bek, in 1834. Upon the death of Hamzád-Bek, Shamíl became Imám and served till his death in 1871. The story of Hadji Murád, a historical figure known to Tolstoy through contemporary published accounts, emerges from this political and religious context. As in *War and Peace* Tolstoy attempts to recreate this context from historical sources, some of which he quotes verbatim.

Hadji Murád is a framed narrative which opens with the narrator returning home through the fields. Much of the frame is devoted to a characteristically detailed nature description designed to give a sense of the variety and vitality of the natural world. On the way through the field the narrator encounters two different thistle plants, of the type known as 'Tatar'. The first he picks for a bouquet and in the process displaces and destroys, the second he sees has survived despite the recent ploughing. This encounter with a 'Tatar' seen as unique and vital as long as it is in its place and determined to hold on to life there in its place triggers the narrator's memory of an 'episode' which he had 'partly seen myself, partly heard of from eye-witnesses, and partly imagined'. The 'episode' that follows takes on a symbolic character, for it tells a historical tale about the human violation of the natural. It reflects Tolstoy's deep respect for indigenous cultures and alien faiths, a respect already latent in the realistic narratological technique used in *The Cossacks*.

The frame that surrounds the recollected 'episode' marks the uniqueness of the form of this novella. Unlike Másha's 'romance' in *Family Happiness* narrated as a first-person *Bildungsroman*, Pózdnyshev's 'story' told in his own words quoted by the narrator of *The Kreutzer Sonata*, or the reworked Romantic 'tale' of Olénin in *The Cossacks*, the inscribed generic marker in *Hadji Murád* does not refer to a literary genre as such. An 'episode' (*istoriya*) is a sequence of events that happened in the past. There are two ordering principles that structure Tolstoy's literary version of this recollected 'episode'. The 'episode' is not designed to explore the development of Hadji Murád's character, as one would expect from a Tolstoyan novel. Rather the character is shown in his complexity, from different angles. To achieve this effect, Tolstoy consciously adopted what was for him a new method of characterization: 'There is an English toy called a peepshow—now one thing, now another is shown through a glass. That is how the man Hadji Murád must be shown, as husband, fanatic, etc.' (liii. 188; 1898). Coupled with this peepshow construction of character, Tolstoy used the device of parallelism that plays such a major role in his novels. The organization of the material is determined not only by the sequence of events, but by representation of parallel figures or situations: Nicholas I and Shamíl, Avdéev and Sado in their family milieu, the deaths of Avdéev and Hadji Murád. These parallelisms help to underline the similarities and differences in attitudes toward patriotism, loyalty, power, war, death, family, and love, which comprise the major thematic focus of the work. The text of this 'episode' thus strives simultaneously for complexity and uniqueness of character and universality of experience, toward realism and emblematic statement.

Just as *Hadji Murád* opens with the narrator's recollection of the 'episode' of many years ago which he then retells, so the whole work is reminiscent of Tolstoy's early war stories and especially *War and Peace*. The representation of Butler entering battle, for example, recalls Nicholas Rostóv's youthful war enthusiasm: 'He was filled with a buoyant sense of the joy of living, the danger of death, a wish for action, and the consciousness of being part of an immense whole directed by a single will' (p. 424). Like the great epic novel, *Hadji Murád* juxtaposes the military and civilian worlds and mixes historical figures drawn from published accounts with the fictional characters drawn from Tolstoy's personal experience of war in the Caucasus. Furthermore, the depiction of Nicholas I recalls the figure of Napoleon in *War and Peace*: 'he no longer saw his own inconsistencies or measured his actions and words by reality, logic, or even simple common sense; but was quite convinced that all his orders, however senseless, unjust, and mutually contradictory they might be, became reasonable, just, and mutually accordant simply because he gave them' (p. 418). Also like Napoleon, whose famous hat Nicholas claims to be rivalled by his own famous cloak, Nicholas I is represented as a man of the flesh:

> his enormous body—with his overgrown stomach tightly laced in—was thrown back, and he gazed at the newcomers with fixed, lifeless eyes. His long pale face, with its enormous receding forehead between the tufts of hair which were brushed forward and skilfully joined to the wig that covered his bald patch, was specially cold and stony that day. His eyes, always dim, looked duller than usual. The compressed lips under his upturned moustaches, the high collar which supported his chin, and his fat freshly shaven cheeks on which symmetrical sausage-shaped bits of whiskers had been left, gave his face a dissatisfied and even irate expression. (p. 413)

The striking parallels between these two figures, one the foreign ruler and the other the Russian Tsar, mark the different ideological and political visions of the two fictions.

Hadji Murád also shares with the earlier fiction the strategic depiction of death and dying. Tolstoy's narrator knows what the Russian officers in this work do not know or learn: 'None of them saw in this death that most important moment of a life, its termination and return to the source whence it sprang' (p. 366). In this work the moment of termination serves to reveal character and meaning. The death of Avdéev, told against the family environment from which he came, is a triumph of simple forgiveness and stoic nobility (pp. 377–83). Most telling in this regard is the death of Hadji Murád himself, which is represented in a dramatic flashback that ends the whole story. In Tolstoy the usual focus in these moments is psychological and moral, as with Avdéev or Iván Ilých. In the early work this could take the form of extended internal monologues, as in the death of Praskúkhin in *Sevastopol in May* or of the more metaphysical Prince Andréy in *War and Peace*. This technique is used in describing Hadji Murád:

> The wound in the side was fatal and he felt that he was dying. Memories and pictures succeeded one another with extraordinary rapidity in his imagination. Now he saw the powerful Abu Nutsal Khan, dagger in hand, and holding up his severed cheek, he rushed at his foe; then he saw the weak, bloodless old Vorontsóv with his cunning white face, and heard his soft voice; then he saw his son Yusúf, his wife Sofiát, and then the pale, red-bearded face of his enemy Shamíl with its half-closed eyes.
>
> All these images passed through his mind without evoking any feeling within him—neither pity nor anger nor any kind of desire: everything seemed so insignificant in comparison with what was beginning, or had already begun, within him. (p. 466)

But this moment is not the death of Hadji Murád. 'His strong body continued the thing that he had commenced.' He fells one of the enemy running towards him and climbs out of the ditch to finish the job. He is shot and falls. 'But the body that seemed to be dead suddenly moved. First the uncovered, bleeding, shaven head rose; then the body with hands holding to the trunk of a tree.' Hadji Murád staggers and falls again, now 'stretched out . . . like a thistle that had been mown down'. The action comes to an end with a gruesome, but Homeric picture of his corpse: 'Crimson blood spurted from the arteries of the neck, and black blood flowed from the head, soaking the grass' (p. 467). In the face of all his own theories of non-violence, Tolstoy in this last major work of fiction celebrates the dignity of righteous battle which he marks with the vital signs of his hero's body. To valorize the heroic feat, the historical 'episode' is placed in the expanse of nature: the events are presented under the stars and punctuated with the singing of the nightingales, and the central emblem of the work, the thistle called a 'Tatar', resurfaces to close the work. The telling of Hadji Murád's death is designed to capture not the metaphysical or religious significance of the moment, but the singular conviction, bravery, and loyal steadfastness of the hero determined to fight for his life and its meaning. In this struggle for a meaningful life, Hadji Murád resembles Másha, Olénin, and even Pózdnyshev, but most importantly he resembles his creator Leo Tolstoy.

NOTE ON THE TEXT

The stories in this edition were first published as follows: *Family Happiness* in 1859, *The Kreutzer Sonata* in 1889, *The Cossacks* in 1863, and *Hadji Murád* posthumously in 1912. J. D. Duff's translation of *Family Happiness* first appeared in 1924 together with Aylmer Maude's translation of *The Kreutzer Sonata*; *The Cossacks* and *Hadji Murád*, translated by Louise and Aylmer Maude, were first published in 1916 and 1935 respectively.

Aylmer Maude was personally acquainted with Tolstoy and he and his wife together translated most of his major work. Tolstoy often expressed his gratitude for their services, and their translations have achieved classic status. For this edition the translations have been correlated with the established Russian texts. Censored and omitted items have been restored, inconsistencies and errors corrected, and, when necessary, certain phrases and expressions have been modernized. English translation has rendered Tolstoy's ethnographic and linguistic footnotes to *The Cossacks* inappropriate; Tolstoy's definitions of local words have been incorporated where appropriate into the Glossary and marked 'LT'.

The 'Afterword to *The Kreutzer Sonata*' was translated by Robert Edwards and is reprinted here in a slightly reworked version from *Tolstoy Studies Journal*, 6 (1993), 111–21, with the kind permision of the translator and the editor.

SELECT BIBLIOGRAPHY

Bayley, John, *Tolstoy and the Novel* (London, 1966).

Berlin, Isaiah, *The Hedgehog and the Fox: An Essay on Tolstoy's View of History* (London, 1954).

Christian, R. F., *Tolstoy: A Critical Introduction* (Cambridge, 1969).

——(ed.), *Tolstoy's Letters*, 2 vols. (New York, 1978).

——(ed.), *Tolstoy's Diaries*, 2 vols. (New York, 1985).

Ciatati, Pietro, *Tolstoy*, trans. Raymond Rosenthal (New York, 1986).

Gifford, Henry (ed.), *Leo Tolstoy: A Critical Anthology* (Harmondsworth, 1971).

Gustafson, Richard F., *Leo Tolstoy, Resident and Stranger* (Princeton, 1986).

Hayman, Ronald, *Tolstoy* (New York, 1970).

Knowles, A. V., *Tolstoy: The Critical Heritage* (London, 1978).

Kornblatt, Judith Deutsch, *The Cossack Hero in Russian Literature* (Madison, 1992).

Layton, Susan, *Russian Literature and Empire: Conquest of the Caucasus from Pushkin to Tolstoy* (Cambridge, 1994).

Matlaw, Ralph E., *Tolstoy: A Collection of Critical Essays* (Englewood Cliffs, NJ, 1967).

Maude, Aylmer, *The Life of Tolstoy*, 2 vols. (London, 1929–30).

Merejkowski, Dmitri, *Tolstoy as Man and Artist, with an Essay on Dostoievski* (New York, 1902).

Moller, Peter Ulf, *Postlude to the Kreutzer Sonata* (Leiden, 1988).

Noyes, George Rapall, *Tolstoy* (New York, 1918).

Orwin, Donna Tussing, *Tolstoy's Art and Thought, 1847–1880* (Princeton, 1993).

Rolland, Romain, *The Life of Tolstoy*, trans. B. Miall (New York, 1911).

Seaton, Albert, *The Horsemen of the Steppes: The Story of the Cossacks* (London, 1985).

Shklovsky, Victor, *Leo Tolstoy*, trans. from Russian (Moscow, 1978).

Simmons, Ernest J., *Leo Tolstoy* (Boston, 1946).

——*Introduction to Tolstoy's Writings* (Chicago, 1968).

Troyat, Henri, *Tolstoy*, trans. Nancy Amphoux (Garden City, NY, 1967).

Wasiolek, Edward, *Tolstoy's Major Fiction* (Chicago, 1978).

Wilson, A. N., *Tolstoy* (London, 1988).

A CHRONOLOGY OF LEO TOLSTOY

1828 28 August (os): born at Yásnaya Polyána, province of Tula, fourth son of Count Nikoláy Tolstoy. Mother dies 1830, father 1837.

1844–7 Studies at University of Kazan (Oriental Languages, then Law). Leaves without graduating.

1851 Goes to Caucasus with elder brother. Participates in army raid on local village. Begins to write *Childhood* (pub. 1852).

1854 Commissioned. *Boyhood*.* Active service on Danube; gets posting to Sevastopol.

1855 After its fall returns to Petersburg, already famous for his first two *Sevastopol Sketches*. Literary and social life in the capital.

1856 Leaves army. *A Landlord's Morning*.

1857 Visits Western Europe. August: returns to Yásnaya Polyána.

1859 His interest and success in literature wane. Founds on his estate a school for peasant children. *Three Deaths*; *Family Happiness*.

1860–1 Second visit to Western Europe, in order to study educational methods.

1861 Serves as Arbiter of the Peace, to negotiate land settlements after Emancipation of Serfs.

1862 Death of two brothers. Marries Sophia Behrs, daughter of a Moscow physician. There were to be thirteen children of the marriage, only eight growing up. Publishes educational magazine *Yásnaya Polyána*.

1863 *The Cossacks*, *Polikúshka*. Begins *War and Peace*.

1865–6 *1805* (first part of *War and Peace*).

1866 Unsuccessfully defends at court martial soldier who had struck officer.

1869 *War and Peace* completed; final vols. published.

1870 Studies drama and Greek.

1871–2 Working on *Primer* for children.

1872 *A Prisoner in the Caucasus*.

1873 Goes with family to visit new estate in Samara. Publicizes Samara famine. Begins *Anna Karénina* (completed 1877).

1877 His growing religious problems. Dismay over Russo-Turkish War.

* Tolstoy's works are dated, unless otherwise indicated, according to the year of publication.

1879 Begins *A Confession* (completed 1882).
1881 Letter to new tsar asking for clemency towards assassins of Alexander II.
1882 *What Men Live By*. Begins *Death of Iván Ilých* and *What Then Must We Do?* (completed 1886).
1883 Meets Chertkóv, afterwards his leading disciple.
1885 Founds with Chertkóv's help the *Intermediary*, to publish edifying popular works, including his own stories. Vegetarian, gives up hunting.
1886 *The Death of Iván Ilých*. Writes play *The Power of Darkness*.
1889 *The Kreutzer Sonata* completed. Begins *Resurrection*.
1891–2 Organizes famine relief.
1893 *The Kingdom of God is Within You* pub. abroad.
1897 Begins *What is Art?* (pub. 1898) and *Hadji Murád*.
1899 *Resurrection*.
1901 Excommunicated from Orthodox Church. Seriously ill. In Crimea meets Chékhov and Górky.
1902 *What is Religion?* completed. Working on play *The Light Shineth in Darkness*.
1903 Denounces pogroms against Jews.
1904 *Shakespeare and the Drama* completed. Also *Hadji Murád* (pub. after his death). Pamphlet on Russo-Japanese War, *Bethink Yourselves!*
1906 Death of favourite daughter Másha. Increasing tension with wife.
1908 *I Cannot Be Silent*, opposing capital punishment. 28 August: celebrations for eightieth birthday.
1909 Frequent disputes with wife. Draws up will relinquishing copyrights. His secretary Gúsev arrested and exiled.
1910 Flight from home, followed by death at Astápovo railway station, 7 November (OS).

THE KREUTZER SONATA AND OTHER STORIES

FAMILY HAPPINESS

PART I

CHAPTER I

We were in mourning for my mother, who had died in the autumn, and I spent all that winter alone in the country with Kátya and Sónya.

Kátya was an old friend of the family, our governess who had brought us all up, and I had known and loved her since my earliest recollections. Sónya was my younger sister. It was a dark and sad winter which we spent in our old house at Pokróvskoe. The weather was cold and so windy that the snowdrifts came higher than the windows; the panes were almost always dimmed by frost, and we seldom walked or drove anywhere throughout the winter. Our visitors were few, and those who came brought no addition of cheerfulness or happiness to the household. They all wore sad faces and spoke low, as if they were afraid of waking someone; they never laughed, but sighed and often shed tears as they looked at me and especially at little Sónya in her black frock. The feeling of death clung to the house; the air was still filled with the grief and horror of death. My mother's room was kept locked; and whenever I passed it on my way to bed, I felt a strange uncomfortable impulse to look into that cold empty room.

I was then seventeen; and in the very year of her death my mother was intending to move to Petersburg, in order to take me into society. The loss of my mother was a great grief to me; but I must confess to another feeling behind that grief—a feeling that though I was young and pretty (so everybody told me), I was wasting a second winter in the solitude of the country. Before the winter ended, this sense of dejection, loneliness, and simple boredom increased to such an extent that I refused to leave my room or open the piano or take up a book. When Kátya urged me to find some occupation, I said that I did not want to or feel able to; but in my heart I said, 'What is the good of it? What is the good of doing anything, when the best part of my life is being wasted like this?' And to this question, tears were my only answer.

I was told that I was growing thin and losing my looks; but even this failed to interest me. What did it matter? For whom? I felt that my whole life was bound to go on in the same loneliness and helpless dreariness, from which I had myself no strength and even no wish to escape. Towards the end of winter Kátya became anxious about me and determined to make an effort to take me abroad. But money was needed for this, and we hardly knew how our affairs stood after my mother's death. Our guardian, who was to come and clear up our position, was expected every day.

In March he arrived.

'Well, thank God!' Kátya said to me one day, when I was walking up and down the room like a shadow, without occupation, without a thought, and without a wish. 'Sergéy Mikháylych has arrived; he has sent to inquire about us and means to come here for dinner. You must rouse yourself, dear Máshechka,' she added, 'or what will he think of you? He was so fond of you all.'

Sergéy Mikháylych was our near neighbour, and, though a much younger man, had been a friend of my father's. His coming was likely to change our plans and to make it possible to leave the country; and also I had grown up in the habit of love and regard for him; and when Kátya begged me to rouse myself, she guessed rightly that it would give me especial pain to show myself to disadvantage before him, more than before any other of our friends. Like everyone in the house, from Kátya and his god-daughter Sónya down to the helper in the stables, I loved him from old habit; and also he had a special significance for me, owing to a remark which my mother had once made in my presence. 'I should like you to marry a man like him,' she said. At the time this seemed to me strange and even unpleasant. My ideal husband was quite different: he was to be thin, pale, and sad; and Sergéy Mikháylych was middle-aged, tall, robust, and always, as it seemed to me, in good spirits. But still my mother's words stuck in my head; and even six years before this time, when I was eleven, and he still said 'thou' to me, and played with me, and called me by the pet-name of 'violet'—even then I sometimes asked myself in a fright, 'What *shall* I do, if he suddenly wants to marry me?'

Before our dinner, to which Kátya made an addition of sweets and a dish of spinach, Sergéy Mikháylych arrived. From the window I watched him drive up to the house in a small sleigh; but as soon as it turned the corner, I hastened to the drawing-room, meaning to pretend that his visit was a complete surprise. But when I heard his tramp and loud voice and Kátya's footsteps in the hall, I lost patience and went to meet him myself. He was holding Kátya's hand, talking loud, and smiling. When he saw me, he stopped and looked at me for a time without bowing. I was uncomfortable and felt myself blushing.

'Can this be really you?' he said in his plain decisive way, walking towards me with his arms apart. 'Is so great a change possible? How grown-up you are! I used to call you "violet", but now you are a rose in full bloom!'

He took my hand in his own large hand and pressed it so hard that it almost hurt. Expecting him to kiss my hand, I bent towards him, but he only pressed it again and looked straight into my eyes with the old firmness and cheerfulness in his face.

It was six years since I had seen him last. He was much changed—older and darker in complexion; and he now wore whiskers which did not become him at all; but much remained the same—his simple manner, the large features of his honest open face, his bright intelligent eyes, his friendly, almost boyish, smile.

Five minutes later he had ceased to be a visitor and had become the friend of us all, even of the servants, whose visible eagerness to wait on him proved their pleasure at his arrival.

He behaved quite unlike the neighbours who had visited us after my mother's death. They had thought it necessary to be silent when they sat with us, and to shed tears. He, on the contrary, was cheerful and talkative, and said not a word about my mother, so that this indifference seemed strange to me at first and even improper on the part of so close a friend. But I understood later that what seemed indifference was sincerity, and I felt grateful for it. In the evening Kátya poured out tea, sitting in her old place in the drawing-room, where she used to sit in my mother's lifetime; Sónya and I sat near him; our old butler Grigóri had hunted out one of my father's pipes and brought it to him; and he began to walk up and down the room as he used to do in past days.

'How many terrible changes there are in this house, when one thinks of it all!' he said, stopping in his walk.

'Yes,' said Kátya with a sigh; and then she put the lid on the samovar and looked at him, quite ready to burst out crying.

'I suppose you remember your father?' he said, turning to me.

'Not clearly,' I answered.

'How happy you would have been together now!' he added in a low voice, looking thoughtfully at my face above the eyes. 'I was very fond of him,' he added in a still lower tone, and it seemed to me that his eyes were shining more than usual.

'And now God has taken her too!' said Kátya; and at once she laid her napkin on the teapot, took out her handkerchief, and began to cry.

'Yes, the changes in this house are terrible,' he repeated, turning away. 'Sónya, show me your toys,' he added after a little and went off to the parlour. When he had gone, I looked at Kátya with eyes full of tears.

'What a splendid friend he is!' she said. And, though he was no relation, I did really feel a kind of warmth and comfort in the sympathy of this good man.

I could hear him moving about in the parlour with Sónya, and the sound of her high childish voice. I sent tea to him there; and I heard him sit down at the piano and strike the keys with Sónya's little hands.

Then his voice came—'Márya Alexándrovna, come here and play something.'

I liked his easy behaviour to me and his friendly tone of command; I got up and went to him.

'Play this,' he said, opening a book of Beethoven's music at the *adagio* of the sonata 'Quasi una fantasia'. 'Let me hear how you play,' he added, and went off to a corner of the room, carrying his cup with him.

I somehow felt that with him it was impossible to refuse or to say beforehand that I played badly: I sat down obediently at the piano and began to play as well as I could; yet I was afraid of criticism, because I knew that he understood and enjoyed music. The *adagio* suited the remembrance of past days evoked by our conversation at tea, and I believe that I played it fairly well. But the would not let me play the *scherzo*. 'No,' he said, coming up to me; 'you don't play that right; don't go on; but the first movement was not bad; you seem to be musical.' This moderate praise pleased me so much that I even reddened. I felt it pleasant and strange that a friend of my father's, and his contemporary, should no longer treat me like a child but speak to me seriously. Kátya now went upstairs to put Sónya to bed, and we were left alone in the parlour.

He talked to me about my father, and about the beginning of their friendship and the happy days they had spent together, while I was still busy with lesson-books and toys; and his talk put my father before me in quite a new light, as a man of simple and delightful character. He asked me too about my tastes, what I read and what I intended to do, and gave me advice. The man of mirth and jest who used to tease me and make me toys had disappeared; here was a serious, simple, and affectionate friend, for whom I could not help feeling respect and sympathy. It was easy and pleasant to talk to him; and yet I felt an involuntary strain also. I was anxious about each word I spoke: I wished so much to earn for my own sake the love which had been given me already merely because I was my father's daughter.

After putting Sónya to bed, Kátya joined us and began to complain to him of my apathy, about which I had said nothing.

'So she never told me the most important thing of all!' he said, smiling and shaking his head reproachfully at me.

'Why tell you?' I said. 'It is very tiresome to talk about, and it will pass off.' (I really felt now, not only that my dejection would pass, but that it had already passed, or rather had never existed.)

'It is a bad thing', he said, 'not to be able to stand solitude. Can it be that you are a young lady?'

'Of course, I am a young lady,' I answered, laughing.

'Well, I can't praise a young lady who is alive only when people are admiring her, but as soon as she is left alone, collapses and finds nothing to her taste—one who is all for show and has no resources in herself.'

'You have a flattering opinion of me!' I said, just for the sake of saying something.

He was silent for a little. Then he said: 'Yes; your likeness to your father means something. There is something in you . . . ,' and his kind attentive look again flattered me and made me feel a pleasant embarrassment.

I noticed now for the first time that his face, which gave one at first the impression of high spirits, had also an expression peculiar to himself—bright at first and then more and more attentive and rather sad.

'You ought not to be bored and you cannot be,' he said; 'you have music, which you appreciate, books, study; your whole life lies before you, and now or never is the time to prepare for it and save yourself future regrets. A year hence it will be too late.'

He spoke to me like a father or an uncle, and I felt that he kept a constant check upon himself, in order to keep on my level. Though I was hurt that he considered me as inferior to himself, I was pleased that for me alone he thought it necessary to try to be different.

For the rest of the evening he talked about business with Kátya.

'Well, good-bye, dear friends,' he said. Then he got up, came towards me, and took my hand.

'When shall we see you again?' asked Kátya.

'In spring,' he answered, still holding my hand. 'I shall go now to Danílovka' (this was another property of ours), 'look into things there and make what arrangements I can; then I go to Moscow on business of my own; and in summer we shall meet again.'

'Must you really be away so long?' I asked, and I felt terribly grieved. I had really hoped to see him every day, and I felt a sudden shock of regret, and a fear that my depression would return. And my face and voice must have made this plain.

'You must find more to do and not get depressed,' he said;

and I thought his tone too cool and unconcerned. 'I shall put you through an examination in spring,' he added, letting go my hand and not looking at me.

When we saw him off in the hall, he put on his fur coat in a hurry and still avoided looking at me. 'He is taking a great deal of trouble for nothing!' I thought. 'Does he think me so anxious for him to look at me? He is a good man, a very good man; but that's all.'

That evening, however, Kátya and I sat up late, talking, not about him but about our plans for the summer, and where we should spend next winter and what we should do then. I had ceased to ask that terrible question—what is the good of it all? Now it seemed quite plain and simple: the proper object of life was happiness, and I promised myself much happiness ahead. It seemed as if our gloomy old house had suddenly become full of light and life.

CHAPTER II

Meanwhile spring arrived. My old dejection passed away and gave place to the unrest which spring brings with it, full of dreams and vague hopes and desires. Instead of living as I had done at the beginning of winter, I read and played the piano and gave lessons to Sónya; but also I often went into the garden and wandered for long alone through the pathways, or sat on a bench there; and Heaven knows what my thoughts and wishes and hopes were at such times. Sometimes at night, especially if there was a moon, I sat by my bedroom window till dawn; sometimes, when Kátya was not watching, I stole out into the garden in just my nightgown and ran through the dew as far as the pond; and once I went all the way to the open fields and walked right round the garden alone at night.

I find it difficult now to recall and understand the dreams which then filled my imagination. Even when I *can* recall them, I find it hard to believe that my dreams were just like that: they were so strange and so remote from life.

Sergéy Mikháylych kept his promise: he returned from his travels at the end of May.

His first visit to us was in the evening and was quite

unexpected. We were sitting on the veranda, preparing for tea. By this time the garden was all green, and the nightingales had taken up their quarters for the whole of St Peter's Fast* in the leafy borders. The tops of the round lilac bushes had a sprinkling of white and purple—a sign that their flowers were ready to open. On the pathway of birches the foliage was all transparent in the light of the setting sun. On the veranda there was shade and freshness. The evening dew was sure to be heavy on the grass. Out of doors beyond the garden the last sounds of day were audible, and the noise of the sheep and cattle, as they were driven home. Níkon, the half-witted boy, was driving his water-cart along the path outside the veranda, and a cold stream of water from the sprinkler made dark circles on the mould round the stems and supports of the dahlias. On our veranda the polished samovar shone and hissed on the white table-cloth; there were cracknels and biscuits and cream on the table. Kátya was busy washing the cups with her plump hands. I was too hungry after bathing to wait for tea, and was eating bread with thick fresh cream. I was wearing a gingham blouse with loose sleeves, and my hair, still wet, was covered with a kerchief. Kátya saw him first, even before he came in.

'You, Sergéy Mikháylych!' she cried. 'Why, we were just talking about you.'

I got up, meaning to go and change my dress, but he caught me just by the door.

'Why stand on such ceremony in the country?' he said, looking with a smile at the kerchief on my head. 'You don't mind the presence of your butler, and I am really the same to you as Grigóri is.' But I felt just then that he was looking at me in a way quite unlike Grigóri's way, and I was uncomfortable.

'I shall come back at once,' I said, as I left them.

'But what is wrong?' he called out after me; 'it's just the dress of a young peasant woman.'

'How strangely he looked at me!' I said to myself as I was quickly changing upstairs. 'Well, I'm glad he has come; things will be more lively.' After a look in the mirror I ran gaily downstairs and onto the veranda; I was out of breath and did not disguise my haste. He was sitting at the table, talking to

Kátya about our affairs. He glanced at me and smiled; then he went on talking. From what he said it appeared that our affairs were in capital shape: it was now possible for us, after spending the summer in the country, to go either to Petersburg for Sónya's education, or abroad.

'If only you would go abroad with us—' said Kátya; 'without you we shall be quite lost there.'

'Oh, I should like to go round the world with you,' he said, half in jest and half in earnest.

'All right,' I said; 'let us start off and go round the world.'

He smiled and shook his head.

'What about my mother? What about my business?' he said. 'But that's not the question just now: I want to know how you have been spending your time. Not depressed again, I hope?'

When I told him that I had been busy and not bored during his absence, and when Kátya confirmed my report, he praised me as if he had a right to do so, and his words and looks were kind, as they might have been to a child. I felt obliged to tell him, in detail and with perfect frankness, all my good actions, and to confess, as if I were in church, all that he might disapprove of. The evening was so fine that we stayed on the veranda after tea was cleared away; and the conversation interested me so much that I did not notice how we ceased by degrees to hear any sound of the servants indoors. The scent of flowers grew stronger and came from all sides; the grass was drenched with dew; a nightingale started trilling in a lilac bush close by and then stopped on hearing our voices; the starry sky seemed to come down lower over our heads.

It was growing dusk, but I did not notice it till a bat suddenly and silently flew in beneath the veranda awning and began to flutter round my white shawl. I shrank back against the wall and nearly cried out; but the bat as silently and swiftly dived out from under the awning and disappeared in the half-darkness of the garden.

'How fond I am of this place of yours!' he said, changing the conversation; 'I wish I could spend all my life here, sitting on this veranda.'

'Well, do then!' said Kátya.

'That's all very well,' he said, 'but life won't sit still.'

'Why don't you marry?' asked Kátya; 'you would make an excellent husband.'

'Because I like sitting still?' and he laughed. 'No, Katerína Kárlovna, too late for you and me to marry. People have long ceased to think of me as a marrying man, and I am even surer of it myself; and I declare I have felt quite comfortable since the matter was settled.'

It seemed to me that he said this in an unnaturally persuasive way.

'Nonsense!' said Kátya; 'a man of thirty-six makes out that he is too old!'

'Too old indeed,' he went on, 'when all one wants is to sit still. For a man who is going to marry that's not enough. Just you ask her,' he added, nodding at me; 'people of her age should marry, and you and I can rejoice in their happiness.'

The sadness and constraint latent in his voice was not lost upon me. He was silent for a little, and neither Kátya nor I spoke.

'Well, just fancy,' he went on, turning a little on his seat; 'suppose that by some mischance I married a girl of seventeen, Másha, if you like—I mean, Márya Alexándrovna. It's a good example; I am glad it has turned up like this; it is the best example.'

I laughed; but I could not understand why he was glad, or what it was that had turned up.

'Just tell me honestly, with your hand on your heart,' he said, turning as if playfully to me, 'would it not be a misfortune for you to unite your life with that of an old worn-out man who only wants to sit still, whereas Heaven knows what wishes are fermenting in that heart of yours?'

I felt uncomfortable and was silent, not knowing how to answer him.

'I am not making you a proposal, you know,' he said, laughing; 'but am I really the kind of husband you dream of when walking alone on the pathway at twilight? It would be a misfortune, would it not?'

'No, not a misfortune,' I began.

'But a bad thing,' he ended my sentence.

'Perhaps; but I may be mistaken . . .' He interrupted me again.

'There, you see! She is quite right, and I am grateful to her for her frankness, and very glad to have had this conversation. And there is something else to be said'—he added: 'for me too it would be a very great misfortune.'

'How odd you are! You have not changed in the least,' said Kátya, and then left the veranda, to order supper to be served.

When she had gone, we were both silent and all was still around us, but for one exception. A nightingale, which had sung last night by fitful snatches, now flooded the garden with a steady stream of song, and was soon answered by another from the dell below, which had not sung till that evening. The nearer bird stopped and seemed to listen for a moment, and then broke out again still louder than before, pouring out his trills in piercing long-drawn cadences. There was a regal calm in the birds' voices, as they floated through the realm of night which belongs to those birds and not to man. The gardener walked past to his sleeping-quarters in the greenhouse, and the noise of his heavy boots grew fainter and fainter along the path. Someone whistled twice sharply at the foot of the hill; and then all was still again. The rustling of leaves could just be heard; the veranda awning flapped; a faint perfume, floating in the air, came down on the veranda and filled it. I felt silence awkward after what had been said, but what to say I did not know. I looked at him. His eyes, bright in the half-darkness, turned towards me.

'How good life is!' he said.

I sighed, I don't know why.

'Well?' he asked.

'Life is good,' I repeated after him.

Again we were silent, and again I felt uncomfortable. I could not help fancying that I had wounded him by agreeing that he was old; and I wished to comfort him but did not know how.

'Well, I must be saying good-bye,' he said, rising; 'my mother expects me for supper; I have hardly seen her all day.'

'I meant to play you the new sonata,' I said.

'That must wait,' he replied; and I thought that he spoke coldly.

'Good-bye.'

I felt still more certain that I had wounded him, and I was sorry. Kátya and I went to the steps to see him off and stood for a while in the open, looking along the road where he had disappeared from view. When we ceased to hear the sound of his horse's hoofs, I walked round the house to the veranda, and again sat looking into the garden; and all I wished to see and hear, I still saw and heard for a long time in the dewy mist filled with the sounds of night.

He came a second time, and a third; and the awkwardness arising from that strange conversation passed away entirely, never to return. During that whole summer he came two or three times a week; and I grew so accustomed to his presence, that, when he failed to come for some time, I missed him and felt angry with him, and thought he was behaving badly in deserting me. He treated me like a boy whose company he liked, asked me questions, invited the most cordial frankness on my part, gave me advice and encouragement, or sometimes scolded and checked me. But in spite of his constant effort to keep on my level, I was aware that behind the part of him which I could understand there remained an entire region of mystery, into which he did not consider it necessary to admit me; and this fact did much to preserve my respect for him and his attraction for me. I knew from Kátya and from our neighbours that he had not only to care for his old mother with whom he lived, and to manage his own estate and our affairs, but was also responsible for some public business which was the source of serious worries; but what view he took of all this, what were his convictions, plans, and hopes, I could not in the least find out from him. Whenever I turned the conversation to his affairs, he frowned in a way peculiar to himself and seemed to imply, 'Please stop! That is no business of yours;' and then he changed the subject. This hurt me at first; but I soon grew accustomed to confining our talk to my affairs, and felt this to be quite natural.

There was another thing which displeased me at first and then became pleasant to me. This was his complete indifference and even contempt for my personal appearance. Never by word or look did he imply that I was pretty; on the contrary, he frowned and laughed, whenever the word was applied to me in his presence. He even liked to find fault with my looks and tease me about them. On special days Kátya liked to dress me out in fine clothes and to arrange my hair effectively; but my finery met only with mockery from him, which pained kind-hearted Kátya and at first disconcerted me. She had made up her mind that he admired me; and she could not understand how a man could help wishing a woman whom he admired to appear to the utmost advantage. But I soon understood what he wanted. He wished to make sure that I had not a trace of affectation. And when I understood this I was really quite free from affectation in the clothes I wore, or the arrangement of my hair, or my movements; but a very obvious form of affectation took its place—an affectation of simplicity, at a time when I could not yet be really simple. That he loved me, I knew; but I did not yet ask myself whether he loved me as a child or as a woman. I valued his love; I felt that he thought me better than all other young women in the world, and I could not help wishing him to go on being deceived about me. Without wishing to deceive him, I did deceive him, and I became better myself while deceiving him. I felt it a better and worthier course to show him the good points of my heart and mind than of my body. My hair, hands, face, ways—all these, whether good or bad, he had appraised at once and knew so well, that I could add nothing to my external appearance except the wish to deceive him. But my mind and heart he did not know, because he loved them, and because they were in the very process of growth and development; and on this point I could and did deceive him. And how easy I felt in his company, once I understood this clearly! My causeless bashfulness and awkward movements completely disappeared. Whether he saw me from in front, or in profile, sitting or standing, with my hair up or my hair down, I felt that he knew me from head to foot, and I fancied, was satisfied with me as I was. If, contrary to his habit, he had suddenly said to me as other people did, that I had a pretty face, I believe that I should not have liked it at all. But, on the other hand, how light and happy my heart was when, after I had said something, he looked hard at me and said, hiding emotion under a mask of raillery:

'Yes, there *is* something in you! you are a fine girl—that I must tell you.'

And for what did I receive such rewards, which filled my heart with pride and joy? Merely for saying that I felt for old Grigóri in his love for his little granddaughter; or because the reading of some poem or novel moved me to tears; or because I like Mozart better than Schulhof.* And I was surprised at my own quickness in guessing what was good and worthy of love, when I certainly did not know then what *was* good and worthy to be loved. Most of my former tastes and habits did not please him; and a mere look of his, or a twitch of his eyebrow was enough to show that he did not like what I was trying to say; and I felt at once that my own standard was changed. Sometimes, when he was about to give me a piece of advice, I seemed to know beforehand what he would say. When he looked in my face and asked me a question, his very look would draw out of me the answer he wanted. All my thoughts and feelings of that time were not really mine: they were his thoughts and feelings, which had suddenly become mine and passed into my life and lighted it up. Quite unconsciously I began to look at everything with different eyes—at Kátya and the servants and Sónya and myself and my occupations. Books, which I used to read merely to escape boredom, now became one of the chief pleasures of my life, merely because he brought me the books and we read and discussed them together. The lessons I gave to Sónya had been a burdensome obligation which I forced myself to go through from a sense of duty; but, after he was present at a lesson, it became a joy to me to watch Sónya's progress. It used to seem to me an impossibility to learn a whole piece of music by heart; but now, when I knew that he would hear it and might praise it, I would play a single movement forty times over without stopping, till poor Kátya stuffed her ears with cotton-wool, while I was still not weary of it. The same old sonatas seemed quite different in their expression, and came out quite changed and much improved. Even Kátya, whom I knew and loved like a second self, became different in my eyes. I now understood for the first time that she was not in the least bound to be the mother, friend, and slave that she was to us. Now I appreciated all the self-sacrifice and devotion of this affectionate creature, and all my obligations to her; and I began to love her even better. It was he too who taught me to take quite a new view of our serfs and servants and maids. It is an absurd confession to make—but I had spent seventeen years among these people and yet knew less about them than about strangers whom I had never seen; it had never once occurred to me that they had their affections and wishes and sorrows, just as I had. Our garden and woods and fields, which I had known so long, became suddenly new and beautiful to me. He was right in saying that the only certain happiness in life is to live for others. At the time his words seemed to me strange, and I did not understand them; but by degrees this became a conviction with me, without thinking about it. He revealed to me a whole new world of joys in the present, without changing anything in my life, without adding anything except himself to each impression in my mind. All that had surrounded me from childhood without saying anything to me, suddenly came to life. The mere sight of him made everything begin to speak and press for admittance to my heart, filling it with happiness.

Often during that summer, when I went upstairs to my room and lay down on my bed, the old unhappiness of spring with its desires and hopes for the future gave place to a passionate happiness in the present. Unable to sleep, I often got up and sat on Kátya's bed, and told her how perfectly happy I was, though I now realize that this was quite unnecessary, as she could see it for herself. But she told me that she was quite content and perfectly happy, and kissed me. I believed her—it seemed to me so necessary and just that everyone should be happy. But Kátya could also think of sleep; and sometimes, pretending to be angry, she drove me from her bed and went to sleep, while I turned over and over in my mind all that made me so happy. Sometimes I got up and said my prayers over again, praying in my own words and thanking God for all the happiness he had given me.

All was quiet in the room; there was only the even breathing of Kátya in her sleep, and the ticking of the clock by her bed, while I turned from side to side and whispered words of prayer, or crossed myself and kissed the cross round my neck. The door was shut and the windows shuttered; perhaps a fly or gnat hung buzzing in the air. I felt a wish never to leave that room—a wish that dawn might never come, that my present frame of mind might never change. I felt that my dreams and thoughts and prayers were live things, living there in the dark with me, hovering about my bed, and standing over me. And every thought was his thought, and every feeling his feeling. I did not know yet that this was love; I thought that things might go on so for ever, and that this feeling involved no consequences.

CHAPTER III

One day when the grain was being harvested, I went with Kátya and Sónya to our favourite seat in the garden, in the shade of the lime-trees and above the dell, beyond which the fields and woods lay open before us. It was three days since Sergéy Mikháylych had been to see us; we were expecting him, all the more because our bailiff reported that he had promised to visit the harvest-field. At two o'clock we saw him ride on to the rye-field. With a smile and a glance at me, Kátya ordered peaches and cherries, of which he was very fond, to be brought; then she lay down on the bench and began to doze. I tore off a crooked flat lime-tree branch, which made my hand wet with its juicy leaves and juicy bark. Then I fanned Kátya with it and went on with my book, breaking off from time to time, to look at the field-path along which he must come. Sónya was making a dolls' house at the root of an old lime-tree. The day was sultry, windless, and steaming; the clouds were thickening and growing blacker; all morning a thunderstorm had been gathering, and I felt restless, as I always did before thunder. But by afternoon the clouds began to part, the sun sailed out into a clear sky, and only in one direction was there a faint rumbling. A single heavy cloud, hanging above the horizon and mingling with the dust from the fields, was rent from time to time by pale zigzags of lightning which ran down to the ground. It was clear that for today the storm would pass off, with us at all events. The road beyond the garden was visible in places, and we could see a procession of high creaking carts slowly moving along it with their load of sheaves, while the empty carts rattled at a faster pace to meet them, with swaying legs and shirts fluttering in them. The thick dust neither blew away nor settled down—it stood still beyond the fence, and we could see it through the transparent foliage of the garden trees. A little farther off, in the stackyard, the same voices and the same creaking of wheels were audible; and the same yellow sheaves that had moved slowly past the fence were now flying aloft, and I could see the oval stacks gradually rising higher, and their conspicuous pointed tops, and the labourers swarming upon them. On the dusty field in front more carts were moving and more yellow sheaves were visible; and the noise of the carts, with the sound of talking and singing, came to us from a distance. At one side the bare stubble, with strips of fallow covered with wormwood, came more and more into view. Lower down, to the right, the gay dresses of the women were visible, as they bent down and swung their arms to bind the sheaves. Here the bare stubble looked untidy; but the disorder was cleared by degrees, as the pretty sheaves were ranged at close intervals. It seemed as if summer had suddenly turned to autumn before my eyes. The dust and heat were everywhere, except in our favourite nook in the garden; and everywhere, in this heat and dust and under the burning sun, the labourers carried on their heavy task with talk and noise.

Meanwhile Kátya slept so sweetly on our shady bench, beneath her white cambric handkerchief, the black juicy cherries glistened so temptingly on the plate, our dresses were so clean and fresh, the water in the jug was so bright with rainbow colours in the sun, and I felt so happy! 'How can I help it?' I thought; 'am I to blame for being happy? And how can I share my happiness? How and to whom can I surrender all myself and all my happiness?'

By this time the sun had sunk behind the tops of the birch pathway, the dust was settling on the fields, the distance became clearer and brighter in the slanting light. The clouds had dispersed altogether; I could see through the trees the thatch of three new corn-stacks. The labourers came down off the stacks; the carts hurried past, evidently for the last time, with a loud noise of shouting; the women, with rakes over their shoulders and straw-bands in their belts, walked home past us, singing loudly; and still there was no sign of Sergéy Mikháylych, though I had seen him ride down the hill long ago. Suddenly he appeared upon the pathway, coming from a direction where I was not looking for him. He had walked round by the dell. He came quickly towards me, with his hat off and radiant with high spirits. Seeing that Kátya was asleep, he bit his lip, closed his eyes, and advanced on tiptoe; I saw at once that he was in that peculiar mood of causeless merriment which I always delighted to see in him, and which we called 'wild ecstasy'. He was just like a schoolboy playing truant; his whole figure, from head to foot, breathed content, happiness, and boyish frolic.

'Well, young violet, how are you? All right?' he said in a whisper, coming up to me and taking my hand. Then, in answer to my question, 'Oh, I'm splendid today, I feel like a boy of thirteen—I want to play at horses and climb trees.'

'Is it wild ecstasy?' I asked, looking into his laughing eyes, and feeling that the 'wild ecstasy' was infecting me.

'Yes,' he answered, winking and checking a smile. 'But I don't see why you need hit Katerína Kárlovna on the nose.'

With my eyes on him I had gone on waving the branch, without noticing that I had knocked the handkerchief off Kátya's face and was now brushing her with the leaves. I laughed.

'She will say she was awake all the time,' I whispered, as if not to awake Kátya; but that was not my real reason—it was only that I liked to whisper to him.

He moved his lips in imitation of me, pretending that my voice was too low for him to hear. Catching sight of the dish of cherries, he pretended to steal it, and carried it off to Sónya under the lime-tree, where he sat down on her dolls. Sónya was angry at first, but he soon made his peace with her by starting a game, to see which of them could eat cherries faster.

'If you like, I will send for more cherries,' I said; 'or let us go ourselves.'

He took the dish and set the dolls on it, and we all three started for the orchard. Sónya ran behind us, laughing and pulling at his coat, to make him surrender the dolls. He gave them up and then turned to me, speaking more seriously.

'You really are a violet,' he said, still speaking low, though there was no longer any fear of waking anybody; 'when I came to you out of all that dust and heat and toil, I positively smelt violets at once. Not the sweet violet—you know, but that early dark violet that smells of melting snow and spring grass.'

'Is harvest going on well?' I asked, in order to hide the happy agitation which his words produced in me.

'First-rate! Our people are always splendid. The more you know them, the better you like them.'

'Yes,' I said; 'before you came I was watching them from the garden, and suddenly I felt ashamed to be so comfortable myself while they were hard at work, and so . . .'

He interrupted me, with a kind but grave look: 'Don't talk like that, my dear; it is too sacred a matter to talk of lightly. God forbid that you should use fine phrases about that!'

'But it is only to *you* I say this.'

'All right, I understand. But what about those cherries?'

The orchard was locked, and no gardener to be seen: he had sent them all off to help with the harvest. Sónya ran to fetch the key. But he would not wait for her: climbing up a corner of the wall, he raised the net and jumped down on the other side.

His voice came over the wall—'If you want some, give me the dish.'

'No,' I said; 'I want to pick for myself. I shall fetch the key; Sónya won't find it.'

But suddenly I felt that I must see what he was doing there and what he looked like—that I must watch his movements while he supposed that no one saw him. Besides I was simply unwilling just then to lose sight of him for a single minute. Running on tiptoe through the nettles to the other side of the orchard where the wall was lower, I mounted on an empty cask, till the top of the wall was on a level with my waist, and then leaned over into the orchard. I looked at the gnarled old trees, with their broad dented leaves and the ripe black cherries hanging straight and heavy among the foliage; then I pushed my head under the net, and from under the knotted bough of an old cherry-tree I caught sight of Sergéy Mikháylych. He evidently thought that I had gone away and that no one was watching him. With his hat off and his eyes shut, he was sitting on the fork of an old tree and carefully rolling into a ball a lump of cherry-tree gum. Suddenly he shrugged his shoulders, opened his eyes, muttered something, and smiled. Both words and smile were so unlike him that I felt ashamed of myself for eavesdropping. It seemed to me that he had said, 'Másha!' 'Impossible,' I thought. 'Darling Másha!' he said again, in a lower and more tender tone. There was no possible doubt about the two words this time. My heart beat hard, and such a passionate joy—illicit joy, as I felt—took hold of me, that I clutched at the wall, fearing to fall and betray myself. Startled by the sound of my movement, he looked round—he dropped his eyes instantly, and his face turned red, even scarlet, like a child's. He tried to speak, but in vain; again and again his face positively flamed up. Still he smiled as he looked at me, and I smiled too. Then his whole face grew radiant with happiness. He had ceased to be the old uncle who spoiled or scolded me; he was a man on my level, who loved and feared me as I loved and feared him. We looked at one another without speaking. But suddenly he frowned; the smile and light in his eyes disappeared, and he resumed his cold paternal tone, just as if we were doing something wrong and he was repenting and calling on me to repent.

'You had better get down, or you will hurt yourself,' he said; 'and do put your hair straight; just think what you look like!'

'What makes him pretend? what makes him want to give me pain?' I thought in my vexation. And the same instant brought an irresistible desire to upset his composure again and test my power over him.

'No,' I said; 'I mean to pick for myself.' I caught hold of the nearest branch and climbed to the top of the wall; then, before he had time to catch me, I jumped down on the other side.

'What foolish things you do!' he muttered, flushing again and trying to hide his confusion under a pretence of annoyance; 'you might really have hurt yourself. But how do you mean to get out of this?'

He was even more confused than before, but this time his confusion frightened rather than pleased me. It infected me too and made me blush; avoiding his eye and not knowing what to say, I began to pick cherries though I had nothing to put them in. I reproached myself, I repented of what I had done, I was frightened; I felt that I had lost his good opinion for ever by my folly. Both of us were silent and embarrassed. From this difficult situation Sónya rescued us by running back with the key in her hand. For some time we both addressed our conversation to her and said nothing to each other. When we returned to Kátya, who assured us that she had never been asleep and was listening all the time, I calmed down, and he tried to drop into his fatherly patronizing manner again, but I was not taken in by it. A discussion which we had some days before came back clear before me.

Kátya had been saying that it was easier for a man to be in love and declare his love than for a woman.

'A man may say that he is in love, and a woman can't,' she said.

'I disagree,' said he; 'a man has no business to say, and can't say, that he is in love.'

'Why not?' I asked.

'Because it never can be true. What sort of a revelation is that, that a man is in love? A man seems to think that whenever he says the word, something will go pop!—that some miracle will be worked, signs and wonders, with all the big guns firing at once! In my opinion,' he went on, 'whoever solemnly brings out the words "I love you" is either deceiving himself or, which is even worse, deceiving others.'

'Then how is a woman to know that a man is in love with her, unless he tells her?' asked Kátya.

'That I don't know,' he answered; 'every man has his own way of telling things. If the feeling exists, it will out somehow. But when I read novels, I always fancy the crestfallen look of Lieut. Strélski or Alfred, when he says, "I love you, Eleanora",* and expects something wonderful to happen at once, and no change at all takes place in either of them—their eyes and their noses and their whole selves remain exactly as they were.'

Even then I had felt that this banter covered something serious that had reference to myself. But Kátya resented his disrespectful treatment of the heroes in novels.

'You are never serious,' she said; 'but tell me truthfully, have you never yourself told a woman that you loved her?'

'Never, and never gone down on one knee,' he answered, laughing; 'and never will.'

This conversation I now recalled, and I reflected that there was no need for him to tell me that he loved me. 'I know that he loves me,' I thought, 'and all his endeavours to seem indifferent will not change my opinion.'

He said little to me throughout the evening, but in every word he said to Kátya and Sónya and in every look and movement of his I saw love and felt no doubt of it. I was only vexed and sorry for him, that he thought it necessary still to hide his feelings and pretend coldness, when it was all so clear, and when it would have been so simple and easy to be boundlessly happy. But my jumping down to him in the orchard weighed on me like a crime. I kept feeling that he would cease to respect me and was angry with me.

After tea I went to the piano, and he followed me.

'Play me something—it is long since I heard you,' he said, catching me up in the parlour.

'I was just going to,' I said. Then I looked straight in his face and said quickly, 'Sergéy Mikháylych, you are not angry with me, are you?'

'What for?' he asked.

'For not obeying you this afternoon,' I said, blushing.

He understood me: he shook his head and made a grimace, which implied that I deserved a scolding but that he did not feel able to give it.

'So it's all right, and we are friends again?' I said, sitting down at the piano.

'Of course!' he said.

In the drawing-room, a large lofty room, there were only two lighted candles on the piano, the rest of the room remaining in half-darkness. Outside the open windows the summer night was bright. All was silent, except when the sound of Kátya's footsteps in the unlighted parlour was heard occasionally, or when his horse, which was tied up under the window, snorted or stamped his hoof on the burdocks that grew there. He sat behind me, where I could not see him; but everywhere—in the half-darkness of the room, in every sound, in myself—I felt his presence. Every look, every movement of his, though I could not see them, found an echo in my heart. I played a sonata of Mozart's which he had brought me and which I had learnt in his presence and for him. I was not thinking at all of what I was playing, but I believe that I played it well, and I thought that he was pleased. I was conscious of his pleasure, and conscious too, though I never looked at him, of the gaze fixed on me from behind. Still moving my fingers mechanically, I turned round quite involuntarily and looked at him. The night had grown brighter, and his head stood out on a background of darkness. He was sitting with his head propped on his hands, and his eyes shone as they gazed at me. Catching his look, I smiled and stopped playing. He smiled too and shook his head reproachfully at the music, for me to go on. When I stopped, the moon had grown brighter and was riding high in the heavens; and the faint light of the candles was supplemented by a new silvery light which came in through the windows and fell on the floor. Kátya called out that it was really too bad—that I had stopped at the best part of the piece, and that I was playing badly. But he declared that I had never played so well; and then he began to walk about the rooms—through the drawing-room to the unlighted parlour and back again to the drawing-room, and each time he looked at me and smiled. I smiled too; I wanted even to laugh with no reason; I was so happy at something that had happened that very day. Kátya and I were standing by the piano; and each time that he vanished through the drawing-room door, I started kissing her in my favourite place, the soft part of her neck under the chin; and each time he came back, I made a solemn face and refrained with difficulty from laughing.

'What is the matter with her today?' Kátya asked him.

He only smiled at me without answering; he knew what was the matter with me.

'Just look what a night it is!' he called out from the parlour, where he had stopped by the open French window looking into the garden.

We joined him; and it really was such a night as I have never seen since. The full moon shone above the house and behind us, so that we could not see it, and half the shadow, thrown by the roof and pillars of the house and by the veranda awning, lay slanting and foreshortened on the gravel-path and the strip of turf beyond. Everything else was bright and saturated with the silver of the dew and the moonlight. The broad garden-path, one side of which was patterned by the slanting shadows of the dahlias and their supports, was all cool and light, and ran on till its uneven glistening gravel vanished in the distant mist. Through the trees the roof of the greenhouse shone bright, and a growing mist rose from the dell. The lilac-bushes, already partly leafless, were bright all through the branches. Each flower was distinguishable apart, and all were drenched with dew. In the pathways light and shade were so mingled that they looked, not like paths and trees but like transparent houses, swaying and moving. To our right, in the shadow of the house, everything was black, indistinguishable, and uncanny. But all the brighter for the surrounding darkness was the top of a poplar, with a fantastic crown of leaves, which for some strange reason remained there close to the house, towering into the bright light, instead of flying away into the dim distance, into the retreating dark-blue of the sky.

'Let us go for a walk,' I said.

Kátya agreed, but said I must put on goloshes.

'I don't want them, Kátya,' I said; 'Sergéy Mikháylych will give me his arm.'

As if that would prevent me from wetting my feet! But to us three this seemed perfectly natural at the time. Though he never used to offer me his arm, I now took it of my own accord, and he saw nothing strange in it. We all went down from the veranda together. That whole world, that sky, that garden, that air, were different from those that I knew.

We were walking along a pathway, and it seemed to me, whenever I looked ahead, that we could go no farther in the same direction, that the world of the possible ended there, and that the whole scene must remain fixed for ever in its beauty. But we still moved on, and the magic wall kept parting to let us in; and still we found the familiar garden with trees and paths and withered leaves. And we were really walking along the paths, treading on patches of light and shade; and a withered leaf was really crackling under my foot, and a live twig brushing my face. And that was really he, walking steadily and slowly at my side, and carefully supporting my arm; and that was really Kátya walking beside us with her creaking shoes. And that must be the moon in the sky, shining down on us through the motionless branches.

But at each step the magic wall closed up again behind us and in front, and I ceased to believe in the possibility of advancing farther—I ceased to believe in the reality of it all.

'Oh, there's a frog!' cried Kátya.

'Who said that? and why?' I thought. But then I realized it was Kátya, and that she was afraid of frogs. Then I looked at the ground and saw a little frog which gave a jump and then stood still in front of me, while its tiny shadow was reflected on the shining clay of the path.

'You're not afraid of frogs, are you?' he asked.

I turned and looked at him. Just where we were there was a gap of one tree in the lime-tree pathway, and I could see his face clearly—it was so handsome and so happy!

Though he had spoken of my fear of frogs, I knew that he meant to say, 'I love you, my dear one!' 'I love you, I love you' was repeated by his look, by his arm; the light, the shadow, and the air all repeated the same words.

We had gone all round the garden. Kátya's short steps had kept up with us, but now she was tired and out of breath. She said it was time to go in; and I felt very sorry for her. 'Poor thing!' I thought; 'why does she not feel as we do? why are we not all young and happy, like this night and like him and me?'

We went in, but it was a long time before he went away, though the cocks had crowed, and everyone in the house was asleep, and his horse, tethered under the window, snorted continually and stamped his hoof on the burdocks. Kátya never reminded us of the hour, and we sat on talking of the merest trifles and not thinking of the time, till it was past two. The cocks were crowing for the third time and the dawn was breaking when he rode away. He said good-bye as usual and made no special allusion; but I knew that from that day he was mine, and that I should never lose him now. As soon as I had confessed to myself that I loved him, I took Kátya into my confidence. She rejoiced in the news and was touched by my telling her; but she was actually able—poor thing!—to go to bed and sleep! For me, I walked for a long, long time about the veranda; then I went down to the garden, where, recalling each word, each movement, I walked along the same avenues through which I had walked with him. I did not sleep at all that night, and saw sunrise and early dawn for the first time in my life. And never again did I see such a night and such a morning. 'Only why does he not tell me plainly that he loves me?' I thought; 'what makes him invent obstacles and call himself old, when all is so simple and so splendid? What makes him waste this golden time which may never return? Let him say "I love you", say it in plain words; let him take my hand in his and bend over it and say "I love you." Let him blush and look down before me; and then I will tell him all. No! not tell him, but throw my arms round him and press close to him and weep.' But then a thought came to me, 'What if I am mistaken and he does not love me?'

I was startled by this fear—God knows where it might have led me. I recalled his embarrassment and mine, when I jumped down to him in the orchard; and my heart grew very heavy. Tears gushed from my eyes, and I began to pray. A strange thought occurred to me, calming me and bringing hope with it. I resolved to begin fasting on that day, to take communion on my birthday,* and on that same day to be betrothed to him.

How this result would come to pass I had no idea; but from that moment I believed and felt sure it would be so. The dawn had fully come and the labourers were getting up when I went back to my room.

CHAPTER IV

The fast of the Dormition falling in August,* no one in the house was surprised by my intention of fasting.

During the whole of the week he never once came to see us; but, far from being surprised or vexed or made uneasy by his absence, I was glad of it—I did not expect him until my birthday. Each day during the week I got up early. While the horses were being harnessed, I walked in the garden alone, turning over in my mind the sins of the day before, and considering what I must do today, so as to be satisfied with my day and not spoil it by a single sin. It seemed so easy to me then to abstain from sin altogether; only a trifling effort seemed necessary. When the horses came round, I got into the carriage with Kátya or one of the maids, and we drove to the church two miles away. While entering the church, I always recalled the prayer for those who 'come unto the Temple in the fear of God', and tried to get just that frame of mind when mounting the two grass-grown steps up to the building. At that hour there were not more than a dozen worshippers—household servants or peasant women keeping the fast. They bowed to me, and I returned their bows with studied humility. Then, with what seemed to me a great effort of courage, I went myself and got candles from the man who kept them, an old soldier and an Elder; and I placed the candles before the icons. Through the central door of the altar-screen I could see the altar-cloth which my mother had embroidered; on the screen were the two angels which had seemed so big to me when I was little, and the dove with a golden halo which had fascinated me long ago. Behind the choir stood the old battered font, where I had been christened myself and had stood godmother to so many of the servants' children. The old priest came out, wearing a cope made of the pall that had covered my father's coffin, and began to read in the same voice that I had heard all my life—at services held in our house, at Sónya's christening, at memorial services for my father, and at my mother's funeral. The same old quavering voice of the deacon rose in the choir; and the same old woman, whom I could remember at every service in that church, crouched by the wall, fixing her streaming eyes on an icon in the choir, pressing her folded fingers against her faded kerchief, and muttering with her toothless gums. And these objects were no longer merely curious to me, merely interesting from old recollections—each had become important and sacred in my eyes and seemed charged with profound meaning. I listened to each word of the prayers and tried to suit my feeling to it; and if I failed to understand, I prayed silently that God would enlighten me, or made up a prayer of my own in place of what I had failed to catch. When the penitential prayers were repeated, I recalled my past life, and that innocent childish past seemed to me so black when compared to the present brightness of my soul, that I wept and was horrified at myself; but I felt too that all these sins would be forgiven, and that if my sins had been even greater, my repentance would be all the sweeter. At the end of the service when the priest said, 'The blessing of the Lord be upon you!' I seemed to feel an immediate sensation of physical well-being, of a mysterious light and warmth that instantly filled my heart. The service over, the priest came and asked me whether he should come to our house to say vespers, and what hour would suit me; and I thanked him for the suggestion, intended, as I thought, to please me, but said that I would come to church instead, walking or driving.

'Is that not too much trouble?' he asked. And I was at a loss for an answer, fearing to commit a sin of pride.

After the service, if Kátya was not with me, I always sent the carriage home and walked back alone, bowing humbly to all who passed, and trying to find an opportunity of giving help or advice. I was eager to sacrifice myself for someone, to help in lifting a fallen cart, to rock a child's cradle, to give up the path to others by stepping into the mud. One evening I heard the bailiff report to Kátya that Simon, one of our serfs, had come to beg some boards to make a coffin for his daughter, and a rouble to pay the priest for the funeral; the bailiff had given what he asked. 'Are they as poor as that?' I asked. 'Very poor, Miss,' the bailiff answered; 'they have no salt for their food.' My heart ached to hear this, and yet I felt a kind of pleasure too. Pretending to Kátya that I was merely going for a walk, I ran upstairs, got out all my money (it was very little but it was all I had), crossed myself, and started off alone, through the veranda and the garden, on my way to Simon's hut. It stood at the end of the village, and no one saw me as I went up to the window, placed the money on the sill, and tapped on the pane. Someone came out, making the door creak, and hailed me; but I hurried home, cold and shaking with fear like a criminal. Kátya asked where I had been and what was the matter with me; but I did not answer, and did not even understand what she was saying. Everything suddenly seemed to me so petty and insignificant. I locked myself up in my own room, and walked up and down alone for a long time, unable to do anything, unable to think, unable to understand my own feelings. I thought of the joy of the whole family, and of what they would say of their benefactor; and I felt sorry that I had not given them the money myself. I thought too of what Sergéy Mikháylych would say, if he knew what I had done; and I was glad to think that no one would ever find out. I was so happy, and I felt myself and everyone else so bad, and yet was so kindly disposed to myself and to all the world, that the thought of death came to me as a dream of happiness. I smiled and prayed and wept, and felt at that moment a burning passion of love for all the world, myself included. Between services I used to read the Gospel; and the book became more and more intelligible to me, and the story of that divine life simpler and more touching; and the depths of thought and feeling I found in studying it became more awful and impenetrable. On the other hand, how clear and simple everything seemed to me when I rose from the study of this book and looked again on life around me and reflected on it! It was so difficult, I felt, to lead a bad life, and so simple to love everyone and be loved. All were so kind and gentle to me; even Sónya, whose lessons I had not broken off, was quite different—trying to understand and please me and not to vex me. Everyone treated me as I treated them. Thinking over my enemies, of whom I must ask pardon before confession, I could only remember one—one of our neighbours, a girl, whom I had made fun of in company a year ago, and who had ceased to visit us. I wrote to her, confessing my fault and asking her forgiveness. She replied that she forgave me and wished me to forgive her. I cried for joy over her simple words, and saw in them, at the time, a deep and touching feeling. My old nurse cried, when I asked her to forgive me. 'What makes them all so kind to me? what have I done to deserve their love?' I asked myself. Sergéy Mikháylych would come into my mind, and I thought for long about him. I could not help it, and I did not consider these thoughts sinful. But my thoughts of him were quite different from what they had been on the night when I first realized that I loved him: he seemed to me now like a second self, and became a part of every plan for the future. The inferiority which I had always felt in his presence had vanished entirely: I felt myself his equal, and could understand him thoroughly from the moral elevation I had reached. What had seemed strange in him was now quite clear to me. Now I could see what he meant by saying that to live for others was the only true happiness, and I agreed with him perfectly. I believed that our life together would be endlessly happy and untroubled. I looked forward, not to foreign tours or fashionable society or display, but to a quite different scene—a quiet family life in the country, with constant self-sacrifice, constant mutual love, and constant recognition in all things of the kind hand of Providence.

I carried out my plan of taking communion on my birthday. When I came back from church that day, my heart was so swelling with happiness that I was afraid of life, afraid of any feeling that might break in on that happiness. We had hardly left the carriage for the steps in front of the house, when there was a sound of wheels on the bridge, and I saw Sergéy Mikháylych drive up in his well-known trap. He congratulated me,* and we went together to the parlour. Never since I had known him had I been so much at my ease with him and so self-possessed as on that morning. I felt in myself a whole new world, out of his reach and beyond his comprehension. I was not conscious of the slightest embarrassment in speaking to him. He must have understood the cause of this feeling; for he was tender and gentle beyond his wont and showed a kind of reverent consideration for me. When I made for the piano, he locked it and put the key in his pocket.

'Don't spoil your present mood,' he said, 'you have the sweetest of all music in your soul just now.'

I was grateful for his words, and yet I was not quite pleased at his understanding too easily and clearly what ought to have been an exclusive secret in my heart. At dinner he said that he had come to congratulate me and also to say good-bye; for he must go to Moscow tomorrow. He looked at Kátya as he spoke; but then he stole a glance at me, and I saw that he was afraid he might detect signs of emotion on my face. But I was neither surprised nor agitated; I did not even ask whether he would be away long. I knew he would say yes, and I knew that he would not go. How did I know? I cannot explain that to myself now; but on that memorable day it seemed that I knew everything that had been and that would be. It was like a delightful dream, when all that happens seems to have happened already and to be quite familiar, and it will all happen over again, and one knows that it will happen.

He meant to go away immediately after dinner; but, as Kátya was tired after church and went to lie down for a little, he had to wait until she woke up in order to say good-bye to her. The sun shone into the drawing-room, and we went out to the veranda. When we were seated, I began at once, quite calmly, the conversation that was bound to fix the fate of my heart. I began to speak, no sooner and no later, but at the very moment when we sat down, before our talk had taken any turn or colour that might have hindered me from saying what I meant to say. I cannot tell myself where it came from—my coolness and determination and preciseness of expression. It was as if something independent of my will was speaking through my lips. He sat opposite me with his elbows resting on the rails of the veranda; he pulled a lilac-branch towards him and stripped the leaves off it. When I began to speak, he let go the branch and leaned his head on one hand. His attitude might have shown either perfect calmness or strong emotion.

'Why are you going?' I asked, significantly, deliberately, and looking straight at him.

He did not answer at once.

'Business!' he muttered at last and dropped his eyes.

I realized how difficult he found it to lie to me, and in reply to such a frank question.

'Listen,' I said; 'you know what today is to me, how important for many reasons. If I question you, it is not to show an interest in your doings (you know that I have become intimate with you and fond of you)—I ask you this question, because I *must* know the answer. Why are you going?'

'It is very hard for me to tell you the true reason,' he said. 'During this week I have thought much about you and about myself, and have decided that I must go. You understand why; and if you care for me, you will ask no questions.' He put up a hand to rub his forehead and cover his eyes. 'I find it very difficult . . . But you will understand.'

My heart began to beat fast.

'I cannot understand you,' I said; 'I *cannot! you* must tell me; in God's name and for the sake of this day tell me what you please, and I shall hear it with calmness,' I said.

He changed his position, glanced at me, and again drew the lilac-twig towards him.

'Well!' he said, after a short silence in a voice that tried in vain to seem steady, 'it is a foolish business and impossible to put into words, and I feel the difficulty, but I will try to explain it to you,' he added, frowning as if in bodily pain.

'Well?' I said.

'Just imagine the existence of a man—let us call him A—who has left youth far behind, and of a woman whom we may call B, who is young and happy and has seen nothing as yet of life or of the world. Family circumstances of various kinds brought them together, and he grew to love her as a daughter, and had no fear that his love would change its nature.'

He stopped, but I did not interrupt him.

'But he forgot that B was so young, that life was still all a May-game to her,' he went on with a sudden swiftness and determination and without looking at me, 'and that it was easy to fall in love with her in a different way, and that this would amuse her. He made a mistake and was suddenly aware of another feeling, as heavy as remorse, making its way into his heart, and he was afraid. He was afraid that their old friendly relations would be destroyed, and he made up his mind to go away before that happened.' As he said this, he began again to rub his eyes, with a pretence of indifference, and to close them.

'Why was he afraid to love differently?' I asked very low; but I restrained my emotion and spoke in an even voice. He evidently thought that I was not serious; for he answered as if he were hurt.

'You are young, and I am not young. You want amusement, and I want something different. Amuse yourself, if you like, but not with me. If you do, I shall take it seriously; and then I shall be unhappy, and you will repent. That is what A said,' he added; 'however, this is all nonsense; but you understand why I am going. And don't let us continue this conversation. Please not!'

'No! no!' I said, 'we must continue it,' and tears began to tremble in my voice 'Did he love her, or not?'

He did not answer.

'If he did not love her, why did he treat her as a child and pretend to her?' I asked.

'Yes, A behaved badly,' he interrupted me quickly; 'but it all came to an end and they parted friends.'

'This is horrible! Is there no other ending?' I said with a great effort, and then felt afraid of what I had said.

'Yes, there is,' he said, showing a face full of emotion and looking straight at me. 'There are two different endings. But, for God's sake, listen to me quietly and don't interrupt. Some say'—here he stood up and smiled with a smile that was heavy with pain—'some say that A went off his head, fell passionately in love with B, and told her so. But she only laughed. To her it was all a jest, but to him a matter of life and death.'

I shuddered and tried to interrupt him—tried to say that he must not dare to speak for me; but he checked me, laying his hand on mine.

'Wait!' he said, and his voice shook. 'The other story is that she took pity on him, and fancied, poor child, from her ignorance of the world, that she really could love him, and so consented to be his wife. And he, in his madness, believed it—believed that his whole life could begin anew; but she saw herself that she had deceived him and that he had deceived her. . . . But let us drop the subject finally,' he ended, clearly unable to say more; and then he began to walk up and down in silence before me.

Though he had asked that the subject should be dropped, I saw that his whole soul was hanging on my answer. I tried to speak, but the pain at my heart kept me dumb. I glanced at him—he was pale and his lower lip trembled. I felt sorry for him. With a sudden effort I broke the bonds of silence which had held me fast, and began to speak in a low inward voice, which I feared would break every moment.

'There is a third ending to the story,' I said, and then paused, but he said nothing; 'the third ending is that he did not love her, but hurt her, hurt her, and thought that he was right; and he left her and was actually proud of himself. You have been pretending, not I; I have loved you since the first day we met, loved you,' I repeated, and at the word 'loved' my low inward voice changed, without intention of mine, to a wild cry which frightened me myself.

He stood pale before me, his lip trembled more and more violently, and two tears came out upon his cheeks.

'It is wrong!' I almost screamed, feeling that I was choking with angry unshed tears. 'Why do you do it?' I cried, and got up to leave him.

But he would not let me go. His head was resting on my knees, his lips were kissing my still trembling hands, and his tears were wetting them. 'My God! if I had only known!' he whispered.

'Why? why?' I kept on repeating, but in my heart there was happiness, happiness which had now come back, after so nearly departing for ever.

Five minutes later Sónya was rushing upstairs to Kátya and proclaiming all over the house that Másha intended to marry Sergéy Mikháylych.

CHAPTER V

There were no reasons for putting off our wedding, and neither he nor I wished for delay. Kátya, it is true, thought we ought to go to Moscow, to buy and order wedding-clothes; and his mother tried to insist that, before the wedding, he must set up a new carriage, buy new furniture, and re-paper the whole house. But we two together carried our point, that all these things, if they were really indispensable, should be done afterwards, and that we should be married within a fortnight after my birthday, quietly, without wedding-clothes, without a party, without best men and supper and champagne, and all the other conventional features of a wedding. He told me how dissatisfied his mother was that there should be no band, no mountain of luggage, no renovation of the whole house—so unlike her own marriage which had cost thirty thousand roubles; and he told of the solemn and secret confabulations which she held in her store-room with her housekeeper, Maryúshka, rummaging the chests and discussing carpets, curtains, and salvers as indispensable conditions of our happiness. At our house Kátya did just the same with my old nurse, Kuzmínichna. It was impossible to treat the matter lightly with Kátya. She was firmly convinced that he and I, when discussing our future, were merely talking the sentimental nonsense natural to people in our position; and that our real future happiness depended on the hemming of table-cloths and napkins and the proper cutting-out and stitching of under-clothing. Several times a day secret information passed between the two houses, to communicate what was going forward in each; and though the external relations between Kátya and his mother were most affectionate, yet a slightly hostile though very subtle diplomacy was already perceptible in their dealings. I now became more intimate with Tatyána Semyónovna, the mother of Sergéy Mikháylych, an old-fashioned lady, strict and formal in the management of her household. Her son loved her, and not merely because she was his mother: he thought her the best, cleverest, kindest, and most affectionate woman in the world. She was always kind to us and to me especially, and was glad that her son should be getting married; but when I was with her after our engagement, I always felt that she wished me to understand that, in her opinion, her son might have looked higher, and that it would be as well for me to keep that in mind. I understood her meaning perfectly and thought her quite right.

During that fortnight he and I met every day. He came to dinner regularly and stayed on till midnight. But though he said—and I knew he was speaking the truth—that he had no life apart from me, yet he never spent the whole day with me, and tried to go on with his ordinary occupations. Our outward relations remained unchanged to the very day of our marriage: we went on saying 'you' and not 'thou' to each other; he did not even kiss my hand; he did not seek, but even avoided, opportunities of being alone with me. It was as if he feared to yield to the harmful excess of tenderness he felt. I don't know which of us had changed; but I now felt myself entirely his equal; I no longer found in him the pretence of simplicity which had displeased me earlier; and I often delighted to see in him, not a grown man inspiring respect and awe but a loving and wildly happy child. 'How mistaken I was about him!' I often thought; 'he is just such another human being as myself!' It seemed to me now, that his whole character was before me and that I thoroughly understood it. And how simple was every feature of his character, and how congenial to my own! Even his plans for our future life together were just my plans, only more clearly and better expressed in his words.

The weather was bad just then, and we spent most of our time indoors. The corner between the piano and the window was the scene of our best intimate talks. The candle-light was reflected on the blackness of the window near us; from time to time drops struck the glistening pane and rolled down. The rain pattered on the roof; the water splashed in a puddle under the spout; it felt damp near the window; but our corner seemed all the brighter and warmer and happier for that.

'Do you know, there is something I have long wished to say to you,' he began one night when we were sitting up late in our corner; 'I was thinking of it all the time you were playing.'

'Don't say it, I know all about it,' I replied.

'All right! mum's the word!'

'No! what is it?' I asked.

'Well, it is this. You remember the story I told you about A and B?'

'I should just think I did! What a stupid story! Lucky that it ended as it did!'

'Yes, I was very near destroying my happiness by my own act. You saved me. But the main thing is that I was always telling lies then, and I'm ashamed of it, and I want to have my say out now.'

'Please don't! you really mustn't!'

'Don't be frightened,' he said, smiling. 'I only want to justify myself. When I began then, I meant to argue.'

'It is always a mistake to argue,' I said.

'Yes, I argued wrong. After all my disappointments and mistakes in life, I told myself firmly when I came to the country this year, that love was no more for me, and that all I had to do was to grow old decently. So for a long time, I was unable to clear up my feeling towards you, or to make out where it might lead me. I hoped, and I didn't hope: at one time I thought you were trifling with me; at another I felt sure of you but could not decide what to do. But after that evening, you remember, when we walked in the garden at night, I got alarmed: the present happiness seemed too great to be real. What if I allowed myself to hope and then failed? But of course I was thinking only of myself, for I am disgustingly selfish.'

He stopped and looked at me.

'But it was not all nonsense that I said then. It was possible and right for me to have fears. I take so much from you and can give so little. You are still a child, a bud that has yet to open; you have never been in love before, and I . . .'

'Yes, do tell me the truth . . . ,' I began, and then stopped, afraid of his answer. 'No, never mind,' I added.

'Have I been in love before? is that it?' he said, guessing my thoughts at once. 'That I can tell you. No, never before—nothing at all like what I feel now.' But a sudden painful recollection seemed to flash across his mind. 'No,' he said sadly; 'in this too I need your compassion, in order to have the right to love you. Well, was I not bound to think twice before saying that I loved you? What do I give you? love, no doubt.'

'And is that little?' I asked, looking him in the face.

'Yes, my dear, it is little to give *you*,' he continued; 'you have youth and beauty. I often lie awake at night from happiness, and all the time I think of our future life together. I have lived through much, and now I think I have found what is needed for happiness. A quiet secluded life in the country, with the possibility of being useful to people to whom it is easy to do good, and who are not accustomed to have it done to them; then work which one hopes may be of some use; then rest, nature, books, music, love for one's neighbour—such is my idea of happiness. And then, on the top of all that, you for a mate, and children, perhaps—what more can the heart of man desire?'

'It should be enough,' I said.

'Enough for me whose youth is over,' he went on, 'but not for you. Life is still before you, and you will perhaps seek happiness, and perhaps find it, in something different. You think now that this is happiness, because you love me.'

'You are wrong,' I said; 'I have always desired just that quiet domestic life and prized it. And you only say just what I have thought.'

He smiled.

'So you think, my dear; but that is not enough for you. You have youth and beauty,' he repeated thoughtfully.

But I was angry because he disbelieved me and seemed to cast my youth and beauty in my teeth.

'Why do you love me then?' I asked angrily; 'for my youth or for myself?'

'I don't know, but I love you,' he answered, looking at me with his attentive and attractive gaze.

I did not reply and involuntarily looked into his eyes. Suddenly a strange thing happened to me: first I ceased to see what was around me; then his face seemed to vanish till only the eyes were left, shining over against mine; next the eyes seemed to be in my own head, and then all became confused—I could see nothing and was forced to shut my eyes, in order to break loose from the feeling of pleasure and fear which his gaze was producing in me . . .

The day before our wedding-day, the weather cleared up towards evening. The rains which had begun in summer gave place to clear weather, and we had our first autumn evening, bright and cold. It was a wet, cold, shining world, and the garden showed for the first time the spaciousness and colour and bareness of autumn. The sky was clear, cold, and pale. I went to bed happy in the thought that tomorrow, our wedding-day, would be fine. I awoke with the sun, and the thought that this very day . . . seemed alarming and surprising. I went out into the garden. The sun had just risen and shone fitfully through the meagre yellow leaves of the lime-tree pathway. The path was strewn with rustling leaves, clusters of mountain-ash berries hung red and wrinkled on the boughs, with a sprinkling of frost-bitten crumpled leaves; the dahlias were black and wrinkled. The first rime lay like silver on the pale green of the grass and on the broken burdock plants round the house. In the clear cold sky there was not, and could not be, a single cloud.

'Can it possibly be today?' I asked myself, incredulous of my own happiness. 'Is it possible that I shall wake tomorrow, not here but in that strange house with the pillars? Is it possible that I shall never again wait for his coming and meet him, and sit up late with Kátya to talk about him? Shall I never sit with him beside the piano in our drawing-room? never see him off and feel uneasy about him on dark nights?' But I remembered that he promised yesterday to pay a last visit, and that Kátya had insisted on my trying on my wedding-dress, and had said 'For tomorrow'. I believed for a moment that it was all real, and then doubted again. 'Can it be that after today I shall be living there with a mother-in-law, without Nadyózha or old Grigóri or Kátya? Shall I go to bed without kissing my old nurse good-night and hearing her say, while she signs me with the cross from old custom, "Good-night, Miss"? Shall I never again teach Sónya and play with her and knock through the wall to her in the morning and hear her hearty laugh? Shall I become from today someone that I myself do not know? and is a new world, that will realize my hopes and desires, opening before me? and will that new world last for ever?' Alone with these thoughts I was depressed and impatient for his arrival. He came early, and it required his presence to convince me that I should really be his wife that very day, and the prospect ceased to frighten me.

Before dinner we walked to our church, to attend a memorial service for my father.

'If only he were living now!' I thought as we were returning and I leant silently on the arm of him who had been the dearest friend of the object of my thoughts. During the service, while I pressed my forehead against the cold stone of the chapel floor, I called up my father so vividly; I was so convinced that he understood me and approved my choice, that I felt as if his spirit were still hovering over us and blessing me. And my recollections and hopes, my joy and sadness, made up one solemn and satisfied feeling which was in harmony with the fresh still air, the silence, the bare fields and pale sky, from which the bright but powerless rays, trying in vain to burn my cheek, fell over all the landscape. My companion seemed to understand and share my feeling. He walked slowly and silently; and his face, at which I glanced from time to time, expressed the same serious mood between joy and sorrow which I shared with nature.

Suddenly he turned to me, and I saw that he intended to speak. 'Suppose he starts some other subject than that which is in my mind?' I thought. But he began to speak of my father and did not even name him.

'He once said to me in jest, "you should marry my Másha",' he began.

'He would have been happy now,' I answered, pressing closer the arm which held mine.

'You were a child then,' he went on, looking into my eyes; 'I loved those eyes then and used to kiss them only because they were like his, never thinking they would be so dear to me for their own sake. I used to call you Másha then.'

'I want you to say "thou"* to me,' I said.

'I was just going to,' he answered; 'I feel for the first time that *thou art* entirely mine;' and his calm happy gaze that drew me to him rested on me.

We went on along the footpath over the beaten and trampled stubble; our voices and footsteps were the only sounds. On the side the brownish stubble stretched over a hollow to a distant leafless wood; across it at some distance a peasant was noiselessly ploughing a black strip which grew wider and wider. A drove of horses scattered under the hill seemed close to us. On the other side, as far as the garden and our house peeping through the trees, a field of winter corn, thawed by the sun, showed black with occasional patches of green. The winter sun shone over everything, and everything was covered with long gossamer spider's webs, which floated in the air round us, lay on the frost-dried stubble, and got into our eyes and hair and clothes. When we spoke, the sound of our voices hung in the motionless air above us, as if we two were alone in the whole world—alone under that azure vault, in which the beams of the winter sun played and flashed without scorching.

I too wished to say 'thou' to him, but I felt ashamed.

'Why *dost thou* walk so fast?' I said quickly and almost in a whisper; I could not help blushing.

He slackened his pace, and the gaze he turned on me was even more affectionate, gay, and happy.

At home we found that his mother and the inevitable guests had arrived already, and I was never alone with him again till we came out of church to drive to Nikólskoe.

The church was nearly empty: I just caught a glimpse of his mother standing up straight on a mat by the choir and of Kátya wearing a cap with purple ribbons and with tears on her cheeks, and of two or three of our servants looking curiously at me. I did not look at him, but felt his presence there beside me. I attended to the words of the prayers and repeated them, but they found no echo in my heart. Unable to pray, I looked listlessly at the icons, the candles, the embroidered cross on the priest's cope, the screen, and the window, and took nothing in. I only felt that something strange was being done to me. At last the priest turned to us with the cross in his hand, congratulated us, and said, 'I christened you and by God's mercy have lived to marry you.' Kátya and his mother kissed us, and Grigóri's voice was heard, calling up the carriage. But I was only frightened and disappointed: all was over, but nothing extraordinary, nothing worthy of the sacrament I had just received, had taken place in myself. He and I exchanged kisses, but the kiss seemed strange and not expressive of our feeling. 'Is this all?' I thought. We went out of church, the sound of wheels reverberated under the vaulted roof, the fresh air blew on my face, he put on his hat and handed me into the carriage. Through the window I could see a frosty moon with a halo round it. He sat down beside me and shut the door after him. I felt a sudden pang. The assurance of his proceedings seemed to me insulting. Kátya called out that I should put something on my head; the wheels rumbled on the stone and then moved along the soft road, and we were off. Huddling in a corner, I looked out at the distant fields and the road flying past in the cold glitter of the moon. Without looking at him, I felt his presence beside me. 'Is this all I have got from the moment, of which I expected so much?' I thought; and still it seemed humiliating and insulting to be sitting alone with him, and so close. I turned to him, intending to speak; but the words would not come, as if my love had vanished, giving place to a feeling of mortification and alarm.

'Till this moment I did not believe it was possible,' he said in a low voice in answer to my look.

'But I am afraid somehow,' I said.

'Afraid of me, my dear?' he said, taking my hand and bending over it.

My hand lay lifeless in his, and the cold at my heart was painful.

'Yes,' I whispered.

But at that moment my heart began to beat faster, my hand trembled and pressed his, I grew hot, my eyes sought his in the half-darkness, and all at once I felt that I did not fear him, that this fear was love—a new love still more tender and stronger than the old. I felt that I was wholly his, and that I was happy in his power over me.

PART II

CHAPTER VI

Days, weeks, two whole months, of seclusion in the country slipped by unnoticed, as we thought then; and yet those two months comprised feelings, emotions, and happiness, sufficient for a lifetime. Our plans for the regulation of our life in the country were not carried out at all in the way that we expected; but the reality was not inferior to our ideal. There was none of that hard work, performance of duty, self-sacrifice, and life for others, which I had pictured to myself before our marriage; there was, on the contrary, merely a selfish feeling of love for one another, a wish to be loved, a constant causeless gaiety and entire oblivion of all the world. It is true that my husband sometimes went to his study to work, or drove to town on business, or walked about attending to the management of the estate; but I saw what it cost him to tear himself away from me. He confessed later that every occupation, in my absence, seemed to him mere nonsense in which it was impossible to take any interest. It was just the same with me. If I read, or played the piano, or passed my time with his mother, or taught in the school, I did so only because each of these occupations was connected with him and won his approval; but whenever the thought of him was not associated with any duty, my hands fell by my sides and it seemed to me absurd to think that anything existed apart from him. Perhaps it was a wrong and selfish feeling, but it gave me happiness and lifted me high above all the world. He alone existed on earth for me, and I considered him the best and most faultless man in the world; so that I could not live for anything else than for him, and my one object was to realize his conception of me. And in his eyes I was the first and most excellent woman in the world, the possessor of all possible virtues; and I strove to be that woman in the opinion of the first and best of men.

He came to my room one day while I was praying. I looked round at him and went on with my prayers. Not wishing to interrupt me, he sat down at a table and opened a book. But I thought he was looking at me and looked round myself. He smiled, I laughed, and had to stop my prayers.

'Have you prayed already?' I asked.

'Yes. But you go on; I'll go away.'

'You do say your prayers, I hope?'

He made no answer and was about to leave the room when I stopped him.

'Darling, for my sake, please repeat the prayers with me!' He stood up beside me, dropped his arms awkwardly, and began, with a serious face and some hesitation. Occasionally he turned towards me, seeking signs of approval and aid in my face.

When he came to the end, I laughed and embraced him.

'I feel just as if I were ten! And you do it all!' he said, blushing and kissing my hands.

Our house was one of those old-fashioned country houses in which several generations have passed their lives together under one roof, respecting and loving one another. It was all redolent of good sound family traditions, which as soon as I entered it seemed to become mine too. The management of the household was carried on by Tatyána Semyónovna, my mother-in-law, on old-fashioned lines. Of grace and beauty there was not much; but, from the servants down to the furniture and food, there was abundance of everything, and a general cleanliness, solidity, and order, which inspired respect. The drawing-room furniture was arranged symmetrically; there were portraits on the walls, and the floor was covered with home-made carpets and mats. In the parlour there was an old piano, with chiffoniers of two different patterns, sofas, and little carved tables with bronze ornaments. My sitting-room, specially arranged by Tatyána Semyónovna, contained the best furniture in the house, of many styles and periods, including an old pier-glass, which I was frightened to look into at first, but came to value as an old friend. Though Tatyána Semyónovna's voice was never heard, the whole household went like a clock. The number of servants was far too large (they all wore soft boots with no heels, because Tatyána Semyónovna had an intense dislike for stamping heels and creaking soles); but they all seemed proud of their calling, trembled before their old mistress, treated my husband and me with an affectionate air of patronage, and performed their duties, to all appearance, with extreme satisfaction. Every Saturday the floors were scoured and the carpets beaten without fail; on the first of every month there was a religious service in the house and holy water was sprinkled; on Tatyána Semyónovna's name-day and on her son's (and on mine too, beginning from that autumn) an entertainment was regularly provided for the whole neighbourhood. And all this had gone on without a break ever since the beginning of Tatyána Semyónovna's life.

My husband took no part in the household management, he attended only to the farm-work and the labourers, and gave much time to this. Even in winter he got up so early that I often woke to find him gone. He generally came back for early tea, which we drank alone together; and at that time, when the worries and vexations of the farm were over, he was almost always in that state of high spirits which we called 'wild ecstasy'. I often made him tell me what he had been doing in the morning, and he gave such absurd accounts that we both laughed till we cried. Sometimes I insisted on a serious account, and he gave it, restraining a smile. I watched his eyes and moving lips and took nothing in: the sight of him and the sound of his voice was pleasure enough.

'Well, what have I been saying? repeat it,' he would sometimes say. But I could repeat nothing. It seemed so absurd that *he* should talk to *me* of any other subject than ourselves. As if it mattered in the least what went on in the world outside! It was at a much later time that I began to some extent to understand and take an interest in his occupations. Tatyána Semyónovna never appeared before dinner: she breakfasted alone and said good-morning to us by deputy. In our exclusive little world of frantic happiness a voice from the staid orderly region in which she dwelt was quite startling: I often lost self-control and could only laugh without speaking, when the maid stood before me with folded hands and made her formal report: 'The mistress bade me inquire how you slept after your walk yesterday evening; and about her I was to report that she had pain in her side all night, and a stupid dog barked in the village and kept her awake: and also I was to ask how you liked the bread this morning, and to tell you that it was not Tarás who baked today, but Nikoláshka who was trying his hand for the first time; and she says his baking is not at all bad, especially the cracknels: but the tea-rusks were over-baked.' Before dinner we saw little of each other: he wrote or went out again while I played the piano or read; but at four o'clock we all met in the drawing-room before dinner. Tatyána Semyónovna sailed out of her own room, and certain poor and pious maiden ladies, of whom there were always two or three living in the house, made their appearance also. Every day without fail my husband by old habit offered his arm to his mother, to take her in to dinner; but she insisted that I should take the other, so that every day, without fail, we stuck in the doors and got in each other's way. She also presided at dinner, where the conversation, if rather solemn, was polite and sensible. The commonplace talk between my husband and me was a pleasant interruption to the formality of those entertainments. Sometimes there were squabbles between mother and son and they bantered with one another; and I especially enjoyed those scenes, because they were the best proof of the strong and tender love which united the two. After dinner Tatyána Semyónovna went to the drawing-room, where she sat in an armchair and ground her snuff or cut the leaves of new books, while we read aloud or went off to the piano in the parlour. We read much together at this time, but music was our favourite and best enjoyment, always evoking fresh chords in our hearts and as it were revealing each afresh to the other. While I played his favourite pieces, he sat on a distant sofa where I could hardly see him. He was ashamed to betray the impression produced on him by the music; but often, when he was not expecting it, I rose from the piano, went up to him, and tried to detect on his face signs of emotion—the unnatural brightness and moistness of the eyes, which he tried in vain to conceal. Tatyána Semyónovna, though she often wanted to take a look at us there, was also anxious to put no constraint upon us. So she always passed through the room with an air of indifference and a pretence of being busy; but I knew that she had no real reason for going to her room and returning so soon. In the evening I poured out tea in the large drawing-room, and all the household met again. This solemn ceremony of distributing cups and glasses before the solemnly shinning samovar made me nervous for a long time. I felt myself still unworthy of such a distinction, too young and frivolous to turn the tap of such a big samovar, to put glasses on Nikíta's salver, saying 'For Peter Ivánovich', 'For Márya Mínichna', to ask 'Is it sweet enough?' and to leave out lumps of sugar for nanny and other deserving persons. 'Wonderful! wonderful! Just like a grown-up person!' was a frequent comment from my husband, which only increased my confusion.

After tea Tatyána Semyónovna played patience or listened to Márya Mínichna telling fortunes by the cards. Then she kissed us both and signed us with the cross, and we went off to our own rooms. But we generally sat up together till midnight, and that was our best and pleasantest time. He told me stories of his past life; we made plans and sometimes even talked philosophy; but we tried always to speak low, for fear we should be heard upstairs and reported to Tatyána Semyónovna, who insisted on our going to bed early. Sometimes we grew hungry; and then we stole off to the pantry, secured a cold supper by the good offices of Nikíta, and ate it in my sitting-room by the light of one candle. He and I lived like strangers in that big old house, where the uncompromising spirit of the past and of Tatyána Semyónovna ruled supreme. Not she only, but the servants, the old ladies, the furniture, even the pictures, inspired me with respect and a little alarm, and made me feel that he and I were a little out of place in that house and must always be very careful and cautious in our doings. Thinking it over now, I see that many things—the pressure of that unvarying routine, and that crowd of idle and inquisitive servants—were uncomfortable and oppressive; but at the time that very constraint made our love for one another still keener. Not I only, but he also, never grumbled openly at anything; on the contrary he shut his eyes to what was amiss. Dmítri Sídorov, one of the footmen, was a great smoker; and regularly every day, when we two were in the parlour after dinner, he went to my husband's study to take tobacco from the jar; and it was a sight to see Sergéy Mikháylych creeping on tiptoe to me with a face between delight and terror, and a wink and a warning forefinger, while he pointed at Dmítri Sídorov, who was quite unconscious of being watched. Then, when Dmítri Sídorov had gone away without having seen us, in his joy that all had passed off successfully, he declared (as he did on every other occasion) that I was a darling, and kissed me. At times his calm connivance and apparent indifference to everything annoyed me, and I took it for weakness, never noticing that I acted in the same way myself. 'It's like a child who dares not show his will,' I thought.

'My dear! my dear!' he said once when I told him that his weakness surprised me; 'how can a man, as happy as I am, be dissatisfied with anything? Better to give way myself than to put compulsion on others; of that I have long been convinced. There is no condition in which one cannot be happy; but our life is such bliss! I simply cannot be angry; to me now nothing seems bad, but only pitiful and amusing. Above all—*le mieux est l'ennemi du bien.*[1] Will you believe it, when I hear a ring at the bell, or receive a letter, or even wake up in the morning, I'm frightened. Life must go on, something may change; and nothing can be better than the present.'

I believed him but did not understand him. I was happy; but I took that as a matter of course, the invariable experience

[1] The better is the enemy of the good.

of people in our position, and believed that there was somewhere, I knew not where, a different happiness, not greater but different.

So two months went by and winter came with its cold and snow; and, in spite of his company, I began to feel lonely, that life was repeating itself, that there was nothing new either in him or in myself, and that we were merely going back to what had been before. He began to give more time to business which kept him away from me, and my old feeling returned, that there was a special department of his mind into which he was unwilling to admit me. His unbroken calmness provoked me. I loved him as much as ever and was as happy as ever in his love; but my love, instead of increasing, stood still; and another new and disquieting sensation began to creep into my heart. To love him was not enough for me after the happiness I had felt in falling in love. I wanted movement and not a calm course of existence. I wanted excitement and danger and the chance to sacrifice myself for my love. I felt in myself a superabundance of energy which found no outlet in our quiet life. I had fits of depression which I was ashamed of and tried to conceal from him, and fits of excessive tenderness and high spirits which alarmed him. He realized my state of mind before I did, and proposed a visit to Petersburg; but I begged him to give this up and not to change our manner of life or spoil our happiness. Happy indeed I was; but I was tormented by the thought that this happiness cost me no effort and no sacrifice, though I was even painfully conscious of my power to face both. I loved him and saw that I was all in all to him; but I wanted everyone to see our love; I wanted to love him in spite of obstacles. My mind, and even my senses, were fully occupied; but there was another feeling of youth and craving for movement, which found no satisfaction in our quiet life. What made him say that, whenever I liked, we could go to town? Had he not said so I might have realized that my uncomfortable feelings were my own fault and dangerous nonsense, and that the sacrifice I desired was there before me, in the task of overcoming these feelings. I was haunted by the thought that I could escape from depression by a mere change from the country; and at the same time I felt ashamed and sorry to tear him away, out of selfish motives, from all he cared for.

So time went on, the snow grew deeper, and there we remained together, all alone and just the same as before, while outside I knew there was noise and glitter and excitement, and hosts of people suffering or rejoicing without one thought of us and our remote existence. I suffered most from the feeling that custom was daily petrifying our lives into one fixed shape, that our minds were losing their freedom and becoming enslaved to the steady passionless course of time. The morning always found us cheerful; we were polite at dinner, and affectionate in the evening. 'It is all right,' I thought, 'to do good to others and lead upright lives, as he says; but there is time for that later; and there are other things, for which the time is now or never.' I wanted, not what I had got, but a life of struggle; I wanted feeling to be the guide of life, and not life to guide feeling. If only I could go with him to the edge of a precipice and say, 'One step, and I shall fall over—one movement, and I shall be lost!' then, pale with fear, he would catch me in his strong arms and hold me over the edge till my blood froze, and then carry me off whither he pleased.

This state of feeling even affected my health, and I began to suffer from nerves. One morning I was worse than usual. He had come back from the estate-office out of sorts, which was a rare thing with him. I noticed it at once and asked what was the matter. He would not tell me and said it was of no importance. I found out afterwards that the police-inspector, out of spite against my husband, was summoning our peasants, making illegal demands on them, and using threats to them. My husband could not swallow this at once; he could not feel it merely 'pitiful and amusing'. He was provoked, and therefore unwilling to speak of it to me. But it seemed to me that he did not wish to speak to me about it because he considered me a mere child, incapable of understanding his concerns. I turned from him and said no more. I then told the servant to ask Márya Mínichna, who was staying in the house, to join us at breakfast. I ate my breakfast very fast and took her to the parlour, where I began to talk loudly to her about some trifle which did not interest me in the least. He walked about the room, glancing at us from time to time. This made me more and more inclined to talk and even to laugh; all that I said myself, and all that Márya Mínichna said, seemed to me laughable. Without a word to me he went off to his study and shut the door behind him. When I ceased to hear him, all my high spirits vanished at once: indeed Márya Mínichna was surprised and asked what was the matter. I sat down on a sofa without answering, and felt ready to cry. 'What has he got on his mind?' I wondered; 'some trifle which he thinks important; but, if he tried to tell it me, I should soon show him it was mere nonsense. But he must needs think that I won't understand, must humiliate me by his majestic composure, and always be in the right as against me. But I too am in the right when I find things tiresome and trivial,' I reflected; 'and I do well to want an active life rather than to stagnate in one spot and feel life flowing past me. I want to move forward, to have some new experience every day and every hour, whereas he wants to stand still and to keep me standing beside him. And how easy it would be for him to gratify me! He need not take me to town; he need only be like me and not compel himself and regulate his feelings, but live simply. That is the advice he gives me, but he is not simple himself. That is what is the matter.'

I felt the tears rising and knew that I was irritated with him. My irritation frightened me, and I went to his study. He was sitting at the table, writing. Hearing my step, he looked up for a moment and then went on writing; he seemed calm and unconcerned. His look vexed me: instead of going up to him, I stood beside his writing-table, opened a book, and began to look at it. He broke off his writing again and looked at me.

'Másha, are you out of sorts?' he asked.

I replied with a cold look, as much as to say, 'You are very polite, but what is the use of asking?' He shook his head and smiled with a tender timid air; but his smile, for the first time, drew no answering smile from me.

'What happened to you today?' I asked; 'why did you not tell me?'

'Nothing much—a trifling nuisance,' he said. 'But I might tell you now. Two of our serfs went off to the town . . .'

But I would not let him go on.

'Why would you not tell me, when I asked you at breakfast?'

'I was angry then and should have said something foolish.'

'I wished to know then.'

'Why?'

'Why do you suppose that I can never help you in anything?'

'Not help me!' he said, dropping his pen. 'Why, I believe that without you I could not live. You not only help me in everything I do, but you do it yourself. You are very wide of the mark,' he said, and laughed. 'My life depends on you. I am pleased with things, only because you are there, because I need you . . .'

'Yes, I know; I am a delightful child who must be humoured and kept quiet,' I said in a voice that astonished him, so that he looked up as if this was a new experience; 'but I don't want to be quiet and calm; that is more in your line, and too much in your line,' I added.

'Well,' he began quickly, interrupting me and evidently afraid to let me continue, 'when I tell you the facts, I should like to know your opinion.'

'I don't want to hear them now,' I answered. I did want to hear the story, but I found it so pleasant to break down his composure. 'I don't want to play at life,' I said, 'but to live, as you do yourself.'

His face, which reflected every feeling so quickly and so vividly, now expressed pain and intense attention.

'I want to share your life, to . . . ,' but I could not go on—his face showed such deep distress. He was silent for a moment.

'But what part of my life do you not share?' he asked; 'is it because I, and not you, have to bother with the inspector and with tipsy labourers?'

'That's not the only thing,' I said.

'For God's sake try to understand me, my dear!' he cried. 'I know that excitement is always painful; I have learnt that from the experience of life. I love you, and I can't but wish to save you from excitement. My life consists of my love for you; so you should not make life impossible for me.'

'You are always in the right,' I said without looking at him.

I was vexed again by his calmness and coolness while I was conscious of annoyance and some feeling akin to penitence.

'Másha, what is the matter?' he asked. 'The question is not, which of us is in the right—not at all; but rather, what grievance have you against me? Take time before you answer, and tell me all that is in your mind. You are dissatisfied with me: and you are, no doubt, right; but let me understand what I have done wrong.'

But how could I put my feeling into words? That he understood me at once, that I again stood before him like a child, that I could do nothing without his understanding and foreseeing it—all this only increased my agitation.

'I have no complaint to make of you.' I said; 'I am merely bored and want not to be bored. But you say that it can't be helped, and, as always, you are right.'

I looked at him as I spoke. I had gained my object: his calmness had disappeared, and I read fear and pain in his face.

'Másha,' he began in a low troubled voice, 'this is no mere trifle: the happiness of our lives is at stake. Please hear me out without answering. Why do you wish to torment me?'

But I interrupted him.

'Oh, I know you will turn out to be right. Words are useless; of course you are right.' I spoke coldly, as if some evil spirit were speaking with my voice.

'If you only knew what you are doing!' he said, and his voice shook.

I burst out crying and felt relieved. He sat down beside me and said nothing. I felt sorry for him, ashamed of myself, and annoyed at what I had done. I avoided looking at him. I felt that any look from him at that moment must express severity or perplexity. At last I looked up and saw his eyes: they were fixed on me with a tender gentle expression that seemed to ask for pardon. I caught his hand and said.

'Forgive me! I don't know myself what I have been saying.'

'But I do; and you spoke the truth.'

'What do you mean?' I asked.

'That we must go to Petersburg,' he said; 'there is nothing for us to do here just now.'

'As you please,' I said.

He took me in his arms and kissed me.

'You must forgive me,' he said; 'for I am to blame.'

That evening I played for him for a long time, while he walked about the room. He had a habit of muttering to himself;

and when I asked him what he was muttering, he always thought for a moment and then told me exactly what it was. It was generally verse, and sometimes mere nonsense, but I could always judge of his mood by it. When I asked him now, he stood still, thought an instant, and then repeated two lines from Lérmontov:

It in its madness prays for storms,
*And dreams that storms will bring it peace.**

'He is really more than human,' I thought; 'he knows everything. How can one help loving him?'

'I got up, took his arm, and began to walk up and down with him, trying to keep step.

'Well?' he asked, smiling and looking at me.

'All right,' I whispered. And then a sudden fit of merriment came over us both: our eyes laughed, we took longer and longer steps, and rose higher and higher on tiptoe. Prancing in this manner, to the profound dissatisfaction of the butler and astonishment of my mother-in-law, who was playing patience in the parlour, we proceeded through the house till we reached the dining-room; there we stopped, looked at one another, and burst out laughing.

A fortnight later, before Christmas, we were in Petersburg.

CHAPTER VII

The journey to Petersburg, a week in Moscow, visits to my own relations and my husband's, settling down in our new quarters, travel, new towns and new faces—all this passed before me like a dream. It was all so new, various, and delightful, so warmly and brightly lighted up by his presence and his love, that our quiet life in the country seemed to me something very remote and unimportant. I had expected to find people in society proud and cold; but to my great surprise, I was received everywhere with unfeigned cordiality and pleasure, not only by relations, but also by strangers. I seemed to be the one object of their thoughts, and my arrival the one thing they wanted, to complete their happiness. I was surprised too to discover in what seemed to me the very best society a number of people acquainted with my husband, though he had never spoken of them to me; and I often felt it odd and disagreeable to hear him now speak disapprovingly of some of these people who seemed to me so kind. I could not understand his coolness towards them or his endeavours to avoid many acquaintances that seemed to me flattering. Surely, the more kind people one knows, the better; and here everyone was kind.

'This is how we must manage, you see,' he said to me before we left the country; 'here we are little Croesuses, but in town we shall not be at all rich. So we must not stay after Easter, or go into society, or we shall get into difficulties. For your sake too I should not wish it.'

'Why should we go into society?' I asked; 'we shall have a look at the theatres, see our relations, go to the opera, hear some good music, and be ready to come home before Easter.'

But these plans were forgotten the moment we got to Petersburg. I found myself at once in such a new and delightful world, surrounded by so many pleasures and confronted by such novel interests, that I instantly, though unconsciously, turned my back on my past life and its plans. 'All that was preparatory, a mere playing at life; but here is the real thing! And there is the future too!' Such were my thoughts. The restlessness and symptoms of depression which had troubled me at home vanished at once and entirely, as if by magic. My love for my husband grew calmer, and I ceased to wonder whether he loved me less. Indeed I could not doubt his love: every thought of mine was understood at once, every feeling shared, and every wish gratified by him. His composure, if it still existed, no longer provoked me. I also began to realize that he not only loved me but was proud of me. If we paid a call, or made some new acquaintance, or gave an evening party at which I, trembling inwardly from fear of disgracing myself, acted as hostess, he often said when it was over: 'Bravo, young woman! wonderful! you needn't be frightened; a real success!' And his praise gave me great pleasure. Soon after our arrival he wrote to his mother and asked me to add a postscript, but refused to let me see his letter; of course I insisted on reading it; and he had said: 'You would not know Másha again, I don't myself. Where does she get that charming graceful self-confidence and ease, such social gifts with such simplicity and charm and kindliness? Everybody is delighted with her. I can't admire her enough myself, and should be more in love with her than ever, if that were possible.'

'Now I know what I am like,' I thought. In my joy and pride I felt that I loved him more than before. My success with all our new acquaintances was a complete surprise to me. I heard on all sides, how this uncle had taken a special fancy for me, and that aunt was raving about me; I was told by one admirer that I had no rival among the Petersburg ladies, and assured by another, a lady, that I might, if I cared, lead the fashion in society. A cousin of my husband's, in particular, a Princess D., middle-aged and very much at home in society, fell in love with me at first sight and paid me compliments which turned my head. The first time that she invited me to a ball and spoke to my husband about it, he turned to me and asked if I wished to go; I could just detect a sly smile on his face. I nodded assent and felt that I was blushing.

'She looks like a criminal when confessing what she wishes,' he said with a good-natured laugh.

'But you said that we must not go into society, and you don't care for it yourself,' I answered, smiling and looking imploringly at him.

'Let us go, if you want to very much,' he said.

'Really, we had better not.'

'Do you want to? very badly?' he asked again.

I said nothing.

'Society in itself is no great harm,' he went on; 'but unsatisfied social aspirations are a bad and ugly business. We must certainly accept, and we will.'

'To tell you the truth,' I said, 'I never in my life longed for anything as much as I do for this ball.'

So we went, and my delight exceeded all my expectations. It seemed to me, more than ever, that I was the centre around which everything revolved, that for my sake alone this great room was lighted up and the band played, and that this crowd of people had assembled to admire me. From the hairdresser and the lady's maid to my partners and the old gentlemen promenading the ball-room, all alike seemed to make it plain that they were in love with me. The general verdict formed at the ball about me and reported by my cousin, came to this: I was quite unlike the other women and had a rural simplicity and charm of my own. I was so flattered by my success that I frankly told my husband I should like to attend two or three more balls during the season, and 'so get thoroughly sick of them', I added; but I did not mean what I said.

He agreed readily; and he went with me at first with obvious satisfaction. He took pleasure in my success, and seemed to have quite forgotten his former warning or to have changed his opinion.

But a time came when he was evidently bored and wearied by the life we were leading. I was too busy, however, to think about that. Even if I sometimes noticed his eyes fixed questioningly on me with a serious attentive gaze, I did not realize its meaning. I was utterly blinded by this sudden affection which I seemed to evoke in all our new acquaintances, and confused by the unfamiliar atmosphere of luxury, refinement, and novelty. It pleased me so much to find myself in these surroundings not merely his equal but his superior, and yet to love him better and more independently than before, that I could not understand what he could object to for me in society life. I had a new sense of pride and self-satisfaction when my entry at a ball attracted all eyes, while he, as if ashamed to confess his ownership of me in public, made haste to leave my side and efface himself in the crowd of black coats. 'Wait a little!' I often said in my heart, when I identified his obscure and sometimes woebegone figure at the end of the room—'Wait till we get home! Then you will see and understand for whose sake I try to be beautiful and brilliant, and what it is I love in all that surrounds me this evening!' I really believed that my success pleased me only because it enabled me to give it up for his sake. One danger I recognized as possible—that I might be carried away by a fancy for some new acquaintance, and that my husband might grow jealous. But he trusted me so absolutely, and seemed so undisturbed and indifferent, and all the young men were so inferior to him, that I was not alarmed by this one danger. Yet the attention of so many people in society gave me satisfaction, flattered my vanity, and made me think that there was some merit in my love for my husband. Thus I became more offhand and self-confident in my behaviour to him.

'Oh, I saw you this evening carrying on a most animated conversation with Mme N.,' I said one night on returning from a ball, shaking my finger at him. He had really been talking to this lady, who was a well-known figure in Petersburg society. He was more silent and depressed than usual, and I said this to rouse him up.

'What is the good of talking like that, for *you* especially, Másha?' he said with half-closed teeth and frowning as if in pain. 'Leave that to others; it does not suit you and me. Pretence of that sort may spoil the true relation between us, which I still hope may come back.'

I was ashamed and said nothing.

'Will it ever come back, Másha, do you think?' he asked.

'It never was spoilt and never will be,' I said; and I really believed this then.

'God grant that you are right!' he said; 'if not, we ought to be going home.'

But he only spoke like this once—in general he seemed as satisfied as I was, and I was so gay and so happy! I comforted myself too by thinking, 'If he is bored sometimes, I endured the same thing for his sake in the country. If the relation between us has become a little different, everything will be the same again in summer, when we shall be alone in our house at Nikólskoe with Tatyána Semyónovna.'

So the winter slipped by, and, in spite of our plans, we stayed on over Easter in Petersburg. A week later we were preparing to start; our packing was all done; my husband, who had bought things—plants for the garden and presents for people at Nikólskoe—was in a specially cheerful and affectionate mood. Just then Princess D. came and begged us to stay till the Saturday, in order to be present at a reception to be given by Countess R. The Countess was very anxious to secure me, because a foreign prince, who was visiting Petersburg and had seen me already at a ball, wished to make my acquaintance; indeed this was his motive for attending the reception, and he declared that

I was the most beautiful woman in Russia. All the world was to be there; and, in a word, it would really be too bad, if I did not go too.

My husband was talking to someone at the other end of the drawing-room.

'So you will go, won't you, Mary?' said the Princess.

'We meant to start for the country the day after to-morrow,' I answered undecidedly, glancing at my husband. Our eyes met, and he turned away at once.

'I must persuade him to stay,' she said, 'and then we can go on Saturday and turn all heads. All right?'

'It would upset our plans; and we have packed,' I answered, beginning to give way.

'She had better go this evening and make her curtsey to the Prince,' my husband called out from the other end of the room; and he spoke in a tone of suppressed irritation which I had never heard from him before.

'I declare he's jealous, for the first time in his life,' said the lady, laughing. 'But it's not for the sake of the Prince I urge it, Sergéy Mikháylych, but for all our sakes. The Countess was so anxious to have her.'

'It rests with her entirely,' my husband said coldly, and then left the room.

I saw that he was much disturbed, and this pained me. I gave no positive promise. As soon as our visitor left, I went to my husband. He was walking up and down his room, thinking, and neither saw nor heard me when I came in on tiptoe.

Looking at him I said to myself: 'He is dreaming already of his dear Nikólskoe, our morning coffee in the bright drawing-room, the land and the labourers, our evenings in the music-room, and our secret midnight suppers.' Then I decided in my own heart: 'Not for all the balls and all the flattering princes in the world will I give up his glad confusion and tender cares.' I was just about to say that I did not wish to go to the ball and would refuse, when he looked round, saw me, and frowned. His face, which had been gentle and thoughtful, changed at once to its old expression of sagacity, penetration, and patronizing composure. He would not show himself to me as a mere man, but had to be a demigod on a pedestal.

'Well, my dear?' he asked, turning towards me with an unconcerned air.

I said nothing. I was provoked, because he was hiding his real self from me, and would not continue to be the man I loved.

'Do you want to go to this reception on Saturday?' he asked.

'I did, but you disapprove. Besides, our things are all packed,' I said.

Never before had I heard such coldness in his tone to me, and never before seen such coldness in his eye.

'I shall order the things to be unpacked,' he said, 'and I shall stay till Tuesday. So you can go to the party, if you like. I hope you will; but I shall not go.'

Without looking at me, he began to walk about the room jerkily, as his habit was when perturbed.

'I simply can't understand you,' I said, following him with my eyes from where I stood. 'You say that you never lose self-control' (he had never really said so); 'then why do you talk to me so strangely? I am ready on your account to sacrifice this pleasure, and then you, in a sarcastic tone which is new from you to me, insist that I should go.'

'So you make a *sacrifice*!' he threw special emphasis on the last word. 'Well, so do I. What could be better? We compete in generosity—what an example of family happiness!'

Such harsh and contemptuous language I had never heard from his lips before. I was not abashed, but mortified by his contempt; and his harshness did not frighten me but made me harsh too. How could *he* speak thus, he who was always so frank and simple and dreaded insincerity in our speech to one another? And what had I done that he should speak so? I really intended to sacrifice for his sake a pleasure in which I could see no harm; and a moment ago I loved him and understood his feelings as well as ever. We had changed parts: now he avoided direct and plain words, and I desired them.

'You are much changed,' I said, with a sigh. 'How am I guilty before you? It is not this party—you have something else, some old count against me. Why this insincerity? You used to be so afraid of it yourself. Tell me plainly what you complain of.' 'What will he say?' thought I, and reflected with some complacency that I had done nothing all winter which he could find fault with.

I went into the middle of the room, so that he had to pass close to me, and looked at him. I thought, 'He will come and clasp me in his arms, and there will be an end of it.' I was even sorry that I should not have the chance of proving him wrong. But he stopped at the far end of the room and looked at me.

'Do you not understand yet?' he asked.

'No, I don't.'

'Then I must explain. What I feel, and cannot help feeling, positively sickens me for the first time in my life.' He stopped, evidently startled by the harsh sound of his own voice.

'What do you mean?' I asked, with tears of indignation in my eyes.

'It sickens me that the Prince admired you, and you therefore run to meet him, forgetting your husband and yourself and womanly dignity; and you wilfully misunderstand what your want of self-respect makes your husband feel for you: you actually come to your husband and speak of the "sacrifice" you are making, by which you mean—"To show myself to His Highness is a great pleasure to me, but I 'sacrifice' it."'

The longer he spoke, the more he was excited by the sound of his own voice, which was hard and rough and cruel. I had never seen him, had never thought of seeing him, like that. The blood rushed to my heart and I was frightened; but I felt that I had nothing to be ashamed of, and the excitement of wounded vanity made me eager to punish him.

'I have long been expecting this,' I said, 'Go on. Go on!'

'What you expected, I don't know,' he went on; 'but I might well expect the worst, when I saw you day after day sharing the dirtiness and idleness and luxury of this foolish society, and it has come at last. Never have I felt such shame and pain as now—pain for myself, when your friend thrusts her unclean fingers into my heart and speaks of my jealousy!—jealousy of a man whom neither you nor I know; and you refuse to understand me and offer to make a sacrifice for me—and what sacrifice? I am ashamed for you, for your degradation! . . . Sacrifice!' he repeated again.

'Ah, so this is a husband's power,' thought I: 'to insult and humiliate a perfectly innocent woman. Such may be a husband's rights, but I will not submit to them.' I felt the blood leave my face and a strange distension of my nostrils, as I said, 'No! I make no sacrifice on your account. I shall go to the party on Saturday without fail.'

'And I hope you may enjoy it. But all is over between us two!' he cried out in a fit of unrestrained fury. 'But you shall not torture me any longer! I was a fool, when I . . .', but his lips quivered, and he refrained with a visible effort from ending the sentence.

I feared and hated him at that moment. I wished to say a great deal to him and punish him for all his insults; but if I had opened my mouth, I should have lost my dignity by bursting into tears. I said nothing and left the room. But as soon as I ceased to hear his footsteps, I was horrified at what we had done. I feared that the tie which had made all my happiness might really be snapped for ever; and I thought of going back. But then I wondered: 'Is he calm enough now to understand me, if I mutely stretch out my hand and look at him? Will he realize my generosity? What if he calls my grief a mere pretence? Or he may feel sure that he is right and accept my repentance and forgive me with unruffled pride. And why, oh why, did he whom I loved so well insult me so cruelly?'

I went not to him but to my own room, where I sat for a long time and cried. I recalled with horror each word of our conversation, and substituted different words, kind words, for those that we had spoken, and added others; and then again I remembered the reality with horror and a feeling of injury. In the evening I went down for tea and met my husband in the presence of a friend who was staying with us; and it seemed to me that a wide gulf had opened between us from that day. Our friend asked me when we were to start; and before I could speak, my husband answered:

'On Tuesday,' he said; 'we have to stay for Countess R.'s reception.' He turned to me: 'I believe you intend to go?' he asked.

His matter-of-fact tone frightened me, and I looked at him timidly. His eyes were directed straight at me with an unkind and scornful expression; his voice was cold and even.

'Yes,' I answered.

When we were alone that evening, he came up to me and held out his hand.

'Please forget what I said to you to-day,' he began.

As I took his hand, a smile quivered on my lips and the tears were ready to flow; but he took his hand away and sat down on an armchair at some distance, as if fearing a sentimental scene. 'Is it possible that he still thinks himself in the right?' I wondered; and, though I was quite ready to explain and to beg that we might not go to the party, the words died on my lips.

'I must write to my mother that we have put off our departure,' he said; 'otherwise she will be uneasy.'

'When do you think of going?' I asked.

'On Tuesday, after the reception,' he replied.

'I hope it is not on my account,' I said, looking into his eyes; but those eyes merely looked—they said nothing, and a veil seemed to cover them from me. His face seemed to me to have grown suddenly old and disagreeable.

We went to the reception, and good friendly relations between us seemed to have been restored, but these relations were quite different from what they had been.

At the party I was sitting with other ladies when the Prince came up to me, so that I had to stand up in order to speak to him. As I rose, my eyes involuntarily sought my husband. He was looking at me from the other end of the room, and now turned away. I was seized by a sudden sense of shame and pain; in my confusion I blushed all over my face and neck under the Prince's eye. But I was forced to stand and listen, while he spoke, eyeing me from his superior height. Our conversation was soon over: there was no room for him beside me, and he, no doubt, felt that I was uncomfortable with him. We talked of the last ball, of where I should spend the summer, and so on. As he left me, he expressed a wish to make the acquaintance of my husband, and I saw them meet and begin a conversation at the far end of the room. The Prince evidently said something about me; for he smiled in the middle of their talk and looked in my direction.

My husband suddenly flushed up. He made a low bow and turned away from the Prince without being dismissed. I blushed too: I was ashamed of the impression which I and, still more, my husband must have made on the Prince. Everyone, I thought, must have noticed my awkward shyness when I was presented, and my husband's eccentric behaviour. 'Heaven knows how they will interpret such conduct? Perhaps they know already about my scene with my husband!'

Princess D. drove me home, and on the way I spoke to her about my husband. My patience was at an end, and I told her the whole story of what had taken place between us owing to this unlucky party. To calm me, she said that such differences were very common and quite unimportant, and that our quarrel would leave no trace behind. She explained to me her view of my husband's character—that he had become very stiff and unsociable. I agreed, and believed that I had learned to judge him myself more calmly and more truly.

But when I was alone with my husband later, the thought that I had sat in judgement upon him weighed like a crime upon my conscience; and I felt that the gulf which divided us had grown still greater.

CHAPTER VIII

From that day there was a complete change in our life and our relations to each other. We were no longer as happy when we were alone together as before. To certain subjects we gave a wide berth, and conversation flowed more easily in the presence of a third person. When the talk turned on life in the country, or on a ball, we were uneasy and shrank from looking at one another. Both of us knew where the gulf between us lay, and seemed afraid to approach it. I was convinced that he was proud and irascible, and that I must be careful not to touch him on his weak point. He was equally sure that I disliked the country and was dying for social distraction, and that he must put up with this unfortunate taste of mine. We both avoided frank conversation on these topics, and each misjudged the other. We had long ceased to think each other the most perfect people in the world; each now judged the other in secret, and measured the offender by the standard of other people. I fell ill before we left Petersburg, and we went from there to a house near town, from which my husband went on alone, to join his mother at Nikólskoe. By that time I was well enough to have gone with him, but he urged me to stay on the pretext of my health. I knew, however, that he was really afraid we should be uncomfortable together in the country; so I did not insist much, and he went off alone. I felt it dull and solitary in his absence; but when he came back, I saw that he did not add to my life what he had added formerly. In the old days every thought and experience weighed on me like a crime till I had imparted it to him; every action and word of his seemed to me a model of perfection; we often laughed for joy at the mere sight of each other. But these relations had changed, so imperceptibly that we had not even noticed their disappearance. Separate interests and cares, which we no longer tried to share, made their appearance, and even the fact of our estrangement ceased to trouble us. The idea became familiar, and, before a year had passed, each could look at the other without confusion. His fits of boyish merriment with me had quite vanished; his mood of calm indulgence to all that passed, which used to provoke me, had disappeared; there was an end of those penetrating looks which used to confuse and delight me, an end of the ecstasies and prayers which we once shared in common. We did not even meet often: he was continually absent, with no fears or regrets for leaving me alone; and I was constantly in society, where I did not need him.

There were no further scenes or quarrels between us. I tried to satisfy him, he carried out all my wishes, and we seemed to love each other.

When we were by ourselves, which we seldom were, I felt neither joy nor excitement nor embarrassment in his company: it seemed like being alone. I realized that he was my husband and no mere stranger, a good man, and as familiar to me as my own self. I was convinced that I knew just what he would say and do, and how he would look; and if anything he did surprised me, I concluded that he had made a mistake. I expected nothing from him. In a word, he was my husband—and that was all. It seemed to me that things must be so, as a matter of course, and that no other relations between us had ever existed. When he left home, especially at first, I was lonely and frightened and felt keenly my need of support; when he came back,

I ran to his arms with joy, though two hours later my joy was quite forgotten, and I found nothing to say to him. Only at moments which sometimes occurred between us of quiet undemonstrative affection, I felt something wrong and some pain at my heart, and I seemed to read the same story in his eyes. I was conscious of a limit to tenderness, which he seemingly would not, and I could not, overstep. This saddened me sometimes; but I had no leisure to reflect on anything, and my regret for a change, which I vaguely realized, I tried to drown in the distractions which were always within my reach. Fashionable life, which had dazzled me at first by its glitter and flattery of my self-love, now took entire command of my nature, became a habit, laid its fetters upon me, and monopolized my capacity for feeling. I could not bear solitude, and was afraid to reflect on my position. My whole day, from late in the morning till late at night, was taken up by the claims of society; even if I stayed at home, my time was not my own. This no longer seemed to me either gay or dull, but it seemed that so, and not otherwise, it always had to be.

So three years passed, during which our relations to one another remained unchanged and seemed to have taken a fixed shape which could not become either better or worse. Though two events of importance in our family life took place during that time, neither of them changed my own life. These were the birth of my first child and the death of Tatyána Semyónovna. At first the feeling of motherhood did take hold of me with such power, and produce in me such a passion of unanticipated joy, that I believed this would prove the beginning of a new life for me. But, in the course of two months, when I began to go out again, my feeling grew weaker and weaker, till it passed into mere habit and the lifeless performance of a duty. My husband, on the contrary, from the birth of our first boy, became his old self again—gentle, composed, and home-loving, and transferred to the child his old tenderness and gaiety. Many a night when I went, dressed for a ball, to the nursery, to bless the child with the cross before he slept, I found my husband there and felt his eyes fixed on me with something of reproof in their serious gaze. Then I was ashamed and even shocked by my own callousness, and asked myself if I was worse than other women. 'But it can't be helped,' I said to myself; 'I love my child, but to sit beside him all day long would bore me; and nothing will make me pretend what I do not really feel.'

His mother's death was a great sorrow to my husband; he said that he found it painful to go on living at Nikólskoe. For myself, although I mourned for her and sympathized with my husband's sorrow, yet I found life in that house easier and pleasanter after her death. Most of those three years we spent in town: I went only once to Nikólskoe for two months; and the third year we went abroad and spent the summer at Baden.

I was then twenty-one; our financial position was, I believed, satisfactory; my domestic life gave me all that I asked of it; everyone I knew, it seemed to me, loved me; my health was good; I was the best-dressed woman in Baden; I knew that I was good-looking; the weather was fine; I enjoyed the atmosphere of beauty and refinement; and, in short, I was in excellent spirits. They had once been even higher at Nikólskoe, when my happiness was in myself and came from the feeling that I deserved to be happy, and from the anticipation of still greater happiness to come. That was a different state of things; but I did very well this summer also. I had no special wishes or hopes or fears; it seemed to me that my life was full and my conscience easy. Among all the visitors at Baden that season there was no one man whom I preferred to the rest, or even to our old ambassador, Prince K., who was assiduous in his attentions to me. One was young, and another old; one was English and fair, another French and wore a beard—to me they were all alike, but all indispensable. Indistinguishable as they were, they together made up the atmosphere which I found so pleasant. But there was one, an Italian marquis, who stood out from the rest by reason of the boldness with which he expressed his admiration. He seized every opportunity of being with me—danced with me, rode with me, and met me at the casino; and everywhere he spoke to me of my charms. Several times I saw him from my windows loitering round our hotel, and the fixed gaze of his bright eyes often troubled me, and made me blush and turn away. He was young, handsome, and well-mannered; and, above all, by his smile and the expression of his brow, he resembled my husband, though much handsomer than he. He struck me by this likeness, though in general, in his lips, eyes, and long chin, there was something coarse and animal which contrasted with my husband's charming expression of kindness and noble serenity. I supposed him to be passionately in love with me, and thought of him sometimes with proud commiseration. When I tried at times to soothe him and change his tone to one of easy, half-friendly confidence, he resented the suggestion with vehemence, and continued to disquiet me by a smouldering passion which was ready at any moment to burst forth. Though I would not own it even to myself, I feared him and often thought of him against my will. My husband knew him, and treated him—even more than other acquaintances of ours who regarded him only as my husband—with coldness and disdain.

Towards the end of the season I fell ill and stayed indoors for a fortnight. The first evening that I went out again to hear the band, I learnt that Lady S., an Englishwoman famous for her beauty, who had long been expected, had arrived in my absence. My return was welcomed, and a group gathered round me; but a more distinguished group attended the beautiful stranger. She and her beauty were the one subject of conversation around me. When I saw her, she was really beautiful, but her self-satisfied expression struck me as disagreeable, and I said so. That day everything that had formerly seemed amusing, seemed dull. Lady S. arranged an expedition to the ruined castle for the next day; but I declined to be of the party. Almost everyone else went; and my opinion of Baden underwent a complete change. Everything and everybody seemed to me stupid and tiresome; I wanted to cry, to break off my cure, to return to Russia. There was some evil feeling in my soul, but I did not yet acknowledge it to myself. Pretending that I was not strong, I ceased to appear at crowded parties; if I went out, it was only in the morning by myself, to drink the waters; and my only companion was Mme M., a Russian lady, with whom I sometimes took drives in the surrounding country. My husband was absent: he had gone to Heidelberg for a time, intending to return to Russia when my cure was over, and only paid me occasional visits at Baden.

One day when Lady S. had carried off all the company on a

hunting-expedition, Mme M. and I drove in the afternoon to the castle. While our carriage moved slowly along the winding road, bordered by ancient chestnut-trees and commanding a vista of the pretty and pleasant country round Baden, with the setting sun lighting it up, our conversation took a more serious turn than had ever happened to us before. I had known my companion for a long time; but she appeared to me now in a new light, as a well-principled and intelligent woman, to whom it was possible to speak without reserve, and whose friendship was worth having. We spoke of our private concerns, of our children, of the emptiness of life at Baden, till we felt a longing for Russia and the Russian countryside. When we entered the castle we were still under the impression of this serious feeling. Within the walls there was shade and coolness; the sunlight played from above upon the ruins. Steps and voices were audible. The landscape, charming enough but cold to a Russian eye, lay before us in the frame made by a doorway. We sat down to rest and watched the sunset in silence. The voices now sounded louder, and I thought I heard my own name. I listened and could not help overhearing every word. I recognized the voices: the speakers were the Italian marquis and a French friend of his whom I knew also. They were talking of me and of Lady S., and the Frenchman was comparing us as rival beauties. Though he said nothing insulting, his words made my pulse quicken. He explained in detail the good points of us both. I was already a mother, while Lady S. was only nineteen; though I had the advantage in hair, my rival had a better figure. 'Besides,' he added, 'Lady S. is a real *grande dame*, and the other is nothing in particular, only one of those obscure Russian princesses who turn up here nowadays in such numbers.' He ended by saying that I was wise in not attempting to compete with Lady S., and that I was completely buried as far as Baden was concerned.

'I am sorry for her—unless indeed she takes a fancy to console herself with you,' he added with a hard ringing laugh.

'If she goes away, I follow her'—the words were blurted out in an Italian accent.

'Happy man! he is still capable of a passion!' laughed the Frenchman.

'Passion!' said the other voice and then was still for a moment. 'It is a necessity to me: I cannot live without it. To make life a romance is the one thing worth doing. And with me romance never breaks off in the middle, and this affair I shall carry through to the end.'

'*Bonne chance, mon ami!*'[1] said the Frenchman.

They now turned a corner, and the voices stopped. Then we heard them coming down the steps, and a few minutes later they came out upon us by a side-door. They were much surprised to see us. I blushed when the marquis approached me, and felt afraid when we left the castle and he offered me his arm. I could not refuse, and we set off for the carriage, walking behind Mme M. and his friend. I was mortified by what the Frenchman had said of me, though I secretly admitted that he had only put in words what I felt myself; but the plain speaking of the Italian had surprised and upset me by its coarseness. I was tormented by the thought that, though I had overheard him, he showed no fear of me. It was hateful to have him so close to me; and I walked fast after the other couple, not looking at him or answering him and trying to hold his arm in such a way as not to hear him. He spoke of the fine view, of the unexpected pleasure of our meeting, and so on; but I was not listening. My thoughts were with my husband, my child, my country; I felt ashamed, distressed, anxious; I was in a hurry to get back to my solitary room in the Hôtel de Bade, there to think at leisure of the storm of feeling that had just risen in my heart. But Mme M. walked slowly, it was still a long way to the carriage, and my escort seemed to loiter on purpose as if he wished to detain me. 'None of that!' I thought, and resolutely quickened my pace. But it soon became unmistakable that he was detaining me and even pressing my arm. Mme M. turned a corner, and we were quite alone. I was afraid.

'Excuse me,' I said coldly and tried to free my arm; but the lace of my sleeve caught on a button of his coat. Bending towards me, he began to unfasten it, and his ungloved fingers touched my arm. A feeling new to me, half horror and half pleasure, sent an icy shiver down my back. I looked at him,

[1] Good luck, my friend!

intending by my coldness to convey all the contempt I felt for him; but my look expressed nothing but fear and excitement. His liquid blazing eyes, right up against my face, stared strangely at me, at my neck and breast; both his hands fingered my arm above the wrist; his parted lips were saying that he loved me, and that I was all the world to him; and those lips were coming nearer and nearer, and those hands were squeezing mine harder and harder and burning me. A fever ran through my veins, my sight grew dim, I trembled, and the words intended to check him died in my throat. Suddenly I felt a kiss on my cheek. Trembling all over and turning cold, I stood still and stared at him. Unable to speak or move, I stood there, horrified, expectant, even desirous. It was over in a moment, but the moment was horrible! In that short time I saw him exactly as he was—the low straight forehead (that forehead so like my husband's!) under the straw hat; the handsome regular nose and dilated nostrils; the long waxed moustache and short beard; the close-shaved cheeks and sunburnt neck. I hated and feared him; he was utterly repugnant and alien to me. And yet the excitement and passion of this hateful strange man raised a powerful echo in my own heart; I felt an irresistible longing to surrender myself to the kisses of that coarse handsome mouth, and to the pressure of those white hands with their delicate veins and jewelled fingers; I was tempted to throw myself headlong into the abyss of forbidden delights that had suddenly opened up before me.

'I am so unhappy already,' I thought; 'let more and more storms of unhappiness burst over my head!'

He put one arm round me and bent towards my face. 'Better so!' I thought: 'let sin and shame cover me ever deeper and deeper!'

'*Je vous aime!*'[1] he whispered in the voice which was so like my husband's. At once I thought of my husband and child, as creatures once precious to me who had now passed altogether out of my life. At that moment I heard Mme M.'s voice; she called to me from round the corner. I came to myself, tore my hand away without looking at him, and almost ran after her: I

[1] I love you.

only looked at him after she and I were already seated in the carriage. Then I saw him raise his hat and ask some commonplace question with a smile. He little knew the inexpressible aversion I felt for him at that moment.

My life seemed so wretched, the future so hopeless, the past so black! When Mme M. spoke, her words meant nothing to me. I thought that she talked only out of pity, and to hide the contempt I aroused in her. In every word and every look I seemed to detect this contempt and insulting pity. The shame of that kiss burnt my cheek, and the thought of my husband and child was more than I could bear. When I was alone in my own room, I tried to think over my position; but I was afraid to be alone. Without drinking the tea which was brought me, and uncertain of my own motives, I got ready with feverish haste to catch the evening train and join my husband at Heidelberg.

I found seats for myself and my maid in an empty carriage. When the train started and the fresh air blew through the window on my face, I grew more composed and pictured my past and future to myself more clearly. The course of our married life from the time of our first visit to Petersburg now presented itself to me in a new light, and lay like a reproach on my conscience. For the first time I clearly recalled our start at Nikólskoe and our plans for the future; and for the first time I asked myself what happiness had my husband had since then. I felt that I had behaved badly to him. 'But why', I asked myself, 'did he not stop me? Why did he make pretences? Why did he always avoid explanations? Why did he insult me? Why did he not use the power of his love to influence me? Or did he not love me?' But whether he was to blame or not, I still felt the kiss of that strange man upon my cheek. The nearer we got to Heidelberg, the clearer grew my picture of my husband, and the more I dreaded our meeting. 'I shall tell him all,' I thought, 'and wipe out everything with tears of repentance; and he will forgive me.' But I did not know myself what I meant by 'everything'; and I did not believe in my heart that he would forgive me.

As soon as I entered my husband's room and saw his calm though surprised expression, I felt at once that I had nothing to tell him, no confession to make, and nothing to ask forgiveness for. I had to suppress my unspoken grief and penitence.

'What put this into your head?' he asked. 'I meant to go to Baden tomorrow.' Then he looked more closely at me and seemed to take alarm. 'What's the matter with you? What has happened?' he said.

'Nothing at all,' I replied, almost breaking down. 'I am not going back. Let us go home, tomorrow if you like, to Russia.'

For some time he said nothing but looked at me attentively. Then he said. 'But do tell me what has happened to you.'

I blushed involuntarily and looked down. There came into his eyes a flash of anger and displeasure. Afraid of what he might imagine, I said with a power of pretence that surprised myself:

'Nothing at all has happened. It was merely that I grew weary and sad by myself; and I have been thinking a great deal of our way of life and of you. I have long been to blame towards you. Why do you take me abroad, when you can't bear it yourself? I have long been to blame. Let us go back to Nikólskoe and settle there for ever.'

'Spare us these sentimental scenes, my dear,' he said coldly. 'To go back to Nikólskoe is a good idea, for our money is running short; but the notion of stopping there "for ever" is fanciful. I know you would not settle down. Have some tea, and you will feel better,' and he rose to ring for the waiter.

I imagined all he might be thinking about me; and I was offended by the horrible thoughts which I ascribed to him when I encountered the dubious and shame-faced look he directed at me. 'He will not and cannot understand me.' I said I would go and look at the child, and I left the room. I wished to be alone, and to cry and cry and cry . . .

CHAPTER IX

The house at Nikólskoe, so long unheated and uninhabited, came to life again; but much of the past was dead beyond recall. Tatyána Semyónovna was no more, and we were now alone together. But far from desiring such close companionship, we even found it irksome. To me that winter was the more trying because I was in bad health, from which I only recovered after the birth of my second son. My husband and I were still on the same terms as during our life in Petersburg: we were coldly friendly to each other; but in the country each room and wall and sofa recalled what he had once been to me, and what I had lost. It was as if some unforgiven grievance held us apart, as if he were punishing me and pretending not to be aware of it. But there was nothing to ask pardon for, no penalty to deprecate; my punishment was merely this, that he did not give his whole heart and mind to me as he used to do; but he did not give it to anyone or to anything; as though he had no longer a heart to give. Sometimes it occurred to me that he was only pretending to be like that, in order to hurt me, and that the old feeling was still alive in his breast; and I tried to call it forth. But I always failed: he always seemed to avoid frankness, evidently suspecting me of insincerity, and dreading the folly of any emotional display. I could read in his face and the tone of his voice, 'What is the good of talking? I know all the facts already, and I know what is on the tip of your tongue, and I know that you will say one thing and do another.' At first I was mortified by his dread of frankness, but I came later to think that it was rather the absence, on his part, of any need of frankness. It would never have occurred to me now, to tell him of a sudden that I loved him, or to ask him to repeat the prayers with me or listen while I played the piano. Our relationship came to be regulated by a fixed code of good manners. We lived our separate lives: he had his own occupations in which I was not needed, and which I no longer wished to share, while I continued my idle life which no longer vexed or grieved him. The children were still too young to form a bond between us.

But spring came round and brought Kátya and Sónya to spend the summer with us in the country. As the house at Nikólskoe was under repair, we went to live at my old home at Pokróvskoe. The old house was unchanged—the veranda, the folding table and the piano in the sunny drawing-room, and my old bedroom with its white curtains and the dreams of my girlhood which I seemed to have left behind me there. In that room there were two beds: one had been mine, and in it now my plump little Kokósha lay sprawling, when I went at night to sign him with the cross; the other was a crib, in which the little face of my baby, Ványa, peeped out from his swaddling-clothes. Often, when I had made the sign over them and remained standing in the middle of the quiet room, suddenly there rose up from all the corners, from the walls and curtains, old forgotten visions of youth. Old voices began to sing the songs of my girlhood. Where were those visions now? where were those dear old sweet songs? All that I had hardly dared to hope for had come to pass. My vague confused dreams had become a reality, and the reality had become an oppressive, difficult, and joyless life. All remained the same—the garden visible through the window, the grass, the path, the very same bench over there above the dell, the same song of the nightingale by the pond, the same lilacs in full bloom, the same moon shining above the house; and yet, in everything such a terrible inconceivable change! Such coldness in all that might have been near and dear! Just as in old times, Kátya and I sit quietly alone together in the parlour and talk, and talk of him. But Kátya has grown wrinkled and pale; and her eyes no longer shine with joy and hope, but express only sympathy, sorrow, and regret. We do not go into raptures as we used to, we judge him coolly; we do not wonder what we have done to deserve such happiness, or long to proclaim our thoughts to all the world. No! we whisper together like conspirators and ask each other for the hundredth time why all has changed so sadly. Yet he was still the same man, save for the deeper furrow between his eyebrows and the whiter hair on his temples; but his serious attentive look was constantly veiled from me by a cloud. And I am the same woman, but without love or desire for love, with no longing for work and no content with myself. My religious ecstasies, my love for my husband, the fullness of my former life—all these now seem utterly remote and visionary. Once it seemed so plain and right that to live for others was happiness; but now it has become unintelligible. Why live for others, when life had no attraction even for oneself?

I had given up my music altogether since the time of our first visit to Petersburg; but now the old piano and the old music tempted me to begin again.

One day I was not well and stayed indoors alone. My husband had taken Kátya and Sónya to see the new buildings at Nikólskoe. Tea was laid; I went downstairs and while waiting for them sat down at the piano. I opened the sonata 'Quasi una fantasia' and began to play. There was no one within sight or sound, the windows were open over the garden, and the familiar sounds floated through the room with a solemn sadness. At the end of the first movement I looked round instinctively to the corner where he used once to sit and listen to my playing. He was not there; his chair, long unmoved, was still in its place; through the window I could see a lilac-bush against the light of the setting sun; the freshness of evening streamed in through the open windows. I rested my elbows on the piano and covered my face with both hands; and so I sat for a long time, thinking. I recalled with pain the irrevocable past, and timidly imagined the future. But for me there seemed to be no future, no desires at all and no hopes. 'Can life be over for me?' I thought with horror; then I looked up, and, trying to forget and not to think, I began playing the same movement over again. 'O God!' I prayed, 'forgive me if I have sinned, or restore to me all that once blossomed in my heart, or teach me what to do and how to live now.' There was a sound of wheels on the grass and before the steps of the house; then I heard cautious and familiar footsteps pass along the veranda and cease; but my heart no longer replied to the sound. When I stopped playing the footsteps were behind me and a hand was laid on my shoulder.

'How clever of you to think of playing that!' he said.

I said nothing.

'Have you had tea?' he asked.

I shook my head without looking at him—I was unwilling to let him see the signs of emotion on my face.

'They'll be here immediately,' he said; 'the horse gave trouble, and they got out on the high road to walk home.'

'Let us wait for them,' I said, and went out to the veranda, hoping that he would follow; but he asked about the children and went upstairs to see them. Once more his presence and simple kindly voice made me doubt if I had really lost anything. What more could I wish? 'He is kind and gentle, a good husband, a good father; I don't know myself what more I want.' I sat down under the veranda awning on the very bench on which I had sat when we became engaged. The sun had set, it was growing dark, and a little spring rain-cloud hung over the house and garden, and only behind the trees the horizon was clear, with the fading glow of twilight, in which one star had just begun to twinkle. The landscape, covered by the shadow of the cloud, seemed waiting for the light spring shower. There was not a breath of wind; not a single leaf or blade of grass stirred; the scent of lilac and bird-cherry was so strong in the garden and veranda that it seemed as if all the air was in flower; it came in wafts, now stronger and now weaker, till one longed to shut both eyes and ears and drink in that fragrance only. The dahlias and rose-bushes, not yet in flower, stood motionless on the black mould of the border, looking as if they were growing slowly upwards on their white-shaved props; beyond the dell, the frogs were making the most of their time before the rain drove them to the pond, croaking busily and loudly. Only the high continuous note of water falling at some distance rose above their croaking. From time to time the nightingales called to one another, and I could hear them flitting restlessly from bush to bush. Again this spring a nightingale had tried to build a nest in a bush under the window, and I heard her fly off across the pathway when I went onto the veranda. From there she whistled once and then stopped; she, too, was expecting the rain.

I tried in vain to calm my feelings: I had a sense of anticipation and regret.

He came downstairs again and sat down beside me.

'I am afraid they will get wet,' he said.

'Yes,' I answered; and we sat for long without speaking.

The cloud came down lower and lower with no wind. The air grew stiller and more fragrant. Suddenly a drop fell on the canvas awning and seemed to rebound from it; then another broke on the gravel path; soon there was a splash on the burdock leaves, and a fresh shower of big drops came down faster and faster. The nightingales and frogs were silent; only the high note of the falling water, though the rain made it seem more distant, still went on; and a bird, which must have sheltered among the dry leaves near the veranda, steadily repeated its two unvarying notes. My husband got up to go in.

'Where are you going?' I asked, trying to keep him; 'it is so pleasant here.'

'We must send them an umbrella and goloshes,' he replied.

'Don't trouble—it will soon be over.'

He thought I was right, and we remained together on the veranda. I rested one hand upon the wet slippery rail and put my head out. The fresh rain wetted my hair and neck in places. The cloud, growing lighter and thinner, was passing overhead; the steady patter of the rain gave place to occasional drops that fell from the sky or dripped from the trees. The frogs began to croak again in the dell; the nightingales woke up and began to call from the dripping bushes from one side and then from another. The whole prospect before us grew clear.

'How delightful!' he said, seating himself on the veranda rail and passing a hand over my wet hair.

This simple caress had on me the effect of a reproach: I felt inclined to cry.

'What more can a man need?' he said; 'I am so content now that I want nothing; I am perfectly happy!'

He told me a different story once, I thought. He had said that, however great his happiness might be, he always wanted more and more. Now he is calm and contented; while my heart is full of unspoken repentance and unshed tears.

'I think it delightful too,' I said; 'but I am sad just because of the beauty of it all. All is so fair and lovely outside me, while my own heart is confused and baffled and full of vague unsatisfied longing. Is it possible that there is no element of pain, no yearning for the past, in your enjoyment of nature?'

He took his hand off my head and was silent for a little.

'I used to feel that too,' he said, as though recalling it, 'especially in spring. I used to sit up all night too, with my hopes and fears for company, and good company they were! But life was all before me then. Now it is all behind me, and I am content with what I have. I find life wonderful,' he added with such careless confidence, that I believed, whatever pain it gave me to hear it, that it was the truth.

'But is there nothing you wish for?' I asked.

'I don't ask for impossibilities,' he said, guessing my thoughts. 'You go and get your head wet,' he added, stroking my head like a child's and again passing his hand over the wet hair; 'you envy the leaves and the grass their wetting from the rain, and you would like yourself to be the grass and the leaves and the rain. But I am content to enjoy them and everything else that is good and young and happy.'

'And do you miss nothing of the past?' I asked, while my heart grew heavier and heavier.

Again he thought for a time before replying. I saw that he wished to reply with perfect frankness.

'Nothing,' he said shortly.

'Not true! not true!' I said, turning towards him and looking into his eyes. 'Do you really not miss the past?'

'No!' he repeated; 'I am grateful for it, but I don't miss it.'

'But would you not like to have it back?' I asked.

He turned away and looked out over the garden.

'No; I might as well wish to have wings. It is impossible.'

'And would you not alter the past? do you not reproach yourself or me?'

'No, never! It was all for the best.'

'Listen to me!' I said, touching his arm to make him look round. 'Why did you never tell me that you wished me to live as you really wished me to? Why did you give me a freedom for which I was unfit? Why did you stop teaching me? If you had wished it, if you had guided me differently, none of all this would have happened!' said I in a voice that increasingly expressed cold displeasure and reproach, in place of the love of former days.

'What would not have happened?' he asked, turning to me in surprise. 'As it is, there is nothing wrong. Things are all right, quite all right,' he added with a smile.

'Does he really not understand?' I thought; 'or, still worse, does he not wish to understand?'

Then I suddenly broke out. 'Had you acted differently, I should not now be punished, for no fault at all, by your indifference and even contempt, and you would not have taken from me unjustly all that I valued in life!'

'What do you mean, my dear one?' he asked—he seemed not to understand me.

'No! don't interrupt me! You have taken from me your confidence, your love, even your respect; for I cannot believe, when I think of the past, that you still love me. No! don't speak! I must once for all say out what has long been torturing me. Is it my fault that I knew nothing of life, and that you left me to learn experience for myself? Is it my fault that now, when I have gained the knowledge and have been struggling for nearly a year to come back to you, you push me away and pretend not to understand what I want? And you always do it so that it is impossible to reproach you, while I am guilty and unhappy. Yes, you wish to drive me out again to that life which might rob us both of happiness.'

'How did I show that?' he asked in evident alarm and surprise.

'No later than yesterday you said, and you constantly say, that I can never settle down here, and that we must spend this winter too at Petersburg; and I hate Petersburg!' I went on. 'Instead of supporting me, you avoid all plain speaking, you never say a single frank affectionate word to me. And then, when I fall utterly, you will reproach me and rejoice in my fall.'

'Stop!' he said with cold severity. 'You have no right to say that. It only proves that you are ill-disposed towards me, that you don't . . .'

'That I don't love you? Don't hesitate to say it!' I cried, and the tears began to flow. I sat down on the bench and covered my face with my handkerchief.

'So that is how he understood me!' I thought, trying to restrain the sobs which choked me. 'Gone, gone is our former love!' said a voice at my heart. He did not come close or try to comfort me. He was hurt by what I had said. When he spoke, his tone was cool and dry.

'I don't know what you reproach me with,' he began. 'If you mean that I don't love you as I once did . . .'

'Did love!' I said, with my face buried in the handkerchief, while the bitter tears fell still more abundantly.

'If so, time is to blame for that, and we ourselves. Each time of life has its own kind of love.' He was silent for a moment.

'Shall I tell you the whole truth, if you really wish for frankness? In that summer when I first knew you, I used to lie awake all night, thinking about you, and I made that love myself, and it grew and grew in my heart. So again, in Petersburg and abroad, in the course of horrible sleepless nights, I strove to shatter and destroy that love, which had come to torture me. I did not destroy it, but I destroyed that part of it which gave me pain. Then I grew calm; and I feel love still, but it is a different kind of love.'

'You call it love, but I call it torture!' I said. 'Why did you allow me to go into society, if you thought so badly of it that you ceased to love me on that account?'

'No, it was not society, my dear,' he said.

'Why did you not exercise your authority?' I went on; 'why did you not lock me up or kill me? That would have been better than the loss of all that formed my happiness. I should have been happy, instead of being ashamed.'

I began to sob again and hid my face.

Just then Kátya and Sónya, wet and cheerful, came out to the veranda, laughing and talking loudly. They were silent as soon as they saw us, and went in again immediately.

We remained silent for a long time. I had had my cry out and felt relieved. I glanced at him. He was sitting with his head resting on his hand; he intended to make some reply to my glance, but only sighed deeply and resumed his former position.

I went up to him and removed his hand. His eyes turned thoughtfully to my face.

'Yes,' he began, as if continuing his thoughts aloud, 'all of us, and especially you women, must have personal experience of all the nonsense of life, in order to get back to life itself; the evidence of other people is no good. At that time you had not got near the end of that charming nonsense which I admired in you. So I let you go through it alone, feeling that I had no right to put pressure on you, though my own time for that sort of thing was long past.'

'If you loved me,' I said, 'how could you stand beside me and allow me to go through it?'

'Because it was impossible for you to take my word for it,

though you would have tried to. Personal experience was necessary, and now you have had it.'

'There was much calculation in all that,' I said, 'but little love.'

Again we were silent.

'What you said just now is severe, but it is true,' he began, rising suddenly and beginning to walk about the veranda. 'Yes, it is true. I was to blame,' he added, stopping opposite me; 'I ought either to have kept myself from loving you at all, or to have loved you in a simpler way.'

'Let us forget it all,' I said timidly.

'No,' he said; 'the past can never come back, never;' and his voice softened as he spoke.

'It is restored already,' I said, laying a hand on his shoulder.

He took my hand away and pressed it.

'I was wrong when I said that I did not miss the past. I do miss it; I weep for that past love which can never return. Who is to blame, I do not know. Love remains, but not the old love; its place remains, but it is all wasted away and has lost all strength and substance; recollections are still left, and gratitude; but . . .'

'Do not say that!' I broke in. 'Let all be as it was before! Surely that is possible?' I asked, looking into his eyes; but their gaze was clear and calm, and did not look deeply into mine.

Even while I spoke, I knew that my wishes and my petition were impossible. He smiled calmly and gently; and I thought it the smile of an old man.

'How young you are still!' he said, 'and I am so old. What you seek in me is no longer there. Why deceive ourselves?' he added, still smiling.

I stood silent opposite to him, and my heart grew calmer.

'Don't let us try to repeat life,' he went on. 'Don't let us make pretences to ourselves. Let us be thankful that there is an end of the old emotions and excitements. The excitement of searching is over for us; our quest is done, and happiness enough has fallen to our lot. Now we must stand aside and make room—for him, if you like,' he said, pointing to the nurse who was carrying Ványa out and had stopped at the veranda door. 'That's the truth, my dear one,' he said, drawing down my head and kissing it, not a lover any longer but an old friend.

The fragrant freshness of the night rose ever stronger and sweeter from the garden; the sounds and the silence grew more solemn; star after star began to twinkle overhead. I looked at him, and suddenly my heart grew light; it seemed that the cause of my suffering had been removed like an aching nerve. Suddenly I realized clearly and calmly that the past feeling, like the past time itself, was gone beyond recall, and that it would be not only impossible but painful and uncomfortable to bring it back. And after all, was that time so good which seemed to me so happy? And it was all so long, long ago!

'Time for tea!' he said, and we went together to the parlour. At the door we met the nurse with the baby. I took him in my arms, covered his bare little red legs, pressed him to me, and kissed him with the lightest touch of my lips. Half asleep, he moved the parted fingers of one creased little hand and opened dim little eyes, as if he was looking for something or recalling something. All at once his eyes rested on me, a spark of consciousness shone in them, the little pouting lips, parted before, now met and opened in a smile. 'Mine, mine, mine!' I thought, pressing him to my breast with such an impulse of joy in every limb that I found it hard to restrain myself from hurting him. I fell to kissing the cold little feet, his stomach and hand and head with its thin covering of down. My husband came up to me, and I quickly covered the child's face and uncovered it again.

'Iván Sergéich!' said my husband, tickling him under the chin. But I made haste to cover Iván Sergéich up again. None but I had any business to look long at him. I glanced at my husband. His eyes smiled as he looked at me; and I looked into them with an ease and happiness which I had not felt for a long time.

That day my romance* with my husband ended; the old feeling became a precious irrecoverable remembrance; but a new feeling of love for my children and the father of my children laid the foundation of a new life and a quite different happiness; and that life and happiness have lasted to the present time.

THE KREUTZER SONATA

> But I say unto you, that every one that looketh on a woman to lust after her hath committed adultery with her already in his heart.
>
> (Matt. 5: 28)

> The disciples say unto him, If the case of the man is so with his wife, it is not expedient to marry. But he said unto them, All men cannot receive this saying, but they to whom it is given. For there are some eunuchs who were so born from their mother's womb, and there are some eunuchs who were made eunuchs of men, and there are eunuchs who have made themselves eunuchs for the kingdom of heaven's sake. Whoever is able to receive this, let him receive it.
>
> (Matt. 19: 10, 11, 12)

I

It was early spring, and the second day of our journey. Passengers going short distances entered and left our carriage, but three others, like myself, had come all the way with the train. One was a lady, plain and no longer young, who smoked, had a harassed look, and wore a mannish coat and cap; another was an acquaintance of hers, a talkative man of about forty, whose things looked neat and new; the third was a rather short man who kept himself apart. He was not old, but his curly hair had gone prematurely grey. His movements were abrupt and his unusually glittering eyes moved rapidly from one object to another. He wore an old overcoat, evidently from a first-rate tailor, with an astrakhan collar, and a tall astrakhan cap. When he unbuttoned his overcoat a sleeveless Russian coat and embroidered shirt showed beneath it. A peculiarity of this man was a strange sound he emitted, something like a clearing of his throat, or a laugh begun and sharply broken off.

All the way this man had carefully avoided making acquaintance or having any conversation with his fellow passengers. When spoken to by those near him he gave short and abrupt answers, and at other times read, looked out of the window, smoked, or drank tea and ate something he took out of an old bag.

It seemed to me that his loneliness depressed him, and I made several attempts to converse with him, but whenever our eyes met, which happened often as he sat nearly opposite me, he turned away and took up his book or looked out of the window.

Towards the second evening, when our train stopped at a large station, this nervous man fetched himself some boiling water and made tea. The man with the neat new things—a lawyer as I found out later—and his neighbour, the smoking lady with the mannish coat, went into the station to drink tea.

During their absence several new passengers entered the carriage, among them a tall, shaven, wrinkled old man, evidently a tradesman, in a coat lined with skunk fur, and a cloth cap with an enormous peak. The tradesman sat down opposite the seats of the lady and the lawyer, and immediately started a conversation with a young man who had also entered at that station and, judging by his appearance, was a tradesman's clerk.

I was sitting the other side of the gangway and as the train was standing still I could hear snatches of their conversation when nobody was passing between us. The tradesman began by saying that he was going to his estate which was only one station farther on; then as usual the conversation turned to prices and trade, and they spoke of the state of business in Moscow and then of the Nízhni-Nóvgorod Fair. The clerk began to relate how a wealthy merchant, known to both of them, had gone on the spree at the fair, but the old man interrupted him by telling of the orgies he had been at in former times at the Kunávin Fair. He evidently prided himself on the part he had played in them, and recounted with pleasure how he and some acquaintances, together with the merchant they had been speaking of, had once got drunk at Kunávin and played such a trick that he had to tell of it in a whisper. The clerk's roar of laughter filled the whole carriage; the old man laughed also, exposing two yellow teeth.

Not expecting to hear anything interesting, I got up to stroll about the platform till the train should start. At the carriage door I met the lawyer and the lady who were talking with animation as they approached.

'You won't have time,' said the sociable lawyer, 'the second bell will ring in a moment.'*

And the bell did ring before I had gone the length of the train. When I returned, the animated conversation between the lady and the lawyer was proceeding. The old tradesman sat silent opposite to them, looking sternly before him, and occasionally mumbled disapprovingly as if chewing something.

'Then she plainly informed her husband,' the lawyer was smilingly saying as I passed him, 'that she was not able, and did not wish, to live with him since . . .'

He went on to say something I could not hear. Several other passengers came in after me. The guard passed, a porter hurried in, and for some time the noise made their voices inaudible. When all was quiet again the conversation had evidently turned from the particular case to general considerations.

The lawyer was saying that public opinion in Europe was occupied with the question of divorce, and that cases of 'that kind' were occurring more and more often in Russia. Noticing that his was the only voice audible, he stopped his discourse and turned to the old man.

'Those things did not happen in the old days, did they?' he said, smiling pleasantly.

The old man was about to reply, but the train moved and he took off his cap, crossed himself, and whispered a prayer. The lawyer looked away and waited politely. Having finished his prayer and crossed himself three times the old man set his cap straight, pulled it well down over his forehead, changed his position, and began to speak.

'They used to happen even then, sir, but less often,' he said. 'As times are now they can't help happening. People have got too educated.'

The train moved faster and faster and jolted over the joints of the rails, making it difficult to hear, but being interested I moved nearer. The nervous man with the glittering eyes opposite me, evidently also interested, listened without changing his place.

'What is wrong with education?' said the lady, with a

scarcely perceptible smile. 'Surely it can't be better to marry as they used to in the old days when the bride and bridegroom did not even see one another before the wedding,' she continued, answering not what her interlocutor had said but what she thought he would say, in the way many ladies have. 'Without knowing whether they loved, or whether they could love, they married just anybody, and were wretched all their lives. And you think that was better?' she said, evidently addressing me and the lawyer chiefly and least of all the old man with whom she was talking.

'They've got so very educated,' the tradesman reiterated, looking contemptuously at the lady and leaving her question unanswered.

'It would be interesting to know how you explain the connexion between education and matrimonial discord,' said the lawyer, with a scarcely perceptible smile.

The tradesman was about to speak, but the lady interrupted him.

'No,' she said, 'those times have passed.' But the lawyer stopped her.

'Yes, but allow the gentleman to express his views.'

'Foolishness comes from education,' the old man said categorically.

'They make people who don't love one another marry, and then wonder that they live in discord,' the lady hastened to say, turning to look at the lawyer, at me, and even at the clerk, who had got up and, leaning on the back of the seat, was smilingly listening to the conversation. 'It's only animals, you know, that can be paired off as their master likes; but human beings have their own inclinations and attachments,' said the lady, with an evident desire to annoy the tradesman.

'You should not talk like that, madam,' said the old man, 'animals are cattle, but human beings have a law given them.'

'Yes, but how is one to live with a man when there is no love?' the lady again hastened to express her argument, which probably seemed very new to her.

'They used not to go into that,' said the old man in an impressive tone, 'it is only now that all this has sprung up. The least thing makes them say: "I will leave you!" The fashion has spread even to the peasants. "Here you are!" she says, "Here, take your shirts and trousers and I will go with Vánka; his hair is curlier than yours." What can you say? The first thing that should be required of a woman is fear!'

The clerk glanced at the lawyers, at the lady, and at me, apparently suppressing a smile and prepared to ridicule or to approve of the tradesman's words according to the reception they met with.

'Fear of what?' asked the lady.

'Why this: Let her fear her husband! That fear!'

'Oh, the time for that, sir, has passed,' said the lady with a certain viciousness.

'No, madam, that time cannot pass. As she, Eve, was made from the rib of a man, so it will remain to the end of time,' said the old man, jerking his head with such sternness and such a victorious look that the clerk at once concluded that victory was on his side, and laughed loudly.

'Ah yes, that's the way you men argue,' said the lady unyieldingly, and turned to us. 'You have given yourselves freedom but want to shut women up in a tower.* You no doubt permit yourselves everything.'

'No one is permitting anything, but a man does not bring offspring into the home; while a woman—a wife—is a leaky vessel,' the tradesman continued insistently. His tone was so impressive that it evidently vanquished his hearers, and even the lady felt crushed but still did not give in.

'Yes, but I think you will agree that a woman is a human being and has feelings as a man has. What is she to do then, if she does not love her husband?'

'Does not love!' said the tradesman severely, moving his brows and lips. 'She'll love, have no fear!' This unexpected argument particularly pleased the clerk, and he emitted a sound of approval.

'Oh, no, she won't!' the lady began, 'and when there is no love you can't force it.'

'Well, and supposing the wife is unfaithful, what then?' asked the lawyer.

'That is not admissible,' said the old man. 'One has to see to that.'

'But if it happens, what then? You know it does occur.'

'It happens among some, but not among us,' said the old man.

All were silent. The clerk moved, came still nearer, and, evidently unwilling to lag behind the others, began with a smile:

'Yes, a young fellow of ours had a scandal. It was a difficult case to deal with. It too was a case of a woman who was a bad lot. She began to play the devil, and the young fellow was respectable and cultured. At first it was with one of the office-clerks. The husband tried to persuade her with kindness. She would not stop, but played all sorts of dirty tricks. Then she began to steal his money. He beat her, but she only grew worse. Carried on intrigues, if I may mention it, with an unchristened Jew. What was he to do? He turned her out altogether and lives as a bachelor, while she gads about.'

'Because he is a fool,' said the old man. 'If he'd pulled her up properly from the first and not let her have her way, she'd be living with him, no fear! It's giving way at first that counts. Don't trust your horse in the field, or your wife in the house.'

At that moment the guard entered to collect the tickets for the next station. The old man gave up his.

'Yes, the female sex must be curbed in time or else all is lost!'

'Yes, but you yourself just now were speaking about the way married men amuse themselves at the Kunávin Fair,' I could not help saying.

'That's a different matter,' said the old man and relapsed into silence.

When the whistle sounded the tradesman rose, got out his bag from under the seat, buttoned up his coat, and slightly lifting his cap went out of the carriage.

II

As soon as the old man had gone several voices were raised.

'A daddy of the old style!' remarked the clerk.

'A living Domostróy!'* said the lady. 'What barbarous views of women and marriage!'

'Yes, we are far from the European understanding of marriage,' said the lawyer.

'The chief thing such people do not understand,' continued the lady, 'is that marriage without love is not marriage; that love alone sanctifies marriage, and that real marriage is only such as is sanctified by love.'

The clerk listened smilingly, trying to store up for future use all he could of the clever conversation.

In the midst of the lady's remarks we heard, behind me, a sound like that of a broken laugh or sob; and on turning round we saw my neighbour, the lonely grey-haired man with the glittering eyes, who had approached unnoticed during our conversation, which evidently interested him. He stood with his arms on the back of the seat, evidently much excited; his face was red and a muscle twitched in his cheek.

'What kind of love . . . love . . . is it that sanctifies marriage?' he asked hesitatingly.

Noticing the speaker's agitation, the lady tried to answer him as gently and fully as possible.

'True love . . . When such love exists between a man and a woman, then marriage is possible,' she said.

'Yes, but how is one to understand what is meant by "true love"?' said the gentleman with the glittering eyes timidly and with an awkward smile.

'Everybody knows what love is,' replied the lady, evidently wishing to break off her conversation with him.

'But I don't,' said the man. 'You must define what you understand . . .'

'Why? It's very simple,' she said, but stopped to consider. 'Love? Love is an exclusive preference for one above everybody else,' said the lady.

'Preference for how long? A month, two days, or half an hour?' said the grey-haired man and began to laugh.

'Excuse me, we are evidently not speaking of the same thing.'

'Oh, yes! Exactly the same.'

'She means,' interposed the lawyer, pointing to the lady, 'that in the first place marriage must be the outcome of attachment—or love, if you please—and only where that exists is marriage sacred, so to speak. Secondly, that marriage when not based on natural attachment—love, if you prefer the word—lacks the element that makes it morally binding. Do I understand you rightly?' he added, addressing the lady.

The lady indicated her approval of his explanation by a nod of her head.

'It follows . . .' the lawyer continued—but the nervous man whose eyes now glowed as if aflame and who had evidently restrained himself with difficulty, began without letting the lawyer finish:

'Yes, I mean exactly the same thing, a preference for one person over everybody else, and I am only asking: a preference for how long?'

'For how long? For a long time; for life sometimes,' replied the lady, shrugging her shoulders.

'Oh, but that happens only in novels and never in real life. In real life this preference for one may last for years (that happens very rarely), more often for months, or perhaps for weeks, days, or hours,' he said, evidently aware that he was astonishing everybody by his views and pleased that it was so.

'Oh, what are you saying?' 'But no . . .' 'No, allow me . . .' we all three began at once. Even the clerk uttered an indefinite sound of disapproval.

'Yes, I know,' the grey-haired man shouted above our voices, 'you are talking about what is supposed to be, but I am speaking of what is. Every man experiences what you call love for every pretty woman.'

'Oh, what you say is awful! But the feeling that is called love does exist among people, and is given not for months or years, but for a lifetime!'

'No, it does not! Even if we should grant that a man might prefer a certain woman all his life, the women in all probability would prefer someone else; and so it always has been and still is in the world,' he said, and taking out his cigarette-case he began to light up.

'But the feeling may be reciprocal,' said the lawyer.

'No, sir, it can't!' rejoined the other. 'Just as it cannot be that in a cartload of peas, two marked peas will lie side by side. Besides, it is not merely this impossibility, but the inevitable satiety. To love one person for a whole lifetime is like saying that one candle will burn a whole life,' he said, greedily inhaling the smoke.

'But you are talking all the time about physical love. Don't you acknowledge love based on identity of ideals, on spiritual affinity?' asked the lady.

'Spiritual affinity! Identity of ideals!' he repeated, emitting his peculiar sound. "But in that case why go to bed together? (Excuse my coarseness!) Or do people go to bed together because of the identity of their ideals?' he said, bursting into a nervous laugh.

'But permit me,' said the lawyer. 'Facts contradict you. We do see that matrimony exists, that all mankind, or the greater part of it, lives in wedlock, and many people honourably live long married lives.'

The grey-haired man again laughed.

'First you say that marriage is based on love, and when I express a doubt as to the existence of a love other than sensual, you prove the existence of love by the fact that marriages exist. But marriages in our days are mere deception!'

'No, allow me!' said the lawyer. 'I only say that marriages have existed and do exist.'

'They do! But why? They have existed and do exist among people who see in marriage something sacramental, a mystery binding them in the sight of God. Among them marriages do exist. Among us, people marry regarding marriage as nothing but copulation, and the result is either deception or coercion. When it is deception it is easier to bear. The husband and wife merely deceive people by pretending to be monogamists, while living polygamously. That is bad, but still bearable. But when, as most frequently happens, the husband and wife have undertaken the external duty of living together all their lives, and begin to hate each other after a month, and wish to part but still continue to live together, it leads to that terrible hell which makes people take to drink, shoot themselves, and kill or poison themselves or one another,' he went on, speaking more and more rapidly, not allowing anyone to put in a word and becoming more and more excited. We all remained silent. It was embarrassing.

'Yes, undoubtedly there are critical episodes in married life,' said the lawyer, wishing to end this disturbingly heated conversation.

'I see you have found out who I am!' said the grey-haired man softly, and with apparent calm.

'No, I have not that pleasure.'

'It is no great pleasure. I am that Pózdnyshev in whose life that critical episode occurred to which you alluded; the episode when he killed his wife,' he said, rapidly glancing at each of us.

No one knew what to say and all remained silent.

'Well, never mind,' he said with that peculiar sound of his. 'However, pardon me. Ah! . . . I won't intrude on you.'

'Oh, no, if you please . . .' said the lawyer, himself not knowing 'if you please' what.

But Pózdnyshev, without listening to him, rapidly turned away and went back to his seat. The lawyer and the lady whispered together. I sat down beside Pózdnyshev in silence, unable to think of anything to say. It was too dark to read, so I shut my eyes pretending that I wished to go to sleep. So we travelled in silence to the next station.

At that station the lawyer and the lady moved into another car, having some time previously consulted the guard about it. The clerk lay down on the seat and fell asleep. Pózdnyshev kept smoking and drinking the tea which he had made at the last station.

When I opened my eyes and looked at him he suddenly addressed me resolutely and irritably:

'Perhaps it is unpleasant for you to sit with me, knowing who I am? In that case I will go away.'

'Oh no, not at all.'

'Well then, won't you have some? Only it's very strong.'

He poured out some tea for me.

'They talk . . . and they always lie . . .' he remarked.

'What are you speaking about?' I asked.

'Always about the same thing. About that love of theirs and what it is! Don't you want to sleep?'

'Not at all.'

'Then would you like me to tell you how that love led to what happened to me?'

'Yes, if it will not be painful for you.'

'No, it is painful for me to be silent. Drink the tea . . . or is it too strong?'

The tea was really like beer, but I drank a glass of it.* Just then the guard entered. Pózdnyshev followed him with angry eyes, and only began to speak after he had left.

III

'Well then, I'll tell you. But do you really want to hear it?'

I repeated that I wanted to very much. He paused, rubbed his face with his hands, and began:

'If I am to tell it, I must tell everything from the beginning: I must tell how and why I married, and the kind of man I was before my marriage.

'Till my marriage I lived as everybody does, that is, everybody in our class. I am a landowner and a graduate of the university, and was a marshal of the gentry. Before my marriage I lived as everyone does, that is, dissolutely; and while living dissolutely I was convinced, like everybody in our class, that I was living as one has to. I thought I was a charming fellow and quite a moral man. I was not a seducer, had no unnatural tastes, did not make that the chief purpose of my life as many of my associates did, but I practised debauchery in a steady, decent way for health's sake. I avoided women who might tie my hands by having a child or by attachment for me. However, there may have been children and attachments, but I acted as if there were not. And this I not only considered moral, but I was even proud of it.'

He paused and gave vent to his peculiar sound, as he evidently did whenever a new idea occurred to him.

'And you know, that is the chief abomination!' he exclaimed. 'Debauchery does not lie in anything physical, debauchery is not any sort of physically outrageous behaviour; real debauchery lies precisely in freeing oneself from moral relations with a woman with whom you have physical intimacy. And such emancipation I regarded as a merit. I remember how I once worried because I had not had an opportunity to pay a woman who gave herself to me (having probably taken a fancy to me) and how I only became tranquil after having sent her some money—thereby intimating that I did not consider myself in any way morally bound to her . . . Don't nod as if you agreed with me,' he suddenly shouted at me. 'Don't I know these things? We all, and you too unless you are a rare exception, hold those same views, just as I used to. Never mind, I beg your pardon, but the fact is that it's horrible, horrible, horrible!'

'What is horrible?' I asked.

'That abyss of delusion in which we live regarding women and our relations with them. No, I can't speak calmly about it, not because of that "episode", as he called it, in my life, but because since that "episode" occurred my eyes have been opened and I have seen everything in quite a different light. Everything is reversed, everything is reversed!'

He lit a cigarette and began to speak, leaning his elbows on his knees.

It was too dark to see his face, but, above the jolting of the train, I could hear his impressive and pleasant voice.

IV

'Yes, only after such torments as I have endured, only by their means, have I understood where the root of the matter lies—understood what ought to be, and therefore seen all the horror of what is.

'So you will see how and when that which led up to my "episode" began. It began when I was not quite sixteen. It happened when I still went to the grammar school and my elder brother was a first-year student at the university. I had not yet known any woman, but, like all the unfortunate children of our class, I was no longer an innocent boy. I had been depraved two years before that by other boys. Already woman, not some particular woman but woman as something to be desired, woman, every woman, woman's nudity, tormented me. My solitude was not pure. I was tormented, as ninety-nine per cent of our boys are. I was horrified, I suffered, I prayed, and I fell. I was already depraved in imagination and in fact, but I had not yet taken the last step. I was perishing, but I had not yet laid hands on another human being. But one day a comrade of my brother's, a jolly student, a so-called good fellow, that is, the worst kind of good-for-nothing, who had taught us to drink and to play cards, persuaded us after a carousal to go *there*. We went. My brother was also still innocent, and he fell that same night. And I, a fifteen-year-old boy, defiled myself and took part in defiling a woman, without at all understanding what I was doing. I had never heard from any of my elders that what I was doing was wrong, you know. And indeed no one hears it now. It is true it is in the Commandments, but then the Commandments are only needed to answer the priest at Scripture examination, and even then they are not very necessary, not nearly as necessary as the commandment about the use of *ut* in conditional clauses in Latin.

'And so I never heard those older persons whose opinions I respected say that it was an evil. On the contrary, I heard people I respected say it was good. I had heard that my struggles and sufferings would be eased after that. I heard this and read it, and heard my elders say it would be good for my health, while from my comrades I heard that it was rather a fine, spirited thing to do. So in general I expected nothing but good from it. The risk of disease? But that too had been foreseen. A paternal government saw to that. It sees to the correct working of the brothels,* and makes profligacy safe for schoolboys. Doctors too deal with it for a consideration. That is proper. They assert that debauchery is good for the health, and they organize proper well-regulated debauchery. I know some mothers who attend to their sons' health in that sense. And science sends them to the brothels.'

'Why do you say "science"?' I asked.

'Why, who are the doctors? The priests of science. Who deprave youths by maintaining that this is necessary for their health? They do. And with awful pomposity they treat syphilis.'

'But why not treat syphilis?'

'Because if a one-hundredth part of the efforts devoted to the cure of syphilis were devoted to the eradication of debauchery, there would long ago not have been a trace of syphilis left. But as it is, efforts are made not to eradicate debauchery but to encourage it and to make debauchery safe. That is not the point however. The point is that with me—and with nine-tenths, if not more, not of our class only but of all classes, even the peasants—this terrible thing happens that happened to me; I fell not because I succumbed to the natural temptation of a particular woman's charm—no, I was not seduced by a woman—but I fell because, in the set around me, what was really a fall was regarded by some as a most legitimate function good for one's health, and by others as a very natural and not only excusable but even innocent amusement for a young man. I did not understand that it was a fall, but simply indulged in that half-pleasure, half-need, which, as was suggested to me, was natural at a certain age. I began to indulge in debauchery as I began to drink and to smoke. Yet in that first fall there was something special and pathetic. I remember that at once, on the spot before I left the room, I felt sad, so sad that I wanted to cry—to cry for the loss of my innocence and for my relationship with women, now sullied for ever. Yes, my natural, simple relationship with women was spoilt for ever. From that time I have not had, and could not have, pure relations with women. I had become what is called a lecher. To be a lecher is a physical condition like that of a morphine addict, a drunkard, or a smoker. As a morphine addict, a drunkard, or a smoker is no longer normal, so too a man who has known several women for his pleasure is not normal but is a man perverted for ever, a lecher. As a drunkard or a morphine addict can be recognized at once by his face and manner, so it is with a lecher. A lecher may restrain himself, may struggle, but he will never have those pure, simple, clear, brotherly relations with a woman. By the way he looks at a young woman and examines her, a lecher can always be recognized. And I had become and I remained a lecher, and it was this that brought me to ruin.'

V

'Ah, yes! After that things went from bad to worse, and there were all sorts of deviations. Oh, God! When I recall the abominations I committed in this respect I am seized with horror! And that is true of me, whom my companions, I remember, ridiculed for my so-called innocence. And when one hears of the "gilded youths", of officers, of the Parisians . . . ! And when all these gentlemen, and I—who have on our souls hundreds of the most varied and horrible crimes against women—when we thirty-year-old profligates, very carefully washed, shaved, perfumed, in clean linen and in evening dress or uniform, enter a drawing-room or ball-room, we are emblems of purity, charming!

'Only think of what ought to be, and of what is! When in society such a gentleman comes up to my sister or daughter, I, knowing his life, ought to go up to him, take him aside, and say quietly, "My dear fellow, I know the life you lead, and how and with whom you pass your nights. This is no place for you. There are pure, innocent girls here. Be off!" That is what ought to be; but what happens is that when such a gentleman comes and dances, embracing our sister or daughter, we are jubilant, if he is rich and well-connected. Maybe after Rigulboche* he will honour my daughter! Even if traces of disease remain, no matter! They are clever at curing that nowadays. Oh, yes, I know several girls in the best society whom their parents enthusiastically gave in marriage to men suffering from a certain disease. Oh, oh . . . the abomination of it! But a time will come when this abomination and falsehood will be exposed!'

He made his strange noise several times and again drank tea. It was fearfully strong and there was no water with which to dilute it. I felt that I was much excited by the two glasses I had drunk. Probably the tea affected him too, for he became more and more excited. His voice grew increasingly mellow and expressive. He continually changed his position, now taking off his cap and now putting it on again, and his face changed strangely in the semi-darkness in which we were sitting.

'Well, so I lived till I was thirty, not abandoning for a moment the intention of marrying and arranging for myself a most elevated and pure family life. With that purpose I observed the girls suitable for that end,' he continued. 'I weltered in a mire of debauchery and at the same time was on the lookout for a girl pure enough to be worthy of me. I rejected many just because they were not pure enough to suit me, but at last I found one whom I considered worthy. She was one of two daughters of a once-wealthy Pénza landowner who had been ruined.

'One evening after we had been out in a boat and had returned by moonlight, and I was sitting beside her admiring her curls and her shapely figure in a tight-fitting blouse, I suddenly decided that it was she! It seemed to me that evening that she understood all that I felt and thought, and that what I felt and thought was very lofty. In reality it was only that the blouse and the curls were particularly becoming to her and that after a day spent near her I wanted to be still closer.

'It is amazing how complete is the delusion that beauty is goodness. A handsome woman talks nonsense, you listen and hear not nonsense but cleverness. She says and does horrid things, and you see only charm. And if a handsome woman does not say stupid or horrid things, you at once persuade yourself that she is wonderfully clever and moral.

'I returned home in rapture, decided that she was the acme of moral perfection, and that therefore she was worthy to be my wife, and I proposed to her next day.

'What a muddle it is! Out of a thousand men who marry (not only among us but unfortunately also among the masses) there is hardly one who has not already been married ten, a hundred, or even, like Don Juan, a thousand times, before his wedding. (It is true as I have heard and have myself observed that there are nowadays some chaste young men who feel and know that this thing is not a joke but an important matter. God help them! But in my time there was not one such in ten thousand.) And everybody knows this and pretends not to know it. In all novels they describe in detail the heroes' feelings and the ponds and bushes beside which they walk, but when their great love for some maiden is described, nothing is said about what has happened to these interesting heroes before: not a word about their frequenting certain houses, or about the servant-girls, cooks, and other people's wives! If there are such improper novels they are not put into the hands of those who most need this information—the unmarried girls. We first pretend to these girls that the profligacy which fills half the life of our towns, and even of the villages, does not exist at all. Then we get so accustomed to this pretence that at last, like the English, we ourselves really begin to believe that we are all moral people and live in a moral world. The girls, poor things, believe this quite seriously. So too did my unfortunate wife. I remember how, when we were engaged, I showed her my diary, from which she could learn something, if but a little, of my past, especially about my last *liaison*, of which she might hear from others, and about which I therefore felt it necessary to inform her. I remember her horror, despair, and confusion, when she learnt of it and understood it. I saw that she then wanted to give me up. And why did she not do so?'

He again made that sound, swallowed another mouthful of tea, and remained silent for a while.

VI

'No, after all, it is better, better so!' he exclaimed. 'It serves me right! But that's not to the point. I meant to say that it is only the unfortunate girls who are deceived.

'The mothers know it, especially mothers educated by their own husbands—they know it very well. While pretending to believe in the purity of men, they act quite differently. They know with what sort of bait to catch men for themselves and for their daughters.

'You see it is only we men who don't know (because we don't wish to know) what women know very well, that the most exalted poetic love, as we call it, depends not on moral qualities but on physical nearness and on the *coiffure*, and the colour and cut of the dress. Ask an expert coquette who has set herself the task of captivating a man, which she would prefer to risk: to be convicted in his presence of lying, of cruelty, or even of dissoluteness, or to appear before him in an ugly and badly made dress—she will always prefer the first. She knows that we are continually lying about high sentiments, but really only want her body and will therefore forgive any abomination except an ugly tasteless costume that is in bad style. A coquette knows that consciously, and every innocent girl knows it unconsciously just as animals do.

'That is why there are those detestable blouses, bustles, and naked shoulders, arms, almost breasts. A woman, especially if she has passed the male school, knows very well that all the talk about elevated subjects is just talk, but that what a man wants is her body and all that presents it in the most deceptive but alluring light; and she acts accordingly. If we only throw aside our familiarity with this indecency, which has become second nature to us, and look at the life of our upper classes as it is, in all its shamelessness—why, it is simply a brothel. You don't agree? Allow me, I'll prove it,' he said, interrupting me. 'You say that the women of our society have other interests in life than prostitutes have, but I say no, and will prove it. If people differ in the aims of their lives, by the inner content of their lives, this difference will necessarily be reflected in externals and their externals will be different. But look at those unfortunate despised women and at the highest society ladies: the same costumes, the same fashions, the same perfumes, the same exposure of arms, shoulders, and breasts, the same tight skirts over prominent bustles, the same passion for little stones, for costly, glittering objects, the same amusements, dances, music, and singing. As the former employ all means to allure, so do these others. There is no difference. Strictly defining the matter, one must say that prostitutes for short terms are usually despised, while prostitutes for long terms are respected.

VII

'Well, so these blouses and curls and bustles caught me! It was very easy to catch me for I was brought up in the conditions in which amorous young people are forced like cucumbers in a hot-bed. You see our stimulating superabundance of food, together with complete physical idleness, is nothing but a systematic excitement of desire. Whether this astonishes you or not, it is so. Why, till quite recently I did not see anything of this myself, but now I have seen it. That is why it torments me that nobody knows this, and people talk such nonsense as that lady did.

'Yes, last spring some peasants were working in our neighbourhood on a railway embankment. The usual food of a young peasant is rye-bread, kvas,* and onions; he keeps alive and is vigorous and healthy; his work is light agricultural work. When he goes to railway-work his rations are buckwheat porridge and a pound of meat a day. But he works off that pound of meat during his sixteen hours' work wheeling barrow-loads of half-a-ton weight, so it is just enough for him. But we who every day consume two pounds of meat, and game, and fish and all sorts of hot foods and strong drinks—where does that go to? Into excesses of sensuality. And if it goes there and the safety-valve is open, all is well; but try and close the safety-valve, as I closed it temporarily, and at once a stimulus arises which, passing through the prism of our artificial life, expresses itself in utter infatuation, sometimes even platonic. And I fell in love as they all do.

'Everything was there to hand: raptures, tenderness, and poetry. In reality that love of mine was the result, on the one hand of her mamma's and the dressmakers' activity, and on the other of the superabundance of food consumed by me while living an idle life. If on the one hand there had been no boating, no dressmaker with her waists and so forth, and had my wife been sitting at home in a shapeless dressing-gown, and had I on the other hand been in circumstances normal to man—consuming just enough food to suffice for the work I did—and had the safety-valve been open—it happened to be closed at the time—I should not have fallen in love and nothing of all this would have happened.

VIII

'Well, and now it so happened that everything succeeded—my condition, her pretty dress, and the boating. It had failed twenty times but now it succeeded. Just like a trap! I am not joking. You see nowadays marriages are arranged that way—like traps. What is the natural way? The lass is ripe, she must be given in marriage. It seems very simple if the girl is not a fright and there are men wanting to marry. That is how it was done in olden times. The lass was grown up and her parents arranged the marriage. So it was done, and is done, among all mankind—Chinese, Hindus, Muhammadans, and among our own working classes; so it is done among at least ninety-nine per cent of the human race. Only among one per cent or less, among us libertines, has it been discovered that that is not right, and something new has been invented. And what is this novelty? It is that the maidens sit round and the men walk about, as at a bazaar, choosing. And the maidens wait and think, but dare not say: "Me, please!" "No, me!" "Not her, but me!" "Look what shoulders and other things I have!" And we men stroll around and look, and are very pleased. "Yes, I know! I won't be caught!" They stroll about and look, and are very pleased that everything is arranged like that for them. And then in an unguarded moment—snap! He is caught!'

'Then how ought it to be done?' I asked. 'Should the woman propose?'

'Oh, I don't know how; only if there's to be equality, let it be equality. If they have discovered that pre-arranged matches are degrading, why this is a thousand times worse! Then the rights and chances were equal, but here the woman is a slave in a bazaar or the bait in a trap. Tell any mother, or the girl herself, the truth, that she is only occupied in catching a husband . . . oh dear! what an insult! Yet they all do it and have nothing else to do. What is so terrible is to see sometimes quite innocent poor young girls engaged in it. And again, if it were but done openly—but it is always done deceitfully. "Ah, the origin of species, how interesting! Oh, Liza takes such an interest in painting! And will you be going to the exhibition? How instructive! And the troyka-drives, and the theatre, and the symphony? Oh! how remarkable! My Liza is mad about music. And why don't you share these convictions? And boating." But their one thought is: "Take me, take my Liza! No, me! Well, try me at least!" Oh, what an abomination! What falsehood!' he concluded, finishing his tea and beginning to put away the tea-things.

IX

'You know,' he began while packing the tea and sugar into his bag. 'The domination by women from which the world suffers all arises from this.'

'What "domination by women"?' I asked. 'The rights, the legal privileges, are on the man's side.'

'Yes, yes! That's just it,' he interrupted me. 'That's just what I want to say. It explains the extraordinary phenomenon that on the one hand woman is reduced to the lowest stage of humiliation, while on the other she dominates. Just like the Jews: as they pay us back for their oppression by financial domination, so it is with women. "Ah, you want us to be traders only—all right, as traders we will dominate you!" say the Jews. "Ah, you want us to be merely objects of sensuality—all right, as objects of sensuality we will enslave you," say the women. Woman's lack of rights arises not from the fact that she may not vote or be a judge—to be occupied with such affairs is no privilege—but from the fact that she is not man's equal in sexual intercourse and has not the right to use a man or abstain from him as she likes—is not allowed to choose a man at her pleasure instead of being chosen by him. You say that is monstrous. Very well! Then a man must not have those rights either. As it is at present, a woman is deprived of that right while a man has it. And to make up for that right she acts on man's sensuality, and through his sensuality subdues him so that he only chooses formally, while in reality it is she who chooses. And once she has obtained these means she abuses them and acquires a terrible power over people.'

'But where is this special power?' I inquired.

'Where is it? Why everywhere, in everything! Go round the shops in any big town. There are goods worth millions and you cannot estimate the human labour expended on them, and look whether in nine-tenths of these shops there is anything for the use of men. All the luxuries of life are demanded and maintained by women. Count all the factories. An enormous proportion of them produce useless ornaments, carriages, furniture, and trinkets, for women. Millions of people, generations of slaves, perish at hard labour in factories merely to satisfy woman's caprice. Women, like queens, keep nine-tenths of mankind in bondage to heavy labour. And all because they have been abased and deprived of equal rights with men. And they revenge themselves by acting on our sensuality and catch us in their nets. Yes, it all comes from that. Women have made of themselves such an instrument for acting upon our sensuality that a man cannot quietly relate to a woman. As soon as a man approaches a woman he succumbs to her stupefying influence and becomes intoxicated and crazy. I used formerly to feel uncomfortable and uneasy when I saw a lady dressed up for a ball, but now I am simply frightened and plainly see her as something dangerous and illicit. I want to call a policeman and ask for protection from the peril, and demand that the dangerous object be removed and put away.

'Ah, you are laughing!' he shouted at me, 'but it is not at all a joke. I am sure a time will come, and perhaps very soon, when people will understand this and will wonder how a society could exist in which actions were permitted which so disturb social tranquillity as those adornments of the body directly evoking sensuality, which we tolerate for women in our society. Why, it's like setting all sorts of traps along the paths and promenades—it is even worse! Why is gambling forbidden while women in costumes which evoke sensuality are not forbidden? They are a thousand times more dangerous!

X

'Well, you see, I was caught that way. I was what is called in love. I not only imagined her to be the height of perfection, but during the time of our engagement I regarded myself also as the height of perfection. You know there is no rascal who cannot, if he tries, find rascals in some respects worse than himself, and who consequently cannot find reasons for pride and self-satisfaction. So it was with me: I was not marrying for money—covetousness had nothing to do with it—unlike the majority of my acquaintances who married for money or connections—I was rich, she was poor. That was one thing. Another thing I prided myself on was that while others married intending to continue in future the same polygamous life they had lived before marriage, I was firmly resolved to be monogamous after marriage, and there was no limit to my pride on that score. Yes, I was a dreadful pig and imagined myself to be an angel.

'Our engagement did not last long. I cannot now think of that time without shame! What nastiness! Love is supposed to be spiritual and not sensual. Well, if the love is spiritual, a spiritual communion, then that spiritual communion should find expression in words, in conversations, in discourse. There was nothing of the kind. It used to be dreadfully difficult to talk when we were left alone. It was the labour of Sisyphus.* As soon as we thought of something to say and said it, we had again to be silent, devising something else. There was nothing to talk about. All that could be said about the life that awaited us, our arrangements and plans, had been said, and what was there more? Now if we had been animals we should have known that speech was unnecessary; but here on the contrary it was necessary to speak, and there was nothing to say, becasue we were not occupied with what finds vent in speech. And moreover there was that ridiculous custom of giving sweets, of coarse gormandizing on sweets, and all those abominable preparations for the wedding: remarks about the house, the bedroom, beds, wraps, dressing-gowns, underclothing, costumes. You must remember that if one married according to the injunctions of Domostróy, as that old fellow was saying, then the feather-beds, the trousseau, and the bedstead—are all but details appropriate to the sacrament. But among us, when of ten who marry there are certainly nine who not only do not believe in the sacrament, but do not even believe that what they are doing entails certain obligations—where scarcely one man out of a hundred has not been married before, and of fifty scarcely one is not preparing in advance to be unfaithful to his wife at every convenient opportunity—when the majority regard the going to church as only a special condition for obtaining possession of a certain woman—think what a dreadful significance all these details acquire. They show that the whole business is only that; they show that it is a kind of sale. An innocent girl is sold to a profligate, and the sale is accompanied by certain formalities.

XI

'That is how everybody marries and that is how I married, and the much vaunted honeymoon began. Why, its very name is vile!' he hissed viciously. 'In Paris I once went to see the sights, and noticing a bearded woman and a water-dog on a signboard, I entered the show. It turned out to be nothing but a man in a woman's low-necked dress, and a dog done up in walrus skin and swimming in a bath. It was very far from being interesting; but as I was leaving, the showman politely saw me out and, addressing the public at the entrance, pointed to me and said, "Ask the gentleman whether it is not worth seeing! Come in, come in, one franc apiece!" I felt ashamed to say it was not worth seeing, and the showman had probably counted on that. It must be the same with those who have experienced the abomination of a honeymoon and who do not disillusion others. Neither did I disillusion anyone, but I do not now see why I should not tell the truth. Indeed, I think it needful to tell the truth about it. One felt awkward, ashamed, repelled, sorry, and above all dull, intolerably dull! It was something like what I felt when I learnt to smoke—when I felt sick and the saliva gathered in my mouth and I swallowed it and pretended that it was very pleasant. Pleasure from smoking, just as from that, if it comes at all, comes later. The husband must cultivate that vice in his wife in order to derive pleasure from it.'

'Why vice?' I said. 'You are speaking of the most natural human functions.'

'Natural?' he said. 'Natural? No, I may tell you that I have come to the conclusion that it is, on the contrary, *un*natural. Yes, quite *un*natural. Ask a child, ask an unperverted girl. My sister, when very young, married a man twice her age and a debauchee. I remember how astonished we were the night of the wedding, when she ran out of her bedroom in tears and, shaking all over, said that she could on no account, on no account, even tell us what he had wanted to do to her.

'Natural, you say! It is natural to eat. And to eat is, from the very beginning, enjoyable, easy, pleasant, and not shameful; but this is horrid, shameful, and painful. No, it is unnatural! And an unspoilt girl, as I have convinced myself, always hates it.'

'But how,' I asked, 'would the human race continue?'

'Yes, would not the human race perish?' he said, irritably and ironically, as if he had expected this familiar and insincere objection. 'Teach abstention from child-bearing so that English lords may always gorge themselves—that is all right. Preach it for the sake of greater pleasure—that is all right; but just hint at abstention from child-bearing in the name of morality—and, my goodness, what a rumpus . . . ! Isn't there a danger that the human race may die out because they want to cease to be swine? But forgive me! This light is unpleasant, may I shade it?' he said, pointing to the lamp. I said I did not mind; and with the haste with which he did everything, he got up on the seat and drew the woollen shade over the lamp.

'All the same,' I said, 'if everyone thought this the right thing to do, the human race would cease to exist.'

He did not reply at once.

'You ask how the human race will continue to exist,' he said, having again sat down in front of me; and spreading his legs far apart he leant his elbows on his knees. 'Why should it continue?'

'Why? If not, we should not exist.'

'And why should we exist?'

'Why? In order to live, of course.'

'But why live? If life has no aim, if life is given us for life's sake, there is no reason for living. And if it is so, then the Schopenhauers, the Hartmanns, and all the Buddhists as well, are quite right. But if life has an aim, it is clear that it ought to come to an end when that aim is reached. And so it turns out,' he said with noticeable agitation, evidently prizing his thought very highly. 'So it turns out. Just think: if the aim of humanity is goodness, righteousness, love—call it what you will—if it is what the prophets have said, that all mankind should be united together in love, that the spears should be beaten into pruning-hooks and so forth, what is it that hinders the attainment of this aim? The passions hinder it. Of all the passions the strongest, cruellest, and most stubborn is the sex-passion, physical love; and therefore if the passions are destroyed, including the strongest of them—physical love—the prophecies will be fulfilled, mankind will be brought into unity, the aim of human existence will be attained, and there will be nothing further to live for. As long as mankind exists the ideal is before it, and of course not the rabbits' and pigs' ideal of breeding as fast as possible, nor that of monkeys or Parisians—to enjoy sex-passion in the most refined manner—but the ideal of goodness attained by continence and purity. Towards that people have always striven and still strive. You see what follows.

'It follows that physical love is a safety-valve. If the present generation has not attained its aim, it has not done so because of its passions, of which the sex-passion is the strongest. And if the sex-passion endures there will be a new generation and consequently the possibility of attaining the aim in the next generation. If the next one does not attain it, then the next after that may, and so on, till the aim is attained, the prophecies fulfilled, and mankind attains unity. If not, what would result? If one admits that God created men for the attainment of a certain aim, and created them mortal but sexless, or created them immortal, what would be the result? Why, if they were mortal but without the sex-passion, and died without attaining the aim, God would have had to create new people to attain his aim. If they were immortal, let us grant that (though it would be more difficult for the same people to correct their mistakes and approach perfection than for those of another generation) they might attain that aim after many thousands of years, but then what use would they be afterwards? What could be done with them? It is best as it is. . . . But perhaps you don't like that way of putting it? Perhaps you are an evolutionist? It comes to the same thing. The highest race of animals, the human race, in order to maintain itself in the struggle with other animals ought to unite into one whole like a swarm of bees, and not breed continually; it should bring up sexless members as the bees do; that is, again, it should strive towards continence and not towards inflaming desire—to which the whole system of our life is now directed.' He paused. 'The human race will cease? But can anyone doubt it, whatever his outlook on life may be? Why, it is as certain as death. According to all the teaching of the Church the end of the world will come, and according to all the teaching of science the same result is inevitable. So what is so strange if moral teaching comes to the same conclusion?'

He remained silent for a long time after that, drank some more tea, smoked a cigarette, and put some new ones that he got out of his sack into his old, soiled cigarette case.

'I understand your views,' I said. 'The Shakers believe something similar.'

'Yes, yes, and they are right,' he said. 'Sexual passion, no matter how it is arranged, is evil, a terrifying evil with which one has to struggle, and not encourage as we do now. The words of the Gospel about the one who looketh on a woman to lust after her hath committed adultery with her already refer not just to the wives of others, but precisely and especially to one's own.

XII

'In our world it is just the reverse: even if a man does think of continence while he is a bachelor, once married he is sure to think continence no longer necessary. You know those wedding tours—the seclusion into which, with their parents' consent, the young couple go—are nothing but licensed debauchery. But a moral law avenges itself when it is violated. Hard as I tried to make a success of my honeymoon, nothing came of it. It was horrid, shameful, and boring, the whole time. And very soon I began also to experience a painful, oppressive feeling. That began very quickly. I think it was on the third or fourth day that I found my wife depressed. I began asking her the reason and embracing her, which in my view was all she could want, but she removed my arm and began to cry. What about? She could not say. But she felt sad and distressed. Probably her exhausted nerves suggested to her the truth as to the vileness of our relation but she did not know how to express it. I began to question her, and she said something about feeling sad without her mother. It seemed to me that this was untrue, and I began comforting her without alluding to her mother. I did not understand that she was simply depressed and her mother was merely an excuse. But she immediately took offence because I had not mentioned her mother, as though I did not believe her. She told me she saw that I did not love her. I reproached her with being capricious, and suddenly her face changed entirely and instead of sadness it expressed irritation, and with the most venomous words she began accusing me of selfishness and cruelty. I gazed at her. Her whole face showed complete coldness and hostility, almost hatred. I remember how horror-struck I was when I saw this. "How? What?" I thought. "Love is a union of souls—and instead of that there is this! Impossible, this is not she!" I tried to soften her, but encountered such an insuperable wall of cold virulent hostility that before I had time to turn round I too was seized with irritation and we said a great many unpleasant things to one another. The impression of that first quarrel was dreadful. I call it a quarrel, but it was not a quarrel but only the disclosure of the abyss that really existed between us. Amorousness was exhausted by the satisfaction of sensuality and we were left confronting one another in our true relation: that is, as two egotists quite alien to each other who wished to get as much pleasure as possible each from the other. I call what took place between us a quarrel, but it was not a quarrel, only the consequence of the cessation of sensuality—revealing our real relations to one another. I did not understand that this cold and hostile relation was our normal state, I did not understand it because at first this hostile attitude was very soon concealed from us by a renewal of driving sensuality, that is by lovemaking.

'I thought we had quarrelled and made it up again, and that it would not recur. But during that same first month of honeymoon a period of satiety soon returned, we again ceased to need one another, and another quarrel supervened. This second quarrel struck me even more painfully than the first. "So the first one was not an accident but was bound to happen and will happen again," I thought. I was all the more staggered by that second quarrel because it arose from such an impossible pretext. It had something to do with money, which I never grudged and could certainly not have grudged to my wife. I only remember that she gave the matter such a twist that some remark of mine appeared to be an expression of a desire on my part to dominate over her by means of money, to which I was supposed to assert an exclusive right—it was something impossibly stupid, mean, and not natural either to me or to her. I became exasperated, and upbraided her with lack of consideration for me. She accused me of the same thing, and it all began again. In her words and in the expression of her face and eyes I again noticed the cruel cold hostility that had so staggered me before. I had formerly quarrelled with my brother, my friends, and my father, but there had never, I remember, been the special venomous malice which there was here. But after a while this mutual hatred was screened by amorousness, that is sensuality, and I still consoled myself with the thought that these two quarrels had been mistakes and could be remedied. But then a third and a fourth quarrel followed and I realized that it was not accidental, but that it was bound to happen and would happen so, and I was horrified at the prospect before me. At the same time I was tormented by the terrible thought that I alone lived on such bad terms with my wife, so unlike what I had expected, whereas this did not happen between other married couples. I did not know then that it is our common fate, but that all imagine, just as I did, that it is their peculiar misfortune, and all conceal this exceptional and shameful misfortune not only from others but even from themselves and do not acknowledge it to themselves.

'It began during the first days and continued all the time, ever increasing and growing more obdurate. In the depths of my soul I felt from the first weeks that I had fallen for it, that things had not turned out as I expected, that marriage was not only no happiness but a very heavy burden; but like everybody else I did not wish to acknowledge this to myself (I should not have acknowledged it even now but for the end that followed) and I concealed it not only from others but from myself too. Now I am astonished that I failed to see my real position. It might have been seen from the fact that the quarrels began on pretexts it was impossible to remember when the fighting was over. Our reason was not quick enough to devise sufficient excuses for the animosity that always existed between us. But more striking still was the insufficiency of the excuses for our reconciliations. Sometimes there were words, explanations, even tears, but sometimes ... oh! it is disgusting even now to think of it—after the most cruel words to one another, came sudden silent glances, smiles, kisses, embraces. . . . Faugh, how horrid! How is it I did not then see all the vileness of it?'

XIII

Two passengers entered and settled down on the farthest seats. He was silent while they were seating themselves but as soon as they had settled down continued, evidently not for a moment losing the thread of his idea.

'You know, what is vilest about it,' he began, 'is that in theory love is something ideal and exalted, but in practice it is something abominable, swinish, which it is horrid and shameful to mention or remember. It is not for nothing that nature has made it disgusting and shameful. And if it is disgusting and shameful one must understand that it is so. But here, on the contrary, people pretend that what is disgusting and shameful is beautiful and lofty. What were the first symptoms of my love? Why that I gave way to animal excesses, not only without shame but being somehow even proud of the possibility of these physical excesses, and without in the least considering either her spiritual or even her physical life. I wondered what embittered us against one another, yet it was perfectly simple: that animosity was nothing but the protest of our human nature against the animal nature that overpowered it.

'I was surprised at our enmity to one another; yet it could not have been otherwise. That hatred was nothing but the mutual hatred of accomplices in a crime—both for the incitement to the crime and for the part taken in it. What was it but a crime when she, poor thing, became pregnant in the first month and our swinish connection continued? You think I am straying from my subject? Not at all! I am telling you how I killed my wife. They asked me at the trial with what and how I killed her. Fools! They thought I killed her with a knife, on the 5th of October. It was not then I killed her, but much earlier. Just as they are all now killing, all of them.'

'But with what?' I asked.

'That is just what is so surprising, that nobody wants to see what is so clear and evident, what doctors ought to know and preach, but are silent about. Yet the matter is very simple. Men and women are created like the animals so that physical love is followed by pregnancy and then by suckling—conditions under which physical love is bad for the woman and for her child. There are an equal number of men and women. What follows from this? It seems clear, and no great wisdom is needed to draw the conclusion that animals do, namely, the need of continence. But no. Science has been able to discover some kind of leucocytes that run about in the blood, and all sorts of useless nonsense, but cannot understand that. At least one does not hear of science teaching it!

'And so a woman has only two ways out: one is to make a monster of herself, to destroy and go on destroying within herself to such degree as may be necessary the capacity of being a woman, that is, a mother, in order that a man may quietly and continuously get his enjoyment; the other way out—and it is not even a way out but a simple, coarse, and direct violation of the laws of nature—practised in all so-called decent families—is that, contrary to her nature, the woman must be her husband's mistress even while she is pregnant or nursing—must be what not even an animal descends to, and for which her strength is insufficient. That is what causes nerve troubles and hysteria in our class, and among the peasants causes what they call being "possessed by the devil"—epilepsy. You will notice that no pure maidens are ever "possessed", but only married women living with their husbands. That is so here, and it is just the same in Europe. All the hospitals for hysterical women are full of those who have violated nature's law. The epileptics and Charcot's* patients are complete wrecks you know, but the world is full of half-crippled women. Just think of it, what great work goes on within a woman when she conceives or when she is nursing an infant. That is growing which will continue us and replace us. And this sacred work is violated—by what? It is terrible to think of it! And they prate about the freedom and the rights of women! It is as if cannibals fattened their captives to be eaten, and at the same time declared that they were concerned about their prisoners' rights and freedom.'

All this was new to me and startled me.

'What is one to do? If that is so,' I said, 'it means that one may love one's wife once in two years, but the man . . .'

'For the man it is necessary!' he interrupted me. 'It is again those precious priests of science who have persuaded everybody of that. Imbue a man with the idea that vodka, tobacco, or opium are necessary for him, and all these things will be necessary. It seems that God did not understand what was needed and therefore, omitting to consult those wizards, arranged things badly. You see matters do not tally. They have decided that it is necessary and needed for a man to satisfy his desires, and the bearing and nursing of children comes and interferes with it and hinders the satisfaction of that need. What is one to do then? Consult the wizards! They will arrange it. And they have devised something. Oh! when will those wizards with their deceptions be dethroned? It is high time! It has come to such a point that people go mad and shoot themselves and all because of this. How could it be otherwise? The animals seem to know that their progeny continue their race, and they keep to a certain law in this matter. Man alone neither knows it nor wishes to know, but is concerned only to get all the pleasure he can. And who is doing that? The lord of nature—man! Animals, you see, only come together at times when they are capable of producing progeny, but the filthy lord of nature is at it any time if only it pleases him! And as if that were not sufficient, he exalts this apish occupation into the most precious pearl of creation, into love. In the name of this love, that is, this filth, he destroys—what? Why, half the human race! All the women who might help the progress of mankind towards truth and goodness he converts, for the sake of his pleasure, into enemies instead of helpmates. See what it is that everywhere impedes the forward movement of mankind. Women! And why are they what they are? Only because of that. Yes, yes . . .' he repeated several times, and began to move about, and to get out his cigarettes and to smoke, evidently trying to calm himself.

XIV

'I too lived like a pig of that sort,' he continued in his former tone. 'The worst thing about it was that while living that horrid life I imagined that, because I did not go after other women, I was living an honest family life, that I was a moral man and in no way blameworthy, and if quarrels occurred it was her fault and resulted from her character.

'Of course the fault was not hers. She was like everybody else—like the majority of women. She had been brought up as the position of women in our society requires, and as therefore all women of the leisured classes without exception are brought up and cannot help being brought up. People talk about some new kind of education for women. It is all empty words: their education is exactly what it has to be in view of our unfeigned, real, general opinion about women.

'The education of women will always correspond to men's opinion about them. Don't we know how men regard women: *Wein, Weib, und Gesang*,[1] and what the poets say in their verses? Take all poetry, all pictures and sculpture, beginning with love poems and the nude Venuses and Phrynes, and you will see that woman is an instrument of enjoyment; she is so on the Trubá and the Grachévka,* and also at the court balls. And note the devil's cunning: if they are here for enjoyment and pleasure, let it be known that it is pleasure and that woman is a sweet morsel. But no, first the knights-errant declare that they worship women (worship her, and yet regard her as an instrument of enjoyment), and now people assure us that they respect women. Some give up their places to her, pick up her handkerchief; others acknowledge her right to occupy all positions and to take part in the government, and so on. They do all that, but their outlook on her remains the same. She is a means of enjoyment. Her body is a means of enjoyment. And she knows this. It is just as it is with slavery. Slavery, you know, is nothing else than the exploitation by some of the unwilling labour of many. Therefore to get rid of slavery it is necessary that people should not wish to profit by the forced labour of others and should consider it a sin and a shame. But they go and abolish the external form of slavery and arrange so that one can no longer buy and sell slaves, and they imagine and assure themselves that slavery no longer exists, and do not see or wish to see that it does, because people still want and consider it good and right to exploit the labour of others. And as long as they consider that good, there will always be people stronger or more cunning than others who will succeed in doing it. So it is with the emancipation of woman: the enslavement of woman lies simply in the fact that people desire, and think it good, to avail themselves of her as a tool of enjoyment. Well, and they

[1] 'Wine, woman, and song.'

liberate woman, give her all sorts of rights equal to man, but continue to regard her as an instrument of enjoyment, and so educate her in childhood and afterwards by public opinion. And there she is, still the same humiliated and depraved slave, and the man still a depraved slave-owner.

'They emancipate women in universities and in law courts, but continue to regard her as an object of enjoyment. Teach her, as she is taught among us, to regard herself as such, and she will always remain an inferior being. Either with the help of those scoundrels the doctors she will prevent the conception of offspring—that is, will be a complete prostitute, lowering herself not to the level of an animal but to the level of a thing—or she will be what the majority of women are, mentally diseased, hysterical, unhappy, and lacking capacity for spiritual development. High schools and universities cannot alter that. It can only be changed by a change in men's outlook on women and women's way of regarding themselves. It will change only when woman regards virginity as the highest state, and does not, as at present, consider the highest state of a human being a shame and a disgrace. While that is not so, the ideal of every girl, whatever her education may be, will continue to be to attract as many men as possible, as many males as possible, so as to have the possibility of choosing.

'But the fact that one of them knows more mathematics, and another can play the harp, makes no difference. A woman is happy and attains all she can desire when she has bewitched man. Therefore the chief aim of a woman is to be able to bewitch him. So it has been and will be. So it is in her maiden life in our society, and so it continues to be in her married life. For a maiden this is necessary in order to have a choice, for the married woman in order to have power over her husband.

'The one thing that stops this or at any rate suppresses it for a time, is children, and then only if the mother is not a monster, that is, if she nurses them herself. But here the doctors again come in.

'My wife, who wanted to nurse, and did nurse the four later children herself, happened to be unwell after the birth of her first child. And those doctors, who cynically undressed her and felt her all over—for which I had to thank them and pay them money—those dear doctors considered that she must not nurse the child; and that first time she was deprived of the only means which might have kept her from coquetry. We engaged a wet nurse, that is, we took advantage of the poverty, the need, and the ignorance of a woman, tempted her away from her own baby to ours, and in return gave her a fine head-dress with gold lace.* But that is not the point. The point is that during that time when my wife was free from pregnancy and from suckling, the feminine coquetry which had lain dormant within her manifested itself with particular force. And coinciding with this the torments of jealousy rose up in me with special force. They tortured me all my married life, as they cannot but torture all husbands who live with their wives as I did with mine, that is, immorally.

XV

'During the whole of my married life I never ceased to be tormented by jealousy, but there were periods when I specially suffered from it. One of these periods was when, after the birth of our first child, the doctors forbade my wife to nurse it. I was particularly jealous at that time, in the first place because my wife was experiencing that unrest natural to a mother which is sure to be aroused when the natural course of life is needlessly violated; and secondly, because seeing how easily she abandoned her moral obligations as a mother, I rightly though unconsciously concluded that it would be equally easy for her to disregard her duty as a wife, especially as she was quite well and in spite of the precious doctors' prohibition was able to nurse her later children admirably.'

'I see you don't like doctors,' I said, noticing a peculiarly malevolent tone in his voice whenever he alluded to them.

'It is not a case of liking or disliking. They have ruined my life as they have ruined and are ruining the lives of thousands and hundreds of thousands of human beings, and I cannot help connecting the effect with the cause. I understand that they want to earn money like lawyers and others, and I would willingly give them half my income, and all who realize what they are doing would willingly give them half of their possessions, if only they would not interfere with our family life and would never come near us. I have not collected evidence, but I know dozens of cases (there are any number of them!) where they have killed a child in its mother's womb asserting that she could not give it birth, though she has had children quite safely later on; or they have killed the mother on the pretext of performing some operation. No one reckons these murders any more than they reckoned the murders of the Inquisition, because it is supposed that it is done for the good of mankind. It is impossible to number all the crimes they commit. But all those crimes are as nothing compared to the moral corruption of materialism they introduce into the world, especially through women. I don't lay stress on the fact that if one is to follow their instructions, then on account of the infections which exist everywhere and in everything, people would not progress towards greater unity but towards separation; for according to their teaching we ought all to sit apart and not remove the carbolic atomizer from our mouths (though now they have discovered that even that is of no avail). But that does not matter either. The principal poison lies in the demoralization of the world, especially of women.

'To-day one can no longer say: "You are not living rightly, live better." One can't say that, either to oneself or to anyone else. If you live a bad life it is caused by the abnormal functioning of your nerves, etc. So you must go to them, and they will prescribe thirty-five kopeks' worth of medicine from a chemist, which you must take! You get still worse: then more medicine and the doctor again. An excellent trick!

'That however is not the point. All I wish to say is that she nursed her babies perfectly well and that only her pregnancy and the nursing of her babies saved me from the torments of jealousy. Had it not been for that it would all have happened sooner. The children saved me and her. In eight years she had five children and nursed all except the first herself.'

'And where are your children now?' I asked.

'The children?' he repeated in a frightened voice.

'Forgive me, perhaps it is painful for you to be reminded of them.'

'No, it does not matter. My wife's sister and brother have

taken them. They would not let me have them. I gave them my estate, but they did not give them up to me. You know I am a sort of lunatic. I have left them now and am going away. I have seen them, but they won't let me have them because I might bring them up so that they would not be like their parents, and they have to be just like them. Oh well, what is to be done? Of course they won't let me have them and won't trust me. Besides, I do not know whether I should be able to bring them up. I think not. I am a ruin, a cripple. Still I have one thing in me. I know! Yes, that is true, I know what others are far from knowing.

'Yes, my children are living and growing up just such savages as everybody around them. I saw them, saw them three times. I can do nothing for them, nothing. I am now going to my place in the south. I have a little house and a small garden there.

'Yes, it will be a long time before people learn what I know. How much of iron and other metal there is in the sun and the stars is easy to find out, but anything that exposes our swinishness is difficult, terribly difficult!

'You at least listen to me, and I am grateful for that.

XVI

'You mentioned my children. There again, what terrible lies are told about children! Children a blessing from God, a joy! That is all a lie. It was so once upon a time, but now it is not so at all. Children are a torment and nothing else. Most mothers feel this quite plainly, and sometimes inadvertently say so. Ask most mothers of our propertied classes and they will tell you that they do not want to have children for fear of their falling ill and dying. They don't want to nurse them if they do have them, for fear of becoming too much attached to them and having to suffer. The pleasure a baby gives them by its loveliness, its little hands and feet, and its whole body, is not as great as the suffering caused by the very fear of its possibly falling ill and dying, not to speak of its actual illness or death. After weighing the advantages and disadvantages it seems disadvantageous, and therefore undesirable, to have children. They say this quite frankly and boldly, imagining that these feelings of theirs arise from their love of children, a good and laudable feeling of which they are proud. They do not notice that by this reflection they plainly repudiate love, and only affirm their own selfishness. They get less pleasure from a baby's loveliness than suffering from fear on its account, and therefore the baby they would love is not wanted. They do not sacrifice themselves for a beloved being, but sacrifice a being whom they might love, for their own sakes.

'It is clear that this is not love but selfishness. But one has not the heart to blame them—the mothers in well-to-do families—for that selfishness, when one remembers how dreadfully they suffer on account of their children's health, again thanks to the influence of those same doctors among our well-to-do classes. Even now, when I do but remember my wife's life and the condition she was in during the first years when we had three or four children and she was absorbed in them, I am seized with horror! We led no life at all, but were in a state of constant danger, of escape from it, recurring danger, again followed by a desperate struggle and another escape—always as if we were on a sinking ship. Sometimes it seemed to me that this was done on purpose and that she pretended to be anxious about the children in order to subdue me. It solved all questions in her favour with such tempting simplicity. It sometimes seemed as if all she did and said on these occasions was pretence. But no! She herself suffered terribly, and continually tormented herself about the children and their health and illnesses. It was torture for her and for me too; and it was impossible for her not to suffer. After all, the attachment to her children, the animal need of feeding, caressing, and protecting them, was there as with most women, but there was not the lack of imagination and reason that there is in animals. A hen is not afraid of what may happen to her chick, does not know all the diseases that may befall it, and does not know all those remedies with which people imagine that they can save from illness and death. And for a hen her young are not a source of torment. She does for them what it is natural and pleasurable for her to do; her young ones are a pleasure to her. When a chick falls ill her duties are quite definite: she warms and feeds it. And doing this she knows that she is doing all that is necessary. If her chick dies she does not ask herself why it died, or where it has gone to; she cackles for a while, and then leaves off and goes on living as before. But for our unfortunate women, my wife among them, it was not so. Not to mention illnesses and how to cure them, she was always hearing and reading from all sides endless rules for the rearing and educating of children, which were continually being superseded by others. This is the way to feed a child: feed it in this way, on such a thing; no, not on such a thing, but in this way; clothes, drinks, baths, putting to bed, walking, fresh air,—for all these things we, especially she, heard of new rules every week, just as if children had only begun to be born into the world since yesterday. And if a child that had not been fed or bathed in the right way or at the right time fell ill, it appeared that we were to blame for not having done what we ought.

'That was so while they were well. It was a torment even then. But if one of them happened to fall ill, it was all up: a regular hell! It is supposed that illness can be cured and that there is a science about it, and people—doctors—who know about it. Ah, but not all of them know—only the very best. When a child is ill one must get hold of the very best one, the one who saves, and then the child is saved; but if you don't get that doctor, or if you don't live in the place where that doctor lives, the child is lost. This was not a creed peculiar to her, it is the creed of all the women of our class, and she heard nothing else from all sides. Catherine Semyónovna lost two children because Iván Zakhárych was not called in in time, but Iván Zakhárych saved Mary Ivánovna's eldest girl, and the Petróvs moved in time to various hotels by the doctor's advice, and the children remained alive; but if they had not been segregated the children would have died. Another who had a delicate child moved south by the doctor's advice and saved the child. How can she help being tortured and agitated all the time, when the lives of the children for whom she has an animal attachment depend on her finding out in time what Iván Zakhárych will say! But what Iván Zakhárych will say nobody knows, and he himself least of all, for he is well aware that he knows nothing and therefore cannot be of any use, but just shuffles about at random so that people should not cease to believe that he knows something or other. You see, had she been wholly an animal she would not have suffered so, and if she had been quite a human being she would have had faith in God and would have said and thought, as a believer does: "The Lord giveth, and the Lord taketh away. From the Lord you cannot escape."* She would have thought that the life and death of her children, as of all people, are not in human control, but only in the hands of God, and then she would not have tormented herself trying to prevent the sickness and death of her children. But she did not do this. Rather her situation was like this. She was granted the most fragile and weak of beings who were subjected to the most innumerable of misfortunes. For these beings she felt a passionate, animal attachment. Besides, these beings were entrusted to her, while the means for the preservation of these beings were hidden from us and revealed to completely alien people whose services and advice we could obtain only at great cost and then not always.

'Our whole life with the children, for my wife and consequently for me, was not a joy but a torment. How could she help torturing herself? She tortured herself incessantly. Sometimes when we had just made peace after some scene of jealousy, or simply after a quarrel, and thought we should be able to live, to read, and to think a little, we had no sooner settled down to some occupation than the news came that Vásya was being sick, or Másha showed symptoms of dysentery, or Andrúsha had a rash, and there was an end to peace, it was not life any more. Where was one to drive to? For what doctor? How isolate the child? And then it's a case of enemas, temperatures, medicines, and doctors. Hardly is that over before something else begins. We had no regular settled family life but only, as I have already said, continual escapes from imaginary and real dangers. It is like that in most families nowadays you know, but in my family it was especially acute. My wife was a child-loving and a credulous woman.

'So the presence of children not only failed to improve our life but poisoned it. Besides, the children were a new cause of dissension. As soon as we had children they became the means and the object of our discord, and more often the older they grew. They were not only the object of discord but the weapons of our strife. We used our children, as it were, to fight one another with. Each of us had a favourite weapon among them for our strife. I used to fight her chiefly through Vásya, the eldest boy, and she me through Lisa. Besides that, as they grew older and their characters became defined, it came about that they grew into allies whom each of us tried to draw to his or her side. They, poor things, suffered terribly from this, but we, with our incessant warfare, had no time to think of that. The girl was my ally, and the eldest boy, who resembled his mother and was her favourite, was often hateful to me.

XVII

'Well, and so we lived. Our relations to one another grew more and more hostile and at last reached a stage where it was not disagreement that caused hostility but hostility that caused disagreement. Whatever she might say I disagreed with beforehand, and it was just the same with her.

'In the fourth year we both, it seemed, came to the conclusion that we could not understand one another or agree with one another. We no longer tried to bring any dispute to a conclusion. We invariably kept to our own opinions even about the most trivial questions, but especially about the children. As I now recall them the views I maintained were not at all so dear to me that I could not have given them up; but she was of the opposite opinion and to yield meant yielding to her, and that I could not do. It was the same with her. She probably considered herself quite in the right towards me, and as for me I always thought myself a saint towards her. When we were alone together we were doomed almost to silence, or to conversations such as I am convinced animals can carry on with one another: "What is the time? Time to go to bed. What is today's dinner? Where shall we go? What is there in the papers? Send for the doctor; Másha has a sore throat." We only needed to go a hairbreadth beyond this impossibly limited circle of conversation for irritation to flare up. We had collisions and acrimonious words about the coffee, a tablecloth, a cab, a lead at bridge, all of them things that could not be of any importance to either of us. In me at any rate there often raged a terrible hatred of her. Sometimes I watched her pouring out tea, swinging her leg, lifting a spoon to her mouth, smacking her lips and drawing in some liquid, and I hated her for these things as though they were the worst possible actions. I did not then notice that the periods of anger corresponded quite regularly and exactly to the periods of what we called love. A period of love—then a period of animosity; an energetic period of love, then a long period of animosity; a weaker manifestation of love, and a shorter period of animosity. We did not then understand that this love and animosity were one and the same animal feeling only at opposite poles. To live like that would have been awful had we understood our position; but we neither understood nor saw it. For man both salvation and punishment lie in the fact that if he lives wrongly he can befog himself so as not to see the misery of his position. And this we did. She tried to forget herself in intense and always hurried occupation with household affairs, busying herself with the arrangements of the house, her own and the children's clothes, their lessons, and their health, while I had my own drunkenness—the drunkenness of the office, the hunt, and of cards. We were both continually occupied, and we both felt that the busier we were the nastier we might be to each other. "It's all very well for you to grimace," I thought, "but you have harassed me all night with your scenes, and I have a meeting on." "It's all very well for you," she not only thought but said, "but I have been awake all night with the baby."

'Thus we lived in a perpetual fog, not seeing the condition we were in. And if what did happen had not happened, I should have gone on living so to old age and should have thought, when dying, that I had led a good life. I should not have realized the abyss of misery and the horrible falsehood in which I wallowed.

'We were like two convicts hating each other and chained together, poisoning one another's lives and trying not to see it. I did not then know that ninety-nine per cent of married people live in a similar hell to the one I was in and that it cannot be otherwise. I did not then know this either about others or about myself.

'It is strange what coincidences there are in regular, or even in irregular, lives! Just when the parents find life together unendurable, it becomes necessary to move to town for the children's education.'

He stopped, and once or twice gave vent to his strange sounds, which were now quite like suppressed sobs. We were approaching a station.

'What is the time?' he asked.

I looked at my watch. It was two o'clock.

'Are you not tired?' he asked.

'No, but you are.'

'I am suffocating. Excuse me, I will walk a bit and drink some water.'

He went unsteadily through the carriage. I remained alone thinking over what he had said, and I was so engrossed in thought that I did not notice when he re-entered by the door at the other end of the carriage.

XVIII

'Yes, I keep diverging,' he began. 'I have thought a great deal about it. I now see many things differently and I want to express it.

'Well, so we lived in town. In town a man can live for a hundred years without noticing that he has long been dead and has rotted away. He has no time to take account of himself, he is always occupied. Business affairs, social intercourse, health, art, the children's health and their education. Now one has to receive so-and-so and so-and-so, go to see so-and-so and so-and-so; now one has to go and look at this, and hear this man or that woman. In town, you know, there are at any given moment one or two, or even three, celebrities whom one must on no account miss seeing. Then one has to undergo a treatment oneself or get someone else attended to, then there are teachers, tutors, and governesses, but one's own life is quite empty. Well, so we lived and felt less the painfulness of living together. Besides at first we had splendid occupations, arranging things in a new place, in new quarters; and we were also occupied in going from the town to the country and back to town again.

'We lived so through one winter, and the next there occurred, unnoticed by anyone, an apparently unimportant thing, but the cause of all that happened later. She was not well and the doctors told her not to have children, and taught her how to avoid it. To me it was disgusting. I struggled against it, but she with frivolous obstinacy insisted on having her own way and I submitted. The last excuse for our swinish life—children—was then taken away, and life became viler than ever.

'To a peasant, a labouring man, children are necessary; though it is hard for him to feed them, still he needs them, and therefore his marital relations have a justification. But to us who have children, more children are unnecessary; they are an additional care and expense, a further division of property, and a burden. So our swinish life has no justification. We either artificially deprive ourselves of children or regard them as a misfortune, the consequences of carelessness, and that is still worse. We have no justification. But we have fallen morally so low that we do not even feel the need of any justification. The majority of the present educated world devote themselves to this kind of debauchery without the least qualm of conscience.

'There is indeed nothing that can feel qualms, for conscience in our society is non-existent, unless one can call public opinion and the criminal law a "conscience". In this case neither the one nor the other is violated: there is no reason to be ashamed of public opinion for everybody acts in the same way—Mary Pávlovna, Iván Zakhárych, and the rest. Why breed paupers or deprive oneself of the possibility of social life? There is no need to fear or be ashamed in face of the criminal law either. Those shameless hussies, or soldiers' wives, throw their babies into ponds or wells, and they of course must be put in prison, but we do it all at the proper time and in a clean way.

'We lived like that for another two years. The means employed by those scoundrel-doctors evidently began to bear fruit; she became physically stouter and handsomer, like the late beauty of summer's end. She felt this and paid attention to her appearance. She developed a provocative kind of beauty which made people restless. She was in the full vigour of a well-fed and excited woman of thirty who is not bearing children.

Her appearance disturbed people. When she passed men she attracted their notice. She was like a fresh, well-fed, harnessed horse, whose bridle has been removed. There was no bridle, as is the case with ninety-nine hundredths of our women. And I felt this—and was terrified.'

XIX

He suddenly rose and sat down close to the window.

'Pardon me,' he muttered and, with his eyes fixed on the window, he remained silent for about three minutes. Then he sighed deeply and moved back to the seat opposite mine. His face was quite changed, his eyes looked pathetic, and his lips puckered strangely, almost as if he were smiling. 'I am rather tired but I will go on with it. We have still plenty of time, it is not dawn yet. Ah, yes,' he began after lighting a cigarette, 'she grew plumper after she stopped having babies, and her malady—that everlasting worry about the children—began to pass . . . at least not actually to pass, but she as it were woke up from an intoxication, came to herself, and saw that there was a whole divine world with its joys which she had forgotten, but a divine world she did not know how to live in and did not at all understand. "I must not miss it! Time is passing and won't come back!" So, I imagine, she thought, or rather felt, nor could she have thought or felt differently: she had been brought up in the belief that there was only one thing in the world worthy of attention—love. She had married and received something of that love, but not nearly what had been promised and was expected. Even that had been accompanied by many disappointments and sufferings, and then this unexpected torment: so many children! The torments exhausted her. And then, thanks to the obliging doctors, she learnt that it is possible to avoid having children. She was very glad, tried it, and became alive again for the one thing she knew—for love. But love with a husband, befouled by jealousy and all kinds of anger, was no longer the thing she wanted. She had visions of some other, clean, new love; at least I thought she had. And she began to look about her as if expecting something. I saw this and could not help feeling anxious. It happened again and again that while talking to me, as usual through other people—that is, telling a third person what she meant for me—she boldly, without remembering that she had expressed the opposite opinion an hour before, declared, though half-jokingly, that a mother's cares are a fraud, and that it is not worth while to devote one's life to children when one is young and can enjoy life. She gave less attention to the children, and less frenziedly than before, but gave more and more attention to herself, to her appearance (though she tried to conceal this), and to her pleasures, even to her accomplishments. She again enthusiastically took to the piano which she had quite abandoned, and it all began from that.'

He turned his weary eyes to the window again but, evidently making an effort, immediately continued once more.

'Yes, that man made his appearance . . .' he became confused and once or twice made that peculiar sound with his nose.

I could see that it was painful for him to name that man, to recall him, or speak about him. But he made an effort and, as if he had broken the obstacle that hindered him, continued resolutely.

'He was a worthless man in my opinion and according to my estimate. And not because of the significance he acquired in my life but because he really was so. However, the fact that he was a poor sort of fellow only served to show how irresponsible she was. If it had not been he then it would have been another. It had to be!'

Again he paused. 'Yes, he was a musician, a violinist; not a professional, but a semi-professional semi-society man.

'His father, a landowner, was a neighbour of my father's. He had been ruined, and his children—there were three boys—had obtained settled positions; only this one, the youngest, had been handed over to his godmother in Paris. There he was sent to the *Conservatoire* because he had a talent for music, and he came out as a violinist and played at concerts. He was a man . . .' Having evidently intended to say something bad about him, Pózdnyshev restrained himself and rapidly said: 'Well, I don't really know how he lived, I only know that he returned to Russia that year and appeared in my house.

'With moist almond-shaped eyes, red smiling lips, a small waxed moustache, hair done in the latest fashion, and an insipidly pretty face, he was what women call "not bad looking". His figure was weak though not misshapen, and he had a specially developed posterior, like a woman's, or such as Hottentots are said to have. They too are reported to be musical. Pushing himself as far as possible into familiarity, but sensitive and always ready to yield at the slightest resistance, he maintained his dignity in externals, wore buttoned boots of a special Parisian fashion, bright-coloured ties, and other things foreigners acquire in Paris, which by their noticeable novelty always attract women. There was an affected external gaiety in his manner. That manner, you know, of speaking about everything in allusions and unfinished sentences, as if you knew it all, remembered it, and could complete it yourself.

'It was he with his music who was the cause of it all. You know at the trial the case was put as if it was all caused by jealousy. No such thing, that is, I don't mean "no such thing", it was and yet it was not. At the trial it was decided that I was a wronged husband and that I had killed her while defending my outraged honour (that is the phrase they employ, you know). That is why I was acquitted. I tried to explain matters at the trial but they took it that I was trying to rehabilitate my wife's honour.

'What my wife's relations with that musician may have been has no meaning for me, or for her either. What has a meaning is what I have told you about—my swinishness. The whole thing was an outcome of the terrible abyss between us of which I have told you—that terrible tension of mutual hatred which made the first excuse sufficient to produce a crisis. The quarrels between us had for some time past become terrifying, and were all the more startling because they alternated with similarly intense animal passion.

'If he had not appeared there would have been someone else. If the occasion had not been jealousy it would have been something else. I maintain that all husbands who live as I did must either live dissolutely, separate, or kill themselves or their wives as I have done. If there is anybody who has not done so, he is a rare exception. Before I ended as I did, I had several times been on the verge of suicide, and she too had repeatedly tried to poison herself.

XX

'Well, that is how things were going not long before it happened. We seemed to be living in a state of truce and had no reason to break it. Then we chanced to speak about a dog which I said had been awarded a medal at an exhibition. She remarked "Not a medal, but an honourable mention." A dispute ensues. We jump from one subject to another, reproach one another, "Oh, that's nothing new, it's always been like that." "You said . . ." "No, I didn't say so." "Then I am telling lies! . . ." You feel that at any moment that dreadful quarrelling which makes you wish to kill yourself or her will begin. You know it will begin immediately, and fear it like fire and therefore wish to restrain yourself, but your whole being is seized with fury. She being in the same or even a worse condition purposely misinterprets every word you say, giving it a wrong meaning. Her every word is venomous; where she alone knows that I am most sensitive, she stabs. It gets worse and worse. I shout: "Be quiet!" or something of that kind. She rushes out of the room and into the nursery. I try to hold her back in order to finish what I was saying, to prove my point, and I seize her by the arm. She pretends that I have hurt her and screams: "Children, your father is striking me!" I shout: "Don't lie!" "But it's not the first time!" she screams, or something like that. The children rush to her. She calms them down. I say, "Don't sham!" She says, "Everything is sham in your eyes, you would kill any one and say they were shamming. Now I have understood you. That's just what you want!" "Oh, I wish you were dead as a dog!" I shout. I remember how those dreadful words horrified me. I never thought I could utter such dreadful, coarse words, and am surprised that they escaped me. I shout them and rush away into my study and sit down and smoke. I hear her go out into the hall preparing to go away. I ask, "Where are you going to?" She does not reply. "Well, devil take her," I say to myself, and go back to my study and lie down and smoke. A thousand different plans of how to revenge myself on her and get rid of her, and how to improve matters and go on as if nothing had happened, come into my head. I think all that and go on smoking and smoking. I think of running away from her, hiding myself, going to America. I get as far as dreaming of how I shall get rid of her, how splendid that will be, and how I shall unite with another, an admirable woman—quite different. I shall get rid of her either by her dying or by a divorce, and I plan how it is to be done. I notice that I am getting confused and not thinking of what is necessary, and to prevent myself from perceiving that my thoughts are not to the point I go on smoking.

'Life in the house goes on. The governess comes in and asks: "Where is madame? When will she be back?" The footman asks whether he is to serve tea. I go to the dining-room. The children, especially Lisa who already understands, gaze inquiringly and disapprovingly at me. We drink tea in silence. She has still not come back. The evening passes, she has not returned, and two different feelings alternate within me. Anger because she torments me and all the children by her absence which will end by her returning; and fear that she will not return but will do something to herself. I would go to fetch her, but where am I to look for her? At her sister's? But it would be so stupid to go and ask. And it's all the better: if she is bent on tormenting someone, let her torment herself. Besides that is what she is waiting for; and next time it would be worse still. But suppose she is not with her sister but is doing something to herself, or has already done it! It's past ten, past eleven! I don't go to the bedroom—it would be stupid to lie there alone waiting—but I'll not lie down here either. I wish to occupy my mind, to write a letter or to read, but I can't do anything. I sit alone in my study, tortured, angry, and listening. It's three o'clock, four o'clock, and she is not back. Towards morning I fall asleep. I wake up, she has still not come!

'Everything in the house goes on in the usual way, but all are perplexed and look at me inquiringly and reproachfully, considering me to be the cause of it all. And in me the same struggle still continues: anger that she is torturing me, and anxiety for her.

'At about eleven in the morning her sister arrives as her envoy. And the usual talk begins. "She is in a terrible state. What does it all mean?" "After all, nothing has happened." I speak of her impossible character and say that I have not done anything.

'"But, you know, it can't go on like this," says her sister.

'"It's all her doing and not mine," I say. "I won't take the first step. If it means separation, let it be separation."

'My sister-in-law goes away having achieved nothing. I had boldly said that I would not take the first step; but after her departure, when I came out of my study and saw the children piteous and frightened, I was prepared to take the first step. I should be glad to do it, but I don't know how. Again I pace up and down and smoke; at lunch I drink vodka and wine and attain what I unconsciously desire—I no longer see the stupidity and humiliation of my position.

'At about three she comes. When she meets me she does not speak. I imagine that she has submitted, and begin to say that I had been provoked by her reproaches. She, with the same stern expression on her terribly harassed face, says that she has not come for explanations but to fetch the children, because we cannot live together. I begin telling her that the fault is not mine and that she provoked me beyond endurance. She looks severely and solemnly at me and says: "Do not say any more, you will repent it." I tell her that I cannot stand comedies. Then she cries out something I don't catch, and rushes into her room. The key clicks behind her,—she has locked herself in. I try the door, but getting no answer, go away angrily. Half-an-hour later Lisa runs in crying. "What is it? Has anything happened?" "We can't hear mama." We go. I pull at the double doors with all my might. The bolt had not been firmly secured, and the two halves both open. I approach the bed, on which she is lying awkwardly in her petticoats and with a pair of high boots on. An empty opium bottle is on the table. She is brought to herself. Tears follow, and a reconciliation. No, not a reconciliation: in the heart of each there is still the old animosity, with the additional irritation produced by the pain of this quarrel which each attributes to the other. But one must of course finish it all somehow, and life goes on in the old way.

And so the same kind of quarrel, and even worse ones, occurred continually: once a week, once a month, or at times every day. It was always the same. Once I had already procured a passport to go abroad—the quarrel had continued for two days. But there was again a partial explanation, a partial reconciliation, and I stayed.

XXI

'So those were our relations when that man appeared. He arrived in Moscow—his name is Trukhachévski—and came to my house. It was in the morning. I received him. We had once been on familiar terms and he tried to maintain a familiar tone by using non-committal expressions, but I definitely adopted a conventional tone and he at once submitted to it. I disliked him from the first glance. But curiously enough a strange and fatal force led me not to repulse him, not to keep him away, but on the contrary to invite him to the house. After all, what could have been simpler than to converse with him coldly, and say good-bye without introducing him to my wife? But no, as if purposely, I began talking about his playing, and said I had been told he had given up the violin. He replied that, on the contrary, he now played more than ever. He referred to the fact that there had been a time when I myself played. I said I had given it up but that my wife played well.

'It is astonishing! From the first day, from the first hour of my meeting him, my relations with him were such as they might have been only after all that subsequently happened. There was something strained in them: I noticed every word, every expression he or I used, and attributed importance to them.

'I introduced him to my wife. The conversation immediately turned to music, and he offered to be of use to her by playing with her. My wife was, as usual of late, very elegant, attractive, and disquietingly beautiful. He evidently pleased her at first sight. Besides she was glad that she would have someone to accompany her on a violin, which she was so fond of that she used to engage a violinist from the theatre for the purpose; and her face reflected her pleasure. But catching sight of me she at once understood my feeling and changed her expression, and a game of mutual deception began. I smiled pleasantly to appear as if I liked it. He, looking at my wife as all lechers look at pretty women, pretended that he was only interested in the subject of the conversation—which no longer interested him at all; while she tried to seem indifferent, though my false smile of jealousy with which she was familiar, and his lustful gaze, evidently excited her. I saw that from their first encounter her eyes were particularly bright and, probably as a result of my jealousy, it seemed as if an electric current had been established between them, evoking as it were an identity of expressions, looks, and smiles. She blushed and he blushed. She smiled and he smiled. We spoke about music, Paris, and all sorts of trifles. Then he rose to go, and stood smilingly, holding his hat against his twitching thigh and looking now at her and now at me, as if in expectation of what we would do. I remember that instant just because at that moment I might not have invited him, and then nothing would have happened. But I glanced at him and at her and said silently to myself, "Don't suppose that I am jealous," "or that I am afraid of you," I added mentally addressing him, and I invited him to come some evening and bring his violin to play with my wife. She glanced at me with surprise, flushed, and as if frightened began to decline, saying that she did not play well enough. This refusal irritated me still more, and I insisted the more on his coming. I remember the curious feeling with which I looked at the back of his head, with the black hair parted in the middle contrasting with the white nape of his neck, as he went out with his peculiar springing gait suggestive of some kind of a bird. I could not conceal from myself that that man's presence tormented me. "It depends on me," I reflected, "to act so as to see nothing more of him. But that would be to admit that I am afraid of him. No, I am not afraid of him; it would be too humiliating," I said to myself. And there in the ante-room, knowing that my wife heard me, I insisted that he should come that evening with his violin. He promised to do so, and left.

'In the evening he brought his violin and they played. But it took a long time to arrange matters—they had not the music they wanted, and my wife could not without preparation play what they had. I was very fond of music and sympathized with their playing, arranging a music-stand for him and turning over the pages. They played a few things, some songs without words, and a little sonata by Mozart. They played splendidly, and he had an exceptionally fine tone. Besides that, he had a refined and elevated taste not at all in correspondence with his character.

'He was of course a much better player than my wife, and he helped her, while at the same time politely praising her playing. He behaved himself very well. My wife seemed interested only in music and was very simple and natural. But though I pretended to be interested in the music I was tormented by jealousy all the evening.

'From the first moment his eyes met my wife's I saw that the animal in each of them, regardless of all conditions of their position and of society, asked, "May I?" and answered, "Oh, yes, certainly." I saw that he had not at all expected to find my wife, a Moscow lady, so attractive, and that he was very pleased. For he had no doubt whatever that she was *willing*. The only issue was whether that unendurable husband could hinder them. Had I been pure I should not have understood this, but, like the majority of men, I had myself regarded women in that way before I married and therefore could read his mind like a book. I was particularly tormented because I saw without doubt that she had no other feeling towards me than a continual irritation only occasionally interrupted by the habitual sensuality; but that this man—by his external refinement and novelty and still more by his undoubtedly great talent for music, by the nearness that comes of playing together, and by the influence music, especially the violin, exercises on impressionable natures—was sure not only to please but certainly and without the least hesitation to conquer, crush, bind her, twist her round his little finger and do whatever he liked with her. I could not help seeing this and I suffered horribly. But for all that, or perhaps on account of it, some force obliged me against my will to be not merely polite but amiable to him. Whether I did it for my wife or for him, to show that I was not afraid of him, or whether I did it to deceive myself—I don't know, but I know that from the first I could not behave naturally with him. In order not to yield to my wish to kill him there and then, I had to make much of him. I gave him expensive wines at supper, went into raptures over his playing, spoke to him with a particularly amiable smile, and invited him to dine and play with my wife again the next Sunday. I told him I would ask a few friends who were fond of music to hear him. And so it ended.'

Greatly agitated, Pózdnyshev changed his position and emitted his peculiar sound.

'It is strange how the presence of that man acted on me,' he began again, with an evident effort to keep calm. 'I come home from the Exhibition a day or two later, enter the ante-room, and suddenly feel something heavy, as if a stone had fallen on my heart, and I cannot understand what it is. It was that passing through the ante-room I noticed something which reminded me of him. I realized what it was only in my study, and went back to the ante-room to make sure. Yes, I was not mistaken, there was his overcoat. A fashionable coat, you know. (Though I did not realize it, I observed everything connected with him with extraordinary attention.) I inquire: sure enough he is there. I pass on to the dancing-room, not through the drawing-room but through the schoolroom. My daughter, Lisa, sits reading a book and the nurse sits with the youngest boy at the table, making a lid of some kind spin round. The door to the dancing-room is shut but I hear the sound of a rhythmic arpeggio and his and her voices. I listen, but cannot make out anything.

'Evidently the sound of the piano is purposely made to drown the sound of their voices, their kisses . . . perhaps. My God! What was aroused in me! Even to think of the beast that then lived in me fills me with horror! My heart suddenly contracted, stopped, and then began to beat like a hammer. My chief feeling, as usual whenever I was enraged, was one of self-pity. "In the presence of the children! of their nurse!" thought I. Probably I looked awful, for Lisa gazed at me with strange eyes. "What am I to do?" I asked myself. "Go in? I can't: heaven only knows what I should do. But neither can I go away." The nurse looked at me as if she understood my position. "But it is impossible not to go in," I said to myself, and I quickly opened the door. He was sitting at the piano playing those arpeggios with his large white upturned fingers. She was standing in the curve of the piano, bending over some open music. She was the first to see or hear, and glanced at me. Whether she was frightened and pretended not to be, or whether she was really not frightened, anyway she did not start or move but only blushed, and that not at once.

'"How glad I am that you have come: we have not decided what to play on Sunday," she said in a tone she would not have used to me had we been alone. This and her using the word "we" of herself and him, filled me with indignation. I greeted him silently.

'He pressed my hand, and at once, with a smile which I thought distinctly ironic, began to explain that he had brought some music to practise for Sunday, but that they disagreed about what to play: a classical but more difficult piece, namely Beethoven's sonata for the violin, or a few little pieces. It was all so simple and natural that there was nothing one could cavil at, yet I felt certain that it was all untrue and that they had agreed to deceive me.

'One of the most distressing conditions of life for a jealous man (and everyone is jealous in our world) are certain society conventions which allow a man and woman the greatest and most dangerous proximity. You would become a laughing-stock to others if you tried to prevent such nearness at balls, or the nearness of doctors to their women-patients, or of people occupied with art, sculpture, and especially music. A couple are occupied with the noblest of arts, music; this demands a certain nearness, and there is nothing reprehensible in that and only a stupid jealous husband can see anything undesirable in it. Yet everybody knows that it is by means of those very pursuits, especially of music, that the greater part of the adulteries in our society occur. I evidently confused them by the confusion I betrayed: for a long time I could not speak. I was like a bottle held upside down from which the water does not flow because it is too full. I wanted to abuse him and to turn him out, but again felt that I must treat him courteously and amiably. And I did so. I acted as though I approved of it all, and again because of the strange feeling which made me behave to him the more amiably the more his presence distressed me. I told him that I trusted his taste and advised her to do the same. He stayed as long as was necessary to efface the unpleasant impression caused by my sudden entrance—looking frightened and remaining silent—and then left, pretending that it was now decided what to play next day. I was however fully convinced that compared to what interested them the question of what to play was quite indifferent.

'I saw him out to the ante-room with special politeness. (How could one do less than accompany a man who had come to disturb the peace and destroy the happiness of a whole family?) And I pressed his soft white hand with particular warmth.

XXII

'I did not speak to her all that day—I could not. Nearness to her aroused in me such hatred of her that I was afraid of myself. At dinner in the presence of the children she asked me when I was going away. I had to go next week to the District Meetings of the Zémstvo.* I told her the date. She asked whether I did not want anything for the journey. I did not answer but sat silent at table and then went in silence to my study. Latterly she used never to come to my room, especially not at that time of day. I lay in my study filled with anger. Suddenly I heard her familiar step, and the terrible, monstrous idea entered my head that she, like Uriah's wife,* wished to conceal the sin she had already committed and that that was why she was coming to me at such an unusual time. "Can she be coming to me?" thought I, listening to her approaching footsteps. "If she is coming here, then I am right," and an inexpressible hatred of her took possession of me. Nearer and nearer came the steps. Is it possible that she won't pass on to the dancing-room? No, the door creaks and in the doorway appears her tall handsome figure, on her face and in her eyes a timid ingratiating look which she tries to hide, but which I see and the meaning of which I know. I almost choked, so long did I hold my breath, and still looking at her I grasped my cigarette-case and began to light up.

'"Now how can you? One comes to sit with you for a bit, and you begin smoking"—and she sat down close to me on the sofa, leaning against me. I moved away so as not to touch her.

'"I see you are dissatisfied at my wanting to play on Sunday," she said.

'"I am not at all dissatisfied," I said.

'"As if I don't see!"

'"Well, I congratulate you on seeing. But I only see that you behave like a coquette. . . . You always find pleasure in all kinds of vileness, but to me it is terrible!"

'"Oh, well, if you are going to scold like a cabman I'll go away."

'"Do, but remember that if you don't value the family honour, I don't value you (the hell with you), but the family honour I do value."

'"But what is the matter? What?"

'"Go away, for God's sake be off!"

'Whether she pretended not to understand what it was about or really did not understand, at any rate she took offence, grew angry, and did not go away but stood in the middle of the room.

'"You have really become impossible," she began. "You have a character that even an angel could not put up with." And as usual trying to sting me as painfully as possible, she reminded me of my conduct to my sister (an incident when, being exasperated, I said rude things to my sister); she knew I was distressed about it and she stung me just on that spot. "After that, nothing from you will surprise me," she said.

'"Yes! Insult me, humiliate me, disgrace me, and then put the blame on me," I said to myself, and suddenly I was seized by such terrible rage as I had never before experienced.

'For the first time I wished to give physical expression to that rage. I jumped up and went towards her; but just as I jumped up I remember becoming conscious of my rage and asking myself: "Is it right to give way to this feeling?" and at once I answered that it was right, that it would frighten her, and instead of restraining my fury I immediately began inflaming it still further, and was glad it burnt yet more fiercely within me.

'"Be off, or I'll kill you!" I shouted, going up to her and seizing her by the arm. I consciously intensified the anger in my voice as I said this. And I suppose I was terrible, for she was so frightened that she had not even the strength to go away, but only said: "Vásya, what is it? What is the matter with you?"

'"Go!" I roared louder still. "No one but you can drive me to fury. I do not answer for myself!"

'Having given rein to my rage, I revelled in it and wished to do something still more unusual to show the extreme degree of my anger. I felt a terrible desire to beat her, to kill her, but knew that this would not do, and so to give vent to my fury I seized a paper-weight from my table, again shouting "Go!" and hurled it to the floor near her. I aimed it very exactly past her. Then she left the room, but stopped at the doorway, and immediately, while she still saw it (I did it so that she might see), I began snatching things from the table—candlesticks and ink-stand—and hurling them on the floor still shouting "Go! Get out! I don't answer for myself!" She went away—and I immediately stopped.

'An hour later the nurse came to tell me that my wife was in hysterics. I went to her; she sobbed, laughed, could not speak, and her whole body was convulsed. She was not pretending, but was really ill.

'Towards morning she grew quiet, and we made peace under the influence of the feeling we called love.

'In the morning when, after our reconciliation, I confessed to her that I was jealous of Trukhachévski, she was not at all embarrassed, but laughed most naturally; so strange did the very possibility of an infatuation for such a man seem to her, she said.

'"Could a decent woman have any other feeling for such a man than the pleasure of his music? Why, if you like I am ready never to see him again . . . not even on Sunday, though everybody has been invited. Write and tell him that I am ill, and there's an end of it! Only it is unpleasant that anyone, especially he himself, should imagine that he is dangerous. I am too proud to allow anyone to think that of me!"

'And you know, she was not lying, she believed what she was saying; she hoped by those words to evoke in herself contempt for him and so to defend herself from him, but she did not succeed in doing so. Everything was against her, especially that accursed music. So it all ended, and on the Sunday the guests assembled and they again played together.

XXIII

'I suppose it is hardly necessary to say that I was very vain: if one is not vain there is nothing to live for in our usual way of life. So on that Sunday I arranged the dinner and the musical evening with much care. I bought the provisions myself and invited the guests.

'Towards six the visitors assembled. He came in evening dress with diamond studs that showed bad taste. He behaved in a free and easy manner, answered everything hurriedly with a smile of agreement and understanding, you know, with that peculiar expression which seems to say that all you may do or say is just what he expected. Everything that was not in good taste about him I noticed with particular pleasure, because it ought all to have had the effect of tranquillizing me and showing that he was so far beneath my wife that, as she had said, she could not lower herself to his level. I did not now allow myself to be jealous. In the first place I was exhausted from that torment and needed rest, and secondly I wanted to believe my wife's assurances and did believe them. But though I was not jealous I was nevertheless not natural with either of them, and at dinner and during the first half of the evening before the music began I still followed their movements and looks.

'The dinner was, as dinners are, dull and pretentious. The music began pretty early. Oh, how I remember every detail of that evening! I remember how he brought in his violin, unlocked the case, took off the cover a lady had embroidered for him, drew out the violin, and began tuning it. I remember how my wife sat down at the piano with pretended unconcern, under which I saw that she was trying to conceal great timidity—chiefly as to her own ability—and then the usual A on the piano began, the pizzicato of the violin, and the arrangement of the music. Then I remember how they glanced at one another, turned to look at the audience who were seating themselves, said something to one another, and began. He took the first chords. His face grew serious, stern, and sympathetic, and listening to the sounds he produced, he touched the strings with careful fingers. The piano answered him. And it began. . . .'

Pózdnyshev paused and produced his strange sound several times in succession. He tried to speak, but sniffed, and stopped.

'They played Beethoven's Kreutzer Sonata,' he continued. 'Do you know the first presto? You do?' he cried. 'Ugh! It is a terrifying thing, that sonata. And especially that part. And in general music is a terrifying thing! What is it? I don't understand it. What is music? What does it do? And why does it do what it does? They say music exalts the soul. Nonsense, it is not true! It is effective, terribly effective—I am speaking of myself—but not in an exalting way. It has neither an exalting nor a debasing effect but an agitating one. How can I put it? Music makes me forget myself, my real position; it transports me to some other position not my own. Under the influence of music it seems to me that I feel what I do not really feel, that I understand what I do not understand, that I can do what I cannot do. I explain it by the fact that music acts like yawning, like laughter: I am not sleepy, but I yawn when I see someone yawning; there is nothing for me to laugh at, but I laugh when I hear people laughing.

'Music carries me immediately and directly into the mental condition of the man who composed it. My soul merges with his and together with him I pass from one condition into another, but why this happens I don't know. You see, he who wrote, let us say, the Kreutzer Sonata—Beethoven—knew of course why he was in that condition; that condition caused him to do certain actions and therefore that condition had a meaning for him, but for me—none at all. That is why music only agitates and doesn't lead to a conclusion. Well, when a military march is played the soldiers march to the music and the music has achieved its goal. A dance is played, I dance and the music has achieved its goal. Mass is sung, I receive communion, and that music too has reached a conclusion. Otherwise it is only agitating, and what ought to be done in that agitation is lacking. That is why music sometimes has such a terrible, horrible effect. In China, music is a state affair. And that is as it should be. How can one allow anyone who pleases to hypnotize another, or many others, and do what he likes with them? And especially that this hypnotist should be the first immoral man who turns up?

'It is a terrifying instrument in the hands of any chance user! Take that Kreutzer Sonata for instance, how can that first presto be played in a drawing-room among ladies in low-necked dresses? To hear that played, to clap a little, and then to eat ices and talk of the latest scandal? Such things should only be played on certain important significant occasions, and then only when certain actions answering to such music are wanted; play it then and do what the music has moved you to. Otherwise an awakening of energy and feeling unsuited both to the time and the place, to which no outlet is given, cannot but act harmfully. At any rate that piece had a horrible effect on me; it was as if quite new feelings, new possibilities, of which I had till then been unaware, had been revealed to me. "That's how it is: not at all as I used to think and live, but that way," something seemed to say within me. What this new thing was that had been revealed to me I could not explain to myself, but the consciousness of this new condition was very joyous. All those same people, including my wife and him, appeared in a new light.

'After that allegro they played the beautiful, but common and unoriginal, andante with trite variations, and the very weak finale. Then, at the request of the visitors, they played Ernst's Elegy* and a few small pieces. They were all good, but they did not produce on me a one-hundredth part of the impression the first piece had. The effect of the first piece formed the background for them all.

'I felt light-hearted and cheerful the whole evening. I had never seen my wife as she was that evening. Those shining eyes, that severe, significant expression while she played, and her melting languor and feeble, pathetic, and blissful smile after they had finished. I saw all that but did not attribute any meaning to it except that she was feeling what I felt, and that to her as to me new feelings, never before experienced, were revealed or, as it were, recalled. The evening ended satisfactorily and the visitors departed.

'Knowing that I had to go away to attend the Zémstvo meetings two days later, Trukhachévski on leaving said he hoped to repeat the pleasure of that evening when he next came to Moscow. From this I concluded that he did not consider it possible to come to my house during my absence, and this pleased me. It turned out that as I should not be back before he left town, we should not see one another again.

'For the first time I pressed his hand with real pleasure, and thanked him for the enjoyment he had given us. In the same way he bade a final farewell to my wife. Their leave-taking seemed to be most natural and proper. Everything was splendid. My wife and I were both very well satisfied with our evening party.

XXIV

'Two days later I left for the meetings, parting from my wife in the best and most tranquil of moods. In the district there was always an enormous amount to do and a quite special life, a special little world of its own. I spent two ten-hour days at the council. A letter from my wife was brought me on the second day and I read it there and then. She wrote about the children, about uncle, about the nurse, about shopping, and among other things she mentioned, as a most natural occurrence, that Trukhachévski had called, brought some music he had promised, and had offered to play again, but that she had refused. I did not remember his having promised any music, but thought he had taken leave for good, and I was therefore unpleasantly struck by this. I was however so busy that I had no time to think of it, and it was only in the evening when I had returned to my lodgings that I re-read her letter. Besides the fact that Trukhachévski had called at my house during my absence, the whole tone of the letter seemed to me unnatural. The mad beast of jealousy began to growl in its kennel and wanted to leap out, but I was afraid of that beast and quickly fastened him in. "What an abominable feeling this jealousy is!" I said to myself. "What could be more natural than what she writes!"

'I went to bed and began thinking about the affairs awaiting me next day. During those meetings, sleeping in a new place, I usually slept badly, but now I fell asleep very quickly. And as sometimes happens, you know, you feel a kind of electric shock and wake up. So I awoke thinking of her, of my physical love for her, and of Trukhachévski, and of everything being accomplished between them. Horror and rage compressed my heart. But I began to reason with myself. "What nonsense!" said I to myself. "There are no grounds to go on, there is nothing and there has been nothing. How can I so degrade her and myself as to imagine such horrors? He is a sort of hired violinist, known as a worthless fellow, and suddenly an honourable woman, the respected mother of a family, *my* wife! What absurdity!" So it seemed to me on the one hand. "How could it help being so?" it seemed on the other. "How could that simplest and most intelligible thing help happening—that for the sake of which I married her, for the sake of which I have been living with her, what alone I wanted of her, and which others including this musician must therefore also want? He is an unmarried man, healthy (I remember how he crunched the gristle of a cutlet and how greedily his red lips clung to the glass of wine), well-fed, plump, and not merely unprincipled but evidently making it a principle to accept the pleasures that present themselves. And they have music, that most exquisite voluptuousness of the senses, as a link between them. What then could make him refrain? She? But who is she? She was, and still is, a mystery. I don't know her. I only know her as an animal. And nothing can or should restrain an animal."

'Only then did I remember their faces that evening when, after the Kreutzer Sonata, they played some impassioned little piece, I don't remember by whom, impassioned to the point of obscenity. "How dared I go away?" I asked myself, remembering their faces. Was it not clear that everything had happened between them that evening? Was it not evident already then that there was not only no barrier between them, but that they both, and she chiefly, felt a certain measure of shame after what had happened? I remember her weak, piteous, and beatific smile as she wiped the perspiration from her flushed face when I came up to the piano. Already then they avoided looking at one another, and only at supper when he was pouring out some water for her, they glanced at each other with the vestige of a smile. I now recalled with horror the glance and scarcely perceptible smile I had then caught. "Yes, it is all over," said one voice, and immediately the other voice said something entirely different. "Something has come over you, it can't be that it is so," said that other voice. It felt uncanny lying in the dark and I struck a light, and felt a kind of terror in that little room with its yellow wall-paper. I lit a cigarette and, as always happens when one's thoughts go round and round in a circle of insoluble contradictions, I smoked, taking one cigarette after another in order to befog myself so as not to see those contradictions.

'I did not sleep all night, and at five in the morning, having decided that I could not continue in such a state of tension, I rose, woke the caretaker who attended me and sent him to get horses. I sent a note to the council saying that I had been recalled to Moscow on urgent business and asking that one of the members should take my place. At eight o'clock I got into my tarantas* and started out.'

XXV

The conductor entered and seeing that our candle had burnt down put it out, without supplying a fresh one. The day was dawning. Pózdnyshev was silent, but sighed deeply all the time the conductor was in the carriage. He continued his story only after the conductor had gone out, and in the semi-darkness of the carriage only the rattle of the windows of the moving carriage and the rhythmic snoring of the clerk could be heard. In the half-light of dawn I could not see Pózdnyshev's face at all, but only heard his voice becoming ever more and more excited and full of suffering.

'I had to travel twenty-four miles by road and eight hours by rail. It was splendid driving. It was frosty autumn weather, bright and sunny. The roads were in that condition when the tyres leave their dark imprint on them, you know. They were smooth, the light brilliant, and the air invigorating. It was pleasant driving in the tarantas. When it grew lighter and I had started I felt easier. Looking at the houses, the fields, and the passers-by, I forgot where I was going. Sometimes I felt that I was simply taking a drive, and that nothing of what was calling me back had taken place. This oblivion was peculiarly enjoyable. When I remembered where I was going to, I said to myself, "We shall see when the time comes; I must not think about it." When we were half-way an incident occurred which detained me and still further distracted my thoughts. The tarantas broke down and had to be repaired. That break-down had a very important effect, for it caused me to arrive in Moscow at midnight, instead of at seven o'clock as I had expected, and to reach home between twelve and one, as I missed the express and had to travel by an ordinary train. Going to fetch a cart, having the tarantas mended, settling up, tea at the inn, a talk with the innkeeper—all this still further diverted my attention. It was twilight before all was ready and I started again. By night it was even pleasanter driving than during the day. There was a new moon, a slight frost, still good roads, good horses, and a jolly driver, and as I went on I enjoyed it, hardly thinking at all of what lay before me; or perhaps I enjoyed it just because I knew what awaited me and was saying good-bye to the joys of life. But that tranquil mood, that ability to suppress my feelings, ended with my drive.

'As soon as I entered the train something entirely different began. That eight-hour journey in a railway carriage was something horrible, which I shall never forget all my life. Whether it was that having taken my seat in the carriage I vividly imagined myself as having already arrived, or that railway travelling has such an exciting effect on people, at any rate from the moment I sat down in the train I could no longer control my imagination, and with extraordinary vividness which inflamed my jealousy it painted incessantly, one after another, pictures of what had gone on in my absence, of how she had been false to me. I burnt with indignation, anger, and a peculiar feeling of intoxication with my own humiliation, as I gazed at those pictures, and I could not tear myself away from them; I could not help looking at them, could not efface them, and could not help evoking them. That was not all. The more I gazed at those imaginary pictures the stronger grew my belief in their reality. The vividness with which they presented themselves to me seemed to serve as proof that what I imagined was real. It was as if some devil against my will invented and suggested to me the most terrible reflections. An old conversation I had had with Trukhachévski's brother came to my mind, and in a kind of ecstasy I rent my heart with that conversation, making it refer to Trukhachévski and my wife.

'That had occurred long before, but I recalled it. Trukhachévski's brother, I remember, in reply to a question whether he frequented houses of ill-fame, had said that a decent man would not go to places where there was danger of infection and it was dirty and nasty, since he could always find a decent woman. And now his brother had found my wife! "True, she is not in her first youth, has lost a side-tooth, and there is a slight puffiness about her; but it can't be helped, one has to take advantage of what one can get," I imagined him to be thinking. "Yes, it is condescending of him to take her for his mistress!" I said to myself. "And she is safe." "No, it is impossible!" I thought horror-struck. "There is nothing of the kind, nothing! There are not even any grounds for suspecting such things. Didn't she tell me that the very thought that I could be jealous of him was degrading to her? Yes, but she is lying, she is always lying!" I exclaimed, and everything began anew. There were only two other people in the carriage; an old woman and her husband, both very taciturn, and even they got out at one of the stations and I was quite alone. I was like a caged animal: now I jumped up and went to the window, now I began to walk up and down trying to speed the carriage up; but the carriage with all its seats and windows went jolting on in the same way, just as ours does.'

Pózdnyshev jumped up, took a few steps, and sat down again.

'Oh, I am afraid, afraid of railway carriages, I am seized with horror. Yes, it is awful!' he continued. 'I said to myself, "I will think of something else. Suppose I think of the innkeeper where I had tea," and there in my mind's eye appears the innkeeper with his long beard and his grandson, a boy of the age of my Vásya! "My Vásya! He will see how the musician kisses his mother. What will happen in his poor soul? But what does she care? She loves" . . . and again the same thing rose up in me. "No, no . . . I will think about the inspection of the District Hospital. Oh, yes, about the patient who complained of the doctor yesterday. The doctor has a moustache like Trukhachévski's. And how impudent he is . . . they both deceived me when he said he was leaving Moscow," and it began afresh. Everything I thought of had some connection with them. I suffered dreadfully. The chief cause of the suffering was my ignorance, my doubt, and the contradictions within me: my not knowing whether I ought to love or hate her. My suffering was of a strange kind. I felt a hateful consciousness of my humiliation and of his victory, but a terrible hatred for her. "It will not do to put an end to myself and leave her; she must at least suffer to some extent, and at least understand that I have suffered," I said to myself. I got out at every station to divert my mind. At one station I saw some people drinking, and I immediately drank some vodka. Beside me stood a Jew who was also drinking. He began to talk, and to avoid being alone in my carriage I went with him into his dirty third-class carriage reeking with smoke and bespattered with shells of sunflower seeds. There I sat down beside him and he chattered a great deal and told anecdotes. I listened to him, but could not take in what he was saying because I continued to think about my own affairs. He noticed this and demanded my attention. Then I rose and went back to my carriage. "I must think it over," I said to myself. "Is what I suspect true, and is there any reason for me to suffer?" I sat down, wishing to think it over calmly, but immediately, instead of calm reflection, the same thing began again: instead of reflection, pictures and fancies. "How often I have suffered like this," I said to myself (recalling former similar attacks of jealousy), "and afterwards it all ended in nothing. So it will be now perhaps, yes certainly it will. I shall find her calmly asleep, she will wake up, be pleased to see me, and by her words and looks I shall know that there has been nothing and that this is all nonsense. Oh, how good that would be! But no, that has happened too often and won't happen again now," some voice seemed to say; and it began again. Yes, that was where the punishment lay! I wouldn't take a young man to a venereal disease clinic to knock the hankering after women out of him, but into my soul, to see the devils that were rending it! What was terrible, you know, was that I considered myself to have a complete right to her body as if it were my own, and yet at the same time I felt I could not control that body, that it was not mine and she could dispose of it as she pleased, and that she wanted to dispose of it not as I wished her to. And I could do nothing either to her or to him. He, like Vánka the Steward,* could sing a song before the gallows of how he kissed the sugared lips and so forth. And he would triumph. If she has not yet done it but wishes to—and I know that she does wish to—it is still worse; it would be better if she had done it and I knew it, so that there would be an end to this uncertainty. I could not have said what it was I wanted. I wanted her not to desire that which she was bound to desire. It was utter insanity.

XXVI

'At the next to the last station, when the conductor came to collect the tickets, I gathered my things together and went out onto the platform, and the consciousness that the crisis was at hand still further increased my agitation. I felt cold, and my jaw trembled so that my teeth chattered. I automatically left the station with the crowd, took a cab, got in, and drove off. I rode looking at the few passers-by, the night-watchmen, and the shadows of my cab thrown by the street lamps, now in front and now behind me, and did not think of anything. When we had gone about half a mile my feet felt cold, and I remembered that I had taken off my woollen stockings in the train and put them in my satchel. "Where is the satchel? Is it here? Yes." And my wicker trunk? I remembered that I had entirely forgotten about my luggage, but finding that I had the luggage-ticket I decided that it was not worth while going back for it, and so continued my way.

'Try now as I will, I cannot recall my state of mind at the time. What did I think? What did I want? I don't know at all. All I remember is a consciousness that something dreadful and very important in my life was imminent. Whether that important event occurred because I thought it would, or whether I had a presentiment of what was to happen, I don't know. It may even be that after what has happened all the foregoing moments have acquired a certain gloom in my mind. I drove up to the front porch. It was past midnight. Some cabmen were waiting in front of the porch expecting, from the fact that there were lights in the windows, to get fares. (The lights were in our flat, in the dancing-room and drawing-room.) Without considering why it was still light in our windows so late, I went upstairs in the same state of expectation of something dreadful, and rang. Egór, a kind, willing, but very stupid footman, opened the door. The first thing my eyes fell on in the hall was a man's cloak hanging on the stand with other outdoor coats. I ought to have been surprised but was not, for I had expected it. "That's it!" I said to myself. When I asked Egór who the visitor was and he named Trukhachévski, I inquired whether there was anyone else. He replied, "Nobody, sir." I remember that he replied in a tone as if he wanted to cheer me and dissipate my doubts of there being anybody else there. "So it is, so it is," I seemed to be saying to myself. "And the children?" "All well. heaven be praised. In bed, long ago."

'I could not breathe, and could not check the trembling of my jaw. "Yes, so it is not as I thought: I used to expect a misfortune but things used to turn out all right and in the usual way. Now it is not as usual, but is all as I pictured to myself. I thought it was only my imagination, but here it is, all real. Here it all is . . .!"

'I almost began to sob, but the devil immediately suggested to me: "Cry, be sentimental, and they will get away quietly. You will have no proof and will continue to suffer and doubt all your life." And my self-pity immediately vanished, and a strange sense of joy arose in me, that my torture would now be over, that now I could punish her, could get rid of her, and could vent my anger. And I gave vent to it—I became a beast, a cruel and cunning beast.

'"Don't!" I said to Egór, who was about to go to the drawing-room. "Here is my luggage-ticket, take a cab as quick as you can and go and get my luggage. Go!" He went down the passage to fetch his overcoat. Afraid that he might alarm them, I went as far as his little room and waited while he put on his overcoat. From the drawing-room, beyond another room, one could hear voices and the clatter of knives and plates. They were eating and had not heard the bell. "If only they don't come out now," thought I. Egór put on his overcoat, which had an astrakhan collar, and went out. I locked the door after him and felt creepy when I knew I was alone and must act at once. How, I did not yet know. I only knew that all was now over, that there could be no doubt as to her guilt, and that I should punish her immediately and end my relations with her.

'Previously I had doubted and had thought: "Perhaps after all it's not true, perhaps I am mistaken." But now it was so no longer. It was all irrevocably decided. "Without my knowledge she is alone with him at night! That is a complete disregard of everything! Or worse still: it is intentional boldness and impudence in crime, that the boldness may serve as a sign of innocence. All is clear. There is no doubt." I only feared one thing—their parting hastily, inventing some fresh lie, and thus depriving me of clear evidence and of the possibility of proving the fact. So as to catch them more quickly I went on tiptoe to the dancing-room where they were, not through the drawing-room but through the passage and nurseries.

'In the first nursery slept the boys. In the second nursery the nurse began to stir and was about to wake, and I imagined to myself what she would think when she knew all; and such pity for myself seized me at that thought that I could not restrain my tears, and not to wake the children I ran on tiptoe into the passage and on into my study, where I fell sobbing on the sofa.

'"I, an honest man, I, the son of my parents, I, who have all my life dreamt of the happiness of married life; I, a man who was never unfaithful to her. . . . And now! Five children, and she is embracing a musician because he has red lips! No, she is not a human being. She is a bitch, an abominable bitch! In the next room to her children whom she has all her life pretended to love. And writing to me as she did! Throwing herself so barefacedly on his neck! But what do I know? Perhaps she long ago carried on with the footmen, and so got the children who are considered mine! To-morrow I should have come back and she would have met me with her fine coiffure, with her elegant waist and her indolent, graceful movements" (I saw all her attractive, hateful face), "and that beast of jealousy would for ever have sat in my heart lacerating it. What will the nurse think? . . . And Egór? And poor little Lisa! She already understands something. Ah, that impudence, those lies! And that animal sensuality which I know so well," I said to myself.

'I tried to get up but could not. My heart was beating so that I could not stand on my feet. "Yes, I shall die of a stroke. She will kill me. That is just what she wants. What is killing to her? But no, that would be too advantageous for her and I will not give her that pleasure. Yes, here I sit while they eat and laugh and . . . Yes, though she was no longer in her first freshness he did not disdain her. For in spite of that she is not bad looking, and above all she is at any rate not dangerous to his precious health. And why did I not throttle her then?" I said to myself, recalling the moment when, the week before, I drove her out of my study and hurled things about. I vividly recalled the state I had then been in; I not only recalled it, but again felt the need to strike and destroy that I had felt then. I remember how I wished to act, and how all considerations except those necessary for action went out of my head. I entered into that condition when an animal or a man, under the influence of physical excitement at a time of danger, acts with precision and deliberation but without losing a moment and always with a single definite aim in view.

XXVII

'The first thing I did was to take off my boots and, in my socks, approach the sofa, on the wall above which guns and daggers were hung. I took down a curved Damascus dagger that had never been used and was very sharp. I drew it out of its scabbard. I remember the scabbard fell behind the sofa, and I remember thinking "I must find it afterwards or it will get lost." Then I took off my overcoat which I was still wearing, and stepping softly in my socks I went there.

'Having crept up stealthily to the door, I suddenly opened it. I remember the expression on their faces. I remember that expression because it gave me a painful pleasure—it was an expression of terror. That was just what I wanted. I shall never forget the look of desperate terror that appeared on both their faces the first instant they saw me. He I think was sitting at the table, but on seeing or hearing me he jumped to his feet and stood with his back to the cupboard. His face expressed nothing but quite unmistakable terror. Her face too expressed terror but there was something else besides. If it had expressed only terror, perhaps what happened might not have happened; but on her face there was, or at any rate so it seemed to me at the first moment, also an expression of regret and annoyance that love's raptures and her happiness with him had been disturbed. It was as if she wanted nothing but that her present happiness should not be interfered with. These expressions remained on their faces but an instant. The look of terror on his face changed immediately to one of inquiry: should I lie or not? If I lie, I'd better begin at once; if I don't, something else will happen. But what? . . . He looked inquiringly at her face. On her face the look of vexation and regret changed as she looked at him (so it seemed to me) to one of solicitude for him.

'For an instant I stood in the doorway holding the dagger behind my back. At that moment he smiled, and in a ridiculously indifferent tone remarked: "And we have been having some music."

'"What a surprise!" she began, falling into his tone. But neither of them finished; the same fury I had experienced the week before overcame me. Again I felt that need for destruction, violence, and a transport of rage, and yielded to it. Neither finished what they were saying. That something else began which he had feared and which immediately destroyed all they were saying. I rushed towards her, still hiding the dagger that he might not prevent my striking her in the side under her breast. I selected that spot from the first. Just as I rushed at her he saw it, and—a thing I never expected of him—seized me by the arm and shouted: "Think what you are doing! Help, someone!"

'I snatched my arm away and rushed at him in silence. His eyes met mine and he suddenly grew as pale as a sheet to his very lips. His eyes flashed in a peculiar way, and—what again I had not expected—he darted under the piano and out at the door. I was going to rush after him, but a weight hung on my left arm. It was she. I tried to free myself, but she hung on yet more heavily and would not let me go. This unexpected hindrance, the weight, and her touch which was loathsome to me, inflamed me still more. I felt that I was quite mad and that I must look frightful, and this delighted me. I swung my left arm with all my might, and my elbow hit her straight in the face. She cried out and let go my arm. I wanted to run after him, but remembered that it is ridiculous to run after one's wife's lover in one's socks; and I did not wish to be ridiculous but terrible. In spite of the fearful frenzy I was in, I was all the time aware of the impression I might produce on others, and was even partly guided by that impression. I turned towards her. She fell on the couch, and holding her hand to her bruised eyes, looked at me. Her face showed fear and hatred of me, the enemy, as a rat's does when one lifts the trap in which it has been caught. At any rate I saw nothing in her expression but this fear and hatred of me. It was just the fear and hatred of me which would be evoked by love for another. But still I might perhaps have restrained myself and not done what I did had she remained silent. But she suddenly began to speak and to catch hold of the hand in which I held the dagger.

'"Get a hold of yourself! What are you doing? What is the matter? There has been nothing, nothing, nothing.... I swear it!"

'I might still have hesitated, but those last words of hers, from which I concluded just the opposite—that everything had happened—called forth a reply. And the reply had to correspond to the temper to which I had brought myself, which continued to crescendo and had to keep on rising. Fury, too, has its laws.

'"Don't lie, you wretch!" I howled, and seized her arm with my left hand, but she wrenched herself away. Then, still without letting go of the dagger, I seized her by the throat with my left hand, threw her backwards, and began throttling her. What a firm neck it was...! She seized my hand with both hers trying to pull it away from her throat, and as if I had only waited for that, I struck her with all my might with the dagger in the side below the ribs.

'When people say they don't remember what they do in a fit of fury, it is rubbish, falsehood. I remembered everything and did not for a moment lose consciousness of what I was doing. The more frenzied I became the more brightly the light of consciousness burnt in me, so that I could not help knowing everything I did. I knew what I was doing every second. I cannot say that I knew beforehand what I was going to do; but I knew what I was doing when I did it, and even I think a little before, as if to make repentance possible and to be able to tell myself that I could stop. I knew I was hitting below the ribs and that the dagger would enter. At the moment I did it I knew I was doing an awful thing such as I had never done before, which would have terrible consequences. But that consciousness passed like a flash of lightning and the deed immediately followed the consciousness. I realized the action with extraordinary clearness. I felt, and remember, the momentary resistance of her corset and of something else, and then the plunging of the dagger into something soft. She seized the dagger with her hands, and cut them, but could not hold it back.

'For a long time afterwards, in prison when the moral change had taken place in me, I thought of that moment, recalled what I could of it, and considered it. I remembered that for an instant, only an instant, before the action, I had a terrible consciousness that I was killing, had killed, a defenceless woman, my wife! I remember the horror of that consciousness and conclude from that, and even dimly remember, that having plunged the dagger in I pulled it out immediately, trying to remedy what had been done and to stop it. I stood for a second motionless waiting to see what would happen, and whether it could be remedied.

'She jumped to her feet and screamed: "Nurse! He has killed me."

'The nurse, who had heard the noise, was standing by the door. I continued to stand waiting, and not believing the truth. But the blood rushed from under her corset. Only then did I understand that it could not be remedied, and I then immediately decided that it was not even necessary, that I had done what I wanted and had to do. I waited till she fell down, and the nurse, crying "Good God!" ran to her, and only then did I throw away the dagger and leave the room.

'"I must not be excited; I must know what I am doing," I said to myself without looking at her and at the nurse. The nurse was screaming—calling for the maid. I went down the passage, sent the maid, and went into my study. "What am I to do now?" I asked myself, and immediately realized what it must be. On entering the study I went straight to the wall, took down a revolver and examined it—it was loaded—I put it on the table. Then I picked up the scabbard from behind the sofa and sat down there. I sat thus for a long time. I did not think of anything or call anything to mind. I heard the sounds of bustling outside. I heard someone drive up, then someone else. Then I heard and saw Egór bring into the room my wicker trunk he had fetched. As if anyone wanted that!

'"Have you heard what has happened?" I asked. "Tell the yard-porter to inform the police." He did not reply, and went away. I rose, locked the door, got out my cigarettes and matches and began to smoke. I had not finished the cigarette before sleep overpowered me. I must have slept for a couple of hours. I remember dreaming that she and I were friendly together, that we had quarrelled but were making up, there was something rather in the way, but we were friends. I was awakened by someone knocking at the door. "That is the police!" I thought, waking up. "I have committed murder, I think. But perhaps it's her, and nothing has happened." There was again a knock at the door. I did not answer, but was trying to solve the question whether it had happened or not. Yes, it had! I remembered the resistance of the corset and the plunging in of the dagger, and a cold shiver ran down my back. "Yes, it has. Yes, and now I must do away with myself too," I thought. But I thought this, knowing that I should *not* kill myself. Still I got up and took the revolver in my hand. But it is strange: I remember how I had many times been near suicide, how even that day on the railway it had seemed easy, easy just because I thought how it would stagger her—now I was not only unable to kill myself but even to think of it. "Why should I do it?" I asked myself, and there was no reply. There was more knocking at the door. "First I must find out who is knocking. There will still be time for this." I put down the revolver and covered it with a newspaper. I went to the door and unlatched it. It was my wife's sister, a kindly, stupid widow. "Vásya, what is this?" and her ever ready tears began to flow.

'"What do you want?" I asked rudely. I knew I ought not to

be rude to her and had no reason to be, but I could think of no other tone to adopt.

'"Vásya, she is dying! Iván Zakhárych says so." Iván Zakhárych was her doctor and adviser.

'"Is he here?" I asked, and all my animosity against her surged up again. "Well, what of it?"

'"Vásya, go to her. Oh, how terrible it is!" said she.

'"Shall I go to her?" I asked myself, and immediately decided that I must go to her. Probably it is always done, when a husband has killed his wife, as I had—he must certainly go to her. "If that is what is done, then I must go," I said to myself. "If necessary I shall always have time." I reflected, referring to the shooting of myself, and I went to her. "Now we shall have words, grimaces, but I will not yield to them," I thought. "Wait," I said to her sister, "it is silly without boots, let me at least put on slippers."

XXVIII

'Wonderful to say, when I left my study and went through the familiar rooms, the hope that nothing had happened again awoke in me; but the smell of that doctor's nastiness—iodoform and carbolic—took me aback. "No, it had happened." Going down the passage past the nursery I saw little Lisa. She looked at me with frightened eyes. It even seemed to me that all the five children were there and all looked at me. I approached the door, and the maid opened it from inside for me and went out. The first thing that caught my eye was her light-grey dress thrown on a chair and all stained black with blood. She was lying on one of the twin beds (on mine because it was easier to get at), with her knees raised. She lay in a very sloping position supported by pillows, with her dressing jacket unfastened. Something had been put on the wound. There was a heavy smell of iodoform in the room. What struck me first and most of all was her swollen and bruised face, blue on part of the nose and under the eyes. This was the result of the blow with my elbow when she had tried to hold me back. There was nothing beautiful about her, but something repulsive as it seemed to me. I stopped on the threshold. "Go up to her, do," said her sister. "Yes, no doubt she wants to confess," I thought. "Shall I forgive her? Yes, she is dying and may be forgiven," I thought, trying to be magnanimous. I went up close to her. She raised her eyes to me with difficulty, one of them was black, and with an effort said falteringly:

'"You've got your way, killed . . ." and through the look of suffering and even the nearness of death her face had the old expression of cold animal hatred that I knew so well. "I shan't . . . let you have . . . the children, all the same . . . She (her sister) will take . . ."

'Of what to me was the most important matter, her guilt, her faithlessness, she seemed to consider it not worthy of mention.

'"Yes, look and admire what you have done," she said looking towards the door, and she sobbed. In the doorway stood her sister with the children. "Yes, see what you have done."

'I looked at the children and at her bruised disfigured face, and for the first time I forgot myself, my rights, my pride, and for the first time saw a human being in her. And so insignificant did all that had offended me, all my jealousy, appear, and so important what I had done, that I wished to fall with my face to her hand, and say: "Forgive me," but dared not do so.

'She lay silent with her eyes closed, evidently too weak to say more. Then her disfigured face trembled and puckered. She pushed me feebly away.

'"Why did it all happen? Why?"

'"Forgive me," I said.

'"Forgive! That's all rubbish! . . . Only not to die! . . ." she cried, raising herself, and her glittering eyes were bent on me. "Yes, you have had your way! . . . I hate you! Ah! Ah!" she cried, evidently already in delirium and frightened at something. "Well, go ahead, kill! I'm not afraid! . . . Only kill everyone, everyone, and him. He has gone! Gone!"

'After that the delirium continued all the time. She did not recognize anyone. She died towards noon that same day. Before that they had taken me to the police-station and from there to prison. There, during the eleven months I remained awaiting trial, I examined myself and my past, and understood it. I began to understand it on the third day: on the third day they took me there . . .'

He was going on but, unable to repress his sobs, he stopped. When he recovered himself he continued:

'I only began to understand when I saw her in her coffin . . .'

He gave a sob, but immediately continued hurriedly:

'Only when I saw her dead face did I understand all that I had done. I realized that I, I, had killed her; that it was my doing that she, living, moving, warm, had now become motionless, waxen, and cold, and that this could never, anywhere, or by any means, be remedied. He who has not lived through it cannot understand. . . . Ugh! Ugh! Ugh! . . .' he cried several times and then was silent.

We sat in silence a long while. He kept sobbing and trembling as he sat in silence opposite me.

'Well, forgive me. . . .'* He turned away from me and lay down on the seat, covering himself up with his plaid. At the station where I had to get out (it was at eight o'clock in the morning) I went up to him to say good-bye. Whether he was asleep or only pretended to be, at any rate he did not move. I touched him with my hand. He uncovered his face, and I could see he had not been asleep.

'Good-bye,' I said, holding out my hand. He gave me his and smiled slightly, but so piteously that I felt ready to weep.

'Yes, forgive me,' he said, repeating the same words with which he had concluded his whole story.

AFTERWORD TO *THE KREUTZER SONATA*

At the suggestion of his secretary V. G. Chertkov, Tolstoy began this Afterword in October 1889, while he was still working on the story. This 'answer to the question, What does the author himself think about the subject of the story' (lxxxvi. 271; 1889) was completed in 1890 and first published in that year.

I have received, and continue to receive, a great deal of letters from people I don't know asking me to explain in clear and simple terms, what I think about the subject of the story I wrote entitled 'Kreutzer Sonata'. I will try to do this; that is in a few words, to express, as far as possible, the essence of what I wanted to say in this story, and of the conclusions which, in my opinion, can be made from it.

First of all, I wanted to say that in our society a firm conviction has been formed, general to all classes and supported by false science, that sexual intercourse is necessary for health, and that since marriage is not always a possibility, then sexual intercourse outside marriage, not obligating a man in any way besides a monetary payment, is a completely natural affair and therefore should be encouraged. This conviction has become so firm and generally accepted that parents, on the advice of their physicians, arrange debauchery for their own children; governments, whose single purpose consists in care for the moral well-being of their citizens, institutionalize debauchery, i.e. they regulate a whole class of women obligated to perish bodily and spiritually for the satisfaction of the passing demands of men, while bachelors with a completely clear conscience abandon themselves to debauchery.

And what I wanted to say here was that it is bad, because it cannot be that it is necessary for the sake of the health of some people to destroy the body and soul of other people, in the same way that it cannot be necessary for the sake of the health of some people to drink the blood of others.

The conclusion which, it seems to me, is natural to draw from this is that it is not necessary to yield to this error and deception. But in order not to yield to this, it is necessary in the first place not to believe in immoral teachings no matter how they are supported by sham science, and in the second place, to understand that to enter a sexual relationship in which people either free themselves from its possible consequences, children, or dump the whole weight of the consequences on the woman, or prevent the possibility of the birth of children is a transgression of the simplest demand of morality. It is baseness, and that is why bachelors not wishing to live basely should not do this.

In order for them to be able to abstain, they should lead a natural way of life: not drink, not overeat, not eat meat, not avoid labour (not gymnastics, but exhausting, real work, not play), not permit thoughts about the possibility of intercourse with other men's wives, in the same way that a man does not permit himself such a possibility between himself and his mother, his sisters, his relatives, and the wives of his friends.

Any man can find hundreds of proofs that abstinence is possible and less dangerous and harmful for health than incontinence. This is the first conclusion.

The second is that in our society as a consequence of seeing amorous relations not only as a necessary condition of health and enjoyment, but also as a poetic and lofty blessing in life, marital infidelity has become a very ordinary phenomenon in all classes of society (in the peasant class especially, due to conscription).

And I think that this is not good. It can be concluded from this that men ought not to behave in this way.

In order for men not to behave this way, it is necessary that carnal love be seen differently, that men and women be educated in their families and through social opinion, so that both before and after marriage they would not regard falling in love and the carnal love connected with it as a poetic and elevated state as they look on it now, but rather as a state of bestiality degrading for a human being, so that the violation of the promise of fidelity given in marriage would be castigated by public opinion at least in the same way that violations of financial obligations and business fraud are castigated by public opinion, rather than praised, as it is now in novels, verse, song, operas, and so forth. This is the second conclusion.

The third is that in our society, again as a consequence of the false significance given to carnal love, the birth of children has lost its significance and, instead of being the goal and justification for relations between spouses, has become an obstacle to the pleasant continuation of amorous relations. And this is why, both outside and within marriage, there has begun, on the advice of the votaries of marital science, the dissemination of the use of means which would deprive a woman of the possibility of childbirth. And something that previously did not exist and still does not among the patriarchal families of peasants has become customary and habitual: marital relations during pregnancy and nursing.

And I think that this is not good. It is not good to employ means to prevent the birth of children, in the first place because this frees people from the care and labour over children which serves as an expiation for carnal love, and secondly, because this is something quite close to an act most offensive to the human conscience—murder. And incontinence during the time of pregnancy and nursing is bad, because it undermines the physical, and, most importantly, the spiritual powers of a woman.

The conclusion which may be drawn from this is that people should not do this. But in order not to do this it is necessary to understand that abstinence, which constitutes a necessary condition of human dignity during the period of the unmarried state, is even more necessary in marriage itself. This is the third conclusion.

The fourth is that in our society in which children are considered to be either an obstacle to pleasure, an unfortunate accident, or an amusement (when limited to a certain predetermined number within a family), these children are educated without a sense of those tasks of human life which await them as rational and loving beings, but only in the light of the amusement which they may afford their parents. As a consequence of this, the children of people are educated like the children of animals, so that the chief care of parents consists not in preparing them to be persons involved in a life of worthy activity (in this the parents are supported by false science, so-called medicine), but in how to feed them better, increase their growth, to make them clean, white, satisfied, and pretty (if this is not done in the lower classes, it is only because need prevents it, but their view of the matter is one and the same). And in pampered children, as in overfed animals, there is an unnaturally early appearance of an insuperable sensuality, which is the occasion of the terrible sufferings of these children in adolescence. Clothes, reading, plays, music, dancing, sweets, the whole environment of their lives, from the pictures on candy boxes to novels and tales and poems, inflame even more this sensuality; as a result, the most terrible sexual vices and diseases, which often persist into maturity, are the norm for children of both sexes.

I think that this is bad. The conclusion which might be made from this is that we need to stop educating the children of people as though they were the children of animals, and to set other goals for the education of human children besides an attractive, well-tended body. This is the fourth conclusion.

The fifth is that in our society, where the falling in love of a young man and a woman has as its basis, essentially, a carnal love that is elevated into the highest poetic goal of people's aspirations (all the art and poetry of our society serve as evidence of this), young people consecrate the better part of their lives, if men, in the searching and hunting for, and possessing of, the finest objects of love in the form of an amorous relationship or marriage, and, if women and girls, in the enticement and alluring of men into an affair or marriage.

And because of this, people's best energy is wasted not only on unproductive but on harmful work. A great deal of the senseless opulence of our life is a result of this. This is also the cause of men's idleness and the shamelessness of women, who do not disdain exhibiting, in fashions consciously borrowed from lewd women, those parts of the body which stimulate men's sensuality. And I think that this is bad.

It is bad because the achievement of the goal of union with the object of one's love, in marriage or outside marriage, no matter how it is made into an object of poetry, is a goal unworthy of human beings in the same way that it is unworthy for human beings to set themselves as the highest good, as many people do, the goal of obtaining for themselves tasty and abundant food.

The conclusion to be drawn from this is that we must stop thinking that carnal love is something especially elevated and must understand that the goal worthy of man, whether it is service to humanity, to country, to science, to art (to say nothing of service to God), no matter what it is, as long as we consider it to be worthy of man, cannot be achieved by means of union with the object of love in marriage or outside it. On the contrary, falling in love and union with the object of love (no matter how we try to prove the contrary in verse and prose) will never facilitate the achievement of a worthy goal for man, but will always impede it. This is the fifth conclusion.

This is the essence of what I wanted to say and what I thought I had said in my story. And it had seemed to me, although one may argue about how to correct the evil indicated in the positions mentioned above, that it is impossible not to agree with them.

It had seemed to me that it is impossible not to agree with these positions, in the first place, because they are in complete agreement with the progress of humanity, which always advances from dissipation towards greater and greater chastity, and with the moral consciousness of society, with our conscience, which always condemns dissipation and praises chastity; and secondly, because these positions are the only inescapable conclusions to be drawn from the teachings of the Gospel, which we profess, or at least, albeit unconsciously, recognize as the foundation of our morality. But this turned out not to be the case.

It is true that no one directly disputes that we should not indulge in debauchery before marriage, that we should not use artificial means to prevent conception, that we should not use our own children as a source of amusement, and that we should not consider an amorous union as the highest good—in a word, no one disputes that chastity is better than dissipation. But people say: 'If celibacy is better than marriage, then it is obvious that people ought to do what is better. However, if people do this, the human race will come to an end, so the ideal of the human race cannot be its own destruction.'

But not to mention that the destruction of the human race is not a new concept for the people of our world, that for the religious it is a doctrine of faith, and for scientists it is the inescapable conclusion to be drawn from observations of the cooling of the sun, this objection veils a widely prevalent and long-standing misconception.

People say: 'If the human race attains the ideal of complete chastity, then it will annihilate itself; this is why the ideal cannot be true.' But those who say this, whether intentionally or unintentionally, are mixing two different things—the rule or injunction and the ideal.

Chastity is neither rule nor injunction, but an ideal, or rather—one of the conditions of this ideal. But the ideal is a true one only when its realization is possible only in an idea, in thought, when it is presented as attainable only in the infinite, and therefore, when the possibility of approaching it is infinite. If an ideal not only could be reached but we could imagine its realization, it would cease to be an ideal. Such was the ideal of Christ—the establishment of the Kingdom of God on earth, an ideal, foretold by the prophets, about how the time will come when all people will be taught by God, will turn their swords into ploughshares, and spears into pruning hooks, when the lion will lie down with the lamb, and all creatures will be united in love. The whole meaning of human life consists in movement towards this ideal. This is why the aspiration towards the Christian ideal in its entirety and towards chastity as one of the conditions of this ideal not only does not exclude the possibility of life, but, on the contrary, the absence of this Christian ideal would have annihilated the forward progress of humanity and therefore the possibility of life.

The opinion that the human race will come to an end if people with all their strength will aspire to chastity is similar to the assertion that has been made (indeed is still being made), that the human race will perish if people, rather than engaging in the struggle for existence, will with all their strength strive for a realization of love towards friends, towards enemies, towards every living thing. These opinions also result from a misunderstanding of the difference between two methods of moral guidance.

Just as there are two ways of indicating to the traveller the path to be travelled, so there are also two methods of moral guidance for the person seeking the truth. One method is to point out objects that the person will meet along the way; thus he orients himself according to these objects. Another method is simply to give a person a direction on the compass which he carries with him, by which he continuously reads an invariable direction and can always make note of any degree of variation from it.

The first kind of moral guidance is provided through a set of external precepts, or rules: a person is provided with a set of defined norms of behaviour, what he should and should not do.

'Observe the Sabbath, circumcise, don't steal, don't drink alcohol, don't kill a living being, tithe, don't commit adultery, perform ritual ablutions, and pray five times a day, be baptized, receive communion, and so forth.' Such are the decrees contained in various external religious teachings: Brahmin, Buddhist, Muslim, Jewish, and church teachings falsely called Christian.

Another means of providing guidance is to indicate to a person that perfection is a state never to be reached, but an aspiration which one recognizes in oneself: the ideal is indicated to the person, and one can always measure oneself by the degree to which one has moved away from it.

'Thou shalt love the Lord thy God with all thy heart, and with all thy soul, and with all thy strength, and with all thy mind, and thy neighbour as thyself. Be ye, therefore, perfect, even as your Father, who is in heaven, is perfect.' Such is the teaching of Christ.

The verification of the fulfilment of external religious teachings is seen in the coincidence of behaviour with the injunctions of these teachings and in the possibility of this coincidence.

The verification of the fulfilment of the teachings of Christ is consciousness of the degree of incongruousness one's behaviour has in relation to ideal perfection. (The degree of approximation is not perceptible; only the degree of variance from perfection is perceptible.)

The person who professes faith in external law is like a man standing in the light of a lamp suspended from a post. He stands in the light of this lamp, it shines on him, and there is nowhere further for him to go. The person professing the teachings of Christ is like someone carrying the light in front of him on a pole of unspecified length; the light is always in front of him and always spurs him to go beyond himself, newly revealing to him a new, illuminated space that attracts him.

The Pharisee thanks God that he fulfils everything required of him. The rich young man also fulfilled everything required of him from childhood and did not understand what he might lack. Such people cannot understand it any other way: in front of them there is nothing towards which they might continue to aspire. They have tithed, observed the Sabbath, honoured their parents, not committed adultery, nor theft, nor murder. What more is there? For the person professing Christian teaching, the achievement of every stage of perfection elicits a demand of entry to a higher stage, from which a still higher one is opened, and so on without end.

The person professing the law of Christ is always in the position of the publican. He always feels himself to be imperfect, he can't see the path behind him which he has passed: rather, he always sees in front of him the path along which he needs to go and which he has yet to travel.

This is what differentiates Christ's teaching from all other religious teachings. The distinction lies not in the difference of moral demands, but in the means by which people are guided. Christ did not make any kind of injunctions concerning how life should be lived; he never established any kind of institutions, not even marriage. But people who do not understand the special nature of the teaching of Christ, having become used to external teachings and desiring to feel themselves righteous, as the Pharisee felt himself righteous contrary to whole spirit of the teaching of Christ, have created an external teaching from the letter of the law, which is called the teaching of the Christian Church, and they have substituted this teaching for the genuine teaching of the ideal of Christ.

The Church teachings which call themselves Christian, instead of the teachings of the ideals of Christ and contrary to the spirit of that teaching, set external standards and rules for all the manifestations of life. This is done in relation to the authority of the state, to the judicial system, to the military, to the Church, to the ritual of worship; it is done also in relation to marriage, although Christ not only never established marriage, but, if you search for external standards, rather denied it ('leave your wife and follow me'). Church teachings, calling themselves Christian, establish marriage as a Christian institution; that is, they set external conditions under which carnal love can be enjoyed without sin by the Christian, and can be completely lawful.

But since in genuine Christian teaching there is no foundation for the institution of marriage, it is as if people of our world have left one shore and not yet reached the other; that is, they essentially don't believe in the Church's definition of marriage, sensing that this institution is not founded in Christian teaching. Moreover, they are not shown the ideal of Christ, the aspiration towards complete chastity which is hidden by the teaching of the Church, and they remain without any kind of guidance with respect to marriage. As a result, a phenomenon occurs which at first seems strange, that among the Jews, the Muslims, the Lamaists, and other groups which recognize religious teachings of a considerably lower level than the Christian, but have exact external injunctions concerning marriage, the principle of the family and the fidelity of the spouses are incomparably more strictly adhered to than among so-called Christians.

These religions have a fixed type of concubinage, a polygamy limited according to known boundaries. Among us there exist complete dissipation and concubinage, polygamy and polyandry, not subject to any kind of rules, hidden under the appearance of a fictitious monogamy.

There cannot be and there never was Christian marriage, as there never was and never can be a Christian ritual of worship

(Matt. 6: 5–12; John 4: 21), nor are there any Christian teachers and fathers (Matt. 28: 8–10). There is no Christian property, no Christian army, judicial system, or state. This has always been understood by genuine Christians from the first century on.

The ideal of the Christian is love toward God and one's neighbour. This constitutes renunciation of self and service for God and one's neighbour. Carnal love and marriage are forms of service to oneself, and that is why in every case these are a hindrance to the service of God and to people; this is why, from the Christian point of view, carnal love and marriage are a degradation and a sin.

Getting married cannot promote the service of God, even in the case of marriage for the purpose of continuing the human race. It would be infinitely simpler if these people, rather than getting married to produce children's lives, would support and save those millions of children who are perishing around us from a lack of material (to say nothing of spiritual) sustenance. A Christian might enter into marriage without consciousness of degradation or sin, only if that person could see and know that the lives of all existing children were provided for.

It is possible not to accept the teaching of Christ, that teaching which has permeated all our life and on which our whole morality is based, but if a person does accept this teaching, it is impossible not to recognize that it points toward the ideal of complete chastity.

In the Gospel, of course, it is stated clearly and without any possibility of misinterpretation, that in the first place, a married man should not divorce his wife in order to take another, but should live with the one originally married (Matt. 5: 31–2; 19: 8); secondly, that consequently, a man in general, whether married, or unmarried, who looks at a woman as an object of pleasure, is sinning (Matt. 5: 28–9), and thirdly, that it is better for the man who is unmarried, to remain unmarried entirely, that is, to be completely chaste (Matt. 19: 10–12).

For a great many people these thoughts appear to be strange and even contradictory. And they actually are contradictory, but not within themselves; these thoughts contradict our whole way of life. Thus, a doubt involuntarily occurs: Who is right? These thoughts, or the lives of millions of people including my own? This is the very feeling I experienced most intensely when I was in the process of coming to those convictions which I am expressing now: I never expected that the path of my thoughts would lead me to where they have led. I was horrified by my own conclusions, I did not want to believe them, but it was impossible not to believe them. And no matter how contradictory these conclusions are to the whole structure of our life, no matter how they contradict what I earlier thought and even expressed, I have been forced to recognize them.

'But these are all general considerations which perhaps are correct. They relate to the teaching of Christ and are obligatory for those who profess it. But life is life, and it is impossible, having shown in advance the unreachable ideal of Christ, to abandon without any kind of guidance people who are facing one of the most urgent problems, one so universal and responsible for the most immense calamities.

'At the beginning a passionate young man will be attracted to the ideal, but will be unable to sustain it, then will fall, and now recognizing no moral laws whatsoever, will fall into complete depravity.' So runs the usual argument. 'The ideal of Christ is unreachable, therefore it cannot serve us as a guide in life; it is possible to discuss it, to dream about it, but it cannot be applied to life, and this is why it is necessary to abandon it. We don't need an ideal, but a rule, a guide set according to our strengths, according to the average level of moral capacity in our society: the honourable marriage according to church definition, or even a not entirely honourable marriage, in which one of the partners, as is the case with us, the man, has already had intimate relations with many women, or if only a marriage with a possibility of a divorce, or if only civil, or (extending the same logic) if only in the Japanese style, just for a specified time—why not extend the notion of marriage all the way to the brothels?' People say that this is better than street debauchery. This is just where the trouble lies; in permitting oneself to lower the ideal to one's own weakness, it becomes impossible to find the limit at which one must stop.

But of course this reasoning is false from the very start; it is false, first of all, to claim that the ideal of infinite perfection cannot serve as a guide in life, and that taking this ideal as a guide, one must throw up one's hands, saying that 'I don't need it, since I also will never reach it, or lower the ideal to the level my weaknesses can tolerate.' To reason in this way is to be like the navigator who tells himself, 'Since I cannot reach a certain destination according to that line which my compass indicates, I will throw out the compass or stop looking at it; that is, I will reject the ideal or I will rivet the arrow of the compass to that place which will correspond in a given moment to the path of my vessel; that is, I will lower the ideal to my weakness.'

The ideal of perfection given by Christ is not a dream or a subject for rhetorical sermons, but is the most necessary and universally accessible guide for the moral life of people, like the compass is a necessary and easily understood tool for the guidance of navigators; it is only necessary to believe in one as it is in the other. No matter what the situation may be, the teaching given by Christ will always be sufficient for a person to receive the truest indication of what actions one should or should not perform. But one must believe this teaching completely, and in this teaching alone, and must stop believing in all the others, exactly in the same way that the navigator needs to believe in the compass, must stop looking at and being guided by what he sees on either side of his craft. One needs to know how to be guided by Christian teaching, as one needs to know how to be guided by a compass. In order to do this one must understand one's own position. One needs to learn how not to be afraid to define with exactitude how far one has moved away from the ideal of the direction given. No matter what level a person occupies, it is always possible for one to come closer to the ideal, and no position can be attained where one may say that the ideal has been reached and that a person cannot aspire to come even closer to it. Such is the aspiration of human beings towards a Christian ideal in general, and towards chastity in particular. If you can imagine the many various positions of people in regard to the sexual problem in which chastity is not observed, from an innocent childhood to marriage, in each stage between these two positions the teaching of Christ with the ideal it represents will always serve as a clear and definite guide for what a person ought and what he ought not to do at each of these stages.

What should the pure young man or woman do? They should keep themselves free of temptations, and in order to be in the position of rendering all their strength to the service of God and people, they should strive towards an ever greater chastity of thought and desires.

What should the young man and woman do, having fallen to temptations, become engulfed by thoughts of aimless love or love for a certain person, and as a result having lost a certain portion of their capacity to serve God and people? They should do the same thing, they should not tolerate a further fall, knowing that such tolerance does not liberate them from temptation, but only strengthens it, and they should still continue to aspire towards an ever increased chastity for the possibility of fuller service of God and people.

What are people to do when the struggle overpowers them and they fall? They should look at their own fall not as a lawful pleasure, as it is now seen, when it is justified by the ceremony of marriage. Neither should they see it as a fleeting pleasure which it is possible to repeat with others, nor as a misfortune, when the fall is accomplished with unequals and without a ceremony, but should look at this first fall as having contracted an indissoluble marriage.

Marriage, with the consequence that attends it, the birth of children, defines, for those entering into it, a new, more limited form of service to God and people. Until marriage takes place, a person can spontaneously, and in the most varied forms, be of service to God and people; entering into marriage limits the sphere of one's activity, obligating one to rear and educate the progeny that result from the marriage, who are future servants of God and people.

What are a man and a woman to do who are living in marriage and fulfilling that limited service of God and people, through the raising and education of children? What follows from their situation?

The same thing. They should aspire together towards a liberation from temptation, to purify themselves, and to cease from sinning, to replace relations which impede the universal and private service of God and people, to substitute for carnal love the pure relations of sister and brother.

This is why it is not true that we cannot be guided by the ideal of Christ because it is too lofty, too perfect and unreachable. We are not able to be guided by it only because we lie to ourselves and deceive ourselves.

Of course, if we say that it is necessary to have rules more practicable than the ideal of Christ, or that otherwise, having fallen short of the ideal of Christ, we will fall into depravity, we are not saying that the ideal of Christ is too high for us, but only that we do not believe in it and do not want to define our behaviour according to this ideal.

Saying that having fallen once we fall into depravity, we of course are only saying by this that we have already decided in advance that falling with one who is not an equal is not a sin, but is an amusement, an entertainment, for which it is unnecessary to make amends through that which we call marriage. If we had understood that the fall is a sin which should and can be redeemed only by the indissolubility of marriage and with the full activity which results from the bringing up of children born from that marriage, then the fall could in no way be the reason for sinking into debauchery.

Of course this is just as if a farmer did not consider the seeds he planted in one place which failed to grow as seeds at all, but having sown in a second and third place, considered only the seeds which produced a yield to be real seeds. Obviously, this is a man who had spoiled a great deal of land and seed without learning how to sow. Only when chastity is set as the ideal, and one recognizes that each fall, no matter with whom it took place, is a unique marriage that remains indissoluble for life, will it become clear that the guidance given by Christ is not only sufficient, but is the only one possible.

People say, 'Human beings are weak, it is necessary to give them a task in accordance with their strength.' This is like saying: 'My hands are weak, and I can't draw a straight line, that is, the shortest between two points. This is why I have to go easy on myself. So, rather than drawing a straight line as I would like to do, I will take as my model a crooked or broken one.' The weaker my hand, the more necessary is a perfect model.

It is impossible, once one is acquainted with the Christian teaching of the ideal, to act as though we do not know it and to replace it with external precepts. The Christian teaching of the ideal has been revealed to humanity because it especially can guide us in the present age. Humanity has already outgrown the period of external religious injunctions, and no one believes in them any longer. The Christian teaching of the ideal is the only teaching that can guide humanity. It is impossible to replace the ideal of Christ with external rules; rather it is necessary firmly to hold this ideal before oneself in all its purity, and above all to believe in it.

It is possible to say to the person navigating not far from shore, 'Steer by that rise, that promontory, that tower', and so forth. But the time is here when the navigators have moved away from shore, and only the unattainable stars and the compass showing them the direction can and ought to serve as a guide. Both have been given to us.

THE COSSACKS

A TALE OF 1852

CHAPTER I

ALL is quiet in Moscow. The squeak of wheels is but seldom heard on the winter street. There are no lights left in the windows and the street lamps have been extinguished. Only the sound of bells, borne over the city from the church towers, suggests the approach of morning. The streets are deserted. But seldom does the night-cabman's sledge knead up the snow and sand in the street as he makes his way to another corner only to fall asleep while waiting for a fare. An old woman passes by on her way to church, where a few wax candles burn with a red light reflected on the gilt mountings of the icons. Workmen are already getting up after the long winter night and going to their work—but for the gentlefolk it is still evening.

From a window in Chevalier's restaurant a light—illegal at that hour—is still to be seen through a chink in the shutter. At the entrance a carriage, a sledge, and a cabman's sledge stand close together with their backs to the kerbstone. A three-horse sledge from the post-station* is there also. A yard-porter muffled up and pinched with cold is sheltering behind the corner of the house.

'And what's the good of all this jawing?' thinks the footman who sits in the hall weary and haggard. 'This always happens when I'm on duty.' From the adjoining room are heard the voices of three young men, sitting there around a table on which are wine and the remains of supper. One, a rather plain, thin, neat little man, sits looking with tired kindly eyes at his friend, who is about to start on a journey. Another, a tall man, is lying on a sofa beside a table on which are empty bottles, and plays with his watch-key. The third, wearing a short, fur-lined coat, is pacing up and down the room stopping now and then to crack an almond between his strong, rather thick, but well-tended fingers. He keeps smiling at something and his face and eyes are all aglow. He speaks warmly and gesticulates, but evidently does not find the words he wants and those that occur to him seem to him inadequate to express what has risen to his heart.

'Now I can speak out fully,' said the traveller. 'I don't want to defend myself, but I should like you at least to understand me as I understand myself, and not look at the matter superficially. You say I have treated her badly,' he continued, addressing the man with the kindly eyes who was watching him.

'Yes, you are to blame,' said the latter, and his look seemed to express still more kindliness and weariness.

'I know why you say that,' rejoined the one who was leaving. 'To be loved is in your opinion as great a happiness as to love, and if a man obtains it, it is enough for his whole life.'

'Yes, quite enough, my dear fellow, more than enough!' confirmed the plain little man, opening and shutting his eyes.

'But why shouldn't the man love too?' said the traveller thoughtfully, looking at his friend with something like pity. 'Why shouldn't one love? Because the love doesn't come. No, to be beloved is a misfortune. It is a misfortune to feel guilty because you do not give something you cannot give. O my God!' he added, with a gesture of his arm. 'If it all happened reasonably, and not all topsy-turvy—not in our way but in a way of its own! Why, it's as if I had stolen that love! You think so too, don't deny it. You must think so. But will you believe it, of all the horrid and stupid things I have found time to do in my life—and there are many—this is one I do not and cannot repent of. Neither at the beginning nor afterwards did I lie to myself or to her. It seemed to me that I had at last fallen in love, but then I saw that it was an involuntary falsehood, and that that was not the way to love, and I could not go on, but she did. Am I to blame that I couldn't? What was I to do?'

'Well, it's ended now!' said his friend, lighting a cigar to master his sleepiness. 'The fact is that you have not yet loved and do not know what love is.'

The man in the fur-lined coat was going to speak again, and put his hands to his head, but could not express what he wanted to say.

'Never loved! Yes, quite true, I never have! But after all, I have within me a desire to love, and nothing could be stronger than that desire! But then, again, does such love exist? There always remains something incomplete. Ah well! What's the use of talking? I've made an awful mess of life! But anyhow it's all over now; you are quite right. And I feel that I am beginning a new life.'

'Which you will again make a mess of,' said the man who lay on the sofa playing with his watch-key. But the traveller did not listen to him.

'I am sad and yet glad to go,' he continued. 'Why I am sad I don't know.'

And the traveller went on talking about himself, without noticing that this did not interest the others as much as it did him. A man is never such an egotist as at moments of spiritual ecstasy. At such times it seems to him that there is nothing on earth more splendid and interesting than himself.

'Dmítri Andréich! The coachman won't wait any longer!' said a young serf, entering the room in a sheepskin coat, with a scarf tied round his head. 'The horses have been standing since twelve, and it's now four o'clock!'

Dmítri Andréich looked at his serf, Vanyúsha. The scarf round Vanyúsha's head, his felt boots and sleepy face, seemed to be calling his master to a new life of labour, hardship, and activity.

'True enough! Good-bye!' said he, feeling for the unfastened hook and eye on his coat.

In spite of advice to mollify the coachman by another tip, he put on his cap and stood in the middle of the room. The friends kissed once, then again, and after a pause, a third time. The man in the fur-lined coat approached the table and emptied a champagne glass, then took the plain little man's hand and blushed.

'Ah well, I will speak out all the same. I must and will be frank with you because I am fond of you. Of course you love her—I always thought so—don't you?'

'Yes,' answered his friend, smiling still more gently.

'And perhaps . . .'

'Please sir, I have orders to put out the candles,' said the sleepy attendant, who had been listening to the last part of the conversation and wondering why gentlefolk always talk about one and the same thing. 'To whom shall I make out the bill? To you, sir?' he added, knowing whom to address and turning to the tall man.

'To me,' replied the tall man. 'How much?'

'Twenty-six rubles.'

The tall man considered for a moment, but said nothing and put the bill in his pocket.

The other two continued their talk.

'Good-bye, you are a wonderful fellow!' said the short plain man with the mild eyes.

Tears filled the eyes of both. They stepped onto the porch.

'Oh, by the way,' said the traveller, turning with a blush to the tall man, 'will you settle Chevalier's bill and write and let me know?'

'All right, all right!' said the tall man, pulling on his gloves. 'How I envy you!' he added quite unexpectedly when they were out on the porch.

The traveller got into his sledge, wrapped his coat about him, and said: 'Well then, come along!' He even moved a little to make room in the sledge for the man who said he envied him—his voice trembled.

'Good-bye, Mítya! I hope that with God's help you . . .' said the tall one. But his wish was that the other would go away quickly, and so he could not finish the sentence.

They were silent a moment. Then someone again said, 'Good-bye,' and a voice cried, 'Ready,' and the coachman touched up the horses.

'Hey, Elisár!' one of the friends called out, and the other coachman and the sledge-drivers began moving, clicking their tongues and pulling at the reins. Then the stiffened carriage-wheels rolled squeaking over the frozen snow.

'A fine fellow, that Olénin!' said one of the friends. 'But what an idea to go to the Caucasus—as a cadet, too! I wouldn't do it for anything. Are you dining at the club to-morrow?'

'Yes.'

They separated.

The traveller felt warm, his fur coat seemed too hot. He sat on the bottom of the sledge and unfastened his coat, and the three shaggy post-horses dragged themselves out of one dark street into another, past houses he had never before seen. It seemed to Olénin that only travellers starting on a long journey went through those streets. All was dark and silent and dull around him, but his soul was full of memories, love, regrets, and a pleasant tearful feeling.

CHAPTER II

'I'm fond of them, very fond! First-rate fellows! Fine!' he kept repeating, and felt ready to cry. But why he wanted to cry, who were the first-rate fellows he was so fond of—was more than he quite knew. Now and then he looked round at some house and wondered why it was so curiously built; sometimes he began wondering why the post-boy and Vanyúsha, who were so different from himself, sat so near, and together with him were being jerked about and swayed by the tugs the side-horses gave at the frozen traces, and again he repeated: 'First rate . . . very fond!' and once he even said: 'And how it seizes one . . . excellent!' and wondered what made him say it. 'Dear me, am I drunk?' he asked himself. He had had a couple of bottles of wine, but it was not the wine alone that was having this effect on Olénin. He remembered all the words of friendship heartily, bashfully, spontaneously (as he believed) addressed to him on his departure. He remembered the clasp of hands, glances, the moments of silence, and the sound of a voice saying, '*Good-bye*, *Mítya*!' when he was already in the sledge. He remembered his own deliberate frankness. And all this had a touching significance for him. Not only friends and relatives, not only people who had been indifferent to him, but even those who did not like him, seemed to have agreed to become fonder of him, or to forgive him, before his departure, as people do before confession or death. 'Perhaps I shall not return from the Caucasus,' he thought. And he felt that he loved his friends and some one besides. He was sorry for himself. But it was not love for his friends that so stirred and uplifted his heart that he could not repress the meaningless words that seemed to rise of themselves to his lips; nor was it love for a woman (he had never yet been in love) that had brought on this mood. Love for himself, love full of hope—warm young love for all that was good in his own soul (and at that moment it seemed to him that there was nothing but good in it)—compelled him to weep and to mutter incoherent words.

Olénin was a youth who had never completed his university course, never served anywhere (having only a nominal post in some government office or other), who had squandered half his fortune and had reached the age of twenty-four without having done anything or even chosen a career. He was what in Moscow society is termed *un jeune homme*.[1]

At the age of eighteen he was free—as only rich young Russians in the 'forties who had lost their parents at an early age could be. Neither physical nor moral fetters of any kind existed for him; he could do as he liked, lacking nothing and bound by nothing. Neither relatives, nor fatherland, nor religion, nor wants, existed for him. He believed in nothing and admitted nothing. But although he believed in nothing he was not a morose or blasé young man, nor self-opinionated, but on the contrary continually let himself be carried away. He had come to the conclusion that there is no such thing as love, yet his heart always overflowed in the presence of any young and attractive woman. He had long been aware that honours and position were nonsense, yet involuntarily he felt pleased when at a ball Prince Sergius came up and spoke to him affably. But he yielded to his impulses only in so far as they did not limit his freedom. As soon as he had yielded to any influence and became conscious of its leading on to labour and struggle, he instinctively hastened to free himself from the feeling or activity into which he was being drawn and to regain his freedom. In this way he experimented with society-life, the civil service, farming, music—to which at one time he intended to devote his life—and even with the love of women in which he did not believe. He meditated on the use to which he should devote that power of youth which is granted to man only once in a lifetime: that force which gives a man the power of making himself, or even—as it seemed to him—of making the universe, into anything he wishes: should it be to art, to science, to love of woman, or to practical activities? It is true that some people

[1] A young man.

are devoid of this impulse, and on entering life at once place their necks under the first yoke that offers itself and honestly labour under it for the rest of their lives. But Olénin was too strongly conscious of the presence of that all-powerful God of Youth—of that capacity to be entirely transformed into an aspiration or idea—the capacity to wish and to do—to throw oneself headlong into a bottomless abyss without knowing why or wherefore. He bore this consciousness within himself, was proud of it and, without knowing it, was happy in that consciousness. Up to that time he had loved only himself, and could not help loving himself, for he expected nothing but good of himself and had not yet had time to be disillusioned. On leaving Moscow he was in that happy state of mind in which a young man, conscious of past mistakes, suddenly says to himself, 'That was not the real thing.' All that had gone before was accidental and unimportant. Till then he had not really tried to live, but now with his departure from Moscow a new life was beginning—a life in which there would be no mistakes, no remorse, and certainly nothing but happiness.

It is always the case on a long journey that till the first two or three stages have been passed imagination continues to dwell on the place left behind, but with the first morning on the road it leaps to the end of the journey and there begins building castles in the air. So it happened to Olénin.

After leaving the town behind, he gazed at the snowy fields and felt glad to be alone in their midst. Wrapping himself in his fur coat, he lay at the bottom of the sledge, became tranquil, and fell into a doze. The parting with his friends had touched him deeply, and memories of that last winter spent in Moscow and images of the past, mingled with vague thoughts and regrets, rose unbidden in his imagination.

He remembered the friend who had seem him off and his relations with the girl they had talked about. The girl was rich. 'How could he love her knowing that she loved me?' thought he, and evil suspicions crossed his mind. 'There is much dishonesty in men when one comes to reflect.' Then he was confronted by the question: 'But really, how is it I have never been in love? Every one tells me that I never have. Can it be that I am a moral monstrosity?' And he began to recall all his infatuations. He recalled his entry into society, and a friend's sister with whom he spent several evenings at a table with a lamp on it which lit up her slender fingers busy with needlework, and the lower part of her pretty delicate face. He recalled their conversations that dragged on like the game in which one passes on a stick which one keeps alight as long as possible, and the general awkwardness and restraint and his continual feeling of rebellion at all that conventionality. Some voice had always whispered: 'That's not it, that's not it,' and so it had proved. Then he remembered a ball and the mazurka he danced with the beautiful D——. 'How much in love I was that night and how happy! And how hurt and vexed I was next morning when I woke and felt myself still free! Why does not love come and bind me hand and foot?' thought he. 'No, there is no such thing as love! That neighbour who used to tell me, as she told Dubróvin and the Marshal, that she loved the stars, was not *it* either.' And now his farming and work in the country recurred to his mind, and in those recollections also there was nothing to dwell on with pleasure. 'Will they talk long of my departure?' came into his head; but who 'they' were he did not quite know. Next came a thought that made him wince and mutter incoherently. It was the recollection of M. Cappele the tailor, and the six hundred and seventy-eight rubles he still owed him, and he recalled the words in which he had begged him to wait another year, and the look of perplexity and resignation which had appeared on the tailor's face. 'Oh, my God, my God!' he repeated, wincing and trying to drive away the intolerable thought. 'All the same and in spite of everything she loved me,' thought he of the girl they had talked about at the farewell supper. 'Yes, had I married her I should not now be owing anything, and as it is I am in debt to Vasílyev.' Then he remembered the last night he had played with Vasílyev at the club (just after leaving her), and he recalled his humiliating requests for another game and the other's cold refusal. 'A year's economizing and they will all be paid, and the devil take them! But despite this assurance he again began calculating his outstanding debts, their dates, and when he could hope to pay them off. 'And I owe something to Morell as well as to Chevalier,' thought he, recalling the night when he had run up so large a debt. It was at a carousal at the gypsies arranged by some fellows from Petersburg: Sáshka B——, an aide-de-camp to the Tsar, Prince D——, and that pompous old ——. 'How is it those gentlemen are so self-satisfied?' thought he, 'and by what right do they form a clique to which they think others must be highly flattered to be admitted? Can it be because they are on the Emperor's staff? Why, it's awful what fools and scoundrels they consider other people to be! But I showed them that I at any rate, on the contrary, do not at all want their intimacy. All the same, I fancy Andréy, the steward, would be amazed to know that I am on familiar terms with a man like Sáshka B——, a colonel and an aide-de-camp to the Tsar! Yes, and no one drank more than I did that evening, and I taught the gypsies a new song and everyone listened to it. Though I have done many foolish things, all the same I am a very good fellow,' thought he.

Morning found him at the third post-stage. He drank tea, and himself helped Vanyúsha to move his bundles and trunks and sat down among them, sensible, erect, and precise, knowing where all his belongings were, how much money he had and where it was, where he had put his passport and the post-horse requisition and toll-gate papers, and it all seemed to him so well arranged that he grew quite cheerful and the long journey before him seemed an extended pleasure-trip.

All that morning and noon he was deep in calculations of how many versts he had travelled, how many remained to the next stage, how many to the next town, to the place where he would dine, to the place where he would drink tea, and to Stavrópol, and what fraction of the whole journey was already accomplished. He also calculated how much money he had with him, how much would be left over, how much would pay off all his debts, and what proportion of his income he would spend each month. Towards evening, after tea, he calculated that to Stavrópol there still remained seven-elevenths of the whole journey, that his debts would require seven months' economy and one-eighth of his whole fortune; and then, set at ease, he wrapped himself up, lay down in the sledge, and again dozed off. His imagination was now turned to the future: to the Caucasus. All his dreams of the future were mingled with pictures of Amalat-Beks,* Circassian* women, mountains, precipices, terrible torrents, and perils. All these things were vague and dim, but the love of fame and the danger of death furnished the interest of that future. Now, with unprecedented courage and a strength that amazed everyone, he slew and subdued an innumerable host of hillsmen; now he was himself a hillsman and with them was maintaining their independence against the Russians. As soon as he pictured anything definite, familiar Moscow figures always appeared on the scene. Sáshka B—— fights with the Russians or the hillsmen against him. Even the tailor Cappele in some strange way takes part in the conqueror's triumph. Amid all this he remembered his former humiliations, weaknesses, and mistakes, and the recollection was not disagreeable. It was clear that there among the mountains, waterfalls, fair Circassians, and dangers, such mistakes could not recur. Having once made full confession to himself there was an end of it all. One other vision, the sweetest of them all, mingled with the young man's every thought of the future—the vision of a woman. And there, among the mountains, she appeared to his imagination as a Circassian slave, a fine figure with a long plait of hair and deep submissive eyes. He pictured a lonely hut in the mountains, and on the threshold *she* stands awaiting him when, tired and covered with dust, blood, and fame, he returns to her. He is conscious of her kisses, her shoulders, her sweet voice, and her submissiveness. She is enchanting, but uneducated, wild, and rough. In the long winter evenings he begins her education. She is clever and gifted and quickly acquires all the knowledge essential. Why not? She can quite easily learn foreign languages, read the French masterpieces and understand them: *Notre Dame de Paris*,* for instance, is sure to please her. She can also speak French. In a drawing-room she can show more innate dignity than a lady of the highest society. She can sing, simply, powerfully, and passionately. 'Oh, what nonsense!' said he to himself. But here they reached a post-station and he had to change into another sledge and give some tips. But his fancy again began searching for the 'nonsense' he had relinquished, and again fair Circassians, glory, and his return to Russia with an appointment as aide-de-camp and a lovely wife rose before his imagination. 'But there's no such thing as love,' said he to himself. 'Fame is all rubbish. But the six hundred and seventy-eight rubles? And the conquered land that will bring me more wealth than I need for a lifetime? It will not be right though to keep all that wealth for myself. I shall have to distribute it. But to whom? Well, six hundred and seventy-eight rubles to Cappele and then we'll see.' Quite vague visions now cloud his mind, and only Vanyúsha's voice and the interrupted motion of the sledge break his healthy youthful slumber. Scarcely conscious, he changes into another sledge at the next stage and continues his journey.

Next morning everything goes on just the same: the same kind of post-stations and tea-drinking, the same moving horses' cruppers, the same short talks with Vanyúsha, the same vague dreams and drowsiness, and the same tired, healthy, youthful sleep at night.

CHAPTER III

The further Olénin travelled from Central Russia the further he left his memories behind, and the nearer he drew to the Caucasus the lighter his heart became. 'I'll stay away for good and never return to show myself in society,' was a thought that sometimes occurred to him. 'These people whom I see here are *not* people. None of them know me and none of them can ever enter the Moscow society I was in or find out about my past. And no one in that society will ever know what I am doing, living among these people.' And quite a new feeling of freedom from his whole past came over him among the rough beings he met on the road whom he did not consider to be *people* in the sense that his Moscow acquaintances were. The rougher the people and the fewer the signs of civilization the freer he felt. Stavrópol, through which he had to pass, irked him. The signboards, some of them even in French, ladies in carriages, cabs in the market-place, and a gentleman wearing a fur cloak and tall hat who was walking along the boulevard and staring at the passers-by, quite upset him. 'Perhaps these people know some of my acquaintances,' he thought; and the club, his tailor, cards, society . . . came back to his mind. But after Stavrópol everything was satisfactory—wild and also beautiful and warlike, and Olénin felt happier and happier. All the Cossacks, post-boys, and post-station masters seemed to him simple folk with whom he could jest and converse simply, without having to consider to what class they belonged. They all belonged to the human race which, without his thinking about it, all appeared dear to Olénin, and they all treated him in a friendly way.

Already in the province of the Don Cossacks* his sledge had been exchanged for a cart, and beyond Stavrópol it became so warm that Olénin travelled without wearing his fur coat. It was already spring—an unexpected joyous spring for Olénin. At night he was no longer allowed to leave the Cossack villages, and they said it was dangerous to travel in the evening. Vanyúsha began to be uneasy, and they carried a loaded gun in the cart. Olénin became still happier. At one of the post-stations the post-master told of a terrible murder that had been committed recently on the high road. They began to meet armed men. 'So this is where it begins!' thought Olénin, and kept expecting to see the snowy mountains of which mention was so often made. Once, towards evening, the Nogáy* driver pointed with his whip to the mountains shrouded in clouds. Olénin looked eagerly, but it was dull and the mountains were almost hidden by the clouds. Olénin made out something grey and white and fleecy, but try as he would he could find nothing beautiful in the mountains of which he had so often read and heard. The mountains and the clouds appeared to him quite alike, and he thought the special beauty of the snow peaks, of which he had so often been told, was as much an invention as Bach's music and the love of women, in which he did not believe. So he gave up looking forward to seeing the mountains. But early next morning, being awakened in his cart by the freshness of the air, he glanced carelessly to the right. The morning was perfectly clear. Suddenly he saw, about twenty paces away as it seemed to him at first glance, pure white gigantic masses with delicate contours, the distinct fantastic outlines of their summits showing sharply against the far-off sky. When he had realized the distance between himself and them and the sky and the whole immensity of the mountains, and felt the infinitude of all that beauty, he became afraid that it was but a phantasm or a dream. He gave himself a shake to rouse himself, but the mountains were still the same.

'What's that! What is it?' he said to the driver.

'Why, the mountains,' answered the Nogáy driver with indifference.

'And I too have been looking at them for a long while,' said Vanyúsha. 'Aren't they fine? They won't believe it at home.'

The quick progress of the three-horsed cart along the smooth road caused the mountains to appear to be running along the horizon, while their rosy crests glittered in the light of the rising sun. At first Olénin was only astonished at the sight, then gladdened by it; but later on, gazing more and more intently at that snow-peaked chain that seemed to rise not from among other black mountains, but straight out of the plain, and to glide away into the distance, he began by slow degrees to be penetrated by their beauty and at length to *feel* the mountains. From that moment all he saw, all he thought, and all he felt, acquired for him a new character, sternly majestic like the mountains! All his Moscow reminiscences, shame, and repentance, and his trivial dreams about the Caucasus, vanished and did not return. 'Now it has begun,' a solemn voice seemed to say to him. The road and the Térek,* just becoming visible in the distance, and the Cossack villages and the people, all no longer appeared to him as a joke. He looked at himself or Vanyúsha, and again thought of the mountains. . . . Two Cossacks ride by, their guns in their cases swinging rhythmically behind their backs, the white and bay legs of their horses mingling confusedly . . . and the mountains! Beyond the Térek rises the smoke from a Tatar* village . . . and the mountains! The sun has risen and glitters on the Térek, now visible beyond the reeds . . . and the mountains! From the village comes a Tatar wagon, and women, beautiful young women, pass by . . . and the mountains! '*Abréks* canter about the plain, and here am I driving along and do not fear them! I have a gun, and strength, and youth . . . and the mountains!'

CHAPTER IV

That whole part of the Térek line (about fifty miles) along which lie the villages of the Grebénsk Cossacks* is uniform in character both as to country and inhabitants. The Térek, which separates the Cossacks from the mountaineers, still flows turbid and rapid though already broad and smooth, always depositing greyish sand on its low reedy right bank and washing away the steep, though not high, left bank, with its roots of century-old oaks, its rotting plane trees, and young brushwood. On the right bank lie the villages of pro-Russian, though still somewhat restless, Tatars. Along the left bank, back half a mile from the river and standing five or six miles apart from one another, are Cossack villages. In olden times most of these villages were situated on the banks of the river; but the Térek, shifting northward from the mountains year by year, washed away those banks, and now there remain only the ruins of the old villages and of the gardens of pear and plum trees and poplars, all overgrown with blackberry bushes and wild vines. No one lives there now, and one only sees the tracks of the deer, the wolves, the hares, and the pheasants, who have learned to love these places. From village to village runs a road cut through the forest as a cannon-shot might fly. Along the roads are cordons of Cossacks and watch-towers with sentinels in them. Only a narrow strip about seven hundred yards wide of fertile wooded soil belongs to the Cossacks. To the north of it begin the sand-drifts of the Nogáy or Mozdók steppes, which stretch far to the north and run, Heaven knows where, into the Trukhmén, Astrakhán, and Kirghíz-Kaisátsk steppes. To the south, beyond the Térek, are the Great Chechnyá river, the Kochkálov range, the Black Mountains, yet another range, and at last the snowy mountains, which can just be seen but have never yet been scaled. In this fertile wooded strip, rich in vegetation, has dwelt as far back as memory runs the fine warlike and prosperous Russian tribe belonging to the sect of Old Believers,* and called the Grebénsk Cossacks.

Long long ago their Old Believer ancestors fled from Russia and settled beyond the Térek among the Chechéns* on the Grében, the first range of wooded mountains of Chechnyá. Living among the Chechéns the Cossacks intermarried with them and adopted the manners and customs of the hill tribes, though they still retained the Russian language in all its purity, as well as their Old Faith. A tradition, still fresh among them, declares that Tsar Iván the Terrible* came to the Térek, sent for their Elders, and gave them the land on this side of the river, exhorting them to remain friendly to Russia and promising not to enforce his rule upon them nor oblige them to change their faith. Even now the Cossack families claim relationship with the Chechéns, and the love of freedom, of leisure, of plunder and of war, still form their chief characteristics. Only the harmful side of Russian influence shows itself—by interference at elections, by confiscation of church bells, and by the troops who are stationed in the country or march through it. A Cossack is inclined to hate less the *dzhigít* hillsman who maybe has killed his brother, than the soldier who is stationed with him to defend his village, but who has defiled his hut with tobacco-smoke. He respects his enemy the hillsman and despises the soldier, who is in his eyes an alien and an oppressor. In reality, from a Cossack's point of view a Russian peasant is a foreign, savage, despicable creature, of whom he sees a sample in the hawkers who come to the country and in the Ukraínian immigrants whom the Cossack contemptuously calls 'wool-beaters'. For him, to be smartly dressed means to be dressed like a Circassian. The best weapons are obtained from the hillsmen and the best horses are bought, or stolen, from them. A dashing young Cossack likes to show off his knowledge of Tatar, and when carousing talks Tatar even to his fellow Cossack. In spite of all these things this small Christian clan stranded in a tiny corner of the earth, surrounded by half-savage Muhammadan tribes and by soldiers, considers itself highly advanced, acknowledges none but Cossacks as human beings, and despises everybody else. The Cossack spends most of his time in the cordon, in action, or in hunting and fishing. He hardly ever works at home. When he stays in the village it is an exception to the general rule and then he is holiday-making. All Cossacks make their own wine, and drunkenness is not so much a general tendency as a rite, the non-fulfilment of which would be considered apostasy. The Cossack looks upon a woman as an instrument for his welfare; only the unmarried girls are allowed to amuse themselves. A married woman has to work for her husband from youth to very old age: his demands on her are the Oriental ones of submission and labour. In consequence of this outlook women are strongly developed both physically and mentally, and though they are—as everywhere in the East—nominally in subjection, they possess far greater influence and importance in family life than Western women. Their exclusion from public life and inurement to heavy male labour give the women all the more power and importance in the household. A Cossack, who before strangers considers it improper to speak affectionately or needlessly to his wife, when alone with her is involuntarily conscious of her superiority. His house and all his property, in fact the entire homestead, has been acquired and is kept together solely by her labour and care. Though firmly convinced that labour is degrading to a Cossack and is only proper for a Nogáy labourer or a woman, he is vaguely aware of the fact that all he makes use of and calls his own is the result of that toil, and that it is in the power of the woman (his mother or his wife), whom he considers his slave, to deprive him of all he possesses. Besides, the continuous performance of man's heavy work and the responsibilities entrusted to her have endowed the Grebénsk women with a peculiarly independent masculine character and have remarkably developed their physical powers, common sense, resolution, and stability. The women are in most cases stronger, more intelligent, more developed, and handsomer than the men. A striking feature of a Grebénsk woman's beauty is the combination of the purest Circassian type of face with the broad and powerful build of Northern women. Cossack women wear the Circassian dress—a Tatar smock, *beshmét*, and *chuvyáki*—but they tie their kerchiefs round their heads in the Russian fashion. Smartness, cleanliness, and elegance in dress and in the arrangement of their huts are with them a custom and a necessity. In their relations with men the women, and especially the unmarried girls, enjoy perfect freedom.

Novomlínsk village was considered the very heart of Grebénsk Cossackdom. In it more than elsewhere the customs of the old Grebénsk population have been preserved, and its women have from time immemorial been renowned all over the Caucasus for their beauty. A Cossack's livelihood is derived from vineyards, fruit-gardens, water melon and pumpkin plantations, from fishing, hunting, maize and millet growing, and from war plunder. Novomlínsk village lies about two and a half miles away from the Térek, from which it is separated by a dense forest. On one side of the road which runs through the village is the river; on the other, green vineyards and orchards, beyond which are seen the driftsands of the Nogáy steppe. The village is surrounded by earth-banks and prickly bramble hedges, and is entered by tall gates hung between posts and covered with little reed-thatched roofs. Beside them on a wooden gun-carriage stands an unwieldy cannon captured by the Cossacks at some time or other, and which has not been fired for a hundred years. A uniformed Cossack sentinel with dagger and gun sometimes stands, and sometimes does not stand, on guard beside the gates, and sometimes presents arms to a passing officer and sometimes does not. Below the roof of the gateway is written in black letters on a white board: 'Houses 266: male inhabitants 897: female 1012.' The Cossacks' houses are all raised on pillars two and a half feet from the ground. They are carefully thatched with reeds and have large carved gables. If not new they are at least all straight and clean, with high porches of different shapes; and they are not built close together but have ample space around them, and are all picturesquely placed along broad streets and lanes. In front of the large bright windows of many of the houses, beyond the kitchen gardens, dark green poplars and acacias with their delicate pale verdure and scented white blossoms overtop the houses, and beside them grow flaunting yellow sunflowers, creepers, and grape vines. In the broad open square are three shops where drapery, sunflower and pumpkin seeds, locust beans and gingerbreads are sold; and surrounded by a tall fence, loftier and larger than the other houses, stands the regimental commander's dwelling with its casement windows, behind a row of tall poplars. Few people are to be seen in the streets of the village on week-days, especially in summer. The young men are on duty in the cordons or on military expeditions; the old ones are fishing or helping the women in the orchards and gardens. Only the very old, the sick, and the children remain at home.

CHAPTER V

It was one of those wonderful evenings that occur only in the Caucasus. The sun had sunk behind the mountains but it was still light. The evening glow had spread over a third of the sky, and against its brilliancy the dull white immensity of the mountains was sharply defined. The air was rarefied, motionless, and full of sound. The shadow of the mountains reached for several miles over the steppe. The steppe, the opposite side of the river, and the roads were all deserted. If very occasionally mounted men appeared, the Cossacks in the cordon and the Chechéns in their *aúl* watched them with surprised curiosity and tried to guess who those questionable men could be. At nightfall people from fear of one another flock to their dwellings, and only birds and beasts fearless of man prowl in those deserted spaces. Talking merrily, the women who have been tying up the vines hurry away from the gardens before sunset. The vineyards, like all the surrounding district, are deserted, but the villages become very animated at that time of the evening. From all sides, walking, riding, or driving in their creaking carts, people move towards the village. Girls with their smocks tucked up and twigs in their hands run chatting merrily to the village gates to meet the cattle that are crowding together in a cloud of dust and mosquitoes which they bring with them from the steppe. The well-fed cows and buffaloes disperse at a run all over the streets and Cossack women in coloured *beshméts* go to and fro among them. You can hear their merry laughter and shrieks mingling with the lowing of the cattle. There an armed and mounted Cossack, on leave from the cordon, rides up to a hut and, leaning towards the window, knocks. In answer to the knock the handsome head of a young woman appears at the window and you can hear caressing, laughing voices. There a tattered Nogáy labourer, with prominent cheekbones, brings a load of reeds from the steppes, turns his creaking cart into the Cossack captain's broad and clean courtyard, and lifts the yoke off the oxen that stand tossing their heads while he and his master shout to one another in Tatar. Past a puddle that reaches nearly across the street, a barefooted Cossack woman with a bundle of firewood on her back makes her laborious way by clinging to the fences, holding her smock high and exposing her white legs. A Cossack returning from shooting calls out in jest: 'Lift it higher, shameless thing!' and points his gun at her. The woman lets down her smock and drops the wood. An old Cossack, returning home from fishing with his trousers tucked up and his hairy grey chest uncovered, has a net across his shoulder containing silvery fish that are still struggling; and to take a short cut climbs over his neighbour's broken fence and gives a tug to his coat which has caught on the fence. There a woman is dragging a dry branch along and from round the corner comes the sound of an axe. Cossack children, spinning their tops wherever there is a smooth place in the street, are shrieking; women are climbing over fences to avoid going round. From every chimney rises the odorous *kizyák* smoke. From every homestead comes the sound of increased bustle, precursor to the stillness of night.

Granny Ulítka, the wife of the Cossack cornet who is also a teacher in the regimental school, goes out to the gates of her yard like the other women, and waits for the cattle which her daughter Maryánka is driving along the street. Before she has had time fully to open the wattle gate in the fence, an enormous buffalo cow surrounded by mosquitoes rushes up bellowing and squeezes in. Several well-fed cows slowly follow her, their large eyes gazing with recognition at their mistress as they swish their sides with their tails. The beautiful and shapely Maryánka enters at the gate and throwing away her switch quickly slams the gate to and rushes with all the speed of her nimble feet to separate and drive the cattle into their sheds. 'Take off your *chuvyáki*, you devil's wench!' shouts her mother, 'you've worn them into holes!' Maryánka is not at all offended at being called a 'devil's wench', but accepting it as a term of endearment cheerfully goes on with her task. Her face is covered with a kerchief tied round her head. She is wearing a pink smock and a green *beshmét*. She disappears inside the shed in the yard, following the big fat cattle; and from the shed comes her voice as she speaks gently and persuasively to the buffalo: 'Won't she stand still? What a creature! Come now, come old dear!' Soon the girl and the old woman pass from the shed to the dairy carrying two large pots of milk, the day's yield. From the dairy chimney rises a thin cloud of *kizyák* smoke: the milk is being used to make *kaymák*. The girl makes up the fire while her mother goes to the gate. Twilight has fallen on the village. The air is full of the smell of vegetables, cattle, and scented *kizyák* smoke. From the gates and along the streets Cossack women come running, carrying lighted rags. From the yards one hears the snorting and quiet chewing of the cattle eased of their milk, while in the street only the voices of women and children sound as they call to one another. It is rare on a week-day to hear the drunken voice of a man.

One of the Cossack wives, a tall, masculine old woman, approaches Granny Ulítka from the homestead opposite and asks her for a light. In her hand she holds a rag.

'Have you finished, Granny?'

'The girl is lighting the fire. Is it fire you want?' says Granny Ulítka, proud of being able to oblige her neighbour.

Both women enter the hut, and coarse hands unused to dealing with small articles tremblingly lift the lid of a match-box, which is a rarity in the Caucasus. The masculine-looking new-comer sits down on the doorstep with the evident intention of having a chat.

'And is your man at the school, Mother?' she asked.

'He's always teaching the youngsters, Mother. But he writes that he'll come home for the holidays,' said the cornet's wife.

'Yes, he's a clever man, one sees; it all comes useful.'

'Of course it does.'

'And my Lukáshka is at the cordon; they won't let him come home,' said the visitor, though the cornet's wife had known all this long ago. She wanted to talk about her Lukáshka whom she had lately fitted out for service in the Cossack regiment, and whom she wished to marry to the cornet's daughter, Maryánka.

'So he's at the cordon?'

'He is, Mother. He's not been home since the last holidays. The other day I had Fómushkin take him some shirts. He says he's all right, and that his superiors are satisfied. He says they are looking out for *abréks* again. Lukáshka is quite happy, he says.'

'Ah well, thank God,' said the cornet's wife. '"Snatcher" is certainly the only word for him.' Lukáshka was surnamed 'the Snatcher' because of his bravery in snatching a boy from a watery grave, and the cornet's wife alluded to this, wishing in her turn to say something agreeable to Lukáshka's mother.

'I thank God, Mother, that he's a good son! He's a fine fellow, everyone praises him,' says Lukáshka's mother. 'All I wish is to get him married; then I could die in peace.'

'Well, aren't there plenty of young women in the village?' answered the cornet's wife slyly as she carefully replaced the lid of the match-box with her horny hands.

'Plenty, Mother, plenty,' remarked Lukáshka's mother, shaking her head. 'There's your girl now, your Maryánka—that's the sort of girl! You'd have to search through the whole place to find such another!'

The cornet's wife knows what Lukáshka's mother is after, but though she believes him to be a good Cossack she hangs back: first because she is a cornet's wife and rich, while Lukáshka is the son of a simple Cossack and fatherless, secondly because she does not want to part with her daughter yet, but chiefly because propriety demands it.

'Well when Maryánka grows up she'll be marriageable too,' she answers soberly and modestly.

'I'll send the matchmakers to you—I'll send them! Only let me get the vineyard done and then we'll come and make our bows to you,' says Lukáshka's mother. 'And we'll make our bows to Elias Vasílich too.'

'Elias, indeed!' says the cornet's wife proudly. 'It's to me you must speak! All in its own good time.'

Lukáshka's mother sees by the stern face of the cornet's wife that it is not the time to say anything more just now, so she lights her rag with the match and says, rising; 'Don't refuse us, think of my words. I'll go, it is time to light the fire.'

As she crosses the road swinging the burning rag, she meets Maryánka, who bows.

'Ah, she's a regular queen, a splendid worker, that girl!' she thinks, looking at the beautiful maiden. 'What need for her to grow any more? It's time she was married and to a good home; married to Lukáshka!'

But Granny Ulítka had her own cares and she remained sitting on the threshold thinking hard about something, till the girl called her.

CHAPTER VI

The male population of the village spend their time on military expeditions and in the cordons, or 'at their posts', as the Cossacks say. Towards evening, that same Lukáshka the Snatcher, about whom the old women had been talking, was standing on a watch-tower of the Nízhni-Protótsk post situated on the very banks of the Térek. Leaning on the railing of the tower and screwing up his eyes, he looked now far into the distance beyond the Térek, now down at his fellow Cossacks, and occasionally he addressed the latter. The sun was already approaching the snowy range that gleamed white above the fleecy clouds. The clouds undulating at the base of the mountains grew darker and darker. The clearness of evening was noticeable in the air. A sense of freshness came from the woods, though round the post it was still hot. The voices of the talking Cossacks vibrated more sonorously than before. The moving mass of the Térek's rapid brown waters contrasted more vividly with its motionless banks. The waters were beginning to subside and here and there the wet sands gleamed drab on the banks and in the shallows. The other side of the river, just opposite the cordon, was deserted; only an immense waste of low-growing reeds stretched far away to the very foot of the mountains. On the low bank, a little to one side, could be seen the flat-roofed clay houses and the funnel-shaped chimneys of a Chechén village. The sharp eyes of the Cossack who stood on the watch-tower followed, through the evening smoke of the pro-Russian village, the tiny moving figures of the Chechén women visible in the distance in their red and blue garments.

Although the Cossacks expected *abréks* to cross over and attack them from the Tatar side at any moment, especially as it was May when the woods by the Térek are so dense that it is difficult to pass through them on foot and the river is shallow enough in places for a horseman to ford it, and despite the fact that a couple of days before a Cossack had arrived with a circular from the commander of the regiment announcing that spies had reported the intention of a party of some eight men to cross the Térek, and ordering special vigilance—no special vigilance was being observed in the cordon. The Cossacks, unarmed and with their horses unsaddled just as if they were at home, spent their time some in fishing, some in drinking, and some in hunting. Only the horse of the man on duty was saddled, and with its feet hobbled was moving about by the brambles near the wood, and only the sentinel had his *cherkéska* on and carried a gun and sword. The corporal, a tall thin Cossack with an exceptionally long back and small hands and feet, was sitting on the earth-bank of a hut with his *beshmét* unbuttoned. On his face was the lazy, bored expression of a superior, and having shut his eyes he dropped his head upon the palm first of one hand and then of the other. An elderly Cossack with a broad greyish-black beard was lying in his shirt, girdled with a black strap, close to the river and gazing lazily at the waves of the Térek as they monotonously foamed and swirled. Others, also overcome by the heat and half naked, were rinsing clothes in the Térek, plaiting a fishing line, or humming tunes as they lay on the hot sand of the river bank. One Cossack, with a thin face much burnt by the sun, lay near the hut evidently dead drunk, by a wall which though it had been in shadow some two hours previously was now exposed to the sun's fierce slanting rays.

Lukáshka, who stood on the watch-tower, was a tall handsome lad about twenty years old and very like his mother. His face and whole build, in spite of the angularity of youth, indicated great strength, both physical and moral. Though he had only lately joined the Cossacks at the front, it was evident from the expression of his face and the calm assurance of his attitude that he had already acquired the somewhat proud and warlike bearing peculiar to Cossacks and to men generally who continually carry arms, and that he felt he was a Cossack and fully knew his own value. His ample *cherkéska* was torn in some places, his cap was on the back of his head Chechén fashion, and his leggings had slipped below his knees. His clothing was not rich, but he wore it with that peculiar Cossack foppishness which consists in imitating the Chechén *dzhigít*. Everything on a real *dzhigít* is ample, ragged, and neglected, only his weapons are costly. But these ragged clothes and these weapons are belted and worn with a certain air and matched in a certain manner, neither of which can be acquired by everybody and which at once strike the eye of a Cossack or a hillsman. Lukáshka had this resemblance to a *dzhigít*. With his hands folded under his sword, and his eyes nearly closed, he kept looking at the distant Tatar village. Taken separately his features were not beautiful, but anyone who saw his stately carriage and his dark-browed intelligent face would involuntarily say 'What a fine fellow!'

'Look at the women, what a lot of them are walking about in the *aúl*,' said he in a sharp voice, languidly showing his brilliant white teeth and not addressing anyone in particular.

Nazárka who was lying below immediately lifted his head and remarked:

'They must be going for water.'

'Supposing one scared them with a gun?' said Lukáshka, laughing. 'Wouldn't they be frightened?'

'It wouldn't reach.'

'What! Mine would carry beyond. Just wait a bit, and when their feast comes round I'll go and visit Giréy Khan and drink *buzá* there,' said Lukáshka, angrily swishing away the mosquitoes which attached themselves to him.

A rustling in the thicket drew the Cossack's attention. A pied mongrel half-setter, searching for a scent and violently wagging its scantily furred tail, came running to the cordon. Lukáshka recognized the dog as one belonging to his neighbour, Uncle Eróshka, a hunter, and saw, following it through the thicket, the approaching figure of the hunter himself.

Uncle Eróshka was a gigantic Cossack with a broad, snow-white beard and such broad shoulders and chest that in the wood, where there was no one to compare him with, he did not look particularly tall, so well proportioned were his powerful limbs. He wore a tattered coat and, over the bands with which his legs were swathed, sandals made of undressed deer's hide tied on with strings; while on his head he had a rough little white cap. He carried over one shoulder a screen to hide behind when shooting pheasants, and a bag containing a hen for luring hawks, and a small falcon; over the other shoulder, attached by a strap, was a wild cat he had killed; and stuck in his belt behind were some little bags containing bullets, gunpowder, and bread, a horse's tail to swish away the mosquitoes, a large dagger in a torn scabbard smeared with old bloodstains, and two dead pheasants. Having glanced at the cordon he stopped.

'Hi, Lyam!' he called to the dog in such a ringing bass that it awoke an echo far away in the wood; and throwing over his shoulder his big gun, of the kind the Cossacks call a 'flint', he raised his cap.

'Had a good day, good people, eh?' he said, addressing the Cossacks in the same strong and cheerful voice, quite without effort, but as loudly as if he were shouting to someone on the other bank of the river.

'Yes, yes, Uncle!' answered from all sides the voices of the young Cossacks.

'What have you seen? Tell us!' shouted Uncle Eróshka, wiping the sweat from his broad red face with the sleeve of his coat.

'Ah, there's a vulture living in the plane tree here, Uncle. As soon as night comes he begins hovering round,' said Nazárka, winking and jerking his shoulder and leg.

'Come, come!' said the old man incredulously.

'Really, Uncle! You must keep watch,' replied Nazárka with a laugh.

The other Cossacks began laughing.

The wag had not seen any vulture at all, but it had long been the custom of the young Cossacks in the cordon to tease and mislead Uncle Eróshka every time he came to them.

'Eh, you fool, always lying!' exclaimed Lukáshka from the tower to Nazárka.

Nazárka was immediately silenced.

'It must be watched. I'll watch,' answered the old man to the great delight of all the Cossacks. 'But have you seen any boars?'

'Watching for boars, are you?' said the corporal, bending forward and scratching his back with both hands, very pleased at the chance of some distraction. 'It's *abréks* one has to hunt here and not boars! You've not heard anything, Uncle, have you?' he added, needlessly screwing up his eyes and showing his close-set white teeth.

'*Abréks*,' said the old man. 'No, I haven't. I say, have you any *chikhír*? Let me have a drink, there's a good man. I'm really quite done up. When the time comes I'll bring you some fresh meat, I really will. Give me a drink!' he added.

'Well, and are you going to watch?' inquired the corporal, as though he had not heard what the other said.

'I did mean to watch tonight,' replied Uncle Eróshka. 'Maybe, with God's help, I shall kill something for the holiday. Then you shall have a share, you shall indeed!'

'Uncle! Hallo, Uncle!' called out Lukáshka sharply from above, attracting everybody's attention. All the Cossacks looked up at him. 'Just go to the upper channel, there's a fine herd of boars there. I'm not making it up, really! The other day one of our Cossacks shot one there. I'm telling you the truth,' added he, readjusting the musket at his back and in a tone that showed he was not joking.

'Ah! Lukáshka the Snatcher is here!' said the old man, looking up. 'Where has he been shooting?'

'Haven't you seen? I suppose you're too young!' said Lukáshka. 'Close by the ditch,' he went on seriously with a shake of the head. 'We were just going along the ditch when all at once we heard something crackling, but my gun was in its case. Elias fired suddenly. But I'll show you the place, it's not far. You just wait a bit. I know every one of their footpaths. Daddy Mósev,' said he, turning resolutely and almost commandingly to the corporal, 'it's time to relieve guard!' and holding aloft his gun he began to descend from the watch-tower without waiting for the order.

'Come down!' said the corporal, after Lukáshka had started, and glanced round. 'Is it your turn, Gúrka? Then go. True enough your Lukáshka has become very skilful,' he went on, addressing the old man. 'He keeps going about just like you, he doesn't stay at home. The other day he killed a boar.'

CHAPTER VII

The sun had already set and the shades of night were rapidly spreading from the edge of the wood. The Cossacks finished their task round the cordon and gathered in the hut for supper. Only the old man still stayed under the plane tree watching for the vulture and pulling the string tied to the falcon's leg, but though a vulture was really perching on the plane tree it declined to swoop down on the lure. Lukáshka, singing one song after another, was leisurely placing nets among the very thickest brambles to trap pheasants. In spite of his tall stature and big hands every kind of work, both rough and delicate, prospered under Lukáshka's fingers.

'Hallo, Luke!' came Nazárka's shrill, sharp voice calling him from the thicket close by. 'The Cossacks have gone in to supper.'

Nazárka, with a live pheasant under his arm, forced his way through the brambles and emerged on the footpath.

'Oh!' said Lukáshka, breaking off in his song, 'where did you get that cock pheasant? I suppose it was in my trap?'

'Nazárka was of the same age as Lukáshka and had also only been at the front since the previous spring.

He was plain, thin, and puny, with a shrill voice that rang in one's ears. They were neighbours and comrades. Lukáshka was sitting on the grass cross-legged like a Tatar, adjusting his nets.

'I don't know whose it was—yours, I expect.'

'Was it beyond the pit by the plane tree? Then it is mine! I set the nets last night.'

'Lukáshka rose and examined the captured pheasant. After stroking the dark burnished head of the bird, which rolled its eyes and stretched out its neck in terror, Lukáshka took the pheasant in his hands.

'We'll have it in a *pilaf* tonight. You go and kill and pluck it.'

'And shall we eat it ourselves or give it to the corporal?'

'He has plenty!'

'I don't like killing them,' said Nazárka.

'Give it here!'

Lukáshka drew a little knife from under his dagger and gave it a swift jerk. The bird fluttered, but before it could spread its wings the bleeding head bent and quivered.

'That's how one should do it!' said Lukáshka, throwing down the pheasant. 'It will make a rich *pilaf*.'

Nazárka shuddered as he looked at the bird.

'I say, Lukáshka, that fiend will be sending us to the ambush again tonight,' he said, taking up the bird. (He was alluding to the corporal.) 'He has sent Fómushkin to get wine, and it ought to be his turn. He always puts it on us.'

Lukáshka went whistling along the cordon.

'Take the string with you,' he shouted.

Nazárka obeyed.

'I'll give him a bit of my mind today, I really will,' continued Nazárka. 'Let's say we won't go; we're tired out and there's an end of it! No, really, you tell him, he'll listen to you. It's too bad!'

'Get along with you! What a thing to make a fuss about!' said Lukáshka, evidently thinking of something else. 'What nonsense! If he made us turn out of the village at night now, that would be annoying: there one can have some fun, but here what is there? It's all one whether we're in the cordon or in ambush. What a fellow you are!'

'And are you going to the village?'

'I'll go for the holidays.'

'Gúrka says your Dunáyka is carrying on with Fómushkin,' said Nazárka suddenly.

'Well, let her go to the devil,' said Lukáshka, showing his regular white teeth, though he did not laugh. 'As if I couldn't find another!'

'Gúrka says he went to her house. Her husband was out and there was Fómushkin sitting and eating pie. Gúrka stopped awhile and then went away, and passing by the window he heard her say, "He's gone, the fiend. . . . Why don't you eat your pie, my dear? You needn't go home for the night," she says. And Gúrka under the window says to himself, "That's fine!"'

'You're making it up.'

'No, quite true, by Heaven!'

'Well, if she's found another let her go to the devil,' said Lukáshka, after a pause. 'There's no lack of girls and I was sick of her anyway.'

'Well, see what a devil you are!' said Nazárka. 'You should make up to the cornet's girl, Maryánka, Why doesn't she go out with any one?'

Lukáshka frowned. 'What of Maryánka? They're all alike,' said he.

'Well, you just try.'

'What do you think? Are girls so scarce in the village?'

And Lukáshka recommenced whistling, and went along the cordon pulling leaves and branches from the bushes as he went. Suddenly, catching sight of a smooth sapling, he drew the knife from the handle of his dagger and cut it down. 'What a ramrod it will make,' he said, swinging the sapling till it whistled through the air.

The Cossacks were sitting round a low Tatar table on the earthen floor of the clay-plastered outer room of the hut, when the question of whose turn it was to lie in ambush was raised. 'Who is to go tonight?' shouted one of the Cossacks through the open door to the corporal in the next room.

'Who is to go?' the corporal shouted back. 'Uncle Burlák has been and Fómushkin too,' said he, not quite confidently. 'You two had better go, you and Nazárka,' he went on, addressing Lukáshka. 'And Ergushóv must go too; surely he has slept it off?'

'You don't sleep it off yourself so why should he?' said Nazárka in a subdued voice.

The Cossacks laughed.

Ergushóv was the Cossack who had been lying drunk and asleep near the hut. He had only that moment staggered into the room rubbing his eyes.

Lukáshka had already risen and was getting his gun ready.

'Be quick and go! Finish your supper and go!' said the corporal; and without waiting for an expression of consent he shut the door, evidently not expecting the Cossack to obey. 'Of course,' thought he, 'if I hadn't been ordered to I wouldn't send anyone, but an officer might turn up at any moment. As it is, they say eight *abréks* have crossed over.'

'Well, I suppose I must go,' remarked Ergushóv, 'it's the regulation. Can't be helped! The times are such. I say, we must go.'

Meanwhile Lukáshka, holding a big piece of pheasant to his mouth with both hands and glancing now at Nazárka now at Ergushóv, seemed quite indifferent to what passed and only laughed at them both. Before the Cossacks were ready to go into ambush, Uncle Eróshka, who had been vainly waiting under the plane tree till night fell, entered the dark outer room.

'Well, lads,' his loud bass resounded through the low-roofed room drowning all the other voices, 'I'm going with you. You'll watch for Chechéns and I for boars!'

CHAPTER VIII

It was quite dark when Uncle Eróshka and the three Cossacks, in their cloaks and shouldering their guns, left the cordon and went towards the place on the Térek where they were to lie in ambush. Nazárka did not want to go at all, but Lukáshka shouted at him and they soon started. After they had gone a few steps in silence the Cossacks turned aside from the ditch and went along a path almost hidden by reeds till they reached the river. On its bank lay a thick black log cast up by the water. The reeds around it had been recently beaten down.

'Shall we lie here?' asked Nazárka.

'Why not?' answered Lukáshka. 'Sit down here and I'll be back in a minute. I'll only show Daddy where to go.'

'This is the best place; here we can see and not be seen,' said Ergushóv, 'so it's here we'll lie. It's a first-rate place!'

Nazárka and Ergushóv spread out their cloaks and settled down behind the log, while Lukáshka went on with Uncle Eróshka.

'It's not far from here, Daddy,' said Lukáshka, stepping softly in front of the old man; 'I'll show you where they've been—I'm the only one that knows, Daddy.'

'Show me! You're a fine fellow, a regular Snatcher!' replied the old man, also whispering.

Having gone a few steps Lukáshka stopped, stooped down over a puddle, and whistled. 'That's where they come to drink, d'you see?' He spoke in a scarcely audible voice, pointing to fresh hoof-prints.

'Christ bless you,' answered the old man. 'The boar will be in the hollow beyond the ditch,' he added. 'I'll watch, and you can go.'

Lukáshka pulled his cloak up higher and walked back alone, throwing swift glances now to the left at the wall of reeds, now to the Térek rushing by below the bank. 'I daresay he's watching or creeping along somewhere,' thought he of a possible Chechén hillsman. Suddenly a loud rustling and a splash in the water made him start and seize his musket. From under the bank a boar leapt up—his dark outline showing for a moment against the glassy surface of the water and then disappearing among the reeds. Lukáshka pulled out his gun and aimed, but before he could fire the boar had disappeared in the thicket. Lukáshka spat with vexation and went on. On approaching the ambuscade he halted again and whistled softly. His whistle was answered and he stepped up to his comrades.

Nazárka, all curled up, was already asleep. Ergushóv sat with his legs crossed and moved slightly to make room for Lukáshka.

'How jolly it is to sit here! It's really a good place,' said he. 'Did you take him there?'

'Showed him where,' answered Lukáshka, spreading out his *búrka*. 'But what a big boar I roused just now close to the water! I expect it was the very one! You must have heard the crash?'

'I did hear a beast crashing through. I knew at once it was a beast. I thought to myself: "Lukáshka has roused a beast,"' Ergushóv said, wrapping himself up in his cloak. 'Now I'll go to sleep,' he added. 'Wake me when the cocks crow. We must have discipline. I'll lie down and have a nap, and then you will have a nap and I'll watch—that's the way.'

'Luckily I don't want to sleep,' answered Lukáshka.

The night was dark, warm, and still. Only on one side of the sky the stars were shining, the other and greater part was overcast by one huge cloud stretching from the mountain-tops. The black cloud, blending in the absence of any wind with the mountains, moved slowly onwards, its curved edges sharply defined against the deep starry sky. Only in front of him could the Cossack discern the Térek and the distance beyond. Behind and on both sides he was surrounded by a wall of reeds. Occasionally the reeds would sway and rustle against one another apparently without cause. Seen from down below, against the clear part of the sky, their waving tufts looked like the feathery branches of trees. Close in front at his very feet was the bank, and at its base the rushing torrent. A little farther on was the moving mass of glassy brown water which eddied rhythmically along the bank and round the shallows. Farther still, the water, the banks, and the cloud all merged together into an impenetrable gloom. Along the surface of the water floated black shadows, in which the experienced eyes of the Cossack detected trees carried down by the current. Only very rarely heat-lightning, mirrored in the water as in a black glass, disclosed the sloping bank opposite. The rhythmic sounds of night—the rustling of the reeds, the snoring of the Cossacks, the hum of mosquitoes, and the rushing water, were every now and then broken by a shot fired in the distance, or by the gurgling of water when a piece of bank slipped down, or the splash of a big fish, or the crashing of an animal breaking through the thick undergrowth in the wood. Once an owl flew past along the Térek, flapping one wing against the other rhythmically at every second beat. Just above the Cossack's head it turned towards the wood and then, striking its wings no longer after every other flap but at every flap, it flew to an old plane tree where it rustled about for a long time before settling down among the branches. At every one of these unexpected sounds the watching Cossack listened intently, straining his hearing, and screwing up his eyes while he deliberately felt for his musket.

The greater part of the night was past. The black cloud that had moved westward revealed the clear starry sky from under its torn edge, and the golden upturned crescent of the moon shone above the mountains with a reddish light. The cold began to be penetrating. Nazárka awoke, spoke a little, and fell asleep again. Lukáshka feeling bored got up, drew the knife from his dagger-handle and began to fashion his stick into a ramrod. His head was full of the Chechéns who lived over there in the mountains, and of how their brave lads were coming over in this direction and were not afraid of the Cossacks, and could be crossing the river at some other spot. He thrust himself out of his hiding-place and looked along the river but could see nothing. And as he continued looking out at intervals upon the river and at the opposite bank, now dimly distinguishable from the water in the faint moonlight, he no longer thought about the Chechéns but only of when it would be time to wake his comrades, and of going home to the village. In the village he imagined Dunáyka, his 'little soul', as the Cossacks call a man's mistress, and thought of her with vexation. Silvery mists, a sign of coming morning, glittered white above the water, and not far from him young eagles were whistling and flapping their wings. At last the crowing of a cock reached him from the distant village, followed by the long-sustained note of another, which was again answered by yet other voices.

'Time to wake them,' thought Lukáshka, who had finished his ramrod and felt his eyes growing heavy. Turning to his comrades he managed to make out which pair of legs belonged to whom, when it suddenly seemed to him that he heard something splash on the other side of the Térek. He turned again towards the horizon beyond the hills, where day was breaking under the upturned crescent, glanced at the outline of the opposite bank, at the Térek, and at the now distinctly visible driftwood upon it. For one instant it seemed to him that he was moving and that the Térek with the drifting wood remained stationary. Again he peered out. One large black log with a branch particularly attracted his attention. The tree was floating in a strange way right down the middle of the stream, neither rocking nor whirling. It even appeared not to be floating altogether with the current, but to be crossing it in the direction of the shallows. Lukáshka stretching out his neck watched it intently. The tree floated to the shallows, stopped, and shifted in a peculiar manner. Lukáshka thought he saw an arm stretched out from beneath the tree. 'Supposing I killed an *abrék* all by myself!' he thought, and seized his gun with a swift, unhurried movement, putting up his gun-rest, placing the gun upon it, and holding it noiselessly in position. Cocking the trigger, with bated breath he took aim, still peering out intently. 'I won't wake them,' he thought. But his heart began beating so fast that he remained motionless, listening. Suddenly the trunk gave a plunge and again began to float across the stream towards our bank. 'Only not to miss . . .' thought he, and now by the faint light of the moon he caught a glimpse of a Tatar's head in front of the floating wood. He aimed straight at the head which appeared to be quite near—just at the end of his rifle's barrel. He glanced across. 'Sure enough it is an *abrék*!' he thought joyfully, and suddenly rising to his knees he again took aim. Having found the sight, barely visible at the end of the long gun, be said: 'To the Father and to the Son', in the Cossack way learnt in his childhood, and pulled the trigger. A flash of lightning lit up for an instant the reeds and the water, and the sharp, abrupt report of the shot was carried across the river, changing into a prolonged roll somewhere in the far distance. The piece of driftwood now floated not across, but with the current, rocking and whirling.

'Stop, I say!' exclaimed Ergushóv, seizing his musket and raising himself behind the log near which he was lying.

'Shut up, you devil!' whispered Lukáshka, grinding his teeth. '*Abréks!*'

'Whom have you shot?' asked Nazárka. 'Who was it, Lukáshka?'

Lukáshka did not answer. He was reloading his gun and watching the floating wood. A little way off it stopped on a sand-bank, and from behind it something large that rocked in the water came into view.

'What did you shoot? Why don't you speak?' insisted the Cossacks.

'*Abréks*, I tell you!' said Lukáshka.

'Cut the boasting! Did the gun go off?'

'I've killed an *abrék*, that's what I fired at,' muttered Lukáshka in a voice choked by emotion, as he jumped to his feet. 'A man was swimming' he said, pointing to the sand-bank. 'I killed him. Just look there.'

'Cut the bragging!' said Ergushóv again, rubbing his eyes.

'Cut what? Look there,' said Lukáshka, seizing him by the shoulders and pulling him with such force that Ergushóv groaned.

He looked in the direction in which Lukáshka pointed, and discerning a body immediately changed his tone.

'O Lord! But I tell you, more will come! I tell you for sure,' said he softly, and began examining his musket. 'That was a scout swimming across: either the others are here already or are not far off on the other side—I tell you for sure!'

Lukáshka was unfastening his belt and taking off his *cherkéska*.

'What are you up to, you idiot?' exclaimed Ergushóv. 'Only show yourself and you're lost all for nothing, I tell you for sure! If you've killed him he won't escape. Let me have a little powder for my musket-pan—do you have some? Nazárka, you go back to the cordon and look alive; but don't go along the bank or you'll be killed—I tell you for sure.'

'Catch me going alone! Go yourself!' said Nazárka angrily.

Having taken off his coat, Lukáshka went down to the bank.

'Don't go in, I tell you!' said Ergushóv, putting some powder on the pan. 'Look, he's not moving. I can see. It's nearly morning; wait till they come from the cordon. You go, Nazárka. You're afraid! Don't be afraid, I tell you.'

'Luke, I say, Lukáshka! Tell us how you did it!' said Nazárka.

Lukáshka changed his mind about going into the water just then. 'Go quick to the cordon and I will watch. Tell the Cossacks to send out the patrol. If the *abréks* are on this side they must be caught,' he said.

'I tell you they'll get away,' said Ergushóv, rising. 'For sure they must be caught!'

Ergushóv and Nazárka rose and, crossing themselves, started off for the cordon—not along the river bank but breaking their way through the brambles to reach a path in the wood.

'Now mind, Lukáshka—they may cut you down here, so you'd best keep a sharp look-out, I tell you!'

'Go along; I know,' muttered Lukáshka; and having examined his gun again he sat down behind the log.

He remained alone and sat gazing at the shallows and listening for the Cossacks; but it was some distance to the cordon and he was tormented by impatience. He kept thinking that the other *abréks* who were with the one he had killed would escape. He was vexed with the *abréks* who were going to escape just as he had been with the boar that had escaped the evening before. He glanced round and at the opposite bank, expecting every moment to see a man, and having arranged his gun-rest he was ready to fire. The idea that he might himself be killed never entered his head.

CHAPTER IX

It was growing light. The Chechén's body which was gently rocking in the shallow water was now clearly visible. Suddenly the reeds rustled not far from Luke and he heard steps and saw the feathery tops of the reeds moving. He set his gun at full cock and muttered: 'To the Father and to the Son,' but when the cock clicked the sound of steps ceased.

'Hullo, Cossacks! Don't kill your Daddy!' said a deep bass voice calmly; and moving the reeds apart Daddy Eróshka came up close to Luke.

'I very nearly killed you, by God I did!' said Lukáshka.

'What have you shot?' asked the old man.

His sonorous voice resounded through the wood and downward along the river, suddenly dispelling the mysterious quiet of night around the Cossack. It was as if everything had suddenly become lighter and more distinct.

'There now, Uncle, you have not seen anything, but I've killed a beast,' said Lukáshka, uncocking his gun and getting up with unnatural calmness.

The old man was staring intently at the white back, now clearly visible, against which the Térek rippled.

'He was swimming with a log on his back. I spied him out! Look there. There! He's got blue trousers, and a gun I think. Do you see?' inquired Luke.

'How can one help seeing?' said the old man angrily, and a serious and stern expression appeared on his face. 'You've killed a *dzhigít*,' he said, apparently with regret.

'Well, I sat here and suddenly saw something dark on the other side. I spied him when he was still over there. It was as if a man had come there and fallen in. Strange! And a piece of driftwood, a good-sized piece, comes floating, not with the stream but across it; and what do I see but a head appearing from under it! Strange! I stretched out of the reeds but could see nothing; then I rose and he must have heard, the beast, and crept out into the shallow and looked about. "No, you don't!" I said, as soon as he landed and looked round, "you won't get away!" Oh, there was something choking me! I got my gun ready but did not stir, and looked out. He waited a little and then swam out again; and when he came into the moonlight I could see his whole back. "To the Father and the Son and the Holy Ghost," and through the smoke I see him struggling. He moaned, or so it seemed to me. "Ah," I thought, "the Lord be thanked, I've killed him!" And when he drifted on to the sand-bank I could see him distinctly: he tried to get up but couldn't. He struggled a bit and then lay down. Everything could be seen. Look, he does not move—he must be dead! The Cossacks have gone back to the cordon in case there should be any more of them.'

'And so you got him!' said the old man. 'He is far away now, my lad!' And again he shook his head sadly.

Just then they heard the sound of breaking bushes and the loud voices of Cossacks approaching along the bank on horse-back and on foot. 'Are you bringing the skiff?' shouted Lukáshka.

'You're a trump, Luke! Lug it to the bank!' shouted one of the Cossacks.

Without waiting for the skiff Lukáshka began to undress, keeping an eye all the while on his prey.

'Wait a bit, Nazárka is bringing the skiff,' shouted the corporal.

'You fool! Maybe he is alive and only pretending! Take your dagger with you!' shouted another Cossack.

'Get along,' cried Luke, pulling off his trousers. He quickly undressed and, crossing himself, jumped, plunging with a splash into the river. Then with long strokes of his white arms, lifting his back high out of the water and breathing deeply, he swam across the current of the Térek towards the shallows. A crowd of Cossacks stood on the bank talking loudly. Three horsemen rode off to patrol. The skiff appeared round a bend. Lukáshka stood up on the sand-bank, leaned over the body, and gave it a couple of shakes. 'Quite dead!' he shouted in a shrill voice.

The Chechén had been shot in the head. He had on a pair of blue trousers, a shirt, and a *cherkéska*, and a gun and dagger were tied to his back. Above all these a large branch was tied, and it was this which at first had misled Lukáshka.

'What a carp you've landed!' cried one of the Cossacks who had assembled in a circle, as the body, lifted out of the skiff, was laid on the bank, pressing down the grass.

'How yellow he is!' said another.

'Where have our fellows gone to search? I expect the rest of them are on the other bank. If this one had not been a scout he would not have swum that way. Why else would he swim alone?' said a third.

'Must have been a smart one to offer himself before the others; obviously a real *dzhigít*!' said Lukáshka mockingly, shivering as he wrung out his clothes that had got wet on the bank.

'His beard is dyed and cropped.'

'And he has tied a bag with a coat in it to his back.'

'That would make it easier for him to swim,' said some one.

'I say, Lukáshka,' said the corporal, who was holding the dagger and gun taken from the dead man. 'Keep the dagger for yourself and the coat too; but I'll give you three rubles for the gun. You see it has a hole in it,' said he, blowing into the muzzle. 'I want it just for a souvenir.'

'Lukáshka did not answer. Evidently this sort of begging vexed him but he knew it could not be avoided.

'See, what a devil!' said he, frowning and throwing down the Chechén's coat. 'If at least it were a good coat, but it's a mere rag.'

'It'll do to fetch firewood in,' said one of the Cossacks.

'Mósev, I'm going home,' said Lukáshka, evidently forgetting his vexation and wishing to get some advantage out of having to give a present to his superior.

'All right, you may go!'

'Take the body beyond the cordon, lads,' said the corporal, still examining the gun, 'and put a shelter over him from the sun. Perhaps they'll send from the mountains to ransom it.'

'It isn't hot yet,' said someone.

'And supposing a jackal tears him apart? Wouldn't that be great?' remarked another Cossack.

'We'll set up a watch; if they should come to ransom him it won't do for him to have been torn up.'

'Well, Lukáshka, whatever you do you must stand a pail of vodka for the lads,' said the corporal gaily.

'Of course! That's the custom,' chimed in the Cossacks. 'See what luck God has sent you! Without ever having seen anything of the kind before, you've killed an *abrék*!'

'Buy the dagger and coat and don't be stingy, and I'll let you have the trousers too,' said Lukáshka. 'They're too tight for me; he was a thin devil.'

One Cossack bought the coat for a ruble and another gave the price of two pails of vodka for the dagger.

'Drink, lads! I'll stand you a pail!' said Luke. 'I'll bring it myself from the village.'

'And cut up the trousers into kerchiefs for the girls!' said Nazárka.

The Cossacks burst out laughing.

'Have done laughing!' said the corporal. 'And take the body away. Why have you put the nasty thing by the hut?'

'What are you standing there for? Haul him along, lads!' shouted Lukáshka in a commanding voice to the Cossacks, who reluctantly took hold of the body, obeying him as though he were their chief. After dragging the body along for a few steps the Cossacks let fall the legs, which dropped with a lifeless jerk, and stepping apart they then stood silent for a few moments. Nazárka came up and straightened the head, which was turned to one side so that the round wound above the temple and the whole of the dead man's face were visible. 'See what a mark he has made right in the brain,' he said. 'He won't get lost. His owners will always know him!' No one answered, and again the angel of silence* flew over the Cossacks.

The sun had risen high and its diverging beams were lighting up the dewy grass. Near by, the Térek murmured in the awakened wood and, greeting the morning, the pheasants called to one another. The Cossacks stood still and silent around the dead man, gazing at him. The brown body, with nothing on but the wet blue trousers held by a girdle over the sunken stomach, was well shaped and handsome. The muscular arms lay stretched straight out by his sides; the blue, freshly shaven, round head with the clotted wound on one side of it was thrown back. The smooth tanned forehead contrasted sharply with the shaven part of the head. The open glassy eyes with lowered pupils stared upwards, seeming to gaze past everything. Under the red trimmed moustache the fine lips, drawn at the corners, seemed stiffened into a smile of good-natured subtle raillery. The fingers of the small hands covered with red hairs were bent inward, and the nails were dyed red.

Lukáshka had not yet dressed. He was wet. His neck was redder and his eyes brighter than usual, his broad jaws twitched, and from his healthy body a hardly perceptible steam rose in the fresh morning air.

'He too was a man!' he muttered, evidently admiring the corpse.

'Yes, if you had fallen into his hands you would have had short shrift,' said one of the Cossacks.

The angel of silence had taken wing. The Cossacks began bustling about and talking. Two of them went to cut brushwood for a shelter, others strolled towards the cordon. Luke and Nazárka ran to get ready to go to the village.

Half and hour later they were both on their way homewards, talking incessantly and almost running through the dense woods which separated the Térek from the village.

'Mind, don't tell her I sent you, but just go and find out if her husband is at home,' Luke was saying in his shrill voice.

'And I'll go round to Yámka too,' said the devoted Nazárka. 'We'll have a spree, shall we?'

'When should we have one if not today?' replied Luke.

When they reached the village the two Cossacks drank, and lay down to sleep till evening.

CHAPTER X

On the third day after the events above described, two companies of a Caucasian infantry regiment arrived at the Cossack village of Novomlínsk. The horses had been unharnessed and the companies' wagons were standing in the square. The cooks had dug a pit, and with logs gathered from various yards (where they had not been sufficiently securely stored) were now cooking the food; the pay-sergeants were settling accounts with the soldiers. The service corps men were driving piles in the ground to which to tie the horses, and the quartermasters were going about the streets just as if they were at home, showing officers and men to their quarters. Here were green ammunition boxes stacked in a line. Here were the company's carts and horses. Here were cauldrons in which buckwheat porridge was being cooked. Here were the captain and the lieutenant and the sergeant-major, Onísim Mikháylovich. And all this was in the Cossack village where it was reported that the companies were ordered to take up their quarters: therefore they were at home here. But why they were stationed there, who the Cossacks were, and whether they wanted the troops to be there, and whether they were Old Believers or not—was all quite immaterial. Having received their pay and been dismissed, tired out and covered with dust, the soldiers noisily and in disorder, like a swarm of bees about to settle, spread over the squares and streets; quite regardless of the Cossacks' ill will, chattering merrily and with their muskets clinking, by twos and threes they entered the huts and hung up their accoutrements, unpacked their bags, and bantered with the women. At their favourite spot, round the porridge-cauldrons, a large group of soldiers assembled and with little pipes between their teeth they gazed, now at the smoke which rose into the hot sky, becoming visible when it thickened into white clouds as it rose, and now at the camp fires which were quivering in the pure air like molten glass, and bantered and made fun of the Cossack men and women because they do not live at all like Russians. In all the yards one could see soldiers and hear their laughter and the exasperated and shrill cries of Cossack women defending their houses and refusing to give the soldiers water or cooking utensils. Little boys and girls, clinging to their mothers and to each other, followed all the movements of the troopers (never before seen by them) with frightened curiosity, or ran after them at a respectful distance. The old Cossacks came out silently and dismally and sat on the earthen embankments of their huts, and watched the soldiers' activity with an air of leaving it all to the will of God without understanding what would come of it.

Olénin, who had joined the Caucasian regiment as a cadet three months before, was quartered in one of the best houses in the village, the house of the cornet, Elias Vasílich—that is to say at Granny Ulítka's.

'Goodness knows what it will be like, Dmítri Andréich,' said the panting Vanyúsha to Olénin, who, dressed in a *cherkéska* and mounted on a Kabardá* horse which he had bought in Grózny,* was after a five-hours' march gaily entering the yard of the quarters assigned to him.

'Why, what's the matter?' he asked, caressing his horse and looking merrily at the perspiring, dishevelled, and worried Vanyúsha, who had arrived with the baggage wagons and was unpacking.

Olénin looked quite a different man. In place of his clean-shaven lips and chin he had a youthful moustache and a small beard. Instead of a sallow complexion, the result of nights turned into day, his cheeks, his forehead, and the skin behind his ears were now red with healthy sunburn. In place of a clean new black suit he wore a dirty white *cherkéska* with a deeply pleated skirt, and he bore arms. Instead of a freshly starched collar, his neck was tightly clasped by the red band of his silk *beshmét*. He wore Circassian dress but did not wear it well, and anyone would have taken him for a Russian but not a *dzhigít*. It was the thing—but not the real thing. Yet for all that, his whole person breathed health, joy, and self-satisfaction.

'Yes, it seems funny to you,' said Vanyúsha, 'but just try to talk to these people yourself: they set themselves against one and there's no end of it. You can't get as much as a word out of them.' Vanyúsha angrily threw down a pail on the threshold. 'Somehow they don't seem like Russians.'

'You should speak to the chief of the village!'

'But I don't know where he lives,' said Vanyúsha in an offended tone.

'Who has upset you so?' asked Olénin, looking round.

'The devil only knows. Faugh! There is no real master here. They say he has gone to some kind of *kríga*, and the old woman is a real devil. God preserve us!' answered Vanyúsha, putting his hands to his head. 'How we shall live here I don't know. They are worse than Tatars, I do declare—though they consider themselves Christians! A Tatar is bad enough, but all the same he is more noble. Gone to the *kríga* indeed! What this *kríga* they have invented is, I don't know!' concluded Vanyúsha, and turned aside.

'It's not as it is in the serfs' quarters at home, eh?' chaffed Olénin without dismounting.

'Please sir, may I have your horse?' said Vanyúsha, evidently perplexed by this new order of things but resigning himself to his fate.

'So a Tatar is more noble, eh, Vanyúsha?' repeated Olénin, dismounting and slapping the saddle.

'Yes, you're laughing! You think it funny,' muttered Vanyúsha angrily.

'Come, don't be angry, Vanyúsha,' replied Olénin, still smiling. 'Wait a minute, I'll go and speak to the people of the house; you'll see I shall arrange everything. You don't know what a jolly life we shall have here. Only don't get upset.'

Vanyúsha did not answer. Screwing up his eyes he looked contemptuously after his master, and shook his head. Vanyúsha regarded Olénin as only his master, and Olénin regarded Vanyúsha as only his servant; and they would both have been much surprised if anyone had told them that they were friends, as they really were without knowing it themselves. Vanyúsha had been taken into his proprietor's house when he was only eleven and when Olénin was the same age. When Olénin was fifteen be gave Vanyúsha lessons for a time and taught him to read French, of which the latter was inordinately proud; and when in specially good spirits he still let off French words, always laughing stupidly when he did so.

Olénin ran up the steps of the porch and pushed open the door of the hut. Maryánka, wearing nothing but a pink smock, as all Cossack women do in the house, jumped away from the door, frightened, and pressing herself against the wall covered the lower part of her face with the broad sleeve of her Tatar smock. Having opened the door wider, Olénin in the semi-darkness of the passage saw the whole tall, shapely figure of the young Cossack girl. With the quick and eager curiosity of youth he involuntarily noticed the firm maidenly form revealed by the fine print smock, and the beautiful black eyes fixed on him with childlike terror and wild curiosity. 'This is *she*,' thought Olénin. 'But there will be many others like her' came at once into his head, and he opened the inner door. Old Granny Ulítka, also dressed only in a smock, was stooping with her back turned to him, sweeping the floor.

'Good-day to you, Mother! I've come about my lodgings,' he began.

The Cossack woman, without unbending, turned her severe but still handsome face towards him.

'What have you come here for? Want to mock us, eh? I'll teach you to mock; may the black plague seize you!' she shouted, looking askance from under her frowning brow at the new-comer.

Olénin had at first imagined that the way-worn, gallant Caucasian army (of which he was a member) would be everywhere received joyfully, and especially by the Cossacks, our comrades in the war; and he therefore felt perplexed by this reception. Without losing presence of mind however he tried to explain that he meant to pay for his lodgings, but the old woman would not give him a hearing.

'What have you come for? Who wants a pest like you, with your scraped face? You just wait a bit; when the master returns he'll show you your place. I don't want your dirty money! A likely thing—just as if we had never seen any! You'll stink the house out with your beastly tobacco and want to put it right with money! Think we've never seen a pest! May you be shot in your bowels and your heart!' shrieked the old woman in a piercing voice, interrupting Olénin.

'It seems Vanyúsha was right!' thought Olénin. '"A Tatar would be nobler",' and followed by Granny Ulítka's abuse he went out of the hut. As he was leaving, Maryánka, still wearing only her pink smock, but with her forehead covered down to her eyes by a white kerchief, suddenly slipped out from the passage past him. Pattering rapidly down the steps with her bare feet she ran from the porch, stopped, and looking round hastily with laughing eyes at the young man, vanished round the corner of the hut.

Her firm youthful step, the untamed look of the eyes glistening from under the white kerchief, and the firm stately build of the young beauty, struck Olénin even more powerfully than before. 'Yes, it must be *she*,' he thought, and troubling his head still less about the lodgings, he kept looking round at Maryánka as he approached Vanyúsha.

'There you see, the girl too is quite savage, just like a wild filly!' said Vanyúsha, who though still busy with the luggage wagon had now cheered up a bit. '*Lafom*!'* he added in a loud triumphant voice and burst out laughing.

CHAPTER XI

Towards evening the master of the house returned from his fishing, and having learnt that the cadet would pay for the lodging, pacified the old woman and satisfied Vanyúsha's demands.

Everything was arranged in the new quarters. Their hosts moved into the winter hut and let their summer hut to the cadet for three rubles a month. Olénin had something to eat and went to sleep. Towards evening he woke up, washed and made himself tidy, dined, and having lit a cigarette sat down by the window that looked onto the street. It was cooler. The slanting shadow of the hut with its ornamental gables fell across the dusty road and even bent upwards at the base of the wall of the house opposite. The steep reed-thatched roof of that house shone in the rays of the setting sun. The air grew fresher. Everything was peaceful in the village. The soldiers had settled down and become quiet. The herds had not yet been driven home and the people had not returned from their work.

Olénin's lodging was situated almost at the end of the village. At rare intervals, from somewhere far beyond the Térek in those parts whence Olénin had just come (the Chechén or the Kumýk plain), came muffled sounds of firing. Olénin was feeling very well contented after three months of bivouac life. His newly washed face was fresh and his powerful body clean (an unaccustomed sensation after the campaign) and in all his rested limbs be was conscious of a feeling of tranquillity and strength. His mind, too, felt fresh and clear. He thought of the campaign and of past dangers. He remembered that he had faced them no worse than other men, and that he was accepted as a comrade among valiant Caucasians. His Moscow recollections were left behind Heaven knows how far! The old life was wiped out and a quite new life had begun in which there were as yet no mistakes. Here as a new man among new men he could gain a new and good reputation. He was conscious of a youthful and causeless joy of life. Looking now out of the window at the boys spinning their tops in the shadow of the house, now round his neat new lodging, he thought how pleasantly he would settle down to this new Cossack village life. Now and then he glanced at the mountains and the blue sky, and an appreciation of the solemn grandeur of nature mingled with his reminiscences and dreams. His new life had begun, not as he imagined it would when he left Moscow, but unexpectedly well. 'The mountains, the mountains, the mountains!': they permeated all his thoughts and feelings.

'He's kissed his dog and licked the jug! Daddy Eróshka has kissed his dog!' suddenly the little Cossacks who had been spinning their tops under the window shouted, looking towards the side street. 'He's drunk his bitch, and his dagger!' shouted the boys, crowding together and stepping backwards.

These shouts were addressed to Daddy Eróshka, who with his gun on his shoulder and some pheasants hanging on his belt was returning from his shooting expedition.

'I have done wrong, lads, I have!' he said, vigorously swinging his arms and looking up at the windows on both sides of the street. 'I have drunk the bitch; it was wrong,' he repeated, evidently vexed but pretending not to care.

Olénin was surprised by the boys' behaviour towards the old hunter, but was still more struck by the expressive, intelligent face and the powerful build of the man whom they called Daddy Eróshka.

'Here Daddy, here Cossack!' he called. 'Come here!'

The old man looked into the window and stopped.

'Good evening, good man,' he said, lifting his little cap off his cropped head.

'Good evening, good man,' replied Olénin. 'What is it the youngsters are shouting at you?'

Daddy Eróshka came up to the window. 'Why they're teasing the old man. No matter, I like it. Let them joke about their old daddy,' he said with those firm musical intonations with which old and venerable people speak. 'Are you an army commander?' he added.

'No, I am a cadet. But where did you kill those pheasants?' asked Olénin.

'I dispatched these three hens in the forest,' answered the old man, turning his broad back towards the window to show the hen pheasants which were hanging with their heads tucked into his belt and staining his coat with blood. 'Haven't you seen any?' he asked. 'Take a brace if you like! Here you are,' and he handed two of the pheasants in at the window. 'Are you a sportsman yourself?' he asked.

'I am. During the campaign I killed four myself.'

'Four? What a lot!' said the old man sarcastically. 'And are you a drinker? Do you drink *chikhír*?'

'Why not? I like a drink.'

'Ah, I see you are a trump! We shall be *kunáks*, you and I,' said Daddy Eróshka.

'Step in,' said Olénin. 'We'll have a drop of *chikhír*.'

'I might as well,' said the old man, 'but take the pheasants.' The old man's face showed that he liked the cadet. He had seen at once that he could get free drinks from him, and that therefore it would be all right to give him a brace of pheasants.

Soon Daddy Eróshka's figure appeared in the doorway of the hut, and it was only then that Olénin became fully conscious of the enormous size and sturdy build of this man, whose red-brown face with its perfectly white broad beard was all furrowed by deep lines produced by age and toil. For an old man, the muscles of his legs, arms, and shoulders were quite exceptionally large and prominent. There were deep scars on his head under the short-cropped hair. His thick sinewy neck was covered with deep intersecting folds like a bull's. His horny hands were bruised and scratched. He stepped lightly and easily over the threshold, unslung his gun and placed it in a corner, and casting a rapid glance round the room noted the value of the goods and chattels deposited in the hut, and with out-turned toes stepped softly, in his sandals of raw hide, into the middle of the room. He brought with him a penetrating but not unpleasant smell of *chikhír* wine, vodka, gunpowder, and congealed blood.

Daddy Eróshka bowed down before the icons, smoothed his beard, and approaching Olénin held out his thick brown hand. '*Koshkíldy*' said he; 'That is Tatar for "Good-day"—"Peace be unto you," it means in their tongue.'

'*Koshkíldy*, I know,' answered Olénin, shaking hands.

'Eh, but you don't, you don't know the customs! Fool!' said Daddy Eróshka, shaking his head reproachfully. 'If anyone says "*Koshkíldy*" to you, you must say "*Allah rasi bo sun*," that is, "God save you." That's the way, my dear fellow, and not "*Koshkíldy*." But I'll teach you all about it. We had a fellow here, Elias Mosévich, one of you Russians, he and I were *kunáks*. He was a trump, a drunkard, a thief, a sportsman—and what a sportsman! I taught him everything.'

'And what will you teach me?' asked Olénin, who was becoming more and more interested in the old man.

'I'll take you hunting and teach you to fish. I'll show you Chechéns and find a girl for you, if you like—even that! That's the sort I am! I'm a wag!'—and the old man laughed. 'I'll sit down. I'm tired. *Kargá*?' he added inquiringly.

'And what does "*Kargá*" mean?' asked Olénin.

'Why, that means "All right" in Georgian. But I say it just so. It is a way I have, it's my favourite word. *Kargá*, *Kargá*. I say it just so; in fun I mean. Well, lad, won't you order the *chikhír*? You've got an orderly, haven't you? Hey, Iván! shouted the old man. 'All your soldiers are Iváns. Is yours Iván?'

'True enough, his name is Iván—Vanyúsha.* Here Vanyúsha! Please get some *chikhír* from our landlady and bring it here.'

'Iván or Vanyúsha, that's all one. Why are all your soldiers Iváns? Iván, old fellow,' said the old man, 'You tell them to give you some from the barrel they have begun. They have the best *chikhír* in the village. But don't give more than thirty kopeks for the quart, mind, because that witch would be only too glad. Our people are anathema people; stupid people,' Daddy Eróshka continued in a confidential tone after Vanyúsha had gone out. 'They do not look upon you as on men, you are worse than a Tatar in their eyes. "Worldly Russians" they say. But as for me, though you are a soldier you are still a man, and have a soul in you. Isn't that right? Elias Mosévich was a soldier, yet what a treasure of a man he was! Isn't that so, my dear fellow? That's why our people don't like me; but I don't care! I'm a merry fellow, and I like everybody. I'm Eróshka; yes, my dear fellow.'

And the old Cossack patted the young man affectionately on the shoulder.

CHAPTER XII

Vanyúsha, who meanwhile had finished his housekeeping arrangements and had even been shaved by the company's barber and had pulled his trousers out of his high boots as a sign that the company was stationed in comfortable quarters, was in excellent spirits. He looked attentively but not benevolently at Eróshka, as at a wild beast he had never seen before, shook his head at the floor which the old man had dirtied and, having taken two bottles from under a bench, went to the landlady.

'Good evening, kind people,' he said, having made up his mind to be very gentle. 'My master has sent me to get some *chikhír*, will you draw some for me, my good folk?'

The old woman gave no answer. The girl, who was arranging the kerchief on her head before a little Tatar mirror, looked round at Vanyúsha in silence.

'I'll pay money for it, honoured people,' said Vanyúsha, jingling the coppers in his pocket. 'Be kind to us and we too will be kind to you,' he added.

'How much?' asked the old woman abruptly. 'A quart.'

'Go, my dear, draw some for them,' said Granny Ulítka to her daughter. 'Take it from the cask that's begun, my precious.'

The girl took the keys and a decanter and went out of the hut with Vanyúsha.

'Tell we, who is that young woman?' asked Olénin, pointing to Maryánka, who was passing the window. The old man winked and nudged the young man with his elbow.

'Wait a bit,' said he and reached out of the window. 'Khm,' he coughed, and bellowed 'Maryánka dear. Hallo, Maryánka, my girlie, won't you love me, darling? I'm a wag,' he added in a whisper to Olénin. The girl, not turning her head and swinging her arms regularly and vigorously, passed the window with the peculiarly smart and bold gait of a Cossack woman and only turned her dark shaded eyes slowly towards the old man.

'Love me and you'll be happy,' shouted Eróshka, winking, and he looked questioningly at the cadet.

'I'm a fine fellow, I'm a wag!' he added. 'She's a regular queen, that girl. Eh?'

'She is lovely,' said Olénin. 'Call her here!'

'No, no,' said the old man. 'For that one a match is being arranged with Lukáshka, Luke, a fine Cossack, a *dzhigít*, who killed an *abrék* the other day. I'll find you a better one. I'll find you one that will be all dressed up in silk and silver. Once I've said it I'll do it. I'll get you a regular beauty!'

'You, an old man—and say such things,' replied Olénin. 'Why, it's a sin!'

'A sin? Where's the sin?' said the old man emphatically. 'A sin to look at a nice girl? A sin to have some fun with her? Or is it a sin to love her? Is that so in your parts? No, my dear fellow, it's not a sin, it's salvation! God made you and God made the girl too. He made it all; so it is no sin to look at a nice girl. That's what she was made for; to be loved and to give joy. That's how I judge it, my good fellow.'

Having crossed the yard and entered a cool dark store-room filled with barrels, Maryánka went up to one of them and repeating the usual prayer plunged a dipper into it. Vanyúsha standing in the doorway smiled as he looked at her. He thought it very funny that she had only a smock on, close-fitting behind and tucked up in front, and still funnier that she wore a necklace of silver coins. He thought this quite un-Russian and that they would all laugh in the serfs' quarters at home if they saw a girl like that. '*La fee coam say tray byen*,[1] for a change,' he thought. 'I'll tell that to my master.'

'What are you standing in the light for, you devil!' the girl suddenly shouted. 'Why don't you pass me the decanter!'

Having filled the decanter with cool red wine, Maryánka handed it to Vanyúsha.

'Give the money to Mother,' she said, pushing away the hand in which he held the money.

[1] How nice the girl is.

Vanyúsha laughed.

'Why are you so cross, little dear?' he said good-naturedly, irresolutely shuffling with his feet while the girl was covering the barrel.

She began to laugh.

'And you! Are you kind?'

'We, my master and I, are very kind,' Vanyúsha answered decidedly. 'We are so kind that wherever we have stayed our hosts were always very grateful. It's because he's generous.'

The girl stood listening.

'And is your master married?' she asked.

'No. The master is young and unmarried, because noble gentlemen can never marry young,' said Vanyúsha didactically.

'A likely thing! See what a well-fed buffalo he is—and too young to marry! Is he the chief of you all?' she asked.

'My master is a cadet; that means he's not yet an officer, but he's more important than a general—he's an important man! Because not only our colonel, but the Tsar himself, knows him,' proudly explained Vanyúsha. 'We are not like those beggars in the line regiment, and our papa himself was a Senator. He had more than a thousand serfs, all his own, and they send us a thousand rubles at a time. That's why everyone likes us. Another may be a captain but have no money. What's the use of that?'

'Go away. I'll lock up,' said the girl, interrupting him.

Vanyúsha brought Olénin the wine and announced that '*La fee say tray jewlee*,'[1] and, laughing stupidly, at once went out.

CHAPTER XIII

Meanwhile the tattoo had sounded in the village square. The people had returned from their work. The herd lowed as in clouds of golden dust it crowded at the village gate. The girls and the women hurried through the streets and yards, turning in their cattle. The sun had quite hidden itself behind the distant snowy peaks. One pale bluish shadow spread over land and sky. Above the darkened gardens stars just discernible were kindling, and the sounds were gradually hushed in the

[1] The girl is very pretty.

village. The cattle having been attended to and left for the night, the women came out and gathered at the corners of the streets and, cracking sunflower seeds with their teeth, settled down on the earthen embankments of the houses. Later on Maryánka, having finished milking the buffalo and the other two cows, also joined one of these groups.

The group consisted of several women and girls and one old Cossack man.

They were talking about the *abrék* who had been killed. The Cossack was telling the story and the women asking questions.

'I expect he'll get a handsome reward,' said one of the women.

'Of course. It's said that they'll send him a cross.'

'Mósev did try to wrong him. Took the gun away from him, but the authorities at Kizlyár heard of it.'

'A mean creature that Mósev is!'

'They say Lukáshka has come home,' remarked one of the girls.

'He and Nazárka are merry-making at Yámka's.' (Yámka was an unmarried, disreputable Cossack woman who kept an illicit tavern.) 'I heard say they had drunk half a pailful.'

'What luck that Snatcher has,' somebody remarked. 'A real snatcher. But there's no denying he's fine lad, smart enough for anything, a right-minded lad! His father was just such another, Daddy Kiryák was: he takes after his father. When he was killed the whole village howled. Look, there they are,' added the speaker, pointing to the Cossacks who were coming down the street towards them. 'And Ergushóv has managed to come along with them too! The drunkard!'

Lukáshka, Nazárka, and Ergushóv, having emptied half a pail of vodka, were coming towards the girls. The faces of all three, but especially that of the old Cossack, were redder than usual. Ergushóv was reeling and kept laughing and nudging Nazárka in the ribs.

'Why are you not singing?' he shouted to the girls. 'Sing to our merry-making, I tell you!'

They were welcomed with the words, 'Had a good day? Had a good day?'

'Why sing? It's not a holiday,' said one of the women. 'You're tight, so you go and sing.'

Ergushóv roared with laughter and nudged Nazárka. 'You'd better sing. And I'll begin too. I'm clever, I tell you.'

'Are you asleep, fair ones?' said Nazárka. 'We've come from the cordon to drink your health. We've already drunk Lukáshka's health.'

Lukáshka, when he reached the group, slowly raised his cap and stopped in front of the girls. His broad cheek-bones and neck were red. He stood and spoke softly and sedately, but in his tranquillity and sedateness there was more of animation and strength than in all Nazárka's loquacity and bustle. He reminded one of a playful colt that with a snort and a flourish of its tail suddenly stops short and stands as though nailed to the ground with all four feet. Lukáshka stood quietly in front of the girls, his eyes laughed, and he spoke but little as he glanced now at his drunken companions and now at the girls. When Maryánka joined the group he raised his cap with a firm deliberate movement, moved out of her way and then stepped in front of her with one foot a little forward and with his thumbs in his belt, fingering his dagger. Maryánka answered his greeting with a leisurely bow of her head, settled down on the earth-bank, and took some seeds out of the bosom of her smock. Lukáshka, keeping his eyes fixed on Maryánka, slowly cracked seeds and spat out the shells. All were quiet when Maryánka joined the group.

'Have you come for long?' asked a woman, breaking the silence.

'Till tomorrow morning,' quietly replied Lukáshka.

'Well, God grant you get something good,' said the Cossack; 'I'm glad of it, as I've just been saying.'

'And I say so too,' put in the tipsy Ergushóv, laughing. 'What a lot of visitors have come,' he added, pointing to a soldier who was passing by. 'The soldiers' vodka is good—I like it.'

'They've sent three of the devils to us,' said one of the women. 'Grandad went to the village Elders, but they say nothing can be done.'

'Ah, ha! Have you met with trouble?' said Ergushóv.

'I expect they have smoked you out with their tobacco?'

asked another woman. 'Smoke as much as you like in the yard, I say, but we won't allow it inside the hut. Not if the Elder himself comes, I won't allow it. Besides, they may rob you. He's not quartered any of them on himself, no fear, that devil's son of an Elder.'

'You don't like it?' Ergushóv began again.

'And I've also heard say that the girls will have to make the soldiers' beds and offer them *chikhír* and honey,' said Nazárka, putting one foot forward and tilting his cap like Lukáshka.

'Ergushóv burst into a roar of laughter, and seizing the girl nearest to him, he embraced her. 'For sure, I say.'

'Now then, you boor!' squealed the girl, 'I'll tell your old woman.'

'Tell her,' shouted he. 'That's quite right what Nazárka says; a circular has been sent round. He can read, you know. Quite true!' And he began embracing the next girl.

'What are you up to, you beast?' squealed the rosy, round-faced Ústenka, laughing and lifting her arm to hit him.

The Cossack stepped aside and nearly fell.

'There, they say girls have no strength, and you nearly killed me.'

'Get away, you boor, what devil has brought you from the cordon?' said Ústenka, and turning away from him she again burst out laughing. 'You were asleep and missed the *abrék*, didn't you? Suppose he had done for you it would have been all the better.'

'You'd have howled I expect,' said Nazárka, laughing.

'Howled! A likely thing.'

'Just look, she doesn't care. She'd howl, Nazárka, eh? Would she?' said Ergushóv.

Lukáshka all this time had stood silently looking at Maryánka. His gaze evidently confused the girl.

'Well, Maryánka! I hear they've stationed one of the chiefs with you?' he said, drawing nearer.

Maryánka, as was her wont, waited before she replied, and slowly raising her eyes looked at the Cossack. Lukáshka's eyes were laughing as if something special, apart from what was said, was taking place between himself and the girl.

'Yes, it's all right for them as they have two huts,' replied an old woman on Maryánka's behalf, 'but at Fómushkin's now they also have one of the chiefs stationed with them and they say one whole corner is packed full with his things, and the family have no room left. Was such a thing ever heard of as that they should turn a whole horde loose in the village?' she said. 'And what the plague are they going to do here?'

'I've heard say they'll build a bridge across the Térek,' said one of the girls.

'And I've been told that they will dig a pit to put the girls in because they don't love the lads,' said Nazárka, approaching Ústenka; and he again made a whimsical gesture which set everybody laughing, and Ergushóv, passing by Maryánka, who was next in turn, began to embrace an old woman.

'Why don't you hug Maryánka? You should do it to each in turn,' said Nazárka.

'No, my old one is sweeter,' shouted the Cossack, kissing the struggling old woman.

'He'll smother me,' she screamed, laughing.

The tramp of regular footsteps at the other end of the street interrupted their laughter. Three soldiers in their cloaks, with their muskets on their shoulders, were marching in step to relieve the guard by the ammunition wagon.

The corporal, an old cavalry man, looked angrily at the Cossacks and led his men straight along the road where Lukáshka and Nazárka were standing, so that they should have to get out of the way. Nazárka moved, but Lukáshka only screwed up his eyes and turned his broad back without moving from his place.

'People are standing here, so you go round,' he muttered, half turning his head and tossing it contemptuously in the direction of the soldiers.

The soldiers passed by in silence, keeping step regularly along the dusty road.

Maryánka began laughing and all the other girls chimed in.

'What swells!' said Nazárka, 'Just like long-skirted choristers,' and he walked a few steps down the road imitating the soldiers.

Again everyone broke into peals of laughter.

Lukáshka came slowly up to Maryánka.

'And where have you put up the chief?' he asked.

Maryánka thought for a moment.

'We've let him have the new hut,' she said.

'And is he old or young,' asked Lukáshka, sitting down beside her.

'Do you think I've asked?' answered the girl. 'I went to get him some *chikhír* and saw him sitting at the window with Daddy Eróshka. Red-headed he seemed. They've brought a whole cartload of things.'

And she dropped her eyes.

'Oh, how glad I am that I got leave from the cordon!' said Lukáshka, moving closer to the girl and looking straight in her eyes all the time.

'And have you come for long?' asked Maryánka, smiling slightly.

'Till the morning. Give me some sunflower seeds,' he said, holding out his hand.

Maryánka now smiled outright and unfastening the neckband of her smock:

'Don't take them all,' she said.

'Really I felt so bored all the time without you, I swear I did,' he said in a calm, restrained whisper, helping himself to some seeds out of the bosom of the girl's smock, and stooping still closer over her he continued with laughing eyes to talk to her in low tones.

'I won't come, I tell you,' Maryánka suddenly said aloud, leaning away from him.

'No really . . . what I wanted to say to you,' . . . whispered Lukáshka. 'By God! Do come!'

Maryánka shook her head, but did so with a smile.

'Nursey Maryánka! Hallo Nursey! Mummy is calling! Supper time!' shouted Maryánka's little brother, running towards the group.

'I'm coming,' replied the girl, 'Go, my dear, go alone—I'll come in a minute.'

Lukáshka rose and raised his cap.

'I expect I had better go home too, that will be best,' he said, trying to appear unconcerned but hardly able to repress a smile, and he disappeared behind the corner of the house.

Meanwhile night had entirely enveloped the village. Bright stars were scattered over the dark sky. The streets became dark and empty. Nazárka remained with the women on the earth-bank and their laughter was still heard, but Lukáshka, having slowly moved away from the girls, crouched down like a cat and then suddenly started running lightly, holding his dagger to steady it: not homeward, however, but towards the cornet's house. Having passed two streets he turned into a lane and lifting the skirt of his coat sat down on the ground in the shadow of a fence. 'A regular cornet's daughter!' he thought about Maryánka. 'Won't even have a lark—the devil! But just wait a bit.'

The approaching footsteps of a woman attracted his attention. He began listening, and laughed all by himself. Maryánka with bowed head, striking the pales of the fences with a switch, was walking with rapid regular strides straight towards him. Lukáshka rose. Maryánka started and stopped.

'What an accursed devil! You frightened me! So you have not gone home?' she said, and laughed aloud.

Lukáshka put one arm round her and with the other hand raised her face. 'What I wanted to tell you, by God!' his voice trembled and broke.

'What are you talking of, at night time!' answered Maryánka. 'Mother is waiting for me, and you'd better go to your sweetheart.'

And freeing herself from his arms she ran away a few steps. When she had reached the wattle fence of her home she stopped and turned to the Cossack who was running beside her and still trying to persuade her to stay a while with him.

'Well, what do you want to say, midnight-gad-about?' and she again began laughing.

'Don't laugh at me, Maryánka! By God! Well, what if I have a sweetheart? May the devil take her! Only say the word and now I'll love *you*—I'll do anything you wish. Here it is!' (And he jingled the money in his pocket.) 'Now we can live splendidly. Others have pleasures, and I? I get no pleasure from you, Maryánka dear!'

The girl did not answer. She stood before him breaking her switch into little bits with the rapid movement of her fingers.

Lukáshka suddenly clenched his teeth and fists.

'And why keep waiting and waiting? Don't I love you, darling? You can do what you like with me,' said he suddenly, frowning angrily and seizing both her hands.

The calm expression of Maryánka's face and voice did not change.

'Don't bluster, Lukáshka, but listen to me,' she answered, not pulling away her hands but holding the Cossack at arm's length. 'It's true I am a girl, but you listen to me! It does not depend on me, but if you love me I'll tell you this. Let go my hands, I'll tell you without.—I'll marry you, but you'll never get any nonsense from me,' said Maryánka without turning her face.

'What, you'll marry me? Marriage does not depend on us. Love me yourself, Maryánka dear,' said Lukáshka, from sullen and furious becoming again gentle, submissive, and tender, and smiling as he looked closely into her eyes.

Maryánka clung to him and kissed him firmly on the lips.

'Brother dear!' she whispered, pressing him convulsively to her. Then, suddenly tearing herself away, she ran into the gate of her house without looking round.

In spite of the Cossack's entreaties to wait another minute to hear what he had to say, Maryánka did not stop.

'Go,' she cried, 'you'll be seen! I do believe that devil, our lodger, is walking about the yard.'

'Cornet's daughter,' thought Lukáshka, 'She will marry me. Marriage is all very well, but you just love me!'

He found Nazárka at Yámka's house, and after having a spree with him went to Dunáyka's house, where, in spite of her not being faithful to him, he spent the night.

CHAPTER XIV

It was quite true that Olénin had been walking about the yard when Maryánka entered the gate, and had heard her say, 'That devil, our lodger, is walking about.' He had spent that evening with Daddy Eróshka on the porch of his new lodging. He had had a table, a samovar, wine, and a candle brought out, and over a cup of tea and a cigar he listened to the tales the old man told seated on the threshold at his feet. Though the air was still, the candle dripped and flickered: now lighting up the post of the porch, now the table and crockery, now the cropped white head of the old man. Moths circled round the flame and, shedding the dust of their wings, fluttered on the table and in the glasses, flew into the candle flame, and disappeared in the black space beyond. Olénin and Eróshka had emptied five bottles of *chikhír*. Eróshka filled the glasses every time, offering one to Olénin, drinking his health, and talking untiringly. He told of Cossack life in the old days: of his father, 'The Broad,' who alone had carried on his back a boar's carcass weighing three hundredweight, and drank two pails of *chikhír* at one sitting. He told of his own days and his chum Gírchik, with whom during the plague he used to smuggle felt cloaks across the Térek. He told how one morning he had killed two deer, and about his 'little soul' who used to run to him at the cordon at night. He told all this so eloquently and picturesquely that Olénin did not notice how time passed.

'Ah yes, my dear fellow,' he said, 'you did not know me in my golden days; then I'd have shown you things. Today it's "Eróshka licks the jug," but then Eróshka was famous in the whole regiment. Whose was the finest horse? Who had a *Gurda* sword? To whom should one go to get a drink? With whom go on a spree? Who should be sent to the mountains to kill Akhmet Khan? Why, always Eróshka! Whom did the girls love? Always Eróshka had to answer for it. Because I was a real *dzhigít*: a drinker, a thief (I used to seize herds of horses in the mountains), a singer; I was a master of every art! There are no Cossacks like that nowadays. It's disgusting to look at them. When they're that high (Eróshka held his hand three feet from the ground) they put on idiotic boots and keep looking at them—that's all the pleasure they know. Or they'll drink themselves foolish, not like men but all wrong. And who was I? I was Eróshka, the thief; they knew me not only in this village but up in the mountains. Tatar princes, my *kunáks*, used to come to see me! I used to be everybody's *kunák*. I was a Tatar—with a Tatar; an Armenian—with an Armenian; a soldier—with a soldier; an officer—with an officer! I didn't care as long as he was a drinker. He says you should cleanse yourself from contact with the world, not drink with soldiers, not eat with a Tatar.'

'Who says all that?' asked Olénin.

'Why, our teacher! But listen to a *múlla* or a Tatar Qadi.* He says, "You unbelieving Giaours, why do you eat pig?" That shows that everyone has his own law. But I think it's all one. God has made everything for the joy of man. There is no sin in any of it. Take example from an animal. It lives in the Tatar's reeds or in ours. Wherever it happens to go, there is its home! Whatever God gives it, that it eats! But our people say we have to lick red-hot plates in hell for that. And I think it's all a fraud,' he added after a pause.

'What is a fraud?' asked Olénin.

'Why, what the preachers say. We had an army captain in Chervlyóna who was my *kunák*: a fine fellow just like me. He was killed in Chechnyá. Well, he used to say that the preachers invent all that out of their own heads. "When you die the grass will grow on your grave and that's all!"' The old man laughed. 'He was a desperate fellow.'

'And how old are you?' asked Olénin.

'The Lord only knows! I must be about seventy. When the Tsaritsa* reigned in Russia I was no longer very small. So you can reckon it out. I must be seventy.'

'Yes you must, but you are still a fine fellow.'

'Well, thank Heaven I am healthy, quite healthy, except that a woman, a witch, has harmed me.'

'How?'

'Oh, just harmed me.'

'And so when you die the grass will grow?' repeated Olénin.

Eróshka evidently did not wish to express his thought clearly. He was silent for a while.

'And what did you think? Drink!' he shouted suddenly, smiling and handing Olénin some wine.

CHAPTER XV

'Well, what was I saying?' he continued, trying to remember. 'Yes, that's the sort of man I am. I am a hunter. There is no hunter to equal me in the whole army. I will find and show you any animal and any bird. What and where, I know it all! I have dogs, and two guns, and nets, and a screen and a hawk. I have everything, thank the Lord! If you are not bragging but are a real sportsman, I'll show you everything. Do you know what a man I am? When I have found a track—I know the animal. I know where he will lie down and where he'll drink or wallow. I make myself a perch and sit there all night watching. What's the good of staying at home? One only gets into mischief, gets drunk. And here women come and chatter, and boys shout at me—enough to drive one mad. It's a different matter when you go out at nightfall, choose yourself a place, press down the reeds and sit there and stay waiting, like a real brave. One knows everything that goes on in the woods. One looks up at the sky: the stars move, you look at them and find out from them how the time goes. One looks round—the wood is rustling; one goes on waiting, now there comes a crackling—a boar comes to rub himself; one listens to hear the young eaglets screech and then the cocks give voice in the village, or the geese. When you hear the geese you know it is not yet midnight. And I know all about it! Or when a gun is fired somewhere far away, thoughts come to me. One thinks, who is that firing? Is it another Cossack like myself who has been watching for some animal? And has he killed it? Or only wounded it so that now the poor thing goes through the reeds smearing them with its blood all for nothing? I don't like that! Oh, I don't like that! Why injure a beast? You fool, you fool! Or one thinks, "Maybe an *abrék* has killed some silly little Cossack." All this passes through one's mind. And once as I sat watching by the river I saw a cradle floating down. It was sound except for one corner which was broken off. Thoughts did come that time! I thought some of your soldiers, the devils, must have got into an *aúl* and seized the Chechén women, and one of the devils has killed the little one: taken it by its legs, and hit its head against a wall. Don't they do such things? Sh! Men have no souls! And thoughts came to me that filled me with pity. I thought: they've thrown away the cradle and driven the wife out, and her *dzhigít* has taken his gun and come across to our side to rob us. One watches and thinks. And when one hears a litter breaking through the thicket, something begins to knock inside one.

Dear one, come this way! "They'll scent me," one thinks; and one sits and does not stir while one's heart goes dun! dun! dun! and simply lifts you. Once this spring a fine litter came near me. I saw something black. "To the Father and to the Son," and I was just about to fire when she grunts to her pigs: "Danger, children," she says, "there's a man here," and off they all ran, breaking through the bushes. And she had been so close I could almost have bitten her.'

'How could a sow tell her brood that a man was there?' asked Olénin.

'What do you think? You think the beast's a fool? No, he is wiser than a man though you do call him a pig! He knows everything. Take this for instance. A man will pass along your track and not notice it; but a pig as soon as it gets onto your track turns and runs at once: that shows there is wisdom in him, since he scents your smell and you don't. And there is this to be said too: you wish to kill it and it wishes to go about the woods alive. You have one law and it has another. It is a pig, but it is no worse than you—it too is God's creature. Ah, dear! Man is foolish, foolish, foolish!' The old man repeated this several times and then, letting his head drop, he sat thinking.

Olénin also became thoughtful, and descending from the porch with his hands behind his back began pacing up and down the yard.

Eróshka, rousing himself, raised his head and began gazing intently at the moths circling round the flickering flame of the candle and burning themselves in it.

'Fool, fool!' he said. 'Where are you flying to? Fool, fool!' He rose and with his thick fingers began to drive away the moths.

'You'll burn, little fool! Fly this way, there's plenty of room.' He spoke tenderly, trying to catch them delicately by their wings with his thick fingers and then letting them fly again. 'You are killing yourself and I am sorry for you!'

He sat a long time chattering and sipping out of the bottle. Olénin paced up and down the yard. Suddenly he was struck by the sound of whispering outside the gate. Involuntarily holding his breath, he heard a woman's laughter, a man's voice, and the sound of a kiss. Intentionally rustling the grass under his feet he crossed to the opposite side of the yard, but after a while the wattle fence creaked. A Cossack in a dark *cherkéska* and a white sheepskin cap passed along the other side of the fence (it was Luke), and a tall woman with a white kerchief on her head went past Olénin. 'You and I have nothing to do with one another' was what Maryánka's firm step gave him to understand. He followed her with his eyes to the porch of the hut, and through the window he even saw her take off her kerchief and sit down. And suddenly a feeling of lonely depression and some vague longings and hopes, and envy of someone or other, overcame the young man's soul.

The last lights had been put out in the huts. The last sounds had died away in the village. The wattle fences and the cattle gleaming white in the yards, the roofs of the houses and the stately poplars, all seemed to be sleeping the labourers' healthy peaceful sleep. Only the incessant ringing voices of frogs from the damp distance reached the young man. In the east the stars were growing fewer and fewer and seemed to be melting in the increasing light, but overhead they were denser and deeper than before. The old man was dozing with his head on his hand. A cock crowed in the yard opposite, but Olénin still paced up and down thinking of something. The sound of a song sung by several voices reached him and he stepped up to the fence and listened. The voices of several young Cossacks carolled a merry song, and one voice was distinguishable among them all by its firm strength.

'Do you know who is singing there?' said the old man, rousing himself. 'It is Lukáshka, the *dzhigít*. He has killed a Chechén and now he rejoices. And what is there to rejoice at? . . . The fool, the fool!'

'And have you ever killed people?' asked Olénin.

'You devil!' shouted the old man. 'What are you asking? One must not talk so. It is a serious thing to destroy a human being. Ah, a very serious thing! Good-bye, my dear fellow. I've eaten my fill and am drunk,' he said rising. 'Shall I come tomorrow to go shooting?'

'Yes, come!'

'Mind, get up early; if you oversleep you will be fined!'

'Never fear, I'll be up before you,' answered Olénin.

The old man left. The song ceased, but one could hear footsteps and merry talk. A little later the singing broke out again but further away, and Eróshka's loud voice chimed in with the other. 'What people, what a life!' thought Olénin with a sigh as he returned alone to his hut.

CHAPTER XVI

Daddy Eróshka was a superannuated and solitary Cossack: twenty years ago his wife had gone over to the Orthodox Church and run away from him and married a Russian sergeant-major, and he had no children. He was not bragging when he spoke of himself as having been the boldest dare-devil in the village when he was young. Everybody in the regiment knew of his old-time prowess. The death of more than one Russian, as well as Chechén, lay on his conscience. He used to go plundering in the mountains, and robbed the Russians too; and he had twice been in prison. The greater part of his life was spent in the forests, hunting. There he lived for days on a crust of bread and drank nothing but water. But on the other hand, when he was in the village he made merry from morning to night. After leaving Olénin he slept for a couple of hours and awoke before it was light. He lay on his bed thinking of the man he had become acquainted with the evening before. Olénin's 'simplicity' (simplicity in the sense of not grudging him a drink) pleased him very much, and so did Olénin himself. He wondered why the Russians were all 'simple' and so rich, and why they were educated, and yet knew nothing. He pondered on these questions and also considered what he might get out of Olénin.

Daddy Eróshka's hut was of a good size and not old, but the absence of a woman was very noticeable in it. Contrary to the usual cleanliness of the Cossacks, the whole of this hut was filthy and exceedingly untidy. A blood-stained coat had been thrown on the table, half a dough-cake lay beside a plucked and mangled crow with which to feed the hawk. Sandals of raw hide, a gun, a dagger, a little bag, wet clothes, and sundry rags lay scattered on the benches. In a corner stood a tub with stinking water, in which another pair of sandals were being steeped, and near by was a gun and a hunting-screen. On the floor a net had been thrown down and several dead pheasants lay there, while a hen tied by its leg was walking about near the table pecking about in the dirt. In the unheated oven stood a broken pot with some kind of milky liquid. On the top of the oven a falcon was screeching and trying to break the cord by which it was tied, and a moulting hawk sat quietly on the edge of the oven, looking askance at the hen and occasionally bowing its head to right and left. Daddy Eróshka himself, in his shirt, lay on his back on a short bed rigged up between the wall and the oven, with his strong legs raised and his feet on the oven. He was picking with his thick fingers at the scratches left on his hands by the hawk, which he was accustomed to carry without wearing gloves. The whole room, especially near the old man, was filled with that strong but not unpleasant mixture of smells that he always carried about with him.

'*Úyde-ma*, Daddy?' (Is Daddy in?) He heard a sharp voice through the window, which he at once recognized as Lukáshka's.

'*Úyde, Úyde, Úyde*. I am in!' shouted the old man. 'Come in, neighbour Mark, Luke Mark. Come to see Daddy? On your way to the cordon?'

At the sound of his master's shout the hawk flapped his wings and pulled at his cord.

The old man was fond of Lukáshka, who was the only man he excepted from his general contempt for the younger generation of Cossacks. Besides that, Lukáshka and his mother, as near neighbours, often gave the old man wine, *kaymák*, and other home produce which Eróshka did not possess. Daddy Eróshka, who all his life had allowed himself to get carried away, always explained his infatuations from a practical point of view. 'Well, why not?' he used to say to himself. 'I'll give them some fresh meat, or a bird, and they won't forget Daddy: they'll sometimes bring a cake or a piece of pie.'

'Good morning, Mark! I am glad to see you,' shouted the old man cheerfully, and quickly putting down his bare feet he jumped off his bed and walked a step or two along the creaking floor, looked down at his out-turned toes, and suddenly, amused by the appearance of his feet, smiled, stamped with his bare heel on the ground, stamped again, and then performed a funny dance-step. 'That's clever, eh?' he asked, his small eyes glistening. Lukáshka smiled faintly. 'Going back to the cordon?' asked the old man.

'I have brought the *chikhír* I promised you when we were at the cordon.'

'May Christ save you!' said the old man, and he took up the extremely wide trousers that were lying on the floor, and his *beshmét*, put them on, fastened a strap round his waist, poured some water from an earthenware pot over his hands, wiped them on the old trousers, smoothed his beard with a bit of comb, and stopped in front of Lukáshka. 'Ready,' he said.

Lukáshka fetched a cup, wiped it and filled it with wine, and then handed it to the old man.

'Your health! To the Father and the Son!' said the old man, accepting the wine with solemnity. 'May you have what you desire, may you always be a hero, and obtain a cross.'

Lukáshka also drank a little after repeating a prayer, and then put the wine on the table. The old man rose and brought out some dried fish which he laid on the threshold, where he beat it with a stick to make it tender; then, having put it with his rough hands on a blue plate (his only one), he placed it on the table.

'I have all I want. I have food, thank God!' he said proudly. 'Well and what of Mósev?' he added.

Lukáshka, evidently wishing to know the old man's opinion, told him how the officer had taken the gun from him.

'Never mind the gun,' said the old man. 'If you don't give the gun you will get no reward.'

'But they say, Daddy, it's little reward a fellow gets when he is not yet a mounted Cossack; and the gun is a fine one, a Crimean, worth eighty rubles.'

'Eh, let it go! I had a dispute like that with an officer, he wanted my horse, "Give it me and you'll be made a cornet," says he. I wouldn't, and I got nothing!'

'Yes, Daddy, but you see I have to buy a horse; and they say you can't get one the other side of the river under fifty rubles, and mother has not yet sold our wine.'

'Eh, we didn't bother,' said the old man; 'when Daddy Eróshka was your age he already stole herds of horses from the Nogáy folk and drove them across the Térek. Sometimes we'd give a fine horse for a quart of vodka or a cloak.'

'Why so cheap?' asked Lukáshka.

'You're a fool, a fool, Mark,' said the old man contemptuously. 'Why, that's what one steals for, so as not to be stingy! As for you, I suppose you haven't so much as seen how one drives off a herd of horses? Why don't you speak?'

'What's one to say, Daddy?' replied Lukáshka. 'It seems we are not the same sort of men as you were.'

'You're a fool, Mark, a fool! "not the same sort of men!"' retorted the old man, mimicking the Cossack lad. 'I was not that sort of Cossack at your age.'

'How's that?' asked Lukáshka.

The old man shook his head contemptuously.

'Daddy Eróshka was *simple*; he did not grudge anything! That's why I was *kunák* with all Chechnyá. A *kunák* would come to visit me and I'd make him drunk with vodka and make him happy and put him to sleep with me, and when I went to see him I'd take him a present—a dagger! That's the way it is done, and not as you do nowadays: the only amusement lads have now is to crack seeds and spit out the shells!' the old man finished contemptuously, imitating the present-day Cossacks cracking seeds and spitting out the shells.

'Yes, I know,' said Lukáshka; 'that's so!'

'If you wish to be a fellow of the right sort, be a *dzhigít* and not a peasant! Because even a peasant can buy a horse—pay the money and take the horse.'

They were silent for a while.

'Well of course it's boring both in the village and the cordon, Daddy: but there's nowhere one can go for a bit of sport. All our fellows are so timid. Take Nazárka. The other day when we went to the *aúl*, Girèy Khan asked us to come to Nogáy to take some horses, but no one went, and how was I to go alone?'

'And what of Daddy? Do you think I am quite dried up? No, I'm not dried up. Let me have a horse and I'll be off to Nogáy at once.'

'What's the good of talking nonsense!' said Luke. 'You'd

better tell me what to do about Giréy Khan. He says, "Only bring horses to the Térek, and then even if you bring a whole herd I'll find a place for them." You see he's also a shaven-headed Tatar—how's one to believe him?'

'You may trust Giréy Khan, all his kin were good people. His father too was a faithful *kunák*. But listen to Daddy and I won't teach you wrong: make him take an oath, then it will be all right. And if you go with him, have your pistol ready all the same, especially when it comes to dividing up the horses. I was nearly killed that way once by a Chechén. I wanted ten rubles from him for a horse. Trusting is all right, but don't go to sleep without a gun.'

Lukáshka listened attentively to the old man.

'I say, Daddy, have you any stone-break grass?' he asked after a pause.

'No, I haven't any, but I'll teach you how to get it. You're a good lad and won't forget the old man. Shall I tell you?'

'Tell me, Daddy.'

'You know a tortoise? She's a devil, the tortoise is!'

'Of course I know!'

'Find her nest and fence it round so that she can't get in. Well, she'll come, go round it, and then will go off to find the stone-break grass and will bring some along and destroy the fence. Anyhow next morning come in good time, and where the fence is broken there you'll find the stone-break grass lying. Take it wherever you like. No lock and no bar will be able to stop you.'

'Have you tried it yourself, Daddy?'

'As for trying, I have not tried it, but I was told of it by good people. I used only one charm: that was to repeat the pilgrim song when mounting my horse; and no one ever killed me!'

'What is the pilgrim song, Daddy?'

'What, don't you know it? Oh, what people! You're right to ask Daddy. Well, listen, and repeat after me:

'Hail! Ye, living in Sion,
This is your King,
Our steeds we shall sit on,

Sophonius is weeping.
Zacharias is speaking,
Father Pilgrim,
Mankind ever loving.

'Kind ever loving,' the old man repeated. 'Do you know it now? Try it.'

Lukáshka laughed.

'Come, Daddy, was it that that hindered their killing you? Maybe it just happened so!'

'You've grown too clever! You learn it all, and say it. It will do you no harm. Well, suppose you have sung "Pilgrim" it's all right,' and the old man himself began laughing. 'But just one thing, Luke, don't you go to Nogáy!'

'Why?'

'Times have changed. You are not the same men. You've become rubbishy Cossacks! And see how many Russians have come down on us! You'd get to prison. Really, give it up! Just as if you could! Now Gírchik and I, we used . . .'

And the old man was about to begin one of his endless tales, but Lukáshka glanced at the window and interrupted him.

'It is quite light, Daddy. It's time to be off. Look us up some day.'

'May Christ save you! I'll go to the officer; I promised to take him out shooting. He seems a good fellow.'

CHAPTER XVII

From Eróshka's hut Lukáshka went home. As he returned, the dewy mists were rising from the ground and enveloped the village. In various places the cattle, though out of sight, could be heard beginning to stir. The cocks called to one another with increasing frequency and insistence. The air was becoming more transparent, and the villagers were getting up. Not till he was close to it could Lukáshka discern the fence of his yard, all wet with dew, the porch of the hut, and the open shed. From the misty yard he heard the sound of an axe chopping wood. Lukáshka entered the hut. His mother was up, and stood at the oven throwing wood into it. His little sister was still lying in bed asleep.

'Well, Lukáshka, had enough holiday-making?' asked his mother softly. 'Where did you spend the night?'

'I was in the village,' replied her son reluctantly, reaching for his musket, which he drew from its cover and examined carefully.

His mother swayed her head.

Lukáshka poured a little gunpowder onto the pan, took out a little bag from which he drew some empty cartridge cases which he began filling, carefully plugging each one with a ball wrapped in a rag. Then, having tested the loaded cartridges with his teeth and examined them, he put down the bag.

'I say, Mother, I told you the bags wanted mending; have they been done?' he asked.

'Oh yes, our dumb one was mending something last night. Why, is it time for you to be going back to the cordon? I haven't seen anything of you!'

'Yes, as soon as I have got ready I shall have to go,' answered Lukáshka, tying up the gunpowder. 'And where is our dumb one? Outside?'

'Chopping wood, I expect. She kept fretting for you. "I shall not see him at all!" she said. She puts her hand to her face like this, and clicks her tongue and presses her hands to her heart as much as to say—"sorry." Shall I call her in? She understood all about the *abrék*.'

'Call her,' said Lukáshka. 'And I had some tallow there; bring it: I must grease my sword.'

The old woman went out, and a few minutes later Lukáshka's dumb sister came up the creaking steps and entered the hut. She was six years older than her brother and would have been extremely like him had it not been for the dull and coarsely changeable expression (common to all deaf and dumb people) of her face. She wore a coarse smock all patched; her feet were bare and muddy, and on her head she had an old blue kerchief. Her neck, arms, and face were sinewy like a peasant's. Her clothing and her whole appearance indicated that she always did the hard work of a man. She brought in a heap of logs which she threw down by the oven. Then she went up to her brother, and with a joyful smile which made her whole face pucker up, touched him on the shoulder and began making rapid signs to him with her hands, her face, and whole body.

'That's right, that's right, Styópka is great!' answered the brother, nodding. 'She's fetched everything and mended everything, she's great! Here, take this for it!' He brought out two pieces of gingerbread from his pocket and gave them to her.

The dumb woman's face flushed with pleasure, and she began making a weird noise for joy. Having seized the gingerbread she began to gesticulate still more rapidly, frequently pointing in one direction and passing her thick finger over her eyebrows and her face. Lukáshka understood her and kept nodding, while he smiled slightly. She was telling him to give the girls dainties, and that the girls liked him, and that one girl, Maryánka—the best of them all—loved him. She indicated Maryánka by rapidly pointing in the direction of Maryánka's home and to her own eyebrows and face, and by smacking her lips and swaying her head. 'Loves' she expressed by pressing her hands to her breast, kissing her hand, and pretending to embrace someone. Their mother returned to the hut, and seeing what her dumb daughter was saying, smiled and shook her head. Her daughter showed her the gingerbread and again made the noise which expressed joy.

'I told Ulítka the other day that I'd send a matchmaker to them,' said the mother. 'She took my words well.'

Lukáshka looked silently at his mother.

'But how about selling the wine, mother? I need a horse.'

'I'll cart it when I have time. I must get the barrels ready,' said the mother, evidently not wishing her son to meddle in domestic matters. 'When you go out you'll find a bag in the passage. I borrowed from the neighbours and got something for you to take back to the cordon; or shall I put it in your saddle-bag?'

'All right,' answered Lukáshka. 'And if Giréy Khan should come across the river send him to me at the cordon, for I shan't get leave again for a long time now; I have some business with him.'

He began to get ready to start.

'I will send him on,' said the old woman. 'It seems you have been spreeing at Yámka's all the time. I went out in the night to see the cattle, and I think it was your voice I heard singing songs.'

Lukáshka did not reply, but went out into the passage, threw the bags over his shoulder, tucked up the skirts of his coat, took his musket, and then stopped for a moment on the threshold.

'Good-bye, mother!' he said as he closed the gate behind him. 'Send me a small barrel of wine with Nazárka. I promised it to the lads, and he'll call for it.'

'May Christ keep you, Lukáshka. God be with you! I'll send you some, some from the new barrel,' said the old woman, going to the fence: 'But listen,' she added, leaning over the fence.

The Cossack stopped.

'You've been making merry here; well, that's all right. Why should not a young man amuse himself? God has sent you luck and that's good. But now look out and mind, my son. Don't you go and get into mischief. Above all, satisfy your superiors: one has to! And I will sell the wine and find money for a horse and will arrange a match with the girl for you.'

'All right, all right!' answered her son, frowning.

His deaf sister shouted to attract his attention. She pointed to her head and the palm of her hand, to indicate the shaved head of a Chechén. Then she frowned, and pretending to aim with a gun, she shrieked and began rapidly humming and shaking her head. This meant that Lukáshka should kill another Chechén.

Lukáshka understood. He smiled, and shifting the gun at his back under his cloak stepped lightly and rapidly, and soon disappeared in the thick mist.

The old woman, having stood a little while at the gate, returned silently to the hut and immediately began working.

CHAPTER XVIII

Lukáshka returned to the cordon and at the same time Daddy Eróshka whistled to his dogs and, climbing over his wattle fence, went to Olénin's lodging, passing by the back of the houses (he disliked meeting women before going out hunting or shooting). He found Olénin still asleep, and even Vanyúsha, though awake, was still in bed and looking round the room considering whether it was not time to get up, when Daddy Eróshka, gun on shoulder and in full hunter's trappings, opened the door.

'A cudgel!' he shouted in his deep voice, 'An alarm! The Chechéns are upon us! Iván! Get the samovar ready for your master, and get up yourself—quick!' cried the old man. 'That's our way, my good man! Why even the girls are already up! Look out of the window. See, she's going for water and you're still sleeping!'

Olénin awoke and jumped up, feeling fresh and light-hearted at the sight of the old man and at the sound of his voice.

'Quick, Vanyúsha, quick!' he cried.

'Is that the way you go hunting?' said the old man. 'Others are having their breakfast and you are asleep! Lyam! Here!' he called to his dog. 'Is your gun ready?' he shouted, as loud as if a whole crowd were in the hut.

'Well, it's true I'm guilty, but it can't be helped! The powder, Vanyúsha, and the wads!' said Olénin.

'A fine!' shouted the old man.

'*Du tay voolay voo?*'[1] asked Vanyúsha, grinning.

'You're not one of us—your gabble is not like our speech, you devil!' the old man shouted at Vanyúsha, showing the stumps of his teeth.

'A first offence must be forgiven,' said Olénin playfully, drawing on his high boots.

'The first offence shall be forgiven,' answered Eróshka, 'but if you oversleep another time you'll be fined a pail of *chikhír*. When it gets warmer you won't find the deer.'

'And even if we do find him he is wiser than we are,' said Olénin, repeating the words spoken by the old man the evening before, 'and you can't deceive him!'

'Yes, laugh away! You kill one first, and then you may talk. Now then, hurry up! Look, there's the master himself coming to see you,' added Eróshka, looking out of the window. 'Just see how he's got himself up. He's put on a new coat so that you should see that he's an officer. Ah, these people, these people!'

Sure enough, Vanyúsha came in and announced that the master of the house wished to see Olénin.

[1] Do you want some tea?

'*Larjan*!'[1] he remarked profoundly, to forewarn his master of the meaning of this visitation. Following him, the master of the house in a new *cherkéska* with an officer's stripes on the shoulders and with polished boots (quite exceptional among Cossacks) entered the room, swaying fom side to side, and congratulated his lodger on his safe arrival.

The cornet, Elias Vasílich, was an *educated* Cossack. He had been to Russia proper, was a regimental school-teacher, and above all he was noble. He wished to appear noble, but one could not help feeling that beneath his grotesque pretence of polish, his affectation, his self-confidence, and his absurd way of speaking, he was just the same as Daddy Eróshka. This could also be clearly seen by his sunburnt face and his hands and his red nose. Olénin asked him to sit down.

'Good morning, Father Elias Vasílich,' said Eróshka, rising with (or so it seemed to Olénin) an ironically low bow.

'Good morning, Daddy. So you're here already,' said the cornet, with a careless nod.

The cornet was a man of about forty, with a grey pointed beard, skinny and lean, but handsome and very fresh-looking for his age. Having come to see Olénin he was evidently afraid of being taken for an ordinary Cossack, and wanted to let Olénin feel his importance from the first.

'That's our Egyptian Nimrod,'* he remarked, addressing Olénin and pointing to the old man with a self-satisfied smile. 'A mighty hunter before the Lord! He's our foremost man on every hand. You've already been pleased to get acquainted with him.'

Daddy Eróshka gazed at his feet in their shoes of wet raw hide and shook his head thoughtfully at the cornet's ability and learning, and muttered to himself: 'Gyptian Nimvrod! What things he invents!'

'Yes, you see we mean to go hunting,' answered Olénin.

'Yes, sir, exactly,' said the cornet, 'but I have a small bit of business with you.'

'What do you want?'

'Seeing that you are a gentleman,' began the cornet, 'and as I may understand myself to be in the rank of an officer too, and

[1] Money!

therefore we may always progressively negotiate, as gentlemen do' (he stopped and looked with a smile at Olénin and at the old man). 'But if you have the desire with my consent, then, as my wife is a foolish woman of our class, she could not quite comprehend your words of yesterday's date. Therefore my quarters might be let for six rubles to the regimental adjutant, without the stables; but I can always avert that from myself free of charge. But, as you desire, therefore I, being myself of an officer's rank, can come to an agreement with you in everything personally, as an inhabitant of this district, not according to our customs, but can maintain the conditions in every way.'

'Speaks clearly!' muttered the old man.

The cornet continued in the same strain for a long time. At last, not without difficulty, Olénin gathered that the cornet wished to let his rooms to him, Olénin, for six rubles a month. The latter gladly agreed to this, and offered his visitor a glass of tea. The cornet declined it.

'According to our silly custom we consider it a sort of sin to drink out of a "worldly" tumbler,' he said. 'Though, of course, with my education I may understand, but my wife from her human weakness . . .'

'Well then, will you have some tea?'

'If you will permit me, I will bring my own particular glass,' answered the cornet, and stepped out onto the porch. 'Bring me my glass!' he cried.

In a few minutes the door opened and a young sunburnt arm in a print sleeve thrust itself in, holding a tumbler in the hand. The cornet went up, took it, and whispered something to his daughter. Olénin poured tea for the cornet into the latter's own 'particular' glass, and for Eróshka into a 'worldly' glass.

'However, I do not desire to detain you,' said the cornet, scalding his lips and emptying his tumbler. 'I too have a great liking for fishing, and I am here, so to say, only on leave of absence for recreation from my duties. I too have the desire to tempt fortune and see whether some *Gifts of the Térek** may not fall to my share. I hope you too will come and see us and have a drink of our wine, according to the custom of our village,' he added.

The cornet bowed, shook hands with Olénin, and went out.

While Olénin was getting ready, he heard the cornet giving orders to his family in an authoritative and sensible tone, and a few minutes later he saw him pass by the window in a tattered coat with his trousers rolled up to his knees and a fishing net over his shoulder.

'A rascal!' said Daddy Eróshka, emptying his 'worldly' tumbler. 'And will you really pay him six rubles? Was such a thing ever heard of? They would let you the best hut in the village for two rubles. What a beast! Why, I'd let you have mine for three!'

'No, I'll remain here,' said Olénin.

'Six rubles! Clearly it's a fool's money. Eh, eh, eh!' answered the old man. 'Let's have some *chikhír*, Iván!'

Having had a snack and a drink of vodka to prepare themselves for the road, Olénin and the old man went out together before eight o'clock.

At the gate they came up against a wagon to which a pair of oxen were harnessed. With a white kerchief tied round her head down to her eyes, a coat over her smock, and wearing high boots, Maryánka with a long switch in her hand was dragging the oxen by a cord tied to their horns.

'Mammy,' said the old man, pretending that he was going to seize her.

Maryánka flourished her switch at him and glanced merrily at them both with her beautiful eyes.

Olénin felt still more light-hearted.

'Now then, come on, come on,' he said, throwing his gun on his shoulder and conscious of the girl's eyes upon him.

'Gee up!' sounded Maryánka's voice behind them, followed by the creak of the moving wagon.

As long as their road lay through the pastures at the back of the village Eróshka went on talking. He could not forget the cornet and kept on abusing him.

'Why are you so angry with him?' asked Olénin.

'He's stingy. I don't like it,' answered the old man. 'He'll leave it all behind when he dies! Then who's he saving up for? He's built two houses, and he's got a second garden from his brother by a law-suit. And in the matter of papers what a dog he is! They come to him from other villages to fill up documents. As he writes it out, exactly so it happens. He gets it quite exact. But who is he saving for? He's only got one boy and the girl; when she's married who'll be left?'

'Well then, he's saving up for her dowry,' said Olénin.

'What dowry? The girl is sought after, she's a fine girl. But he's such a devil that he must yet marry her to a rich fellow. He wants to get a big price for her. There's Luke, a Cossack, a neighbour and a nephew of mine, a fine lad. It's he who killed the Chechén—he has been wooing her for a long time, but he hasn't let him have her. He's given one excuse, and another, and a third. "The girl's too young," he says. But I know what he is thinking. He wants to keep them bowing to him. He's been acting shamefully about that girl. Still, they will get Lukáshka for her, because he is the best Cossack in the village, a *dzhigít*, who has killed an *abrék* and will be rewarded with a cross.'

'But how about this? When I was walking up and down the yard last night, I saw my landlord's daughter and some Cossack kissing,' said Olénin.

'You're pretending!' cried the old man, stopping.

'On my word,' said Olénin.

'Women are the devil,' said Eróshka pondering. 'But what Cossack was it?'

'I couldn't see.'

'Well, what sort of a cap had he, a white one?'

'Yes.'

'And a red coat? About your height?'

'No, a bit taller.'

'It's him!' and Eróshka burst out laughing. 'It's him, it's Mark. He is Luke, but I call him Mark for a joke. It's him himself! I love him. I was just such a one myself. What's the good of minding them? My sweetheart used to sleep with her mother and her sister-in-law, but I managed to get in. She used to sleep upstairs; that witch her mother was a regular demon; it's awful how she hated me. Well, I used to come with a chum, Gírchik his name was. We'd come under her window and I'd climb on his shoulders, push up the window and begin groping about. She used to sleep just there on a bench. Once I woke her up and she nearly called out. She hadn't recognized me. "Who is there?" she said and I could not answer. Her mother was even beginning to stir, but I took off my cap and shoved it over her mouth; and she at once knew it by the seam in it, and ran out to me. I used not to want for anything then. She'd bring along *kaymák* and grapes and everything,' added Eróshka (who always explained things practically), 'and she wasn't the only one. It was a life!'

'And what now?'

'Now we'll follow the dog, get a pheasant to settle on a tree, and then you may fire.'

'Would you have made up to Maryánka?'

'Attend to the dogs. I'll tell you tonight,' said the old man, pointing to his favourite dog, Lyam.

After a pause they continued talking, while they went about a hundred paces. Then the old man stopped again and pointed to a twig that lay across the path.

'What do you think of that?' he said. 'You think it's nothing? It's bad that this stick is lying so.'

'Why is it bad?'

He smiled.

'Ah, you don't know anything. Just listen to me. When a stick lies like that don't you step across it, but go round it or throw it off the path this way, and pray "To the Father and the Son and the Holy Ghost," and then go on with God's blessing. Nothing will happen to you. That's what the old men used to teach me.'

'Come, what rubbish!' said Olénin. 'You'd better tell me more about Maryánka. Does she carry on with Lukáshka?'

'Hush, . . . be quiet now!' the old man again interrupted in a whisper: 'just listen, we'll go round through the forest.'

And the old man, stepping quietly in his soft shoes, led the way by a narrow path leading into the dense, wild, overgrown forest. Now and again with a frown he turned to look at Olénin, who rustled and clattered with his heavy boots and, carrying his gun carelessly, several times caught the twigs of trees that grew across the path.

'Don't make a noise. Step softly, soldier!' the old man whispered angrily.

There was a feeling in the air that the sun had risen. The mist was dissolving but it still enveloped the tops of the trees. The forest looked terribly high. At every step the view changed: what had appeared like a tree proved to be a bush, and a reed looked like a tree.

CHAPTER XIX

The mist had partly lifted, showing the wet reed thatches, and was now turning into dew that moistened the road and the grass beside the fence. Smoke rose everywhere in clouds from the chimneys. The people were going out of the village, some to their work, some to the river, and some to the cordon. The hunters walked together along the damp, grass-grown path. The dogs, wagging their tails and looking at their masters, ran on both sides of them. Myriads of gnats hovered in the air and pursued the hunters, covering their backs, eyes, and hands. The air was fragrant with the grass and with the dampness of the forest. Olénin continually looked round at the ox-cart in which Maryánka sat urging on the oxen with a long switch.

It was calm. The sounds from the village, audible at first, now no longer reached the sportsmen. Only the brambles cracked as the dogs ran under them, and now and then birds called to one another. Olénin knew that danger lurked in the forest, that *abréks* always hid in such places. But he knew too that in the forest, for a man on foot, a gun is a great protection. Not that he was afraid, but he felt that another in his place might be; and looking into the damp misty forest and listening to the rare and faint sounds with strained attention, he changed his hold on his gun and experienced a pleasant feeling that was new to him. Daddy Eróshka went in front, stopping and carefully scanning every puddle where an animal had left a double track, and pointing it out to Olénin. He hardly spoke at all and only occasionally made remarks in a whisper. The path they were following had once been made by wagons, but the grass had long overgrown it. The elm and plane-tree forest on both sides of them was so dense and overgrown with brushwood that it was impossible to see anything through it. Nearly every tree was enveloped from top to bottom with wild grape vines, and dark bramble bushes covered the ground thickly. Every little glade was overgrown with blackberry bushes and grey feathery reeds. In places, large hoof-prints and small funnel-shaped pheasant-trails led from the path into the thicket. The vigour of the growth of this forest, untrampled by cattle, struck Olénin at every turn, for he had never seen anything like it. This forest, the danger, the old man and his mysterious whispering, Maryánka with her virile upright bearing, and the mountains—all this seemed to him like a dream.

'A pheasant has settled,' whispered the old man, looking round and pulling his cap over his face—'Cover your mug! A pheasant!' he waved his arm angrily at Olénin and pushed forward almost on all fours. 'He don't like a man's mug.'

Olénin was still behind him when the old man stopped and began examining a tree. A cock-pheasant on the tree clucked at the dog that was barking at it, and Olénin saw the pheasant; but at that moment a report, as of a cannon, came from Eróshka's enormous gun, the bird fluttered up and, losing some feathers, fell to the ground. Coming up to the old man Olénin disturbed another, and raising his gun he aimed and fired. The pheasant flew swiftly up and then, catching at the branches as he fell, dropped like a stone to the ground.

'Good man!' the old man (who could not hit a flying bird) shouted laughing.

Having picked up the pheasants they went on. Olénin, excited by the exercise and the praise, kept addressing remarks to the old man.

'Stop! Come this way,' the old man interrupted. 'I noticed a deer track here yesterday.'

After they had turned into the thicket and gone some three hundred paces they scrambled through into a glade overgrown with reeds and partly under water. Olénin failed to keep up with the old huntsman and presently Daddy Eróshka, some twenty paces in front, stooped down, nodding and beckoning with his arm. On coming up with him Olénin saw a man's footprint to which the old man was pointing.

'D'you see?'

'Yes, well?' said Olénin, trying to speak as calmly as he could. 'A man's footprint!'

Involuntarily a thought of Cooper's *Pathfinder** and of

abréks flashed through Olénin's mind, but noticing the mysterious manner with which the old man moved on, he hesitated to question him and remained in doubt whether this mysteriousness was caused by fear of danger or by the sport.

'No, it's my own footprint,' the old man said quietly, and pointed to some grass under which the track of an animal was just perceptible.

The old man went on, and Olénin kept up with him. Descending to lower ground some twenty paces farther on they came upon a spreading pear-tree, under which, on the black earth, lay the fresh dung of some animal.

The spot, all covered over with wild vines, was like a cosy arbour, dark and cool.

'He's been here this morning,' said the old man with a sigh; 'the lair is still damp, quite fresh.'

Suddenly they heard a terrible crash in the forest some ten paces from where they stood. They both started and seized their guns, but they could see nothing and only heard the branches breaking. The rhythmical rapid thud of galloping was heard for a moment and then changed into a hollow rumble which resounded farther and farther off, re-echoing in wider and wider circles through the forest. Olénin felt as though something had snapped in his heart. He peered carefully but vainly into the green thicket and then turned to the old man. Daddy Eróshka with his gun pressed to his breast stood motionless; his cap was thrust backwards, his eyes gleamed with an unwonted glow, and his open mouth, with its worn yellow teeth, seemed to have stiffened in that position.

'A horned stag!' he muttered, and throwing down his gun in despair he began pulling at his grey beard. 'Here it stood. We should have come round by the path. Fool! fool!' and he gave his beard an angry tug. 'Fool! Pig!' he repeated, pulling painfully at his own beard. Through the forest something seemed to fly away in the mist, and ever farther and farther off was heard the sound of the flight of the stag.

It was already dusk when, hungry, tired, but full of vigour, Olénin returned with the old man. Dinner was ready. He ate and drank with the old man till he felt warm and merry. Olénin then went out onto the porch. Again, to the west, the mountains rose before his eyes. Again the old man told his endless stories of hunting, of *abréks*, of sweethearts, and of all that free and reckless life. Again the fair Maryánka went in and out and across the yard, her beautiful powerful form outlined by her smock.

CHAPTER XX

The next day Olénin went alone to the spot where he and the old man had startled the stag.* Instead of passing round through the gate he climbed over the prickly hedge, as everybody else did, and before he had had time to pull out the thorns that had caught in his coat, his dog, which had run on in front, startled two pheasants. He had hardly walked into the briers when the pheasants flew up wherever he stepped (the old man had not shown him that place the day before as he meant to keep it for shooting from behind the screen). Olénin fired twelve times and killed five pheasants, but clambering after them through the briers he got so fatigued that he was drenched with perspiration. He called off his dog, uncocked his gun, put in a bullet above the small shot, and brushing away the mosquitoes with the wide sleeve of his *cherkéska* he went slowly to the spot where they had been the day before. It was however impossible to keep back the dog, who found trails on the very path, and Olénin killed two more pheasants, so that after being detained by this it was getting towards noon before he began to find the place he was looking for.

The day was perfectly clear, calm, and hot. The morning moisture had dried up even in the forest, and myriads of mosquitoes literally covered his face, his back, and his arms. His dog had turned from black to grey, its back being covered with mosquitoes, and so had Olénin's coat through which the insects thrust their stings. Olénin was ready to run away from them and it seemed to him that it was impossible to live in this country in the summer. He was about to go home, but remembering that other people managed to endure such pain he resolved to bear it and gave himself up to being devoured. And strange to say, by noontime the feeling became actually pleasant. He even felt that without this mosquito-filled atmosphere around him, and that mosquito-paste mingled with perspiration which his hand smeared over his face, and that unceasing irritation all over his body, the forest would lose for him some of its character and charm. These myriads of insects were so well suited to this monstrously lavish wild vegetation, these multitudes of birds and beasts which filled the forest, this dark foliage, this hot scented air, these runlets filled with turbid water which everywhere soaked through from the Térek and gurgled here and there under the overhanging leaves, that the very thing which had at first seemed to him dreadful and intolerable now seemed pleasant. After going round the place where yesterday they had found the animal and not finding anything, he felt inclined to rest. The sun stood right above the forest and poured its perpendicular rays down on his back and head whenever he came out into a glade or onto the road. The seven heavy pheasants dragged painfully at his waist. Having found the hoofprints of yesterday's stag he crept under a bush into the thicket just where the stag had lain, and lay down in its lair. He examined the dark foliage around him, the place marked by the stag's perspiration and yesterday's dung, the imprint of the stag's knees, the bit of black earth it had kicked up, and his own footprints of the day before. He felt cool and comfortable and did not think of or wish for anything. And suddenly he was overcome by such a strange feeling of causeless joy and of love for everything, that from an old habit of his childhood he began crossing himself and thanking someone. Suddenly, with extraordinary clarity, he thought: 'Here am I, Dmítri Olénin, a being quite distinct from every other being, now lying all alone Heaven only knows where—where a stag used to live—an old stag, a beautiful stag who perhaps had never seen a man, and in a place where no human being has ever sat or thought these thoughts. Here I sit, and around me stand old and young trees, one of them festooned with wild grape vines, and pheasants are fluttering, driving one another about and perhaps scenting their murdered brothers.' He felt his pheasants, examined them, and wiped the warm blood off his hand onto his coat. 'Perhaps the jackals scent them and with dissatisfied faces go off in another direction: above me, flying in among the leaves which to them seem enormous islands, mosquitoes hang in the air and buzz: one, two, three, four, a hundred, a thousand, a million mosquitoes, and around me all of them buzz something and for some reason and each one of them is just such a Dmítri Olénin separate from all as I am myself.' He vividly imagined what the mosquitoes buzzed: 'This way, this way, lads! Here's some one we can eat!' They buzzed and stuck to him. And it was clear to him that he was not a Russian nobleman, a member of Moscow society, the friend and relation of so-and-so and so-and-so, but just such a mosquito, or pheasant, or stag, as those that were now living all around him. 'Just as they, just as Daddy Eróshka, I shall live awhile and die, and as he says truly: "just the grass will grow".'

'But so what that the grass will grow?' he continued thinking, 'Still I must live and be happy, because happiness is all I desire. Never mind what I am—an animal like all the rest, above whom the grass will grow and nothing more, or a frame in which a bit of the one God has been set—still I must live in the very best way. How then must I live to be happy, and why was I not happy before?' And he began to recall his former life and he felt disgusted with himself. He appeared to himself to have been a terribly exacting egoist, though he really needed nothing for himself. And he looked round at the foliage with the light shining through it, at the setting sun and the clear sky, and he felt just as happy as before. 'Why am I happy, and what did I use to live for?' thought he. 'How exacting I was for myself; how I schemed and did not manage to gain anything but shame and sorrow! and, here now, I require nothing to be happy;' and suddenly a new light seemed to reveal itself to him. 'Happiness is this!' he said to himself, 'Happiness lies in living for others. That is evident. The desire for happiness is innate in every man; therefore it is legitimate. When trying to satisfy it egoistically—that is, by seeking for oneself riches, fame, comforts, or love—it may happen that circumstances arise which make it impossible to satisfy these desires. It follows that it is these desires that are illegitimate, but not the need for happiness. But what desires can always be satisfied despite external circumstances? What are they? Love, self-sacrifice.' He was so glad and excited when he had discovered this, as it seemed to him, new truth, that he jumped up and began impatiently seeking some one to sacrifice himself for, to do good to and to love. 'Since one wants nothing for oneself,' he kept thinking, 'why not live for others?' He took up his gun with the intention of returning home quickly to think this out and to find an opportunity of going good. He made his way out of the thicket. When he had come out into the glade he looked around him; the sun was no longer visible above the tree-tops. It had grown cooler and the place seemed to him quite strange and not like the country round the village. Everything seemed changed—the weather and the character of the forest; the sky was wrapped in clouds, the wind was rustling in the tree-tops, and all around nothing was visible but reeds and dying broken-down trees. He called to his dog who had run away to follow some animal, and his voice came back as in a desert. And suddenly he became terrified and awestruck. He grew frightened. He remembered the *abréks* and the murders he had been told about, and he expected every moment that an *abrék* would spring from behind every bush and he would have to defend his life and die, or be a coward. He thought of God and of the future life as he had not thought about them for a long time. And all around was that same gloomy stern wild nature. 'And is it worth while living for oneself,' thought he, 'when at any moment you may die, and die without having done any good, and so that no one will know of it?' He went in the direction where he fancied the village lay. Of his hunting he had no further thought; but he felt tired to death and peered round at every bush and tree with particular attention and almost with terror, expecting every moment to be called to account for his life. After having wandered about for a considerable time he came upon a ditch down which was flowing cold sandy water from the Térek, and, not to go astray any longer, he decided to follow it. He went on without knowing where the ditch would lead him. Suddenly the reeds behind him crackled. He shuddered and seized his gun, and then felt ashamed of himself: the over-excited dog, panting hard, had thrown itself into the cold water of the ditch and was lapping it!

He too had a drink, and then followed the dog in the direction it wished to go, thinking it would lead him to the village. But despite the dog's company everything around him seemed still more dreary. The forest grew darker and the wind grew stronger and stronger in the tops of the broken old trees. Some large birds circled screeching round their nests in those trees. The vegetation grew poorer and he oftener came upon rustling reeds and bare sandy spaces covered with animal footprints. To the howling of the wind was added another kind of cheerless monotonous roar. Altogether his spirits became gloomy. Putting his hand behind him he felt his pheasants, and found one missing. It had broken off and was lost, and only the bleeding head and beak remained sticking in his belt. He felt more frightened than he ever had before. He began to pray to God, and feared above all that he might die without having done anything good or kind; and he so wanted to live, and to live so as to perform a feat of self-sacrifice.

CHAPTER XXI

Suddenly it was as though the sun had shone into his soul. He heard Russian being spoken, and also heard the rapid smooth flow of the Térek, and a few steps farther in front of him saw the brown moving surface of the river, with the dim-coloured wet sand of its banks and shallows, the distant steppe, the cordon watch-tower outlined above the water, a saddled and hobbled horse among the brambles, and then the mountains opening out before him. The red sun appeared for an instant from under a cloud and its last rays glittered brightly along the river over the reeds, on the watch-tower, and on a group of Cossacks, among whom Lukáshka's vigorous figure attracted Olénin's involuntary attention.

Olénin felt that he was again, without any apparent cause, perfectly happy. He had come upon the Nízhni-Protótsk post on the Térek, opposite a pro-Russian *aúl* on the other side of the river. He accosted the Cossacks, but not finding as yet any excuse for doing anyone a kindness, he entered the hut; nor in the hut did he find any such opportunity. The Cossacks received him coldly. On entering the mud hut he lit a cigarette. The Cossacks paid little attention to him, first because he was smoking a cigarette, and secondly because they had something else to divert them that evening. Some hostile Chechéns, relatives of the *abrék* who had been killed, had come from the hills with a scout to ransom the body; and the Cossacks were waiting for their commanding officer's arrival from the village. The dead man's brother, tall and well shaped with a short cropped beard which was dyed red, despite his very tattered coat and cap was calm and majestic as a king. His face was very like that of the dead *abrék*. He did not deign to look at anyone and never once glanced at the dead body, but sitting on his heels in the shade he spat as he smoked his short pipe, and occasionally uttered a few guttural sounds of command, which were respectfully listened to by his companion. He was evidently a *dzhigít* who had met Russians more than once before in quite other circumstances, and nothing about them could astonish or even interest him. Olénin was about to approach the dead body and had begun to look at it when the brother, looking up at him from under his brows with calm contempt, said something sharply and angrily. The scout hastened to cover the dead man's face with his coat. Olénin was struck by the dignified and stern expression of the *dzhigít's* face. He began to speak to him, asking from what *aúl* he came, but the Chechén, scarcely giving him a glance, spat contemptuously and turned away. Olénin was so surprised at the Chechén not being interested in him that he could only put it down to the man's stupidity or ignorance of Russian; so he turned to the scout, who also acted as interpreter. The scout was as ragged as the other, but instead of being red haired he was black haired, restless, with extremely white gleaming teeth and sparkling black eyes. The scout willingly entered into conversation and asked for a cigarette.

'There were five brothers,' began the scout in his broken Russian. 'This is the third brother the Russians have killed, only two are left. He is a *dzhigít*, a great *dzhigít*!' he said, pointing to the Chechén. 'When they killed Akhmet Khan (that was the dead *abrék*'s name) this one was sitting on the opposite bank among the reeds. He saw it all. Saw him laid in the skiff and brought to the bank. He sat there till the night and wished to kill the old man, but the others would not let him.'

Lukáshka went up to the speaker, and sat down.

'Of what *aúl*?' he asked.

'From there in the hills,' replied the scout, pointing to the misty bluish gorge beyond the Térek. 'Do you know Suuk-su? It is about eight miles beyond that.'

'Do you know Giréy Khan in Suuk-su?' asked Lukáshka, evidently proud of the acquaintance. 'He is my *kunák*.'

'He is my neighbour,' answered the scout.

'He's a fine fellow!' and Lukáshka, evidently much interested, began talking to the scout in Tatar.

Presently a Cossack captain, with the head of the village, arrived on horseback with a suite of two Cossacks. The captain—one of the new type of Cossack officers—wished the Cossacks 'Good health,' but no one shouted in reply, 'Hail! Good health to your honour,' as is customary in the army, and only a few replied with a bow. Some, and among them Lukáshka, rose and stood erect. The corporal replied that all was well at the outposts. All this seemed ridiculous: it was as if these Cossacks were playing at being soldiers. But these formalities soon gave place to ordinary ways of behaviour, and the captain, who was a smart Cossack just like the others, began speaking fluently in Tatar to the interpreter. They filled in some document, gave it to the scout, and received from him some money. Then they approached the body.

'Which of you is Luke Gavrílov?' asked the captain.

Lukáshka took off his cap and came forward.

'I have reported your exploit to the commander. I don't know what will come of it. I have recommended you for a cross; you're too young to be made a sergeant. Can you read?'

'I can't.'

'But what a fine fellow to look at!' said the captain, again playing the commander. 'Put on your cap. Which Gavrílov does he come from? The Broad, eh?'

'His nephew,' replied the corporal.

'I know, I know. Well, lend a hand, help them,' he said, turning to the Cossacks.

Lukáshka's face shone with joy and seemed handsomer than usual. He moved away from the corporal, and having put on his cap sat down beside Olénin.

When the body had been carried to the skiff the brother Chechén descended to the bank. The Cossacks involuntarily stepped aside to let him pass. He jumped into the boat and pushed off from the bank with his powerful leg, and now, as Olénin noticed, for the first time threw a rapid glance at all the Cossacks and then abruptly asked his companion a question. The latter answered something and pointed to Lukáshka. The Chechén looked at him and, turning slowly away, gazed at the opposite bank. That look expressed not hatred but cold contempt. He again made some remark.

'What is he saying?' Olénin asked of the fidgety interpreter.

'Yours kill ours, ours slay yours. It's always the same *khúrda-múrda*,' replied the scout, evidently deceiving, and he smiled, showing his white teeth, as he jumped into the skiff.

The dead man's brother sat motionless, gazing at the opposite bank. He was so full of hatred and contempt that there was nothing on this side of the river that moved his curiosity. The scout, standing up at one end of the skiff and dipping his paddle now on one side now on the other, steered skilfully while talking incessantly. The skiff became smaller and smaller as it moved obliquely across the stream, the voices became scarcely audible, and at last, still within sight, they landed on the opposite bank where their horses stood waiting. There they lifted out the corpse and (though the horse shied) laid it across one of the saddles, mounted, and rode at a foot-pace along the road past an *aúl* from which a crowd came out to look at them. The Cossacks on the Russian side of the river were highly satisfied and jovial. Laughter and jokes were heard on all sides. The captain and the head of the village entered the mud hut to regale themselves. Lukáshka, vainly striving to impart a sedate expression to his merry face, sat down with his elbows on his knees beside Olénin and whittled away at a stick.

'Why do you smoke?' he said with assumed curiosity. 'Is it good?'

He evidently spoke because he noticed Olénin felt ill at ease and isolated among the Cossacks.

'It's just a habit,' answered Olénin. 'Why?'

'H'm, if one of us were to smoke there would be a row! Look there now, the mountains are not far off,' continued Lukáshka, 'yet you can't get there! How will you get back alone? It's getting dark. I'll take you, if you like. You ask the corporal to give me leave.'

'What a fine fellow!' thought Olénin, looking at the Cossack's bright face. He remembered Maryánka and the kiss he had heard by the gate, and he was sorry for Lukáshka and his want of culture. 'How confusing it is,' he thought. 'A man kills another and is happy and satisfied with himself as if he had done something excellent. Can it be that nothing tells him that it is not a reason for rejoicing, and that happiness lies not in killing, but in sacrificing oneself?'

'Well, you had better not meet him again now, mate!' said one of the Cossacks who had seen the skiff off, addressing Lukáshka. 'Did you hear him asking about you?'

Lukáshka raised his head.

'My godson?' said Lukáshka, meaning by that word the dead Chechén.

'Your godson won't rise, but the red one is the godson's brother!'

'Let him thank God that he got off whole himself,' replied Lukáshka.

'What are you glad about?' asked Olénin. 'Supposing your brother had been killed would you be glad?'

The Cossack looked at Olénin with laughing eyes. He seemed to have understood all that Olénin wished to say to him, but to be above such considerations.

'Well, that happens too! Don't our fellows get killed sometimes?'

CHAPTER XXII

The captain and the head of the village rode away, and Olénin, to please Lukáshka as well as to avoid going back alone through the dark forest, asked the corporal to give Lukáshka leave, and the corporal did so. Olénin thought that Lukáshka wanted to see Maryánka and he was also glad of the companionship of such a pleasant-looking and sociable Cossack. Lukáshka and Maryánka he involuntarily united in his mind, and he found pleasure in thinking about them. 'He loves

Maryánka,' thought Olénin, 'and I could love her,' and a new and powerful emotion of tenderness overcame him as they walked homewards together through the dark forest. Lukáshka too felt happy; something akin to love made itself felt between these two very different young men. Every time they glanced at one another they wanted to laugh.

'By which gate do you enter?' asked Olénin.

'By the middle one. But I'll see you as far as the marsh. After that you have nothing to fear.'

Olénin laughed.

'Do you think I am afraid? Go back, and thank you. I can get on alone.'

'It's all right! What have I to do? And how can you help being afraid? Even we are afraid,' said Lukáshka to set Olénin's self-esteem at rest, and he laughed too.

'Then come in with me. We'll have a talk and a drink and in the morning you can go back.'

'You think I couldn't find a place to spend the night?' laughed Lukáshka. 'But the corporal asked me to go back.'

'I heard you singing last night, and also saw you.'

'Every one . . .' and Luke swayed his head.

'Is it true you are getting married?' asked Olénin.

'Mother wants me to marry. But I have not got a horse yet.'

'Aren't you in the regular service?'

'Oh dear no! I've only just joined, and have not got a horse yet, and don't know how to get one. That's why I haven't got married.'

'And what would a horse cost?'

'We were bargaining for one beyond the river the other day and they would not take sixty rubles for it, though it is a Nogáy horse.'

'Will you come and be my drabánt?' (A drabánt was a kind of orderly attached to an officer when campaigning.) 'I'll get it arranged and will give you a horse,' said Olénin suddenly. 'Really now, I have two and I don't want both.'

'How—don't want it?' Lukáshka said, laughing. 'Why should you make me a present? We'll get on by ourselves by God's help.'

'No, really! Or don't you want to be a drabánt?' said Olénin, glad that it had entered his head to give a horse to Lukáshka, though, without knowing why, he felt uncomfortable and confused and did not know what to say when he tried to speak.

Lukáshka was the first to break the silence.

'Have you a house of your own in Russia?' he asked.

Olénin could not refrain from replying that he had not only one, but several houses.

'A good house? Bigger than ours?' asked Lukáshka good-naturedly.

'Much bigger; ten times as big and three stories high,' replied Olénin.

'And have you horses such as ours?'

'I have a hundred horses, worth three or four hundred rubles each, but they are not like yours. They are trotters, you know. But still, I like the horses here best.'

'Well and did you come here of your own free will, or were you sent?' said Lukáshka, laughing at him. 'Look! that's where you lost your way,' he added, 'you should have turned to the right.'

'I came by my own wish,' replied Olénin. 'I wanted to see these parts and to join some expeditions.'

'I would go on an expedition any day,' said Lukáshka. 'D'you hear the jackals howling?' he added, listening.

'I say, don't you feel any horror at having killed a man?' asked Olénin.

'What's there to be frightened about? But I should like to join an expedition,' Lukáshka repeated. 'How I want to! How I want to!'

'Perhaps we may be going together. Our company is going before the holidays, and your "hundred" too.'

'And what did you want to come here for? You've a house and horses and serfs. In your place I'd do nothing but make merry! And what is your rank?'

'I am a cadet, but have been recommended for a commission.'

'Well, if you're not bragging about your home, if I were you I'd never have left it! Yes, I'd never have gone away anywhere. Do you find it pleasant living among us?'

'Yes, very pleasant,' answered Olénin.

It had grown quite dark before, talking in this way, they approached the village. They were still surrounded by the deep gloom of the forest. The wind howled through the tree-tops. The jackals suddenly seemed to be crying close beside them, howling, chuckling, and sobbing; but ahead of them in the village the sounds of women's voices and the barking of dogs could already be heard; the outlines of the huts were clearly to be seen; lights gleamed and the air was filled with the peculiar smell of *kizyák* smoke. Olénin felt keenly, that night especially, that here in this village was his home, his family, all his happiness, and that he never had and never would live so happily anywhere as he did in this village. He was so fond of everybody and especially of Lukáshka that night. On reaching home, to Lukáshka's great surprise, Olénin with his own hands led out of the shed a horse he had bought in Grózny—it was not the one he usually rode but another—not a bad horse though no longer young, and gave it to Lukáshka.

'Why should you give me a present?' said Lukáshka, 'I have not yet done anything for you.'

'Really it is nothing,' answered Olénin. 'Take it, and you will give me a present, and we'll go on an expedition against the enemy together.'

Lukáshka became confused.

'But what d'you mean by it? As if a horse were of little value,' he said without looking at the horse.

'Take it, take it! If you don't you will offend me. Vanyúsha! Take the grey horse to his house.'

Lukáshka took hold of the halter.

'Well then, thank you! This is something unexpected, undreamt of.'

Olénin was as happy as a boy of twelve.

'Tie it up here. It's a good horse. I bought it in Grózny; it gallops splendidly! Vanyúsha, bring us some *chikhír*. Come into the hut.'

The wine was brought. Lukáshka sat down and took the wine-bowl.

'God willing I'll find a a way to repay you,' he said, finishing his wine. 'What's your name?'

'Dmítri Andréich.'

'Well, 'Mítry Andréich, God bless you. We will be *kunáks*. Now you must come to see us. Though we are not rich people still we can treat a *kunák*, and I will tell mother in case you need anything—*kaymák* or grapes—and if you come to the cordon I'm your servant to go hunting or to go across the river, anywhere you like! There now, only the other day, what a boar I killed, and I divided it among the Cossacks, but if I had only known I'd have given it to you.'

'That's all right, thank you! But don't harness the horse, it has never been in harness.'

'Why harness the horse? And there is something else I'll tell you if you like,' said Lukáshka, bending his head. 'I have a *kunák*, Giréy Khan. He asked me to lie in ambush by the road where they come down from the mountains. Shall we go together? I'll not betray you. I'll be your *muríd*.'

'Yes, we'll go; we'll go some day.'

Lukáshka seemed quite to have quieted down and to have understood Olénin's attitude towards him. His calmness and the ease of his behaviour surprised Olénin, and he did not even quite like it. They talked long, and it was late when Lukáshka, not tipsy (he never was tipsy) but having drunk a good deal, left Olénin after shaking hands.

Olénin looked out of the window to see what he would do. Lukáshka went out, hanging his head. Then, having led the horse out of the gate, he suddenly shook his head, threw the reins of the halter over its head, sprang onto its back like a cat, gave a wild shout, and galloped down the street. Olénin expected that Lukáshka would go to share his joy with Maryánka, but though he did not do so Olénin still felt his soul more at ease than ever before in his life. He was as delighted as a boy, and could not refrain from telling Vanyúsha not only that he had given Lukáshka the horse, but also why he had done it, as well as his new theory of happiness. Vanyúsha did not approve of his theory, and announced that '*larjan eelnyapa*'[1] and that therefore it was all nonsense.

Lukáshka rode home, jumped off the horse, and handed it over to his mother, telling her to let it out with the communal

[1] There is no money!

Cossack herd. He himself had to return to the cordon that same night. His deaf sister undertook to take the horse, and explained by signs that when she saw the man who had given the horse, she would bow down at his feet. The old woman only shook her head at her son's story, and decided in her own mind that he had stolen it. She therefore told the deaf girl to take it to the herd before daybreak.

Lukáshka went back alone to the cordon pondering over Olénin's action. Though he did not consider the horse a good one, yet it was worth at least forty rubles and Lukáshka was very glad to have the present. But why it had been given him he could not at all understand, and therefore he did not experience the least feeling of gratitude. On the contrary, vague suspicions that the cadet had some evil intentions filled his mind. What those intentions were he could not decide, but neither could he admit the idea that a stranger would give him a horse worth forty rubles for nothing, just out of kindness; it seemed impossible. Had he been drunk one might understand it! He might have wished to show off. But the cadet had been sober, and therefore must have wished to bribe him to do something wrong. 'Nonsense!' thought Lukáshka. 'Haven't I got the horse and we'll see later on. I'm not a fool myself and we shall see who'll get the better of the other,' he thought, feeling the necessity of being on his guard, and therefore arousing in himself unfriendly feelings towards Olénin. He told no one how he had got the horse. To some he said he had bought it, to others he replied evasively. However, the truth soon got about in the village, and Lukáshka's mother and Maryánka, as well as Elias Vasílich and other Cossacks, when they heard of Olénin's unnecessary gift, were perplexed, and began to be on their guard against the cadet. But despite their fears his action aroused in them a great respect for his simplicity and wealth.

'Have you heard,' said one, 'that the cadet quartered on Elias Vasílich has thrown a fifty-ruble horse at Lukáshka? He's rich!'

'Yes, I heard of it,' replied another profoundly, 'he must have done him some great service. We shall see what will come of this cadet. Eh! what luck that Snatcher has!'

'Those cadets are crafty, awfully crafty,' said a third. 'See if he don't go setting fire to a building, or doing something!'

CHAPTER XXIII

Olénin's life went on with monotonous regularity. He had little to do with the commanding officers or with his equals. The position of a rich cadet in the Caucasus was peculiarly advantageous in this respect. He was not sent out to work, or for training. As a reward for going on an expedition he was recommended for a commission, and meanwhile he was left in peace. The officers regarded him as an aristocrat and behaved towards him with dignity. Card-playing and the officers' carousals accompanied by the soldier-singers, of which he had had experience when he was with the detachment, did not seem to him attractive, and he also avoided the society and life of the officers in the village. The life of officers stationed in a Cossack village has long had its own definite form. Just as every cadet or officer when in a fort regularly drinks porter, plays cards, and discusses the rewards given for taking part in the expeditions, so in the Cossack villages he regularly drinks *chikhír* with his hosts, treats the girls to sweetmeats and honey, dangles after the Cossack women, and falls in love, and occasionally marries there. Olénin always took his own path and had an unconscious objection to the beaten tracks. And here, too, he did not follow the ruts of a Caucasian officer's life.

It came quite naturally to him to wake up at daybreak. After drinking tea and admiring from his porch the mountains, the morning, and Maryánka, he would put on a tattered ox-hide coat, sandals of soaked raw hide, buckle on a dagger, take a gun, put cigarettes and some lunch in a little bag, call his dog, and soon after five o'clock would start for the forest beyond the village. Towards seven in the evening he would return tired and hungry with five or six pheasants hanging from his belt (sometimes with some other animal) and with his bag of food and cigarettes untouched. If the thoughts in his head had lain like the lunch and cigarettes in the bag, one might have seen that during all those fourteen hours not a single thought had moved in it. He returned morally fresh, strong, and perfectly happy, and he could not tell what he had been thinking about all the time. Were they ideas, memories, or dreams that had been flitting through his mind? They were frequently all three. He would rouse himself and ask what he had been thinking about; and would see himself as a Cossack working in a vineyard with his Cossack wife, or an *abrék* in the mountains, or a boar running away from himself. And all the time he kept peering and watching for a pheasant, a boar, or a deer.

In the evening Daddy Eróshka would be sure to be sitting with him. Vanyúsha would bring a jug of *chikhír*, and they would converse quietly, drink, and separate to go quite contentedly to bed. The next day he would again go shooting, again be healthily weary, again they would sit conversing and drink their fill, and again be happy. Sometimes on a holiday or day of rest Olénin spent the whole day at home. Then his chief occupation was watching Maryánka, whose every movement, without realizing it himself, he followed greedily from his window or his porch. He regarded Maryánka and loved her (so he thought) just as he loved the beauty of the mountains and the sky, and he had no thought of entering into any relations with her. It seemed to him that between him and her such relations as there were between her and the Cossack Lukáshka could not exist, and still less such as often existed between rich officers and other Cossack girls. It seemed to him that if he tried to do as his fellow officers did, he would exchange his complete enjoyment of contemplation for an abyss of suffering, disillusionment, and remorse. Besides, he had already achieved a triumph of self-sacrifice in connection with her which had given him great pleasure, and above all he was in a way afraid of Maryánka and would not for anything have ventured to utter a word of love to her lightly.

Once during the summer, when Olénin had not gone out shooting but was sitting at home, quite unexpectedly a Moscow acquaintance, a very young man whom he had met in society, came in.

'Ah, *mon cher*,[1] my dear fellow, how glad I was when I heard

[1] My dear.

that you were here!' he began in his Moscow French, and he went on intermingling French words in his remarks. 'They said, "Olénin". What Olénin? And I was so pleased. Fancy fate bringing us together here! Well and how are you? How? Why?' and Prince Belétski told his whole story: how he had temporarily entered the regiment, how the commander-in-chief had offered to take him as an adjutant, and how he would take up the post after this campaign although personally he felt quite indifferent about it.

'Living here in this hole one must at least make a career—get a cross—or a rank—be transferred to the guards. That is quite indispensable, not for myself but for the sake of my relations and friends. The prince received me very well; he is a very decent fellow,' said Belétski, and went on unceasingly. 'I have been recommended for the St Anna Cross for the expedition. Now I shall stay here a bit until we start on the campaign. It's great here. What women! Well and how are you getting on? I was told by our captain, Stártsev you know, a kind-hearted stupid creature. . . . Well, he said you were living like an awful savage, seeing no one! I quite understand you don't want to be mixed up with the set of officers we have here. I am so glad now you and I will be able to see something of one another. I have put up at the Cossack corporal's house. There is such a girl there, Ústenka! I tell you she's just charming.'

And more and more French and Russian words came pouring forth from that world which Olénin thought he had left for ever. The general opinion about Belétski was that he was a nice, good-natured fellow. Perhaps he really was; but in spite of his pretty, good-natured face, Olénin thought him extremely unpleasant. He just seemed to exhale that filth which Olénin had forsworn. What vexed him most was that he could not—had not the strength—abruptly to repulse this man who came from that world: as if that old world he used to belong to had an irresistible claim on him. Olénin felt angry with Belétski and with himself, yet against his wish he introduced French phrases into his own conversation, was interested in the commander-in-chief and in their Moscow acquaintances, and because in this Cossack village he and Belétski both spoke French, he spoke contemptuously of their fellow officers and of the Cossacks, and was friendly with Belétski, promising to visit him and inviting him to drop in to see him. Olénin however did not himself go to see Belétski. Vanyúsha for his part approved of Belétski, remarking that he was a real gentleman.

Belétski at once adopted the customary life of a rich officer in a Cossack village. Before Olénin's eyes, in one month he came to be like an old resident of the village; he made the old men drunk, arranged evening parties, and himself went to parties arranged by the girls—bragged of his conquests, and even got so far that, for some unknown reason, the woman and girls began calling him grandad, and the Cossacks, to whom a man who loved wine and women was clearly understandable, got used to him and even liked him better than they did Olénin, who was a puzzle to them.

CHAPTER XXIV

It was five in the morning. Vanyúsha was on the porch heating the samovar, and using the leg of a long boot instead of bellows. Olénin had already ridden off to bathe in the Térek. (He had recently invented a new amusement: to swim his horse in the river.) His landlady was in her shed, and the dense smoke of the kindling fire rose from the chimney. The girl was milking the buffalo-cow in the shed. 'Can't keep quiet, the damned thing!' came her impatient voice, followed by the rhythmical sound of milking.

From the street in front of the house horses' hoofs were heard clattering briskly, and Olénin, riding bareback on a handsome dark-grey horse which was still wet and shining, rode up to the gate. Maryánka's handsome head, tied round with a red kerchief, appeared from the shed and again disappeared. Olénin was wearing a red silk shirt, a white *cherkéska* girdled with a strap which carried a dagger, and a tall cap. He sat on his well-fed wet horse with a slightly conscious elegance and, holding his gun at his back, stooped to open the gate. His hair was still wet, and his face shone with youth and health. He thought himself handsome, agile, and like a *dzhigít*; but he was mistaken. To any experienced Caucasian he was still only a soldier. When he noticed that the girl had put out her head he stooped with particular smartness, threw open the gate and, tightening the reins, swished his whip and entered the yard. 'Is tea ready, Vanyúsha?' he cried gaily, not looking at the door of the shed. He felt with pleasure how his fine horse, pressing down its flanks, pulling at the bridle and with every muscle quivering and with each foot ready to leap over the fence, pranced on the hard clay of the yard. '*Say prey*,'[1] answered Vanyúsha. Olénin felt as if Maryánka's beautiful head was still looking out of the shed but he did not turn to look at her. As he jumped down from his horse he made an awkward movement and caught his gun against the porch, and turned a frightened look towards the shed, where there was no one to be seen and whence the sound of milking could still be heard.

Soon after he had entered the hut he came out again and sat down with his pipe and a book on the side of the porch which was not yet exposed to the rays of the sun. He meant not to go anywhere before dinner that day, and to write some long-postponed letters; but somehow he felt disinclined to leave his place on the porch, and he was as reluctant to go back into the hut as if it had been a prison. The housewife had heated her oven, and the girl, having driven the cattle, had come back and was collecting *kizyák* and heaping it up along the fence. Olénin went on reading, but did not understand a word of what was written in the book that lay open before him. He kept lifting his eyes from it and looking at the powerful young woman who was moving about. Whether she stepped into the moist morning shadow thrown by the house, or went out into the middle of the yard lit up by the joyous young light, so that the whole of her stately figure in its bright coloured garment gleamed in the sunshine and cast a black shadow—he always feared to lose any one of her movements. It delighted him to see how freely and gracefully her figure bent: into what folds her only garment, a pink smock, draped itself on her bosom and along her shapely legs; how she drew herself up and her tight-drawn smock showed the outline of her heaving bosom, how the soles of her narrow feet in her worn red slippers rested on the ground without altering their shape; how her strong arms with the sleeves rolled up, exerting the muscles, used the spade almost as if in anger, and how her deep dark eyes

[1] It's ready.

sometimes glanced at him. Though the delicate brows frowned, yet her eyes expressed pleasure and a knowledge of her own beauty.

'I say, Olénin, have you been up long?' said Belétski as he entered the yard dressed in the coat of a Caucasian officer.

'Ah, Belétski,' replied Olénin, holding out his hand. 'How is it you are out so early?'

'I had to. I was driven out; we are having a ball to-night. Maryánka, of course you'll come to Ústenka's?' he added, turning to the girl.

Olénin felt surprised that Belétski could address this woman so easily. But Maryánka, as though she had not heard him, bent her head, and throwing the spade across her shoulder went with her firm masculine tread towards the shed.

'She's shy, the wench is shy,' Belétski called after her. 'Shy of you,' he added as, smiling gaily, he ran up the steps of the porch.

'How is it you are having a ball and have been driven out?'

'The ball is at Ústenka's, at my landlady's, and you two are invited. A ball, that's a pie and a gathering of girls.'

'What should we do there?'

Belétski smiled knowingly and winked, jerking his head in the direction of the shed into which Maryánka had disappeared.

Olénin shrugged his shoulders and blushed.

'Well, really you are a strange fellow!' said he.

'Come now, don't pretend!'

Olénin frowned, and Belétski noticing this smiled insinuatingly. 'Oh, come, what do you mean?' he said, 'living in the same house—and such a fine girl, a splendid girl, a perfect beauty—'

'Wonderfully beautiful! I never saw such a woman before,' replied Olénin.

'Well then?' said Belétski, quite unable to understand the situation.

'It may be strange,' replied Olénin, 'but why should I not say what is true? Since I have lived here women don't seem to exist for me. And it is so good, really! Now what can there be in common between us and women like these? Eróshka—

that's a different matter! He and I have a passion in common—sport.'

'There now! In common! And what have I in common with Amália Ivánovna? It's the same thing! You may say they're not very clean—that's another matter. *À la guerre, comme à la guerre!*'[1]

'But I have never known any Amália Ivánovnas, and have never known how to behave with women of that sort,' replied Olénin. 'One cannot respect them, but these I do respect.'

'Well go on respecting them! Who wants to prevent you?'

Olénin did not reply. He evidently wanted to complete what he had begun to say. It was very near his heart.

'I know I am an exception.' He was visibly confused. 'But my life has so shaped itself that I not only see no necessity to renounce my rules, but I could not live here, let alone live as happily as I am doing, were I to live as you do. Therefore I look for something quite different from what you look for.'

Belétski raised his eyebrows incredulously. 'Anyhow, come to me this evening; Maryánka will be there and I will make you acquainted. Do come, please! If you feel bored you can go away. Will you come?'

'I would come, but to speak frankly I am afraid of being seriously carried away.'

'Oh, oh, oh!' shouted Belétski. 'Only come, and I'll see that you aren't. Will you? On your word?'

'I would come, but really I don't understand what we shall do; what part we shall play!'

'Please, I beg of you. You will come?'

'Yes, perhaps I'll come,' said Olénin.

'Really now! Charming women such as one sees nowhere else, and to live like a monk! What an idea! Why spoil your life and not make use of what is at hand? Have you heard that our company is ordered to Vozdvízhensk?'

'Hardly. I was told the 8th Company would be sent there,' said Olénin.

'No. I have had a letter from the adjutant there. He writes that the Prince himself will take part in the campaign. I am very

[1] War is war!

glad I shall see something of him. I'm beginning to get tired of this place.'

'I hear we shall start on a raid soon.'

'I have not heard of it; but I have heard that Krinovítsin has received the Order of St Anna for a raid. He expected a lieutenancy,' said Belétski laughing. 'He was had! He has set off for headquarters.'

It was growing dusk and Olénin began thinking about the party. The invitation he had received worried him. He felt inclined to go, but what might take place there seemed strange, absurd, and even rather alarming. He knew that neither Cossack men nor older women, nor anyone besides the girls, were to be there. What was going to happen? How was he to behave? What would they talk about? What connection was there between him and those wild Cossack girls? Belétski had told him of such curious, cynical, and yet rigid relations. It seemed strange to think that he would be there in the same hut with Maryánka and perhaps might have to talk to her. It seemed to him impossible when he remembered her majestic bearing. But Belétski spoke of it as if it were all perfectly simple. 'Is it possible that Belétski will treat Maryánka in the same way? That is interesting,' thought he. 'No, better not go. It's all so horrid, so vulgar, and above all—it leads to nothing!' But again he was worried by the question of what would take place; and besides he felt as if bound by a promise. He went out without having made up his mind one way or the other, but he walked as far as Belétski's, and went in there.

The hut in which Belétski lived was like Olénin's. It was raised nearly five feet from the ground on wooden piles, and had two rooms. In the first (which Olénin entered by the steep flight of steps) feather beds, rugs, blankets, and cushions were tastefully and handsomely arranged, Cossack fashion, along the main wall. On the side wall hung brass basins and weapons, while on the floor, under a bench, lay water-melons and pumpkins. In the second room there was a big brick oven, a table, and Old-Believer icons. It was here that Belétski was quartered, with his camp-bed and his pack and trunks. His weapons hung on the wall with a little rug behind them, and on the table were his toilet articles and some portraits. A silk dressing-gown had been thrown on the bench. Belétski himself, clean and good looking, lay on the bed in his underclothing, reading *Les Trois Mousquetaires*.*

He jumped up.

'There, you see how I have arranged things. Fine! Well, it's good that you have come. They are working furiously. Do you know what the pie is made of? Dough with a stuffing of pork and grapes. But that's not the point. You just look at the commotion out there!'

And really, on looking out of the window they saw an unusual bustle going on in the hut. Girls ran in and out, now for one thing and now for another.

'Will it soon be ready?' cried Belétski.

'Very soon! Why? Is Grandad hungry?' and from the hut came the sound of ringing laughter.

Ústenka, plump, small, rosy, and pretty, with her sleeves turned up, ran into Belétski's hut to fetch some plates.

'Get away or I shall smash the plates!' she squeaked, escaping from Belétski. 'You'd better come and help,' she shouted to Olénin, laughing. 'And don't forget to get some refreshments for the girls.' ('Refreshments' meaning spice-bread and sweets.)

'And has Maryánka come?'

'Of course! She brought some dough.'

'Do you know,' said Belétski, 'if one were to dress Ústenka up and clean and polish her up a bit, she'd be better than all our beauties. Have you ever seen that Cossack woman who married a colonel; she was charming! Bórsheva? What dignity! Where do they get it?'

'I have not seen Bórsheva, but I think nothing could be better than the costume they wear here.'

'Ah, I'm first rate at fitting into any kind of life,' said Belétski with a sigh of pleasure. 'I'll go and see what they are up to.'

He threw his dressing-gown over his shoulders and ran out, shouting, 'And you look after the "refreshments".'

Olénin sent Belétski's orderly to buy spice-bread and honey; but it suddenly seemed to him so disgusting to give money (as if he were bribing someone) that he gave no definite reply to the orderly's question: 'How much spice-bread with peppermint, and how much with honey?'

'Just as you please.'

'Shall I spend all the money?' asked the old soldier impressively. 'The peppermint is dearer. It's sixteen kopeks.'

'Yes, yes, spend it all,' answered Olénin and sat down by the window, surprised that his heart was thumping as if he were preparing himself for something serious and wicked.

He heard screaming and shrieking in the girls' hut when Belétski went there, and a few moments later saw how he jumped out and ran down the steps, accompanied by shrieks, bustle, and laughter.

'Turned out,' he said.

A little later Ústenka entered and solemnly invited her visitors to come in: announcing that all was ready.

When they came into the room they saw that everything was really ready. Ústenka was rearranging the cushions along the wall. On the table, which was covered by a disproportionately small cloth, was a decanter of *chikhír* and some dried fish. The room smelt of dough and grapes. Some half-dozen girls in smart tunics, with their heads not covered as usual with kerchiefs, were huddled together in a corner behind the oven, whispering, giggling, and spluttering with laughter.

'I humbly beg you to do honour to my patron saint,' said Ústenka, inviting her guests to the table.

Olénin noticed Maryánka among the group of girls, who without exception were all handsome, and he felt vexed and hurt that he met her in such vulgar and awkward circumstances. He felt stupid and awkward, and made up his mind to do what Belétski did. Belétski stepped to the table somewhat solemnly yet with confidence and ease, drank a glass of wine to Ústenka's health, and invited the others to do the same. Ústenka announced that girls don't drink.

'We might with a little honey,' exclaimed a voice from among the group of girls.

The orderly, who had just returned with the honey and spice-cakes, was called in. He looked askance (whether with envy or with contempt) at the gentlemen, who in his opinion were *on a spree*; and carefully and conscientiously handed over to them a piece of honeycomb and the cakes wrapped up in a piece of greyish paper, and began explaining circumstantially all about the price and the change, but Belétski sent him away.

Having mixed honey with wine in the glasses, and having lavishly scattered the three pounds of spice-cakes on the table, Belétski dragged the girls from their corners by force, made them sit down at the table, and began distributing the cakes among them. Olénin involuntarily noticed how Maryánka's sunburnt but small hand closed on two round peppermint nuts and one brown one, and that she did not know what to do with them. The conversation was halting and constrained, in spite of Ústenka's and Belétski's free and easy manner and their wish to enliven the company. Olénin faltered, and tried to think of something to say, feeling that he was exciting curiosity and perhaps provoking ridicule and infecting the others with his shyness. He blushed, and it seemed to him that Maryánka in particular was feeling uncomfortable. 'Most likely they are expecting us to give them some money,' thought he. 'How are we to do it? And how can we manage quickest to give it and get away?'

CHAPTER XXV

'How is it you don't know your own lodger?' said Belétski, addressing Maryánka.

'How is one to know him if he never comes to see us?' answered Maryánka, with a look at Olénin.

Olénin felt frightened, he did not know of what. He flushed and, hardly knowing what he was saying, remarked; 'I'm afraid of your mother. She gave me such a scolding the first time I went in.'

Maryánka burst out laughing.

'And so you were frightened?' she said, and glanced at him and turned away.

It was the first time Olénin had seen the whole of her beautiful face. Till then he had seen her with her kerchief covering her to the eyes. It was not for nothing that she was reckoned the beauty of the village. Ústenka was a pretty girl, small, plump, rosy, with merry brown eyes, and red lips which were perpetually smiling and chattering. Maryánka on the contrary was certainly not pretty but beautiful. Her features might have been considered too masculine and almost harsh had it not been for her tall stately figure, her powerful chest and shoulders, and especially the severe yet tender expression of her long dark eyes which were darkly shadowed beneath their black brows, and for the gentle expression of her mouth and smile. She rarely smiled, but her smile was always striking. She seemed to radiate virginal strength and health. All the girls were good-looking, but they themselves and Belétski, and the orderly when he brought in the spice-cakes, all involuntarily gazed at Maryánka, and anyone addressing the girls was sure to address her. She seemed a proud and happy queen among them.

Belétski, trying to keep up the spirit of the party, chattered incessantly, made the girls hand round *chikhír*, fooled about with them, and kept making improper remarks in French about Maryánka's beauty to Olénin, calling her 'yours' (*la vôtre*), and advising him to behave as he did himself. Olénin felt more and more uncomfortable. He was devising an excuse to get out and run away when Belétski announced that Ústenka, whose saint's day it was, must offer *chikhír* to everybody with a kiss. She consented on condition that they should put money on her plate, as is the custom at weddings. 'What fiend brought me to this disgusting feast?' thought Olénin, rising to go away.

'Where are you off to?'

'I'll fetch some tobacco,' he said, meaning to escape, but Belétski seized his hand.

'I have some money,' he said to him in French.

'One can't go away, one has to pay here,' thought Olénin bitterly, vexed at his own awkwardness. 'Can't I really behave like Belétski? I ought not to have come, but once I am here I must not spoil their fun. I must drink like a Cossack,' and taking the wooden bowl (holding about eight tumblers) he almost filled it with *chikhír* and drank it almost all. The girls looked at him, surprised and almost frightened, as he drank. It seemed to them strange and not right. Ústenka brought them another glass each, and kissed them both. 'There girls, now we'll have some fun,' she said, clinking on the plate the four rubles the men had put there.

Olénin no longer felt awkward, but became talkative.

'Now, Maryánka, it's your turn to offer us wine and a kiss,' said Belétski, seizing her hand.

'Yes, I'll give you such a kiss!' she said playfully, preparing to strike at him.

'One can kiss Grandad without payment,' said another girl.

'There's a sensible girl,' said Belétski, kissing the struggling girl. 'No, you must offer it,' he insisted, addressing Maryánka. 'Offer a glass to your lodger.'

And taking her by the hand he led her to the bench and sat her down beside Olénin.

'What a beauty,' he said, turning her head to see it in profile.

Maryánka did not resist but proudly smiling turned her long eyes towards Olénin.

'A beautiful girl,' repeated Belétski.

'Yes, see what a beauty I am,' Maryánka's look seemed to endorse. Without considering what he was doing Olénin embraced Maryánka and was going to kiss her, but she suddenly extricated herself, upsetting Belétski and pushing the top off the table, and sprang away towards the oven. There was much shouting and laughter. Then Belétski whispered something to the girls and suddenly they all ran out into the passage and locked the door behind them.

'Why did you kiss Belétski and won't kiss me?' asked Olénin.

'Oh, just so. I don't want to, that's all!' she answered, pouting and frowning. 'He's Grandad,' she added with a smile. She went to the door and began to bang at it. 'Why have you locked the door, you devils?'

'Well, let them be there and us here,' said Olénin, drawing closer to her.

She frowned, and sternly pushed him away with her hand. And again she appeared so majestically handsome to Olénin that he came to his senses and felt ashamed of what he was doing. He went to the door and began pulling at it himself.

'Belétski! Open the door! What a stupid joke!'

Maryánka again gave a bright happy laugh. 'Ah, you're afraid of me?' she said.

'Yes, you know you're as cross as your mother.'

'Spend more of your time with Eróshka; that will make the girls love you!' And she smiled, looking straight and close into his eyes.

He did not know what to reply. 'And if I were to come to see you—' he let fall.

'That would be a different matter,' she replied, tossing her head.

At that moment Belétski pushed the door open, and Maryánka sprang away from Olénin and in doing so her thigh struck his leg.

'It's all nonsense what I have been thinking about—love and self-sacrifice and Lukáshka. Happiness is the only thing. He who is happy is right,' flashed through Olénin's mind, and with a strength unexpected to himself he seized and kissed the beautiful Maryánka on her temple and her cheek. Maryánka was not angry, but only burst into a loud laugh and ran out to the other girls.

That was the end of the party. Ústenka's mother, returned from her work, gave all the girls a scolding, and turned them all out.

CHAPTER XXVI

'Yes,' thought Olénin, as he walked home. 'I need only slacken the reins a bit and I might fall desperately in love with this Cossack girl.' He went to bed with these thoughts, but expected it all to blow over and that he would continue to live as before.

But the old life did not return. His relations to Maryánka were changed. The wall that had separated them was broken down. Olénin now greeted her every time they met.

The master of the house having returned to collect the rent, on hearing of Olénin's wealth and generosity invited him to his hut. The old woman received him kindly, and from the day of the party onwards Olénin often went in of an evening and sat with them till late at night. He seemed to be living in the village just as he used to, but within him everything had changed. He spent his days in the forest, and towards eight o'clock, when it began to grow dusk, he would go to see his hosts, alone or with

Daddy Eróshka. They grew so used to him that they were surprised when he stayed away. He paid well for his wine and was a quiet fellow. Vanyúsha would bring him his tea and he would sit down in a corner near the oven. The old woman did not mind him but went on with her work, and over their tea or their *chikhír* they talked about Cossack affairs, about the neighbours, or about Russia: Olénin relating and the others inquiring. Sometimes he brought a book and read to himself. Maryánka crouched like a wild goat with her feet drawn up under her, sometimes on the top of the oven,* sometimes in a dark corner. She did not take part in the conversations, but Olénin saw her eyes and face and heard her moving or cracking sunflower seeds, and he felt that she listened with her whole being when he spoke, and was aware of his presence while he silently read to himself. Sometimes he thought her eyes were fixed on him, and meeting their radiance he involuntarily became silent and gazed at her. Then she would instantly hide her face and he would pretend to be deep in conversation with the old woman, while he listened all the time to her breathing and to her every movement and waited for her to look at him again. In the presence of others she was generally bright and friendly with him, but when they were alone together she was shy and rough. Sometimes he came in before Maryánka had returned home. Suddenly he would hear her firm footsteps and catch a glimmer of her blue cotton smock at the open door. Then she would step into the middle of the hut, catch sight of him, and her eyes would give a scarcely perceptible kindly smile, and he would feel happy and frightened.

He neither sought for nor wished for anything from her, but every day her presence became more and more necessary to him.

Olénin had entered into the life of the Cossack village so fully that his past seemed quite foreign to him. As to the future, especially a future outside the world in which he was now living, it did not interest him at all. When he received letters from home, from relatives and friends, he was offended by the evident distress with which they regarded him as a lost man, while he in his village considered those as lost who did not live as he was living. He felt sure he would never repent of having broken away from his former surroundings and of having settled down in this village to such a solitary and original life. When out on expeditions, and when quartered at one of the forts, he felt happy too; but it was here, from under Daddy Eróshka's wing, from the forest and from his hut at the end of the village, and especially when he thought of Maryánka and Lukáshka, that he seemed to see the falseness of his former life. That falseness used to rouse his indignation even before, but now it seemed inexpressibly vile and ridiculous. Here he felt freer and freer every day and more and more of a human being. The Caucasus now appeared entirely different to what his imagination had painted it. He had found nothing at all like his dreams, nor like the descriptions of the Caucasus he had heard and read. 'There are none of all those chestnut steeds, precipices, Amalet Beks, heroes or villains,' thought he. 'The people live as nature lives: they die, are born, copulate, and more are born—they fight, eat and drink, rejoice and die, without any restrictions but those that nature imposes on sun and grass, on animal and tree. They have no other laws.' Therefore these people, compared to himself, appeared to him beautiful, strong, and free, and the sight of them made him feel ashamed and sorry for himself. Often it seriously occurred to him to throw up everything, to get registered as a Cossack, to buy a hut and cattle and marry a Cossack woman (only not Maryánka, whom he conceded to Lukáshka), and to live with Daddy Eróshka and go shooting and fishing with him, and go with the Cossacks on their expeditions. 'Why ever don't I do it? What am I waiting for?' he asked himself, and he egged himself on and shamed himself. 'Am I afraid of doing what I hold to be reasonable and right? Is the wish to be a simple Cossack, to live close to nature, not to injure anyone but even to do good to others, more stupid than my former dreams, such as those of becoming a minister of state or a colonel?' but a voice seemed to say that he should wait, and not take any decision. He was held back by a dim consciousness that he could not live altogether like Eróshka and Lukáshka because he had a different idea of happiness—he was held back by the thought that happiness lies in self-sacrifice. What he had done for Lukáshka continued to give him joy. He kept looking for occasions to sacrifice himself for others, but did not meet with them. Sometimes he forgot this newly discovered recipe for happiness and considered himself capable of identifying his life with Daddy Eróshka's, but then he quickly bethought himself and promptly clutched at the idea of conscious self-sacrifice, and from that basis looked calmly and proudly at all men and at their happiness.

CHAPTER XXVII

Just before the vintage Lukáshka came on horseback to see Olénin. He looked more dashing then ever.

'Well? Are you getting married?' asked Olénin, greeting him merrily.

Lukáshka gave no direct reply.

'There, I've exchanged your horse across the river. This *is* a horse! A Kabardá horse from the Lov* stud. I know horses.'

They examined the new horse and made him caracole about the yard. The horse really was an exceptionally fine one, a broad and long gelding, with glossy coat, thick silky tail, and the soft fine mane and crest of a thoroughbred. He was so well fed that 'you might go to sleep on his back' as Lukáshka expressed it. His hoofs, eyes, teeth, all were exquisitely shaped and sharply outlined, as one only finds them in very pure-bred horses. Olénin could not help admiring the horse, he had not yet met with such a beauty in the Caucasus.

'And how it moves!' said Lukáshka, patting its neck. 'What a step! And so clever—he simply runs after his master.'

'Did you have to add much to make the exchange?' asked Olénin.

'I did not count it,' answered Lukáshka with a smile. 'I got him from a *kunák*.'

'A wonderfully beautiful horse! What would you take for it?' asked Olénin.

'I have been offered a hundred and fifty rubles for it, but I'll give it to you for nothing,' said Lukáshka, merrily. 'Only say the word and it's yours. I'll unsaddle it and you may take it. Only give me some sort of a horse for my duties.'

'No, on no account.'

'Well then, here is a *peshkésh* I've brought you,' said Lukáshka, unfastening his girdle and taking out one of the two daggers which hung from it. 'I got it from across the river.'

'Oh, thank you!'

'And mother has promised to bring you some grapes herself.'

'That's quite unnecessary. We'll balance up some day. You see I don't offer you any money for the dagger!'

'How could you? We are *kunáks*. It's just the same as when Giréy Khan across the river took me into his home and said, "Choose what you like!" So I took this sword. It's our custom.'

They went into the hut and had a drink.

'Are you staying here awhile?' asked Olénin.

'No, I have come to say good-bye. They are sending me from the cordon to a company beyond the Térek. I am going tonight with my comrade Nazárka.'

'And when is the wedding to be?'

'I shall be coming back for the betrothal, and then I shall return to the company again,' Lukáshka replied reluctantly.

'What, and see nothing of your betrothed?'

'Just so—what is the good of looking at her? When you go on campaign ask in our company for Lukáshka the Broad. But what a lot of boars there are in our parts! I've killed two. I'll take you.'

'Well, good-bye! Christ save you.'

Lukáshka mounted his horse, and without calling on Maryánka, rode *dzhigíting* down the street, where Nazárka was already awaiting him.

'What? aren't we going to stop in?' asked Nazárka, winking in the direction of Yámka's house.

'That's a good one!' said Lukáshka. 'Here, take my horse to her and if I don't come soon give him some hay. I shall reach the company by the morning any way.'

'Hasn't the cadet given you anything more?'

'I am thankful to have paid him back with a dagger—he was going to ask for the horse,' said Lukáshka, dismounting and handing over the horse to Nazárka.

He darted into the yard past Olénin's very window, and

came up to the window of the cornet's hut. It was already quite dark. Maryánka, wearing only her smock, was combing her hair preparing for bed.

'It's me—' whispered the Cossack.

Maryánka's look was severely indifferent, but her face suddenly brightened up when she heard her name. She opened the window and leant out, frightened and joyous.

'What—what do you want?' she said.

'Open!' uttered Lukáshka. 'Let me in for a minute. I am so sick of waiting! It's awful!'

He took hold of her head through the window and kissed her.

'Really, do open!'

'Why do you talk nonsense? I've told you I won't! Have you come for long?'

He did not answer but went on kissing her, and she did not ask again.

'There, through the window one can't even hug you properly,' said Lukáshka.

'Maryánka dear!' came the voice of her mother, 'who is that with you?'

Lukáshka took off his cap, which might have been seen, and crouched down by the window.

'Go, be quick!' whispered Maryánka.

'Lukáshka stopped by,' she answered; 'he was asking for Daddy.'

'Well then send him here!'

'He's gone; said he was in a hurry.'

In fact, Lukáshka, all stooped over, ran out under the windows into the yard and towards Yámka's house unseen by anyone but Olénin. After drinking two bowls of *chikhír* he and Nazárka rode away to the outpost. The night was warm, dark, and calm. They rode in silence, only the footfall of their horses was heard. Lukáshka started a song about the Cossack, Mingál, but stopped before he had finished the first verse, and after a pause, turning to Nazárka, said:

'I say, she wouldn't let me in!'

'Oh?' rejoined Nazárka. 'I knew she wouldn't. D'you know what Yámka told me? The cadet has begun going to their house. Daddy Eróshka brags that he got a gun from the cadet for getting him Maryánka.'

'He lies, the old devil!' said Lukáshka, angrily. 'She's not such a girl. If he does not look out I'll wallop that old devil's sides,' and he began his favourite song:

'From the village of Izmáylov,
From the master's favourite garden,
Once escaped a keen-eyed falcon.
Soon after him a huntsman came a-riding,
And he beckoned to the falcon that had strayed,
But the bright-eyed bird thus answered:
"In gold cage you could not keep me,
On your hand you could not hold me,
So now I fly to blue seas far away.
There a white swan I will kill,
Of sweet swan-flesh have my fill."'

CHAPTER XXVIII

The betrothal was taking place in the cornet's hut. Lukáshka had returned to the village, but had not been to see Olénin, and Olénin had not gone to the betrothal though he had been invited. He was sadder than he had ever been since he settled in this Cossack village. He had seen Lukáshka earlier in the evening and was worried why Lukáshka was so cold towards him. Olénin shut himself up in his hut and began writing in his diary as follows:

'Many things have I pondered over lately and much have I changed,' Olénin wrote, 'and I have come back to the copy-book maxim: The one way to be happy is to love, to love self-denyingly, to love everybody and everything; to spread a web of love* on all sides and to take all who come into it. In this way I caught Vanyúsha, Daddy Eróshka, Lukáshka, and Maryánka.'

As Olénin was finishing this sentence Daddy Eróshka entered the room.

Eróshka was in the happiest frame of mind. A few evenings before this, Olénin had gone to see him and had found him with a proud and happy face deftly skinning the carcass of a boar with a small knife in the yard. The dogs (Lyam his pet among them) were lying close by watching what he was doing and gently wagging their tails. The little boys were respectfully looking at him through the fence and not even teasing him as was their wont. His women neighbours, who were as a rule not too gracious towards him, greeted him and brought him, one a jug of *chikhír*, another some *kaymák*, and a third a little flour. The next day Eróshka sat in his store-room all covered with blood, and distributed pounds of boar-flesh, taking in payment money from some and wine from others. His face clearly expressed, 'God has sent me luck. I have killed a boar, so now I am wanted. Consequently he naturally began to drink, and had gone on for four days never leaving the village. Besides which he had had something to drink at the betrothal.

He came to Olénin quite drunk: his face red, his beard tangled, but wearing a new *beshmét* trimmed with gold braid; and he brought with him a *balaláyka** which he had obtained beyond the river. He had long promised Olénin this treat, and felt in the mood for it, so that he was sorry to find Olénin writing.

'Write on, write on, my lad,' he whispered, as if he thought that a spirit sat between him and the paper and must not be frightened away, and he softly and silently sat down on the floor. When Daddy Eróshka was drunk his favourite position was on the floor. Olénin looked round, ordered some wine to be brought, and continued to write. Eróshka found it boring to drink by himself and he wished to talk.

'I've been to the betrothal at the cornet's. But there! They're shwine!—Don't want them!—Have come to you.'

'And where did you get your *balaláyka*?' asked Olénin, still writing.

'I've been beyond the river and got it there, my friend,' he answered, also very quietly. 'I'm a master at it. Tatar or Cossack, squire or soldiers' songs, any kind you please.'

Olénin looked at him again, smiled, and went on writing.

That smile emboldened the old man.

'Come, leave off my lad, leave off!' he said with sudden firmness.

'Well, perhaps I will.'

'Come, people have injured you but leave them alone, spit at them! Come, what's the use of writing and writing, what's the good?'

And he tried to mimic Olénin by tapping the floor with his thick fingers, and then twisted his big face to express contempt.

'What's the good of writing quibbles. Better have a spree and show you're a man!'

No other conception of writing found place in his head except that of legal chicanery.

Olénin burst out laughing and so did Eróshka. Then, jumping up from the floor, the latter began to show off his skill on the *balaláyka* and to sing Tatar songs.

'Why write, my good fellow! You'd better listen to what I'll sing to you. When you're dead you won't hear any more songs. Make merry now!'

First he sang a song of his own composing accompanied by a dance:

> 'Ah, dee, dee, dee, dee, dee, dim,
> Say where did they last see him?
> In a booth, at the fair,
> He was selling pins, there.'

Then he sang a song he had learnt from his former sergeant-major:

> 'Deep I fell in love on Monday,
> Tuesday nothing did but sigh,
> Wednesday I popped the question,
> Thursday waited her reply.
> Friday, late, it came at last,
> Then all hope for me was past!
> Saturday my life to take
> I determined like a man,
> But for my salvation's sake
> Sunday morning changed my plan!'

Then he sang again:

> 'Oh dee, dee, dee, dee, dee, dim,
> Say where did they last see him.'

And after that, winking, twitching his shoulders, and footing it to the tune, he sang:

'I will kiss you and embrace,
Ribbons red twine round you;
And I'll call you little Grace.
Oh! you little Grace now do
Tell me, do you love me true?'

And he became so excited that with a sudden dashing movement he started dancing around the room accompanying himself the while.

Songs like 'Dee, dee, dee'—'gentlemen's songs'—he sang for Olénin's benefit, but after drinking three more tumblers of *chikhír* he remembered old times and began singing real Cossack and Tatar songs. In the midst of one of his favourite songs his voice suddenly trembled and he ceased singing, and only continued strumming on the *balaláyka*.

'Oh, my dear friend!' he said.

The peculiar sound of his voice made Olénin look round. The old man was weeping. Tears stood in his eyes and one tear was running down his cheek.

'You are gone, my young days, and will never come back!' he said, blubbering and halting. 'Drink, why don't you drink!' he suddenly shouted with a deafening roar, without wiping away his tears.

There was one Tatar song that specially moved him. It had few words, but its charm lay in the sad refrain. 'Ay day, dalalay!' Eróshka translated the words of the song: 'A youth drove his sheep from the *aúl* to the mountains: the Russians came and burnt the *aúl*, they killed all the men and took all the women into bondage. The youth returned from the mountains. Where the *aúl* had stood was an empty space; his mother was not there, nor his brothers, nor his house; one tree alone was left standing. The youth sat beneath the tree and wept. "Alone like thee, alone am I left,"' and Eróshka began singing: 'Ay day, dalalay!' and the old man repeated several times this wailing, heart-rending refrain.

When he had finished the refrain Eróshka suddenly seized a gun that hung on the wall, rushed hurriedly out into the yard and fired off both barrels into the air. Then again he began, more dolefully, his 'Ay day, dalalay—ah, ah,' and ceased.

Olénin followed him onto the porch and looked up into the starry sky in the direction where the shots had flashed. In the cornet's house there were lights and the sound of voices. In the yard girls were crowding round the porch and the windows, and running backwards and forwards between the hut and the shed. Some Cossacks rushed out of the hut and could not refrain from shouting, re-echoing the refrain of Daddy Eróshka's song and his shots.

'Why are you not at the betrothal?' asked Olénin.

'Never mind them! Never mind them!' muttered the old man, who had evidently been offended by something there. 'Don't like them, I don't. Oh, those people! Come back into the hut! Let them make merry by themselves and we'll make merry by ourselves.'

Olénin went in.

'And Lukáshka, is he happy? Won't he come to see me?' he asked.

'What, Lukáshka? They've lied to him and said I am getting his girl for you,' whispered the old man. 'But what's the girl? She will be ours if we want her. Give enough money—and she's ours. I'll fix it up for you. Really!'

'No, Daddy, money can do nothing if she does not love me. You'd better not talk like that!'

'We are not loved, you and I. We are forlorn,' said Daddy Eróshka suddenly, and again he began to cry.

Listening to the old man's talk Olénin had drunk more than usual. 'So now my Lukáshka is happy,' thought he; yet he felt sad. The old man had drunk so much that evening that he fell down on the floor and Vanyúsha had to call soldiers in to help, and spat as they dragged the old man out. He was so angry with the old man for his bad behaviour that he did not even say a single French word.

CHAPTER XXIX

It was August. For days the sky had been cloudless, the sun scorched unbearably and from early morning the warm wind raised a whirl of hot sand from the sand-drifts and from the road, and bore it in the air through the reeds, the trees, and the village. The grass and the leaves on the trees were covered with dust, the roads and dried-up salt marshes were baked so hard that they rang when trodden on. The water had long since subsided in the Térek and rapidly vanished and dried up in the ditches. The slimy banks of the pond near the village were trodden bare by the cattle and all day long you could hear the splashes and shouts of girls and boys bathing. The sand-drifts and the reeds were already drying up in the steppes, and the cattle, lowing, ran into the fields in the day-time. The boars migrated into the distant reed-beds and to the hills beyond the Térek. Mosquitoes and gnats swarmed in thick clouds over the low lands and villages. The snow-peaks were hidden in grey mist. The air was rarefied and smoky. It was said that *abréks* had crossed the now shallow river and were prowling on this side of it. Every night the sun set in a glowing red blaze. It was the busiest time of the year. The villagers all swarmed in the melon-fields and the vineyards. The vineyards thickly overgrown with twining verdure lay in cool, deep shade. Everywhere between the broad translucent leaves, ripe, heavy, black clusters peeped out. Along the dusty road from the vineyards the creaking carts moved slowly, heaped up with black grapes. Clusters of them, crushed by the wheels, lay in the dirt. Boys and girls in smocks stained with grape-juice, with grapes in their hands and mouths, ran after their mothers. On the road you continually came across tattered labourers with baskets of grapes on their powerful shoulders; Cossack maidens, veiled with kerchiefs to their eyes, drove bullocks harnessed to carts laden high with grapes. Soldiers who happened to meet these carts asked for grapes, and the maidens, clambering up without stopping their carts, would take an armful of grapes and drop them into the skirts of the soldiers' coats. In some homesteads they had already begun pressing the grapes; and the smell of the emptied skins filled the air. The blood-red troughs were visible under the overhangs and Nogáy labourers with their trousers rolled up and their legs stained with the juice were visible in the yard. Grunting pigs gorged themselves with the empty skins and rolled about in them. The flat roofs of the sheds were all spread over with the dark amber clusters drying in the sun. Daws and magpies crowded round the roofs, picking the seeds and fluttering from one place to another.

The fruits of the year's labour were being merrily gathered in, and this year the fruit was unusually fine and plentiful.

In the shady green vineyards amid a sea of vines, laughter, songs, merriment, and the voices of women were to be heard on all sides, and glimpses of their bright-coloured garments could be seen.

Just at noon Maryánka was sitting in their vineyard in the shade of a peach-tree, getting out the family dinner from under an unharnessed cart. Opposite her, on a spread-out horse-cloth, sat the cornet (who had returned from the school) washing his hands by pouring water on them from a little jug. Her little brother, who had just come straight out of the pond, stood wiping his face with his wide sleeves, and gazed anxiously at his sister and his mother and breathed deeply, awaiting his dinner. The old mother, with her sleeves rolled up over her strong sunburnt arms, was arranging grapes, dried fish, and *kaymák* on a little low, circular Tatar table. The cornet wiped his hands, took off his cap, crossed himself, and moved nearer to the table. The boy seized the jug and eagerly began to drink. The mother and daughter crossed their legs under them and sat down by the table. Even in the shade it was intolerably hot. The air above the vineyard smelt unpleasant: the strong warm wind passing amid the branches brought no coolness, but only monotonously bent the tops of the pear, peach, and mulberry trees with which the vineyard was sprinkled. The cornet, having crossed himself once more, took a little jug of *chikhír* that stood behind him covered with a vine-leaf, and having had a drink from the mouth of the jug passed it to the old woman. He had nothing on over his shirt, which was unfastened at the neck and showed his shaggy muscular chest. His fine-featured cunning face looked cheerful; neither in his attitude nor in his words was his usual wiliness to be seen, he was cheerful and natural.

'Shall we finish the bit beyond the shed tonight?' he asked, wiping his wet beard.

'We'll manage it,' replied his wife, 'if only the weather does not hinder us. The Dyómkins have not half finished yet,' she added. 'Only Ústenka is at work there, wearing herself out.'

'What can you expect of them?' said the old man proudly.

'Here, have a drink, Maryánka dear!' said the old woman, passing the jug to the girl. 'God willing we'll have enough to pay for the wedding feast,' she added.

'That's not yet awhile,' said the cornet with a slight frown.

The girl hung her head.

'Why shouldn't we mention it?' said the old woman. 'the affair is settled, and the time is drawing near too.'

'Don't make plans beforehand,' said the cornet. 'Now we have the harvest to get in.'

'Have you seen Lukáshka's new horse?' asked the old woman. 'The one Dmítri Andréich Olénin gave him is gone—he's exchanged it.'

'No, I have not; but I spoke with the servant today,' said the cornet, 'and he said his master has again received a thousand rubles.'

'Rolling in riches, in short,' said the old woman.

The whole family felt cheerful and contented.

The work was progressing successfully. The grapes were more abundant and finer than they had expected.

After dinner Maryánka threw some grass to the oxen, folded her *beshmét* for a pillow, and lay down under the wagon on the juicy down-trodden grass. She had on only a red kerchief over her head and a faded blue print smock, yet she felt unbearably hot. Her face was burning, and she did not know where to put her feet, her eyes were moist with sleepiness and weariness, her lips parted involuntarily, and her chest heaved heavily and deeply.

The busy time of year had begun a fortnight ago and the continuous heavy labour had filled the girl's life. At dawn she jumped up, washed her face with cold water, wrapped herself in a shawl, and ran out barefoot to see to the cattle. Then she hurriedly put on her shoes and her *beshmét* and, taking a small bundle of bread, she harnessed the bullocks and drove away to the vineyards for the whole day. There she cut the grapes and carried the baskets with only an hour's interval for rest, and in the evening she returned to the village, bright and not tired, dragging the bullocks by a rope or driving them with a long stick. After attending to the cattle, she took some sunflower seeds in the wide sleeve of her smock and went to the corner of the street to crack them and have some fun with the other girls. But as soon as it was dusk she returned home, and after having supper with her parents and her brother in the dark shed, she went into the hut, healthy and free from care, and climbed onto the oven, where half drowsing she listened to their lodger's conversation. As soon as he went away she would throw herself down on her bed and sleep soundly and quietly till morning. And so it went on day after day. She had not seen Lukáshka since the day of their betrothal, but calmly awaited the wedding. She had got used to their lodger and felt his intent looks with pleasure.

CHAPTER XXX

Although there was no escape from the heat and the mosquitoes swarmed in the cool shadow of the wagons, and her little brother tossing about beside her kept pushing her, Maryánka having drawn her kerchief over her head was just falling asleep, when suddenly their neighbour Ústenka came running towards her and, diving under the wagon, lay down beside her.

'Sleep, girls, sleep!' said Ústenka, making herself comfortable under the wagon. 'Wait a bit,' she exclaimed, 'this won't do!'

She jumped up, plucked some green branches, and stuck them through the wheels on both sides of the wagon and hung her *beshmét* over them.

'Let me in,' she shouted to the little boy as she again crept under the wagon. 'Is this the place for a Cossack—with the girls? Go away!'

When alone under the wagon with her friend, Ústenka suddenly put both her arms round her, and clinging close to her began kissing her cheeks and neck.

'Darling, sweetheart,' she kept repeating, between bursts of shrill, clear laughter.

'Why, you've learnt it from Grandad,' said Maryánka, struggling. 'Stop it!'

And they both broke into such peals of laughter that Maryánka's mother shouted to them to be quiet.

'Are you jealous?' asked Ústenka in a whisper.

'What nonsense! Let me sleep. What have you come for?'

But Ústenka kept on, 'But I really have something to tell you.'

Maryánka raised herself on her elbow and arranged the kerchief which had slipped off.

'Well, what is it?'

'I know something about your lodger!'

'There's nothing to know,' said Maryánka.

'Oh, you naughty girl!' said Ústenka, nudging her with her elbow and laughing. 'Won't tell anything. Does he come to you?'

'He does. What of that?' said Maryánka with a sudden blush.

'Now I'm a simple lass. I tell everybody. Why should I pretend?' said Ústenka, and her bright rosy face suddenly became pensive. 'Whom do I hurt? I love him, that's all there is to it.'

'Grandad, do you mean?'

'Well, yes!'

'And the sin?'

'Ah, Maryánka! When is one to have a good time if not while one's still free? When I marry a Cossack I shall bear children and shall have cares. There now, when you get married to Lukáshka not even a thought of joy will enter your head: children will come, and work!'

'Well? Some who are married live happily. It makes no difference!' Maryánka replied quietly.

'Do tell me just this once what has passed between you and Lukáshka?'

'What has passed? A match was proposed. Father put it off for a year, but now it's been settled and they'll marry us in autumn.'

'But what did he say to you?'

Maryánka smiled.

'What should he say? He said he loved me. He kept asking me to come to the vineyards with him.'

'Just see what a boor! But you didn't go, did you? And what a dare-devil he has become: the first among the *dzhigíts*. He makes merry out there in the army too! The other day our Kírka came home; he says: What a horse Lukáshka's got in exchange! But all the same I expect he frets after you. And what else did he say?'

'Must you know everything?' said Maryánka laughing. 'One night he came to my window tipsy, and asked me to let him in.'

'And you didn't let him?'

'Let him, indeed! Once I have said a thing I keep to it firm as a rock,' answered Maryánka seriously.

'A fine fellow! If he wanted her, no girl would refuse him.'

'Well, let him go to the others,' replied Maryánka proudly.

'You don't pity him?'

'I do pity him, but I'll have no nonsense. It is wrong.'

Ústenka suddenly dropped her head on her friend's breast, seized hold of her, and shook with smothered laughter. 'You silly fool!' she exclaimed, quite out of breath. 'You don't want to be happy,' and she began tickling Maryánka.

'Oh, leave off!' said Maryánka, screaming and laughing. 'You've crushed Lazútka.'

'Hark at those young devils! Quite frisky! Not tired yet!' came the old woman's sleepy voice from the wagon.

'Don't want happiness,' repeated Ústenka in a whisper, insistently. 'But you are lucky, that you are! How they love you! You are so crusty, and yet they love you. Ah, if I were in your place I'd soon turn the lodger's head! I noticed him when you were at our house. He was ready to eat you with his eyes. What things Grandad has given me! And yours they say is the richest of the Russians. His orderly says they have serfs of their own.'

Maryánka raised herself, and after thinking a moment, smiled.

'Do you know what he once told me: the lodger I mean?' she said, biting a bit of grass. 'He said, I'd like to be Lukáshka the Cossack, or your brother Lazútka—. What do you think he meant?'

'Oh, just chattering what came into his head,' answered Ústenka. 'What does mine not say! Just as if he was possessed!'

Maryánka dropped her head on her folded *beshmét*, threw her arm over Ústenka's shoulder, and shut her eyes.

'He wanted to come and work in the vineyard today: father invited him,' she said, and after a short silence she fell asleep.

CHAPTER XXXI

The sun had come out from behind the pear-tree that had shaded the wagon, and even through the branches that Ústenka had fixed up it scorched the faces of the sleeping girls. Maryánka woke up and began arranging the kerchief on her head. Looking about her, beyond the pear-tree she noticed their lodger, who with his gun on his shoulder stood talking to her father. She nudged Ústenka and smilingly pointed him out to her.

'I went yesterday and didn't find a single one,' Olénin was saying as he looked about uneasily, not seeing Maryánka through the branches.

'Ah, you should go out there in that direction, go right as by compasses, there in an abandoned vineyard denominated as the Waste, hares are always to be found,' said the cornet, having at once changed his manner of speech.

'A fine thing to go looking for hares in these busy times! You had better come and help us, and do some work with the girls,' the old woman said merrily. 'Now then, girls, up with you!' she cried.

Maryánka and Ústenka under the cart were whispering and could hardly restrain their laughter.

Since it had become known that Olénin had given a horse worth fifty rubles to Lukáshka, his hosts had become more amiable and the cornet in particular saw with pleasure his daughter's growing intimacy with Olénin.

'But I don't know how to do the work,' replied Olénin, trying not to look through the green branches under the wagon where he had now noticed Maryánka's blue smock and red kerchief.

'Come, I'll give you some peaches,' said the old woman.

'It's only according to the ancient Cossack hospitality. It's her old woman's silliness,' said the cornet, explaining and apparently correcting his wife's words. 'In Russia, I expect, it's not so much peaches as pineapple jam and preserves you have been accustomed to eat at your pleasure.'

'So you say hares are to be found in the abandoned vineyard?' asked Olénin. 'I will go there,' and throwing a hasty glance through the green branches he raised his cap and disappeared between the regular rows of green vines.

The sun had already sunk behind the fence of the vineyards, and its broken rays glittered through the translucent leaves when Olénin returned to his host's vineyard. The wind was falling and a cool freshness was beginning to spread around. By some instinct Olénin recognized from afar Maryánka's blue smock among the rows of vine, and, picking grapes on his way, he approached her. His highly excited dog also now and then seized a low-hanging cluster of grapes in his slobbering mouth. Maryánka, her face flushed, her sleeves rolled up, and her kerchief down below her chin, was rapidly cutting the heavy clusters and laying them in a basket. Without letting go of the vine she had hold of, she stopped to smile pleasantly at him and resumed her work. Olénin drew near and threw his gun behind his back to have his hands free. 'Where are your people? May God aid you! Are you alone?' he meant to say but did not say, and only raised his cap in silence.

He was ill at ease alone with Maryánka, but as if purposely to torment himself he went up to her.

'You'll be shooting the women with your gun like that,' said Maryánka.

'No, I shan't shoot them.'

They were both silent.

Then after a pause she said: 'You should help me.'

He took out his knife and began silently to cut off the clusters. From under the leaves low down he pulled out a thick bunch weighing about three pounds the grapes of which grew so close that they flattened each other for want of space. He showed it to Maryánka.

'Must they all be cut? Isn't this one too green?'

'Give it here.'

Their hands touched. Olénin took her hand, and she looked at him smiling.

'Are you going to be married soon?' he asked.

She did not answer, but turned away with a stern look.

'Do you love Lukáshka?'

'What's that to you?'

'I envy him!'

'Very likely!'

'No really. You are so beautiful!'

And he suddenly felt terribly ashamed of having said it, so commonplace did the words seem to him. He flushed, lost control of himself, and seized both her hands.

'Whatever I am, I'm not for you. Why do you make fun of me?' replied Maryánka, but her look showed how certainly she knew he was not making fun.

'Making fun? If you only knew how I—'

The words sounded still more commonplace, they accorded still less with what he felt, but yet he continued, 'I don't know what I would not do for you—'

'Leave me alone, you boor!'

But her face, her shining eyes, her swelling bosom, her shapely legs, said something quite different. It seemed to him that she understood how petty were all things he had said, but that she was superior to such considerations. It seemed to him she had long known all he wished and was not able to tell her, but wanted to hear how he would say it. 'And how can she help knowing,' he thought, 'since I only want to tell her all that she herself is? But she does not wish to understand, does not wish to reply.'

'Hullo!' suddenly came Ústenka's high voice from behind the vine at no great distance, followed by her shrill laugh. 'Come and help me, Dmítri Andréich. I am all alone,' she cried, thrusting her round, naïve little face through the vines.

Olénin did not answer nor move from his place.

Maryánka went on cutting and continually looked up at Olénin. He was about to say something, but stopped, shrugged his shoulders and, having jerked up his gun, walked out of the vineyard with rapid strides.

CHAPTER XXXII

He stopped once or twice, listening to the ringing laughter of Maryánka and Ústenka who, having come together, were shouting something. Olénin spent the whole evening hunting in the forest and returned home at dusk without having killed anything. When crossing the road he noticed her open the door of the shed, and her blue smock showed through it. He called to Vanyúsha very loud so as to let her know that he was back, and then sat down on the porch in his usual place. His hosts now returned from the vineyard; they came out of the shed and into their hut, but did not ask him in. Maryánka went twice out of the gate. Once in the twilight it seemed to him that she was looking at him. He eagerly followed her every movement, but could not make up his mind to approach her. When she disappeared into the hut he left the porch and began pacing up and down the yard, but Maryánka did not come out again. Olénin spent the whole sleepless night out in the yard listening to every sound in his hosts' hut. He heard them talking early in the evening, heard them having their supper and pulling out their cushions, and going to bed; he heard Maryánka laughing at something, and then heard everything growing gradually quiet. The cornet and his wife talked a while in whispers, and someone was breathing. Olénin re-entered his hut. Vanyúsha lay asleep in his clothes. Olénin envied him, and again went out to pace the yard, always expecting something, but no one came, no one moved, and he only heard the regular breathing of three people. He knew Maryánka's breathing and listened to it and to the beating of his own heart. In the village everything was quiet. The waning moon rose late, and the deep-breathing cattle in the yard became more visible as they lay down and slowly rose. Olénin angrily asked himself, 'What is it I want?' but could not tear himself away from the enchantment of the night. Suddenly he thought he distinctly heard the floor creak and the sound of footsteps in his hosts' hut. He rushed to the door, but all was silent again except for the sound of regular breathing, and in the yard the buffalo-cow, after a deep sigh, again moved, rose on her foreknees and then on her feet, swished her tail, and something splashed steadily on the dry clay ground; then she lay down again in the dim moonlight. He asked himself: 'What am I to do?' and definitely decided to go to bed, but again he heard a sound, and in his imagination there arose the image of Maryánka coming out into this moonlit misty night, and again he rushed to her window and again heard the sound of footsteps. Not till just before dawn did he go up to her window and push at the shutter and then run to the door, and this time he really heard Maryánka's deep breathing and her footsteps. He took hold of the latch and knocked. The floor hardly creaked under the bare cautious footsteps which approached the door. The latch clicked, the door creaked, and he noticed a faint smell of marjoram and pumpkin, and Maryánka's whole figure appeared in the doorway. He saw her only for an instant in the moonlight. She slammed the door and, muttering something, ran lightly back again. Olénin began rapping softly but nothing responded. He ran to the window and listened. Suddenly he was startled by a shrill, squeaky man's voice.

'Just great!' exclaimed a rather small young Cossack in a white cap, coming across the yard close to Olénin. 'I saw . . . Just great!'

Olénin recognized Nazárka, and was silent, not knowing what to do or say.

'Just great! I'll go and tell them at the office, and I'll tell her father! What a cornet's daughter! One's not enough for her.'

'What do you want of me, what are you after?' uttered Olénin.

'Nothing; only I'll tell them at the office.'

Nazárka spoke very loud, and evidently did so intentionally, adding: 'Just see what a clever cadet!'

Olénin trembled and grew pale.

'Come here, here!' He seized the Cossack firmly by the arm and drew him towards his hut.

'Nothing happened, she did not let me in, and I too mean no harm. She is an honest girl.'

'You can discuss it there.'

'Yes, but all the same I'll give you something now. Wait a bit!'

Nazárka said nothing. Olénin ran into his hut and brought out ten rubles, which he gave to the Cossack.

'Nothing happened, but still I was to blame, so I give this!—Only for God's sake don't let anyone know, for nothing happened.'

'I wish you joy,' said Nazárka laughing, and went away.

Nazárka had come to the village that night at Lukáshka's bidding to find a place to hide a stolen horse, and now, passing by on his way home, had heard the sound of footsteps. When he returned next morning to his company he bragged to his chum, and told him how cleverly he had got ten rubles. Next morning Olénin met his hosts and they knew nothing about the events of the night. He did not speak to Maryánka, and she only laughed a little when she looked at him. Next night he also passed without sleep, vainly wandering about the yard. The day after he purposely spent shooting, and in the evening he went to see Belétski to escape from his own thoughts. He was afraid of himself, and promised himself not to go to his hosts' hut any more.

That night he was roused by the sergeant-major. His company was ordered to start at once on a raid. Olénin was glad this had happened, and thought he would not again return to the village.

The raid lasted four days. The commander, who was a relative of Olénin's, wished to see him and offered to let him remain with the staff, but this Olénin declined. He found that he could not live away from the village, and asked to be allowed to return to it. For having taken part in the raid he received a soldier's cross, which he had formerly greatly desired. Now he was quite indifferent about it, and even more indifferent about his promotion, the order for which had still not arrived. Accompanied by Vanyúsha he rode back to the cordon without any accident several hours in advance of the rest of the company. He spent the whole evening on his porch watching Maryánka, and he again walked about the yard, without aim or thought, all night.

CHAPTER XXXIII

It was late when he awoke the next day. His hosts were no longer in. He did not go shooting, but now took up a book, and now went out onto the porch, and now again re-entered the hut and lay down on the bed. Vanyúsha thought he was ill.

Towards evening Olénin got up, resolutely began writing, and wrote on till late at night. He wrote a letter, but did not post it because he felt that no one would have understood what he wanted to say, and besides it was not necessary that anyone but himself should understand it. This is what he wrote:

'I receive letters of condolence from Russia. They are afraid that I shall perish, buried in these wilds. They say about me: "He will become coarse; he will be behind the times in everything; he will take to drink, and who knows but that he may marry a Cossack girl." It was not for nothing, they say, that Ermólov* declared: "Anyone serving in the Caucasus for ten years either becomes a confirmed drunkard or marries a loose woman." How terrible! Indeed it won't do for me to ruin myself when I might have the great happiness of even becoming the Countess B——'s husband, or a court chamberlain, or a marshal of my district. Oh, how repulsive and pitiable you all seem to me! You do not know what happiness is and what life is! One must taste life once in all its natural beauty, must see and understand what I see every day before me—those eternally unapproachable snowy peaks, and a majestic woman in that primitive beauty in which the first woman must have come from her creator's hands—and then it becomes clear who is ruining himself and who is living truly or falsely—you or I. If you only knew how despicable and pitiable you, in your delusions, seem to me! When I picture to myself—in place of my hut, my forests, and my love—those drawing-rooms, those women with their pomatum-greased hair eked out with false curls, those unnaturally grimacing lips, those hidden, feeble, distorted limbs, and that chatter of obligatory drawing-room conversation which has no right to the name—I feel unendurably revolted. I then see before me those obtuse faces, those rich eligible girls whose looks seem to say: "It's all right, you may come near though I am rich and eligible"—and that arranging and rearranging of seats, that shameless matchmaking and that eternal tittle-tattle and pretence; those rules—with whom to shake hands, to whom only to nod, with whom to converse (and all this done deliberately with a conviction of its inevitability), that continual ennui in the blood passing on from generation to generation. Try to understand or believe just this one thing: you need only see and comprehend what truth and beauty are, and all that you now say and think and all your wishes for me and for yourselves will scatter to the winds! Happiness is being with nature, seeing her, and conversing with her. "He may even (God forbid) marry a common Cossack girl, and be quite lost socially" I can imagine them saying of me with sincere pity! Yet the one thing I desire is to be quite "lost" in your sense of the word. I wish to marry a Cossack girl, and dare not because it would be a height of happiness of which I am unworthy.

'Three months have passed since I first saw the Cossack girl, Maryánka. The views and prejudices of the world I had left were still fresh in me. I did not then believe that I could love that woman. I delighted in her beauty just as I delighted in the beauty of the mountains and the sky, nor could I help delighting in her, for she is as beautiful as they. I found that the sight of her beauty had become a necessity of my life and I began asking myself whether I did not love her. But I could find nothing within myself at all like love as I had imagined it to be. Mine was not the restlessness of loneliness and desire for marriage, nor was it platonic, still less a carnal love such as I have experienced. I needed only to see her, to hear her, to know that she was near—and if I was not happy, I was at peace.

'After an evening gathering at which I met her and touched her, I felt that between that woman and myself there existed an indissoluble though unacknowledged bond against which I could not struggle, yet I did struggle. I asked myself: "Is it possible to love a woman who will never understand the profoundest interests of my life? Is it possible to love a woman simply for her beauty, to love the statue of a woman?" But I was already in love with her, though I did not yet trust to my feelings.

'After that evening when I first spoke to her our relations changed. Before that she had been to me an extraneous but majestic object of external nature: but since then she has become a human being. I began to meet her, to talk to her, and sometimes to go to work for her father and to spend whole evenings with them, and in this intimate intercourse she remained still in my eyes just as pure, inaccessible, and majestic. She always responded with equal calm, pride, and cheerful equanimity. Sometimes she was friendly, but generally her every look, every word, and every movement expressed equanimity—not contemptuous, but crushing and bewitching. Every day with a feigned smile on my lips I tried to play a part, and with torments of passion and desire in my heart I spoke banteringly to her. She saw that I was dissembling, but looked straight at me cheerfully and simply. This position became unbearable. I wished not to deceive her but to tell her all I thought and felt. I was extremely agitated. We were in the vineyard when I began to tell her of my love, in words I am now ashamed to remember. I am ashamed because I ought not to have dared to speak so to her because she stood far above such words and above the feeling they were meant to express. I said no more, but from that day my position has been intolerable. I did not wish to demean myself by continuing our former flippant relations, and at the same time I felt that I had not yet reached the level of straight and simple relations with her. I asked myself despairingly, "What am I to do?" In foolish dreams I imagined her now as my mistress and now as my wife, but rejected both ideas with disgust. To make her a wanton woman would be dreadful. It would be murder. To turn her into a fine lady, the wife of Dmítri Andréich Olénin, like a Cossack woman here who is married to one of our officers, would be still worse. Now could I turn Cossack like Lukáshka, and steal horses, get drunk on *chikhír*, sing rollicking songs, kill people, and when drunk climb in at her window for the night without a thought of who and what I am, it would be different: then we might understand one another and I might be happy.

'I tried to throw myself into that kind of life but was still more conscious of my own weakness and artificiality. I cannot forget myself and my complex distorted past, and my future appears to me still more hopeless. Every day I have before me the distant snowy mountains and this majestic, happy woman. But not for me is the only happiness possible in the world; I cannot have this woman! What is most terrible and yet sweetest in my condition is that I feel that I understand her but that she will never understand me; not because she is inferior: on the contrary she ought not to understand me. She is happy, she is like nature: consistent, calm, and self-contained; and I, a weak distorted being, want her to understand my deformity and my torments! I have not slept at night, but have aimlessly passed under her windows not rendering account to myself of what was happening to me. On the 18th our company started on a raid, and I spent three days away from the village. I was sad and apathetic, the usual songs, cards, drinking-bouts, and talk of rewards in the regiment, were more repulsive to me than usual. Yesterday I returned home and saw her, my hut, Daddy Eróshka, and the snowy mountains, from my porch, and was seized by such a strong, new feeling of joy that I understood it all. I love this woman; I feel real love for the first and only time in my life. I know what has befallen me. I do not fear to be degraded by this feeling, I am not ashamed of my love, I am proud of it. It is not my fault that I love. It has come about against my will. I tried to escape from my love by self-renunciation, and tried to devise a joy in the Cossack Lukáshka's and Maryánka's love, but thereby only stirred up my own love and jealousy. This is not the ideal, the so-called exalted love which I have known before, not that feeling of attraction in which you admire your own love, feel that the source of your emotion is within yourself, and do everything yourself. I have felt that too. It is still less a desire for pleasure. It is something different. Perhaps in her I love nature, the personification of all that is beautiful in nature. Yet I am not acting by my own will, but some elemental force loves her through me; the whole of God's world, all nature, presses this love into my soul and says, "Love her." I love her not with my mind or my imagination, but with my whole being. Loving her I feel myself to be an integral part of all God's joyous world. I wrote before about the new convictions to which my solitary life had brought me, but no one knows with what labour they shaped themselves within me and with what joy I realized them and saw a new way of life opening out before me; nothing was dearer to me than those convictions. Well! Love has come and neither they nor any regrets for them remain! It is even difficult for me to believe that I could prize such a one-sided, cold, and abstract state of mind. Beauty came and scattered to the winds all that laborious inward toil, and no regret remains for what has vanished! Self-renunciation is all nonsense and absurdity!

That is pride, a refuge from well-merited unhappiness, and salvation from the envy of others' happiness: "Live for others, and do good!"—Why? when in my soul there is only love for myself and the desire to love her and to live her life with her? Not for others, not for Lukáshka, I now desire happiness. I do not now love those others. Formerly I should have told myself that this is wrong. I should have tormented myself with the questions: What will become of her, of me, and of Lukáshka? Now I don't care. I do not live my own life, there is something stronger than me which directs me. I suffer; but formerly I was dead and only now do I live. Today I will go to their house and tell her everything.'

CHAPTER XXXIV

Late that evening, after writing this letter, Olénin went to his hosts' hut. The old woman was sitting on a bench behind the oven unwinding cocoons. Maryánka with her head uncovered sat sewing by the light of a candle. On seeing Olénin she jumped up, took her kerchief and stepped to the oven.

'Maryánka dear,' said her mother, 'won't you sit here with me a bit?'

'No, I'm bareheaded,' she replied, and sprang up on the oven.

Olénin could only see a knee, and one of her shapely legs hanging down from the oven. He treated the old woman to tea. She treated her guest to *kaymák* which she sent Maryánka to fetch. But having put a plateful on the table Maryánka again sprang on the oven from whence Olénin felt her eyes upon him. They talked about household matters. Granny Ulítka became animated and went into raptures of hospitality. She brought Olénin preserved grapes and a grape tart and some of her best wine, and pressed him to eat and drink with the rough yet proud hospitality of country folk, only found among those who produce their bread by the labour of their own hands. The old woman, who had at first struck Olénin so much by her rudeness, now often touched him by her simple tenderness towards her daughter.

'Yes, we need not offend the Lord by grumbling! We have

enough of everything, thank God. We have pressed sufficient *chikhír* and have preserved and shall sell three or four barrels of grapes and have enough left to drink. Don't be in a hurry to leave us. We will make merry together at the wedding.'

'And when is the wedding to be?' asked Olénin, feeling his blood suddenly rush to his face while his heart beat irregularly and painfully.

He heard a movement on the oven and the sound of seeds being cracked.

'Well, you know, it ought to be next week. We are quite ready,' replied the old woman, as simply and quietly as though Olénin did not exist. 'I have prepared and have procured everything for Maryánka. We will give her away properly. Only there's one thing not quite right. Our Lukáshka has been running rather wild. He has been too much on the spree! He's up to tricks! The other day a Cossack came here from his company and said he had been to the Nogáys.'

'He must mind he does not get caught,' said Olénin.

'Yes, that's what I tell him. "Mind, Lukáshka, don't you get into mischief. Well of course a young fellow naturally wants to cut a dash. But there's a time for everything. Well, you've captured or stolen something and killed an *abrék*! Well, you're a fine fellow! But now you should live quietly for a bit, or else there'll be trouble."'

'Yes, I saw him a time or two in the division, he was always merry-making. He has sold another horse,' said Olénin, and glanced towards the oven.

A pair of large, dark, and hostile eyes glittered as they gazed severely at him.

He became ashamed of what he had said. 'What of it? He does no one any harm,' suddenly remarked Maryánka. 'He makes merry with his own money,' and lowering her legs she jumped down from the oven and went out banging the door.

Olénin followed her with his eyes as long as she was in the hut, and then looked at the door and waited, understanding nothing of what Granny Ulítka was telling him.

A few minutes later some visitors arrived: an old man, Granny Ulítka's brother, with Daddy Eróshka, and following them came Maryánka and Ústenka.

'Good evening,' squeaked Ústenka. 'Still on holiday?' she added, turning to Olénin.

'Yes, still on holiday,' he replied, and felt, he did not know why, ashamed and ill at ease.

He wished to go away but could not. It also seemed to him impossible to remain silent. The old man helped him by asking for a drink, and they had a drink. Olénin drank with Eróshka, with the other Cossack, and again with Eróshka, and the more he drank the heavier was his heart. But the two old men grew merry. The girls climbed onto the oven, where they sat whispering and looking at the men, who drank till it was late. Olénin did not talk, but drank more than the others. The Cossacks were shouting. The old woman would not let them have any more *chikhír*, and at last turned them out. The girls laughed at Daddy Eróshka, and it was past ten when they all went out onto the porch. The old men invited themselves to finish their merry-making at Olénin's. Ústenka ran off home and Eróshka led the old Cossack to Vanyúsha. The old woman went out to tidy up the shed. Maryánka remained alone in the hut. Olénin felt fresh and joyous, as if he had only just woken up. He noticed everything, and having let the old men pass ahead he turned back to the hut where Maryánka was preparing for bed. He went up to her and wished to say something, but his voice broke. She moved away from him, sat down cross-legged on her bed in the corner, and looked at him silently with wild and frightened eyes. She was evidently afraid of him. Olénin felt this. He felt sorry and ashamed of himself, and at the same time proud and pleased that he aroused even that feeling in her.

'Maryánka!' he said, 'Will you never take pity on me? I can't tell you how I love you.'

She moved still farther away.

'Just hear how the wine is speaking! . . . You'll get nothing from me!'

'No, it is not the wine. Don't marry Lukáshka. I will marry you.' ('What am I saying,' he thought as he uttered these words. 'Shall I be able to say the same tomorrow?' 'Yes, I shall, I am sure I shall, and I will repeat them now,' replied an inner voice.)

'Will you marry me?'

She looked at him seriously and her fear seemed to have passed.

'Maryánka, I shall go out of my mind! I am not myself. I will do whatever you command,' and madly tender words came from his lips of their own accord.

'Now then, what are you drivelling about?' she interrupted, suddenly seizing the arm he was stretching towards her. She did not push his arm away but pressed it firmly with her strong hard fingers. 'Do gentlemen marry Cossack girls? Go away!'

'But will you? Everything . . .'

'And what shall we do with Lukáshka?' said she, laughing.

He snatched away the arm she was holding and firmly embraced her young body, but she sprang away like a fawn and ran barefoot onto the porch. Olénin came to his senses and was terrified at himself. He again felt himself inexpressibly vile compared to her, yet not repenting for an instant of what he had said he went home, and without even glancing at the old men who were drinking in his room he lay down and fell asleep more soundly than he had done for a long time.

CHAPTER XXXV

The next day was a holiday. In the evening all the villagers, their holiday clothes shining in the sunset, were out in the street. That season more wine than usual had been produced, and the people were now free from their labours. In a month the Cossacks were to start on a campaign and in many families preparations were being made for weddings.

Most of the people were standing in the square in front of the Cossack Government Office and near the two shops, in one of which cakes and pumpkin seeds were sold, in the other kerchiefs and cotton prints. On the earth-embankment of the office-building sat or stood the old men in sober grey, or black coats without gold trimmings or any kind of ornament. They conversed among themselves quietly in measured tones, about the harvest, about the young folk, about village affairs, and about old times, looking with dignified equanimity at the younger generation. Passing by them, the women and girls stopped and bent their heads. The young Cossacks respectfully slackened their pace and raised their caps, holding them for a while over their heads. The old men then stopped speaking. Some of them watched the passers-by severely, others kindly, and in their turn slowly took off their caps and put them on again.

The Cossack girls had not yet started their circle dance,* but having gathered in groups, in their bright-coloured *beshméts* with white kerchiefs on their heads pulled down to their eyes, they sat either on the ground or on the earth-banks about the huts sheltered from the oblique rays of the sun, and laughed and chattered in their ringing voices. Little boys and girls playing in the square sent their balls high up into the clear sky, and ran about squealing and shouting. The half-grown girls had started their circle dance, and were timidly singing in their thin shrill voices. Clerks, lads not in the service, or home for the holiday, bright faced and wearing smart white or new red, gold-trimmed *cherkéskas*, went about arm in arm in twos or threes from one group of women or girls to another, and stopped joking and chatting with the Cossack girls. The Armenian shopkeeper, in a gold-trimmed coat of fine blue cloth, stood at the open door through which piles of folded bright-coloured kerchiefs were visible and, conscious of his own importance and with the pride of an oriental tradesman, waited for customers. Two red-bearded, bare-footed Chechéns, who had come from beyond the Térek to see the fête, sat on their heels outside the house of a friend, negligently smoking their little pipes and occasionally spitting, watching the villagers and exchanging remarks with one another in their rapid guttural speech. Occasionally a workaday-looking soldier in an old overcoat passed across the square among the bright-clad girls. Here and there the songs of tipsy Cossacks who were merry-making could already be heard. All the huts were closed; the porches had been scrubbed clean the day before. Even the old women were out in the street, which was everywhere sprinkled with the shells of pumpkin and melon seeds. The air was warm and still, the sky deep and clear. Beyond the roofs the dead-white mountain range, which seemed very near, was turning rosy in the glow of the evening sun. Now and then from the other side of the river came the distant roar of a cannon, but above the village, mingling with one another, floated all sorts of merry holiday sounds.

Olénin had been pacing the yard all that morning hoping to see Maryánka. But she, having put on holiday clothes, went to Mass at the chapel and afterwards sat with the other girls on an earth-embankment cracking seeds; sometimes again, together with her companions, she ran home, and each time gave the lodger a bright and kindly look. Olénin felt afraid to address her playfully or in the presence of others. He wished to finish telling her what he had begun to say the night before, and to get her to give him a definite answer. He waited for another moment like that of yesterday evening, but the moment did not come, and he felt that he could not remain any longer in this uncertainty. She went out into the street again, and after waiting awhile he too went out and without knowing where he was going he followed her. He passed by the corner where she was sitting in her shining blue satin *beshmét*, and with an aching heart he heard behind him the girls laughing.

Belétski's hut looked out onto the square. As Olénin was passing it he heard Belétski's voice calling to him, 'Come in,' and in he went.

After a short talk they both sat down by the window and were soon joined by Eróshka, who entered dressed in a new *beshmét* and sat down on the floor beside them.

'There, that's the aristocratic party,' said Belétski, pointing with his cigarette to a brightly coloured group at the corner. 'Mine is there too. Do you see her? in red. That's a new *beshmét*.' 'Why don't you start the circle dance?' he shouted, leaning out of the window. 'Wait a bit, and then when it grows dark let us go too. Then we will invite them to Ústenka's. We must arrange a ball for them!'

'And I will come to Ústenka's,' said Olénin in a decided tone. 'Will Maryánka be there?'

'Yes, she'll be there. Do come!' said Belétski, without the least surprise. 'But isn't it a pretty picture?' he added, pointing to the motley crowds.

'Yes, very!' Olénin assented, trying to appear indifferent. 'Holidays of this kind,' he added, 'always make me wonder why all these people should suddenly be contented and jolly. Today for instance, just because it happens to be the fifteenth of the month, everything is festive. Eyes and faces and voices and movements and garments, and the air and the sun, are all in a holiday mood. And we no longer have any holidays!'

'Yes,' said Belétski, who did not like such reflections. 'And why are you not drinking, old fellow?' he said, turning to Eróshka.

Eróshka winked at Olénin, pointing to Belétski. 'Eh, he's a proud one that *kunák* of yours,' he said.

Belétski raised his glass. '*Allah birdy*' he said, emptying it. (*Allah birdy*, 'God has given!'—the usual greeting of Caucasians when drinking together.)

'*Saubul*' ('Your health'), answered Eróshka smiling, and emptied his glass.

'Speaking of holidays!' he said, turning to Olénin as he rose and looked out of the window, 'What sort of holiday is that! You should have seen them make merry in the old days! The women used to come out in their gold-trimmed *sarafáns*. Two rows of gold coins hanging round their necks and gold-cloth diadems on their heads, and when they passed they made a noise, "flu, flu", with their dresses. Every woman looked like a princess. Sometimes they'd come out, a whole herd of them, and begin singing songs so that the air seemed to rumble, and they went on making merry all night. And the Cossacks would roll out a barrel into the yards and sit down and drink till break of day, or they would go hand-in-hand sweeping the village. Whoever they met they seized and took along with them, and went from house to house. Sometimes they used to make merry for three days on end. Father used to come home—I still remember it—quite red and swollen, without a cap, having lost everything: he'd come and lie down. Mother knew what to do: she would bring him some fresh caviar and a little *chikhír* to sober him up, and would herself run about in the village looking for his cap. Then he'd sleep for two days! That's the sort of fellows they were then! But now what are they?'

'Well, and the girls in the *sarafáns*, did they make merry all by themselves?' asked Belétski.

'Yes, they did! Sometimes Cossacks would come on foot or

on horse and say, "Let's break up the circle dance," and they'd go, but the girls would take up cudgels. Carnival week, some young fellow would come galloping up, and they'd cudgel his horse and cudgel him too. But he'd break through, seize the one he loved, and carry her off. And his sweetheart would love him to his heart's content! Yes, the girls in those days they were regular queens!'

CHAPTER XXXVI

Just then two men rode out of the side street into the square. One of them was Nazárka. The other, Lukáshka, sat slightly sideways on his well-fed bay Kabardá horse which stepped lightly over the hard road jerking its beautiful head with its fine glossy mane. The well-adjusted gun in its cover, the pistol at his back, and the cloak rolled up behind his saddle showed that Lukáshka had not come from a peaceful place or from one near by. The smart way in which he sat a little sideways on his horse, the careless motion with which he touched the horse under its belly with his whip, and especially his half-closed black eyes, glistening as he looked proudly around him, all expressed the conscious strength and self-confidence of youth. 'Ever seen as fine a lad?' his eyes, looking from side to side, seemed to say. The elegant horse with its silver ornaments and trappings, the weapons, and the handsome Cossack himself attracted the attention of everyone in the square. Nazárka, lean and short, was much less well dressed. As he rode past the old men, Lukáshka paused and raised his curly white sheepskin cap above his closely cropped black head.

'Well, have you carried off many Nogáy horses?' asked a lean old man with a frowning, lowering look.

'Have you counted them, Grandad, that you ask?' replied Lukáshka, turning away.

'That's all very well, but you need not take my lad along with you,' the old man muttered with a still darker frown.

'Just see the old devil, he knows everything,' muttered Lukáshka to himself, and a worried expression came over his face; but then, noticing a corner where a number of Cossack girls were standing, he turned his horse towards them.

'Hallo, girls!' he shouted in his powerful, resonant voice, suddenly checking his horse. 'You've grown old without me, you witches!' and he laughed.

'Hallo, Lukáshka! Hallo, old pal!' the merry voices answered. 'Have you brought much money? Buy some sweets for the girls! Have you come for long? True enough it's long since we saw you.'

'Nazárka and I have just flown across to make a night of it,' replied Lukáshka, raising his whip and riding straight at the girls.

'Why, Maryánka has quite forgotten you,' said Ústenka, nudging Maryánka with her elbow and breaking into a shrill laugh.

Maryánka moved away from the horse and throwing back her head calmly looked at the Cossack with her large sparkling eyes.

'True enough you have not been around for a long time! Why are you trampling us under your horse?' she remarked dryly, and turned away.

Lukáshka seemed especially merry. His face shone with audacity and joy. Obviously staggered by Maryánka's cold reply he suddenly knitted his brow.

'Step up on my stirrup and I'll carry you away to the mountains, Mummy!' he suddenly exclaimed, and as if to disperse his dark thoughts he *dzhigíted* among the girls. Stooping down towards Maryánka he said, 'I'll kiss, oh, how I'll kiss you!'

Maryánka's eyes met his and she suddenly blushed and stepped back.

'Oh, bother you! you'll crush my feet,' she said, and bending her head looked at her well-shaped feet in their tightly fitting light blue stockings and her new red *chuvyáki* trimmed with narrow silver braid.

Lukáshka turned towards Ústenka, and Maryánka sat down next to a woman with a baby in her arms. The baby stretched his plump little hands towards the girl and seized a necklace string that hung down onto her blue *beshmét*. Maryánka bent towards the child and glanced at Lukáshka from the corner of her eyes. Lukáshka just then was getting out from under his coat, from the pocket of his black *beshmét*, a bundle of sweetmeats and seeds.

'There, I give them to all of you,' he said, handing the bundle to Ústenka and smiling at Maryánka.

A confused expression again appeared on the girl's face. It was as though a mist gathered over her beautiful eyes. She drew her kerchief down below her lips, and leaning her head over the fair-skinned face of the baby that still held her by her coin necklace she suddenly began to kiss it greedily. The baby pressed his little hands against the girl's high breasts, and opening his toothless mouth screamed loudly.

'You're smothering the boy!' said the little one's mother, taking him away; and she unfastened her *beshmét* to give him the breast. 'You'd better have a chat with the young fellow.'

'I'll only go and put up my horse and then Nazárka and I will come back; we'll make merry all night,' said Lukáshka, touching his horse with his whip and riding away from the girls.

Turning into a side street, he and Nazárka rode up to two huts that stood side by side.

'Here we are all right, old fellow! Be quick and come soon!' called Lukáshka to his comrade, dismounting in front of one of the huts; then he carefully led his horse in at the gate of the wattle fence of his own home.

'How d'you do, Styópka?' he said to his dumb sister, who, smartly dressed like the others, came in from the street to take his horse; and he made signs to her to take the horse to the hay, but not to unsaddle it.

The dumb girl made her usual humming noise, smacked her lips as she pointed to the horse and kissed it on the nose, as much as to say that she loved it and that it was a fine horse.

'How d'you do, mother? How is it that you have not gone out yet?' shouted Lukáshka, holding his gun in place as he mounted the steps of the porch.

His old mother opened the door.

'Dear me! I never expected, never thought, you'd come,' said the old woman. 'Why, Kírka said you wouldn't be here.'

'Go and bring some *chikhír*, mother. Nazárka is coming here and we will celebrate the feast day.'

'Right away, Lukáshka, right away!' answered the old woman. 'Our women are making merry. I expect our dumb one has gone too.'

She took her keys and hurriedly went to the shed.

Nazárka, after putting up his horse and taking the gun off his shoulder, returned to Lukáshka's house and went in.

CHAPTER XXXVII

'Your health!' said Lukáshka, taking from his mother's hands a cup filled to the brim with *chikhír* and carefully raising it to his bowed head.

'A bad business!' said Nazárka. 'You heard how Daddy Burlák said, "Have you stolen many horses?" He seems to know!'

'A regular wizard!' Lukáshka replied shortly. 'But what of it!' he added, tossing his head. 'They are across the river by now. Go and find them!'

'Still it's a bad lookout.'

'What's a bad lookout? Go and take some *chikhír* to him to-morrow and nothing will come of it. Now let's make merry. Drink!' shouted Lukáshka, just in the tone in which old Eróshka uttered the word. 'We'll go out into the street and make merry with the girls. You go and get some honey; or no, I'll send our dumb wench. We'll make merry till morning.'

Nazárka smiled.

'Are we stopping here long?' he asked.

'Till we've had a bit of fun. Run and get some vodka. Here's the money.'

Nazárka ran off obediently to get the vodka from Yámka's.

Daddy Eróshka and Ergushóv, like birds of prey, scenting where the merry-making was going on, tumbled into the hut one after the other, both tipsy.

'Bring us another half-pail,' shouted Lukáshka to his mother, by way of reply to their greeting.

'Now then, tell us where did you steal them, you devil?' shouted Eróshka. 'Fine fellow, I'm fond of you!'

'Fond indeed,' answered Lukáshka laughing, 'carrying sweets from cadets to lasses! Eh, you old . . .'

'That's not true, not true! Oh, Mark,' and the old man burst out laughing. 'And how that devil begged me. "Go," he said, "and arrange it." He offered me a gun! But no. I'd have managed it, but I feel for you. Now tell us where have you been?' And the old man began speaking in Tatar.

Lukáshka answered him promptly.

Ergushóv, who did not know much Tatar, only occasionally put in a word in Russian:

'What I say is he's driven away the horses. I know it for a fact,' he chimed in.

'Giréy and I went together.' (His speaking of Giréy Khan as 'Giréy' was, to the Cossack mind, evidence of his boldness.) 'Just beyond the river he kept bragging that he knew the whole of the steppe and would lead the way straight, but we rode on and the night was dark, and my Giréy lost his way and began wandering in a circle without getting anywhere: couldn't find the village, and there we were. We must have gone too much to the right. I believe we wandered about wellnigh till midnight. Then, thank goodness, we heard dogs howling.'

'Fools!' said Daddy Eróshka. 'There now, we too used to lose our way in the steppe. (Who the devil can follow it?) But I used to ride up a hillock and start howling like the wolves, like this!' He placed his hands before his mouth, and howled like a pack of wolves, all on one note. 'The dogs would answer at once. Well, go on—so you found them?'

'We soon led them away! Nazárka was nearly caught by some Nogáy women, he was!'

'Caught indeed,' Nazárka, who had just come back, said in an injured tone.

'We rode off again, and again Giréy lost his way and almost landed us among the sand-drifts. We thought we were just getting to the Térek but we were riding away from it all the time!'

'You should have steered by the stars,' said Daddy Eróshka.

'That's what I say,' interjected Ergushóv.

'Yes, steer when all is black; I tried and tried all about . . . and at last I put the bridle on one of the mares and let my own horse go free—thinking he'll lead us out, and what do you think! he just gave a snort or two with his nose to the ground, galloped ahead, and led us straight to our village. Thank goodness! It was getting quite light. We barely had time to hide them in the forest. Nagím came across the river and took them away.'

Ergushóv shook his head. 'It's just what I said. Smart. Did you get much for them?'

'It's all here,' said Lukáshka, slapping his pocket.

Just then his mother came into the room, and Lukáshka did not finish what he was saying.

'Drink!' he shouted.

'We too, Gírich and I, rode out late one night,' began Eróshka.

'Oh bother, we'll never hear the end of you!' said Lukáshka. 'I am going.' And having emptied his cup and tightened the strap of his belt he went out.

CHAPTER XXXVIII

It was already dark when Lukáshka went out into the street. The autumn night was fresh and calm. The full golden moon floated up behind the tall dark poplars that grew on one side of the square. From the chimneys of the outhouses smoke rose and spread above the village, mingling with the mist. Here and there lights shone through the windows, and the air was laden with the smell of *kizyák*, grape-pulp, and mist. The sounds of voices, laughter, songs, and the cracking of seeds mingled just as they had done in the daytime, but were now more distinct. Clusters of white kerchiefs and caps gleamed through the darkness near the houses and by the fences.

In the square, before the shop door which was lit up and open, the black and white figures of Cossack men and maids showed through the darkness, and one heard from afar their loud songs and laughter and talk. The girls, hand in hand, went round and round in a circle stepping lightly in the dusty square. A skinny girl, the plainest of them all, set the tune:

> From beyond the wood, from the forest dark,
> From the garden green and the shady park,
> There came out one day two young lads so gay.
> Young bachelors, hey! brave and smart were they!
> And they walked and walked, then stood still, each man,

And they talked and soon to dispute began!
Then a maid came out; as she came along,
Said, 'To one of you I shall soon belong!'
'Twas the fair-faced lad got the maiden fair,
Yes, the fair-faced lad with the golden hair!
Her right hand so white in his own took he,
And he led her round for his mates to see!
And said, 'Have you ever in all your life,
Met a lass as fair as my sweet little wife?'

The old women stood round listening to the songs. The little boys and girls ran about chasing one another in the dark. The men stood by, catching at the girls as the latter moved round, and sometimes breaking the ring and entering it. On the dark side of the door-way stood Belétski and Olénin, in their *cherkéskas* and sheepskin caps, and talked together in a style of speech unlike that of the Cossacks, in low but distinct tones, conscious that they were attracting attention. Next to one another in the circle dance moved plump little Ústenka in her red *beshmét* and the stately Maryánka in her new smock and *beshmét*. Olénin and Belétski were discussing how to snatch Ústenka and Maryánka out of the ring. Belétski thought that Olénin wished only to amuse himself, but Olénin was expecting his fate to be decided. He wanted at any cost to see Maryánka alone that very day and to tell her everything, and ask her whether she could and would be his wife. Although that question had long been answered in the negative in his own mind, he hoped he would be able to tell her all he felt, and that she would understand him.

'Why did you not tell me sooner?' said Belétski. 'I would have got Ústenka to arrange it for you. You are such a queer fellow!'

'What's to be done! Some day, very soon, I'll tell you all about it. Only now for Heaven's sake arrange so that she should come to Ústenka's.'

'All right, that's easily done! Well, Maryánka, will you belong to the "fair-faced lad", and not to Lukáshka?' said Belétski, speaking to Maryánka first for propriety's sake, but having received no reply he went up to Ústenka and begged her to bring Maryánka home with her. He had hardly time to finish what he was saying before the leader began another song and the girls started pulling each other round in the ring by the hand.

They sang:

Past the garden, by the garden,
A young man came strolling down,
Up the street and through the town.
And the first time as he passed
He did wave his strong right hand.
As the second time he passed
Waved his hat with silken band.
But the third time as he went
He stood still: before her bent.

'How is it that thou, my dear,
My reproaches dost not fear?
In the park don't come to walk
That we there might have a talk?

'Come now, answer me, my dear,
Dost thou hold me in contempt?
Later on, thou knowest, dear,
Thou'lt get sober and repent.
Soon to woo thee I will come,
And when we shall married be
Thou wilt weep because of me!'

'Though I knew what to reply,
Yet I dared not him deny,
No, I dared not him deny!
So into the park went I,
In the park my lad to meet,
There my dear one I did greet.'

'Maiden dear, I bow to thee!
Take this handkerchief from me.
In thy white hand take it, see!
Say I am beloved by thee.
I don't know at all, I fear,
What I am to give thee, dear!
To my dear I think I will
Of a shawl a present make—
And five kisses for it take.'

Lukáshka and Nazárka broke into the circle dance and started walking about among the girls. Lukáshka joined in the singing, taking seconds in his clear voice as he walked in the middle of the circle dance swinging his arms. 'Well come in, one of you!' he said. The other girls pushed Maryánka, but she would not go. The sound of shrill laughter, slaps, kisses, and whispers mingled with the singing.

As he went past Olénin, Lukáshka gave a friendly nod.

'Dmítri Andréich! Have you too come to have a look?' he said.

'Yes,' answered Olénin drily.

Belétski stooped and whispered something into Ústenka's ear. She had not time to reply till she came round again, when she said:

'All right, we'll come.'

'And Maryánka too?'

Olénin stooped towards Maryánka. 'You'll come? Please do, if only for a minute. I must speak to you.'

'If the other girls come, I will.'

'Will you answer my question?' said he, bending towards her. 'You are in good spirits today.'

She had already moved past him. He went after her.

'Will you answer?'

'Answer what?'

'The question I asked you the other day,' said Olénin, stooping to her ear. 'Will you marry me?'

Maryánka thought for a moment.

'I'll tell you,' said she, 'I'll tell you tonight.'

And through the darkness her eyes gleamed brightly and kindly at the young man.

He still followed her. He enjoyed stooping closer to her.

But Lukáshka, without ceasing to sing, suddenly seized her firmly by the hand and pulled her from her place in the ring of girls into the middle. Olénin had only time to say, 'Come to Ústenka's,' and stepped back to his companion. The song came to an end. Lukáshka wiped his lips, Maryánka did the same, and they kissed. 'No, no, five times!' said Lukáshka. Chatter, laughter, and running about, succeeded to the rhythmic movements and sound. Lukáshka, who seemed to have drunk a great deal, began to distribute sweetmeats to the girls.

'I offer them to everyone!' he said with proud, comically pathetic self-admiration. 'But anyone who goes after soldiers goes out of the ring!' he suddenly added, with an angry glance at Olénin.

The girls grabbed his sweetmeats from him, and, laughing, struggled for them among themselves. Belétski and Olénin stepped aside.

Lukáshka, as if ashamed of his generosity, took off his cap and wiping his forehead with his sleeve came up to Maryánka and Ústenka.

'Answer me, my dear, dost thou hold me in contempt?' he said in the words of the song they had just been singing, and turning to Maryánka he angrily repeated the words: 'Dost thou hold me in contempt? When we shall married be thou wilt weep because of me!' he added, embracing Ústenka and Maryánka both together.

Ústenka tore herself away, and swinging her arm gave him such a blow on the back that she hurt her hand.

'Well, are you going to have another turn?' he asked.

'The other girls may if they like,' answered Ústenka, 'but I am going home and Maryánka was coming to our house too.'

With his arm still round her, Lukáshka led Maryánka away from the crowd to the darker corner of a house.

'Don't go, Maryánka,' he said, 'let's have some fun for the last time. Go home and I will come to you!'

'What am I to do at home? Holidays are meant for merry-making. I am going to Ústenka's', replied Maryánka.

'I'll marry you all the same, you know!'

'All right,' said Maryánka, 'we shall see when the time comes.'

'So you are going,' said Lukáshka sternly, and, pressing her close, he kissed her on the cheek.

'There, leave off! Don't bother,' and Maryánka, wrenching herself from his arms, moved away.

'Ah my girl, it will turn out badly,' said Lukáshka reproachfully and stood still, shaking his head. 'Thou wilt weep because of me . . .' and turning away from her he shouted to the other girls:

'Now then! Play away!'

What he had said seemed to have frightened and vexed Maryánka. She stopped. 'What will turn out badly?'

'Why, that!'

'That what?'

'Why, that you keep company with a soldier-lodger and no longer care for me!'

'I'll care just as long as I choose. You're not my father, nor my mother. What do you want? I'll care for whom I like!'

'Well all right,' said Lukáshka, 'but remember!' He moved towards the shop. 'Girls!' he shouted, 'why have you stopped? Go on dancing. Nazárka, fetch some more *chikhír*.'

'Well, will they come?' asked Olénin, addressing Belétski.

'They'll come directly,' replied Belétski. 'Come along, we must prepare the ball.'

CHAPTER XXXIX

It was already late in the night when Olénin came out of Belétski's hut following Maryánka and Ústenka. He saw in the dark street before him the gleam of the girl's white kerchief. The golden moon was descending towards the steppe. A silvery mist hung over the village. All was still; there were no lights anywhere and one heard only the receding footsteps of the young women. Olénin's heart beat fast. The fresh moist atmosphere cooled his burning face. He glanced at the sky and turned to look at the hut he had just come out of: the candle was already out. Then he again peered through the darkness at the girls' retreating shadows. The white kerchief disappeared in the mist. He was afraid to remain alone, he was so happy. He jumped down from the porch and ran after the girls.

'Bother you, someone may see,' said Ústenka.

'Never mind!'

Olénin ran up to Maryánka and embraced her.

Maryánka did not resist.

'Haven't you kissed enough yet?' said Ústenka. 'Marry and then kiss, but now you'd better wait.'

'Good-night, Maryánka, tomorrow I will come to see your father and tell him. Don't you say anything.'

'Why should I!' answered Maryánka.

Both the girls started running. Olénin went on by himself thinking over all that had happened. He had spent the whole evening alone with her in a corner by the oven. Ústenka had not left the hut for a single moment, but had romped about with the other girls and with Belétski all the time. Olénin had talked in whispers to Maryánka.

'Will you marry me?' he had asked.

'You'd deceive me and not have me,' she replied cheerfully and calmly.

'But do you love me? Tell me for God's sake!'

'Why shouldn't I love you? You don't squint,' answered Maryánka, laughing and with her hard hands squeezing his.

'What whi-ite, whi-i-ite, soft hands you've got—just like *kaymák*,' she said.

'I am in earnest. Tell me, will you marry me?'

'Why not, if father gives me to you?'

'Well then remember, I shall go mad if you deceive me. To-morrow I will tell your mother and father. I shall come and propose.'

Maryánka suddenly burst out laughing.

'What's the matter?'

'It seems so funny!'

'It's true! I will buy a vineyard and a house and will enroll myself as a Cossack.'

'Mind you don't go after other women then. I am severe about that.'

Olénin joyfully repeated all these words to himself. The memory of them now gave him pain and now such joy that it took his breath away. The pain was because she had remained as calm as usual while talking to him. She did not seem at all agitated by these new conditions. It was as if she did not trust him and did not think of the future. It seemed to him that she only loved him for the present moment, and that in her mind there was no future with him. He was happy because her words sounded to him true, and she had consented to be his. 'Yes,' thought he to himself, 'we shall only understand one another when she is quite mine. For such love there are no words. It needs life—the whole of life. Tomorrow everything will be cleared up. I cannot live like this any longer; tomorrow I will tell everything to her father, to Belétski, and to the whole village.'

Lukáshka, after two sleepless nights, had drunk so much at the fête that for the first time in his life his feet would not carry him, and he slept in Yámka's house.

CHAPTER XL

The next day Olénin awoke earlier than usual, and immediately remembered what lay before him, and he joyfully recalled her kisses, the pressure of her hard hands, and her words, 'What white hands you have!' He jumped up and wished to go at once to his hosts' hut to ask for their consent to his marriage with Maryánka. The sun had not yet risen, but it seemed that there was an unusual bustle in the street and side-street: people were moving about on foot and on horseback, and talking. He threw on his *cherkéska* and hastened out onto the porch. His hosts were not yet up. Five Cossacks were riding past and talking loudly together. In front rode Lukáshka on his broad-backed Kabardá horse. The Cossacks were all speaking and shouting so that it was impossible to make out exactly what they were saying.

'Ride to the Upper Post,' shouted one.

'Saddle and catch us up, be quick,' said another.

'It's nearer through the other gate!'

'What are you talking about?' cried Lukáshka. 'We must go through the middle gates, of course.'

'So we must, it's nearer that way,' said one of the Cossacks who was covered with dust and rode a perspiring horse. Lukáshka's face was red and swollen after the drinking of the previous night and his cap was pushed to the back of his head. He was calling out with authority as though he were an officer.

'What is the matter? Where are you going?' asked Olénin, with difficulty attracting the Cossacks' attention.

'We are off to catch *abréks*. They're hiding among the sand-drifts. We are just off, but there are not enough of us yet.'

And the Cossacks continued to shout, more and more of them joining as they rode down the street. It occurred to Olénin that it would not look well for him to stay behind; besides he thought he could soon come back. He dressed, loaded his gun with bullets, jumped onto his horse which

Vanyúsha had saddled more or less well, and overtook the Cossacks at the village gates. The Cossacks had dismounted, and filling a wooden bowl with *chikhír* from a little cask which they had brought with them, they passed the bowl round to one another and drank to the success of their expedition. Among them was a smartly dressed young cornet, who happened to be in the village and who took command of the group of nine Cossacks who had joined for the expedition. All these Cossacks were privates, and although the cornet assumed the airs of a commanding officer, they only obeyed Lukáshka. Of Olénin they took no notice at all, and when they had all mounted and started, and Olénin rode up to the cornet and began asking him what was taking place, the cornet, who was usually quite friendly, treated him with marked condescension. It was with great difficulty that Olénin managed to find out from him what was happening. Scouts who had been sent out to search for *abréks* had come upon several hillsmen some six miles from the village. These *abréks* had taken shelter in pits and had fired at the scouts, declaring they would not surrender. A corporal who had been scouting with two Cossacks had remained to watch the *abréks*, and had sent one Cossack back to get help.

The sun was just rising. Three miles beyond the village the steppe spread out and nothing was visible except the dry, monotonous, sandy, dismal plain covered with the hoofprints of cattle, and here and there with tufts of withered grass, with low reeds in the flats, and rare, little-trodden footpaths, and the camps of the nomad Nogáy tribe just visible far away. The absence of shade and the austere aspect of the place were striking. The sun always rises and sets red in the steppe. When it is windy whole hills of sand are carried by the wind from place to place. When it is calm, as it was that morning, the silence, uninterrupted by any movement or sound, is peculiarly striking. That morning in the steppe it was quiet and dull, though the sun had already risen. It all seemed specially soft and desolate. The air was hushed, the footfalls and the snorting of the horses were the only sounds to be heard, and even they quickly died away.

The men rode almost silently. A Cossack always carries his

weapons so that they neither jingle nor rattle. Jingling weapons are a terrible disgrace to a Cossack. Two other Cossacks from the village caught the party up and exchanged a few words. Lukáshka's horse either stumbled or caught its foot in some grass, and became restive—which is a sign of bad luck among the Cossacks, and at such a time was of special importance. The others exchanged glances and turned away, trying not to notice what had happened. Lukáshka pulled at the reins, frowned sternly, set his teeth, and flourished his whip above his head. His good Kabardá horse, prancing from one foot to another not knowing with which to start, seemed to wish to fly upwards on wings. But Lukáshka hit its well-fed sides with his whip once, then again, and a third time, and the horse, showing its teeth and spreading out its tail, snorted and reared and stepped on its hind legs a few paces away from the others.

'Ah, a good steed that!' said the cornet.

That he said *steed* instead of *horse* indicated special praise.

'A lion of a horse,' assented one of the others, an old Cossack.

The Cossacks rode forward silently, now at a foot-pace, then at a trot, and these changes were the only incidents that interrupted for a moment the stillness and solemnity of their movements.

Riding through the steppe for about six miles, they passed nothing but one Nogáy tent, placed on a cart and moving slowly along at a distance of about a mile from them. A Nogáy family was moving from one part of the steppe to another. Afterwards they met two tattered Nogáy women with high cheekbones, who with baskets on their backs were gathering dung left by the cattle that wandered over the steppe. The cornet, who did not know their language well, tried to question them, but they did not understand him and, obviously frightened, looked at one another.

Lukáshka rode up to them both, stopped his horse, and promptly uttered the usual greeting. The Nogáy women were evidently relieved, and began speaking to him quite freely as to a brother.

'*Ay-ay, kop abrék!*' they said plaintively, pointing in the direction in which the Cossacks were going. Olénin understood that they were saying, 'Many *abréks.*'

Never having seen an engagement of that kind, and having formed an idea of them only from Daddy Eróshka's tales, Olénin wished not to be left behind by the Cossacks, but wanted to see it all. He admired the Cossacks, and was on the watch, looking and listening and making his own observations. Though he had brought his sword and a loaded gun with him, when he noticed that the Cossacks avoided him he decided to take no part in the action, as in his opinion his courage had already been sufficiently proved when he was with his detachment, and also because he was very happy.

Suddenly a shot was heard in the distance.

The cornet became excited, and began giving orders to the Cossacks as to how they should divide and from which side they should approach. But the Cossacks did not appear to pay any attention to these orders, listening only to what Lukáshka said and looking to him alone. Lukáshka's face and figure were expressive of calm solemnity. He put his horse to a trot with which the others were unable to keep pace, and screwing up his eyes kept looking ahead.

'There's a man on horseback,' he said, reining in his horse and keeping in line with the others.

Olénin looked intently, but could not see anything. The Cossacks soon distinguished two riders and quietly rode straight towards them.

'Are those the *abréks*?' asked Olénin.

The Cossacks did not answer his question, which appeared quite meaningless to them. The *abréks* would have been fools to venture across the river on horseback.

'That's friend Ródka waving to us, I do believe,' said Lukáshka, pointing to the two mounted men who were now clearly visible. 'Look, he's coming to us.'

A few minutes later it became plain that the two horsemen were the Cossack scouts. The corporal rode up to Lukáshka.

CHAPTER XLI

'Are they far?' was all Lukáshka said.

Just then they heard a sharp shot some thirty paces off. The corporal smiled slightly.

'Our Gúrka is taking shots at them,' he said, nodding in the direction of the shot.

Having gone a few paces farther they saw Gúrka sitting behind a sand-hillock and loading his gun. To while away the time he was exchanging shots with the *abréks*, who were behind another sand-heap. A bullet came whistling from their side.

The cornet was pale and grew confused. Lukáshka dismounted from his horse, threw the reins to one of the other Cossacks, and went up to Gúrka. Olénin also dismounted and, bending down, followed Lukáshka. They had hardly reached Gúrka when two bullets whistled above them. Lukáshka looked around laughing at Olénin and stooped a little.

'Look out or they will kill you, Dmítri Andréich,' he said. 'You'd better go away—you have no business here.'

But Olénin wanted absolutely to see the *abréks*.

From behind the mound he saw caps and muskets some two hundred paces off. Suddenly a little cloud of smoke appeared from thence, and again a bullet whistled past. The *abréks* were hiding in a marsh at the foot of the hill. Olénin was much impressed by the place in which they sat. In reality it was very much like the rest of the steppe, but because the *abréks* sat there it seemed to detach itself from all the rest and to have become distinguished. Indeed it appeared to Olénin that it was the very spot for *abréks* to occupy. Lukáshka went back to his horse and Olénin followed him.

'We must get a hay-cart,' said Lukáshka, 'or they will be killing some of us. There behind that mound is a Nogáy cart with a load of hay.'

The cornet listened to him and the corporal agreed. The cart of hay was fetched, and the Cossacks, hiding behind it, pushed it forward. Olénin rode up a hillock from whence he could see everything. The hay-cart moved on and the Cossacks crowded together behind it. The Cossacks advanced, but the Chechéns, of whom there were nine, sat with their knees in a row and did not fire.

All was quiet. Suddenly from the Chechéns arose the sound of a mournful song, something like Daddy Eróshka's 'Ay day, dalalay'. The Chechéns knew that they could not escape, and to prevent themselves from being tempted to take to flight they had strapped themselves together, knee to knee, had got their guns ready, and were singing their death-song.

The Cossacks with their hay-cart drew closer and closer, and Olénin expected the firing to begin at any moment, but the silence was only broken by the *abréks*' mournful song. Suddenly the song ceased; there was a sharp report, a bullet struck the front of the cart, and Chechén curses and yells broke the silence and shot followed on shot and one bullet after another struck the cart. The Cossacks did not fire and were now only five paces distant.

Another moment passed and the Cossacks with a whoop rushed out on both sides from behind the cart—Lukáshka in front of them. Olénin heard only a few shots, then shouting and moans. He thought he saw smoke and blood, and abandoning his horse and quite beside himself he ran towards the Cossacks. Horror seemed to blind him. He could not make out anything, but understood that all was over. Lukáshka, pale as death, was holding a wounded Chechén by the arms and shouting, 'Don't kill him. I'll take him alive!' The Chechén was the red-haired man who had fetched his brother's body away after Lukáshka had killed him. Lukáshka was twisting his arms. Suddenly the Chechén wrenched himself free and fired his pistol. Lukáshka fell, and blood began to flow from his stomach. He jumped up, but fell again, swearing in Russian and in Tatar. More and more blood appeared on his clothes and under him. Some Cossacks approached him and began loosening his girdle. One of them, Nazárka, before beginning to help, fumbled for some time unable to put his sword in its sheath: it would not go the right way. The blade of the sword was bloodstained.

The Chechéns with their red hair and clipped moustaches lay dead and hacked about. Only the one we know of, who had fired at Lukáshka, though wounded in many places was still alive. Like a wounded hawk all covered with blood (blood was flowing from a wound under his right eye), pale and gloomy, he looked about him with wide-open excited eyes and clenched teeth as he crouched, dagger in hand, still prepared to defend himself. The cornet went up to him as if intending to pass by, and with a quick movement shot him in the ear. The Chechén started up, but it was too late, and he fell.

The Cossacks, quite out of breath, dragged the bodies aside and took the weapons from them. Each of the red-haired Chechéns had been a man, and each one had his own individual expression. Lukáshka was carried to the cart. He continued to swear in Russian and in Tatar.

'No fear, I'll strangle him with my hands. *Ana seni!*' he cried, struggling. But he soon became quiet from weakness.

Olénin rode home. In the evening he was told that Lukáshka was at death's door, but that a Tatar from beyond the river had undertaken to cure him with herbs.

The bodies were brought to the village office. The women and the little boys hastened to look at them.

It was growing dark when Olénin returned, and he could not collect himself after what he had seen. But towards night memories of the evening before came rushing to his mind. He looked out of the window; Maryánka was passing to and fro from the house to the cowshed, putting things straight. Her mother had gone to the vineyard and her father to the office. Olénin could not wait till she had quite finished her work, but went out to meet her. She was in the hut standing with her back towards him. Olénin thought she felt shy.

'Maryánka,' said he, 'I say, Maryánka! May I come in?'

She suddenly turned. There was a scarcely perceptible trace of tears in her eyes and her face was beautiful in its sadness. She looked at him in silent dignity.

Olénin again said:

'Maryánka, I have come—'

'Leave me alone!' she said. Her face did not change but the tears ran down her cheeks.

'What are you crying for? What is it?'

'What?' she repeated in a rough voice. 'Cossacks have been killed, that's what for.'

'Lukáshka?' said Olénin.

'Go away! What do you want?'

'Maryánka!' said Olénin, approaching her.

'You will never get anything from me!'

'Maryánka, don't speak like that,' Olénin entreated.

'Get away. I'm sick of you!' shouted the girl, stamping her foot, and moved threateningly towards him. And her face expressed such abhorrence, such contempt, and such anger that Olénin suddenly understood that there was no hope for him, and that his first impression of this woman's inaccessibility had been perfectly correct.

Olénin said nothing more, but ran out of the hut.

CHAPTER XLII

For two hours after returning home he lay on his bed motionless. Then he went to his company commander and obtained leave to visit the staff. Without taking leave of anyone, and sending Vanyúsha to settle his accounts with his landlord, he prepared to leave for the fort where his regiment was stationed. Daddy Eróshka was the only one to see him off. They had a drink, and then a second, and then yet another. Again as on the night of his departure from Moscow, a three-horsed conveyance stood waiting at the door. But Olénin did not confer with himself as he had done then, and did not say to himself that all he had thought and done here was 'not it'. He did not promise himself a new life. He loved Maryánka more than ever, and knew that he could never be loved by her.

'Well, good-bye, my lad!' said Daddy Eróshka. 'When you go on an expedition, be wise and listen to my words—the words of an old man. When you are out on a raid or the like (you know I'm an old wolf and have seen things), and when they begin firing, don't get into a crowd where there are many men. When you fellows get frightened you always try to get close together with a lot of others. You think it is merrier to be with others, but that's where it is worst of all! They always aim at a crowd. Now I used to keep farther away from the others and went alone, and I've never been wounded. Yet what things haven't I seen in my day?'

'But you've got a bullet in your back,' remarked Vanyúsha, who was clearing up the room.

'That was the Cossacks fooling about,' answered Eróshka.

'Cossacks? How was that?' asked Olénin.

'Oh, just so. We were drinking. Vánka Sítkin, one of the

Cossacks, got merry, and puff! he gave me one from his pistol right here.'

'Yes, and did it hurt?' asked Olénin. 'Vanyúsha, will you soon be ready?' he added.

'Ah, where's the hurry! Let me tell you. When he banged into me, the bullet did not break the bone but remained here. And I say: "You've killed me, brother. Eh! What have you done to me? I won't let you off! You'll have to stand me a pailful!"'

'Well, but did it hurt?' Olénin asked again, scarcely listening to the tale.

'Let me finish. He stood a pailful, and we drank it, but the blood went on flowing. The whole room was drenched and covered with blood. Grandad Burlák, he says, "The lad will give up the ghost. Stand a bottle of the sweet sort, or we shall have you taken up!" They bought more drink, and boozed and boozed—'

'Yes, but did it hurt you much?' Olénin asked once more.

'Hurt, indeed! Don't interrupt: I don't like it. Let me finish. We boozed and boozed till morning, and I fell asleep on the top of the oven, drunk. When I woke in the morning I could not unbend myself anyhow—'

'Was it very painful?' repeated Olénin, thinking that now he would at last get an answer to his question.

'Did I tell you it was painful? I did not say it was painful, but I could not bend and could not walk.'

'And then it healed up?' said Olénin, not even laughing, so heavy was his heart.

'It healed up, but the bullet is still there. Just feel it!' And lifting his shirt he showed his powerful back, where just near the bone a bullet could be felt and rolled about.

'Feel how it rolls,' he said, evidently amusing himself with the bullet as with a toy. 'There now, it has rolled to the back.'

'And Lukáshka, will he recover?' asked Olénin.

'Heaven only knows! There's no doctor. They've gone for one.'

'Where will they get one? From Grózny?' asked Olénin.

'No, my lad. Were I the Tsar I'd have hung all your Russian doctors long ago. Cutting is all they know! There's our Cossack Bakláshka, no longer a real man now that they've cut off his leg! That shows they're fools. What's Bakláshka good for now? No, my lad, in the mountains there are real doctors. There was my chum, Vórchik, he was on an expedition and was wounded just here in the chest. Well, your doctors gave him up, but one of theirs came from the mountains and cured him! They understand herbs, my lad!'

'Come, stop talking rubbish,' said Olénin. 'I'd better send a doctor from head-quarters.'

'Rubbish!' the old man said mockingly. 'Fool, fool! Rubbish. You'll send a doctor!—If yours cured people, Cossacks, and Chechéns would go to you for treatment, but as it is your officers and colonels send to the mountains for doctors. Yours are all fakes, all fakes.

Olénin did not answer. He agreed only too fully that all was fake in the world in which he had lived and to which he was now returning.

'How is Lukáshka? You've been to see him?' he asked.

'He just lies as if he were dead. He does not eat nor drink. Vodka is the only thing his soul accepts. But as long as he drinks vodka it's well. I'd be sorry to lose the lad. A fine lad—a *dzhigit*, like me. I too lay dying like that once. The old women were already wailing. My head was burning. They had already laid me out under the holy icons. So I lay there, and above me on the oven little drummers, no bigger than this, beat the tattoo. I shout at them and they drum all the harder.' (The old man laughed.) 'The women brought our church elder. They were getting ready to bury me. They said, "he defiled himself with worldly unbelievers; he made merry with women; he ruined people; he did not fast, and he played the *balaláyka*." "Confess," they said. So I began to confess. "I've sinned!" I said. Whatever the priest said, I always answered "I've sinned." He began to ask me about the *balaláyka*. "Where is the accursed thing," he says. "Show it me and smash it." But I say, "I've not got it." I'd hidden it myself in a net in the shed. I knew they could not find it. So they left me. Yet after all I recovered. When I went for my *balaláyka*—What was I saying?' he continued. 'Listen to me, and keep farther away from the other men or you'll get killed foolishly. I feel for you, truly:

you are a drinker—I love you! And fellows like you like riding up the mounds. There was one who lived here who had come from Russia, he always would ride up the mounds (he called the mounds so delightfully, "hillocks"). Whenever he saw a mound, off he'd gallop. Once he galloped off that way and rode to the top quite pleased, but a Chechén fired at him and killed him! Ah, how well they shoot from their gun-rests, those Chechéns! Some of them shoot even better than I do. I don't like it when a fellow gets killed so foolishly! Sometimes I used to look at your soldiers and wonder at them. There's foolishness for you! They go, the poor fellows, all in a clump, and even sew red collars to their coats! How can they help being hit! One gets killed, they drag him away and another takes his place! What foolishness!' the old man repeated, shaking his head. 'Why not scatter, and go one by one? So you just go like that and they won't notice you. That's what you must do.'

'Well, thank you! Good-bye, Daddy. God willing we may meet again,' said Olénin, getting up and moving towards the passage.

The old man, who was sitting on the floor, did not rise.

'Is that the way one says "Good-bye"? Fool, fool!' he began. 'Oh dear, what have people come to? We've kept company, kept company for wellnigh a year, and now "Good-bye!" and off he goes! Why, I love you, and how I pity you! You are so forlorn, always alone, always alone. You're somehow so unsociable. At times I can't sleep for thinking about you. I am so sorry for you. As the song has it:

> It is very hard, dear brother,
> In a foreign land to live.

So it is with you.'

'Well, good-bye,' said Olénin again.

The old man rose and held out his hand. Olénin pressed it and turned to go.

'Give us your mug, your mug!'

And the old man took Olénin by the head with both hands and kissed him three times with wet moustaches and lips, and began to cry.

'I love you, good-bye!'

Olénin got into the cart.

'Well, is that how you're going? You might give me something for a remembrance. Give me a gun! What do you want two for?' said the old man, sobbing quite sincerely.

Olénin got out a musket and gave it to him.

'What a lot you've given the old fellow,' murmured Vanyúsha, 'he'll never have enough! A regular old beggar. They are all such irregular people,' he remarked, as he wrapped himself in his overcoat and took his seat on the box.

'Hold your tongue, swine!' exclaimed the old man, laughing. 'What a stingy fellow!'

Maryánka came out of the cowshed, glanced indifferently at the cart, bowed and went towards the hut.

'*La fee!*'[1] said Vanyúsha, with a wink and burst out into a silly laugh.

'Drive on!' shouted Olénin, angrily.

'Good-bye, my lad! Good-bye. I won't forget you!' shouted Eróshka.

Olénin turned round. Daddy Eróshka was talking to Maryánka, evidently about his own affairs, and neither the old man nor the girl looked at Olénin.

[1] The girl!

HADJI MURÁD

I WAS returning home by the fields. It was midsummer, the hay harvest was over and they were just beginning to reap the rye. At that season of the year there is a delightful variety of flowers—red, white, and pink scented tufty clover; milk-white oxeye daisies with their bright yellow centres and pleasant spicy smell; yellow honey-scented rape blossoms; tall campanulas with white and lilac bells, tulip-shaped; creeping vetch; yellow, red, and pink scabious; faintly scented, neatly arranged purple plantains with blossoms slightly tinged with pink; cornflowers, the newly opened blossoms bright blue in the sunshine but growing paler and redder towards evening or when growing old; and delicate almond-scented dodder flowers that withered quickly. I gathered myself a large nosegay and was going home when I noticed in a ditch, in full bloom, a beautiful thistle plant of the crimson variety, which in our neighbourhood they call 'Tatar' and carefully avoid when mowing—or, if they do happen to cut it down, throw out from among the grass for fear of pricking their hands. Thinking to pick this thistle and put it in the centre of my nosegay, I climbed down into the ditch, and after driving away a velvety bumble-bee that had penetrated deep into one of the flowers and had there fallen sweetly asleep, I set to work to pluck the flower. But this proved a very difficult task. Not only did the stalk prick on every side—even through the handkerchief I wrapped round my hand—but it was so tough that I had to struggle with it for nearly five minutes, breaking the fibres one by one; and when I had at last plucked it, the stalk was all frayed and the flower itself no longer seemed so fresh and beautiful. Moreover, owing to its coarseness and stiffness, it did not seem in place among the delicate blossoms of my nosegay. I threw it away feeling sorry to have vainly destroyed a flower that looked beautiful in its proper place.

'But what energy and tenacity! With what determination it defended itself, and how dearly it sold its life!' thought I, remembering the effort it had cost me to pluck the flower. The way home led across black-earth fields that had just been ploughed up. I ascended the dusty path. The ploughed field belonged to a landed proprietor and was so large that on both sides and before me to the top of the hill nothing was visible but evenly furrowed and moist earth. The land was well tilled and nowhere was there a blade of grass or any kind of plant to be seen, it was all black. 'Ah, what a destructive creature is man.... How many different plant-lives he destroys to support his own existence!' thought I, involuntarily looking around for some living thing in this lifeless black field. In front of me to the right of the road I saw some kind of little clump, and drawing nearer I found it was the same kind of thistle as that which I had vainly plucked and thrown away. This 'Tatar' plant had three branches. One was broken and stuck out like the stump of a mutilated arm. Each of the other two bore a flower, once red but now blackened. One stalk was broken, and half of it hung down with a soiled flower at its tip. The other, though also soiled with black mud, still stood erect. Evidently a cartwheel had passed over the plant but it had risen again, and that was why, though erect, it stood twisted to one side, as if a piece of its body had been torn from it, its bowels drawn out, an arm torn off, and one of its eyes plucked out. Yet it stood firm and did not surrender to man who had destroyed all its brothers around it....

'What vitality!' I thought. 'Man has conquered everything and destroyed millions of plants, yet this one won't submit.'

And I remembered a Caucasian episode of years ago, which I had partly seen myself, partly heard of from eye-witnesses, and partly imagined. The episode, as it has taken shape in my memory and imagination, was as follows.

I

It happened towards the end of 1851.

On a cold November evening Hadji Murád rode into Makhmet, a hostile Chechén* *aúl* that lay some fifteen miles from Russian territory and was filled with the scented smoke of burning *kizyák*. The strained chant of the *muézzin* had just ceased, and through the clear mountain air, impregnated with *kizyák* smoke, above the lowing of the cattle and the bleating of the sheep that were dispersing among the *sáklyas* (which were crowded together like the cells of a honeycomb), could be clearly heard the guttural voices of disputing men, and sounds of women's and children's voices rising from near the fountain below.

This Hadji Murád was Shamíl's *naíb*, famous for his exploits, who used never to ride out without his banner and some dozens of *muríds*, who *dzhigíted* and showed off before him. Now wrapped in hood and *búrka*, from under which protruded a rifle, he rode, a fugitive, with one *muríd* only, trying to attract as little attention as possible and peering with his quick black eyes into the faces of those he met on his way.

When he entered the *aúl*, instead of riding up the road leading to the open square, he turned to the left into a narrow side street, and on reaching the second *sáklya*, which was cut into the hill-side, he stopped and looked round. There was no one under the overhang in front, but on the roof of the *sáklya* itself, behind the freshly plastered clay chimney, lay a man covered with a sheepskin. Hadji Murád touched him with the handle of his leather-plaited whip and clicked his tongue, and an old man, wearing a greasy old *beshmét* and a nightcap, rose from under the sheepskin. His moist red eyelids had no lashes, and he blinked to get them unstuck. Hadji Murád, repeating the customary '*Selaam aleikum!*' uncovered his face. '*Aleikum, selaam!*' said the old man, recognizing him, and smiling with his toothless mouth. And raising himself on his thin legs he began thrusting his feet into the wooden-heeled slippers that stood by the chimney. Then he leisurely slipped his arms into the sleeves of his crumpled sheepskin, and going to the ladder that leant against the roof he descended backwards. While he dressed and as he climbed down he kept shaking his head on its thin, shrivelled sunburnt neck and mumbling something with his toothless mouth. As soon as he reached the ground he hospitably seized Hadji Murád's bridle and right stirrup; but the strong active *muríd* had quickly dismounted and, motioning the old man aside, took his place. Hadji Murád also dismounted, and walking with a slight limp, entered under the overhang. A boy of fifteen, coming quickly out of the door, met him and wonderingly fixed his sparkling eyes, black as ripe sloes, on the new arrivals.

'Run to the mosque and call your father,' ordered the old man as he hurried forward to open the thin, creaking door into the *sáklya*.

As Hadji Murád entered the outer door, a slight, spare, middle-aged woman in a yellow smock, red *beshmét*, and wide blue trousers came through an inner door carrying cushions.

'May thy coming bring happiness!' she said, and bending nearly double began arranging the cushions along the front wall for the guest to sit on.

'May thy sons live!' answered Hadji Murád, taking off his *búrka*, his rifle, and his sword, and handing them to the old man who carefully hung the rifle and sword on a nail beside the weapons of the master of the house, which were suspended between two large basins that glittered against the clean clay-plastered and carefully whitewashed wall.

Hadji Murád adjusted the pistol at his back, came up to the cushions, and wrapping his *cherkéska* closer round him, sat down. The old man squatted on his bare heels beside him, closed his eyes, and lifted his hands palms upwards. Hadji Murád did the same; then after repeating a prayer they both stroked their faces, passing their hands downwards till the palms joined at the end of their beards.

'*Ne habar*?' ('Is there anything new?') asked Hadji Murád, addressing the old man.

'*Habar yok*' ('Nothing new'), replied the old man, looking with his lifeless red eyes not at Hadji Murád's face but at his breast. 'I live at the apiary and have only today come to see my son. . . . He knows.'

Hadji Murád, understanding that the old man did not wish to say what he knew and what Hadji Murád wanted to know, slightly nodded his head and asked no more questions.

'There is no good news,' said the old man. 'The only news is that the hares keep discussing how to drive away the eagles, and the eagles tear first one and then another of them. The other day the Russian dogs burnt the hay in the Mitchit *aúl*. . . . May their faces be torn!' he added hoarsely and angrily.

Hadji Murád's *muríd* entered the room, his strong legs striding softly over the earthen floor. Retaining only his dagger and pistol, he took off his *búrka*, rifle, and sword as Hadji Murád had done, and hung them up on the same nails as his leader's weapons.

'Who is he?' asked the old man, pointing to the newcomer.

'My *muríd*. Eldár is his name,' said Hadji Murád.

'All right,' said the old man, and motioned Eldár to a place on a piece of felt beside Hadji Murád. Eldár sat down, crossing his legs and fixing his fine ram-like eyes on the old man who, having now started talking, was telling how their brave fellows had caught two Russian soldiers the week before and had killed one and sent the other to Shamíl in Vedén.

Hadji Murád heard him absently, looking at the door and listening to the sounds outside. Under the overhang steps were heard, the door creaked, and Sado, the master of the house, came in. He was a man of about forty, with a small beard, long nose, and eyes as black, though not as glittering, as those of his fifteen-year-old son who had run to call him home and who now entered with his father and sat down by the door. The master of the house took off his wooden slippers at the door, and pushing his old and much-worn cap to the back of his head (which had remained unshaved so long that it was beginning to be overgrown with black hair), at once squatted down in front of Hadji Murád.

He too lifted his hands palms upwards, as the old man had done, repeated a prayer, and then stroked his face downwards. Only after that did he begin to speak. He told how an order had come from Shamíl to seize Hadji Murád alive or dead, that Shamíl's envoys had left only the day before, that the people were afraid to disobey Shamíl's orders, and that therefore it was necessary to be careful.

'In my house,' said Sado, 'no one shall injure my *kunák* while I live, but how will it be in the open fields? . . . We must think it over.'

Hadji Murád listened with attention and nodded approvingly. When Sado had finished he said:

'Very well. Now we must send a man with a letter to the Russians. My *muríd* will go but he will need a guide.'

'I will send brother Bata,' said Sado. 'Go and call Bata,' he added, turning to his son.

The boy instantly bounded to his nimble feet as if he were on springs, and swinging his arms, rapidly left the *sáklya*. Some ten minutes later he returned with a sinewy, short-legged Chechén, burnt almost black by the sun, wearing a worn and tattered yellow *cherkéska* with frayed sleeves, and crumpled black leggings.

Hadji Murád greeted the newcomer, and again without wasting a single word, immediately asked:

'Canst thou conduct my *muríd* to the Russians?'

'I can,' gaily replied Bata. 'I can certainly do it. There is not another Chechén who would pass as I can. Another might agree to go and might promise anything, but would do nothing; but I can do it!'

'All right,' said Hadji Murád. 'Thou shalt receive three for thy trouble,' and he held up three fingers.

Bata nodded to show that he understood, and added that it was not money he prized, but that he was ready to serve Hadji Murád for the honour alone. Every one in the mountains knew Hadji Murád, and how he slew the Russian swine.

'Very well. A rope should be long but a speech short,' said Hadji Murád.

'Well then I'll hold my tongue,' said Bata.

'Where the river Argun bends by the cliff,' said Hadji Murád, 'there are two stacks in a glade in the forest—thou knowest?'

'I know.'

'There my four horsemen are waiting for me,' said Hadji Murád.

'Aye,' answered Bata, nodding.

'Ask for Khan Mahomá. He knows what to do and what to say. Canst thou lead him to the Russian commander, Prince Vorontsóv?'

'Yes, I'll take him.'

'Canst thou take him and bring him back again?'

'I can.'

'Then take him there and return to the wood. I shall be there too.'

'I will do it all,' said Bata, rising, and putting his hands on his heart he went out.

Hadji Murád turned to his host.

'A man must also be sent to Gekhi,' he began, and took hold of one of the cartridge pouches of his *cherkéska*, but let his hand drop immediately and became silent on seeing two women enter the *sáklya*.

One was Sado's wife—the thin middle-aged woman who had arranged the cushions. The other was quite a young girl, wearing red trousers and a green *beshmét*. A necklace of silver coins covered the whole front of her dress, and at the end of the short but thick plait of hard black hair that hung between her thin shoulder-blades a silver ruble was suspended. Her eyes, as sloe-black as those of her father and brother, sparkled brightly in her young face which tried to be stern. She did not look at the visitors, but evidently felt their presence.

Sado's wife brought in a low round table on which were tea, pancakes in butter, cheese, *churék* (that is, thinly rolled out bread), and honey. The girl carried a basin, a ewer, and a towel.

Sado and Hadji Murád kept silent as long as the women, with their coin ornaments tinkling, moved softly about in their red soft-soled *chuvyáki*, setting out before the visitors the things they had brought. Eldár sat motionless as a statue, his ram-like eyes fixed on his crossed legs, all the time the women were in the *sáklya*. Only after they had gone and their soft footsteps could no longer be heard behind the door, did he give a sigh of relief.

Hadji Murád having pulled out a bullet from one of the cartridge-pouches of his *cherkéska*, and having taken out a rolled-up note that lay beneath it, held it out, saying:

'To be handed to my son.'

'Where must the answer be sent?'

'To thee; and thou must forward it to me.'

'It shall be done,' said Sado, and placed the note in a cartridge-pocket of his own coat. Then he took up the metal ewer and moved the basin towards Hadji Murád.

Hadji Murád turned up the sleeves of his *beshmét* on his white muscular arms, held out his hands under the clear cold water which Sado poured from the ewer, and having wiped them on a clean unbleached towel, turned to the table. Eldár did the same. While the visitors ate, Sado sat opposite and thanked them several times for their visit. The boy sat by the door never taking his sparkling eyes off Hadji Murád's face, and smiled as if in confirmation of his father's words.

Though he had eaten nothing for more than twenty-four hours Hadji Murád ate only a little bread and cheese; then, drawing out a small knife from under his dagger, he spread some honey on a piece of bread.

'Our honey is good,' said the old man, evidently pleased to see Hadji Murád eating his honey. 'This year, above all other years, it is plentiful and good.'

'I thank thee,' said Hadji Murád and turned from the table. Eldár would have liked to go on eating but he followed his leader's example, and having moved away from the table, handed him the ewer and basin.

Sado knew that he was risking his life by receiving such a guest in his house, for after his quarrel with Shamíl the latter had issued a proclamation to all the inhabitants of Chechnyá forbidding them to receive Hadji Murád on pain of death. He knew that the inhabitants of the *aúl* might at any moment become aware of Hadji Murád's presence in his house and might demand his surrender. But this not only did not frighten Sado, it even gave him pleasure: he considered it his duty to protect his guest though it should cost him his life, and he was proud and pleased with himself because he was doing his duty.

'Whilst thou art in my house and my head is on my shoulders no one shall harm thee,' he repeated to Hadji Murád.

Hadji Murád looked into his glittering eyes and understanding that this was true, said with some solemnity—

'Mayest thou receive joy and life!'

Sado silently laid his hand on his heart in token of thanks for these kind words.

Having closed the shutters of the *sáklya* and laid some sticks in the fireplace, Sado, in an exceptionally bright and animated mood, left the room and went into that part of his *sáklya* where his family all lived. The women had not yet gone to sleep, and were talking about the dangerous visitors who were spending the night in their guest-chamber.

II

At Vozdvízhensk, the advanced fort situated some ten miles from the *aúl* in which Hadji Murád was spending the night, three soldiers and a non-commissioned officer left the fort and went beyond the Shahgirínsk Gate. The soldiers, dressed as Caucasian soldiers used to be in those days, wore sheepskin coats and caps, and boots that reached above their knees, and they carried their cloaks tightly rolled up and fastened across their shoulders. Shouldering arms, they first went some five hundred paces along the road and then turned off it and went some twenty paces to the right—the dead leaves rustling under their boots—till they reached the blackened trunk of a broken plane tree just visible through the darkness. There they stopped. It was at this plane tree that an ambush party was usually placed.

The bright stars, that had seemed to be running along the tree-tops while the soldiers were walking through the forest, now stood still, shining brightly between the bare branches of the trees.

'Thank God it's dry,' said the non-commissioned officer Panóv, bringing down his long gun and bayonet with a clang from his shoulder and placing it against the plane tree.

The three soldiers did the same.

'Sure enough I've lost it!' muttered Panóv crossly. 'Must have left it behind or I've dropped it on the way.'

'What are you looking for?' asked one of the soldiers in a bright, cheerful voice.

'The bowl of my pipe. Where the devil has it got to?'

'Have you got the stem?' asked the cheerful voice.

'Here it is.'

'Then why not stick it straight into the ground?'

'Not worth bothering!'

'We'll manage that in a minute.'

Smoking in ambush was forbidden, but this ambush hardly deserved the name. It was rather an outpost to prevent the mountaineers from bringing up a cannon unobserved and firing at the fort as they used to. Panóv did not consider it necessary to forgo the pleasure of smoking, and therefore accepted the cheerful soldier's offer. The latter took a knife from his pocket and made a small round hole in the ground. Having smoothed it, he adjusted the pipe-stem to it, then filled the hole with tobacco and pressed it down, and the pipe was ready. A sulphur match flared and for a moment lit up the broad-cheeked face of the soldier who lay on his stomach, the air whistled in the stem, and Panóv smelt the pleasant odour of burning tobacco.

'Fixed it up?' said he, rising to his feet.

'Why, of course!'

'What a smart chap you are, Avdéev! As wise as a judge! Now then, lad.'

Avdéev rolled over on his side to make room for Panóv, letting smoke escape from his mouth.

Panóv lay down prone, and after wiping the mouthpiece with his sleeve, began to inhale.

When they had had their smoke the soldiers began to talk.

'They say the commander has had his fingers in the cash-box again,' remarked one of them in a lazy voice. 'He lost at cards, you see.'

'He'll pay it back again,' said Panóv.

'Of course he will! He's a good officer,' assented Avdéev.

'Good! good!' gloomily repeated the man who had started the conversation. 'In my opinion the company ought to speak to him. "If you've taken the money, tell us how much and when you'll repay it."'

'That will be as the company decides,' said Panóv, tearing himself away from the pipe.

'Of course. "A commune is a strong man,"' assented Avdéev, quoting the proverb.

'There will be oats to buy and boots to get towards spring. Money will be needed, and what shall we do if he's pocketed it?' insisted the dissatisfied one.

'I tell you it will be as the company wishes,' repeated Panóv. 'It's not the first time: he takes it and gives it back.'

In the Caucasus in those days each company chose men to manage its own commissariat. They received 6 rubles 50 kopeks a month per man from the treasury, and catered for the company. They planted cabbages, made hay, had their own carts, and prided themselves on their well-fed horses. The company's money was kept in a chest of which the commander had the key, and it often happened that he borrowed from the chest. This had just happened again, and the soldiers were talking about it. The morose soldier, Nikítin, wished to demand an account from the commander, while Panóv and Avdéev considered that unnecessary.

After Panóv, Nikítin had a smoke, and then spreading his cloak on the ground sat down on it leaning against the trunk of the plane tree. The soldiers were silent. Far above their heads the crowns of the trees rustled in the wind and suddenly, above this incessant low rustling, rose the howling, whining, weeping, and chuckling of jackals.

'Just listen to those accursed creatures—how they caterwaul!'

'They're laughing at you because your mouth's all on one side,' remarked the high voice of the third soldier, a Ukrainian.

All was silent again, except for the wind that swayed the branches, now revealing and now hiding the stars.

'I say, Panóv,' suddenly asked the cheerful Avdéev, 'do you ever feel down?'

'Down, why?' replied Panóv reluctantly.

'Well, I do. I feel so down sometimes that I don't know what I might not be ready to do to myself.'

'There now!' was all Panóv replied.

'That time when I drank all the money it was from feeling down. It took hold of me . . . took hold of me till I thought to myself, "I'll just get blind drunk!"'

'But sometimes drinking makes it still worse.'

'Yes, that's happened to me too. But what is a man to do with himself?'

'But what makes you feel so down?'

'What, me? Why, it's longing for home.'

'Is yours a wealthy home then?'

'No; we weren't wealthy, but things went properly—we lived well.' And Avdéev began to relate what he had already told Panóv many times.

'You see, I went as a soldier of my own free will, instead of my brother,' he said. 'He has children. They were five in the family and I had only just married. Mother began begging me to go. So I thought, "Well, maybe they will remember what I've done." So I went to our proprietor . . . he was a good master and he said, "You're a fine fellow, go!" So I went instead of my brother.'

'Well, that was right,' said Panóv.

'And yet, will you believe me, Panóv, it's chiefly because of that that I feel so down now? "Why did you go instead of your brother?" I say to myself. "He's living like a king now over there, while you have to suffer here;" and the more I think of it the worse I feel. . . . It seems just a piece of ill-luck!'

Avdéev was silent.

'Perhaps we'd better have another smoke,' said he after a pause.

'Well then, fix it up!'

But the soldiers were not to have their smoke. Hardly had Avdéev risen to fix the pipe-stem in its place when above the rustling of the trees they heard footsteps along the road. Panóv took his gun and pushed Nikítin with his foot.

Nikítin rose and picked up his cloak.

The third soldier, Bondarénko, rose also, and said:

'And I have dreamt such a dream, mates. . . .'

'Sh!' said Avdéev, and the soldiers held their breath, listening. The footsteps of men in soft-soled boots were heard approaching. The fallen leaves and dry twigs could be heard rustling clearer and clearer through the darkness. Then came the peculiar guttural tones of Chechén voices. The soldiers could now not only hear men approaching, but could see two shadows passing through a clear space between the trees; one shadow taller than the other. When these shadows had come in line with the soldiers, Panóv, gun in hand, stepped out on to the road, followed by his comrades.

'Who goes there?' cried he.

'Me, friendly Chechén,' said the shorter one. This was Bata. 'Gun, *yok!* Sword, *yok!*' said he, pointing to himself. 'Prince, want!'

The taller one stood silent beside his comrade. He too was unarmed.

'He means he's a scout, and wants the colonel,' explained Panóv to his comrades.

'Prince Vorontsóv . . . much want! Big business!' said Bata.

'All right, all right! We'll take you to him,' said Panóv. 'I say, you'd better take them,' said he to Avdéev, 'you and Bondarénko; and when you've given them up to the officer on duty come back again. Mind,' he added, 'be careful to make them keep in front of you!'

'And what of this?' said Avdéev, moving his gun and bayonet as though stabbing someone. 'I'd just give a dig, and let the steam out of him!'

'What'll he be worth when you've stuck him?' remarked Bondarénko.

'Now, march!'

When the steps of the two soldiers conducting the scouts could no longer be heard, Panóv and Nikítin returned to their post.

'What the devil brings them here at night?' said Nikítin.

'Seems it's necessary,' said Panóv. 'But it's getting chilly,' he added, and unrolling his cloak he put it on and sat down by the tree.

About two hours later Avdéev and Bondarénko returned.

'Well, have you handed them over?'

'Yes. They weren't yet asleep at the colonel's—they were taken straight in to him. And do you know, mates, those shaven-headed lads are fine!' continued Avdéev. 'Yes, really. What a talk I had with them!'

'Of course you'd talk,' remarked Nikítin disapprovingly.

'Really they're just like Russians. One of them is married. "Marústika," says I, "*bar?*" "*Bar*," he says. Bondarénko, didn't I say "*bar?*" "Many *bar?*" "A couple," says he. A couple! Such a good talk we had! Such nice fellows!'

'Nice, indeed!' said Nikítin. 'If you met him alone he'd soon let the guts out of you.'

'It will be getting light before long,' said Panóv.

'Yes, the stars are beginning to go out,' said Avdéev, sitting down and making himself comfortable.

And the soldiers were silent again.

III

The windows of the barracks and the soldiers' houses had long been dark in the fort; but there were still lights in the windows of the best house.

In it lived Prince Semyón Mikháylovich Vorontsóv,* commander of the Kurín regiment, an imperial aide-de-camp and son of the commander-in-chief. Vorontsóv's wife, Márya Vasílevna, a famous Petersburg beauty, was with him and they lived in this little Caucasian fort more luxuriously than any one had ever lived there before. To Vorontsóv, and even more to his wife, it seemed that they were not only living a very modest life, but one full of privations, while to the inhabitants of the place their luxury was surprising and extraordinary.

Just now, at midnight, the host and hostess sat playing cards with their visitors, at a card-table lit by four candles, in the spacious drawing-room with its carpeted floor and rich curtains drawn across the windows. Vorontsóv, who had a long face and wore the insignia and gold cords of an aide-de-camp, was partnered by a shaggy young man of gloomy appearance, a graduate of Petersburg University whom Princess Vorontsóva had lately had sent to the Caucasus to be tutor to her little son (born of her first marriage). Against them played two officers: one a broad, red-faced man, Poltorátski,* a company commander who had exchanged out of the guards; and the other the regimental adjutant, who sat very straight on his chair with a cold expression on his handsome face.

Princess Márya Vasílevna, a large-built, large-eyed, black-browed beauty, sat beside Poltorátski—her crinoline touching his legs—and looked over his cards. In her words, her looks, her smile, her perfume, and in every movement of her body, there was something that reduced Poltorátski to obliviousness of everything except the consciousness of her nearness, and he made blunder after blunder, trying his partner's temper more and more.

'No . . . that's too bad! You've wasted an ace again,' said the regimental adjutant, flushing all over as Poltorátski threw out an ace.

Poltorátski turned his kindly, wide-set black eyes towards

the dissatisfied adjutant uncomprehendingly, as though just aroused from sleep.

'Do forgive him!' said Márya Vasílevna, smiling. 'There, you see! Didn't I tell you so?' she went on, turning to Poltorátski.

'But that's not at all what you said,' replied Poltorátski, smiling.

'Wasn't it?' she queried, with an answering smile, which excited and delighted Poltorátski to such a degree that he blushed crimson and seizing the cards began to shuffle.

'It isn't your turn to deal,' said the adjutant sternly, and with his white ringed hand he began to deal himself, as though he wished to get rid of the cards as quickly as possible.

The prince's valet entered the drawing-room and announced that the officer on duty wanted to speak to him.

'Excuse me, gentlemen,' said the prince, speaking Russian with an English accent. 'Will you take my place, Márya?'

'Do you all agree?' asked the princess, rising quickly and lightly to her full height, rustling her silks, and smiling the radiant smile of a happy woman.

'I always agree to everything,' replied the adjutant, very pleased that the princess—who could not play at all—was now going to play against him.

Poltorátski only spread out his hands and smiled.

The rubber was nearly finished when the prince returned to the drawing-room, animated and obviously very pleased.

'Do you know what I propose?'

'What?'

'That we have some champagne.'

'I am always ready for that,' said Poltorátski.

'Why not? We shall be delighted!' said the adjutant.

'Bring some, Vasíli!' said the Prince.

'What did they want you for?' asked Márya Vasílevna.

'It was the officer on duty and another man.'

'Who? What about?' asked Márya Vasílevna quickly.

'I mustn't say,' said Vorontsóv, shrugging his shoulders.

'You mustn't say!' repeated Márya Vasílevna. 'We'll see about that.'

When the champagne was brought each of the visitors drank a glass, and having finished the game and settled the scores they began to take their leave.

'Is it your company that's ordered to the forest tomorrow?' the prince asked Poltorátski as they said good-bye.

'Yes, mine . . . why?'

'Then we shall meet tomorrow,' said the prince, smiling slightly.

'Very pleased,' replied Poltorátski, not quite understanding what Vorontsóv was saying to him and preoccupied only by the thought that he would in a minute be pressing Márya Vasílevna's hand.

Márya Vasílevna, according to her wont, not only pressed his hand firmly but shook it vigorously, and again reminding him of his mistake in playing diamonds, she gave him what he took to be a delightful, affectionate, and meaningful smile.

Poltorátski went home in an ecstatic condition only to be understood by people like himself who, having grown up and been educated in society, meet a woman belonging to their own circle after months of isolated military life, and moreover a woman like Princess Vorontsóv.

When he reached the little house in which he and his comrade lived he pushed the door, but it was locked. He knocked, with no result. He felt vexed, and began kicking the door and banging it with his sword. Then he heard a sound of footsteps and Vovílo—a domestic serf of his—undid the cabin-hook which fastened the door.

'What do you mean by locking yourself in, blockhead?'

'But how is it possible, sir?'

'You're tipsy again! I'll show you "how it is possible!"' and Poltorátski was about to strike Vovílo but changed his mind. 'Oh, go to the devil! Light a candle.'

'In a minute.'

Vovílo was really tipsy. He had been drinking at the name-day party of the ordnance-sergeant, Iván Petróvich. On returning home he began comparing his life with that of the latter. Iván Petróvich had a salary, was married, and hoped in a year's time to get his discharge.

Vovílo had been taken 'up' when a boy—that is, he had been taken into his owner's household service—and now although he was already over forty he was not married, but lived a campaigning life with his harum-scarum young master. He was a good master, who seldom struck him, but what kind of a life was it? 'He promised to free me when we return from the Caucasus, but where am I to go with my freedom? It's a dog's life!' thought Vovílo, and he felt so sleepy that, afraid lest someone should come in and steal something, he fastened the hook of the door and fell asleep.

Poltorátski entered the bedroom which he shared with his comrade Tíkhonov.

'Well, have you lost?' asked Tíkhonov, waking up.

'No, as it happens, I haven't. I've won seventeen rubles, and we drank a bottle of Clicquot!'*

'And you've looked at Márya Vasílevna?'

'Yes, and I've looked at Márya Vasílevna,' repeated Poltorátski.

'It will soon be time to get up,' said Tíkhonov. 'We are to start at six.'

'Vovílo!' shouted Poltorátski, 'see that you wake me up properly tomorrow at five!'

'How can I wake you if you fight?'

'I tell you you're to wake me! Do you hear?'

'All right.' Vovílo went out, taking Poltorátski's boots and clothes with him. Poltorátski got into bed and smoked a cigarette and put out his candle, smiling the while. In the dark he saw before him the smiling face of Márya Vasílevna.

The Vorontsóvs did not go to bed at once. When the visitors had left, Márya Vasílevna went up to her husband and standing in front of him, said severely—

'*Eh bien! Vous allez me dire ce que c'est.*'

'*Mais, ma chère . . .*'

'*Pas de "ma chère"! C'était un émissaire, n'est-ce pas?*'

'*Quand même, je ne puis pas vous le dire.*'

'*Vous ne pouvez pas? Alors, c'est moi qui vais vous le dire!*'

'*Vous?*'[1]

[1] 'Well now! You're going to tell me what it is.'
'But, my dear. . . .'
'Don't "my dear" me! It was an emissary, wasn't it?'
'Supposing it was, still I must not tell you.'
'You must not? Well then, I will tell you!'
'You?'

'It was Hadji Murád, wasn't it?' said Márya Vasílevna, who had for some days past heard of the negotiations and thought that Hadji Murád himself had been to see her husband. Vorontsóv could not altogether deny this, but disappointed her by saying that it was not Hadji Murád himself but only an emissary to announce that Hadji Murád would come to meet him next day at the spot where a wood-cutting expedition had been arranged.

In the monotonous life of the fortress the young Vorontsóvs, both husband and wife, were glad of this occurrence, and it was already past two o'clock when, after speaking of the pleasure the news would give his father, they went to bed.

IV

After the three sleepless nights he had passed flying from the *muríds* Shamíl had sent to capture him, Hadji Murád fell asleep as soon as Sado, having bid him good-night, had gone out of the *sáklya*. He slept fully dressed with his head on his hand, his elbow sinking deep into the red down-cushions his host had arranged for him.

At a little distance, by the wall, slept Eldár. He lay on his back, his strong young limbs stretched out so that his high chest, with the black cartridge-pouches sewn into the front of his white *cherkéska*, was higher than his freshly shaven, blue-gleaming head, which had rolled off the pillow and was thrown back. His upper lip, on which a little soft down was just appearing, pouted like a child's now contracting and now expanding, as though he were sipping something. Like Hadji Murád he slept with pistol and dagger in his belt. The sticks in the grate burnt low, and a night-light in a niche in the wall gleamed faintly.

In the middle of the night the floor of the guest-chamber creaked, and Hadji Murád immediately rose, putting his hand to his pistol. Sado entered, treading softly on the earthen floor.

'What is it?' asked Hadji Murád, as if he had not been asleep at all.

'We must think,' replied Sado, squatting down in front of him. 'A woman from her roof saw you arrive and told her husband, and now the whole *aúl* knows. A neighbour has just been to tell my wife that the Elders have assembled in the mosque and want to detain you.'

'I must be off!' said Hadji Murád.

'The horses are saddled,' said Sado, quickly leaving the *sáklya*.

'Eldár!' whispered Hadji Murád. And Eldár, hearing his name, and above all his master's voice, leapt to his feet, setting his cap straight as he did so.

Hadji Murád put on his weapons and then his *búrka*. Eldár did the same, and they both went silently out of the *sáklya* to underneath the overhang. The black-eyed boy brought their horses. Hearing the clatter of hoofs on the hard-beaten road, someone stuck his head out of the door of a neighbouring *sáklya*, and a man ran up the hill towards the mosque, clattering with his wooden shoes. There was no moon, but the stars shone brightly in the black sky so that the outlines of the *sáklya* roofs could be seen in the darkness, the mosque with its minarets in the upper part of the village rising above the other buildings. From the mosque came a hum of voices.

Quickly seizing his gun, Hadji Murád placed his foot in the narrow stirrup, and silently and easily throwing his body across, swung himself on to the high cushion of the saddle.

'May God reward you!' he said, addressing his host while his right foot felt instinctively for the stirrup, and with his whip he lightly touched the lad who held his horse, as a sign that he should let go. The boy stepped aside, and the horse, as if it knew what it had to do, started at a brisk pace down the lane towards the principal street. Eldár rode behind him. Sado in his sheepskin followed, almost running, swinging his arms and crossing now to one side and now to the other of the narrow side-street. At the place where the streets met, first one moving shadow and then another appeared in the road.

'Stop. Who's that? Stop!' shouted a voice, and several men blocked the path.

Instead of stopping, Hadji Murád drew his pistol from his belt and increasing his speed rode straight at those who blocked the way. They separated, and without looking round he started down the road at a swift canter. Eldár followed him at a sharp trot. Two shots cracked behind them and two bullets whistled past without hitting either Hadji Murád or Eldár. Hadji Murád continued riding at the same pace, but having gone some three hundred yards he stopped his slightly panting horse and listened.

In front of him, lower down, there gurgled rapidly running water. Behind him in the *aúl* cocks crowed, answering one another. Above these sounds he heard behind him the approaching tramp of horses and the voices of several men. Hadji Murád touched his horse and rode on at an even pace. Those behind him galloped and soon overtook him. They were some twenty mounted men, inhabitants of the *aúl*, who had decided to detain Hadji Murád or at least to make a show of detaining him in order to justify themselves in Shamíl's eyes. When they came near enough to be seen in the darkness, Hadji Murád stopped, let go his bridle, and with an accustomed movement of his left hand unbuttoned the cover of his rifle, which he drew forth with his right. Eldár did the same.

'What do you want?' cried Hadji Murád. 'Do you wish to take me? Take me, then!' and he raised his rifle. The men from the *aúl* stopped, and Hadji Murád, rifle in hand, rode down into the ravine. The mounted men followed him but did not draw any nearer. When Hadji Murád had crossed to the other side of the ravine the men shouted to him that he should hear what they had to say. In reply he fired his rifle and put his horse to a gallop. When he reined it in his pursuers were no longer within hearing and the crowing of the cocks could also no longer be heard; only the murmur of the water in the forest sounded more distinctly and now and then came the cry of an owl. The black wall of the forest appeared quite close. It was in this forest that his *muríds* awaited him.

On reaching it Hadji Murád paused, and drawing much air into his lungs he whistled and then listened silently. The next minute he was answered by a similar whistle from the forest. Hadji Murád turned from the road and entered it. When he had gone about a hundred paces he saw among the trunks of the trees a bonfire, the shadows of some men sitting round it, and, half lit-up by the firelight, a hobbled horse which was saddled. Four men were seated by the fire.

One of them rose quickly, and coming up to Hadji Murád took hold of his bridle and stirrup. This was the Avar Khanéfi, Hadji Murád's sworn brother, who managed his household affairs for him.

'Put out the fire,' said Hadji Murád, dismounting.

The men began scattering the pile and trampling on the burning branches.

'Has Bata been here?' asked Hadji Murád, moving towards a *búrka* that was spread on the ground.

'Yes, he went away long ago with Khan Mahomá.'

'Which way did they go?'

'That way,' answered Khanéfi pointing in the opposite direction to that from which Hadji Murád had come.

'All right,' said Hadji Murád, and unslinging his rifle he began to load it.

'We must take care—I have been pursued,' he said to a man who was putting out the fire.

This was Gamzálo, a Chechén. Gamzálo approached the *búrka*, took up a rifle that lay on it wrapped in its cover, and without a word went to that side of the glade from which Hadji Murád had come.

When Eldár had dismounted he took Hadji Murád's horse, and having reined up both horses' heads high, tied them to two trees. Then he shouldered his rifle as Gamzálo had done and went to the other side of the glade. The bonfire was extinguished, the forest no longer looked as black as before, but in the sky the stars still shone, though faintly.

Lifting his eyes to the stars and seeing that the Pleiades had already risen half-way up the sky, Hadji Murád calculated that it must be long past midnight and that his nightly prayer was long overdue. He asked Khanéfi for a ewer (they always carried one in their packs), and putting on his *búrka* went to the water.

Having taken off his shoes and performed his ablutions, Hadji Murád stepped onto the *búrka* with bare feet and then squatted down on his calves, and having first placed his fingers in his ears and closed his eyes, he turned to the east and recited the usual prayer.

When he had finished he returned to the place where the saddle-bags lay, and sitting down on the *búrka* he leant his elbows on his knees and bowed his head and fell into deep thought.

Hadji Murád always had great faith in his own fortune. When planning anything he always felt in advance firmly convinced of success, and fate smiled on him. It had been so, with a few rare exceptions, during the whole course of his stormy military life; and so he hoped it would be now. He pictured to himself how—with the army Vorontsóv would place at his disposal—he would march against Shamíl and take him prisoner, and revenge himself on him; and how the Russian Tsar would reward him and how he would again rule not only over Avaria,* but over the whole of Chechnyá, which would submit to him. With these thoughts he unwittingly fell asleep.

He dreamt how he and his brave followers rushed at Shamíl with songs and with the cry. 'Hadji Murád is coming!' and how they seized him and his wives and how he heard the wives crying and sobbing. He woke up. The song, *Lya-il-allysha*, and the cry, 'Hadji Murád is coming!' and the weeping of Shamíl's wives, was the howling, weeping, and laughter of jackals that awoke him. Hadji Murád lifted his head, glanced at the sky which, seen between the trunks of the trees, was already growing light in the east, and inquired after Khan Mahomá of a *muríd* who sat at some distance from him. On hearing that Khan Mahomá had not yet returned, Hadji Murád again bowed his head and at once fell asleep.

He was awakened by the merry voice of Khan Mahomá returning from his mission with Bata. Khan Mahomá at once sat down beside Hadji Murád and told him how the soldiers had met them and had led them to the prince himself, and how pleased the prince was and how he promised to meet them in the morning where the Russians would be felling trees beyond Mitchík in the Shalín glade. Bata interrupted his fellow-envoy to add details of his own.

Hadji Murád asked particularly for the words with which Vorontsóv had answered his offer to go over to the Russians, and Khan Mahomá and Bata replied with one voice that the prince promised to receive Hadji Murád as a guest and to make him feel comfortable.

Then Hadji Murád questioned them about the road, and

when Khan Mahomá assured him that he knew the way well and would conduct him straight to the spot, Hadji Murád took out some money and gave Bata the promised three rubles. Then he ordered his men to take out of the saddle-bags his gold-ornamented weapons and his turban, and to clean themselves up so as to look good when they arrived among the Russians.

While they cleaned their weapons, harness, and horses, the stars faded away, it became quite light, and an early morning breeze sprang up.

V

Early in the morning, while it was still dark, two companies carrying axes and commanded by Poltorátski marched six miles beyond the Shahgirínsk Gate, and having thrown out a line of sharpshooters set to work to fell trees as soon as the day broke. Towards eight o'clock the mist which had mingled with the perfumed smoke of the hissing and crackling damp green branches on the bonfires began to rise and the wood-fellers—who till then had not seen five paces off but had only heard one another—began to see both the bonfires and the road through the forest, blocked with fallen trees. The sun now appeared like a bright spot in the fog and now again was hidden.

In the glade, some way from the road, Poltorátski, his subaltern Tíkhonov, two officers of the third company, and Baron Freze, an ex-officer of the guards and a fellow-student of Poltorátski's at the cadet college, who had been reduced to the ranks for fighting a duel, were sitting on drums. Bits of paper that had contained food, cigarette stumps, and empty bottles lay scattered around them. The officers had had some vodka and were now eating, and drinking porter. A drummer was uncorking their third bottle.

Poltorátski, although he had not had enough sleep, was in that peculiar state of elation and kindly careless gaiety which he always felt when he found himself among his soldiers and with his comrades where there was a possibility of danger.

The officers were carrying on an animated conversation, the subject of which was the latest news: the death of General Sleptsóv. None of them saw in this death that most important moment of a life, its termination and return to the source whence it sprang—they saw in it only the valour of a gallant officer who rushed at the mountaineers sword in hand and hacked them desperately.

Though all of them—and especially those who had been in action—knew and could not help knowing that in those days in the Caucasus, and in fact anywhere and at any time, such hand-to-hand hacking as is always imagined and described never occurs (or if hacking with swords and bayonets ever does occur, it is only those who are running away that get hacked), that fiction of hand-to-hand fighting endowed them with the calm pride and cheerfulness with which they sat on the drums, some with a jaunty air, others on the contrary in a very modest pose, and drank and joked without troubling about death, which might overtake them at any moment as it had overtaken Sleptsóv. And in the midst of their talk, as if to confirm their expectations, they heard to the left of the road the pleasant stirring sound of a rifle-shot; and a bullet, merrily whistling somewhere in the misty air, flew past and crashed into a tree.

'Hullo!' exclaimed Poltorátski in a merry voice; 'why that's at our line. There now, Kóstya,' and he turned to Freze, 'now's your chance. Go back to the company. I will lead the whole company to support the cordon and we'll arrange a battle that will be simply delightful, and then we'll make a report.'

Freze jumped to his feet and went at a quick pace towards the smoke-enveloped spot where he had left his company.

Poltorátski's little Kabardá* dapple-bay was brought to him, and he mounted and drew up his company and led it in the direction of the shots. The outposts stood on the skirts of the forest in front of the bare descending slope of a ravine. The wind was blowing in the direction of the forest, and not only was it possible to see the slope of the ravine, but the opposite side of it was also distinctly visible. When Poltorátski rode up to the line the sun came out from behind the mist, and on the other side of the ravine, by the outskirts of a young forest, a few horsemen could be seen at a distance of a quarter of a mile. These were the Chechéns who had pursued Hadji Murád and wanted to see him meet the Russians. One of them fired at the line. Several soldiers fired back. The Chechéns retreated and the firing ceased.

But when Poltorátski and his company came up he nevertheless gave orders to fire, and scarcely had the word been passed than along the whole line of sharpshooters the incessant, merry, stirring rattle of our rifles began, accompanied by pretty dissolving cloudlets of smoke. The soldiers, pleased to have some distraction, hastened to load and fired shot after shot. The Chechéns evidently caught the feeling of excitement, and leaping forward one after another fired a few shots at our men. One of these shots wounded a soldier. It was that same Avdéev who had lain in ambush the night before.

When his comrades approached him he was lying prone, holding his wounded stomach with both hands, and rocking himself with a rhythmic motion moaned softly. He belonged to Poltorátski's company, and Poltorátski, seeing a group of soldiers collected, rode up to them.

'What is it, lad? Been hit?' said Poltorátski. 'Where?'

Avdéev did not answer.

'I was just going to load, your honour, when I heard a click,' said a soldier who had been with Avdéev; 'and I look and see he's dropped his gun.'

'Tut, tut, tut!' Poltorátski clicked his tongue. 'Does it hurt much, Avdéev?'

'It doesn't hurt but it stops me walking. A drop of vodka now, your honour!'

Some vodka (or rather the spirit drunk by the soldiers in the Caucasus) was found, and Panóv, severely frowning, brought Avdéev a can-lid full. Avdéev tried to drink it but immediately handed back the lid.

'My soul turns against it,' he said. 'Drink it yourself.'

Panóv drank up the spirit.

Avdéev raised himself but sank back at once. They spread out a cloak and laid him on it.

'Your honour, the colonel is coming,' said the sergeant-major to Poltorátski.

'All right. Then will you see to him?' said Poltorátski, and flourishing his whip he rode at a fast trot to meet Vorontsóv.

Vorontsóv was riding his thoroughbred English chestnut gelding, and was accompanied by the adjutant, a Cossack, and a Chechén interpreter.

'What's happening here?' asked Vorontsóv.

'Why, a skirmishing party attacked our advanced line,' Poltorátski answered.

'Come, come—you arranged the whole thing yourself!'

'Oh no, Prince, not I,' said Poltorátski with a smile; 'they pushed forward of their own accord.'

'I hear a soldier has been wounded?'

'Yes, it's a great pity. He's a good soldier.'

'Seriously?'

'Seriously, I believe . . . in the stomach.'

'And do you know where I am going?' Vorontsóv asked.

'I don't.'

'Can't you guess?'

'No.'

'Hadji Murád has surrendered and we are now going to meet him.'

'You don't mean to say so?'

'His envoy came to me yesterday,' said Vorontsóv, with difficulty repressing a smile of pleasure. 'He will be waiting for me at the Shalín glade in a few minutes. Place sharpshooters as far as the glade, and then come and join me.'

'I understand,' said Poltorátski, lifting his hand to his cap, and rode back to his company. He led the sharpshooters to the right himself, and ordered the sergeant-major to do the same on the left side.

The wounded Avdéev had meanwhile been taken back to the fort by some of the soldiers.

On his way back to rejoin Vorontsóv, Poltorátski noticed behind him several horsemen who were overtaking him. In front on a white-maned horse rode a man of imposing appearance. He wore a turban and carried weapons with gold ornaments. This man was Hadji Murád. He approached Poltorátski and said something to him in Tatar.* Raising his eyebrows, Poltorátski made a gesture with his arms to show that he did not understand, and smiled. Hadji Murád gave him smile for smile, and that smile struck Poltorátski by its childlike kindliness. Poltorátski had never expected to see the terrible mountain chief look like that. He had expected to see a morose, hard-featured man, and here was a vivacious person whose smile was so kindly that Poltorátski felt as if he were an old acquaintance. He had only one peculiarity: his eyes, set wide apart, which gazed from under their black brows calmly, attentively, and penetratingly into the eyes of others.

Hadji Murád's suite consisted of five men; among them was Khan Mahomá, who had been to see Prince Vorontsóv that night. He was a rosy, round-faced fellow with black lashless eyes and a beaming expression, full of the joy of life. Then there was the Avar Khanéfi, a thick-set, hairy man, whose eyebrows met. He was in charge of all Hadji Murád's property and led a stud-bred horse which carried tightly packed saddle-bags. Two men of the suite were particularly striking. The first was a Lesgian:* a youth, broad-shouldered but with a waist as slim as a woman's, beautiful ram-like eyes, and the beginnings of a brown beard. This was Eldár. The other, Gamzálo, was a Chechén with a short red beard and no eyebrows or eyelashes; he was blind in one eye and had a scar across his nose and face. Poltorátski pointed out Vorontsóv, who had just appeared on the road. Hadji Murád rode to meet him, and putting his right hand on his heart said something in Tatar and stopped. The Chechén interpreter translated.

'He says, "I surrender myself to the will of the Russian Tsar. I wish to serve him," he says. "I wished to do so long ago but Shamíl would not let me."'

Having heard what the interpreter said, Vorontsóv stretched out his hand in its wash-leather glove to Hadji Murád. Hadji Murád looked at it hesitatingly for a moment and then pressed it firmly, again saying something and looking first at the interpreter and then at Vorontsóv.

'He says he did not wish to surrender to any one but you, as you are the son of the *sirdar* and he respects you much.'

Vorontsóv nodded to express his thanks. Hadji Murád again said something, pointing to his suite.

'He says that these men, his henchmen, will serve the Russians as well as he.'

Vorontsóv turned towards them and nodded to them too. The merry, black-eyed, lashless Chechén, Khan Mahomá, also nodded and said something which was probably amusing, for the hairy Avar drew his lips into a smile, showing his ivory-white teeth. But the red-haired Gamzálo's one red eye just glanced at Vorontsóv and then was again fixed on the ears of his horse.

When Vorontsóv and Hadji Murád with their retinues rode back to the fort, the soldiers released from the lines gathered in groups and made their own comments.

'What a lot of men that damned fellow has destroyed! And now see what a fuss they will make of him!'

'Naturally. He was Shamíl's right hand, and now—no fear!'

'Still there's no denying it! he's a fine fellow—a regular *dzhigít!*'

'And the red one! He squints at you like a beast!'

'Ugh! He must be a hound!'

They had all specially noticed the red one.

Where the wood-felling was going on the soldiers nearest to the road ran out to look. Their officer shouted to them, but Vorontsóv stopped him.

'Let them have a look at their old friend.'

'You know who that is?' he added, turning to the nearest soldier, and speaking the words slowly with his English accent.

'No, your Excellency.'

'Hadji Murád. . . . Heard of him?'

'How could we help it, your Excellency? We've beaten him many a time!'

'Yes, and we've had it from him too.'

'Yes, that's true, your Excellency,' answered the soldier, pleased to be talking with his chief.

Hadji Murád understood that they were speaking about him, and smiled brightly with his eyes.

Vorontsóv returned to the fort in a very cheerful mood.

VI

Young Vorontsóv was much pleased that it was he, and no one else, who had succeeded in winning over and receiving Hadji Murád—next to Shamíl Russia's chief and most active enemy. There was only one unpleasant thing about it: General Meller-

Zakomélsky was in command of the army at Vozdvízhensk, and the whole affair ought to have been carried out through him. As Vorontsóv had done everything himself without reporting it there might be some unpleasantness, and this thought rather interfered with his satisfaction. On reaching his house he entrusted Hadji Murád's henchmen to the regimental adjutant and himself showed Hadji Murád into the house.

Princess Márya Vasílevna, elegantly dressed and smiling, and her little son, a handsome curly-headed child of six, met Hadji Murád in the drawing-room. The latter placed his hands on his heart, and through the interpreter, who had entered with him, said with solemnity that he regarded himself as the prince's *kunák*, since the prince had brought him into his own house; and that a *kunák's* whole family was as sacred as the *kunák* himself.

Hadji Murád's appearance and manners pleased Márya Vasílevna, and the fact that he flushed when she held out her large white hand to him inclined her still more in his favour. She invited him to sit down, and having asked him whether he drank coffee, had some served. He, however, declined it when it came. He understood a little Russian but could not speak it. When something was said which he could not understand he smiled, and his smile pleased Márya Vasílevna just as it had pleased Poltorátski. The curly-haired, keen-eyed little boy (whom his mother called Búlka) standing beside her did not take his eyes off Hadji Murád, whom he had always heard spoken of as a great warrior.

Leaving Hadji Murád with his wife, Vorontsóv went to his office to do what was necessary about reporting the fact of Hadji Murád's having come over to the Russians. When he had written a report to the general in command of the left flank, General Kozlóvski at Grózny,* and a letter to his father, Vorontsóv hurried home, afraid that his wife might be vexed with him for forcing on her this terrible stranger, who had to be treated in such a way that he should not take offence, and yet not too kindly. But his fears were needless. Hadji Murád was sitting in an armchair with little Búlka, Vorontsóv's stepson, on his knee, and with bent head was listening attentively to the interpreter who was translating to him the words of the laughing Márya Vasílevna. Márya Vasílevna was telling him that if every time a *kunák* admired anything of his he made him a present of it, he would soon have to go about like Adam.

When the prince entered, Hadji Murád rose at once and, surprising and offending Búlka by putting him off his knee, changed the playful expression of his face to a stern and serious one. He only sat down again when Vorontsóv had himself taken a seat.

Continuing the conversation he answered Márya Vasílevna by telling her that it was a law among his people that anything your *kunák* admired must be presented to him.

'Thy son, *kunák!*' he said in Russian, patting the curly head of the boy who had again climbed on his knee.

'He is delightful, your brigand!' said Márya Vasílevna to her husband in French. 'Búlka has been admiring his dagger, and he has given it to him.'

Búlka showed the dagger to his father. '*C'est un objet de prix!*'[1] she added.

'*Il faudra trouver l'occasion de lui faire cadeau,*'[2] said Vorontsóv.

Hadji Murád, his eyes turned down, sat stroking the boy's curly hair and saying: '*Dzhigít, dzhigít!*'

'A beautiful, beautiful dagger,' said Vorontsóv, half drawing out the sharpened blade which had a ridge down the centre. 'I thank thee!'

'Ask him what I can do for him,' he said to the interpreter.

The interpreter translated, and Hadji Murád at once replied that he wanted nothing but that he begged to be taken to a place where he could say his prayers.

Vorontsóv called his valet and told him to do what Hadji Murád desired.

As soon as Hadji Murád was alone in the room allotted to him his face altered. The pleased expression, now kindly and now stately, vanished, and a look of anxiety showed itself. Vorontsóv had received him far better than Hadji Murád had expected. But the better the reception the less did Hadji Murád

[1] It is a thing of value.

[2] We must find an opportunity to make him a present.

trust Vorontsóv and his officers. He feared everything: that he might be seized, chained, and sent to Siberia, or simply killed; and therefore he was on his guard. He asked Eldár, when the latter entered his room, where his *muríds* had been put and whether their arms had been taken from them, and where the horses were. Eldár reported that the horses were in the prince's stables; that the men had been placed in a barn; that they retained their arms, and that the interpreter was giving them food and tea.

Hadji Murád shook his head in doubt, and after undressing said his prayers and told Eldár to bring him his silver dagger. He then dressed, and having fastened his belt sat down on the divan with his legs tucked under him, to await what might befall him.

At four in the afternoon the interpreter came to call him to dine with the prince.

At dinner he hardly ate anything except some *pilaf*, to which he helped himself from the very part of the dish from which Márya Vasílevna had helped herself.

'He is afraid we shall poison him,' Márya Vasílevna remarked to her husband. 'He has helped himself from the place where I took my helping.' Then instantly turning to Hadji Murád she asked him through the interpreter when he would pray again. Hadji Murád lifted five fingers and pointed to the sun. 'Then it will soon be time,' and Vorontsóv drew out his watch and pressed a spring. The watch struck four and one quarter. This evidently surprised Hadji Murád, and he asked to hear it again and to be allowed to look at the watch.

'*Voilà l'occasion! Donnez-lui la montre*,'[1] said the Princess to her husband.

Vorontsóv at once offered the watch to Hadji Murád.

The latter placed his hand on his breast and took the watch. He touched the spring several times, listened, and nodded his head approvingly.

After dinner, Meller-Zakomélski's aide-de-camp was announced.

The aide-de-camp informed the prince that the general, hav-

[1] This is the opportunity! Give him the watch.

ing heard of Hadji Murád's arrival, was highly displeased that this had not been reported to him, and required Hadji Murád to be brought to him without delay. Vorontsóv replied that the general's command should be obeyed, and through the interpreter informed Hadji Murád of these orders and asked him to go to Meller with him.

When Márya Vasílevna heard what the aide-de-camp had come about, she at once understood that unpleasantness might arise between her husband and the general, and in spite of all her husband's attempts to dissuade her, decided to go with him and Hadji Murád.

'*Vous feriez bien mieux de rester—c'est mon affaire, non pas la vôtre. . . .*'

'*Vous ne pouvez pas m'empêcher d'aller voir madame la générale!*'[1]

'You could go some other time.'

'But I wish to go now!'

Nothing could be done, so Vorontsóv agreed, and they all three went.

When they entered, Meller with sombre politeness conducted Márya Vasílevna to his wife and told his aide-de-camp to show Hadji Murád into the waiting-room and not let him out till further orders.

'Please,' he said to Vorontsóv, opening the door of his study and letting the prince enter before him.

Having entered the study he stopped in front of Vorontsóv and, without offering him a seat, said:

'I am in command here and therefore all negotiations with the enemy have to be carried on through me! Why did you not report to me that Hadji Murád had come over?'

'An emissary came to me and announced his wish to capitulate only to me,' replied Vorontsóv growing pale with excitement, expecting some rude expression from the angry general and at the same time becoming infected with his anger.

'I ask you why I was not informed?'

'I intended to inform you, Baron, but . . .'

[1] 'You would do much better to remain at home . . . this is my business, and not yours.'

'You cannot prevent my going to see the general's wife!'

'You are not to address me as "Baron", but as "Your Excellency"!' And here the baron's pent-up irritation suddenly broke out and he uttered all that had long been boiling in his soul.

'I have not served my sovereign twenty-seven years in order that men who began their service yesterday, relying on family connections, should give orders under my very nose about matters that do not concern them!'

'Your Excellency, I request you not to say things that are incorrect!' interrupted Vorontsóv.

'I am saying what is correct, and I won't allow . . .' said the general, still more irritably.

But at that moment Márya Vasílevna entered, rustling with her skirts and followed by a modest-looking little lady, Meller-Zakomélski's wife.

'Come, come, Baron! Semyón did not wish to displease you,' began Márya Vasílevna.

'I am not speaking about that, Princess.'

'Well, well, let's forget it all! You know, "A bad peace is better than a good quarrel!" Oh dear, what am I saying?' and she laughed.

The angry general capitulated to the enchanting laugh of the beauty. A smile hovered under his moustache.

'I confess I was wrong,' said Vorontsóv, 'but—'

'And I too got rather carried away,' said Meller, and held out his hand to the prince.

Peace was re-established, and it was decided to leave Hadji Murád with the general for the present, and then to send him to the commander of the left flank.

Hadji Murád sat in the next room and though he did not understand what was said, he understood what it was necessary for him to understand—namely, that they were quarrelling about him, that his desertion of Shamíl was a matter of immense importance to the Russians, and that therefore not only would they not exile or kill him, but that he would be able to demand much from them. He also understood that though Meller-Zakomélski was the commanding-officer, he had not as much influence as his subordinate Vorontsóv, and that Vorontsóv was important and Meller-Zakomélski unimportant; and therefore when Meller-Zakomélski sent for him and began to question him, Hadji Murád bore himself proudly and ceremoniously, saying that he had come from the mountains to serve the White Tsar and would give account only to his *sirdar*, meaning the commander-in-chief, Prince Vorontsóv senior, in Tiflis.*

VII

The wounded Avdéev was taken to the hospital, a small wooden building roofed with boards at the entrance of the fort, and was placed on one of the empty beds in the common ward. There were four patients in the ward: one ill with typhus and in high fever; another, pale, with dark shadows under his eyes, who had ague, was just expecting another attack and yawned continually; and two more who had been wounded in a raid three weeks before: one in the hand—he was up—and the other in the shoulder. The latter was sitting on a bed. All of them except the typhus patient surrounded and questioned the newcomer and those who had brought him.

'Sometimes they fire as if they were spilling peas over you, and nothing happens . . . and this time only about five shots were fired,' related one of the bearers.

'Each man gets what fate sends!'

'Oh!' groaned Avdéev loudly, trying to master his pain when they began to place him on the bed; but he stopped groaning when he was on it, and only frowned and moved his feet continually. He held his hands over his wound and looked fixedly before him.

The doctor came, and gave orders to turn the wounded man over to see whether the bullet had passed out behind.

'What's this?' the doctor asked, pointing to the large white scars that crossed one another on the patient's back and loins.

'That was done long ago, your honour!' replied Avdéev with a groan.

They were scars left by the flogging Avdéev had received for the money he drank.

Avdéev was again turned over, and the doctor probed in his stomach for a long time and found the bullet, but failed to extract it. He put a dressing on the wound, and having stuck plaster over it went away. During the whole time the doctor was probing and bandaging the wound Avdéev lay with clenched teeth and closed eyes, but when the doctor had gone he opened them and looked around as though amazed. His eyes were turned on the other patients and on the surgeon's orderly, though he seemed to see not them but something else that surprised him.

His friends Panóv and Serógin came in, but Avdéev continued to lie in the same position looking before him with surprise. It was long before he recognized his comrades, though his eyes gazed straight at them.

'I say, Pyótra,* have you no message to send home?' said Panóv.

Avdéev did not answer, though he was looking Panóv in the face.

'I say, haven't you any orders to send home?' again repeated Panóv, touching Avdéev's cold, large-boned hand.

Avdéev seemed to come to.

'Ah? Panóv!'

'Yes, I'm here. I've come! Have you nothing for home? Serógin would write a letter.'

'Serógin,' said Avdéev moving his eyes with difficulty towards Serógin, 'will you write? Well then, write: "Your son," say, "Petrúkha, has given orders that you should live long".* I envied my brother. I told you about that today. But now I myself am glad. Don't worry him, let him live. God grant it him. I am glad! Write that.'

Having said this he was silent for some time with his eyes fixed on Panóv.

'And did you find your pipe?' he suddenly asked.

Panóv did not reply.

'Your pipe, your pipe! I mean, have you found it?' Avdéev repeated.

'It was in my bag.'

'That's right! Well, and now give me a candle to hold. I am going to die,' said Avdéev.

Just then Poltorátski came in to inquire after his soldier.

'How goes it, my lad! Badly?' said he.

Avdéev closed his eyes and shook his head negatively. His broad-cheeked face was pale and stern. He did not reply, but again said to Panóv:

'Bring a candle. I am going to die.'

A wax taper was placed in his hand but his fingers would not bend, so it was placed between them and held up for him.

Poltorátski went away, and five minutes later the orderly put his ear to Avdéev's heart and said that all was over.

Avdéev's death was described in the following manner in the report sent to Tiflis:

'*23rd Nov.*—Two companies of the Kurín regiment advanced from the fort on a wood-felling expedition. At midday a considerable number of mountaineers suddenly attacked the wood-fellers. The sharpshooters began to retreat, but the 2nd Company charged with their bayonets and overthrew the mountaineers. In this affair two privates were slightly wounded and one killed. The mountaineers lost about a hundred men killed and wounded.'

VIII

On the day Petrúkha Avdéev died in the hospital at Vozdvízhensk, his old father with the wife of the brother in whose stead he had enlisted, and that brother's daughter—who was already approaching womanhood and almost of age to get married—were threshing oats on the hard-frozen threshing-floor.

There had been a heavy fall of snow the previous night, followed towards morning by a severe frost. The old man woke when the cocks were crowing for the third time, and seeing the bright moonlight through the frozen window-panes got down from the stove, put on his boots, his sheepskin coat and cap, and went out to the threshing-floor. Having worked there for a couple of hours he returned to the hut and awoke his son and the women. When the woman and the girl came to the threshing-floor they found it ready swept, with a wooden shovel sticking in the dry white snow, beside which were birch brooms with the twigs upwards and two rows of oat-sheaves laid ears to ears in a long line the whole length of the clean threshing-floor. They chose their flails and started threshing, keeping time with their triple blows. The old man struck powerfully with his heavy flail, breaking the straw, the girl struck the ears from above with measured blows, and the daughter-in-law turned the oats over with her flail.

The moon had set, dawn was breaking, and they were finishing the line of sheaves when Akím, the eldest son, in his sheepskin and cap, joined the threshers.

'What are you lazing about for?' shouted his father to him, pausing in his work and leaning on his flail.

'The horses had to be seen to.'

'"Horses seen to!"' the father repeated, mimicking him. 'The old woman will look after them. Take your flail! You're getting too fat, you drunkard!'

'Well, have you been treating me?' muttered the son.

'What?' said the old man, frowning sternly and missing a stroke.

The son silently took a flail and they began threshing with four flails.

'Trak, tapatam . . . trak, tapatam . . . trak . . .' came down the old man's heavy flail after the three others.

'Why, you've got a neck like a goodly gentleman! Look here, my trousers have hardly anything to hang on!' said the old man, omitting his stroke and only swinging his flail in the air so as not to get out of time.

They had finished the row, and the women began removing the straw with rakes.

'Petrúkha was a fool to go in your stead. They'd have knocked the nonsense out of you in the army, and he was worth five of such as you at home!'

'That's enough, father,' said the daughter-in-law, as she threw aside the binders that had come off the sheaves.

'Yes, feed the six of you and get no work out of a single one! Petrúkha used to work for two. He was not like . . .'

Along the trodden path from the house came the old man's wife, the frozen snow creaking under the new bark shoes she wore over her tightly wound woollen leg-bands. The men were shovelling the unwinnowed grain into heaps, the woman and the girl sweeping up what remained.

'The Elder has been and orders everybody to go and work for the master, carting bricks,' said the old woman. 'I've got breakfast ready. Come along, won't you?'

'All right. Harness the roan and go,' said the old man to Akím, 'and you'd better look out that you don't get me into trouble as you did the other day! . . . I can't help missing Petrúkha!'

'When he was at home you used to scold him,' retorted Akím. 'Now he's away you keep nagging at me.'

'That shows you deserve it,' said his mother in the same angry tones. 'You'll never be Petrúkha's equal.'

'Oh, all right,' said the son.

'"All right," indeed! You've drunk the meal, and now you say "all right!"'

'Let bygones by bygones!' said the daughter-in-law.

The disagreements between father and son had begun long ago—almost from the time Peter went as a soldier. Even then the old man felt that he had parted with an eagle for a cuckoo. It is true that it was right—as the old man understood it—for a childless man to go in place of a family man. Akím had four children and Peter had none; but Peter was a worker like his father, skilful, observant, strong, enduring, and above all industrious. He was always at work. If he happened to pass by where people were working he lent a helping hand as his father would have done, and took a turn or two with the scythe, or loaded a cart, or felled a tree, or chopped some wood. The old man regretted his going away, but there was no help for it. Conscription in those days was like death. A soldier was a severed branch, and to think about him at home was to tear one's heart uselessly. Only occasionally, to prick his elder son, did the father mention him, as he had done that day. But his mother often thought of her younger son, and for a long time—more than a year now—she had been asking her husband to send Petrúkha a little money, but the old man had made no response.

The Avdéevs were a well-to-do family and the old man had some savings hidden away, but he would on no account have consented to touch what he had laid by. Now however the old woman having heard him mention their younger son, made up her mind to ask him again to send him at least a ruble after selling the oats. This she did. As soon as the young people had gone to work for the proprietor and the old folk were left alone together, she persuaded him to send Petrúkha a ruble out of the oats-money. So when ninety-six bushels of the winnowed oats had been packed onto three sledges lined with sacking carefully pinned together at the top with wooden skewers, she gave her husband a letter the church clerk had written at her dictation, and the old man promised when he got to town to enclose a ruble and send it off to the right address.

The old man, dressed in a new sheepskin with a homespun cloak over it, his legs wrapped round with warm white woollen leg-bands, took the letter, placed it in his wallet, said a prayer, got into the front sledge, and drove to town. His grandson drove in the last sledge. When he reached town the old man asked the innkeeper to read the letter to him, and listened to it attentively and approvingly.

In her letter Petrúkha's mother first sent him her blessing, then greetings from everybody and the news of his godfather's death, and at the end she added that Aksínya (Peter's wife) had not wished to stay with them but had gone into service, where they heard she was living honestly and well. Then came a reference to the present of a ruble, and finally a message which the old woman, yielding to her sorrow, had dictated with tears in her eyes and the church clerk had taken down exactly, word for word:

'One thing more, my darling child, my sweet dove, my own Petrúshenka! I have wept my eyes out lamenting for you, oh light of my eyes. To whom have you left me?' At this point the old woman had sobbed and wept, and said: 'That will do!' So the words stood in the letter; but it was not fated that Petrúkha should receive the news of his wife's having left home, nor the present of the ruble, nor his mother's last words. The letter with the money in it came back with the announcement that Petrúkha had been killed in the war, 'defending his Tsar, his Fatherland, and the Orthodox Faith.' That is how the army clerk expressed it.

The old woman, when this news reached her, wept for as long as she could spare time, and then set to work again. The very next Sunday she went to church and had a requiem chanted and Peter's name entered among those for whose souls prayers were to be said, and she distributed bits of holy bread 'to all the good people in memory of Peter, the servant of God'.

Aksínya, his widow, also lamented loudly when she heard of the death of her 'beloved husband with whom she had lived but one short year'. She regretted her husband and her own ruined life, and in her lamentations mentioned 'Peter Mikháylovich's brown locks and his love, and the sadness of her life with her little orphaned Vánka', and bitterly reproached 'Petrúsha for having had pity on his brother but none on her—obliged to wander among strangers!'

But in the depth of her soul Aksínya was glad of her husband's death. She was pregnant a second time by the shopman with whom she was living, and no one would now have a right to scold her, and the shopman could marry her as he had said he would when he was persuading her to yield.

IX

Michael Semyónovich Vorontsóv,* being the son of the Russian ambassador, had been educated in England and possessed a European education quite exceptional among the higher Russian officials of his day. He was ambitious, gentle and kind in his manner with inferiors, and a finished courtier with superiors. He did not understand life without power and submission. He had obtained all the highest ranks and decorations and was looked upon as a clever commander, and even as the conqueror of Napoleon at Krásnoe.*

In 1852 he was over seventy, but young for his age, he moved briskly, and above all was in full possession of a facile, refined, and agreeable intellect which he used to maintain his power and strengthen and increase his popularity. He possessed large means—his own and his wife's (who had been a Countess Branítski)—and received an enormous salary as viceroy, and he spent a great part of his means on building a palace and laying out a garden on the south coast of the Crimea.

On the evening of 4 December 1852, a courier's troyka drew up before his palace in Tiflis. An officer, tired and black with dust, sent by General Kozlóvski with the news of Hadji Murád's surrender to the Russians, entered the wide porch, stretching the stiffened muscles of his legs as he passed the sentinel. It was six o'clock, and Vorontsóv was just going in to dinner when he was informed of the courier's arrival. He received him at once, and was therefore a few minutes late for dinner.

When he entered the drawing-room the thirty persons invited to dine, who were sitting beside Princess Elizabeth Ksavérevna Vorontsóva, or standing in groups by the windows, turned their faces towards him. Vorontsóv was dressed in his usual black military coat, with shoulder-straps but no epaulets, and wore the White Cross of the Order of St George at his neck.

His clean-shaven, foxlike face wore a pleasant smile as, screwing up his eyes, he surveyed the assembly. Entering with quick soft steps he apologized to the ladies for being late, greeted the men, and approaching Princess Manana Orbelyáni—a tall, fine, handsome woman of oriental type about forty-five years of age—he offered her his arm to take her in to dinner. Princess Elizabeth Ksavérevna Vorontsóva gave her arm to a red-haired general with bristly moustaches who was visiting Tiflis. A Georgian prince offered his arm to Princess Vorontsóva's friend, Countess Choiseuil. Doctor Andréevski, the aide-de-camp, and others, with ladies or without, followed these first couples. Footmen in livery and knee-breeches drew back and replaced the guests' chairs when they sat down, while the major-domo ceremoniously ladled out steaming soup from a silver tureen.

Vorontsóv took his place in the centre of one side of the long table, and his wife sat opposite, with the general on her right. On the prince's right sat his lady, the beautiful Orbelyáni; and on his left was a graceful, dark, red-cheeked Georgian woman, glittering with jewels and incessantly smiling.

'*Excellentes, chère amie!*'[1] replied Vorontsóv to his wife's inquiry about what news the courier had brought him. '*Simon a eu de la chance!*'[2] And he began to tell aloud, so that everyone could hear, the striking news (for him alone not quite unex-

[1] Excellent, my dear! [2] Simon has had good luck.

pected, because negotiations had long been going on) that Hadji Murád, the bravest and most famous of Shamíl's officers, had come over to the Russians and would in a day or two be brought to Tiflis.

Everybody—even the young aides-de-camp and officials who sat at the far ends of the table and who had been quietly laughing at something among themselves—became silent and listened.

'And you, General, have you ever met this Hadji Murád?' asked the princess of her neighbour, the carroty general with the bristly moustaches, when the prince had finished speaking.

'More than once, Princess.'

And the general went on to tell how Hadji Murád, after the mountaineers had captured Gergebel in 1843, had fallen upon General Pahlen's detachment and killed Colonel Zolotúkhin almost before their very eyes.

Vorontsóv listened to the general and smiled amiably, evidently pleased that the latter had joined in the conversation. But suddenly his face assumed an absent-minded and depressed expression.

The general, having started talking, had begun to tell of his second encounter with Hadji Murád.

'Why, it was he, if your Excellency will please remember,' said the general, 'who arranged the ambush that attacked the rescue party in the "Biscuit" expedition.'

'Where?' asked Vorontsóv, screwing up his eyes.

What the brave general spoke of as the 'rescue' was the affair in the unfortunate Dargo campaign in which a whole detachment, including Prince Vorontsóv who commanded it, would certainly have perished had it not been rescued by the arrival of fresh troops. Every one knew that the whole Dargo campaign under Vorontsóv's command, in which the Russians lost many killed and wounded and several cannon—had been a shameful affair, and therefore if any one mentioned it in Vorontsóv's presence they did so only in the manner in which Vorontsóv had reported it to the Tsar, as a brilliant achievement of the Russian army. But the word 'rescue' plainly indicated that it was not a brilliant victory but a blunder costing many lives. Everybody understood this and some pretended not to notice the meaning of the general's words, others nervously waited to see what would follow, while a few exchanged glances and smiled. Only the carroty general with the bristly moustaches noticed nothing, and carried away by his narrative quietly replied:

'At the rescue, your Excellency.'

Having started on his favourite theme, the general recounted circumstantially how Hadji Murád had so cleverly cut the detachment in two that if the rescue party had not arrived (he seemed to be particularly fond of repeating the word 'rescue') not a man in the division would have escaped, because . . . He did not finish his story, for Manana Orbelyáni having understood what was happening, interrupted him by asking if he had found comfortable quarters in Tiflis. The general, surprised, glanced at everybody all round and saw his aides-de-camp from the end of the table looking fixedly and significantly at him, and he suddenly understood! Without replying to the princess's question, he frowned, became silent, and began hurriedly swallowing the delicacy that lay on his plate, the appearance and taste of which both completely mystified him.

Everybody felt uncomfortable, but the awkwardness of the situation was relieved by the Georgian prince—a very stupid man but an extraordinarily refined and artful flatterer and courtier—who sat on the other side of Princess Vorontsóva. Without seeming to have noticed anything he began to relate how Hadji Murád had carried off the widow of Akhmet Khan of Mekhtulí.

'He came into the village at night, seized what he wanted, and galloped off again with the whole party.'

'Why did he want that particular woman?' asked the princess.

'Oh, he was her husband's enemy, and pursued him but could never once succeed in meeting him right up to the time of his death, so he revenged himself on the widow.'

The princess translated this into French for her old friend Countess Choiseuil, who sat next to the Georgian prince.

'*Quelle horreur!*'[1] said the countess, closing her eyes and shaking her head.

[1] How horrible!

'Oh no!' said Vorontsóv, smiling. 'I have been told that he treated his captive with chivalrous respect and afterwards released her.'

'Yes, for a ransom!'

'Well, of course. But all the same he acted honourably.'

These words of Vorontsóv's set the tone for the further conversation. The courtiers understood that the more importance was attributed to Hadji Murád the better the prince would be pleased.

'The man's audacity is amazing. A remarkable man!'

'Why, in 1849 he dashed into Temir Khan Shurá and plundered the shops in broad daylight.'

An Armenian sitting at the end of the table, who had been in Temir Khan Shurá at the time, related the particulars of that exploit of Hadji Murád's.

In fact, Hadji Murád was the sole topic of conversation during the whole dinner.

Everybody in succession praised his courage, his ability, and his magnanimity. Someone mentioned his having ordered twenty-six prisoners to be killed, but that too was met by the usual rejoinder, 'What's to be done? *À la guerre, comme à la guerre!*'[1]

'He is a great man.'

'Had he been born in Europe he might have been another Napoleon,' said the stupid Georgian prince with a gift of flattery.

He knew that every mention of Napoleon was pleasant to Vorontsóv, who wore the White Cross at his neck as a reward for having defeated him.

'Well, not Napoleon perhaps, but a gallant cavalry general if you like,' said Vorontsóv.

'If not Napoleon, then Murat.'*

'And his name is Hadji *Murád!*'

'Hadji Murád has surrendered and now there'll be an end to Shamíl too,' someone remarked.

'They feel that now' (this 'now' meant under Vorontsóv) 'they can't hold out,' remarked another.

[1] War is war.

'*Tout cela est grâce à vous!*'[1] said Manana Orbelyáni.

Prince Vorontsóv tried to moderate the waves of flattery which began to flow over him. Still, it was pleasant, and in the best of spirits he led his lady back into the drawing-room.

After dinner, when coffee was being served in the drawing-room, the prince was particularly amiable to everybody, and going up to the general with the red bristly moustaches he tried to appear not to have noticed his blunder.

Having made a round of the visitors he sat down to the card-table. He only played the old-fashioned game of ombre. His partners were the Georgian prince, an Armenian general (who had learnt the game of ombre from Prince Vorontsóv's valet), and Doctor Andréevski, a man remarkable for the great influence he exercised.

Placing beside him his gold snuff-box with a portrait of Alexander I on the lid, the prince tore open a pack of highly glazed cards and was going to spread them out, when his Italian valet, Giovanni, brought him a letter on a silver tray.

'Another courier, your Excellency.'

Vorontsóv laid down the cards, excused himself, opened the letter, and began to read.

The letter was from his son, who described Hadji Murád's surrender and his own encounter with Meller-Zakomélski.

The princess came up and inquired what their son had written.

'It's all about the same matter. *Il a eu quelques désagréments avec le commandant de la place. Simon a eu tort.*[2] But "All's well that ends well",' he added in English, handing the letter to his wife; and turning to his respectfully waiting partners he asked them to draw cards.

When the first round had been dealt Vorontsóv did what he was in the habit of doing when in a particularly pleasant mood: with his white, wrinkled old hand he took out a pinch of French snuff, carried it to his nose, and released it.

[1] All this is thanks to you!

[2] He has had some unpleasantness with the commandant of the place. Simon was in the wrong.

X

When Hadji Murád appeared at the prince's palace next day, the waiting-room was already full of people. Yesterday's general with the bristly moustaches was there in full uniform with all his decorations, having come to take leave. There was the commander of a regiment who was in danger of being court-martialled for misappropriating commissariat money, and there was a rich Armenian (patronized by Doctor Andréevski) who wanted to obtain from the government a renewal of his monopoly for the sale of vodka. There, dressed in black, was the widow of an officer who had been killed in action. She had come to ask for a pension, or for free education for her children. There was a ruined Georgian prince in a magnificent Georgian costume who was trying to obtain for himself some confiscated church property. There was an official with a large roll of paper containing a new plan for subjugating the Caucasus. There was also a khan who had come solely to be able to tell his people at home that he had called on the prince.

They all waited their turn and were one by one shown into the prince's cabinet and out again by the aide-de-camp, a handsome, fair-haired youth.

When Hadji Murád entered the waiting-room with his brisk though limping step all eyes were turned towards him and he heard his name whispered from various parts of the room.

He was dressed in a long white *cherkéska* over a brown *beshmét* trimmed round the collar with fine silver lace. He wore black leggings and *chuvyáki* of the same colour which were stretched over his instep as tight as gloves. On his head he wore a high cap draped turban-fashion—that same turban for which, on the denunciation of Akhmet Khan, he had been arrested by General Klügenau* and which had been the cause of his going over to Shamíl.

He stepped briskly across the parquet floor of the waiting-room, his whole slender figure swaying slightly in consequence of his lameness in one leg which was shorter than the other. His eyes, set far apart, looked calmly before him and seemed to see no one.

The handsome aide-de-camp, having greeted him, asked him

to take a seat while he went to announce him to the prince, but Hadji Murád declined to sit down and, putting his hand on his dagger, stood with one foot advanced, looking round contemptuously at all those present.

The prince's interpreter, Prince Tarkhánov, approached Hadji Murád and spoke to him. Hadji Murád answered abruptly and unwillingly. A Kumýk* prince, who was there to lodge a complaint against a police official, came out of the prince's room, and then the aide-de-camp called Hadji Murád, led him to the door of the cabinet, and showed him in.

The commander-in-chief received Hadji Murád standing beside his table, and his old white face did not wear yesterday's smile but was rather stern and solemn.

On entering the large room with its enormous table and great windows with green venetian blinds, Hadji Murád placed his small sunburnt hands on his chest just where the front of his white coat overlapped, and lowering his eyes began, without hurrying, to speak distinctly and respectfully, using the Kumýk dialect which he spoke well.

'I place myself under the powerful protection of the great Tsar and of yourself,' said he, 'and promise to serve the White Tsar in faith and truth to the last drop of my blood, and I hope to be useful to you in the war with Shamíl who is my enemy and yours.'

Having heard the interpreter out, Vorontsóv glanced at Hadji Murád and Hadji Murád glanced at Vorontsóv.

The eyes of the two men met, and expressed to each other much that could not have been put into words and that was not at all what the interpreter said. Without words they told each other the whole truth. Vorontsóv's eyes said that he did not believe a single word Hadji Murád was saying, and that he knew he was and always would be an enemy to everything Russian and had surrendered only because he was obliged to. Hadji Murád understood this and yet continued to give assurances of his fidelity. His eyes said, 'That old man ought to be thinking of his death and not of war, but though he is old he is cunning, and I must be careful.' Vorontsóv understood this also, but nevertheless spoke to Hadji Murád in the way he considered necessary for the success of the war.

'Tell him,' said Vorontsóv, 'that our sovereign is as merciful as he is mighty and will probably at my request pardon him and take him into his service. Have you told him?' he asked, looking at Hadji Murád. 'Until I receive my master's gracious decision, tell him I take it on myself to receive him and make his sojourn among us pleasant.'

Hadji Murád again pressed his hands to the centre of his chest and began to say something with animation.

'He says,' the interpreter translated, 'that formerly, when he governed Avaria in 1839, he served the Russians faithfully and would never have deserted them had not his enemy, Akhmet Khan, wishing to ruin him, calumniated him to General Klügenau.'

'I know, I know,' said Vorontsóv (though if he had ever known he had long forgotten it). 'I know,' he repeated, sitting down and motioning Hadji Murád to the divan that stood beside the wall. But Hadji Murád did not sit down. Shrugging his powerful shoulders as a sign that he could not bring himself to sit in the presence of so important a man, he went on, addressing the interpreter:

'Akhmet Khan and Shamíl are both my enemies. Tell the prince that Akhmet Khan is dead and I cannot revenge myself on him, but Shamíl lives and I will not die without taking vengeance on him,' he said, knitting his brows and tightly closing his mouth.

'Yes, yes; but how does he want to revenge himself on Shamíl?' said Vorontsóv quietly to the interpreter. 'And tell him he may sit down.'

Hadji Murád again declined to sit down, and in answer to the question replied that his object in coming over to the Russians was to help them to destroy Shamíl.

'Very well, very well,' said Vorontsóv; 'but what exactly does he wish to do? Sit down, sit down!'

Hadji Murád sat down, and said that if only they would send him to the Lesgian line and would give him an army, he would guarantee to raise the whole of Dagestan* and Shamíl would then be unable to hold out.

'That would be excellent. I'll think it over,' said Vorontsóv.

The interpreter translated Vorontsóv's words to Hadji Murád.

Hadji Murád pondered.

'Tell the *sirdar* one thing more,' Hadji Murád began again, 'that my family are in the hands of my enemy, and that as long as they are in the mountains I am bound and cannot serve him. Shamíl would kill my wife and my mother and my children if I went openly against him. Let the prince first exchange my family for the prisoners he has, and then I will destroy Shamíl or die!'

'All right, all right,' said Vorontsóv. 'I will think it over. Now let him go to the chief of the staff and explain to him in detail his position, intentions, and wishes.'

Thus ended the first interview between Hadji Murád and Vorontsóv.

That evening an Italian opera was performed at the new theatre, which was decorated in oriental style. Vorontsóv was in his box when the striking figure of the limping Hadji Murád wearing a turban appeared in the stalls. He came in with Lóris-Mélikov,* Vorontsóv's aide-de-camp, in whose charge he was placed, and took a seat in the front row. Having sat through the first act with oriental Muhammadan dignity, expressing no pleasure but only obvious indifference, he rose and looking calmly round at the audience went out, drawing to himself everybody's attention.

The next day was Monday and there was the usual evening party at the Vorontsóvs'. In the large brightly lighted hall a band was playing, hidden among trees. Young women and women not very young wearing dresses that displayed their bare necks, arms, and breasts, turned round and round in the embrace of men in bright uniforms. At the buffet, footmen in red swallow-tail coats and wearing shoes and knee-breeches, poured out champagne and served sweetmeats to the ladies. The '*sirdar*'s' wife also, in spite of her age, went about half-dressed among the visitors smiling affably, and through the interpreter said a few amiable words to Hadji Murád who glanced at the visitors with the same indifference he had shown yesterday in the theatre. After the hostess, other half-naked women came up to him and all of them stood shamelessly before him and smilingly asked him the same question: How he liked what he saw? Vorontsóv himself, wearing gold epaulets and gold shoulder-knots with his white cross and ribbon at his neck, came up and asked him the same question, evidently feeling sure, like all the others, that Hadji Murád could not help being pleased at what he saw. Hadji Murád replied to Vorontsóv as he had replied to them all, that among his people nothing of the kind was done, without expressing an opinion as to whether it was good or bad that it was so.

Here at the ball Hadji Murád tried to speak to Vorontsóv about buying out his family, but Vorontsóv, pretending that he had not heard him, walked away, and Lóris-Mélikov afterwards told Hadji Murád that this was not the place to talk about business.

When it struck eleven Hadji Murád, having made sure of the time by the watch the Vorontsóvs had given him, asked Lóris-Mélikov whether he might now leave. Lóris-Mélikov said he might, though it would be better to stay. In spite of this Hadji Murád did not stay, but drove in the phaeton placed at his disposal to the quarters that had been assigned to him.

XI

On the fifth day of Hadji Murád's stay in Tiflis Lóris-Mélikov, the viceroy's aide-de-camp, came to see him at the latter's command.

'My head and my hands are glad to serve the *sirdar*,' said Hadji Murád with his usual diplomatic expression, bowing his head and putting his hands to his chest. 'Command me!' he said, looking amiably into Lóris-Mélikov's face.

Lóris-Mélikov sat down in an arm-chair placed by the table and Hadji Murád sank onto a low divan opposite and, resting his hands on his knees, bowed his head and listened attentively to what the other said to him. Lóris-Mélikov, who spoke Tatar fluently, told him that though the prince knew about his past life, he yet wanted to hear the whole story from himself.

'Tell it to me, and I will write it down and translate it into Russian and the prince will send it to the Emperor.'

Hadji Murád remained silent for a while (he never interrupted anyone but always waited to see whether his collocutor had not something more to say), then he raised his head, shook back his cap, and smiled the peculiar childlike smile that had captivated Márya Vasílevna.

'I can do that,' said he, evidently flattered by the thought that his story would be read by the Emperor.

'Thou must tell me' (in Tatar nobody is addressed as 'you') 'everything, deliberately from the beginning,' said Lóris-Mélikov drawing a notebook from his pocket.

'I can do that, only there is much—very much—to tell! Many events have happened!' said Hadji Murád.

'If thou canst not do it all in one day thou wilt finish it another time,' said Lóris-Mélikov.

'Shall I begin at the beginning?'

'Yes, at the very beginning . . . where thou wast born and where thou didst live.'

Hadji Murád's head sank and he sat in that position for a long time. Then he took a stick that lay beside the divan, drew a little knife with an ivory gold-inlaid handle, sharp as a razor, from under his dagger, and started whittling the stick with it and speaking at the same time.

'Write: Born in Tselméss, a small *aúl*, "the size of an ass's head," as we in the mountains say,' he began. 'Not far from it, about two cannon-shots, lies Khunzákh* where the khans lived. Our family was closely connected with them. My mother nursed the eldest khan, Abu Nutsal Khan. Because of that I became close to the khans. There were three young khans: Abu Nutsal Khan my brother Osman's foster-brother; Umma Khan my own sworn brother; and Bulách Khan the youngest—whom Shamíl threw over the precipice. But that happened later.

'I was about sixteen when *muríds* began to visit the *aúls*. They beat the stones with wooden scimitars and cried, "Muslims, *ghazavát!*" The Chechéns all went over to murídism and the Avars began to go over too. I was then living in the palace like a brother of the khans. I could do as I liked, and I became rich. I had horses and weapons and money. I lived for pleasure and had no care, and went on like that till the time when Kazi-Mulla, the Imám, was killed and Hamzád* succeeded him. Hamzád sent envoys to the khans to say that if they did not join the *ghazavát* he would destroy Khunzákh.

'This needed consideration. The khans feared the Russians, but were also afraid to join in the holy war. The old khansha sent me with her second son, Umma Khan, to Tiflis to ask the Russian commander-in-chief for help against Hamzád. The commander-in-chief at Tiflis was Baron Rosen.* He did not receive either me or Umma Khan. He sent word that he would help us, but did nothing. Only his officers came riding to us and played cards with Umma Khan. They made him drunk with wine and took him to bad places, and he lost all he had to them at cards. His body was as strong as a bull's and he was as brave as a lion, but his soul was weak as water. He would have gambled away his last horses and weapons if I had not made him come away. 'After visiting Tiflis my ideas changed and I advised the old khansha and the khans to join the *ghazavát*.'

'Why didst thou change thy mind?' asked Lóris-Mélikov. 'Did the Russians displease thee?'

Hadji Murád paused.

'No, I was not pleased,' he answered decidedly, closing his eyes. 'And there was also another reason why I wished to join the *ghazavát*.'

'What was that?'

'Why, near Tselméss the khan and I encountered three *muríds*, two of whom escaped but the third one I shot with my pistol.

'He was still alive when I approached to take his weapons. He looked up at me, and said, "Thou hast killed me. I am happy; but thou art a Muslim, young and strong. Join the *ghazavát!* God wills it!"'

'And didst thou join it?'

'I did not, but it made me think,' said Hadji Murád, and he went on with his tale.

'When Hamzád approached Khunzákh we sent our Elders to him to say that we would agree to join the *ghazavát* if the Imám would send a learned man to explain it to us. Hamzád had our Elders' moustaches shaved off, their nostrils pierced, and cakes hung to their noses, and in that condition he sent them back to us.

'The Elders brought word that Hamzád was ready to send a sheik to teach us the *ghazavát*, but only if the khansha sent him her youngest son as a hostage. She took him at his word and sent her youngest son, Bulách Khan. Hamzád received him well and sent to invite the two elder brothers also. He sent word that he wished to serve the khans as his father had served their father. . . . The khansha was a weak, stupid, and conceited woman, as all women are when they are not under control. She was afraid to send away both sons and sent only Umma Khan. I went with him. We were met by *muríds* about a mile before we arrived and they sang and shot and *dzhigíted* around us, and when we drew near, Hamzád came out of his tent and went up to Umma Khan's stirrup and received him as a khan. He said, "I have not done any harm to thy family and do not wish to do any. Only do not kill me and do not prevent my bringing the people over to the *ghazavát*, and I will serve you with my whole army as my father served your father! Let me live in your house and I will help you with my advice, and you shall do as you like!"

'Umma Khan was slow of speech. He did not know how to reply and remained silent. Then I said that if this was so, let Hamzád come to Khunzákh and the khansha and the khans would receive him with honour. But I was not allowed to finish—and here I first encountered Shamíl, who was beside the Imám. He said to me, "Thou hast not been asked. It was the khan!"

'I was silent, and Hamzád led Umma Khan into his tent. Afterwards Hamzád called me and ordered me to go to Khunzákh with his envoys. I went. The envoys began persuading the khansha to send her eldest son also to Hamzád. I saw there was treachery and told her not to send him; but a woman has as much sense in her head as an egg has hair. She ordered her son to go. Abu Nutsal Khan did not wish to. Then she said, "I see thou art afraid!" Like a bee she knew where to sting him most painfully. Abu Nutsal Khan flushed and did not speak to her any more, but ordered his horse to be saddled. I went with him.

'Hamzád met us with even greater honour than he had shown Umma Khan. He himself rode out two rifle-shot lengths down the hill to meet us. A large party of horsemen with their banners followed him, and they too sang, shot, and *dzhigíted* .

'When we reached the camp, Hamzád led the khan into his tent and I remained with the horses.

'I was some way down the hill when I heard shots fired in Hamzád's tent. I ran there and saw Umma Khan lying prone in a pool of blood, and Abu Nutsal was fighting the *muríds.* One of his cheeks had been hacked off and hung down. He supported it with one hand and with the other stabbed with his dagger at all who came near him. I saw him strike down Hamzád's brother and aim a blow at another man, but then the *muríds* fired at him and he fell.'

Hadji Murád stopped and his sunburnt face flushed a dark red and his eyes became bloodshot.

'I was seized with fear and ran away.'

'Really? I thought thou never wast afraid,' said Lóris-Mélikov.

'Never after that. Since then I have always remembered that shame, and when I recalled it I feared nothing!'

XII

'But enough! It is time for me to pray,' said Hadji Murád drawing from an inner breast-pocket of his *cherkéska* Vorontsóv's repeater watch and carefully pressing the spring. The repeater struck twelve and a quarter. Hadji Murád listened with his head on one side, repressing a childlike smile.

'*Kunák* Vorontsóv's present,' he said, smiling.

'It is a good watch,' said Lóris-Mélikov. 'Well then, go thou and pray, and I will wait.'

'*Yakshí.* Very well,' said Hadji Murád and went to his bedroom.

Left by himself, Lóris-Mélikov wrote down in his notebook the chief things Hadji Murád had related, and then lighting a cigarette began to pace up and down the room. On reaching the door opposite the bedroom he heard animated voices speaking rapidly in Tatar. He guessed that the speakers were Hadji Murád's *muríds*, and opening the door he went in to them.

The room was impregnated with that special leathery acid smell peculiar to the mountaineers. On a *búrka* spread out on the floor sat the one-eyed, red-haired Gamzálo, in a tattered greasy *beshmét*, plaiting a bridle. He was saying something excitedly, speaking in a hoarse voice, but when Lóris-Mélikov entered he immediately became silent and continued his work without paying any attention to him.

In front of Gamzálo stood the merry Khan Mahomá showing his white teeth, his black lashless eyes glittering, and saying something over and over again. The handsome Eldár, his sleeves turned up on his strong arms, was polishing the girths of a saddle suspended from a nail. Khanéfi, the principal worker and manager of the household, was not there, he was cooking their dinner in the kitchen.

'What were you disputing about?' asked Lóris-Mélikov after greeting them.

'Why, he keeps on praising Shamíl,' said Khan Mahomá giving his hand to Lóris-Mélikov. 'He says Shamíl is a great man, learned, holy, and a *dzhigít*.'

'How is it that he has left him and still praises him?'

'He has left him and still praises him,' repeated Khan Mahomá, his teeth showing and his eyes glittering.

'And does he really consider him a saint?' asked Lóris-Mélikov.

'If he were not a saint the people would not listen to him,' said Gamzálo rapidly.

'Shamíl is no saint, but Mansúr* was!' replied Khan Mahomá. 'He was a real saint. When he was Imám the people were quite different. He used to ride through the *aúls* and the people used to come out and kiss the hem of his coat and confess their sins and vow to do no evil. Then all the people, so the old men say, lived like saints: not drinking, nor smoking, nor neglecting their prayers, and forgiving one another their sins even when blood had been spilt. If anyone then found money or anything, he tied it to a stake and set it up by the roadside. In those days God gave the people success in everything—not as now.'

'In the mountains they don't smoke or drink now,' said Gamzálo.

'Your Shamíl is a *lamoréy*,' said Khan Mahomá, winking at Lóris-Mélikov. (*Lamoréy* was a contemptuous term for a mountaineer.)

'Yes, *lamoréy* means mountaineer,' replied Gamzálo. 'It is in the mountains that the eagles dwell.'

'Smart fellow! Well hit!' said Khan Mahomá with a grin, pleased at his adversary's apt retort.

Seeing the silver cigarette-case in Lóris-Mélikov's hand, Khan Mahomá asked for a cigarette, and when Lóris-Mélikov remarked that they were forbidden to smoke, he winked with one eye and jerking his head in the direction of Hadji Murád's bedroom replied that they could do it as long as they were not seen. He at once began smoking, not inhaling, and pouting his red lips awkwardly as he blew out the smoke.

'That is wrong!' said Gamzálo severely, and left the room. Khan Mahomá winked in his direction, and while smoking asked Lóris-Mélikov where he could best buy a silk *beshmét* and a white cap.

'Why, hast thou so much money?'

'I have enough,' replied Khan Mahomá with a wink.

'Ask him where he got the money,' said Eldár, turning his handsome smiling face towards Lóris-Mélikov.

'Oh, I won it!' said Khan Mahomá quickly, and related how while walking in Tiflis the day before he had come upon a group of men, Russians and Armenians, playing at *orlyánka* (a kind of heads-and-tails). The stake was a large one: three gold pieces and much silver. Khan Mahomá at once saw what the game consisted in, and jingling the coppers he had in his pocket he went up to the players and said he would stake the whole amount.

'How couldst thou do it? Hadst thou so much?' asked Lóris-Mélikov.

'I had only twelve kopeks,' said Khan Mahomá, grinning.

'But if thou hadst lost?'

'Why, this!' said Khan Mahomá pointing to his pistol.

'Wouldst thou have given that?'

'Give it indeed! I should have run away, and if anyone had tried to stop me I should have killed him—that's all!'

'Well, and didst thou win?'

'Yes, I won it all and went away!'

Lóris-Mélikov quite understood what sort of men Khan Mahomá and Eldár were. Khan Mahomá was a merry fellow, carefree and ready for any spree. He did not know what to do with his superfluous vitality. He was always gay and reckless, and played with his own and other people's lives. For the sake of that sport with life he had now come over to the Russians, and for the same sport he might go back to Shamíl to-morrow. Eldár was also quite easy to understand. He was a man entirely devoted to his *murshíd*; calm, strong, and firm.

The red-haired Gamzálo was the only one Lóris-Mélikov did not understand. He saw that that man was not only loyal to Shamíl but felt an insuperable aversion, contempt, repugnance, and hatred for all Russians, and Lóris-Mélikov could therefore not understand why he had come over to them. It occurred to him that, as some of the higher officials suspected, Hadji Murád's surrender and his tales of hatred of Shamíl might be false, and that perhaps he had surrendered only to spy out the Russians' weak spots that, after escaping back to the mountains, he might be able to direct his forces accordingly. Gamzálo's whole person strengthened this suspicion.

'The others, and Hadji Murád himself, know how to hide their intentions, but this one betrays them by his open hatred,' he thought.

Lóris-Mélikov tried to speak to him. He asked whether he did not feel bored. 'No, I don't!' he growled hoarsely without stopping his work, and glancing at his questioner out of the corner of his one eye. He replied to all Lóris-Mélikov's other questions in a similar manner.

While Lóris-Mélikov was in the room Hadji Murád's fourth *muríd* came in, the Avar Khanéfi; a man with a hairy face and neck and an arched chest as rough as if it were overgrown with moss. He was strong and a hard worker, always engrossed in his duties, and like Eldár unquestioningly obedient to his master.

When he entered the room to fetch some rice, Lóris-Mélikov stopped him and asked where he came from and how long he had been with Hadji Murád.

'Five years,' replied Khanéfi. 'I come from the same *aúl* as he. My father killed his uncle and they wished to kill me,' he said calmly, looking from under his joined eyebrows straight into Lóris-Mélikov's face. 'Then I asked them to adopt me as a brother.'

'What do you mean by "adopt as a brother"?'

'I did not shave my head nor cut my nails for two months, and then I came to them. They let me in to Patimát, his mother, and she gave me the breast and I became his brother.'

Hadji Murád's voice could be heard from the next room and Eldár, immediately answering his call, promptly wiped his hands and went with large strides into the drawing-room.

'He asks thee to come,' he said, coming back.

Lóris-Mélikov gave another cigarette to the merry Khan Mahomá and went into the drawing-room.

XIII

When Lóris-Mélikov entered the drawing-room Hadji Murád received him with a bright face.

'Well, shall I continue?' he asked, sitting down comfortably on the divan.

'Yes, certainly,' said Lóris-Mélikov. 'I have been in to have a talk with thy henchmen. One is a jolly fellow!' he added.

'Yes, Khan Mahomá is a frivolous fellow,' said Hadji Murád.

'I liked the young handsome one.'

'Ah, that's Eldár. He's young but firm—made of iron!'

They were silent for a while.

'So I am to go on?'

'Yes, yes!'

'I told thee how the khans were killed. Well, having killed them Hamzád rode into Khunzákh and took up his quarters in their palace. The khansha was the only one of the family left alive. Hamzád sent for her. She reproached him, so he winked to his *muríd* Aseldár, who struck her from behind and killed her.'

'Why did he kill her?' asked Lóris-Mélikov.

'What could he do? Where the forelegs have gone the hind legs must follow! He killed off the whole family. Shamíl killed the youngest son—threw him over a precipice.

'Then the whole of Avaria surrendered to Hamzád. But my brother and I would not surrender. We wanted his blood for the blood of the khans. We pretended to yield, but our only thought was how to get his blood. We consulted our grandfather and decided to await the time when he would come out of his palace, and then to kill him from an ambush. Someone overheard us and told Hamzád, who sent for grandfather and said, "Mind, if it be true that thy grandsons are planning evil against me, thou and they shall hang from one rafter. I do God's work and cannot be hindered. Go, and remember what I have said!"

'Our grandfather came home and told us.

'Then we decided not to wait but to do the deed on the first day of the feast in the mosque. Our comrades would not take part in it but my brother and I remained firm.

'We took two pistols each, put on our *búrkas*, and went to the mosque. Hamzád entered the mosque with thirty *muríds*. They all had drawn swords in their hands. Aseldár, his favourite *muríd* (the one who had cut off khansha's head), saw us, shouted to us to take off our *búrkas*, and came towards me. I had my dagger in my hand and I killed him with it and rushed at Hamzád; but my brother Osman had already shot him. He was still alive and rushed at my brother dagger in hand, but I gave him a finishing blow on the head. There were thirty *muríds* and we were only two. They killed my brother Osman, but I kept them at bay, leapt through the window, and escaped.

'When it was known that Hamzád had been killed all the people rose. The *muríds* fled and those of them who did not flee were killed.'

Hadji Murád paused, and breathed heavily.

'That was very good,' he continued, 'but afterwards everything was spoilt.

'Shamíl succeeded Hamzád. He sent envoys to me to say that I should join him in attacking the Russians, and that if I refused he would destroy Khunzákh and kill me.

'I answered that I would not join him and would not let him come to me.'

'Why didst thou not go with him?' asked Lóris-Mélikov.

Hadji Murád frowned and did not reply at once.

'I could not. The blood of my brother Osman and of Abu Nutsal Khan was on his hands. I did not go to him. General Rosen sent me an officer's commission and ordered me to govern Avaria. All this would have been well but that Rosen appointed as khan of Kazi-Kumúkh, first Mahómet-Murza, and afterwards Akhmet Khan, who hated me. He had been trying to get the khansha's daughter, Sultanetta, in marriage for his son, but she would not give her to him, and he believed me to be the cause of this. Yes, Akhmet Khan hated me and sent his henchmen to kill me, but I escaped from them. Then he spoke ill of me to General Klügenau. He said that I told the Avars not to supply wood to the Russian soldiers, and he also said that I had donned a turban—this one' (Hadji Murád touched his turban) 'and that this meant that I had gone over to Shamíl. The general did not believe him and gave orders that I should not be touched. But when the general went to Tiflis, Akhmet Khan did as he pleased. He sent a company of soldiers to seize me, put me in chains, and tied me to a cannon.

'So they kept me six days,' he continued. 'On the seventh day they untied me and started to take me to Temir-Khan-Shurá. Forty soldiers with loaded guns had me in charge. My hands were tied and I knew that they had orders to kill me if I tried to escape.

'As we approached Mansokha the path became narrow, and on the right was an abyss about a hundred and twenty yards deep. I went to the right, to the very edge. A soldier wanted to stop me, but I jumped down and pulled him with me. He was killed outright but I, as you see, remained alive.

'Ribs, head, arms, and leg—all were broken! I tried to crawl but grew giddy and fell asleep. I awoke wet with blood. A shepherd saw me and called some people who carried me to an *aúl*. My ribs and head healed, and my leg too, only it has remained short,' and Hadji Murád stretched out his crooked leg. 'It still serves me, however, and even rather well,' he said.

'The people heard the news and began coming to me. I recovered and went to Tselméss. The Avars again called on me to rule over them,' he went on, with tranquil, confident pride, 'and I agreed.'

He rose quickly and taking a portfolio out of a saddle-bag,

drew out two discoloured letters and handed one of them to Lóris-Mélikov. They were from General Klügenau. Lóris-Mélikov read the first letter, which was as follows:

'Lieutenant Hadji Murád, thou hast served under me and I was satisfied with thee and considered thee a good man.

'Recently Akhmet Khan informed me that thou art a traitor, that thou hast donned a turban and hast contact with Shamíl, and that thou hast taught the people to disobey the Russian Government. I ordered thee to be arrested and brought before me but thou fledst. I do not know whether this is for thy good or not, as I do not know whether thou art guilty or not.

'Now hear me. If thy conscience is pure, if thou art not guilty in anything towards the great Tsar, come to me, fear no one. I am thy defender. The khan can do nothing to thee, he is himself under my command, so thou hast nothing to fear.'

Klügenau added that he always kept his word and was just, and he again exhorted Hadji Murád to appear before him.

When Lóris-Mélikov had read this letter Hadji Murád, before handing him the second one, told him what he had written in reply to the first.

'I wrote that I wore a turban not for Shamíl's sake but for my soul's salvation; that I neither wished nor could go over to Shamíl, because he had caused the death of my father, my brothers, and my relations; but that I could not join the Russians because I had been dishonoured by them. (In Khunzákh, a scoundrel had spat on me while I was bound, and I could not join your people until that man was killed.) But above all I feared that liar, Akhmet Khan.

'Then the general sent me this letter,' said Hadji Murád, handing Lóris-Mélikov the other discoloured paper.

'Thou hast answered my first letter and I thank thee,' read Lóris-Mélikov. 'Thou writest that thou art not afraid to return but that the insult done thee by a certain giaour prevents it, but I assure thee that Russian law is just and that thou shalt see him who dared to offend thee punished before thine eyes. I have already given orders to investigate the matter.

'Hear me, Hadji Murád! I have a right to be displeased with thee for not trusting me and my honour, but I forgive thee, for I know how suspicious mountaineers are in general. If thy conscience is pure, if thou hast put on a turban only for thy soul's salvation, then thou art right and mayst look me and the Russian government boldly in the eye. He who dishonoured thee shall, I assure thee, be punished and *thy property shall be restored to thee*, and thou shalt see and know what Russian law is. Moreover we Russians look at things differently, and thou hast not sunk in our eyes because some scoundrel has dishonoured thee.

'I myself have consented to the Gimrints* wearing turbans, and I regard their actions in the right light, and therefore I repeat that thou hast nothing to fear. Come to me with the man by whom I am sending thee this letter. He is faithful to me and is not the slave of thy enemies, but is the friend of a man who enjoys the special favour of the government.'

Further on Klügenau again tried to persuade Hadji Murád to come over to him.

'I did not believe him,' said Hadji Murád when Lóris-Mélikov had finished reading, 'and did not go to Klügenau. The chief thing for me was to revenge myself on Akhmet Khan, and that I could not do through the Russians. Then Akhmet Khan surrounded Tselméss and wanted to take me or kill me. I had too few men and could not drive him off, and just then came an envoy with a letter from Shamíl promising to help me to defeat and kill Akhmet Khan and making me ruler over the whole of Avaria. I considered the matter for a long time and then went over to Shamíl, and from that time I have fought the Russians continually.'

Here Hadji Murád related all his military exploits, of which there were very many and some of which were already familiar to Lóris-Mélikov. All his campaigns and raids had been remarkable for the extraordinary rapidity of his movements and the boldness of his attacks, which were always crowned with success.

'There never was any friendship between me and Shamíl,' said Hadji Murád at the end of his story, 'but he feared me and needed me. But it so happened that I was asked who should be Imám after Shamíl, and I replied: "He will be Imám whose sword is sharpest!"

'This was told to Shamíl and he wanted to get rid of me. He

sent me into Tabasarán. I went, and captured a thousand sheep and three hundred horses, but he said I had not done the right thing and dismissed me from being *naíb*, and ordered me to send him all the money. I sent him a thousand gold pieces. He sent his *muríds* and they took from me all my property. He demanded that I should go to him, but I knew he wanted to kill me and I did not go. Then he sent to take me. I resisted and went over to Vorontsóv. Only I did not take my family. My mother, my wives, and my son are in his hands. Tell the *sirdar* that as long as my family is in Shamíl's power I can do nothing.'

'I will tell him,' said Lóris-Mélikov.

'Take pains, try hard! . . . What is mine is thine, only help me with the prince! I am tied up and the end of the rope is in Shamíl's hands,' said Hadji Murád concluding his story.

XIV

On 20 December Vorontsóv wrote to Chernyshóv, the Minister of War. The letter was in French:*

'I did not write to you by the last post, dear Prince, as I wished first to decide what we should do with Hadji Murád, and for the last two or three days I have not been feeling quite well.

'In my last letter I informed you of Hadji Murád's arrival here. He reached Tiflis on the 8th, and next day I made his acquaintance, and during the following seven or eight days have spoken to him and considered what use we can make of him in the future, and especially what we are to do with him at present, for he is much concerned about the fate of his family, and with every appearance of perfect frankness says that while they are in Shamíl's hands he is paralysed and cannot render us any service or show his gratitude for the friendly reception and forgiveness we have extended to him.

'His uncertainty about those dear to him makes him restless, and the persons I have appointed to live with him assure me that he does not sleep at night, eats hardly anything, prays continually, and asks only to be allowed to ride out accompanied by several Cossacks—the sole recreation and exercise possible for him and made necessary to him by lifelong habit.

Every day he comes to me to find out whether I have any news of his family, and to ask me to have all the prisoners in our hands collected and offered to Shamíl in exchange for them. He would also give a little money. There are people who would let him have some for that purpose. He keeps repeating to me: "Save my family and then give me a chance to serve thee" (preferably, in his opinion, on the Lesgian line), "and if within a month I do not render you great service, punish me as you think fit." I reply that to me all this appears very just, and that even many among us would not trust him so long as his family remain in the mountains and are not in our hands as hostages, and that I will do everything possible to collect the prisoners on our frontier, that I have no power under our laws to give him money for the ransom of his family in addition to the sum he may himself be able to raise, but that I may perhaps find some other means of helping him. After that I told him frankly that in my opinion Shamíl would not in any case give up the family, and that Shamíl might tell him so straight out and promise him a full pardon and his former posts, and might threaten, if Hadji Murád did not return, to kill his mother, his wives, and his six children. I asked him whether he could say frankly what he would do if he received such an announcement from Shamíl. He lifted his eyes and arms to heaven, and said that everything is in God's hands, but that he would never surrender to his foe, for he is certain Shamíl would not forgive him and he would therefore not have long to live. As to the destruction of his family, he did not think Shamíl would act so rashly: firstly, to avoid making him a yet more desperate and dangerous foe, and secondly, because there were many people, and even very influential people, in Dagestan, who would dissuade Shamíl from such a course. Finally, he repeated several times that whatever God might decree for him in the future, he was at present interested in nothing but his family's ransom, and he implored me in God's name to help him and allow him to return to Grózny, where he could, with the help and consent of our commanders, have some contact with his family and regular news of their condition and of the best means to liberate them. He said that many people, and even some *naíbs* in that part of the enemy's territory, were more or less attached to him, and that among the whole of the population already subjugated by Russia or neutral it would be easy with our help to establish relations very useful for the attainment of the aim which gives him no peace day or night, and the attainment of which would set him at ease and make it possible for him to act for our good and win our confidence. He asks to be sent back to Grózny with a convoy of twenty or thirty picked Cossacks who would serve him as a protection against foes and us as a guarantee of his good faith.

'You will understand, dear Prince, that I have been much perplexed by all this, for do what I will a great responsibility rests on me. It would be in the highest degree rash to trust him entirely, yet in order to deprive him of all means of escape we should have to lock him up, and in my opinion that would be both unjust and impolitic. A measure of that kind, the news of which would soon spread over the whole of Dagestan, would do us great harm by keeping back those who are now inclined more or less openly to oppose Shamíl (and there are many such), and who are keenly watching to see how we treat the Imám's bravest and most adventurous officer now that he has found himself obliged to place himself in our hands. If we treat Hadji Murád as a prisoner all the good effect of the situation will be lost.

'Therefore I think that I could not act otherwise than as I have done, though at the same time I feel that I may be accused of having made a great mistake if Hadji Murád should take it into his head to escape again. In the service, and especially in a complicated situation such as this, it is difficult, not to say impossible, to follow any one straight path without risking mistakes and without accepting responsibility, but once a path seems to be the right one I must follow it, happen what may.

'I beg of you, dear Prince, to submit this to his Majesty the Emperor for his consideration; and I shall be happy if it pleases our most august monarch to approve my action. All that I have written above I have also written to Generals Zavodóvski and Kozlóvski, to guide the latter when communicating direct with Hadji Murád whom I have warned not to act or go anywhere without Kozlóvski's consent. I also told him that it would be all the better for us if he rode out with our convoy, as otherwise Shamíl might spread a rumour that we were keeping him prisoner, but at the same time I made him promise never to go to Vozdvízhensk, because my son, to whom he first surrendered and whom he looks upon as his *kunák* (friend), is not the commander of that place and some unpleasant misunderstanding might easily arise. In any case Vozdvízhensk lies too near a thickly populated hostile settlement, while for the contact with his friends which he desires, Grózny is in all respects suitable.

'Besides the twenty chosen Cossacks who at his own request are to keep close to him, I am also sending Captain Lóris-Mélikov—a worthy, excellent, and highly intelligent officer who speaks Tatar, and knows Hadji Murád well and apparently enjoys his full confidence. During the ten days that Hadji Murád has spent here, he has, however, lived in the same house with Lieutenant-Colonel Prince Tarkhánov, who is in command of the Shoushín district and is here on business connected with the service. He is a truly worthy man whom I trust entirely. He also has won Hadji Murád's confidence, and through him alone—as he speaks Tatar perfectly—we have discussed the most delicate and secret matters. I have consulted Tarkhánov about Hadji Murád, and he fully agrees with me that it was necessary either to act as I have done, or to put Hadji Murád in prison and guard him in the strictest manner (for if we once treat him badly he will not be easy to hold), or else to remove him from the country altogether. But these two last measures would not only destroy all the advantage accruing to us from Hadji Murád's quarrel with Shamíl, but would inevitably check any growth of the present insubordination, and possible future revolt, of the people against Shamíl's power. Prince Tarkhánov tells me he himself has no doubt of Hadji Murád's truthfulness, and that Hadji Murád is convinced that Shamíl will never forgive him but would have him executed in spite of any promise of forgiveness. The only thing Tarkhánov has noticed in his contact with Hadji Murád that might cause any anxiety, is his attachment to his religion. Tarkhánov does not deny that Shamíl might influence Hadji Murád from that side. But as I have already said, he will never persuade Hadji Murád that he will not take his life sooner or later should the latter return to him.

'This, dear Prince, is all I have to tell you about this episode in our affairs here.'

XV

The report was dispatched from Tiflis on 24 December 1851, and on New Year's Eve a courier, having overdriven a dozen horses and beaten a dozen drivers till they bled, delivered it to Prince Chernyshóv who at that time was Minister of War; and on 1 January 1852 Chernyshóv took Vorontsóv's report, among other papers, to the Emperor Nicholas.

Chernyshóv disliked Vorontsóv because of the general respect in which the latter was held and because of his immense wealth, and also because Vorontsóv was a real aristocrat while Chernyshóv, after all, was a *parvenu*,[1] but especially because the Emperor was particularly well disposed towards Vorontsóv. Therefore at every opportunity Chernyshóv tried to injure Vorontsóv.

When he had last presented a report about Caucasian affairs he had succeeded in arousing Nicholas's displeasure against Vorontsóv because—through the carelessness of those in command—almost the whole of a small Caucasian detachment had been destroyed by the mountaineers. He now intended to present the steps taken by Vorontsóv in relation to Hadji Murád in an unfavourable light. He wished to suggest to the Emperor that Vorontsóv always protected and even indulged the natives to the detriment of the Russians, and that he had acted unwisely in allowing Hadji Murád to remain in the Caucasus for there was every reason to suspect that he had only come over to spy on our means of defence, and that it would therefore be better to transport him to Central Russia and make use of him only after his family had been rescued from the mountaineers and it had become possible to convince ourselves of his loyalty.

Chernyshóv's plan did not succeed merely because on that

[1] Social climber, upstart.

New Year's Day Nicholas was in particularly bad spirits, and out of perversity would not have accepted any suggestion whatever from anyone, least of all from Chernyshóv whom he only tolerated, regarding him as indispensable for the time being but looking upon him as a blackguard, for Nicholas knew of his endeavours at the trial of the Decembrists* to secure the conviction of Zacháry Chernyshóv,* and of his attempt to obtain Zacháry's property for himself. So thanks to Nicholas's ill temper Hadji Murád remained in the Caucasus, and his circumstances were not changed as they might have been had Chernyshóv presented his report at another time.

It was half-past nine o'clock when through the mist of the cold morning (the thermometer showed 13 degrees below zero Fahrenheit) Chernyshóv's fat, bearded coachman, sitting on the box of a small sledge (like the one Nicholas drove about in) with a sharp-angled, cushion-shaped azure velvet cap on his head, drew up at the entrance of the Winter Palace* and gave a friendly nod to his chum, Prince Dolgorúki's coachman, who having brought his master to the palace had himself long been waiting outside, in his big coat with the thickly wadded skirts, sitting on the reins and rubbing his numbed hands together. Chernyshóv had on a long cloak with a large cape and a fluffy collar of silver beaver, and a regulation three-cornered hat with cocks' feathers. He threw back the bearskin apron of the sledge and carefully disengaged his chilled feet, on which he had no over-shoes (he prided himself on never wearing any). Clanking his spurs with an air of bravado he ascended the carpeted steps and passed through the hall door which was respectfully opened for him by the porter, and entered the hall. Having thrown off his cloak which an old court lackey hurried forward to take, he went to a mirror and carefully removed the hat from his curled wig. Looking at himself in the mirror, he arranged the hair on his temples and the tuft above his forehead with an accustomed movement of his old hands, and adjusted his cross, the shoulder-knots of his uniform, and his large-initialled epaulets, and then went up the gently ascending carpeted stairs, his not very reliable old legs feebly mounting the shallow steps. Passing the court lackeys in gala livery who stood obsequiously bowing, Chernyshóv entered the waiting-room. He was respectfully met by a newly appointed aide-de-camp of the Emperor's in a shining new uniform with epaulets and shoulder-knots, whose face was still fresh and rosy and who had a small black moustache, and the hair on his temples brushed towards his eyes in the same way as the Emperor.

Prince Vasíli Dolgorúki, Assistant-Minister of War, with an expression of *ennui* on his dull face—which was ornamented with similar whiskers, moustaches, and temple tufts brushed forward like Nicholas's—greeted him.

'*L'empereur?*' said Chernyshóv, addressing the aide-de-camp and looking inquiringly towards the door leading to the cabinet.

'*Sa majesté vient de rentrer*,'[1] replied the aide-de-camp, evidently enjoying the sound of his own voice; and stepping so softly and steadily that had a tumbler of water been placed on his head none of it would have been spilt, he approached the door and disappeared, his whole body evincing reverence for the spot he was about to visit.

Dolgorúki meanwhile opened his portfolio to see that it contained the necessary papers, while Chernyshóv, frowning, paced up and down to restore the circulation in his numbed feet, and thought over what he was about to report to the Emperor. He was near the door of the cabinet when it opened again and the aide-de-camp, even more radiant and respectful than before, came out and with a gesture invited the minister and his assistant to enter.

The Winter Palace had been rebuilt after a fire some considerable time before this, but Nicholas was still occupying rooms in the upper storey. The cabinet in which he received the reports of his ministers and other high officials was a very lofty apartment with four large windows. A big portrait of the Emperor Alexander I hung on the front side of the room. Two bureaux stood between the windows, and several chairs were ranged along the walls. In the middle of the room was an enormous writing-table, with an arm-chair before it for Nicholas, and other chairs for those to whom he gave audience.

Nicholas sat at the table in a black coat with shoulder-straps

[1] His Majesty has just returned.

but no epaulets, his enormous body—with his overgrown stomach tightly laced in—was thrown back, and he gazed at the newcomers with fixed, lifeless eyes. His long pale face, with its enormous receding forehead between the tufts of hair which were brushed forward and skilfully joined to the wig that covered his bald patch, was specially cold and stony that day. His eyes, always dim, looked duller than usual. The compressed lips under his upturned moustaches, the high collar which supported his chin, and his fat freshly shaven cheeks on which symmetrical sausage-shaped bits of whiskers had been left, gave his face a dissatisfied and even irate expression. His bad mood was caused by fatigue, due to the fact that he had been to a masquerade the night before, and while walking about as was his wont in his Horse Guards' uniform with a bird on the helmet, among the public which crowded round and timidly made way for his enormous, self-assured figure, he had again met the mask who at the previous masquerade had aroused his senile sensuality by her whiteness, her beautiful figure, and her tender voice. At that former masquerade she had disappeared after promising to meet him at the next one.

At yesterday's masquerade she had come up to him, and this time he had not let her go, but had led her to the box specially kept ready for that purpose, where he could be alone with her. Having arrived in silence at the door of the box Nicholas looked round to find the attendant, but he was not there. He frowned and pushed the door open himself, letting the lady enter first.

'*Il y a quelqu'un!*'[1] said the mask, stopping short.

And the box actually was occupied. On the small velvet-covered sofa, close together, sat an Uhlan officer and a pretty, fair curly-haired young woman in a domino, who had removed her mask. On catching sight of the angry figure of Nicholas drawn up to its full height, she quickly replaced her mask, but the Uhlan officer, rigid with fear, gazed at Nicholas with fixed eyes without rising from the sofa.

Used as he was to the terror he inspired in others, that terror always pleased Nicholas, and by way of contrast he sometimes

[1] There's someone there!

liked to astound those plunged in terror by addressing kindly words to them. He did so on this occasion.

'Well, friend!' he said to the officer, 'You are younger than I and might give up your place to me.'

The officer jumped to his feet, and growing first pale and then red and bending almost double, he followed his partner silently out of the box, leaving Nicholas alone with his lady.

She proved to be a pretty, twenty-year-old virgin, the daughter of a Swedish governess. She told Nicholas how when quite a child she had fallen in love with him from his portraits; how she adored him and had made up her mind to attract his attention at any cost. Now she had succeeded and wanted nothing more—so she said.

The girl was taken to the place where Nicholas usually had rendezvous with women, and there he spent more than an hour with her.

When he returned to his room that night and lay on the hard narrow bed about which he prided himself, and covered himself with the cloak which he considered to be (and spoke of as being) as famous as Napoleon's hat, it was a long time before he could fall asleep. He thought now of the frightened and elated expression on that girl's fair face, and now of the full, powerful shoulders of his established mistress, Nelídova, and he compared the two. That profligacy in a married man was a bad thing did not once enter his head, and he would have been greatly surprised had anyone censured him for it. Yet though convinced that he had acted rightly, some kind of unpleasant after-taste remained, and to stifle that feeling he dwelt on a thought that always tranquillized him, the thought of his own greatness.

Though he had fallen asleep so late, he rose before eight, and after attending to his toilet in the usual way—rubbing his big well-fed body all over with ice—and saying his prayers (repeating those he had been used to from childhood, the prayer to the Virgin, the Apostles' Creed, and the Lord's Prayer, without attaching any kind of meaning to the words he uttered), he went out through the smaller portico of the palace onto the embankment in his military cloak and cap.

On the embankment he met a student in the uniform of the

School of Jurisprudence, who was as enormous as himself. On recognizing the uniform of that school, which he disliked for its freedom of thought, Nicholas frowned, but the stature of the student and the painstaking manner in which he drew himself up and saluted, ostentatiously sticking out his elbow, mollified his displeasure.

'Your name?' said he.

'Polosátov, your Imperial Majesty.'

'. . . fine fellow!'

The student continued to stand with his hand lifted to his hat.

Nicholas stopped.

'Do you wish to enter the army?'

'Not at all, your Imperial Majesty.'

'Blockhead!' And Nicholas turned away and continued his walk, and began uttering aloud the first words that came into his head.

'Koperwein, Koperwein,' he repeated several times (it was the name of yesterday's girl). 'Horrid, horrid.' He did not think of what he was saying, but stifled his feelings by listening to the words.

'Yes, what would Russia be without me?' said he, feeling his former dissatisfaction returning. 'What would, not Russia alone, but Europe be, without me?' and calling to mind the weakness and stupidity of his brother-in-law the King of Prussia, he shook his head.

As he was returning to the small portico, he saw the carriage of Helena Pávlovna,* with a red-liveried footman, approaching the Saltykóv entrance of the palace.

Helena Pávlovna was to him the personification of that futile class of people who discussed not merely science and poetry, but even the ways of governing men: imagining that they could govern themselves better than he, Nicholas, governed them! He knew that however much he crushed such people they reappeared again and again, and he recalled his brother, Michael Pávlovich, who had died not long before. A feeling of sadness and vexation came over him and with a dark frown he again began whispering the first words that came into his head, which he only ceased doing when he re-entered the palace.

On reaching his apartments he smoothed his whiskers and the hair on his temples and the wig on his bald patch, and twisted his moustaches upwards in front of the mirror, and then went straight to the cabinet in which he received reports.

He first received Chernyshóv, who at once saw by his face, and especially by his eyes, that Nicholas was in a particularly bad humour that day, and knowing about the adventure of the night before he understood the cause. Having coldly greeted him and invited him to sit down, Nicholas fixed on him a lifeless gaze. The first matter Chernyshóv reported upon was a case of embezzlement by commissariat officials which had just been discovered; the next was the movement of troops on the Prussian frontier; then came a list of rewards to be given at the New Year to some people omitted from a former list; then Vorontsóv's report about Hadji Murád; and lastly some unpleasant business concerning an attempt by a student of the Academy of Medicine on the life of a professor.

Nicholas heard the report of the embezzlement silently with compressed lips, his large white hand—with one ring on the fourth finger—stroking some sheets of paper, and his eyes steadily fixed on Chernyshóv's forehead and on the tuft of hair above it.

Nicholas was convinced that everybody stole. He knew he would have to punish the commissariat officials now, and decided to send them all to serve in the ranks, but he also knew that this would not prevent those who succeeded them from acting in the same way. It was a characteristic of officials to steal, but it was his duty to punish them for doing so, and tired as he was of that duty he conscientiously performed it.

'It seems there is only one honest man in Russia!' said he.

Chernyshóv at once understood that this one honest man was Nicholas himself, and smiled approvingly.

'It looks like it, your Imperial Majesty,' said he.

'Leave it. I will give a decision,' said Nicholas, taking the document and putting it on the left side of the table.

Then Chernyshóv reported about the rewards to be given and about moving the army on the Prussian frontier.

Nicholas looked over the list and struck out some names,

and then briefly and firmly gave orders to move two divisions to the Prussian frontier. He could not forgive the King of Prussia for granting a constitution to his people after the events of 1848,* and therefore while expressing most friendly feelings to his brother-in-law in letters and conversation, he considered it necessary to keep an army near the frontier in case of need. He might want to use these troops to defend his brother-in-law's throne if the people of Prussia rebelled (Nicholas saw a readiness for rebellion everywhere) as he had used troops to suppress the uprising in Hungary a few years previously. They were also of use to give more weight and influence to such advice as he gave to the King of Prussia.

'Yes, what would Russia be like now if it were not for me?' he again thought.

'Well, what else is there?' said he.

'A courier from the Caucasus,' said Chernyshóv, and he reported what Vorontsóv had written about Hadji Murád's surrender.

'Well, well!' said Nicholas. 'It's a good beginning!'

'Evidently the plan devised by your Majesty begins to bear fruit,' said Chernyshóv.

This approval of his strategic talents was particularly pleasant to Nicholas because, though he prided himself upon them, at the bottom of his heart he knew that they did not really exist, and he now desired to hear more detailed praise of himself.

'How do you mean?' he asked.

'I mean that if your Majesty's plans had been adopted before, and we had moved forward slowly and steadily, cutting down forests and destroying the supplies of food, the Caucasus would have been subjugated long ago. I attribute Hadji Murád's surrender entirely to his having come to the conclusion that they can hold out no longer.'

'True,' said Nicholas.

Although the plan of a gradual advance into the enemy's territory by means of felling forests and destroying the food supplies was Ermólov's* and Velyamínov's plan, and was quite contrary to Nicholas's own plan of seizing Shamíl's place of residence and destroying that nest of robbers—which was the plan on which the Dargo expedition in 1845 (that cost so many lives) had been undertaken—Nicholas nevertheless attributed to himself also the plan of a slow advance and a systematic felling of forests and devastation of the country. It would seem that to believe the plan of a slow movement by felling forests and destroying food supplies to have been his own would have necessitated hiding the fact that he had insisted on quite contrary operations in 1845. But he did not hide it and was proud of the plan of the 1845 expedition as well as of the plan of a slow advance, though the two were obviously contrary to one another. Continual brazen flattery from everybody round him in the teeth of obvious facts had brought him to such a state that he no longer saw his own inconsistencies or measured his actions and words by reality, logic, or even simple common sense, but was quite convinced that all his orders, however senseless, unjust, and mutually contradictory they might be, became reasonable, just, and mutually accordant simply because he gave them. His decision in the case next reported to him, that of the student of the Academy of Medicine, was of that senseless kind.

The case was as follows: A young man who had twice failed in his examinations was being examined a third time, and when the examiner again would not pass him, the young man, whose nerves were deranged, considering this to be an injustice, seized a pen-knife from the table in a paroxysm of fury, and rushing at the professor inflicted on him several trifling wounds.

'What's his name?' asked Nicholas.

'Bzhezóvski.'

'A Pole?'

'Of Polish descent and a Roman Catholic,' answered Chernyshóv.

Nicholas frowned. He had done much evil to the Poles. To justify that evil he had to feel certain that all Poles were rascals, and he considered them to be such and hated them in proportion to the evil he had done them.

'Wait a little,' he said, closing his eyes and bowing his head.

Chernyshóv, having more than once heard Nicholas say so, knew that when the Emperor had to take a decision it was only necessary for him to concentrate his attention for a few moments and the spirit moved him, and the best possible decision presented itself as though an inner voice had told him what to do. He was now thinking how most fully to satisfy the feeling of hatred against the Poles which this incident had stirred up within him, and the inner voice suggested the following decision. He took the report and in his large handwriting wrote on its margin with three orthographical mistakes:

'*Diserves deth, but, thank God, we have no capitle punishment, and it is not for me to introduce it. Make him run the gauntlet of a thousand men twelve times.—Nicholas.*'

He signed, adding his unnaturally huge flourish.

Nicholas knew that twelve thousand strokes with the regulation rods were not only certain death from torture, but were a superfluous cruelty, for five thousand strokes were sufficient to kill the strongest man. But it pleased him to be ruthlessly cruel and it also pleased him to think that we have abolished capital punishment in Russia.

Having written his decision about the student, he pushed it across to Chernyshóv.

'There,' he said, 'read it.'

Chernyshóv read it, and bowed his head as a sign of respectful amazement at the wisdom of the decision.

'Yes, and let all the students be present on the drill-ground at the punishment,' added Nicholas.

'It will do them good! I will abolish this revolutionary spirit and will tear it up by the roots!' he thought.

'It shall be done,' replied Chernyshóv; and after a short pause he straightened the tuft on his forehead and returned to the Caucasian report.

'What do you command me to write in reply to Prince Vorontsóv's dispatch?'

'To keep firmly to my system of destroying the dwellings and food supplies in Chechnyá and to harass them by raids,' answered Nicholas.

'And what are your Majesty's commands with reference to Hadji Murád?' asked Chernyshóv.

'Why, Vorontsóv writes that he wants to make use of him in the Caucasus.'

'Is it not dangerous?' said Chernyshóv, avoiding Nicholas's gaze. 'Prince Vorontsóv is too confiding, I am afraid.'

'And you—what do you think?' asked Nicholas sharply, detecting Chernyshóv's intention of presenting Vorontsóv's decision in an unfavourable light.

'Well, I should have thought it would be safer to deport him to Central Russia.'

'You would have thought!' said Nicholas ironically. 'But I don't think so, and agree with Vorontsóv. Write to him accordingly.'

'It shall be done,' said Chernyshóv, rising and bowing himself out.

Dolgorúki also bowed himself out, having during the whole audience only uttered a few words (in reply to a question from Nicholas) about the movement of the army.

After Chernyshóv, Nicholas received Bíbikov, General-Governor of the Western Provinces. Having expressed his approval of the measures taken by Bíbikov against the mutinous peasants who did not wish to accept the Orthodox faith, he ordered him to have all those who did not submit tried by court-martial. That was equivalent to sentencing them to run the gauntlet. He also ordered the editor of a newspaper to be sent to serve in the ranks of the army for publishing information about the transfer of several thousand state peasants to the imperial estates.

'I do this because I consider it necessary,' said Nicholas, 'and I will not allow it to be discussed.'

Bíbikov saw the cruelty of the order concerning the Uniate* peasants and the injustice of transferring state peasants (the only free peasants in Russia in those days) to the crown, which meant making them serfs of the imperial family. But it was impossible to express dissent. Not to agree with Nicholas's decisions would have meant the loss of that brilliant position which it had cost Bíbikov forty years to attain and which he now enjoyed; and he therefore submissively bowed his dark head (already touched with grey) to indicate his submission and his readiness to fulfil the cruel, insensate, and dishonest supreme will.

Having dismissed Bíbikov, Nicholas stretched himself, with a sense of duty well fulfilled, glanced at the clock, and went to get ready to go out. Having put on a uniform with epaulets, orders, and a ribbon, he went out into the reception hall where more than a hundred persons—men in uniforms and women in elegant low-necked dresses, all standing in the places assigned to them—awaited his arrival with agitation.

He came out to them with a lifeless look in his eyes, his chest expanded, his stomach bulging out above and below his belt, and feeling everybody's gaze tremulously and obsequiously fixed upon him he assumed an even more triumphant air. When his eyes met those of people he knew, remembering who was who, he stopped and addressed a few words to them sometimes in Russian and sometimes in French, and transfixing them with his cold glassy eye listened to what they said.

Having received all the New Year congratulations he passed on to church, where God, through his servants the priests, greeted and praised Nicholas just as worldly people did; and weary as he was of these greetings and praises Nicholas duly accepted them. All this was as it should be, because the welfare and happiness of the whole world depended on him, and wearied though he was he would still not refuse the universe his assistance.

When at the end of the service the magnificently arrayed deacon, his long hair crimped and carefully combed, began the chant *Many Years*,* which was heartily caught up by the splendid choir, Nicholas looked round and noticed Nelídova, with her fine shoulders, standing by a window, and he decided the comparison with yesterday's girl in her favour.

After the service he went to the Empress and spent a few minutes in the bosom of his family, joking with the children and his wife. Then passing through the Hermitage,* he visited the Minister of the Court, Volkónski, and among other things ordered him to pay out of a special fund a yearly pension to the mother of yesterday's girl. From there he went for his customary drive.

Dinner that day was served in the Pompeian Hall. Besides the younger sons of Nicholas and Michael there were also invited Baron Lieven, Count Rzhévski, Dolgorúki, the Prussian ambassador, and the King of Prussia's aide-de-camp.

While waiting for the appearance of the Emperor and Empress an interesting conversation took place between Baron Lieven and the Prussian ambassador concerning the disquieting news from Poland.

'*La Pologne et le Caucase, ce sont les deux cautères de la Russie*,' said Lieven. '*Il nous faut cent mille hommes à peu près, dans chacun de ces deux pays*.'[1]

The ambassador expressed a fictitious surprise that it should be so.

'*Vous dites, la Pologne—*' began the ambassador.

'*Oh, oui, c'était un coup de maître de Metternich de nous en avoir laissé l'embarras*.'[2]

At this point the Empress, with her trembling head and fixed smile, entered followed by Nicholas.

At dinner Nicholas spoke of Hadji Murád's surrender and said that the war in the Caucasus must now soon come to an end in consequence of the measures he was taking to limit the scope of the mountaineers by felling their forests and by his system of erecting a series of small forts.

The ambassador, having exchanged a rapid glance with the aide-de-camp—to whom he had only that morning spoken about Nicholas's unfortunate weakness for considering himself a great strategist—warmly praised this plan which once more demonstrated Nicholas's great strategic ability.

After dinner Nicholas drove to the ballet where hundreds of women marched round in tights and scanty clothing. One of them specially attracted him, and he had the German ballet-master sent for and gave orders that a diamond ring should be presented to him.

The next day when Chernyshóv came with his report, Nicholas again confirmed his order to Vorontsóv, that now that Hadji Murád had surrendered, the Chechéns should be more actively harassed than ever and the cordon round them tightened.

Chernyshóv wrote in that sense to Vorontsóv; and another

[1] Poland and the Caucasus are Russia's two sores. We need about 100,000 men in each of those two countries.

[2] 'You say that Poland—' 'Oh yes, it was a masterstroke of Metternich's to leave us the bother of it.'

courier, overdriving more horses and bruising the faces of more drivers, galloped to Tiflis.

XVI

In obedience to this command of Nicholas a raid was immediately made in Chechnyá that same month, January 1852.

The detachment ordered for the raid consisted of four infantry battalions, two companies of Cossacks, and eight guns. The column marched along the road; and on both sides of it in a continuous line, now mounting, now descending, marched *Jägers** in high boots, sheepskin coats, and tall caps, with rifles on their shoulders and cartridges in their belts.

As usual when marching through a hostile country, silence was observed as far as possible. Only occasionally the guns jingled jolting across a ditch, or an artillery horse snorted or neighed, not understanding that silence was ordered, or an angry commander shouted in a hoarse subdued voice to his subordinates that the line was spreading out too much or marching too near or too far from the column. Only once was the silence broken, when from a bramble patch between the line and the column a gazelle with a white breast and grey back jumped out followed by a buck of the same colour with small backward-curving horns. Doubling up their forelegs at each big bound they took, the beautiful timid creatures came so close to the column that some of the soldiers rushed after them laughing and shouting, intending to bayonet them, but the gazelles turned back, slipped through the line of *Jägers*, and pursued by a few horsemen and the company's dogs, fled like birds to the mountains.

It was still winter, but towards noon, when the column (which had started early in the morning) had gone three miles, the sun had risen high enough and was powerful enough to make the men quite hot, and its rays were so bright that it was painful to look at the shining steel of the bayonets or at the reflections, like little suns, on the brass of the cannons.

The clear and rapid stream the detachment had just crossed lay behind, and in front were tilled fields and meadows in shallow valleys. Farther in front were the dark mysterious forest-clad hills with crags rising beyond them, and farther still on the lofty horizon were the ever-beautiful ever-changing snowy peaks that played with the light like diamonds.

At the head of the 5th Company, Butler, a tall handsome officer who had recently exchanged from the guards, marched along in a black coat and tall cap, shouldering his sword, He was filled with a buoyant sense of the joy of living, the danger of death, a wish for action, and the consciousness of being part of an immense whole directed by a single will. This was his second time of going into action and he thought how in a moment they would be fired at, and he would not only not stoop when the shells flew overhead, or heed the whistle of the bullets, but would carry his head even more erect than before and would look round at his comrades and the soldiers with smiling eyes, and begin to talk in a perfectly calm voice about quite other matters.

The detachment turned off the good road onto a little-used one that crossed a stubbly cornfield, and they were drawing near the forest when, with an ominous whistle, a shell flew past amid the baggage wagons—they could not see from where—and tore up the ground in the field by the roadside.

'It's beginning,' said Butler with a bright smile to a comrade who was walking beside him.

And so it was. After the shell a thick crowd of mounted Chechéns appeared with their banners from under the shelter of the forest. In the midst of the crowd could be seen a large green banner, and an old and very far-sighted sergeant-major informed the short-sighted Butler that Shamíl himself must be there. The horsemen came down the hill and appeared to the right, at the highest part of the valley nearest the detachment, and began to descend. A little general in a thick black coat and tall cap rode up to Butler's company on his ambler, and ordered him to the right to encounter the descending horsemen. Butler quickly led his company in the direction indicated, but before he reached the valley he heard two cannon shots behind him. He looked round: two clouds of grey smoke had risen above two cannon and were spreading along the valley. The mountaineers' horsemen, who had evidently not expected to meet artillery, retired. Butler's company began firing at them and the whole ravine was filled with the gunpowder smoke. Only higher up above the ravine could the mountaineers be seen hurriedly retreating, though still firing back at the Cossacks who pursued them. The company followed the mountaineers farther, and on the slope of a second ravine came in view of an *aúl*.

Following the Cossacks, Butler and his company entered the *aúl* at a run, to find it deserted. The soldiers were ordered to burn the corn and the hay as well as the *sáklyas*, and the whole *aúl* was soon filled with pungent smoke amid which the soldiers rushed about dragging out of the *sáklyas* what they could find, and above all catching and shooting the fowls the mountaineers had not been able to take away with them. The officers sat down at some distance beyond the smoke, and lunched and drank. The sergeant-major brought them some honeycombs on a board. There was no sign of any Chechéns and early in the afternoon the order was given to retreat. The companies formed into a column behind the *aúl* and Butler happened to be in the rearguard. As soon as they started Chechéns appeared, following and firing at the detachment, but they ceased this pursuit as soon as they came out into an open space. Not one of Butler's company was wounded, and he returned in a most happy and energetic mood.

After fording the same stream it had crossed in the morning, the detachment spread over the cornfields and the meadows, and the singers of each company came forward, filling the air with songs.

There was no wind, the air was fresh and clear and so transparent that the snow hills nearly a hundred miles away seemed quite near, and in the intervals between the songs the regular sound of the footsteps and the jingle of the guns was heard as a background on which each song began and ended. The song that was being sung in Butler's company was composed by a cadet in honour of the regiment, and went to a dance tune. The chorus was: 'Very diff'rent, very diff'rent, *Jägers* are, *Jägers* are!'

Butler rode beside the officer next in rank above him, Major Petróv, with whom he lived, and he felt he could not be thankful enough to have exchanged from the Guards and come to the

Caucasus. His chief reason for exchanging was that he had lost all he had at cards and was afraid that if he remained there he would be unable to resist playing though he had nothing more to lose. Now all that was over, his life was quite changed and was such a pleasant and brave one! He forgot that he was ruined, and forgot his unpaid debts. The Caucasus, the war, the soldiers, the officers, those tipsy, brave, good-natured fellows, and Major Petróv himself, all seemed so delightful that sometimes it appeared too good to be true that he was not in Petersburg, in a room filled with tobacco-smoke, turning down the corners of cards* and gambling, hating the holder of the bank and feeling a dull pain in his head, but was really here in this glorious region among these brave Caucasians.

'Very diff'rent, very diff'rent, *Jägers* are, *Jägers* are!' sang Butler's singers, and his horse stepped merrily to the music. Trezórka, the shaggy grey dog belonging to the company, ran in front, with his tail curled up with an air of responsibility like a commander. Butler felt buoyant, calm, and joyful. War presented itself to him as consisting only in his exposing himself to danger and to possible death, thereby gaining rewards and the respect of his comrades here, as well as of his friends in Russia. Strange to say, his imagination never pictured the other aspect of war: the death and wounds of the soldiers, officers, and mountaineers. To retain his poetic conception he even unconsciously avoided looking at the dead and wounded. So that day when we had three dead and twelve wounded, he passed by a corpse lying on its back and did not stop to look, seeing only with one eye the strange position of the waxen hand and a dark red spot on the head. The hillsmen appeared to him only as mounted *dzhigíts* from whom he had to defend himself.

'You see, my dear sir,' said his major in an interval between two songs, 'it's not as it is with you in Petersburg. "Dress right! Dress left!" And we have done our job, and then we go home and Másha will set a pie and some nice cabbage soup before us. That's life! don't you think so? Now then! *As the Dawn was Breaking!*' He called for his favourite song.

The major and the daughter of a surgeon's orderly, formerly known as Másha, but now generally called by the more respectful name of Márya Dmítrievna, lived together as man and wife. Márya Dmítrievna was a handsome, fair-haired, very freckled, childless woman of thirty. Whatever her past may have been she was now the major's faithful companion and looked after him like a nurse—a very necessary matter, since he often drank himself into oblivion.

When they reached the fort everything happened as the major had foreseen. Márya Dmítrievna gave him and Butler, and two other officers of the detachment who had been invited, a nourishing and tasty dinner, and the major ate and drank till he was unable to speak, and then went off to his room to sleep.

Butler, having drunk rather more *chikhír* than was good for him, went to his bedroom, tired but contented, and hardly had time to undress before he fell into a sound, dreamless, and unbroken sleep with his hand under his handsome curly head.

XVII

The *aúl* which had been destroyed was that in which Hadji Murád had spent the night before he went over to the Russians. Sado and his family had left the *aúl* on the approach of the Russian detachment, and when he returned he found his *sáklya* in ruins—the roof fallen in, the door and the posts supporting the penthouse burned, and the interior filthy. His son, the handsome bright-eyed boy who had gazed with such ecstasy at Hadji Murád, was brought dead to the mosque on a horse covered with a *búrka*: he had been stabbed in the back with a bayonet. The dignified woman who had served Hadji Murád when he was at the house now stood over her son's body, her smock torn in front, her withered old breasts exposed, her hair down, and she dug her nails into her face till it bled, and wailed incessantly. Sado, taking a pick-axe and spade, had gone with his relatives to dig a grave for his son. The old grandfather sat by the wall of the ruined *sáklya* cutting a stick and gazing stolidly in front of him. He had only just returned from the apiary. The two stacks of hay there had been burnt, the apricot and cherry trees he had planted and reared were broken and scorched, and worse still all the beehives and bees had been burnt. The wailing of the women and the little children, who cried with their mothers, mingled with the lowing of the hungry cattle for whom there was no food. The bigger children, instead of playing, followed their elders with frightened eyes. The fountain was polluted, evidently on purpose, so that the water could not be used. The mosque was polluted in the same way, and the *múlla* and his assistants were cleaning it out. No one spoke of hatred of the Russians. The feeling experienced by all the Chechéns, from the youngest to the oldest, was stronger than hate. It was not hatred, for they did not regard those Russian dogs as human beings, but it was such repulsion, disgust, and perplexity at the senseless cruelty of these creatures, that the desire to exterminate them, like the desire to exterminate rats, poisonous spiders, or wolves, was as natural an instinct as that of self-preservation.

The inhabitants of the *aúl* were confronted by the choice of remaining there and restoring with frightful effort what had been produced with such labour and had been so lightly and senselessly destroyed, facing every moment the possibility of a repetition of what had happened; or to submit to the Russians, contrary to their religion and despite the repulsion and contempt they felt for them. The old men prayed, and unanimously decided to send envoys to Shamíl asking him for help. Then they immediately set to work to restore what had been destroyed.

XVIII

On the morning after the raid, not very early, Butler left the house by the back porch meaning to take a stroll and a breath of fresh air before breakfast, which he usually had with Petróv. The sun had already risen above the hills and it was painful to look at the brightly lit-up white walls of the houses on the right side of the street. But then as always it was cheerful and soothing to look to the left, at the dark receding and ascending forest-clad hills and at the dim line of snow peaks, which as usual pretended to be clouds. Butler looked at these mountains, inhaling deep breaths and rejoicing that he was alive, that it was just he that was alive, and that he lived in this beautiful place.

He was also rather pleased that he had behaved so well in yesterday's affair both during the advance and especially during the retreat when things were pretty hot; he was also pleased to remember how Másha (or Márya Dmítrievna), Petróv's mistress, had treated them at dinner on their return after the raid, and how she had been particularly nice and simple with everybody, but specially kind—as he thought—to him.

Márya Dmítrievna with her thick plait of hair, her broad shoulders, her high bosom, and the radiant smile on her kindly freckled face, involuntarily attracted Butler, who was a healthy young bachelor. It sometimes even seemed to him that she wanted him, but he considered that that would be doing his good-natured simple-hearted comrade a wrong, and he maintained a simple, respectful attitude towards her and was pleased with himself for doing so.

He was thinking of this when his meditations were disturbed by the tramp of many horses' hoofs along the dusty road in front of him, as if several men were riding that way. He looked up and saw at the end of the street a group of horsemen coming towards him at a walk. In front of a score of Cossacks rode two men: one in a white *cherkéska* with a tall turban on his head, the other an officer in the Russian service, dark, with an aquiline nose, and much silver on his uniform and weapons. The man with the turban rode a fine chestnut horse with mane and tail of a lighter shade, a small head, and beautiful eyes. The officer's was a large, handsome Karabákh horse. Butler, a lover of horses, immediately recognized the great strength of the first horse and stopped to learn who these people were.

The officer addressed him. 'This the house of commanding officer?' he asked, his foreign accent and his words betraying his foreign origin.

Butler replied that it was. 'And who is that?' he added, coming nearer to the officer and indicating the man with the turban.

'That Hadji Murád. He come here to stay with the commander,' said the officer.

Butler knew about Hadji Murád and about his having come over to the Russians, but he had not at all expected to see him here in this little fort. Hadji Murád gave him a friendly look.

'Good-day, *kotkíldy*,' said Butler, repeating the Tatar greeting he had learnt.

'*Saubul!*' replied Hadji Murád, nodding. He rode up to Butler and held out his hand, from two fingers of which hung his whip.

'The chief?' he asked.

'No, the chief is in here. I will go and call him,' said Butler addressing the officer, and he went up the steps and pushed the door. But the door of the visitors' entrance, as Márya Dmítrievna called it, was locked, and as it still remained closed after he had knocked, Butler went round to the back door. He called his orderly but received no reply, and finding neither of the two orderlies he went into the kitchen, where Márya Dmítrievna—flushed, with a kerchief tied round her head and her sleeves rolled up on her plump white arms—was rolling pastry, white as her hands, and cutting it into small pieces to make pies of.

'Where have the orderlies gone to?' asked Butler.

'Gone to drink,' replied Márya Dmítrievna. 'What do you want?'

'To have the front door opened. You have a whole horde of mountaineers in front of your house. Hadji Murád has come!'

'Invent something else!' said Márya Dmítrievna, smiling.

'I am not joking, he is really waiting by the porch!'

'Is it really true?' said she.

'Why should I wish to deceive you? Go and see, he's just at the porch!'

'Well, this is an event!' said Márya Dmítrievna pulling down her sleeves and putting up her hand to feel whether the hairpins in her thick plait were all in order. 'Then I will go and wake Iván Matvéich.'

'No, I'll go myself. And you Bondarénko, go and open the door,' said he to Petróv's orderly who had just appeared.

'Well, so much the better!' said Márya Dmítrievna and returned to her work.

When he heard that Hadji Murád had come to his house, Iván Matvéich Petróv, the major, who had already heard that Hadji Murád was in Grózny, was not at all surprised. Sitting up in bed he rolled a cigarette, lit it, and began to dress, loudly clearing his throat and grumbling at the authorities who had sent 'that devil' to him.

When he was ready he told his orderly to bring him some

medicine. The orderly knew that 'medicine' meant vodka, and brought some.

'There is nothing so bad as mixing,' muttered the major when he had drunk the vodka and taken a bite of rye bread. 'Yesterday I drank a little *chikhír* and now I have a headache. . . . Well, I'm ready,' he added, and went to the parlour, into which Butler had already shown Hadji Murád and the officer who accompanied him.

The officer handed the major orders from the commander of the left flank to the effect that he should receive Hadji Murád and should allow him to have contact with the mountaineers through spies, but was on no account to allow him to leave the fort without a convoy of Cossacks.

Having read the order the major looked intently at Hadji Murád and again scrutinized the paper. After passing his eyes several times from one to the other in this manner, he at last fixed them on Hadji Murád and said:

'*Yakshí, Bek; yakshí!* ('Very well, sir, very well!') Let him stay here, and tell him I have orders not to let him out—and what is commanded is sacred! Well, Butler, where do you think we'd better lodge him? Shall we put him in the office?'

Butler had not time to answer before Márya Dmítrievna, who had come from the kitchen and was standing in the doorway, said to the major:

'Why? Keep him here! We will give him the guest-chamber and the storeroom. Then at any rate he will be within sight,' she said, glancing at Hadji Murád; but meeting his eyes she turned quickly away.

'Do you know, I think Márya Dmítrievna is right,' said Butler.

'Now then, now then, get away! Women have no business here,' said the major frowning.

During the whole of this discussion Hadji Murád sat with his hand on the hilt of his dagger and a faint smile of contempt on his lips. He said it was all the same to him where he lodged, and that he wanted nothing but what the *sirdar* had permitted, namely, to have communication with the mountaineers, and that he therefore wished they should be allowed to come to him.

The major said this should be done, and asked Butler to

entertain the visitors till something could be got for them to eat and their rooms prepared. Meantime he himself would go across to the office to write what was necessary and to give some orders.

Hadji Murád's relations with his new acquaintances were at once very clearly defined. From the first he was repelled by and contemptuous of the major, to whom he always behaved very haughtily. Márya Dmítrievna, who prepared and served up his food, pleased him particularly. He liked her simplicity and especially the—to him—foreign type of her beauty, and he was influenced by the attraction she felt towards him and unconsciously conveyed. He tried not to look at her or speak to her, but his eyes involuntarily turned towards her and followed her movements. With Butler, from their first acquaintance, he immediately made friends and talked much and willingly with him, questioning him about his life, telling him of his own, communicating to him the news the spies brought him of his family's condition, and even consulting him as to how he ought to act.

The news he received through the spies was not good. During the first four days of his stay in the fort they came to see him twice and both times brought bad news.

XIX

Hadji Murád's family had been removed to Vedenó soon after his desertion to the Russians, and were there kept under guard awaiting Shamíl's decision. The women, his old mother Patimát and his two wives with their five little children, were kept under guard in the *sáklya* of the officer Ibrahim Raschid, while Hadji Murád's son Yusúf, a youth of eighteen, was put in prison, that is, into a pit more than seven feet deep, together with seven criminals, who like himself were awaiting a decision as to their fate.

The decision was delayed because Shamíl was away on a campaign against the Russians.

On 6 January 1852, he returned to Vedenó after a battle, in which according to the Russians he had been vanquished and had fled to Vedenó; but in which according to him and all the *muríds* he had been victorious and had repulsed the Russians. In this battle he himself fired his rifle, a thing he seldom did, and drawing his sword would have charged straight at the Russians had not the *muríds* who accompanied him held him back. Two of them were killed on the spot at his side.

It was noon when Shamíl, surrounded by a party of *muríds* who *dzhigíted* around him firing their rifles and pistols and continually singing *Lya illyah il Allah!* rode up to his place of residence.

All the inhabitants of the large *aúl* were in the street or on their roofs to meet their ruler, and as a sign of triumph they also fired off rifles and pistols. Shamíl rode a white Arab steed which pulled at its bit as it approached the house. The horse had no gold or silver ornaments, its equipment was of the simplest, a delicately worked red leather bridle with a stripe down the middle, metal cup-shaped stirrups, and a red saddle-cloth showing a little from under the saddle. The Imám wore a brown cloth cloak lined with black fur showing at the neck and sleeves, and was tightly girded round his long thin waist with a black strap which held a dagger. On his head he wore a tall cap with flat crown and black tassel, and round it was wound a white turban, one end of which hung down on his neck. He wore green slippers, and black leggings trimmed with plain braid.

He wore nothing bright, no gold or silver, and his tall, erect, powerful figure, clothed in garments without any ornaments, surrounded by *muríds* with gold and silver on their clothes and weapons, produced on the people just the impression and influence he desired and knew how to produce. His pale face framed by a closely trimmed reddish beard, with his small eyes always screwed up, was as immovable as though hewn out of stone. As he rode through the *aúl* he felt the gaze of a thousand eyes turned eagerly on him, but he himself looked at no one.

Hadji Murád's wives had come out under the overhang with the rest of the inmates of the *sáklya* to see the Imám's entry. Only Patimát, Hadji Murád's old mother, did not go out but remained sitting on the floor of the *sáklya* with her grey hair down, her long arms encircling her thin knees, blinking with her fiery black eyes as she watched the dying embers in the fireplace. Like her son she had always hated Shamíl, and now she hated him more than ever and had no wish to see him. Neither did Hadji Murád's son see Shamíl's triumphal entry. Sitting in the dark and fetid pit he heard the firing and singing, and endured tortures such as can only be felt by the young who are full of vitality and deprived of freedom. He only saw his unfortunate, dirty, and exhausted fellow-prisoners, who were embittered and for the most part filled with hatred of one another. He now passionately envied those who, enjoying fresh air and light and freedom, *dzhigíted* on fiery steeds around their chief, shooting and heartily singing: *Lya illyah il Allah!*

When he had crossed the *aúl* Shamíl rode into the large courtyard adjoining the inner court where his seraglio was. Two armed Lesgians met him at the open gates of this outer court, which was crowded with people. Some had come from distant parts about their own affairs, some had come with petitions, and some had been summoned by Shamíl to be tried and sentenced. As the Imám rode in, they all respectfully saluted him with their hands on their breasts, some of them kneeling down and remaining on their knees while he rode across the court from the outer to the inner gates. Though he recognized among the people who waited in the court many whom he disliked, and many tedious petitioners who wanted his attention, Shamíl passed them all with the same immovable, stony expression on his face, and having entered the inner court dismounted at the entrance hall in front of his apartment, to the left of the gate. He was worn out, mentally rather than physically, by the strain of the campaign, for in spite of the public declaration that he had been victorious he knew very well that his campaign had been unsuccessful, that many Chechén *aúls* had been burnt down and ruined, and that the unstable and fickle Chechéns were wavering and those nearest the border line were ready to go over to the Russians.

All this had to be dealt with, and it oppressed him, for at that moment he did not wish to think at all. He only desired one thing: rest and the delights of family life, and the caresses of his favourite wife, the black-eyed quick-footed eighteen-year-old Aminal, who at that very moment was close at hand behind the fence that divided the inner court and separated the men's from the women's quarters (Shamíl felt sure she was there with his other wives, looking through a chink in the fence while he dismounted). But not only was it impossible for him to go to her, he could not even lie down on his feather cushions and rest from his fatigue; he had first of all to perform the midday rites for which he had just then not the least inclination, but which as the religious leader of the people he could not omit, and which moreover were as necessary to him himself as his daily food. So he performed his ablutions and said his prayers and summoned those who were waiting for him.

The first to enter was Jemal Eddin, his father-in-law and teacher, a tall grey-haired good-looking old man with a beard white as snow and a rosy red face. He said a prayer and began questioning Shamíl about the incidents of the campaign and telling him what had happened in the mountains during his absence.

Among events of many kinds, including murders connected with blood-feuds, cattle-stealing, people accused of disobeying the rules of the *Tarikáh** (by smoking and drinking wine), Jemal Eddin related how Hadji Murád had sent men to bring his family over to the Russians, but that this had been detected and the family had been brought to Vedenó where they were kept under guard and awaited the Imám's decision. In the next room, the guest-chamber, the Elders were assembled to discuss all these affairs, and Jemal Eddin advised Shamíl to finish with them and let them go that same day, as they had already been waiting three days for him.

After eating his dinner, which was served to him in his room by Zeidát, a dark, sharp-nosed, disagreeable-looking woman whom he did not love but who was his eldest wife, Shamíl passed into the guest-chamber.

The six old men who made up his council—white-, grey-, or red-bearded, with tall caps on their heads, some with turbans and some without, wearing new *beshméts* and *cherkéskas* girdled with straps on which their daggers were suspended—rose to greet him on his entrance. Shamíl towered a head above them all. On entering the room he, as well as all the others, lifted his hands, palms upwards, closed his eyes and recited a prayer, and then stroked his face downwards with both hands, uniting them at the end of his beard. Having done this they all sat down, Shamíl on a larger cushion than the others, and discussed the various cases before them.

In the case of the criminals the decisions were given according to the *Shariáh*:* two were sentenced to have a hand cut off for stealing, one man to be beheaded for murder, and three were pardoned. Then they came to the principal business, how to stop the Chechéns from going over to the Russians. To counteract that tendency Jemal Eddin drew up the following proclamation:

'I wish you eternal peace with God the Almighty!

'I hear that the Russians flatter you and invite you to surrender to them. Do not believe what they say, and do not surrender but endure. If ye be not rewarded for it in this life ye shall receive your reward in the life to come. Remember what happened before when they took your arms from you! If God had not brought you to reason then, in 1840, ye would now be soldiers, and your wives would be dishonoured and would no longer wear trousers.

'Judge of the future by the past. It is better to die in enmity with the Russians than to live with the Unbelievers. Endure for a little while and I will come with the Koran and the sword and will lead you against the enemy. But now I strictly command you not only to entertain no intention, but not even a thought, of submitting to the Russians!'

Shamíl approved this proclamation, signed it, and had it sent out.

After this business they considered Hadji Murád's case. This was of the utmost importance to Shamíl. Although he did not wish to admit it, he knew that if Hadji Murád, with his agility, boldness, and courage, had been with him, what had now happened in Chechnyá would not have occurred. It would therefore be well to make it up with Hadji Murád and have the benefit of his services again. But as this was not possible it would never do to allow him to help the Russians, and therefore he must be enticed back and killed. They might accomplish this either by sending a man to Tiflis who would kill him there, or by inducing him to come back and then killing him.

The only means of doing the latter was by making use of his family and especially his son, whom Shamíl knew he loved passionately. Therefore they must act through the son.

When the councillors had talked all this over, Shamíl closed his eyes and sat silent.

The councillors knew that this meant that he was listening to the voice of the Prophet, who spoke to him and told him what to do.

After five minutes of solemn silence Shamíl opened his eyes, and narrowing them more than usual, said:

'Bring Hadji Murád's son to me.'

'He is here,' replied Jemal Eddin, and in fact Yusúf, Hadji Murad's son, thin, pale, tattered, and evil-smelling, but still handsome in face and figure, with black eyes that burnt like his grandmother Patimát's, was already standing by the gate of the outside court waiting to be called in.

Yusúf did not share his father's feelings towards Shamíl. He did not know all that had happened in the past, or if he knew it, not having lived through it he still did not understand why his father was so obstinately hostile to Shamíl. To him who wanted only one thing—to continue living the easy, loose life that, as the *naíb's* son, he had led in Khunzákh—it seemed quite unnecessary to be at enmity with Shamíl. Out of defiance and a spirit of contradiction to his father he particularly admired Shamíl, and shared the ecstatic adoration with which he was regarded in the mountains. With a peculiar feeling of tremulous veneration of the Imám he now entered the guest-chamber. As he stopped by the door he met the steady gaze of Shamíl's half-closed eyes. He paused for a moment, and then approached Shamíl and kissed his large, long-fingered hand.

'Thou art Hadji Murád's son?'

'I am, Imám.'

'Thou knowest what he has done?'

'I know, Imám, and deplore it.'

'Canst thou write?'

'I was preparing myself to be a *múlla*.'

'Then write to thy father that if he will return to me now, before the feast of Bairam,* I will forgive him and everything shall be as it was before; but if not, and if he remains with the

Russians'—and Shamíl frowned sternly—'I will send thy grandmother and thy mother to different *aúls*, and thee I will behead!'

Not a muscle of Yusúf's face stirred, and he bowed his head to show that he understood Shamíl's words.

'Write that and give it to my messenger.'

Shamíl ceased speaking, and looked at Yusúf for a long time in silence.

'Write that I have had pity on thee and will not kill thee, but will put out thine eyes as I do to all traitors! Go!'

While in Shamíl's presence Yusúf appeared calm, but when he had been led out of the guest-chamber he rushed at his attendant, snatched the man's dagger from its sheath and tried to stab himself, but he was seized by the arms, bound, and led back to the pit.

That evening at dusk after he had finished his evening prayers, Shamíl put on a white fur-lined cloak and passed out to the other side of the fence where his wives lived, and went straight to Aminal's room, but he did not find her there. She was with the older wives. Then Shamíl, trying to remain unseen, hid behind the door and stood waiting for her. But Aminal was angry with him because he had given some silk stuff to Zeidát and not to her. She saw him come out and go into her room looking for her, and she purposely kept away. She stood a long time at the door of Zeidát's room, laughing softly at Shamíl's white figure that kept going in and out of her room.

Having waited for her in vain, Shamíl returned to his own apartments when it was already time for the midnight prayers.

XX

Hadji Murád had been a week in the major's house at the fort. Although Márya Dmítrievna quarrelled with the shaggy Khanéfi (Hadji Murád had only brought two of his *muríds*, Khanéfi and Eldár, with him) and had turned him out of her kitchen, for which he nearly killed her, she evidently felt a particular respect and sympathy for Hadji Murád. She now no longer served him his dinner, having handed that duty over to Eldár, but she seized every opportunity of seeing him and rendering him service. She always took the liveliest interest in the negotiations about his family, knew how many wives and children he had, and their ages, and each time a spy came to see him she inquired as best she could into the results of the negotiations.

Butler during that week had become quite friendly with Hadji Murád. Sometimes the latter came to Butler's room, sometimes Butler went to Hadji Murád's, sometimes they conversed by the help of the interpreter, and sometimes they got on as best they could with signs and especially with smiles.

Hadji Murád had evidently taken a fancy to Butler, as could be gathered from Eldár's relations with the latter. When Butler entered Hadji Murád's room Eldár met him with a pleased smile showing his glittering teeth, and hurried to put down a cushion for him to sit on and to relieve him of his sword if he was wearing one.

Butler also got to know, and became friendly with, the shaggy Khanéfi, Hadji Murád's sworn brother. Khanéfi knew many mountain songs and sang them well, and to please Butler, Hadji Murád often made Khanéfi sing, choosing the songs he considered best. Khanéfi had a high tenor voice and sang with extraordinary clearness and expression. One of the songs Hadji Murád specially liked impressed Butler by its solemnly mournful tone and he asked the interpreter to translate it.

The subject of the song was the very blood-feud that had existed between Khanéfi and Hadji Murád. It ran as follows:

'The earth will dry on my grave,
    Mother, my Mother!
  And thou wilt forget me!
And over me rank grass will wave,
    Father, my Father!
  Nor wilt thou regret me
When tears cease thy dark eyes to lave,
    Sister, dear Sister!
  No more will grief fret thee!

'But thou, my Brother the elder, wilt never forget,
  With vengeance denied me!

And thou, my Brother the younger, wilt ever regret,
Till thou liest beside me!

'Hotly thou camest, O death-bearing ball that I spurned,
For thou wast my slave!
And thou, black earth, that battle-steed trampled and churned,
Wilt cover my grave!

'Cold art Thou, O Death, yet I was thy Lord and thy Master!
My body sinks fast to the earth, my soul to Heaven flies faster.'

Hadji Murád always listened to this song with closed eyes and when it ended on a long gradually dying note he always remarked in Russian, 'Good song! Wise song!'

After Hadji Murád's arrival and his intimacy with him and his *muríds*, the poetry of the stirring mountain life took a still stronger hold on Butler. He procured for himself a *beshmét* and a *cherkéska* and leggings, and imagined himself a mountaineer living the life those people lived.

On the day of Hadji Murád's departure the major invited several officers to see him off. They were sitting, some at the table where Márya Dmítrievna was pouring out tea, some at another table on which stood vodka, *chikhír*, and light refreshments, when Hadji Murád dressed for the journey came limping into the room with soft, rapid footsteps.

They all rose and shook hands with him. The major offered him a seat on the divan, but Hadji Murád thanked him and sat down on a chair by the window.

The silence that followed his entrance did not at all abash him. He looked attentively at all the faces and fixed an indifferent gaze on the tea-table with the samovar and refreshments. Petróvski, a lively officer who now met Hadji Murád for the first time, asked him through the interpreter whether he liked Tiflis.

'*Alya!*' he replied.

'He says "Yes",' translated the interpreter.

'What did he like there?'

Hadji Murád said something in reply.

'He liked the theatre best of all.'

'And how did he like the ball at the house of the commander-in-chief?'

Hadji Murád frowned. 'Every nation has its own customs!

Our women do not dress in such a way,' said he, glancing at Márya Dmítrievna.

'Well, didn't he like it?'

'We have a proverb,' said Hadji Murád to the interpreter, '"The dog gave meat to the ass and the ass gave hay to the dog, and both went hungry,"' and he smiled. 'Its own customs seem good to each nation.'

The conversation went no further. Some of the officers took tea, some other refreshments. Hadji Murád accepted the tumbler of tea offered him and put it down before him.

'Won't you have cream and a bun?' asked Márya Dmítrievna, offering them to him.

Hadji Murád bowed his head.

'Well, I suppose it is good-bye!' said Butler, touching his knee. 'When shall we meet again?'

'Good-bye, good-bye!' said Hadji Murád, in Russian, with a smile. '*Kunák* be. Strong *kunák* to thee! Time, oh how go!' and he jerked his head in the direction in which he had to go.

Eldár appeared in the doorway carrying something large and white across his shoulder and a sword in his hand. Hadji Murád beckoned to him and he crossed the room with big strides and handed him a white *búrka* and the sword. Hadji Murád rose, took the *búrka*, threw it over his arm, and saying something to the interpreter handed it to Márya Dmítrievna.

'He says thou hast praised the *búrka*, so accept it,' said the interpreter.

'Oh, why?' said Márya Dmítrievna blushing.

'It is necessary,' said Hadji Murád.

'Well, thank you,' sand Márya Dmítrievna, taking the *búrka*. 'God grant that you rescue your son,' she added. '*Ulan yakshi*. Tell him that I wish him success in releasing his family.'

Hadji Murád glanced at Márya Dmítrievna and nodded his head approvingly. Then he took the sword from Eldár and handed it to the major. The major took it and said to the interpreter, 'Tell him to take my chestnut gelding. I have nothing else to give him.'

Hadji Murád waved his hand in front of his face to show that he did not want anything and would not accept it. Then, pointing first to the mountains and then to his heart, he went out.

All the household followed him as far as the door, while the officers who remained inside the room drew the sword from its scabbard, examined its blade, and decided that it was a real *Gurda*.

Butler accompanied Hadji Murád to the porch, and then came a very unexpected incident which might have ended fatally for Hadji Murád had it not been for his quick observation, determination, and agility.

The inhabitants of the Kumýk *aúl*, Tash-Kichu, which was friendly to the Russians, respected Hadji Murád greatly and had often come to the fort merely to look at the famous *naíb*. They had sent messengers to him three days previously to ask him to visit their mosque on the Friday. But the Kumýk princes who lived in Tash-Kichu hated Hadji Murád because there was a blood-feud between them, and on hearing of this invitation they announced to the people that they would not allow him to enter the mosque. The people became excited and a fight occurred between them and the princes' supporters. The Russian authorities pacified the mountaineers and sent word to Hadji Murád not to go to the mosque.

Hadji Murád did not go and everyone supposed that the matter was settled.

But at the very moment of his departure, when he came out into the porch before which the horses stood waiting, Arslán Khan, one of the Kumýk princes and an acquaintance of Butler and the major, rode up to the house.

When he saw Hadji Murád he snatched a pistol from his belt and took aim, but before he could fire, Hadji Murád in spite of his lameness rushed down from the porch like a cat towards Arslán Khan who missed him.

Seizing Arslán Khan's horse by the bridle with one hand, Hadji Murád drew his dagger with the other and shouted something to him in Tatar.

Butler and Eldár both ran at once towards the enemies and caught them by the arms. The major, who had heard the shot, also came out.

'What do you mean by it, Arslán, starting such a nasty business on my premises?' said he, when he heard what had happened. 'It's not right, friend! "To the foe in the field you need not yield", but to start this kind of slaughter in front of my house—'

Arslán Khan, a little man with black moustaches, got off his horse pale and trembling, looked angrily at Hadji Murád, and went into the house with the major. Hadji Murád, breathing heavily and smiling, returned to the horses.

'Why did he want to kill him?' Butler asked the interpreter.

'He says it is a law of theirs,' the interpreter translated Hadji Murád's reply. 'Arslán must avenge a relation's blood and so he tried to kill him.'

'And supposing he overtakes him on the road?' asked Butler.

Hadji Murád smiled.

'Well, if he kills me it will prove that such is Allah's will. Good-bye,' he said again in Russian, taking his horse by the withers. Glancing round at everybody who had come out to see him off, his eyes rested kindly on Márya Dmítrievna.

'Good-bye, my lass,' said he to her. 'I thank you.'

'God help you. God help you to rescue your family!' repeated Márya Dmítrievna.

He did not understand her words, but felt her sympathy for him and nodded to her.

'Mind, don't forget your *kunák*,' said Butler.

'Tell him I am his true friend and will never forget him,' answered Hadji Murád to the interpreter, and in spite of his short leg he swung himself lightly and quickly into the high saddle, barely touching the stirrup, and automatically feeling for his dagger and adjusting his sword. Then, with that peculiarly proud look with which only a Caucasian hill-man sits on his horse, as though he were one with it, he rode away from the major's house. Khanéfi and Eldár also mounted and having taken a friendly leave of their hosts and of the officers, rode off at a trot, following their *murshíd*.

As usual after a departure, those who remained behind began to discuss those who had left.

'Plucky fellow! He rushed at Arslán Khan like a wolf! His face quite changed!'

'But he'll be up to tricks. He's a terrible rogue, I should say,' remarked Petróvski.

'It's a pity there aren't more Russian rogues of such a kind!'

suddenly put in Márya Dmítrievna with vexation. 'He has lived a week with us and we have seen nothing but good from him. He is courteous, wise, and just,' she added.

'How did you find that out?'

'No matter, I did find it out!'

'She's quite smitten, and that's a fact!' said the major, who had just entered the room.

'Well, and if I am smitten? What's that to you? Why run him down if he's a good man? Though he's a Tatar he's still a good man!'

'Quite true, Márya Dmítrievna,' said Butler, 'and you're quite right to take his part!'

XXI

Life in our advanced forts in the Chechén lines went on as usual. Since the events last narrated there had been two alarms when the companies were called out and militiamen galloped about; but both times the mountaineers who had caused the excitement got away, and once at Vozdvízhensk they killed a Cossack and succeeded in carrying off eight Cossack horses that were being watered. There had been no further raids since the one in which the *aúl* was destroyed, but an expedition on a large scale was expected in consequence of the appointment of a new commander of the left flank, Prince Baryátinski.* He was an old friend of the viceroy's and had been in command of the Kabardá regiment. On his arrival at Grózny as commander of the whole left flank he at once mustered a detachment to continue to carry out the Tsar's commands as communicated by Chernyshóv to Vorontsóv. The detachment mustered at Vozdvízhensk left the fort and took up a position towards Kurín, where the troops were encamped and were felling the forest. Young Vorontsóv lived in a splendid cloth tent, and his wife, Márya Vasílevna, often came to the camp and stayed the night. Baryátinski's relations with Márya Vasílevna were no secret to anyone, and the officers who were not in the aristocratic set and the soldiers abused her in coarse terms, for her presence in camp caused them to be sent off to lie in ambush at night. The mountaineers were in the habit of bringing guns within range and firing shells at the camp. The shells generally missed their aim and therefore at ordinary times no special measures were taken to prevent such firing, but now men were placed in ambush to hinder the mountaineers from injuring or frightening Márya Vasílevna with their cannon. To have to be always lying in ambush at night to save a lady from being frightened offended and annoyed them, and therefore the soldiers, as well as the officers not admitted to the higher society, called Márya Vasílevna bad names.

Having obtained leave of absence from his fort, Butler came to the camp to visit some old mess-mates from the cadet corps and fellow officers of the Kurín regiment who were serving as adjutants and orderly officers. When he first arrived he had a very good time. He put up in Poltorátski's tent and there met many acquaintances who gave him a hearty welcome. He also called on Vorontsóv, whom he knew slightly, having once served in the same regiment with him. Vorontsóv received him very kindly, introduced him to Prince Baryátinski, and invited him to the farewell dinner he was giving in honour of General Kozlóvski, who until Baryátinski's arrival had been in command of the left flank.

The dinner was magnificent. Special tents were erected in a line, and along the whole length of them a table was spread as for a dinner-party, with dinner-services and bottles. Everything recalled life in the guards in Petersburg. Dinner was served at two o'clock. Kozlóvski sat in the middle on one side, Baryátinski on the other. At Kozlóvski's right and left hand sat the Vorontsóvs, husband and wife. All along the table on both sides sat the officers of the Kabardá and Kurín regiments. Butler sat next to Poltorátski and they both chatted merrily and drank with the officers around them. When the roast was served and the orderlies had gone round and filled the champagne glasses, Poltorátski said to Butler, with real anxiety:

'Our "how" will disgrace himself!'

'Why?'

'Why, he'll have to make a speech, and what good is he at that? It's not as easy as capturing entrenchments under fire! And with a lady beside him too, and these aristocrats!'

'Really it's painful to look at him,' said the officers to one another. And now the solemn moment had arrived. Baryátinski rose and lifting his glass, addressed a short speech to Kozlóvski. When he had finished, Kozlóvski rose and with a rather firm voice began:

'In compliance with the august will of his Majesty I am leaving you—parting from you, gentlemen,' he said. 'But consider me as always remaining among you. The truth of the proverb, how "One man in the field is no warrior", is well known to you, gentlemen. Therefore, how every reward I have received, how all the benefits showered on me by the great generosity of our sovereign the Emperor, how all my position, how my good name, how everything decidedly, how' (here his voice trembled) 'how I am indebted to you for it, to you alone, my friends!' The wrinkled face puckered up still more, he gave a sob and tears came into his eyes. 'How from my heart I offer you my sincerest, heartfelt gratitude!'

Kozlóvski could not go on but turned round and began to embrace the officers. The princess hid her face in her handkerchief. The prince blinked, with his mouth drawn awry. Many of the officers' eyes grew moist and Butler, who had hardly known Kozlóvski, could also not restrain his tears. He liked all this very much. Then followed toasts to Baryátinski, Vorontsóv, the officers, and the soldiers, and the visitors left the table intoxicated with wine and with the military elation to which they were always so prone.

The weather was wonderful, sunny and calm, and the air fresh and bracing. Bonfires crackled and songs resounded on all sides. It might have been thought that everybody was celebrating some joyful event. Butler went to Poltorátski's in the happiest, most emotional mood. Several officers had gathered there and a card-table was set. An adjutant set up a bank with a hundred rubles. Two or three times Butler left the tent with his hand gripping the purse in his trousers-pocket, but at last he could resist the temptation no longer, and despite the promise he had given to his brother and to himself not to play, he began to do so. Before an hour was past, very red, perspiring, and soiled with chalk, he was sitting with both elbows on the table and writing on it, under cards bent for 'corners' and 'transports', the figures of his stakes. He had already lost so much that he was afraid to count up what was scored against him. But he knew without counting that all the pay he could draw in advance, added to the value of his horse, would not suffice to pay what the adjutant, a stranger to him, had written down against him. He would still have gone on playing, but the adjutant sternly laid down the cards he held in his large clean hands and added up the chalked figures of the score of Butler's losses. Butler, in confusion, began to make excuses for being unable to pay the whole of his debt at once, and said he would send it from home. When he said this he noticed that everybody pitied him and that they all, even Poltorátski, avoided meeting his eye. That was his last evening there. He reflected that he need only have refrained from playing and gone to the Vorontsóvs who had invited him, and all would have been well, but now it was not only not well—it was terrible.

Having taken leave of his comrades and acquaintances he rode home and went to bed, and slept for eighteen hours as people usually sleep after losing heavily. From the fact that he asked her to lend him fifty kopeks to tip the Cossack who had escorted him, and from his sorrowful looks and short answers, Márya Dmítrievna guessed that he had lost at cards and she reproached the major for having given him leave of absence.

When he woke up at noon next day and remembered the situation he was in he longed again to plunge into the oblivion from which he had just emerged, but it was impossible. Steps had to be taken to repay the four hundred and seventy rubles he owed to the stranger. The first step he took was to write to his brother, confessing his sin and imploring him, for the last time, to lend him five hundred rubles on the security of the mill they still owned in common. Then he wrote to a stingy relative asking her to lend him five hundred rubles at whatever rate of interest she liked. Finally he went to the major, knowing that he, or rather Márya Dmítrievna, had some money, and asked him to lend him five hundred rubles.

'I'd let you have them at once,' said the major, 'but Másha won't! These women are so close-fisted, who the devil can understand them? And yet you must get out of it somehow, devil take him! Hasn't that brute the canteen-keeper got something?'

But it was no use trying to borrow from the canteen-keeper, so Butler's salvation could only come from his brother or his stingy relative.

XXII

Not having attained his aim in Chechnyá, Hadji Murád returned to Tiflis and went every day to Vorontsóv's, and whenever he could obtain audience he implored the viceroy to gather together the mountaineer prisoners and exchange them for his family. He said that unless that were done his hands were tied and he could not serve the Russians and destroy Shamíl as he desired to do. Vorontsóv vaguely promised to do what he could, but put it off, saying that he would decide when General Argutínski reached Tiflis and he could talk the matter over with him.

Then Hadji Murád asked Vorontsóv to allow him to go to live for a while in Nukhá, a small town in Transcaucasia where he thought he could better carry on negotiations about his family with Shamíl and with the people who were attached to himself. Moreover Nukhá, being a Muhammadan town, had a mosque where he could more conveniently perform the rites of prayer demanded by the Muhammadan law. Vorontsóv wrote to Petersburg about it but meanwhile gave Hadji Murád permission to go to Nukhá.

For Vorontsóv and the authorities in Petersburg, as well as for most Russians acquainted with Hadji Murád's history, the whole episode presented itself as a lucky turn in the Caucasian war, or simply as an interesting event. For Hadji Murád it was a terrible crisis in his life, especially of late. He had escaped from the mountains partly to save himself and partly out of hatred of Shamíl, and difficult as this flight had been he had attained his object, and for a time was glad of his success and really devised a plan to attack Shamíl, but the rescue of his family, which he had thought would be easy to arrange, had proved more difficult than he expected.

Shamíl had seized the family and kept them prisoners, threatening to hand the women over to different *aúls* and to blind or kill the son. Now Hadji Murád had gone to Nukhá intending to try by the aid of his adherents in Dagestan to rescue his family from Shamíl by force or by cunning. The last spy who had come to see him in Nukhá informed him that the Avars, who were devoted to him, were preparing to capture his family and themselves bring them over to the Russians, but that there were not enough of them and they could not risk making the attempt in Vedenó, where the family was at present imprisoned, but could do so only if the family were moved from Vedenó to some other place, in which case they promised to rescue them on the way.

Hadji Murád sent word to his friends that he would give three thousand rubles for the liberation of his family.

At Nukhá a small house of five rooms was assigned to Hadji Murád near the mosque and the khan's palace. The officers in charge of him, his interpreter, and his henchmen, stayed in the same house. Hadji Murád's life was spent in the expectation and reception of messengers from the mountains and in rides he was allowed to take in the neighbourhood.

On 24 April, returning from one of these rides, Hadji Murád learnt that during his absence an official sent by Vorontsóv had arrived from Tiflis. In spite of his longing to know what message the official had brought him he went to his bedroom and repeated his noonday prayer before going into the room where the officer in charge and the official were waiting. This room served him both as drawing- and reception-room. The official who had come from Tiflis, Councillor Kiríllov, informed Hadji Murád of Vorontsóv's wish that he should come to Tiflis on the 12th to meet General Argutínski.

'*Yakshi!*' said Hadji Murád angrily. The councillor did not please him. 'Have you brought money?'

'I have,' answered Kiríllov.

'For two weeks now,' said Hadji Murád, holding up first both hands and then four fingers. 'Give here!'

'We'll give it you at once,' said the official, getting his purse out of his travelling-bag. 'What does he want with the money?' he went on in Russian, thinking that Hadji Murád would not understand. But Hadji Murád had understood, and glanced angrily at him. While getting out the money the councillor, wishing to begin a conversation with Hadji Murád in order to have something to tell Prince Vorontsóv on his return, asked through the interpreter whether he was not feeling bored there. Hadji Murád glanced contemptuously out of the corner of his eye at the fat, unarmed little man dressed as a civilian, and did not reply. The interpreter repeated the question.

'Tell him that I cannot talk with him! Let him give me the money!' and having said this, Hadji Murád sat down at the table ready to count it.

Hadji Murád had an allowance of five gold pieces a day, and when Kiríllov had got out the money and arranged it in seven piles of ten gold pieces each and pushed them towards Hadji Murád, the latter poured the gold into the sleeve of his *cherkéska*, rose, quite unexpectedly smacked Councillor Kiríllov on his bald pate, and turned to go.

The councillor jumped up and ordered the interpreter to tell Hadji Murád that he must not dare to behave like that to him who held a rank equal to that of colonel! The officer in charge confirmed this, but Hadji Murád only nodded to signify that he knew, and left the room.

'What is one to do with him?' said the officer in charge. 'He'll stick his dagger into you, that's all! One cannot talk with those devils! I see that he is getting exasperated.'

As soon as it began to grow dusk two spies with hoods covering their faces up to their eyes came to him from the hills. The officer in charge led them to Hadji Murád's room. One of them was a fleshy, swarthy Tavlinian, the other a thin old man. The news they brought was not cheering. Hadji Murád's friends who had undertaken to rescue his family now definitely refused to do so, being afraid of Shamíl, who threatened to punish with most terrible tortures anyone who helped Hadji Murád. Having heard the messengers he sat with his elbows on his crossed legs, and bowing his turbaned head remained silent a long time.

He was thinking and thinking resolutely. He knew that he was now considering the matter for the last time and that it was necessary to come to a decision. At last he raised his head, gave each of the messengers a gold piece, and said: 'Go!'

'What answer will there be?'

'The answer will be as God pleases. Go!'

The messengers rose and went away, and Hadji Murád continued to sit on the carpet leaning his elbows on his knees. He sat thus a long time and pondered.

'What am I to do? To take Shamíl at his word and return to him?' he thought. 'He is a fox and will deceive me. Even if he did not deceive me it would still be impossible to submit to that red liar. It is impossible, because now that I have been with the Russians he will not trust me,' thought Hadji Murád; and he remembered a Tavlinian fable about a falcon who had been caught and lived among men and afterwards returned to his own kind in the hills. He returned, wearing jesses with bells, and the other falcons would not receive him. 'Fly back to where they hung those silver bells on thee!' said they. 'We have no bells and no jesses.' The falcon did not want to leave his home and remained, but the other falcons did not wish to let him stay there and pecked him to death.

'And they would peck me to death in the same way,' thought Hadji Murád. 'Shall I remain here and conquer Caucasia for the Russian Tsar and earn renown, titles, riches?'

'That could be done,' he thought, recalling his interviews with Vorontsóv and the flattering things the prince had said; 'but I must decide at once, or Shamíl will destroy my family.'

That night he remained awake, thinking.

XXIII

By midnight his decision had been formed. He had decided that he must fly to the mountains, and break into Vedenó with the Avars still devoted to him, and either die or rescue his family. Whether after rescuing them he would return to the Russians or escape to Khunzákh and fight Shamíl, he had not made up his mind. All he knew was that first of all he must escape from the Russians into the mountains, and he at once began to carry out his plan.

He drew his black wadded *beshmét* from under his pillow and went into his henchmen's room. They lived on the other side of the hall. As soon as he entered the hall, the outer door of which stood open, he was at once enveloped by the dewy freshness of the moonlit night and his ears were filled by the whistling and trilling of several nightingales in the garden by the house.

Having crossed the hall he opened the door of his henchmen's room. There was no light there, but the moon in its first quarter shone in at the window. A table and two chairs were standing on one side of the room, and four of his henchmen were lying on carpets or on *búrkas* on the floor. Khanéfi slept outside with the horses. Gamzálo heard the door creak, rose, turned round, and saw him. On recognizing him he lay down again, but Eldár, who lay beside him, jumped up and began putting on his *beshmét*, expecting his master's orders. Khan Mahomá and Bata slept on. Hadji Murád put down the *beshmét* he had brought on the table, which it hit with a dull sound, caused by the gold sewn up in it.

'Sew these in too,' said Hadji Murád, handing Eldár the gold pieces he had received that day. Eldár took them and at once went into the moonlight, drew a small knife from under his dagger and started unstitching the lining of the *beshmét*. Gamzálo raised himself and sat up with his legs crossed.

'And you, Gamzálo, tell the men to examine the rifles and pistols and get the ammunition ready. To-morrow we shall go far,' said Hadji Murád.

'We have bullets and powder, everything shall be ready,' replied Gamzálo, and roared out something incomprehensible. He understood why Hadji Murád had ordered the rifles to be loaded. From the first he had desired only one thing, to slay and stab as many Russians as possible and to escape to the hills, and this desire had increased day by day. Now at last he saw that Hadji Murád also wanted this and he was satisfied.

When Hadji Murád went away Gamzálo roused his comrades, and all four spent the rest of the night examining their rifles, pistols, flints, and accoutrements, replacing what was damaged, sprinkling fresh powder onto the pans, and stoppering with bullets wrapped in oiled rags packets filled with the right amount of powder for each charge, sharpening their swords and daggers and greasing the blades with tallow.

Before daybreak Hadji Murád again came out into the hall to

get water for his ablutions. The songs of the nightingales that had burst into ecstasy at dawn were now even louder and more incessant, while from his henchmen's room, where the daggers were being sharpened, came the regular screech and rasp of iron against stone.

Hadji Murád got himself some water from a tub, and was already at his own door when above the sound of the grinding he heard from his *muríds*' room the high tones of Khanéfi's voice singing a familiar song. He stopped to listen. The song told of how a *dzhigít*, Hamzád, with his brave followers captured a herd of white horses from the Russians, and how a Russian prince followed him beyond the Térek and surrounded him with an army as large as a forest; and then the song went on to tell how Hamzád killed the horses, entrenched his men behind this gory bulwark, and fought the Russians as long as they had bullets in their rifles, daggers in their belts, and blood in their veins. But before he died Hamzád saw some birds flying in the sky and cried to them:

> 'Fly on, ye winged ones, fly to our homes!
> Tell ye our mothers, tell ye our sisters,
> Tell the white maidens, that fighting we died
> For *ghazavát*! Tell them our bodies
> Never will lie and rest in a tomb!
> Wolves will devour and tear them to pieces,
> Ravens and vultures will pluck out our eyes.'

With that the song ended, and at the last words, sung to a mournful air, the merry Bata's vigorous voice joined in with a loud shout of '*Lya-il-lyakha-il Allakh!*' finishing with a shrill shriek. Then all was quiet again, except for the *tchuk*, *tchuk*, *tchuk*, *tchuk* and whistling of the nightingales from the garden and from behind the door the even grinding, and now and then the whiz, of iron sliding quickly along the whetstone.

Hadji Murád was so full of thought that he did not notice how he tilted his jug till the water began to pour out. He shook his head at himself and re-entered his room. After performing his morning ablutions he examined his weapons and sat down on his bed. There was nothing more for him to do. To be allowed to ride out he would have to get permission from the officer in charge, but it was not yet daylight and the officer was still asleep.

Khanéfi's song reminded him of the song his mother had composed just after he was born, the song addressed to his father that Hadji Murád had repeated to Lóris-Mélikov.

And he seemed to see his mother before him, not wrinkled and grey-haired, with gaps between her teeth, as he had lately left her, but young and handsome, and strong enough to carry him in a basket on her back across the mountains to her father's when he was a heavy five-year-old boy.

And the recollection of himself as a little child reminded him of his beloved son, Yusúf, whose head he himself had shaved for the first time; and now this Yusúf was a handsome young *dzhigít*. He pictured him as he was when last he saw him on the day he left Tselméss. Yusúf brought him his horse and asked to be allowed to accompany him. He was ready dressed and armed, and led his own horse by the bridle, and his rosy handsome young face and the whole of his tall slender figure (he was taller than his father) breathed of daring, youth, and the joy of life. The breadth of his shoulders, though he was so young, the very wide youthful hips, the long slender waist, the strength of his long arms, and the power, flexibility, and agility of all his movements had always rejoiced Hadji Murád, who admired his son.

'Thou hadst better stay. Thou wilt be alone at home now. Take care of thy mother and thy grandmother,' said Hadji Murád. And he remembered the spirited and proud look and the flush of pleasure with which Yusúf had replied that as long as he lived no one should injure his mother or grandmother. All the same, Yusúf had mounted and accompanied his father as far as the stream. There he turned back, and since then Hadji Murád had not seen his wife, his mother, or his son. And it was this son whose eyes Shamíl threatened to put out! Of what would be done to his wife Hadji Murád did not wish to think.

These thoughts so excited him that he could not sit still any longer. He jumped up and went limping quickly to the door, opened it, and called Eldár. The sun had not yet risen, but it was already quite light. The nightingales were still singing.

'Go and tell the officer that I want to go out riding, and saddle the horses,' he said.

XXIV

Butler's only consolation all this time was the poetry of warfare, to which he gave himself up not only during his hours of service but also in private life. Dressed in his Circassian* costume, he *dzhigíted* about on horseback, and twice went into ambush with Bogdanóvich, though neither time did they discover or kill anyone. This closeness to and friendship with Bogdanóvich, famed for his courage, seemed pleasant and warlike to Butler. He had paid his debt, having borrowed the money from a Jew at an enormous rate of interest, which is to say, he had postponed his difficulties but had not solved them. He tried not to think of his position, and to find oblivion not only in the poetry of warfare but also in wine. He drank more and more every day, and day by day grew morally weaker. He was now no longer the chaste Joseph he had been towards Márya Dmítrievna, but on the contrary began courting her grossly, meeting to his surprise with a strong and decided repulse which put him to shame.

At the end of April there arrived at the fort a detachment with which Baryátinski intended to effect an advance right through Chechnyá, which had till then been considered impassable. In that detachment were two companies of the Kabardá regiment, and according to Caucasian custom these were treated as guests by the Kurín companies. The soldiers were lodged in the barracks, and were treated not only to supper, consisting of buckwheat-porridge and beef, but also to vodka. The officers shared the quarters of the Kurín officers, and as usual those in residence gave the newcomers a dinner at which the regimental singers performed and which ended up with a drinking-bout. Major Petróv, very drunk and no longer red but ashy pale, sat astride a chair and, drawing his sword, hacked at imaginary foes, alternately swearing and laughing, now embracing someone and now dancing to the tune of his favourite song.

'Shamíl, he began to riot
In the days gone by;
Try, ry, rataty,
In the years gone by!'

Butler was there too. He tried to see the poetry of warfare in this also, but in the depth of his soul he was sorry for the major. To stop him, however, was quite impossible; and Butler, feeling that the fumes were mounting to his own head, quietly left the room and went home.

The moon lit up the white houses and the stones on the road. It was so light that every pebble, every straw, every little heap of dust was visible. As he approached the house he met Márya Dmítrievna with a shawl over her head and neck. After the rebuff she had given him Butler had avoided her, feeling rather ashamed, but now in the moonlight and after the wine he had drunk he was pleased to meet her and wished to make up to her again.

'Where are you off to?' he asked.

'Why, to see after my old man,' she answered pleasantly. Her rejection of Butler's advances was quite sincere and decided, but she did not like his avoiding her as he had done lately.

'Why bother about him? He'll soon come back.'

'But will he?'

'If he doesn't they'll bring him.'

'Just so. That's not right, you know! But you think I'd better not go?'

'Yes, I do. We'd better go home.'

Márya Dmítrievna turned back and walked beside him. The moon shone so brightly that a halo seemed to move along the road round the shadows of their heads. Butler was looking at this halo and making up his mind to tell her that he liked her as much as ever, but he did not know how to begin. She waited for him to speak, and they walked on in silence almost to the house, when some horsemen appeared from round the corner. These were an officer with an escort.

'Who's that coming now?' said Márya Dmítrievna, stepping aside. The moon was behind the rider so that she did not recognize him until he had almost come up to them. It was Peter Nikoláevich Kámenev, an officer who had formerly served with the major and whom Márya Dmítrievna therefore knew.

'Is that you, Peter Nikoláevich?' said she, addressing him.

'It's me,' said Kámenev. 'Ah, Butler, how d'you do? Not

asleep yet? Having a walk with Márya Dmítrievna! You'd better look out or the major will give it you. Where is he?'

'Why, there. Listen!' replied Márya Dmítrievna pointing in the direction whence came the sounds of a *tulúmbas* and songs. 'They're on a spree.'

'Why? Are your people having a spree on their own?'

'No, some officers have come from Hasav-Yurt, and they are being entertained.'

'Ah, that's good! I shall be in time. I just want the major for a moment.'

'On business?' asked Butler.

'Yes, just a little business matter.'

'Good or bad?'

'It all depends. Good for us but bad for some people,' and Kámenev laughed.

By this time they had reached the major's house.

'Chikhiryóv,' shouted Kámenev to one of his Cossacks, come here!'

A Don Cossack rode up from among the others. He was dressed in the ordinary Don Cossack uniform with high boots and a mantle, and carried saddle-bags behind.

'Well, take the thing out,' said Kámenev, dismounting.

The Cossack also dismounted, and took a sack out of his saddle-bag. Kámenev took the sack from him and inserted his hand.

'Well, shall I show you a novelty? You won't be frightened, Márya Dmítrievna?'

'Why should I be frightened?' she replied.

'Here it is!' said Kámenev taking out a man's head and holding it up in the light of the moon. 'Do you recognize it?'

It was a shaven head with salient brows, black short-cut beard and moustaches, one eye open and the other half-closed. The shaven skull was cleft, but not right through, and there was congealed blood in the nose. The neck was wrapped in a blood-stained towel. Notwithstanding the many wounds on the head, the blue lips still bore a kindly childlike expression.

Márya Dmítrievna looked at it, and without a word turned away and went quickly into the house.

Butler could not tear his eyes from the terrible head. It was the head of that very Hadji Murád with whom he had so recently spent his evenings in such friendly conversation.

'What does this mean? Who has killed him?' he asked.

'He wanted to give us the slip, but was caught,' said Kámenev, and he gave the head back to the Cossack and went into the house with Butler.

'He died like a hero,' he added.

'But however did it all happen?'

'Just wait a bit. When the major comes I'll tell you all about it. That's what I am sent for. I take it round to all the forts and *aúls* and show it.'

The major was sent for, and came back accompanied by two other officers as drunk as himself, and began embracing Kámenev.

'And I have brought you Hadji Murád's head,' said Kámenev.

'No? Killed?'

'Yes, wanted to escape.'

'I always said he would bamboozle them! And where is it? The head, I mean. Let's see it.'

The Cossack was called, and brought in the bag with the head. It was taken out and the major looked long at it with drunken eyes.

'All the same, he was a fine fellow,' he said. 'Let me kiss him!'

'Yes, it's true. It was a valiant head,' said one of the officers.

When they had all looked at it, it was returned to the Cossack who put it in his bag, trying to let it bump against the floor as gently as possible.

'I say, Kámenev, what speech do you make when you show the head?' asked an officer.

'No! Let me kiss him. He gave me a sword!' shouted the major.

Butler went out onto the porch.

Márya Dmítrievna was sitting on the second step. She looked round at Butler and at once turned angrily away again.

'What's the matter, Márya Dmítrievna?' he asked.

'You're all murderers! . . . I hate it! You're murderers, really,' and she got up.

'It might happen to anyone,' remarked Butler, not knowing what to say. 'That's war.'

'War? War, indeed! Murderers and nothing else. A dead body should be given back to the earth, and they're grinning at it there! Murderers, really,' she repeated, as she descended the steps and entered the house by the back door.

Butler returned to the room and asked Kámenev to tell them in detail how the thing had happened.

And Kámenev told them.

This is what had happened.

XXV

Hadji Murád was allowed to go out riding in the neighbourhood of the town, but never without a convoy of Cossacks. There was only half a troop of them altogether in Nukhá, ten of whom were employed by the officers, so that if ten were sent out with Hadji Murád (according to the orders received) the same men would have had to go every other day. Therefore after ten had been sent out the first day, it was decided to send only five in the future and Hadji Murád was asked not to take all his henchmen with him. But on 25 April he rode out with all five. When he mounted, the commander, noticing that all five henchmen were going with him, told him that he was forbidden to take them all, but Hadji Murád pretended not to hear, touched his horse, and the commander did not insist.

With the Cossacks rode a non-commissioned officer, Nazárov, who had received the Cross of St George for bravery. He was a young, healthy, brown-haired lad, as fresh as a rose. He was the eldest of a poor family belonging to the sect of Old Believers, had grown up without a father, and had maintained his old mother, three sisters, and two brothers.

'Mind, Nazárov, keep close to him!' shouted the commander.

'All right, your honour!' answered Nazárov, and rising in his stirrups and adjusting the rifle that hung at his back he started his fine large roan gelding at a trot. Four Cossacks followed him: Ferapóntov, tall and thin, a regular thief and plunderer (it was he who had sold gunpowder to Gamzálo); Ignátov, a sturdy peasant who boasted of his strength, though he was no longer young and had nearly completed his service; Míshkin, a weakly lad at whom everybody laughed; and the young fair-haired Petrakóv, his mother's only son, always amiable and jolly.

The morning had been misty, but it cleared up later on and the opening foliage, the young virgin grass, the sprouting corn, and the ripples of the rapid river just visible to the left of the road, all glittered in the sunshine.

Hadji Murád rode slowly along followed by the Cossacks and by his henchmen. They rode out along the road beyond the fort at a walk. They met women carrying baskets on their heads, soldiers driving carts, and creaking wagons drawn by buffaloes. When he had gone about a mile and a half Hadji Murád touched up his white Kabardá horse, which started at an amble that obliged the henchmen and Cossacks to ride at a quick trot to keep up with him.

'Ah, he's got a fine horse under him,' said Ferapóntov. 'If only he were still an enemy I'd soon bring him down.'

'Yes, mate. Three hundred rubles were offered for that horse in Tiflis.'

'But I can get ahead of him on mine,' said Nazárov.

'You get ahead? A likely thing!'

Hadji Murád kept increasing his pace.

'Hey, *kunák*, you mustn't do that. Steady!' cried Nazárov, starting to overtake Hadji Murád.

Hadji Murád looked round, said nothing, and continued to ride at the same pace.

'Mind, they're up to something, the devils!' said Ignátov. 'See how they are tearing along.'

So they rode for the best part of a mile in the direction of the mountains.

'I tell you you mustn't do that!' shouted Nazárov.

Hadji Murád did not answer or look round, but only increased his pace to a gallop.

'Liar! You won't get away!' shouted Nazárov, stung to the quick. He gave his big roan gelding a cut with his whip and, rising in his stirrups and bending forward, flew full speed in pursuit of Hadji Murád.

The sky was so bright, the air so clear, and life played so joyously in Nazárov's soul as, becoming one with his fine strong horse, he flew along the smooth road behind Hadji Murád, that the possibility of anything sad or dreadful happening never occurred to him. He rejoiced that with every step he was gaining on Hadji Murád.

Hadji Murád judged by the approaching tramp of the big horse behind him that he would soon be overtaken, and seizing his pistol with his right hand, with his left he began slightly to rein in his Kabardá horse which was excited by hearing the tramp of hoofs behind it.

'You mustn't, I tell you!' shouted Nazárov, almost level with Hadji Murád and stretching out his hand to seize the latter's bridle. But before he reached it a shot was fired. 'What are you doing?' he screamed, clutching at his breast. 'At them, lads!' and he reeled and fell forward on his saddle-bow.

But the mountaineers took to their weapons before the Cossacks, and fired their pistols at the Cossacks and hewed at them with their swords.

Nazárov hung on the neck of his horse, which careered round his comrades. The horse under Ignátov fell, crushing his leg, and two of the mountaineers, without dismounting, drew their swords and hacked at his head and arms. Petrakóv was about to rush to his comrade's rescue when two shots—one in his back and the other in his side—stung him, and he fell from his horse like a sack.

Míshkin turned round and galloped off towards the fortress. Khanéfi and Khan Mahomá rushed after him, but he was already too far away and the mountaineers could not catch him.

When they saw that they could not overtake the Cossack Khanéfi and Khan Mahomá returned to the others. Gamzálo, having finished off Ignátov with his sword, gave a cut to Nazárov too and threw him from his horse. Khan Mahomá took the cartridge-pouches from the slain. Khanéfi wanted to take Nazárov's horse, but Hadji Murád called out to him to leave it, and dashed forward along the road. His *muríds* galloped after him, driving away Petrakóv's horse that tried to follow them. They were already among rice-fields more than six miles from Nukhá when a shot was fired from the tower of that place to give the alarm.

Petrakóv lay on his back, his stomach ripped open, his young face turned to the sky, and while dying he gasped for breath like a fish.

'O good Lord! O God! my God! What have they done?' cried the commander of the fort seizing his head with his hands when he heard of Hadji Murád's escape. 'They've done me in! They've let him escape, the villains!' he cried, listening to Míshkin's account.

An alarm was raised everywhere and not only the Cossacks of the place were sent after the fugitives but also all the militia that could be mustered from the pro-Russian *aúls*. A thousand rubles reward was offered for the capture of Hadji Murád alive or dead, and two hours after he and his followers had escaped from the Cossacks more than two hundred mounted men were following the officer in charge at a gallop to find and capture the runaways.

After riding some miles along the high road Hadji Murád checked his panting horse, which, wet with sweat, had turned from white to grey.

To the right of the road could be seen the *sáklyas* and minarets of the *aúl* Benerdzhík, on the left lay some fields, and beyond them the river. Although the way to the mountains lay to the right, Hadji Murád turned to the left, in the opposite direction, assuming that his pursuers would be sure to go to the right, while he, abandoning the road, would cross the Alazán and come out onto the high road on the other side where no one would expect him, ride along it to the forest, and then after recrossing the river make his way to the mountains.

Having come to this conclusion he turned to the left; but it proved impossible to reach the river. The rice-field which had to be crossed had just been flooded, as is always done in spring, and had become a bog in which the horses' legs sank above their pasterns. Hadji Murád and his henchmen turned now to the left, now to the right, hoping to find drier ground, but the field they were in had been equally flooded all over and was now saturated with water. The horses drew their feet out of the sticky mud into which they sank, with a pop like that of a cork drawn from a bottle, and stopped, panting, after every few steps. They struggled in this way so long that it began to grow dusk and they had still not reached the river. To their left lay a patch of higher ground overgrown with shrubs and Hadji Murád decided to ride in among these clumps and remain there till night to rest their exhausted horses and let them graze. The men themselves ate some bread and cheese they had brought with them. At last night came on and the moon that had been shining at first, hid behind the hill and it became dark. There were a great many nightingales in that neighbourhood and there were two of them in these shrubs. As long as Hadji Murád and his men were making a noise among the bushes the nightingales had been silent, but when they became still the birds again began to call to one another and to sing.

Hadji Murád, awake to all the sounds of night, listened to them involuntarily, and their trills reminded him of the song about Hamzád which he had heard the night before when he went to get water. He might now at any moment find himself in the position in which Hamzád had been. He fancied that it would be so, and suddenly his soul became serious. He spread out his *búrka* and performed his ablutions, and scarcely had he finished before a sound was heard approaching their shelter. It was the sound of many horses' feet plashing through the bog.

The keen-sighted Khan Mahomá ran out to one edge of the clump, and peering through the darkness saw black shadows, which were men on foot and on horseback. Khanéfi discerned a similar crowd on the other side. It was Kargánov, the military commander of the district, with his militia.

'Well, then, we shall fight like Hamzád,' thought Hadji Murád.

When the alarm was given, Kargánov with a troop of militiamen and Cossacks had rushed off in pursuit of Hadji Murád, but had been unable to find any trace of him. He had already lost hope and was returning home when, towards evening, he met an old man and asked him if he had seen any horsemen about. The old man replied that he had. He had seen six horsemen floundering in the rice-field, and then had seen them enter the clump where he himself was getting wood. Kargánov turned back, taking the old man with him, and seeing the hobbled horses he made sure that Hadji Murád was there. In the night he surrounded the clump and waited till morning to take Hadji Murád alive or dead.

Having understood that he was surrounded, and having discovered an old ditch among the shrubs, Hadji Murád decided to entrench himself in it and to resist as long as strength and ammunition lasted. He told his comrades this, and ordered them to throw up a bank in front of the ditch, and his henchmen at once set to work to cut down branches, dig up the earth with their daggers, and make an entrenchment. Hadji Murád himself worked with them.

As soon as it began to grow light the commander of the militia troop rode up to the clump and shouted:

'Hey! Hadji Murád, surrender! We are many and you are few!'

In reply came the report of a rifle, a cloudlet of smoke rose from the ditch and a bullet hit the militiaman's horse, which staggered under him and began to fall. The rifles of the militiamen who stood at the outskirt of the clump of shrubs began cracking in their turn, and their bullets whistled and hummed, cutting off leaves and twigs and striking the embankment, but not the men entrenched behind it. Only Gamzálo's horse, that had strayed from the others, was hit in the head by a bullet. It did not fall, but breaking its hobbles and rushing among the bushes it ran to the other horses, pressing close to them and watering the young grass with its blood. Hadji Murád and his men fired only when any of the militiamen came forward, and rarely missed their aim. Three militiamen were wounded, and the others, far from making up their minds to rush the entrenchment, retreated farther and farther back, only firing from a distance and at random.

So it continued for more than an hour. The sun had risen to about half the height of the trees, and Hadji Murád was already thinking of leaping on his horse and trying to make his way to the river, when the shouts were heard of many men who had just arrived. These were Hadji Aga of Mekhtulí with his followers. There were about two hundred of them. Hadji Aga had once been Hadji Murád's *kunák* and had lived with him in the mountains, but he had afterwards gone over to the Russians.

With him was Akhmet Khan, the son of Hadji Murád's old enemy.

Like Kargánov, Hadji Aga began by calling to Hadji Murád to surrender, and Hadji Murád answered as before with a shot.

'Swords out, my men!' cried Hadji Aga, drawing his own, and a hundred voices were raised by men who rushed shrieking in among the shrubs.

The militiamen ran in among the shrubs, but from behind the entrenchment came the crack of one shot after another. Some three men fell, and the attackers stopped at the outskirts of the clump and also began firing. As they fired they gradually approached the entrenchment, running across from behind one shrub to another. Some succeeded in getting across, others fell under the bullets of Hadji Murád or of his men. Hadji Murád fired without missing; Gamzálo too rarely wasted a shot, and shrieked with joy every time he saw that his bullet had hit its aim. Kurbán sat at the edge of the ditch singing '*Il lyakha il Allakh!*' and fired leisurely, but often missed. Eldár's whole body trembled with impatience to rush dagger in hand at the enemy, and he fired often and at random, constantly looking round at Hadji Murád and stretching out beyond the entrenchment. The shaggy Khanéfi, with his sleeves rolled up, did the duty of a servant even here. He loaded the guns which Hadji Murád and Kurbán passed to him, carefully driving home with a ramrod the bullets wrapped in greasy rags, and pouring dry powder out of the powder-flask onto the pans. Khan Mahomá did not remain in the ditch as the others did, but kept running to the horses, driving them away to a safer place and, shrieking incessantly, fired without using a prop for his gun. He was the first to be wounded. A bullet entered his neck and he sat down spitting blood and swearing. Then Hadji Murád was wounded, the bullet piercing his shoulder. He tore some cotton wool from the lining of his *beshmét*, plugged the wound with it, and went on firing.

'Let us fly at them with our swords!' said Eldár for the third time, and he looked out from behind the bank of earth ready to rush at the enemy, but at that instant a bullet struck him and he reeled and fell backwards onto Hadji Murád's leg. Hadji Murád glanced at him. His eyes, beautiful like those of a ram, gazed intently and seriously at Hadji Murád. His mouth, the upper lip pouting like a child's, twitched without opening. Hadji Murád drew his leg away from under him and continued firing. Khanéfi bent over the dead Eldár and began taking the unused ammunition out of the cartridge-cases of his coat. Kurbán meanwhile continued to sing, loading leisurely and firing.

The enemy ran from shrub to shrub, hallooing and shrieking and drawing ever nearer and nearer. Another bullet hit Hadji Murád in the left side. He lay down in the ditch and again pulled some cotton wool out of his *beshmét* and plugged the wound. This wound in the side was fatal and he felt that he was dying. Memories and pictures succeeded one another with extraordinary rapidity in his imagination. Now he saw the powerful Abu Nutsal Khan, dagger in hand, and holding up his severed cheek, he rushed at his foe; then he saw the weak, bloodless old Vorontsóv with his cunning white face, and heard his soft voice; then he saw his son Yusúf, his wife Sofiát, and then the pale, red-bearded face of his enemy Shamíl with its half-closed eyes.

All these images passed through his mind without evoking any feeling within him, neither pity nor anger nor any kind of desire. Everything seemed so insignificant in comparison with what was beginning, or had already begun, within him. Yet his strong body continued the thing that he had commenced. Gathering together his last strength he rose from behind the bank, fired his pistol at a man who was just running towards him, and hit him. The man fell. Then Hadji Murád climbed right out of the ditch, and limping heavily went dagger in hand straight at the foe. Some shots cracked and he reeled and fell. Several militiamen with triumphant shrieks rushed towards the fallen body. But the body that seemed to be dead suddenly moved. First the uncovered, bleeding, shaven head rose, then the body with hands holding to the trunk of a tree. He seemed so terrible, that those who were running towards him stopped short. But suddenly a shudder passed through him, he staggered away from the tree and fell on his face, stretched out at full length like a thistle that had been mown down, and he moved no more.

He did not move, but still he felt. When Hadji Aga, who was the first to reach him, struck him on the head with a large dagger, it seemed to Hadji Murád that someone was striking him with a hammer and he could not understand who was doing it or why. That was his last consciousness of any connection with his body. He felt nothing more and his enemies kicked and hacked at what had no longer anything in common with him. Hadji Aga placed his foot on the back of the corpse and with two blows cut off the head, and carefully, not to soil his shoes with blood, rolled it away with his foot. Crimson blood spurted from the arteries of the neck, and black blood flowed from the head, soaking the grass.

Kargánov and Hadji Aga and Akhmet Khan and all the militiamen gathered together, like sportsmen round a slaughtered animal, near the bodies of Hadji Murád and his men (Khanéfi, Kurbán, and Gamzálo they bound), and amid the gunpowder-smoke which hung over the bushes they triumphed in their victory.

The nightingales, that had hushed their songs while the firing lasted, now started their trills once more, first one quite close, then others in the distance.

It was of this death that I was reminded by the crushed thistle in the midst of the ploughed field.

EXPLANATORY NOTES

FAMILY HAPPINESS

10 *St Peter's Fast*: a two- to five-week fast preceding the feast of St Peter and St Paul (29 June, OS).

16 *Schulhof*: Julius Schulhoff (1825–98), a noted Bohemian pianist and composer best known for his piano transcriptions of works by Mozart, Beethoven, and Haydn.

23 *Strélski . . . Eleanora*: characteristic names used in popular sentimentalist and romantic tales.

28 *fasting . . . birthday*: it was customary in the nineteenth century to prepare oneself for the sacrament of holy communion by a week-long fast during which one attended services and went to confession; ordinarily one received communion only a few times a year.

August: the Fast of the Dormition lasted for the two weeks preceding the Feast of the Dormition (15 August, OS); the Dormition of the *Bogoroditsa* ('birth-giver of God') is called the Assumption in the West.

32 *He congratulated me*: because the reception of communion was relatively rare and marked by special preparation, the offering of congratulations was customary, as it was for one's birthday.

42 *'thou'*: in Russian, as in many Indo-European languages, there is still a special, second-person form of the verb, used in the nineteenth century to address intimates and God, as well as servants and animals.

55 *It . . . peace*: a well-known quotation from an equally well-known poem, 'The Sail' (*Parus*, 1832) by Mikhaíl Lérmontov (1814–41), a writer whose poetry and prose had a special attraction for Tolstoy; the lyric uses the common Romantic topos of the boat at sea to explore the psychology of passions.

84 *romance*: the Russian word means both 'romance' and 'novel', thus suggesting the literary, even generic aspect of love conceived as romance.

THE KREUTZER SONATA

87 *moment*: a first, second, and third bell were rung before the departure of a train.

89 *tower*: the 'tower' (*terem*) refers to the women's quarters where in olden days Russian women were secluded, as was the custom in many Eastern countries.

90 *Domostróy*: *Household Management*, a sixteenth-century manual on religion, family life, and housekeeping compiled by the monk Silvester; the work reflects sixteenth-century Moscovite ideology which aimed to establish rules and rituals for all facets of social life.

95 *glass of it*: in Russia tea is drunk from a glass held by the handle of the metal holder in which the glass is set.

97 *brothels*: in Russia, as in many other countries, houses of prostitution were under government supervision; doctors were employed to establish and maintain hygenic conditions.

99 *Rigulboche*: the nickname adopted by Margarita Bodelle, a popular singer and cancan dancer in Paris during the 1850s and 1860s; the name (derived from *rigolo*, 'funny', and *bauche*, 'crude') came to be used pejoratively for cancan dancers.

102 *kvas*: a mild, fermented drink made from bread.

107 *Sisyphus*: mythical king of Corinth who earned Zeus' wrath and was condemned to eternal torment in Hades, having to try forever to roll uphill a rock which forever rolled back upon him.

115 *Charcot's*: Jean Charcot (1825–93), French neuropathologist and author of books on hypnotism.

117 *Trubá . . . Grachévka*: streets in Moscow where there were numerous brothels.

119 *lace*: wet nurses were commonly used; their employers often provided them with elaborate costumes in the native style.

124 *The Lord . . . escape*: an approximate quotation from the Book of Job.

140 *Zémstvo*: an elective district council for local administration; established in 1864 and abolished in 1917.

Uriah's wife: a biblical reference (2. Sam. 11). King David caught sight of Bathsheba, the wife of Uriah the Hittite, while she was bathing, and, struck with her beauty, he sent for her and had intercourse with her. Bathsheba conceived and notified David, who then tried to get Uriah to sleep with her in order to cover up the misdeed. When Uriah failed to do this, David sent him to his death and married Bathsheba.

145 *Ernst's Elegy*: Heinrich Wilhelm Ernst (1814–65), Moravian violinist and composer; wrote some thirty pieces for violin of which 'Élégie' (op. 10, 1840) is one of the better known.

148 *tarantas*: a four-wheel, springless carriage.

152 *Vánka the Steward*: a character in folk poetry; Vánka seduces his master's wife, boasts of it, and is hanged.

162 *forgive me*: the perfective aspect of the imperative *prostíte* ('forgive me') was sometimes used in place of the imperfective imperative of the same verb *proshcháite* ('good-bye').

THE COSSACKS

178 *post-station*: in the days before railways travellers relied on vehicles hired at posting stations.

186 *Amalat-Beks*: Amalat-Bek is the eponymous hero of a popular novel about the Caucasus written by A. Bestúzhev-Marlínski (1797–1837); the name became associated with the Romantic image of the exotic, 'Oriental' Caucasus.

Circassian: properly called the Adygs, the Circassians lived in the north-west Caucasus, in the Kuban River region; closely related to the Abkházians and the Kabardíns. Their language belongs to the Abkházo-Adyg group of Caucasian languages.

187 *Notre Dame de Paris*: *The Hunchback of Notre Dame*, a novel by Victor Hugo (1802–85), published in 1831.

189 *Don Cossacks*: mainly of Russian origin, settled in the sixteenth century in the Don River region; known for their bravery and love of freedom. The Don Cossacks were often pressed into service for the Tsar.

Nogáy: a steppe people of Mongol origin, tracing their history back to Prince Nogáy, grandson of Chengis Khan; they dwell in the Kuban region and speak a Turkic language. In this period they were often made to do menial labour for the Russians.

190 *Térek*: a river in the east Caucasus region; it flows into the Caspian Sea.

Tatar: a Turco-Mongolian people who speak a variety of Turkic dialects; they were mainly nomads known for their military system and ferocious warriors, who acquired wealth through raiding and tribute. The word tends to be used to describe various Mongol peoples.

Grebénsk Cossacks: probably the original Cossacks in the Térek River region. A mixture of Russian and Tatar, with a great deal of intermarriage with local mountain peoples, especially the Chechéns, Circassians, Kabardíns, and Kumýks. Tolstoy's description of the Grebénsk Cossacks is quite accurate and demonstrates the detailed knowledge he acquired while he lived in the Caucasus in the early 1850s.

191 *Old Believers*: general name for those sects that separated from the Russian Orthodox Church in the seventeenth century, mostly over disagreements about ritual; their rules prohibit the use of tobacco.

Chechéns: an indigenous mountain people of the northern Caucasus settled in the middle Térek region, whose land is called Chechnyá in Russian and Ichkíria in their own language, which is of Turkic origin; they are Islamic.

Iván the Terrible: Iván IV, the first tsar of Russia, ruled 1547–84. He granted autonomy to the Grebénsk Cossacks in return for their repelling marauders from across the river.

216 *angel of silence*: in the culture of Russian Orthodoxy a silence which comes over a group is imagined as an angel of silence (*tikhii angel*) which has descended upon them.

219 *Kabardá*: territory in north central area of Greater Caucasus inhabited by the Karbardíns, who are closely related to the Circassians. From the time of Iván IV, who married a Karbardín princess, Karbardá was closely allied with Russia.

Grózny: the capital of Chechnyá.

222 *Lafom*: i.e. *la femme* ('women!'). Vanyúsha's French pronunciation suffers from a Russian accent. Tolstoy renders this by transliterating the French words into Cyrillic. Throughout this translation Vanyúsha's French will be rendered by an approximate phonetic transcription of the Cyrillic transcription.

225 *Vanyúsha*: a diminutive form of Iván usually used for servants; without the class distinction, the diminutive would be Ványa.

237 *Qadi*: a judge in a Muslim community, whose decisions are based on Islamic religious law.

Tsaritsa: Catherine the Great, who reigned 1762–96.

251 *Nimrod*: the great-grandson of Noah who became proverbial: 'Like Nimrod, a mighty hunter before the Lord' (Gen. 10: 9).

252 *Gifts . . . Térek*: a poem by Lérmontov, written in 1839; the gifts

of the Térek are its waves bearing the body of a young Cossack woman to the old man of the Caspian Sea.

257 *Pathfinder*: a novel by the American novelist James Fenimore Cooper (1789–1851), published in 1840; one of Cooper's *Leatherstocking Tales* of native Americans and the dangers of life in early America, all of which were very popular in nineteenth-century Russia.

259 *stag*: in Russian 'stag' is '*olén*'', the root of Olénin. This linguistic resemblance underlines the theme of identity that is at issue here.

281 *Les Trois Mousquetaires*: *The Three Musketeers*, a novel by Alexandre Dumas, *père* (1802–70), published in 1844.

287 *oven*: the top of the large oven of a Russian stove served as a warm shelf where one could rest.

289 *Lov*: 'the Lov stud farm for breeding Kabardá horses is considered one of the best in the Caucasus', LT.

292 *web of love*: Olénin's diary note reflects Tolstoy's own diary entry of 17 May 1856: 'The best means for true happiness in life is, without any laws, to put forth from yourself in all directions, like a spider, a sticky web of love and to catch everything that falls into it' (*Complete Works*, xlvii. 41). Tolstoy got the idea of a web of love from Laurence Sterne (see xlvi. 110).

293 *balaláyka*: a three-stringed guitar similar to a banjo.

309 *Ermólov*: General Alekséy Petróvich Ermólov (1777–1861) served as 'proconsul' of the Caucasus under Alexander I. In 1818 he undertook a campaign of 'pacification' of Chechnyá and Dagestan, which consisted of the destruction of villages, theft of cattle and goods, clear-cutting of forests, and the resettlement of the people.

317 *circle dance*: a characteristic Slavic folk dance style; girls, lined up in a ring, dance round in a circle, while singing.

HADJI MURÁD

345 *Chechén*: see note to p. 191.

357 *Vorontsóv*: Semyón Mikháylovich Vorontsóv (1823–82), son of the governor-general of the Caucasus; an aide-de-camp and commander of the Kurín regiment of the chasseurs.

Poltorátski: Second Lieutenant Vladímir Alekséevich Poltorátski (1828–89); Tolstoy used his memoirs, published between 1893 and 1895, when writing *Hadji Murád*.

360 *Clicquot*: 'Veuve Clicquot', an expensive champagne popular with the aristocracy and royalty.

365 *Avaria*: the area of the Avar Khanate in the north-east Caucasus region. The Avars lived mainly in the mountainous regions of Dagestan. Their language is of Turkic origin and they are Muslims. The Avar Khanate ruled from the twelfth to the nineteenth centuries. In 1864 the Tsarist regime eliminated the Khanate and took control of the area.

367 *Kabardá*: see note to p. 219.

369 *Tatar*: see note to p. 190.

370 *Lesgian*: Muslim people living mainly in the south-eastern part of the Dagestan region and in neighbouring Azerbaijan. They speak a Caucasian language.

372 *Grózny*: see note to p. 219.

377 *Tiflis*: the capital of Georgia, now Tbilisi.

378 *Pyótra*: note the gradations of emotion reflected in the variations on Peter's name, from the formal Peter Mikháylovich to Pyótra, Petrúkha, Petrúsha, Petrúshenka, where each morphological change indicates a different level of intimacy.

live long: a popular expression meaning that the sender of the message is already dead.

383 *Vorontsóv*: Michael Semyónovich Vorontsóv (1782–1856), governor-general of the Caucasus (1844–56), where he ruled with virtually unlimited power. Tolstoy based his portrait on Vorontsóv's published correspondence.

Krásnoe: a town thirty miles south-west of Smolensk at which, in November 1812, the rearguard of Napoleon's army was defeated during the retreat from Moscow.

387 *Murat*: Joachim Murat (1771–1815), one of Napoleon's marshals. Murat and Murád are pronounced the same in Russian.

389 *Klügenau*: Franz Karlovich Klüki von Klügenau (1791–1851) commanded the Russian armies in northern Dagestan. Tolstoy used his published notes and correspondence while writing *Hadji Murád*.

390 *Kumýk*: a people living mainly in the plains and foothills of the Dagestan region. Their language is of Turkic origin and their religion is Muslim; in culture they are similar to other peoples of the region.

391 *Dagestan*: a region in the eastern part of the northern Caucasus, bounded in the east by the Caspian Sea. Populated by numerous

ethnic groups, including the Avars, Chechéns, Kumýks, and Lesgians.

392 *Lóris-Mélikov*: Mikhail Tarnélovich Lóris-Mélikov (1825–88) later became Minister of the Interior. Tolstoy used his published account of Hadji Murád's story as the basis for Chapters XI and XIII.

394 *Khunzákh*: the capital of Avaria.

Kazi-Mulla . . . Hamzád: Kazi-Mulla (1794–1832), Imám of Chechnyá and Dagestan, the first to declare a jihad against the Russians, was killed by forces commanded by General Rosen in 1832. Hamzád-Bek (1789–1834), who succeeded him, attempted to conquer Avaria, but was killed in 1834 in an attack on Khunzákh. He was succeeded by Shamíl (1798–1871).

395 *Baron Rosen*: G. V. Rosen, commander-in-chief in the Caucasus 1831–8; led expeditions against Kazi-Mulla.

398 *Mansúr*: Sheik Hass Mohamed Mansúr, a Muslim leader from Chechnyá who in the 1780s led his people against the Russians. The revolt failed and he joined the Turks in the Russo-Turkish War of 1787–91.

405 *Gimrints*: people from Gimry, an Avar village in the Gimry mountain range district; Shamíl was born in Gimry in 1798.

406 *French*: the text that follows is Tolstoy's direct Russian translation of M. S. Vorontsóv's original French letter.

411 *Decembrists*: a group of aristocratic young men who attempted to put an end to absolutism in Russia by means of a military revolt at the time of the accession of Nicholas I in December 1825. The failure of the revolt led to their arrest; those who were not executed were exiled to Siberia.

Chernyshóv: Count Zacháry Grigóryevich Chernyshóv (1797–1867), associated with the Decembrists, although he did not take part directly in the events of 14 December; sentenced to four years in prison and then exile. It was believed that this severe sentence was the result of the machinations of his relative Prince A. I. Chernyshóv, the Minister of War close to Nicholas I. Prince Chernyshóv hoped to benefit from the inheritance which was denied Count Chernyshóv.

Winter Palace: the Tsar's Palace in St Petersburg, completed in 1762. One thousand rooms, with façades on the Neva, the Admiralty, and the Palace Square. Now part of the Hermitage Museum.

415 *Helena Pávlovna*: widow of Nicholas's brother Michael; a clever, well-educated woman interested in science, art, and public affairs.

417 *events of 1848*: the publication of the *Communist Manifesto* (1847) inspired students and workers in Paris to seize control of the city and proclaim a new republic. This new revolutionary impulse spread quickly to Berlin, Vienna, Budapest, Prague, Milan, and Rome.

plan . . . Ermólov: Ermólov was removed from power by Nicholas I, who was dissatisfied with the slow pace of his protracted campaign in the war with Persia. See also note to p. 309.

420 *Uniate*: those Eastern Christian churches which retain the traditions of the Orthodox Church, but have re-established ties with Rome.

421 *Many Years*: a hymn of good wishes for long life sung at a prayer service (*moleben*); often sung in non-liturgical circumstances.

Hermitage: in the nineteenth century referred to the halls of the Winter Palace that housed art collections and were open to the élite.

423 *Jägers*: squadrons of sharpshooters.

426 *turning . . . cards*: in the game of *shtos* one signals the doubling of the stakes by turning down the corner of a card.

435 *Tarikáh*: 'road' or 'path'; brotherhood devoted to the mystical life in the Sufi tradition. Of the more than 200 that existed, one, the Nakshbandiyya, played an important role in the nationalist movements in the Caucasus.

436 *Shariáh*: the system of laws and precepts for daily action and living revealed in the Koran.

437 *Bairam*: in Islam a three-day festival (*Shaker-Bairam*, the 'feasts of sweets') follows the month of fasting, Ramadan. Marked by official receptions, visitation of friends, relatives, and the graves of deceased family, as well as the exchange of gifts.

444 *Baryátinski*: Prince Aleksándr Ivánovich Baryátinski (1814–79), an important general during the war in the Caucasus, governor-general of the Caucasus from 1856. Tolstoy met him a number of times while serving in the military.

455 *Circassian*: see note to p. 186.

GLOSSARY

The Glossary includes Tatar words for which no English equivalent is readily available, and which recur in *The Cossacks* and *Hadji Murád*; other foreign phrases are glossed in the Notes. LT indicates Tolstoy's original notes.

abrék 'a hostile Chechén who comes onto the Russian side of the Térek to rob and pilfer', LT
ana seni a coarse swear word
aúl a Tatar village
bar have
beshmét a Tatar waistcoat with sleeves; men wear it under a *cherkéska*
búrka a long, water-repellent felt cape made of sheep's wool or camel or goat hair
buzá 'Tatar beer made from wheat', LT
cherkéska a frock-coat-like tunic, open in the front and reaching below the knees, with cartridge pockets at the breast
chikhír home-made Caucasian wine
chuvyáki 'footwear', LT; like a soft sandal or slipper
dzhigít a warrior or, as among native Americans, a 'brave'; implies skilful horsemanship. Used as noun and verb
ghazavát an expedition against the infidels; now often called jihad
Gurda 'the name of the maker of swords and daggers most highly valued in the Caucasus', LT
Imám leader of ritual prayer in a mosque; may also be social or political figure of authority
kaymák a dairy product something like yogurt or clotted cream
khan a hereditary chief of a tribe or lord of a territorial domain
khansha the wife of a khan
khúrda-múrda stuff
kizyák 'fuel made of straw and manure', LT
kríga 'a protected place on the bank of a river for catching fish', LT
kunák 'special friend, blood brother', LT
muézzin in Islamic communities, the crier who intones aloud the call to prayer (*salat*) five times a day from the minaret of a mosque
múlla title of respect, function, and/or rank for one who is learned in Islamic sacred law
muríd 'he who seeks'; a disciple attached to a teacher in the Sufi tradition; name given to followers of Shamíl

murídism an ascetic and mystical teaching in the Sufi tradition
murshíd in *murídism* the teacher who 'shows the way' to the *muríd*
naíb a Tatar lieutenant or governor
peshkésh a dagger
pilaf a Middle Eastern dish prepared with rice and lamb or chicken
sáklya a Caucasian house built of dirt and plastered with clay
sarafán a peasant dress without sleeves or buttons at the front; worn over a blouse of different material
Saubul a greeting or toast, 'be well', 'your health'
selaam aleikum peace be with you
sirdar leader; head of tribe
tulúmbas a kind of kettledrum
yakshí fine, agreed
yok no, not

MORE ABOUT **OXFORD WORLD'S CLASSICS**

American Literature

British and Irish Literature

Children's Literature

Classics and Ancient Literature

Colonial Literature

Eastern Literature

European Literature

History

Medieval Literature

Oxford English Drama

Poetry

Philosophy

Politics

Religion

The Oxford Shakespeare